Life Mask

ALSO BY EMMA DONOGHUE

FICTION

Stir-Fry

Hood

Kissing the Witch

Slammerkin

The Woman Who Gave Birth to Rabbits

LITERARY HISTORY

Passions Between Women:
British Lesbian Culture 1668–1801

What Sappho Would Have Said:
Four Centuries of Love Poems Between Women (ED.)

We Are Michael Field

The Mammoth Book of Lesbian Short Stories

DRAMA

Ladies and Gentlemen

EMMA DONOGHUE

Life Mask

HARCOURT, INC.
Orlando   Austin   New York   San Diego   Toronto   London

www.HarcourtBooks.com

Published in Great Britain by Virago Press.

Library of Congress Cataloging-in-Publication Data
Donoghue, Emma, 1969-
Life mask/Emma Donoghue.
p.   cm.
ISBN 0-15-100943-0
1. Derby, Edward Smith Stanley, Earl of, 1752–1834—Fiction. 2. London (England)—
History—18th century—Fiction. 3. Damer, Anne Seymour, 1748–1828—Fiction.
4. Triangles (Interpersonal relations)—Fiction. 5. Farren, Elizabeth, 1762–1829—Fiction.
6. Courts and courtiers—Fiction. 7. Women sculptors—Fiction. 8. Actresses—Fiction.
9. Nobility—Fiction.   I. Title.
PR6054.O547L54 2004
823'.914—dc22   2004003190

Text set in ACaslon
Designed by Cathy Riggs

Printed in the United States of America

First U.S. edition
A C E G I K J H F D B

Life Mask is dedicated with gratitude
to my three best teachers
of writing and theatre:

Arthur Alexander,
Joan Winston,
and Betty Ann Norton.

How tired I am of keeping
a mask on my countenance.
How tight it sticks—it makes me sore.
There's metaphor for you.

—WILLIAM BECKFORD
Lisbon Diary, 27 MAY 1787

Contents

I	Primary View	1
II	Struts	92
III	Life Mask	156
IV	*Cire Perdue*	202
V	Multiple View	268
VI	Tool Marks	336
VII	*Écorché*	421
VIII	Armature	492
IX	Relict Cast	573
	AUTHOR'S NOTE	641
	DRAMATIS PERSONAE	645

Life Mask

Primary View

*The angle from which a sculpture yields
its most pleasing and comprehensive view.
Some sculptures appear fragmentary or implausible
when seen from any angle but the primary view.*

SEVERAL of our Correspondents have written to enquire exactly what is meant by that familiar phrase, the World. Allow us to reply that those who must ask the nature of the Beau Monde (alias the Quality, the Bon Ton, or simply the Ton) thereby prove themselves to be excluded from it.

This select band call themselves the World, being convinced that there is no other—or none that matters. Their number is composed of the great and grand: gentlemen and ladies of note (of family and name, of fortune and distinction, of fashion and figure). There are two points of controversy. The first, whether persons of no Breeding, who have achieved high fame and elevated station through their own merits, can be considered members of the World? The second, conversely, whether those members of the higher orders (by which we distinguish the Gentry and the Peerage) who have failed to inherit any of the fortune, elegance or other distinguished qualities of their Ancestors should be considered to have forfeited their membership? To put it in simpler terms, who is the true lady of the Beau Monde: the lovely Miss F-rr-n, whose birth is shamefully low but whose shining talents have

won her unfading laurels on the stage of Dr-ry L-ne, or old
Baroness Dung-Hill, who starves and mumbles in her
brother's west wing and hasn't been to town for a new gown
since the last Coronation?

—THE BEAU MONDE INQUIRER, March 1787

THE THAMES WAS LOOSENING, ITS THIN SKIN OF ICE CRACKED
open by thousands of small boats, as if spring were on its way. The
carriage with the Derby arms gilded on the side forced its way
down Whitehall through a tangle of vehicles and pedestrians. 'The
traffic, these days.' The Earl of Derby sighed.

Eliza Farren leaned across her mother to pull open the blue velvet curtain. The sun splashed her face like water. 'The Richmonds
must have a marvellous view, right across to St Paul's and south to
Surrey.'

'Mm. I'd never choose to live anywhere but Mayfair myself,' said
Derby, 'but I suppose the Duke needs to be close to Parliament.'

Only a few minutes to Richmond House, now; Eliza's stomach
was as tight as a nut. Despite the fur-lined mask, her cheekbones
ached with the cold; she withdrew into the hood of her cloak and
her hands crept deeper into her muff. Had it been a mistake? She'd
bought it only yesterday on Oxford Street; it struck her now as lu-
dicrously large, like a fluffy, bloated dog squatting in her lap. Her
mother was right that the muff was all the ton, but that didn't mean
it would please the people Eliza was going to meet today. How fine
the line between fashion and vulgarity and how easy to stray across
it. Perhaps she should leave the thing in the carriage.

'Of course, the one I've been longing to have you meet is the
Duchess's half-sister, Mrs Damer,' said Derby. 'She's an original;
reads Latin better than most of us Etonians. Her parents were enlightened and hired the best of tutors for the girls. I've known
Anne Damer all my life and never experienced a moment's tedium
in her company.'

On Eliza's other side her mother pressed her lined face to the glass, then recoiled from its bite. The women's feet sat together on the pewter warmer; the daughter's in pointed yellow silks, the mother's in brown leather. Over the years, Eliza had pressed some recently fashionable skirts and bodices on Mrs Farren, calling them cast-offs, but she'd never been able to persuade her to give up her boots. Eliza untied her mask now, tapped her mother's wrist and mouthed the word *mirror*. Mrs Farren fished it out of her skirts, as blank-faced as a pickpocket. Head turned away from Derby, Eliza checked her face in the small oval of glass. Had she rouged a trifle too high for three o'clock? The handkerchief was ready in her mother's hand. Eliza gave each cheek a quick wipe.

Her stomach made a discreet grumble; she'd had nothing since her morning cup of chocolate, though her mother had brought up toast, devilled eggs and cold beef on a tray. Eliza, who had the bene-fit of her mother's constant service and company, often reminded herself to be grateful. Mrs Farren had seen two daughters in the grave already; fifteen years ago she'd thrown in her lot with Eliza, the one with a chance of making the family's fortune. Peggy, the other surviving daughter and a toiling actress up in York, quite understood.

Derby was still singing the praises of the Honourable Mrs Anne Seymour Conway Damer. 'They say she's the first female ever to take up sculpture in a serious way. Did you see her gorgeous spaniels in the last Exhibition? You're both such geniuses, I'm rather hoping you might become great friends.'

Eliza smiled, doubting it. She'd always been too busy for inti-macy. Besides, she wasn't driving to Richmond House to make friends, exactly, but to step into a magic circle of protection. To spin herself a tough and glittering web.

Today was work, though the kind for which it was impossible to name a fee. In their initial interview the Duke of Richmond had murmured something about a recompense for Miss Farren's exper-tise, for the great deal of time she would be missing from Drury Lane. But Eliza's instincts hadn't let her down; she'd looked mildly offended and changed the subject. This had clearly gratified the Duke—a big spender with a frugal streak. So today she would step over the threshold of Richmond House not as a hired theatre manager but as a lady; she could mix with these titles and Honourables on equal terms, knowing that she hadn't been paid, and that they would know it too. Derby hadn't mentioned the matter—money was taboo between them—but she guessed he would be pleased.

Over the years she'd got to know some of the Earl's more easygoing friends—Party men like Fox and drinking companions from Brooks's Club—but the ladies were a different matter. When the very word *actress* still carried murky associations, how was someone who earned her living on the stage to shake them off? The thought caused Eliza a prickle of something like shame, which was ridiculous; wasn't she proud of having clawed her way up from her father's strolling troupe to reign as one of the three Queens of Drury Lane? The problem was her colleagues, that whole slipshod line of them stretching back more than a century to Nelly Gwyn.

Take Mrs Robinson, for instance, who rode around town in her own carriage with an invented coat of arms on it these days; when the Prince of Wales had offered an annuity of £500 a year, hadn't she given up the stage as quick as a blink, as if she'd only chosen it in the first place as a vast shop window where she could show off her goods to the bidders? And even more genuine talents, like Mrs Jordan—much as Eliza disliked her rival, she had to grant that the woman knew how to deliver a line—Dora Jordan, too, lived with a man who enjoyed only the courtesy title of *husband*. Actresses, apart from the odd drab wife or spinster—and, of course, the sternly virtuous Mrs Siddons, Queen of Tragedy—all had keepers; it was the done thing.

Eliza's objection wasn't a moral one. She rarely concerned herself with the state of her soul, or anyone else's, but what did matter to her was her dignity. She knew she was widely respected for her character as well as her professional talents; she'd carved herself a place in London society with considerable effort and she didn't mean to lose it.

This winter at last the Richmond House theatricals seemed to present the perfect opportunity for Derby to introduce Eliza to some of his oldest connections, letting her penetrate a closed circle of the well-born and well-bred. Everything depended on whether she could charm the Richmonds and their friends close to; her future might turn on what kind of a welcome she won herself today. Derby would present her to his friends with the most respectful delicacy—but then, *Derby is still a married man.* No, it wasn't shame Eliza felt there, and certainly she had nothing to reproach herself with, but the fact remained. It irritated her stomach like grit in an oyster, half pearled over by the years.

The carriage had stopped; Eliza glanced through the window at the imposing pediment of Richmond House. Derby jumped down and his thin shoes slithered on the icy cobbles. He came round to the other door, which the coachman was already holding open. Below her, Derby looked like a thickset midget, got up in impeccable grey silk. When this young coachman had first entered the Earl's service—replacing his father, whose sight had gone—he'd tried to hand Eliza into and out of the carriage himself, as convention dictated. She'd been amused to watch Derby make it quite clear, without words, that when he was present no one should help Miss Farren except himself. Eliza took the Earl's hand now, exchanging a brief heat through the kid of her glove.

The slush left a little tidemark on the toe of her shoe. 'My dear, you forgot your muff!' Her mother hurried up the steps to hand over the enormous ball of fur. Eliza suppressed her irritation and gave her a gracious smile, practising.

ANNE DAMER, at a second-floor window at the back of the house, was looking across the sloping lawns to the ballustraded terrace and the Thames. She lifted off her huge hat and handed it to the footman; she shook her curls, making a faint cloud. Under the powder, her hair was still chestnut brown, though she was thirty-eight. She didn't know, yet, what part she was to play, but she hoped it would be something to get her teeth into.

The balding Duke of Richmond came in with his wife on his arm. She spun to meet them. 'Let the games begin.'

'Very classical, my dear Anne,' said Richmond.

'And very prompt.' Lady Mary kissed her sister, cheek to powdered cheek.

'I'm the first, then?'

Lady Mary's ivory fan made a sweeping gesture at the empty chairs lined up against the pea-green papered walls.

'I thought perhaps you'd had each of us shown into a different room.' Anne laughed. 'So as to engorge our lines before the rehearsal.'

'Oh, we're only your hosts, we'll leave everything to your manager,' said Richmond.

'It'll be the first time we've ever had an actress in the house,' said Lady Mary with a sidelong smile, 'but really, as I was telling Mother the other day, Miss Farren and Mrs Siddons are the two exceptions to the rule. Their natural delicacy and good connections have somehow kept them out of the mud.'

After almost a decade of watching her from the Richmond box at Drury Lane, Anne thought of the actress as *Farren,* as the newspapers called her; not so much a woman as a muse or a goddess. She and Jordan were called the two Queens of Comedy, but to Anne's mind there was no comparison; Dora Jordan made a good show in broad humour and breeches parts, but she couldn't rival Farren when it came to fine lady roles and the kind of elegant comedy that combined pathos with laughter.

'Yes, Richmond's only job is to admire and pay,' said Lady Mary and the Duke grimaced.

'But what can cost so much,' asked Anne, 'since none of the players is hired?'

The Richmonds rolled their eyes in tandem. 'Your sister has the unworldliness of the true artist,' the Duke told his wife. 'Why, everything costs, my dear Anne; the scenes, the costumes, the musicians, and as for Wyatt's plans for our little theatre itself—you must look over them later, lend us your exquisite eye—why, the decorations alone will run over £500.'

Anne sucked in her upper lip; she could live on that for a season. 'I thought we were to make do with the saloon.'

'The sightlines were impossible,' said Lady Mary.

'There'll be no *making do*,' said Richmond with melancholy
pleasure. 'Whatever it costs to raise a little private temple to the
Muses of Theatre I sacrifice on their altar.'

'The centrepiece will be a Diana that Sir William Hamilton
picked up for us. Do you hear from him often, Anne?' asked her
sister.

That one slid in like a knife in the ribs. 'No.'

'You must visit him again. Such a treasury of antiquarian knowledge and you like a warm climate,' said Lady Mary disconnectedly.

'Not that warm,' lied Anne. For God's sake, it had been two
years since her last visit to Naples; what was the point of these little
hints? Once a proposal had been turned down it should be buried
in oblivion. When a widow had passed thirty-five, shouldn't her
friends give up all attempts to marry her off again?

A footman announced the Earl of Derby, with Miss Farren and
Mrs Farren. Anne spun round. The actress was a tall doll with a
mask for a face. Her hands were untying a ribbon behind her head
as she walked across the room; the fur mask fell. The perfect features were so familiar, but Anne had the strange sensation of never
having seen this woman before; Eliza Farren had such a liquid, pro-
tean beauty that it transformed itself from portrait to portrait, from
role to role. She had to be in her mid-twenties at least, but today
she had the air of a girl as she undid the ribbons that held her kid
gloves above her elbows, shedding her layers for the waiting footman to catch. She was a shining cloud of blonde hair, two cheeks
faintly pink from the warmth of the mask, her body one long serpentine line from the pale fingernails to the furred hem of her
cloak. She smiled and her lips parted like cut glass.

'Derby,' said Anne, recovering herself, and shaking his hand.
Though the papers called him the ugliest peer in England, Anne
usually thought of her friend as the pleasant-faced, curly-haired
little boy of her childhood. But she had to admit that in his early

thirties his small eyes had receded and so had his hair, leaving him with the large waxy face of a broad bean. And today, beside the long-necked Miss Farren, he looked like a Velazquez dwarf.

'May I, might I present to you, Your Grace,' said Derby to his host, too fast, 'and to Your Ladyship, and you, Mrs Damer—since she's been so kind as to lend her professional expertise to our humble efforts in the thespian line—Miss Eliza Farren, Miss Farren, I should say—'

Bows and curtsies all round. *He's blushing,* marvelled Anne. Edward Smith-Stanley had the oldest earldom in England and the unimaginable income of £50,000 a year; he was equally at home in a smoky inn or the House of Lords, checking hooves in a paddock or whipping in votes for the Foxites. And here he was, avoiding the eyes of his old friends. She'd never seen a man so blatantly in love. Anne inclined to think him noble for having spared his runaway Countess, the adulteress, the public punishment divorce, in an era when shocking ruptures and quick remarriages had become so common in the World. The adulterous Lady Derby was now an invalid and one could only wish for her death to release him to his reward. Anne felt sure that his leberal principles would let him rise above all snobbery and marry the actress in the teeth of his ancestors.

'*Enchantée*,' she said, sliding her hand into the younger woman's. Then she remembered and pulled it back. 'Excuse the roughness; I've been modelling clay all morning.'

'A new piece, Mrs Damer?' asked Miss Farren. 'I so admired your spaniels at the Royal Academy.'

'This one is an eagle,' Anne told her, gratified, and the actress's eyes lit up with interest, like candles. Were they green or blue? She didn't look Irish at all, Anne thought; of course, she was English on her mother's side and born here, so she had none of Mrs Jordan's wildness or brogue.

'I wish you luck, Miss Farren,' Lady Mary said with a tilt of her russet eyebrows, when they were sitting down, glasses in hand. 'Trained actors are one thing, but as for ungovernable amateurs...'

Miss Farren murmured something about the enormous honour, and tasted her madeira.

'Entirely ours,' said the Duke, 'as your worshipful spectators.' He was wearing a sheepishly flirtatious smile.

Anne had finally noticed the mother, an odd, limp-jowled creature who sat behind her magnificent daughter like a shadow. She kept her head too low to catch anyone's eye and sipped her weak peach ratafia as if it were medicine.

'I've often seen you at Drury Lane,' Miss Farren assured the Richmonds, 'and been grateful for your patronage.'

'I've always wondered that very thing,' Anne jumped in, rather too loud, 'whether, caught up in the flow of the play, the players are oblivious?'

'It would be hard not to notice an audience so visible and audible,' said Miss Farren, with a hint of laughter.

'They press too near, to my way of thinking,' complained Derby.

'It's true,' said the actress, 'the amateur critics in the pit frequently lean on the edge of the stage to get a closer view, so one has to take care not to tread on their fingers. As for the more distinguished inhabitants of the boxes, I do recognise faces, but I'm often far from sure whether they notice me, since they arrive so late and keep so busy with nods and bows and quizzing glasses that I wonder how they follow the plot at all.'

She's satirising us, Anne thought, *and we're lapping it up. Does she see this as an audition?* Eliza Farren had all the sparkling enunciation of the ladies she played in comedies; she was the real thing. She sat with her closed fan balanced between her index fingers, with never an awkward glance at the Rubens hung behind her or the Titian to her left, as if she'd been brought up in great reception rooms just like this one, instead of…well, squalid inns, Anne supposed with an inward shiver; barns, even.

'Yes, Richmond and I eat so late and entertain such shocking numbers, ever since he's been Master-General of the Ordnance, we rarely get to Drury Lane before the third act,' said Lady Mary with a sigh.

'But I dine at four, on a few plain dishes, to be in the box by five,' Anne admitted, 'since an unfashionable widow can consult her own pleasure.'

The others laughed at her description of herself.

'Luckily,' said Richmond, 'the stage is so clogged with old plays these days, we know the plots by heart. Is your proprietor *ever* going to write you a new part?'

'Ah, Mr Sheridan's a busy man,' said Miss Farren. 'He was our best playwright since Shakespeare, but now—'

'I admit, it's all the fault of us Foxites,' said Derby with a chuckle. 'The theatre engrossed Sherry's talents long enough and now they're required for a higher stage.'

'The Party?' Anne asked.

'The country, I should say.'

A little snort from Richmond. Anne was suddenly reminded that by inviting a Foxite politician like Derby to take part in these theatricals her brother-in-law was making a rather gracious gesture across Party lines.

'But I live in hope,' Miss Farren added, smoothly filling the gap in the conversation. 'Perhaps Sheridan will write me a new role by the time I'm forty.'

At that they all broke out laughing again. Was it the delivery that gave the simple joke such a glittering spin? Anne thought, *This girl will never be forty.*

It had been an uncomfortable moment between Richmond and Derby, though. Anne was only too aware that these men shared a painful history. Derby, Richmond and his nephew Fox, her father Conway, they'd all been idealistic Whigs in the glory days of the Party, protesting against the King's misbegotten war, wearing the 'buff and blue' of the brave Americans. Anne remembered feeling so proud of her eloquent friends and relations, united in the most noble of causes: Reform. To her, the word was a shining banner; it meant reform not just of Parliament—the broadening of the franchise (which currently let only one man in a hundred vote), the freeing of the Commons from bribery and bullying by the Crown—but also the end of all oppressions, such as censorship, poverty and slavery. Then, five years ago, the Whigs had got their moment in the sun, swept into government...and after three months of wrangling, Fox had resigned, taking half their Members with him, and the Party had broken like a china plate.

These days Richmond served in young Pitt's Tory Cabinet, which grieved Anne when she let herself think about it; how could he have discarded his passion for Reform? But it touched her that he held no personal animosity towards the Foxites (well, except for Fox himself). These theatricals were a proof of something she'd always believed: that political differences shouldn't be allowed to strain the delicate fabric of social life.

'Now in a few months, Mrs Damer,' said Miss Farren, her voice deepening as she began to take charge of the little group, 'it's you who'll have to brave the lights as Mrs Lovemore in the Richmond House Theatre.'

Anne's pulse skidded; she drained her wine. 'Is that my role?'

Derby grinned at her. 'Among my whole acquaintance I'd pick no other leading lady.'

So it was to him that she owed it. 'But I'm the least experienced of our number—'

'If it comes to that,' said Richmond, 'I've trod the boards more than any of you, but forty-one is high time to retire gracefully.'

'Besides, it's character that matters,' Derby told her.

'And your face, which promises much,' said Miss Farren with a slowly ripening smile. 'Besides, you're already so celebrated for your sculpture, you can't shrink at the prospect of a little more fame.'

'Oh, I can, I assure you,' said Anne, laughing.

THE EARL OF DERBY and Sir Charles Bunbury were roasting their boots at the Green Hawk in Croydon. After riding all this way to see a promising two-year-old—as prominent members of the Jockey Club, they vied with each other to buy up good stock—they'd found the road cut off by snowdrifts. 'But how can you stand it?' asked Bunbury, thumping his punch glass down on the table.

Derby gave a languid shrug.

'You love the fair damsel. Am I right? I'm right. I know it, even an old sportsman like me.' Approaching fifty, the Baronet still had broad shoulders, a strong mouth and plenty of short wiry hair. He wiped his mouth with the back of his hand. 'Every scandal sheet from Land's End to John o'Groats knows it. How long's it been? Five years?' The caricaturists were cruel to Derby; the latest print on display in a shop window showed him as a swollen toddler on a horse, floundering along behind his carriage in which Miss Farren sat with elegant, averted head, her mother a grim-faced duenna at her side.

Derby allowed his mind to float back. 'I first saw her walk on stage in the role of Lady Teazle in Sherry's *School for Scandal*.'

'I mean when did you and she start—or rather, when did you start *not*—'

To forestall him Derby said, 'I've been on visiting terms since '81.'

'Six years. Gad,' said Bunbury, ladling some more punch into his glass and topping up Derby's with a splash, 'that's a long stretch to waste. A man never knows how long he has left.'

'I wouldn't call it a waste,' objected Derby. 'I see a great deal of the lady; she often dines with me and stays to play whist. She uses my carriage.'

'Sounds much like being married.'

'Except that we never quarrel.'

Bunbury let out a bark of laughter.

That wasn't quite true, Derby reflected. He and the actress never spoke in heat, but there were significant silences. He was still smarting from yesterday's mistake. He knew the unspoken rules—that they were never to be alone without Mrs Farren, nor use first names, and that Eliza wouldn't accept anything from him but fruit sent down from his greenhouses at Knowsley in Lancashire, or an occasional brace of partridges after the annual Foxite shooting party in Norfolk. But in celebration of her successful début at

Richmond House (where it was clear to Derby that everyone had adored her at once), he'd taken the risk of ordering a little basket of hothouse white currants and hiding a string of pearls among their translucent beads. He'd convinced himself that Eliza might let it pass, on this special occasion, if she were amused by the visual joke. Her mother, though often an irksome presence to Derby, never seemed to oppose his cause—he sometimes thought her a mute supporter of it—and might she not clasp the pearls round her daughter's slim neck and hush her protests? But last night, after dinner, Derby had been shaken out of the warm haze of brandy by the return of the untouched basket. He'd realised how fatuous his self-delusion had been when he read the note: *Mrs Farren & Miss Farren are much obliged, but don't find white currants agree with them.*

'So you get nothing from her, you swear?' Bunbury was banging on. 'The famed Farren remains icy—'

'No names, please,' said Derby with a glance through the fug at the other customers: only a handful of farmers and tradesmen sucking their pipes, or playing quoits in the corner, but one never knew.

Bunbury was trying to annoy him. But in the long years of their friendship Derby had learned not to rise to the bait. He flicked some mud off his leather breeches, and reached into his pocket for his snuffbox. He used to be a smoker till it went out of fashion; he found snuff so much handier and more elegant.

'So what does she say when you put it to her—as it were?' Bunbury let out a filthy chuckle. 'What possible argument can she have against a good settlement?'

'I've never asked her.' Derby flicked open the little ivory lid, which bore a memorial painting of his best gamecock and put a pinch on the back of his hand. It was a strong Maltese variety; when he snorted, he felt that delicious burning in the back of his nose and throat.

'I don't quite know how to put this,' said the Baronet, 'but is the *little sword* of the Smith-Stanleys of Derby by any chance rusted in the scabbard?'

Derby felt a pang of nostalgia for the days of his youth when they'd still worn swords with full dress; he could have put his to Bunbury's throat. 'Would you like to say that a trifle louder?' he growled.

'No disrespect intended.' Bunbury took a long swig of punch.

Relenting, Derby put away his snuffbox and told him, 'There are easier ways of meeting that particular need; London's full of amenable females.' He knew he was making it sound as if he had these females driven to his house in Grosvenor Square every night, whereas the truth was he very rarely resorted to that trade. 'As for offering the young lady in question a settlement—I've never found a suitable moment.'

'In six years?'

'She's not like other women; she has remarkable powers of turning the conversation. And of course I've never been alone with her,' said Derby, wondering if he sounded tragic or only pathetic. 'I once hinted that I'd something important to say and she suddenly remembered a rehearsal.'

'Gad, remarkable staying power, that filly! But what you get out of the exchange is harder to see,' said the Baronet.

'Oh, come, man. You know yourself that in the middle years one can take a calmer attitude than when one was a young stallion, galloping around the Continent.'

'You don't need to tell me that,' said Bunbury, frowning down at his old deer-hide breeches, sticky with spilled punch. 'Believe me, I didn't trouble Lady Sarah much that way—but then, we were married! And the cheek of her: when I offered to give the baby girl my name and say no more, she turned me down and ran away with her paramour...No, that divorce was the best £300 I ever spent, even if I had to sell two good stud-horses to pay for it. Not that I meant to marry again,' he added with a snort, 'I just wanted to be done with the business, in spite of Richmond begging me not to cast off his little sister. No, the whole sex is null and void to me these days.' The Baronet held up his glass as if making a toast.

'Cuckolding whores, the lot of them! And blueblood wives are the worst. I've never understood why you went no further than separation from Lady Derby, yourself—'

On that subject we can't agree,' snapped Derby, 'so let's drop it.' Whenever someone dared to mention the Countess in his hearing, he felt his heart contract to a little chip of ice. It would be nine years this summer since he'd had his wife's portrait taken down from over the fireplace, at Knowsley, and put on a bonfire. It had been quite a fine picture—a Reynolds—but there were times when art wasn't worth a farthing.

The punch had loosened Bunbury's tongue. 'Come, Derby, haven't we shared enough days in the saddle to speak man to man? Dorset's a damn rogue; why has no one ever called him out and speared him like an eel?'

Derby didn't comment. Any grudge he'd borne against the seductive Duke of Dorset had worn off years ago. Men would always take what women didn't refuse them; Derby was a man himself, so he knew. No, the unforgivable crime had been the lovely Lady Betty Derby's, for running off with the Duke like some cheap harlot. No discretion, no dignity. For the last nine years Derby had refused to answer her maudlin letters except through his lawyers, refused to see her, even though her lodgings in Marylebone were only five minutes the wrong side of Oxford Street. The Countess's descent into invalidism had caused him a secret gratification. She lived in a sort of social twilight; she'd clung on to much of her acquaintance, especially the old rakes, but Queen Charlotte still barred her from Court and of course she'd lost her children. That generally hit women hard. It was different for men; Derby was perfectly fond of Edward, Charlotte and Elizabeth, and liked to think of them doing well up at Knowsley, but it wouldn't cause him pain not to lay eyes on them for a year at a time.

Bunbury was wagging one finger. 'But what puzzles me is for a fellow like you—still much the fresh side of forty, aren't you?'

'Thirty-four,' Derby conceded.

'Is that all?—to spend so long in thrall, in bondage, damn it, to one member of the female persuasion without the slightest reward for his efforts.'

'I can afford to wait,' said Derby. 'The company of a brilliant and beautiful lady offers other pleasures. There are many forms of *reward*, as you put it.'

'What, you mean she pays you?' asked Bunbury, innocent. 'You're a hired *cicisbeo*, kept on to remind the World of the lady's charms?'

Derby let out a roar of laughter and drained his glass to the sugary dregs. 'I don't think I'm handsome enough to get that job.'

'As a foil, then?' suggested Bunbury.

'That's more like it. *La Belle et la Bête!*'

THE THAMES was high with melt-water and along the fashionable strip of villas at Twickenham gardens were flooding. The ten miles from Mayfair took Anne's carriage less than an hour, since the road had been improved. She drew up outside the wall of Strawberry Hill. The first glimpse through the trees of Horace Walpole's little castle always made her smile: the quatrefoil windows, spires and pinnacles, twin towers and battlements. She'd been coming to stay with her godfather since before she could walk, before she could re-member; Strawberry Hill felt not so much like home as a place of perpetual holiday. 'We're here, Fidelle,' she murmured to the miniature Italian greyhound asleep in her lap.

As the courtyard already held Walpole's carriage and phaeton, Anne got down outside the gate, under the coat of arms and motto from Horace, which she translated in her head: *The skies above the traveller change, but not the traveller.* She brushed down the cloth skirts of her travelling costume. In the courtyard a gilded angel stood in his niche; she looked through the arches into the tiny cloisters, where a blue-and-white bowl sat on a pedestal, inscribed with Mr Gray's poem on the occasion of Walpole's cat Selina drowning in it. Fidelle was the weight of a baby in Anne's arms; she stirred and scrabbled a little.

One of Walpole's footmen opened the door with a bow. The

hall always reduced visitors to silence; it was the most startling space in the building, a sort of set for a Gothic novel. (Well, after all, her cousin had written the first, Anne thought, and had *The Castle of Otranto* ever been bettered in the twenty-year craze?) A single candle glimmered in a japanned lantern and the grey walls were smeared with the coloured light that came through roundels of painted glass. The wooden balustrade was a fretwork of giant flowers and, on the posts, small golden antelopes holding shields seemed to watch Anne as she climbed the steps. In a high niche on her left François I's suit of armour stood sentinel, visor down, spear ready; as a child she'd scared herself with the idea that it came to life at night. Walpole had designed Strawberry Hill to have an immemorial gloom—not melancholy, but the gloomy warmth of cathedrals, *gloomth* as he called it. It was all pretence and *trompe l'oeil*, she knew—wallpaper painted to look like stone, papier mâché shaped like wood—but it still worked its spell on her.

In the armoury, with its pointed arches and cases of scimitars and quivers, Anne almost tripped over some workmen; the place was never free of them. She found Walpole in his favourite room, the library, in a tizzy. Tonton had jumped into the Thames, 'like one of the mad Gadarene swine,' lamented his master, then raced up the meadows through some cow-pats, run all over the house, and finally lain down and rubbed filth into the Louis XIV carpet in the library. 'Why I ever accepted such a trying legacy from my dear Madame du Deffand I cannot recall.' Walpole lay on the sofa like a shrivelled mannequin, watching his housekeeper towel down the fat black spaniel by the fire.

Anne had often wondered the same thing. 'Tonton's done worse, in his youth,' she pointed out. 'That time he bit Richmond's favourite hound—'

A shaft of merriment lit up Walpole's face. 'Ah, that was different, my dear. Every dog has his day of battle. What is their life if not a struggle for ascendancy?'

'Fidelle's isn't,' she said, looking down at the tight coil of silvery grey in her lap.

'That's true, she's a perfect gentlewoman. But how these creatures tyrannise over our hearts! Madame du Deffand used to tell a good story about a lady whose poodle bit a piece out of a gentleman's leg and ate it.'

Anne had heard this one before, but still smiled.

Walpole's face was a mask of anxiety. 'The lady cried, "I do hope it won't make her sick!"'

His delivery was impeccable. Her cousin would have brought the house down at Drury Lane, Anne thought, if his destiny had ever required him to earn a living. He'd been pleasing enough, in his youth, as the portraits on the walls proved, even if by now he was a morsel of a man with a monkey's face, all skin and nose. He wore the limp remains of his own hair, curled into little old-fashioned rolls at the sides, with a queue at the back.

'There,' said the housekeeper, releasing the spaniel.

'But is he quite warm and dry?'

'Quite, sir.' Margaret Young was on her knees mopping up the puddles.

'Come to Papa.' Walpole flung his arms open, but Tonton ran straight out of the door of the library to bark at the workmen. His master sighed like a lover. 'Well, at least there are no droves of visitors today to burst in upon us,' he told Anne. 'Such constant requests for tickets as I've had this winter! My toy castle is not my own. Margaret shows them round, as long as the daylight lasts; I hide in here and take the odd peep down at them through the balusters. Though it must be said that they give her a guinea apiece,' he added, watching the housekeeper carrying off the wet towels. 'She earns far more from the visitors than from me. I've a good mind to marry the woman myself,' he whispered, wriggling upright on his sofa so spasmodically that Anne thought he might dislocate something, 'to get back all the monies I've sacrificed to this silly house.'

Anne looked round at the pierced and pointed arches filled with leather volumes, the oval portraits above them, the fantastical ceiling inset with scenes of Walpole's ancestors fighting the infidels and a repeated heraldic device of a Saracen's head. (He'd always amused Anne by claiming, on no evidence, to be descended from Crusaders.) The library was choice; there were only about 7000 volumes. Out of unrepentant snobbery, he kept all those written by royal or noble authors in a bookcase of their own. Her godfather was a magpie; he collected as easily as breathing. In a locked case in the corner he kept Pope's own copy of Homer, a Second Folio Shakespeare, some obscenities that Anne had never been allowed to look at and two rare works on the marking of swans' bills. The library was full of her own work: an early bust of the young Paris, and the terracotta models of her masks of Thames and Isis for the bridge at Henley, as well as one of Dick Cosway's sketches of her at work.

'Speaking of monies,' she said, 'Richmond's having to spend very high on our theatre.'

'Ah, yes, you never told me who else is involved in *The Way to Keep Him*, apart from Farren's unalterable Earl? Faithful as the east wind, Derby is, like his family motto.'

Anne looked puzzled.

'*Sans changer*, don't you know. You must study your heraldry,' he scolded.

'As well as Derby, we have Dick Edgcumbe—'

'Dear fellow,' cried Walpole, 'but an insect, like myself. You'll have to pad his calves.'

'He plays Sir Brilliant Fashion; tries to force me in Act Four.'

'Politely?'

'Feebly.'

Walpole nodded in approval.

Fidelle shifted in her lap, coming undone like a sash; her tiny pointed paws chopped at the air. Anne released her and she jumped down. 'Major Arabin plays Sir Bashful Constant, who's pretending not to love his own wife, since it's out of fashion; he's a marvellous mimic of Garrick. We—Derby and I—would have loved to invite Fox to take a role, but we knew there was no point.'

Walpole was wearing a lopsided smile. 'My dear, will you never give up your hero-worship? As a Minister in Pitt's Cabinet,

Richmond has to put up with constant harrying from his slovenly rake of a nephew; he shouldn't have to suffer Fox in private too.'

'Oh, come, you're not fair,' protested Anne. 'Slovenly, I'll grant you, but to my mind that's better than those gaudy costumes Fox used to sport in the '70s, with the high heels, velvet frills and blue wigs.'

Walpole snorted reminiscently.

'And he lives a very settled life with Mrs Armistead.'

Walpole pursed his dry lips. 'Since when has devoting oneself to one very shop-soiled courtesan been a domestic virtue?'

'My point is that he's hardly a rake at all these days.'

'Less of a puddle still muddies one's boots. I'd imagine Fox has no time for private theatricals, anyway.' Walpole yawned. 'Probably too busy giving his creditors the slip!'

Anne decided to change the subject. Fidelle was sniffing at Tonton's traces on the carpet. 'Come on to my lap,' Anne called. She didn't need to make a gesture; the dog leapt up her skirts.

'What a clever creature,' remarked Walpole. 'Italian grey-hounds aren't noted for their intelligence, but Fidelle understands English perfectly.'

'Well, she knows *lap*, at least, and *dinner*.' Anne rubbed the narrow head with her thumb and cupped the pointed jaw.

'The two essentials of a dog's life. Now, whom have we on the distaff side of the Richmond House cast?'

'Mrs Hobart—'

'Fat as ever?' asked Walpole.

'Fatter. She keeps advising Miss Farren to eat more whey, the cheek of her! Oh, and she's got her own faro table these days, so she can fleece her friends without going out in the cold.'

'Back in the knife drawer, Miss Sharp,' cried Walpole with a shiver of enjoyment.

Anne grinned at him. 'Then there's Mrs Blouse and a Mrs Bruce—'

'Who's that?'

'You don't know her.'

'I know everyone,' he said reprovingly.

'A cousin of Lady Mary's,' Anne told him, 'from Wales.'

'Oh, well. *Wales.*'

'And I forgot Sir Harry Englefield.'

'Many do,' said Walpole regretfully. 'I believe he's taken up astronomy.'

'Has he really? Where did you hear that?'

He extended one swollen-knuckled finger towards his mahogany bureau. 'I write twenty letters a day, or dictate them to Kirgate; I spin my web from Boston to St Petersburg.'

'Very well, I bow to your authority,' said Anne.

He shifted to move his right foot higher on its cushion.

'Have you the gout very badly today?' she asked.

'Of course not, my dear; the gout has me. Now let's drink some tea'—reaching for his silver bell. 'The Way to Keep Him's a hackneyed thing, don't you find?'

'Oh, I don't know,' said Anne, who'd sat up late last night rereading it with a rapid pulse. 'Isn't Mrs Lovemore a rather splendid creature, the way she falls into melancholy and rage, and then refashions herself to win back her husband's love?'

Walpole shrugged. 'How many plays do we need about the *longueurs* of marriage? The point is proven, surely! Oh, my dear, I'm as weak as small beer today'—with a yawn that split his face.

THE SPRING Season was in full flow, now, and the tiny diamond that was Mayfair (tucked between Hyde Park, Oxford Street, Bond Street and Piccadilly) was criss-crossed every night with carriages lit up like fireflies, taking their occupants to routs, drums and assemblies, ridottos of 10,000 or musical evenings for a dozen. There were alfresco breakfasts (everyone still in their furs) and calls to pay from afternoon into evening. The World watched a balloon ascent in Hyde Park, and kept an eye out for the sumptuously dressed Prince of Wales and his pink-cheeked Mrs Fitzherbert dashing by in an open phaeton with a pair of bays. Mayfair residents roamed outside their preserve only for certain purposes: the gentlemen to debates at the Lords or Commons in Westminster Palace, or to gamble at their clubs on St James's, perhaps to buy a hat at Lock's, or wine at Berry's; the ladies to shop on the Strand or admire the crocuses at Kew. And, of course, everyone drove east to attend the Opera House and the two patent theatres of Covent Garden and Drury Lane.

Every few days, now, the Richmond House Players (as they affected to call themselves) made their way south-east, on horseback, in sedan-chairs or carriages, from their Mayfair homes to the great house in Whitehall. Already they were experiencing that united delusion, that derangement of the senses known as theatre. On waking, or during the tedious hours it took for them to be dressed for dinner, they muttered their lines, sketched their gestures on the air. They'd never worked so hard in their lives, or felt so necessary.

Today they were to rehearse in Richmond's library, where all the furniture was white and gold. Eliza found Mrs Damer standing at the window, looking remarkably handsome for nearly forty. Everything about the sculptor was pointed—a long chin and aristocratic nose, sharp cheekbones, precisely etched eyelids—which should have been off-putting, but wasn't; her vitality warmed and softened all her lines. Eliza looked past her, to the Privy Garden's constant traffic of Members of Parliament, clerks, messenger boys and lovers. 'A sort of stage on which all London struts and frets its hour.'

Mrs Damer spun round, her brown eyes lively. 'Exactly. All so busy—and so aware of being looked at—'

'But restless, as if they might forget their lines at any moment.' Eliza stared past the Banqueting House to where she could pick out the clean white spire of St Martin-in-the-Fields. A gentleman, Derby had once remarked, was a man with no visible means of support. In her mind's eye a little fellow deftly walked the high-wire between two spires, tiptoeing across the abyss as if to fall was inconceivable because he had invisible means of support: angels, perhaps, holding up his hands and feet. Eliza sometimes felt like that herself these days. Yesterday, for instance, when the Duke had mentioned how lucky they were to have secured the aid of *a lady of such genius,* Eliza had felt the thin wire vibrate under her foot and wondered what tiny, unseen fingers were bearing her up.

'Are you lost in admiration of the Medici Faun?'

Eliza's head turned. 'Oh. Indeed,' she lied. That must be the statue standing in the window.

'The one that moves me is the Apollo Belvedere,' said Mrs Damer, reaching out to touch the shoulder of a handsome curly-haired god shown from the waist up, gazing to one side.

'What a quantity of lovely antiquities your brother-in-law has collected,' said Eliza, looking around the library.

Only the tiny pause told her that she'd made a faux pas. 'Yes,' said Mrs Damer breezily, 'it was back in the days of his sculpture academy that Richmond commissioned these copies for students to work from.'

'Oh, was that when you took up your art?' asked Eliza, a little hot-faced, but she didn't think it showed. Well, how could she have known? Richmond was certainly rich enough to buy a dozen old statues.

'No, I was only a child at the time,' said Mrs Damer, 'this was back in the late '50s. The students were rather wild and, if the casts were plaster, they'd break off the fingers and toes, just for devilment.'

Eliza produced one of her tinkling laughs.

'That's why Richmond had to invest in marble copies. But when I took up carving myself, after I was widowed, I did find them very useful to study. That's from the *David,* of course,' Mrs Damer murmured, pointing to a large, graceful foot.

Eliza thought it looked odd, standing there on a plinth as if it had been ripped from a giant's corpse, but she nodded respectfully.

Here came Derby at last, hurrying into the library but without any unseemly scramble. That was the aristocratic walk that her colleague Jack Palmer caught so well when he was playing lords: a swan's glide. Today Derby was elegant in blue silk. 'My apologies,' he murmured and Eliza let him kiss her hand, but her cheeks flamed up a little again, because really he should have gone to Mrs Damer first, then to Mrs Bruce and so on down, distributing his *politesse* according to rank. She knew how to be with Derby in public and how to be with him in private (with her mother for a chaperone), but these rehearsals at Richmond House were something peculiarly in between.

When he began his scene as Lovemore, the yawning rakish husband, Eliza stiffened a little, as usual, but actually he was remarkably good. Of course, Derby had a fine-toned voice and plenty of spirit, but what surprised her was that he took so naturally to the role of a callous husband. (She herself had never known him as anything but quietly, relentlessly gallant.) His looks gave an extra twist to the role, Eliza thought; it was quite sinister that this ugly little man should be so indifferent to a wife as tall and handsome as Mrs Damer.

At the moment when Mrs Hobart bustled into the room, Derby was being *ennuyé* in an armchair. 'Ah, at last,' he said, breaking off his speech to rise.

'What can you mean, *at last*?' asked Mrs Hobart, emerging from her vast wrappings. 'The streets are a morass of brown slush; I thought we'd never get through Piccadilly. Besides, it's very à la mode to be late, Derby, didn't you know?'

Anne kissed the older woman on the cheek. She thought, *No one past forty should wear rouge before dusk.* She hadn't seen so much of Albinia Hobart since three summers ago, when they'd both campaigned on the hustings but on opposite sides. It had been a riotous and shrill spring, and Anne had almost wanted a vote herself, for the sheer pleasure of casting it in Fox's favour. She remembered one night at the Opera House, when Mrs Hobart and Lady Salisbury in their boxes had roared out *Damn Fox,* and Anne and the Duchess of Devonshire had shouted back *Damn Pitt.*

Her involvement had caused some painful family discussions that she preferred not to remember. Mercifully, her father had retired from Parliament years ago, but Richmond, as a Cabinet Minister in Pitt's new government, had scolded his sister-in-law as if she were a child, for shaming him by campaigning for the Foxite Opposition. It was true that she and her friends had gone rather too far; the papers had rebuked them for their *immodest and Amazonian behaviour*, and caricatures had shown them carrying Fox piggyback; the *Morning Post* had even spread an absurd rumour that Georgiana (as everyone called the Duchess of Devonshire) was sprouting a beard. It had been a secret relief to Anne when the election had ended and they'd all remembered their manners.

'Shall we get on with Scene Four?' asked Miss Farren musically.

Mrs Bruce and Mrs Blouse scuttled back to their places. Dick Edgcumbe assumed the foppish pose of Sir Brilliant Fashion, one finger in his waistcoat, the other hand at his ear. Anne flicked through her bundle of sewn foolscap to find her place. It had taken her a week to get used to having only her cues, business and lines written out, without the rest of the play.

'Besides, I knew I wouldn't be needed yet,' said Mrs Hobart in a tone of faint injury, 'as the Widow Bellmour doesn't come in till late.'

'Count yourself lucky you don't have as many lines as I to learn,' remarked Anne, fanning herself with her thick script.

Mrs Hobart gave her a hard smile and Anne regretted the quip.

'The widow's such a witty character, though,' put in Miss Farren soothingly. 'I've often played her myself at Drury Lane.'

'Yes, and really the story's as much about her as Mrs Lovemore,' Mrs Hobart remarked, brightening, 'since she's the one Lovemore's courting in disguise.'

Sir Harry Englefield clapped his hands to his powdered curls. 'I've toiled over my part, in preparation for this *répétition*, but half the time I take my cue for my speech and my speech for my cue.'

'It'll get easier,' the actress told him. 'And after all, you've only the one part, so you can't confuse it with any other.'

'Yes,' Anne put in, 'we should pity Miss Farren and her fellows, who must permanently store dozens of roles in their heads, to be performed at a day's notice on the proprietor's whim.'

Mrs Bruce let out a cry of horror.

'Mm, it's quite a bedlam scene in my dressing room,' said Miss Farren, 'with myself, Mrs Siddons and Mrs Hopkins all standing around muttering our different lines.'

'Oh, do you share with Siddons?' asked Sir Harry, star-struck.

'Such a commodious brain you must have, in such a pretty little head,' offered Major Arabin.

Miss Farren smiled back at him, but Anne, watching, thought she detected a steeliness. *She's like me, his hackneyed flattery sets her teeth on edge.* 'Shall we get on?'

Sir Brilliant made his lewd proposition. Anne turned on her heel. '*Sir! This liberty, sir*—'

She stopped, because their manager was holding up one slim finger. 'Let me teach you all a helpful rule: never speak as you walk. It dissipates the force of the line.' Miss Farren looked at Dick Edgcumbe severely. '*Sir!*' She swivelled and took three paces, then turned her head back. '*This liberty, sir*—' She stopped, as if overcome, and averted her gaze again.

They all clapped, which seemed to embarrass her somehow. Strange, Anne thought, since Miss Farren had spent so much of her life with the roar of applause in her ears.

'Oh, tush,' the actress protested. 'Some of you must remember how the late great Garrick would have delivered a line like that, with at least a dozen exquisite changes of emotion.'

'I always found the fellow rather twitchy,' said Major Arabin.

'Yes, for my money I prefer young Mr Kemble,' Mrs Hobart declared.

'So much more declamatory grandeur,' murmured Mrs Bruce.

'What about his faddish pronunciations of Shakespeare—not *my heart aches,* but *it aitches*?' said Dick Edgcumbe.

'But such a daring approach when he takes over a role,' said Sir Harry. 'Remember his Hamlet two years ago, when instead of "*Did you not* speak *to it?*" he said to Horatio, "*Did* you *not speak to it?*"'

'Oh, but his sister Siddons is twice as original,' argued Anne. 'Wasn't she the first Lady Macbeth to put her candle down and wring her hands?'

'For my money,' said Derby, 'there's too much long-faced pomposity at Drury Lane these days and Tragedy is elbowing Comedy into a corner. You're of the good old Garrick school, aren't you, Miss Farren?—you and Palmer, Tom King, the Bannisters. Quickness and delicacy, that's the key.'

Miss Farren clapped sternly, her mouth hiding a smile. 'Gentlemen! Ladies! Are we here to argue about theatre or to create it?'

The actress's mother was in the corner as usual, head down over her workbag. It was odd, Anne had thought at first, to have what looked like a fierce old housemaid planted on one of Mr Chippendale's yellow grosgrain chairs. But soon the Players paid Mrs Farren no more attention than if she'd been a fire screen or a hatstand, which seemed to be what she preferred.

AFTER EACH rehearsal Eliza felt relief whenever Derby's carriage dropped the Farrens off at their respectable but unfashionable second-floor lodgings on Great Queen Street, just round the corner from Drury Lane. She was always tired out. She'd come this far by pleasing, but still she couldn't risk failing to please. She knew it was absurd to complain of the strain, given that her whole life since coming to London at fifteen had been aimed like an arrow at the ranks of the Beau Monde. 'They're strange beings, though, carriage folk,' she told her mother over a dish of ragout. *Carriage folk* was what her father used to call them, in caustic homage: people who had their own carriages.

'But you're one of them, Betsy, or as near as makes no matter.'

Eliza shook her head. 'I only borrow Lord Derby's carriage, I don't own it, and you and I still ride in hackneys on occasion. Besides, I'll never be *one of them* if you keep saddling me with *Betsy*.'

'Eliza,' Mrs Farren corrected herself. 'I do try, really; I never call you the old name in company at least.'

'Thank heaven for that! *Betsy Farren* sounds like the kind of jolly hoyden Mrs Jordan might play, who pops into breeches for Act Three to play a trick on her lover; I don't know how I bore it so long.'

'I rather favour what we christened you: Elizabeth; you can't go wrong with a good old saint's name.'

Eliza's mouth set; she thought she'd won this skirmish years ago. 'Eliza's vastly more elegant. Your chin, Mother—'

Mrs Farren snatched up her napkin to wipe away a trace of ragout.

Eliza did feel slightly guilty for her impatience with her mother. After all, should she—as a public figure—not be considered a sort of business, a joint enterprise in which Mrs Margaret Farren, no less than her eldest daughter, had sunk all her energies and resources? Hadn't the woman invested in Eliza's rise all the pragmatic cunning gained in a long hard career as an untalented actress in a barnstorming troupe and wife to its drunkard manager—and now this new business was so flourishing, wasn't she even to be consulted about the name under which it traded? The two partners might disagree on small points, but they had a common goal: the fame and lasting fortune of Miss Farren of Drury Lane.

'Don't you like 'em, then, the titles and Honourables at Richmond House?' asked her mother, mopping her plate with a crust.

Eliza hesitated. 'The Richmonds are very kind and Mrs Damer's delightfully enthusiastic; she's the only one who's learned most of her lines. But all in all...I don't know, Mother, it's like a tasty dish that's hard on the stomach.'

'Ah.' Mrs Farren nodded in sympathy.

'And how tiring! These *soi-disant* Players know nothing, they can't tell Prompt Side from Opposite Side and Sir Harry's mispronounced the opening line of the play a dozen times now. They've never done a day's work in their lives—well, except for Mrs Damer, I think she's learned discipline from her sculpting. But the fact remains I can't click my fingers or lose my temper with them as if they were apprentices at Drury Lane; I have to hint and request and *if it wouldn't be too much trouble, sir and madam, might I suggest*? And Mrs Hobart's always asking for "a brief respite", and then Dick Edgcumbe suggests she might feel the better for "some restorative cordial", meaning port all round at two in the afternoon!'

'They're charming people, though,' said Mrs Farren with a foolish smile. 'How they dress and deport themselves, and how they converse...'

'And how they drink and gluttonise, and gamble their fortunes away,' added Eliza, grinning despite herself. 'But seriously, I admit all the charms of the well-born. Isn't it odd, though, with what relish they take the lowest roles?'

'That's right,' said her mother. 'Who'd have thought that stiff Mrs Bruce could stoop to play a saucy maid like Muslin?'

'She adores it! Whereas I've always played higher than myself at Drury Lane and even now I dread making an uncouth gesture or a slip of the tongue. Do you remember that cruel critic who said my laugh *still smacked of the barnyard*?'

'Oh, my sweet, that must be seven years back, now,' protested her mother.

'I remember, I practised in the parlour,' said Eliza, 'laughing as musically as I could.'

'Until I begged you to stop, in case the neighbours thought we had a madwoman locked up in the house!'

Eliza let out a small sigh. 'I don't dislike the Richmond House Players, but I'm not at ease among them. Being their manager is the hardest part I've ever taken on and I'm not getting a shilling for it.'

'Ah, but it's sure to pay off in the long run,' said her mother with a wink that screwed up half her face.

Eliza wished she wouldn't do that; it was like something out of a burletta or pantomime. 'You mean that with these new connections I'm on the brink of entering the World?'

'I mean, my dear child, that you're on the brink of becoming the next Countess of Derby!'

'Mother,' said Eliza, 'you mean to annoy me.'

'I don't—'

'We've agreed, haven't we, that such speculations are both pointless and tasteless as long as the person in question has a wife still living?'

Mrs Farren's mouth was sulky. 'She's said to be in very poor health. I see a lot, during rehearsals, over my sewing; his Lordship's showing you off to his old friends and they couldn't be more enchanted.'

Eliza got to her feet.

'Oh, won't you take some more ragout? Or a custard? Some nuts, to finish? You'll need your strength tonight for your Ben. You never seem to keep any fat on,' fretted her mother.

'I'm perfectly well,' said Eliza, giving her an exasperated half-smile.

DERBY HAD been obliged to spend the afternoon in his study on Lord-Lieutenant of Lancashire business; although the position would really only become important if Britain were at war, he made a point of answering all correspondence by return of post. Above his Queen Anne desk in heavily carved mahogany a marble life mask of his grandfather looked down. An only child, left mother-less at seven, Derby had been raised by and among sporting men. His father had been a bad-tempered fellow who'd married a for-tune—hence the adding of his wife's name *Smith* to *Stanley*—and died of apoplexy in his fifties without ever succeeding to the Derby title. The boy's grandfather, the eleventh Earl, had combined in one plain but aristocratic face all the serene strengths of manhood, until his death at the great age of eighty-seven. Every milestone in Derby's youth—Preston Grammar School, Eton, Cambridge, election to Commons and marriage at twenty-two—had earned his grandfather's nod and the strangest thing about inheriting the title, at twenty-three, was that the old man had not been there to approve.

The traffic was like treacle; it seemed half the evening was gone when Derby's carriage finally crawled up Drury Lane, but it was only half past seven. Under the scented wax, he could still smell singed hair from the Parisian coiffeur's tongs; how ironic that wear-ing one's natural hair took so much more work than wigs used to do. He shifted his left shoulder a little in his tight brown frock coat;

it got harder to breathe in these things every year. Clothes might be simpler these days than they used to be—which suited an ugly man better—but they were so much tighter that once a fellow was in full evening wear, he was good for nothing but conversation. If Derby tried to climb a hill in these sleek breeches, for instance, he'd geld himself.

Glancing out of the window on to Drury Lane, his attention was caught by a crudely painted message: DAMN THE DUKE OF RICHMOND. Such wall scrawling was becoming rather common, now that more of the lower orders could read and write—but Derby'd had no idea the patron of their private theatricals was so widely hated. Of course, the Foxite newspapers had been stirring things up against Cabinet Ministers recently, he remembered with a twinge of guilt—pointing out to their readers, for instance, that Charles II had granted the first Duke of Richmond a perpetual duty on New-castle coal, which meant that every time they bought a hod the tax went straight into the Master-General of the Ordnance's personal purse. Still, that was a fact—not the kind of low abuse of Fox and Sheridan with which Pitt's hacks filled the government-funded papers.

The carriage turned into Russell Street, where the sight of the tall, slim theatre always lifted his spirits; it had been remodelled by Mr Adam, who'd done such a marvellous job on Derby House. For the past six years, ever since he'd met Eliza Farren, Derby had sub-scribed to the same box, no. 3. Tonight, when he walked down the corridor to the little partition door—his footman rushing to hold it open, with the Earl's greatcoat, gloves, hat and cane under one arm—Derby's eyes took a moment to adjust to the dazzle of hun-dreds of candles from the chandeliers that hung low over the audi-torium. This was probably the brightest space in London. The house was almost full tonight; at least 1800 heads, he estimated. He looked up to the lower gallery, where tradesmen and out-of-towners sat peeling oranges or reading a printed sheet of the story of the play—though Derby couldn't imagine how they could be ig-norant of such a famous plot as Sheridan's *School for Scandal*. Near the ceiling, in the upper gallery, sat the real troublemakers, in his view—labourers and servants, who thought paying their shilling entitled them to shout out for music or repetition of speeches at any point.

Fox popped his bushy head into the box. 'How's England's pre-eminent sportsman?'

'Sit down, man. You're looking well.' Derby meant healthy rather than handsome. Fox had a face like a mountain, jowls flowing into his collar, with an absurd dimpled chin. Wings of hair hung out of his wide-topped black hat and his eyebrows were like furze bushes. As he fell into a chair, his old-fashioned long waistcoat gaped where a button had popped and his shirt gave off a whiff of sweat. Derby saw his friend for a moment as if for the first time. *And here,* he marvelled, *is our Party's leader, the Champion of the People, chief mentor to the Prince of Wales; this grubby fellow is the great liberal thinker of our age and future saviour of our country...* A surge of fondness went through him. In the long years of committee meetings and frustrating campaigns, as the Foxites chafed out their time on the Opposition benches while George III and his pet minister Pitt ruled on implacably, nothing had shaken Derby's loyalty to this man—and it seemed unlikely that anything ever would.

'How's the lovely Mrs A.?'

'In the pink,' Fox assured him with a grin. 'It was hard to tear myself away from the rural delights of St Anne's Hill for dear Miss Farren's Benefit Night, but as a former thespian herself, dear Liz quite understood.'

'I must pay you another visit when the weather warms up.'

'Do, do! The house may be poky but somehow we can always cram in enough beds for our friends. Our crocuses are up in the beech wood and daffodils too.'

'So you've been gardening?'

'Yes and reading Ariosto,' said Fox, 'and looking into the origins of Whiggery; I've started drafting an account of the reign of James II and the Glorious Revolution.'

'Splendid; I've always thought you a scholar manqué.'

'Really'—he sighed—'I couldn't ask more of life than fine weather and the company of a lady I love more and more every year.'

Derby was pricked by envy. After his own marriage had broken apart he'd had the good fortune to meet Liz Armistead. She'd already withdrawn from the stage to be the most expensive courtesan in London, but she was worth every guinea; she had a good heart that her new profession had done nothing to coarsen. Derby had set her up in a villa in Hampstead and insisted she learn to ride, which she grumbled about at the time but was glad of later. At the end of the summer Mrs A. had moved on to another keeper, with no sore feelings on either side.

It was when she'd taken up with Fox that she'd retired from being a courtesan; they were a love match (well, he'd never had the funds for it to be any other way). For years, now, she'd looked after the great man with a passionate fidelity that few wives could match and his friends were all grateful to her. Derby sometimes found himself wishing the impossible, that he could introduce Liz Armistead to Eliza Farren as a living proof that to give in to the pleasures of the flesh was not to become disgusting. But ladies never met Mrs A.; she was a gentleman's woman, having been passed between princes and lords and Honourables for so long like a cup of good cheer.

'I see the afterpiece is about ballooning,' said Fox, glancing up from the playbill. 'D'you recall, a few years ago, when they were all the rage? I wagered you I'd fuck a woman in a balloon 1000 feet above the earth.'

'I never forget a bet,' said Derby with a grin. 'Two guineas to 500, I believe. Why, have you done it?' he asked, pretending to beckon to his footman for his pocketbook. 'Simply produce your witness.'

'Ha ha!' Fox's drooping hazel eyes were as warm as a dog's. 'I don't think m'dear Liz would be on for it nowadays; it's a bit draughty in the clouds, don't you know.'

Derby savoured a brief, discreet memory of Mrs A.'s warm thighs. A knock at the door. 'That'll be Mrs Damer,' said Derby, and Fox jumped up and tried to straighten his waistcoat.

One thing Derby liked about Anne Damer was that there was never any awkward consciousness of sex between them; he wasn't constantly reminded that she was a woman. Not that she was some old dowdy; she dressed well and Derby had a bias towards slimness, even if curves were more fashionable nowadays. Mrs Damer was looking very tall and handsome tonight, with her aristocratic nose and her dark hair powdered white to match the voluminous fichu that filled the neck of her bodice.

'Lo, the Muse of Sculpture.' Fox kissed her hand three times.

She smiled at him. 'How *very* good to see you.' Mrs Damer was devoted to Fox, Derby knew; her feelings seemed rather like the Magdalene's for Christ, if that wasn't too blasphemous a comparison. If she'd had the luck to be born as a son to Field Marshal Conway instead of a daughter, it occurred to Derby now, she might very well have ended up an MP in the Foxite camp. The thought was slightly disconcerting.

'We've seen nothing of either of you since Christmas,' Fox was complaining to his friends, 'and Georgiana's *vewy cwoss* about it.'

Derby was never quite sure whether Fox, like many of the Duchess of Devonshire's intimates, had picked up her baby talk, or was gently parodying her.

'Miss Farren's working us like mules at Richmond House,' Derby explained.

'Oo, yes, I can't wait to see *The Way to Keep Him*. Might I spy on a rehearsal?'

'You might not,' said Derby.

'The presence of the Champion of the People would throw us off entirely,' Mrs Damer told Fox with a hint of mockery. 'Now, you must report to Georgiana that I'm wearing this wide red sash she gave me. I never need to waste my time reading fashion magazines, I just follow the Devonshire party line.'

'Yes, she's a marvellous whip when it comes to style, no less than politics.' Fox laughed.

The prompter's bell rang three times and the orchestra struck up; Fox rushed off to the Devonshire box. A moment later Horace Walpole let himself in the door, tall but stooped in an old-fashioned black silk coat with skirts down to his knees. He always tiptoed, as if afraid of a wet floor, Derby thought.

'Coz, I feared you were laid low with gout in your toe again,' said Mrs Damer, kissing his cheek.

'Not a bit of it,' said Walpole, struggling with a chair. The footman glided forward to move it for him. 'I was paying calls on my friends in the other boxes.'

'Heavens, that could have gone on all night,' remarked Derby.

'Well, indeed, I'm rich in that respect,' Walpole murmured as he settled his narrow frame on the chair, 'but I tore myself away, for fear I'd lose dear Miss Farren's opening lines.'

'She'll be so grateful for your support,' Derby told him. He knew the two cousins would be sure to send the actress at least 5 guineas each and the house was sprinkled with the other Richmond House Players who'd received his reminder notes. Subtracting house expenses of, say, £140, Eliza might hope to clear £400 from tonight's Ben. Absurd, the devices Derby had to use to help the woman he loved earn what he considered a meagre living.

Now there was a stir in the house. Out came Bannister the Younger to speak the prologue, with its satire of a tea-sipping gossip slavering over the morning papers.

A School for Scandal! tell me, I beseech you,
Needs there a school this modish art to teach you?

At last the green baize curtain twitched and began to rise. Behind the arch, flats showed Lady Sneerwell's dressing room. The oil lamps in the wings, lighting up the actors, couldn't compete with the glare of hot light on the audience's faces.

Lady Sneerwell was a snide, indiscreet version of Viscountess

Melbourne, Derby remembered, and Snake the creeping journalist was thought to be Sheridan's caricature of himself. The funniest role—written for, and based on, Jack Palmer—was that of Joseph Surface, the wicked brother who wore a mask of piety. The tall, bow-legged fellow's winking asides to the audience made Derby weep with laughter. Tom King was making quite a good job of Sir Peter Teazle, the cross old husband whose bride had thrown off her innocent country ways and turned worldly within months of the wedding. King was once known as the Monarch of Comedy, Derby remembered, but these days his forces were rather faded; being manager of Drury Lane under Sheridan's rule seemed to be wearing him out.

Eliza came on at the top of Act Two, in a stylish blue redingote with big red buttons, and to Derby it seemed as if the whole audience sat up a little straighter. He joined in the cheer. '*Authority!*' she repeated pertly to her husband.

> *No, to be sure:—if you wanted authority over me, you should have adopted me, and not married me: I am sure you were old enough.*

Derby let out an enormous laugh and Eliza glanced up at him with a flick of the eyelashes that made his heart thump.

Lady Teazle, with her flower-filled rooms and new hats, her quick repartee and giddy goodwill, was really the most charming of the woman-of-fashion roles that were Eliza Farren's forte. (No wonder Georgiana had been flattered when Sheridan had based the role on her.) Derby could easily imagine being Sir Peter, who tried to hide how much he doted on his bride: '*With what a charming air she contradicts everything I say!*' He realised he was falling into a fantasy of being married to Eliza; he shook himself. If he didn't pay attention he'd miss the best jokes. '*She has a charming fresh colour,*' remarked Mrs Candour. '*Yes,*' replied Lady Teazle, letting the pause stretch, making the crowd wait for it...'*when it is fresh put on!*'

Between the second and third acts there was an entr'acte, with a comic dance; Derby had his footman fetch some bowls of lemon ice. 'There's no one like Miss Farren,' said Mrs Damer. 'How she sparkles and glints, and mints every line anew! Isn't it strange, though, how different one feels about someone's performance when one knows her, even a little?'

Walpole was considering her with a slight squint. 'You mean you enjoy it more?'

'Not quite,' she said, wrinkling her high forehead. 'The pleasure's no longer unmixed with anxiety.'

'But she's never given a bad performance,' Derby couldn't help saying.

Walpole looked him in the eye with a sort of compassion. Everyone in this hot, crammed building knew Derby's position; sometimes he felt his heart was being sliced open for public exhibition under the white lights.

In Act Three came one of Derby's favourite scenes, in which the Teazles behaved very sweetly to each other, and then fell into a quarrel about who had begun their previous quarrel and ended by demanding a divorce. But some of the sharpest dialogue was spoiled by the yowl of a fellow in the pit, when one of the chandeliers spilt hot wax into his collar. Had Derby a less famous face, he would sometimes have liked to go incognito and sit on a bench in the pit, as Sir Harry Englefield was boasting of doing the other day. That way he'd be able to catch his beloved's every subtle intonation and expression.

'Isn't the volume of chit-chat shocking?' said Mrs Damer, in the interval.

'Mm,' Walpole agreed, 'poor King's quite drowned out at times.'

'My friend Bunbury once quipped', said Derby, 'that he preferred the theatre to the opera, because there they sing so loud that one can't hear oneself talk.'

The cousins laughed. Below, there was a surge of bodies into the auditorium, which meant that the unsold tickets had been knocked down for half price. 'Now, you youngsters won't remember this,' said Walpole, 'but back in '63 Garrick tried to abolish half-price tickets;

he thought it was an insult to the play to come in for the last two acts only. Well, my dears, the crowd ran amok. Tore up the benches, ripped the fronts off our boxes, smashed the harpsichord...'

'What an appalling scene,' said Mrs Damer, her eyes shining.

'Sheridan always says never trust an audience,' Derby put in. 'They'll clap politely for nine years and then riot like lunatics in the tenth.'

When the curtain rose again Derby enjoyed the picture auction, but really he was waiting in taut anticipation for the famous screen scene. Thrown into a panic by the arrival of her husband at Joseph Surface's house, Lady Teazle couldn't bear to be found in a tête-à-tête, so she hid behind a screen in the library. *I'm ruined,*' she stage-whispered. *I'm quite undone!*'

Joseph's bluff brother, convinced there was some minx of a milliner hidden in the library, toppled the screen—and there stood Lady Teazle, exposed to her husband and the world. At this moment the audience, though they knew just what was coming, always let out a howl of shocked delight. It wasn't simply the fun of seeing a married lady shamed by discovery, Derby realised now; it was about the ripping of all veils, the exposure of all forms of sleight and craft. Eliza stood frozen into a statue, like Job's wife, pinned rigid by the crowd's mocking gaze.

Walpole was whispering in his ear. 'Fanny Abington used to play it for laughs. She'd wring her hands and clutch at her skirts.'

Derby shook his head. That was the difference between talent and genius. Out of the corner of his eye he saw that Mrs Damer was motionless, gripping the edge of the box.

At the end of the comedy, while Eliza was taking her bows and the crowd roared and whistled, she looked up at the Derby box and gave the three of them a smiling nod.

'Derby, you must be—' Mrs Damer broke off. 'I'm sure we all feel so proud of her.'

Walpole sighed pleasurably. 'The man's a rascal, but he can write.'

'Such rudeness!' Mrs Damer threatened to smack Walpole's knuckles with her folded fan.

Derby grinned; he would have liked to explain that his friendship with Sheridan was an unsentimental one and that he'd heard him called much worse than *rascal*.

Mrs Damer was consulting the smeared print of her programme. 'The crowds are still pushing in for the ballooning piece.'

Walpole trembled to his feet. 'While I'd very much like to experience aerial locomotion before I die, I've no wish to watch it mimed on stage and it's near midnight. Fairies, let's away.'

Derby's footman went ahead to clear them a passage through the packed corridors.

LADY MARY was all blithe humour and never meddled with the preparations for the theatricals at Richmond House, Eliza noticed, but she never let them put her out either. One night, when the dining room was full of props and scenery, she went down to the steward's room quietly and ate her supper there. Eliza was studying the Duchess's serene self-containment; there was a trick Lady Mary had, of smiling beatifically as she said something critical, which Eliza was memorising to use on stage.

Mrs Damer couldn't have been more different from her sister. Well, they had different fathers, after all; Anne Damer was said to take after hers, the veteran soldier and politician Field Marshal Conway. She could be tactful, but also startlingly frank. The sculptor struck Eliza as a natural for tragedy, with her tireless vitality, her bony hands and long diamond-cut face. Unfortunately, *The Way to Keep Him* was a comedy.

'Say the line for me, would you, Miss Farren?' asked Mrs Damer.

Eliza hadn't got enough sleep after her Ben and her head was aching. There were still all the comic servant scenes to run throug^h Sir Harry and Mrs Bruce hadn't spoken a line yet today. She down at Mrs Lovemore's imaginary tea table, in the corner c pink saloon, and began with a careless shrug. *'This trash of tea! I don't know why I drink so much of it. Heigho!'* Major Arabin clapped; Eliza ignored him.

'Oh, I see,' said Mrs Damer. 'I never knew quite how to do the *Heigho.'*

Behind them, Dick Edgcumbe failed to suppress a yawn; Mrs Hobart was lecturing Mrs Blouse on hairstyles in a whisper.

'Lighter, simpler, that's what you must remember,' said Eliza. 'From the top—'

This time Mrs Damer began merrily enough with the tea line, but then sank into lugubriousness on *'Surely never was an unhappy woman treated with such cruel indifference.'*

'The audience must pity you, but don't give way to self-pity,' Eliza told her, 'and for sorrow, by the way, one touches the right hand to one's heart, not the left.'

Mrs Damer switched hands, frowning in concentration. *'I care not what they say. I am tired of the World, and the World may be tired of me, if it will.'* Her tone was guarded, almost bitter.

Eliza nodded. When this woman got it right, she could act the rest of the Richmond House Players off the stage. 'Now let's try your transformation scene.'

The others leafed through their parts, but Mrs Damer simply closed her eyes for a moment to summon up the lines, then took up position down front. *'Adieu to melancholy, and welcome pleasure, wit and gaiety,'* she pronounced, sardonic. She marched from side to side of the saloon, singing *'La, la, la'.* The effect was oddly intimidating.

Eliza took a breath. 'Might I ask you to stroll rather more slowly and more flirtatiously?'

'With whom should I flirt?'

'With no one in particular; with the air. And you could seem more gay.'

'But Mrs Lovemore's not really gay,' said Mrs Damer, confused.

'Of course not, but we assume that, being an intelligent woman, she does a good job of acting it.'

Mrs Damer hesitated. 'I don't know that intelligence is enough. I'm sure she tries, but with her heart so full of rage and shame—'

'Shame?' asked Eliza. She realised that the background gossip had stopped; the other Players were watching, like a silent chorus.

'Yes,' said Mrs Damer, 'mortification that she must pose as a shallow lady of the town to win back the love of Mr Lovemore, who doesn't deserve her! That she must contradict her true sensibility, act a mad pantomime, all for a man who'll never be content, never think she's amusing enough, easy enough—'

'But we know he does love her by the end of the comedy,' objected Derby.

Mrs Damer shrugged. 'I don't believe it.'

'But that's what happens, my dear Mrs D.,' chipped in Major Arabin, 'and your *douces charmes* offer motive enough!'

Mrs Damer had two red spots on her cheekbones. 'I know that's what Mr Murphy wrote, but it rings false to me. How could a sensitive woman ever be happy with a husband like that?'

Several of the Players were looking at Eliza as if they expected her to intervene, but she didn't understand. At Drury Lane it was never like this, there wasn't enough time in the day. The very idea of arguing over whether a play was true or false to the human heart!

Derby broke the strained silence. 'That's enough toing and froing over this scene, surely,' he said. 'Should we have another go at the business in Act Three?'

Mrs Hobart sidled up to Mrs Damer. 'If something's amiss, if you're unhappy with your part, I could be prevailed upon—for your sake—to exchange it with the Widow Bellmour's—'

'Nonsense,' said Eliza, too sharply, 'Mrs Damer plays our heroine very well. Nothing's wrong. Is there?'

Mrs Damer put her hand over her mouth. Then she said, 'Do please be good enough to excuse me' and ran from the room.

Eliza's heart was thudding. What kind of manager was she, t make her leading actress flee the scene? She put her hand agai her mouth, instinctively learning Mrs Damer's gesture: the pre on her upper lip, the hot breath on her fingers. 'Well,' she said in as light a voice as she could manage, 'she must have remembered another engagement.'

'Remembered her past, you mean,' said Mrs Hobart with dark relish, flopping down in a pink-and-gilt chair.

In the silence Eliza felt a hammer knocking against her temples. She looked over at her mother, whose needle was motionless in the air.

'You could have had no idea, of course, Miss Farren,' said Derby, pulling up a chair for Eliza, 'as it was all over before you came to town.' His small eyes were dark with apology.

'What was?' she asked, too shrill. 'I know Mrs Damer's husband died young—'

Mrs Hobart let out a snort. 'They were unhappy from the start. It'd seemed a good match at the time—'

'Well, yes,' contributed Mrs Blouse, 'since she was the Countess of Ailesbury's daughter, and John Damer had £30,000 a year and the Earl of Dorchester for a father.'

Sir Harry Englefield shook his head. 'He was a wild young buck, though. After the first few years they lived apart.'

'Like in our play!' said Mrs Blouse with a squeal of insight. 'Poor Mrs D. couldn't seem to win his love back, no matter what she did.'

'I'm not sure it was ever a question of love in the first place,' put in Dick Edgcumbe.

'Or that she tried very hard to win him back,' added Mrs Hobart with a sniff.

Eliza's cheeks were scalding. What a disaster. How had she got herself tangled up in the secrets of these people? They were a little School for Scandal of their own. What did they think of her peculiar relation to Lord Derby; did they consider her a flirt with her eye on a countess's coronet? What did they say about her as soon as she went home?

'The fact of the matter is,' Derby told Eliza grimly, 'that the fellow got into such deep debt, together with his brothers, that the

Damers were going to have to flee to France—but instead he shot himself in a tavern.'

'No!' Eliza looked round at the lit faces; they seemed to her like pedigree hawks. She was reminded once again of how long they'd all known each other and how little she knew them.

'It was the Bedford Arms in Covent Garden,' put in Major Arabin. 'But oh, dear, now you'll shudder whenever you have to pass it, a woman of sensibility like yourself.' He laid a sympathetic paw on her shoulder.

'People were most unkind to Mrs Damer afterwards,' murmured Mrs Hobart. 'Really, it was quite extraordinary, the things that were said!'

'No need to repeat them,' said Derby.

'I've no intention of doing so,' she snapped.

Eliza had managed to edge away from Major Arabin's hand. 'So you see, in today's rehearsal,' murmured Mrs Bruce in her ear, 'to oblige our friend to explain her feelings on the subject of a cold-hearted husband and a shamed wife...well, you couldn't have known, of course.'

Eliza bit her lip hard.

'Don't distress yourself, my dear,' said Derby.

She stiffened at the phrase and averted her head. He knew he was never to use endearments in public.

'Might this be a suitable interval for tea?' The Duchess of Richmond stood in the door of the saloon, blithe as always.

They all shot up. Had she heard them talking about her sister? If she had you wouldn't know it. The members of the World had such self-mastery, Eliza thought. But then, so had she, once she'd got over her mortification. 'Perfectly suitable, your Ladyship,' she carolled, leading the group to the door.

SNOW WAS beginning to fall that afternoon, as if the mildness of March had shrunk backwards into winter. The Derby coach turned on to Grosvenor Square, the largest and most impressive of the three squares in Mayfair. It was more like a parade ground than a place to live, Eliza always thought, but it was popular; she'd once heard Derby mention that more than half its residents were titled. The oval park was thick with trees; the iron railings had a fresh coat of black paint, she noticed, and the statue of George I as a Roman emperor had been regilded.

'Are you sure it's wise to follow Mrs Damer?' Mrs Farren was clutching her workbag. 'His Lordship himself said it was none of your fault, the little upset.'

'You go on home, Mother, I won't be long,' said Eliza instead of answering.

'Well. If you're sure. I suppose it gives you an excuse to pay a call and get on visiting terms,' she added, brightening.

Eliza suppressed her irritation. Everything was policy for Margaret Farren; every step was an inch further up the ladder.

As they passed the irregular roof line of the north side she rapped on the ceiling, but the driver didn't rein in till fifty yards on, where the imposing arches and half-columns of Derby House stood out from the terrace.

'It was no. 8 I wanted,' she said, as he opened the door and unfurled a large canvas umbrella.

'No. 8?' He repeated it as if it were a vastly inferior address. 'Ah, Mrs Damer's. Very good, madam.'

It nettled Eliza, somehow, to have him guess the name of the person she was visiting, but on the other hand what use was a coachman who didn't know where everybody lived? 'It's all right,' said Eliza, stepping down, 'I'll walk from here.'

'M'Lord wouldn't like that, not in this weather,' said the coachman, so she sighed and climbed back in. He cracked the whip and turned the horses round; this was the only square where there was enough room for such a manoeuvre without tangling the traces. They were a splendid pair of bays, highly trained as well as handsome, she could tell that much; Derby always had the best carriage horses money and sense could buy.

'Could you please bring my mother home to Great Queen Street?'

'Certainly, madam. And I'll be back here whenever you need me,' he said indulgently.

Mrs Farren stuck her head out of the window as Eliza got down. 'Shall I wait dinner?'

'No, no.'

'I'll keep something warm at least,' she cried as the carriage pulled away. The coat of arms, with the motto in Gothic lettering, *Sans changer*, had already grown a faint mould of snow.

Eliza's stomach was tight with tension as she rapped on the door of no. 8, a narrow four-storey house in red brick with stone facings and a patterned fanlight. A black footman ushered her into the reception room and took her wraps, which were sprinkled with wet flakes. It was all much smaller than Derby House, of course— just two rooms deep. The furniture was mostly satinwood, with slim legs and an airy, modern feel, and there were shiny brass knobs on all the doors. Eliza noted a marble chimney piece and curtains of striped linen on the tall windows; she relished the crisp feel of the stuff between finger and thumb. 'Excuse me, madam.' Eliza spun round to see a flat-faced woman who had to be the house-keeper. 'Mrs Damer is in her workshop and can't leave off; would you care to come through?'

Eliza felt oddly honoured. She followed the housekeeper through the wainscoted dining room, which was fitted with Turkey carpet and had the inevitable flattering portrait of Charles James Fox in oils. Eliza was very fond of Fox, whom she'd met even before she'd known Derby, but she couldn't share in the general Whig adulation of their leader. Though he was a marvellous speaker, wasn't his Party still languishing in opposition? Eliza couldn't help but pick up bits and scraps of political information from Derby, but it struck her as being as peculiar and closed a world as his horse rac-ing or cockfighting.

Without a word the housekeeper opened a door to show a close-stool and Eliza went in to use it; she actually preferred close-stools to the new water closets at Derby House, with their cold marble seats and unpredictable flushes.

Out she went into the small wet yard and the workshop beyond. It was as plain and crude as any shed, but it glowed with
warmth from a stove. Anne Damer stood beside a large angry bird
in damp clay. Eliza barely recognised her: gone were the curls, the
elegant rings, the sweeping muslin skirts of an hour ago. It was a
working woman who looked up, with filthy cuffs, a muddy apron
with pockets full of dangerous-looking tools and her head swathed
in a sort of bag. There was a smear of something white on the
bridge of the long nose. 'Miss Farren! You'll excuse my not shaking
hands, won't you, as I'm all over clay?'

Eliza's prepared words were forgotten. The workship, the
clothes, were wrong for an exquisitely tactful speech meant to be
delivered in a pale-blue reception room over Meissen teacups. 'Oh,
Mrs Damer,' she said, walking up to her, 'it's you who must excuse
me for distressing you so at our rehearsal. I had no idea—so stupidly ill-informed—'

The sharp face wore a curious expression.

'At Drury Lane we're accustomed to making a glib show of
every human emotion,' Eliza babbled. 'When I think of the number of times I've played an unhappy wife—'

The sculptor had taken Eliza's hands between her own. 'Calm
yourself, my dear girl. You've done no harm.'

Eliza held on to them as if she were drowning. They were such
lean, powerful hands; that must come from the sculpting. 'But you
ran from the room—'

Mrs Damer smiled awkwardly. 'It was a shocking demonstra-
tion, wasn't it, in front of my fellow Players?'

'Not at all, they know your situation. They're old friends.'

'Well, Derby is; the rest are acquaintances, really.'

Eliza persisted. 'They must think me a tactless and ignorant
stranger who broke in upon your most painful memories.'

'Hardly a stranger,' said Mrs Damer, smiling. She looked down.
'I've muddied you with my dreadful paws.'

'It doesn't matter.'

The sculptor spread her bony fingers in front of her. 'Even when they're clean, how they age me! Chicken claws, Mr Damer used to call them.'

'Did he?' asked Eliza, a little fierce. 'They may not be smooth, or plump, but they're most expressive.'

'Oh, excuse me while I moisten my osprey.' Mrs Damer stepped over to the clay model and dabbed it with a sponge from a bucket. 'My work's been so interrupted by our rehearsals—not that I'm complaining.'

Eliza recognised a change of subject. 'I've never seen a statue of a bird before,' she said, walking round it.

'Oh, hardly a statue yet,' the sculptor answered ruefully. 'It's a fishing eagle I'm modelling in terracotta for my cousin Walpole, to go with his ancient Roman one. Terracotta's not as noble as marble, of course, but he dotes on the stuff. It has a quickness and verisimilitude about it that's hard to match in stone.'

Eliza drew closer, inhaling the cool earthiness of the clay. 'Do you always work with your fingers?'

'And with anything that comes to hand. Knives, spoons, gouges and wires...This, for instance,' said Mrs Damer, holding up what looked like a thin embroidery hook. 'I filched from my mother.'

'Lady Ailesbury's famed for her needlework, isn't she?' Eliza was fumbling for details.

Mrs Damer made a little face. 'Pictures in worsted. She enjoys it vastly. But our work has little in common; my mother makes copies of Van Dycks and Rubenses, while I try to create an original image which will live longer than the creature that inspired it. *Actum ne agas,* as Terence puts it.'

Eliza nodded as if she'd caught the allusion and looked the bird in its roughly formed eye. 'You must have studied an eagle close to.'

Mrs Damer stood beside her, arms crossed. 'It was before Christmas, at my friend Lady Melbourne's seat in Hertfordshire. The gamekeeper was a fool; almost cut the magnificent creature's wing off as he netted it and pulled it down.'

'Was it in pain, then?'

'Yes, but I don't want to focus on its helplessness,' Mrs Damer told her, a line of concentration appearing between her eyebrows. 'What I'm trying to capture is rage, I suppose. Or outrage.'

'It's not a bit like your carvings of women, which are so very smooth and Grecian,' said Eliza. She felt the need to prove her knowledge of Mrs Damer's work.

'Ah, yes, I aim for the true ancient style when I sculpt the human face, a beauty that will stand for all time. But animals'— Mrs Damer smiled at the rough clay bird as if it were a pet of hers—'they seem to demand a more everyday look. When I model my dog Fidelle, for instance—Fidelle? Where've you gone?—I often find her curled up like a hedgehog; Italian greyhounds are great nesters, especially the bitches.' She walked through the workshop and pulled aside some sacking. 'Aha! Fidelle, come out and make your obeisance to the Queen of Comedy.' The miniature dog streaked out and ran in circles, chasing her own tail, barking shrilly. 'She's just nervous of strangers.'

'What a little beauty,' said Eliza, watching the loop of smooth silvery flesh and hoping it wouldn't attack her shoes.

'What dogs have you, Miss Farren?'

'None.'

The brown eyes went wide. 'Are your cats afraid of them?'

'I've no cats either, I must confess.'

'Aren't you fond of the brute creation, then?'

Eliza decided to be frank. 'I can appreciate their beauty—in a case like your darling Fidelle's,' she said, aiming her sweetest smile at the dog who was now on two legs, scraping at Eliza's skirts and whimpering. 'But I confess I'm perfectly indifferent to them as beings.'

'Stop that,' scolded Mrs Damer, scooping the greyhound up in her arms and rubbing its head.

'I imagine pet keeping is a taste one must acquire in childhood.'

'You surprise me; I'd always assumed it came naturally.'

Perhaps you've never known anyone who didn't grow up with lap dogs, thought Eliza sardonically. 'No, I won't even have a canary in my dressing room at Drury Lane. Lord Derby despairs of this lack of sensibility, he says I have a very hard heart.'

Mrs Damer gave her a peculiar smile.

Why had she brought that up? Eliza wondered. Of course, Derby had other good reasons for thinking her cold; didn't the nastier papers call her an *icy prude*? She turned towards the clay eagle, now, to hide her face. 'This bird has nothing in common with a tiny greyhound; you must have a great talent for entering into their different natures.'

Mrs Damer smiled at the compliment. 'The ancients would have shown the osprey at his noble best, of course—wings spread, eyes on the horizon.' She spoke as if her visitor only needed reminding. 'But this one is captured, with a smashed wing. I want to seize him in the moment—to make the moment of his fury last for ever. I've shaped his beak very hooked, see? I've taken for my inspiration Giambologna's marvellous turkey-cock in the Grand Duke's Uffizi Gallery—like a shaken bag of feathers—you must know it.'

Eliza nodded vaguely, not wanting to admit that she'd never been any further from England than a visit to her father's relatives in Cork. An odd pause came between them and Eliza couldn't think how to fill it. Mrs Damer picked up a large damp cloth and draped it over the bird. Eliza wondered whether she should take her leave.

'Have a seat, Miss Farren,' said the sculptor, pulling a shabby chair away from the wall and dusting it off. 'I'll be perfectly frank with you, as if I've known you ten years instead of a few weeks. Shall I?'

Eliza had a slightly giddy sensation, as if she was high on a ladder. 'Please do,' she said, sitting down.

'I fled the rehearsal today because I was in danger of laughter.'

'Laughter?' It came out almost as a squeak.

'Yes,' said Mrs Damer, her mouth twisted. 'I wasn't *sad* when I was talking about unworthy husbands and how little good it does to waste all one's womanly wiles on them, but caught up in angry memories. Then, when I saw the ring of concerned faces around me, all thinking I was grieving for John Damer, I felt bubbling up in my throat a sort of dreadful giggle.'

'Oh.' Eliza felt very naïve.

'That's why I had to clap my hand over my mouth and make a run for it,' Mrs Damer told her. 'Though people think me eccentric already, they'd be far more shocked if I were to burst out laughing at the memory of my *dear departed*. Even to admit I had the impulse sounds shocking, though we're in private here and you've such a sympathetic eye. You aren't shocked?'—and Mrs Damer glanced sideways at her guest.

'No.' The dog had tucked herself between Eliza's hip pad and the edge of the chair; she wasn't so much of a nuisance when she'd quietened down. Eliza added, more as a statement than a question, 'You don't miss him, then.'

'Not for a moment,' said Mrs Damer and went on picking some dried mud off her sculpting hook.

Eliza felt oddly comfortable in the workshop, despite the draughts and dirt. She put one hand on Fidelle's warm neck. 'Tell me more, if you don't mind? Your parents made the match?'

'Well, yes, but that's only to be expected among people of birth. You, Miss Farren, for instance, would be so much freer to pick and choose.' A pause. 'You're not offended by the observation?'

'No, no,' said Eliza. She never forgot her low origins, of course, but these days it was rare for anyone to remind her of them so baldly.

'Your life is your own, that's all I mean. Whether and whom to marry is no one's decision but yours.'

Eliza felt doubtful on this point. 'I consult my mother on all important points. And it sometimes seems to me as if I have two thousand parents.'

'Your audience.'

Mrs Damer was quick, thought Eliza. 'Two thousand fathers, mothers, brothers, sisters...'

'Lovers.'

'Well, suitors, perhaps,' said Eliza. 'All interested in my actions, all concerned about my reputation, all waiting to see what I'll do next.'

'I never thought of it that way,' said Mrs Damer. 'I suppose we do make a claim on you, when we sit there in our boxes night after night, raising our spyglasses...But at least you have intelligence and experience, to chart your own course,' she added, suddenly sweeping the leftover scraps of clay into a bucket and turning a winch to lower the work table the eagle stood on. 'At eighteen I had neither. Perhaps I'd read too much Rousseau; I was more interested in tenderness and sensibility than in per cent per annum. And, unfortunately, whereas my elder sister got Richmond, with all his sterling qualities, the boy my mother chose for me proved a dunderhead, a wastrel and a philistine.'

Eliza pressed her fingers against her smiling mouth. What outrageous words to describe a dead husband.

'In Florence,' Mrs Damer groaned, 'we visited the Uffizi with one of John's brothers. I was enraptured by the statues, I felt as if I'd been lifted to Olympus to consort with the gods. But the East Gallery is so vastly long, John and his brother decided they were weary of art, and laid 50 guineas on the result of a hopping race. They nearly toppled a fourth-century Venus Pudica,' she said through her teeth. 'I couldn't tell what I saw after that—the art was hidden in a mist of shame for me—because all I could hear was the crash, crash, crash of two earl's sons pounding like gigantic one-legged hares down the gallery.'

Eliza released a giggle. 'Who won?'

'I didn't look.'

'The winner must have boasted. The loser must have cried foul.'

'Oh, I'm sure, but it's one of many details I've managed to forget. I was married for the best part of ten years, Miss Farren, but my memories probably amount to three months. It's rather terrible', she added, 'to wish away one's prime years.'

'But they weren't.'

'Well, the twenties—aren't they meant to be one's best? But

you're right,' she said with a smile. 'I think perhaps these are my prime years, now, past thirty-five!'

Just then a maid came in to say that Mrs Moll was ready to serve the tea. 'I should go,' said Eliza, glancing at the window, where a crust of snow had built up. She tried to collect her skirts without disturbing the dog, but Fidelle exploded off the chair and ran into a corner. 'You've been very kind.'

'Have you another engagement, or are you needed at Drury Lane?'

'Well, no, but—'

'Then you must stay for a dish of tea. Tell Mrs Moll we'll have it in the library,' said Mrs Damer to the maid. 'I'll join you, my dear, as soon as I've made myself respectable'—pulling off her makeshift turban as she spoke and releasing a shock of unpowdered brown curls—'and we can wait out this snowstorm together.'

'OH, THIS is so much better,' said Mrs Damer, moving round the circular ante-room in the Earl's opulent mansion on Grosvenor Square. 'Aren't we favoured, Derby, to have our own private rehearsal with Miss Farren? Is your dear mother not to join us today?' she asked, turning to the actress.

Eliza gave her a slightly wry smile, seeing through the pretence. 'I left her at Great Queen Street overseeing a thorough spring-cleaning. Let's begin with the scene of the Lovemores meeting by accident at Lady Constant's,' she suggested.

Derby leapt into action. When his wife asked him for the second time that day to come home for dinner, he turned his face away sharply and sneered, *'The question is entertaining, but as it was settled this morning, I think it has lost the graces of novelty.'*

What pleasure he took in such refined spite, thought Eliza. She was seeing a face of the Earl's that she'd never glimpsed before. Did Derby have a secret envy of the rogues and rakes he knew from Brooks's Club, who never wasted an hour thinking of an unattainable beauty, but broke hearts every month and laughed into their brandy glasses?

She was enjoying this rehearsal *à trois* far more than the big ones at Richmond House. Next they tried the dinner scene, in which Mrs Lovemore talked so earnestly that her husband fell asleep in his chair. 'No, no injured looks, not yet,' Eliza instructed Mrs Damer, 'don't throw away the joke.'

'But wouldn't Mrs Lovemore feel hurt to have her husband snoozing over the soup?'

'In real life, yes,' said Eliza, 'but it's more painful and funnier if she doesn't notice yet. At the very end of the scene you turn to him—freeze at the sight—he lets out a gentle snore'—Eliza clicked her fingers and Derby snored—'and you pull yourself up and roar, *"Unfeeling man!"*'

The other two burst out laughing.

'But mightn't Mrs Lovemore seem obtuse?' asked Mrs Damer.

'No, no, just wrapped up in her own woes,' Derby put in. 'That's the very meat of a marriage gone bad, I suppose: the two of them might as well be speaking different languages.'

Eliza blinked and looked away. Given his situation, she thought it tasteless of him to speechify about marital breakdown.

'Derby,' Mrs Damer asked when the ladies were putting on their cloaks at the end of the morning, 'I wonder will you be at the Commons on Tuesday for Sheridan's first sally against Hastings?'

'Mm, d'you need a ticket? I'd be delighted to escort you, if you can be up before seven,' he told her.

'How kind, that's exactly what I was hoping—and I never rise after six, I'll have you know! Miss Farren?'

Eliza looked up from buttoning her satin glove, startled. 'I wasn't planning to go; I get enough of Sheridan at Drury Lane.'

'Oh, but if Hastings of the East India Company is impeached for his bribe taking and warmongering, by means of Foxite eloquence,' said Mrs Damer, 'it'll be a wonderful blow against corruption in high places.'

'I must confess I've little head for politics,' said Eliza.

'That's right,' joked Derby, 'when I rabbit on about by-elections and Third Readings and divisions, her eyes fog over.'

'Miss Farren,' said Mrs Damer as the ladies came down the steps of Derby House, 'this won't do.'

Eliza half laughed at the grave tone.

Mrs Damer put her hand on Eliza's elbow. 'You may think I've no right to say this, but...no one with intelligence and a feeling heart can remain aloof from politics today. Least of all a woman, since our sex is too often confined to ignorance and triviality. Why, my dear, the stakes haven't been as high in a century! Is Britain to languish on under the corrupt and stagnant rule of Old George and his puppet Pitt, or will our Foxite friends seize their chance and drag the country—the Empire—into an era of liberal modernity?' Her eyes were shiny with enthusiasm.

Eliza, at a loss, found herself saying, 'Perhaps I will come with you to the Hastings impeachment, then, if I may.'

'Splendid. By the way, on a sillier matter,' said Mrs Damer, leafing through the papers in her leather pocketbook, 'my sister came across this in last week's *Chronicle*. Did you ever see such tosh?'

Eliza read the limp cutting.

> Some say a certain hippophile Earl must be at least half in love with Mrs D-r, to play his part so well at the R-ch—d House Theatre. If she can bring cold Marble to life, perhaps she can win his heart from her Thespian Rival, Miss F——n.

'Oh, they'll never leave off their inventing, will they?' said Eliza, aiming for as light a tone as Mrs Damer's.

'Sometimes I suspect they throw all our names into a bowl—'

'—pluck out two or three, and compose a fiction accordingly!'

From the Derby carriage Eliza waved goodbye. *Mrs Damer wanted to be the one to show it to me*, she was thinking. *It was her way of saying I've nothing to fear from her.*

IN THEORY, ladies were banned from St Stephen's Chapel, where the Commons sat, as too distracting a presence, but the doorkeepers of the End Gallery turned a blind eye as long as they got a few shillings from each visitor. Today the building was packed like a barrel of cod by eleven in the morning. The Members were squeezed on to their green benches and into the Side Galleries that were supported on slim white pillars, and the End Gallery was thick with visitors a good hour before Richard Brinsley Sheridan was scheduled to speak on the barbarous treatment of the Begums of Oudh (a phrase everyone in the World had by now learned to pronounce).

'I've never seen the House like this,' Mrs Damer marvelled to Eliza. 'Usually there's not a soul in here till two in the afternoon, and less than 200 out of the 558 Members show up at all.'

'I haven't been here in years. How carelessly they're dressed, considering they're running the country,' murmured Eliza. Most of the MPs were in the standard gentleman's uniform of dark coat and breeches with white shirt and stockings, but she saw riding coats, boots, the odd wide-crowned black hat or old-fashioned tricorne, and some of them had even brought in their young sons.

'Speaker Cornwall looks awake, for once,' remarked Derby, pointing out a man in an enormous wig, hat and cloak. 'He's a shocking dozer; he always has a pot of porter on the arm of the Chair.'

The Chair was more like a pulpit, Eliza thought. The many-branched chandeliers overhead blazed with wax candles; already it was uncomfortably hot and the air whirred with the sound of ladies fanning themselves. The building was ridiculously small, it couldn't be more than sixty feet long. 'I'd refuse to act in a theatre as cramped to this,' she remarked and Derby laughed.

'Excuse me, ladies,' said a Norfolk accent behind them, 'but might I beg favour of you to remove your hats? Only that I've ridden through the night to see this show, but the headgear this year is so ridiculous high—'

Derby bristled, but Eliza put her gloved hand on his arm. Mrs Damer had already lifted off her hat; it sat in her lap like a wedding cake. 'We beg your pardon, sir,' said Eliza.

'No, no, I beg yours'—and the stranger sank back on to his bench.

Even bareheaded, she and Mrs Damer towered above the Earl sitting between them. 'We couldn't have you defending our honour in such a scrum,' Eliza whispered in his ear.

Derby's lower lip twitched in amusement. 'Oh, here's the PM, as cool as ever.'

William Pitt sat down on the front government bench, his long ungainly legs crossed before him like kindling, his pointed chin as hairless as a boy's.

'Hard to believe he's been running the country for three years and he's still only twenty-seven,' murmured Mrs Damer resentfully. 'Has any nation ever been tyrannised over by one so young?'

It would have been comical, thought Eliza, if Pitt hadn't been such a very serious character. 'How old-fashioned he dresses,' she murmured, 'embroidered silks and lace ruffles!'

'Oh, but that's Court dress; he'll have been with His Majesty at St James's this morning.'

Was it impossible for Eliza to spend more than five minutes in Mrs Damer's company without exhibiting her ignorance?

Now the young widow was bowing to friends at the other end of the Gallery: Lady Melbourne (vastly pregnant), the Devonshire House set, the Richmonds. Eliza felt a prickle of embarrassment. It was a fact that she and Mrs Damer were becoming friends—somehow, despite the disparities between them—so why did Eliza feel such a fraud, sitting here by her side?

'Why is it that you almost never speak in the Lords, Derby?' Mrs Damer was asking. 'You're proving such a splendid Lovemore—'

'Oh, it's easy among friends, when the lines are in my hand,' he said ruefully. 'No, my job is to canvass for Foxite votes behind the scenes. Quiet influence, civil manners, a word in the right ear at the right moment, that's the thing.'

Eliza smiled, wondering if this was something Derby regretted slightly.

'I suppose, considering the eloquence of Fox and Sheridan and Burke, our Party hardly needs another orator,' said Mrs Damer. 'The vast majority of Members and peers are as mute as slugs,' she told Eliza. 'They come—if they bother to come at all—to vote as their leaders, or the King, or whim directs them.'

It sounded to Eliza as if the two Houses were much like the two patent theatres: a handful of stirring speakers and a sea of listeners.

'Do you ever wish you'd been a second son,' Mrs Damer asked Derby, 'so you could have sat in the Commons instead of the Lords?'

'Oh, this is a more exciting arena,' he admitted with a smile. 'In the Upper House we only tinker and polish. Fox lives in dread of his nephew dying young, which would foist a barony on him and bump him upstairs! But you know, we peers have an immense influence; the Commons is full of our sons and brothers and chosen candidates,' he said, encompassing the benches with a wave of his finger. 'A good half of these seats are under patronage.'

'Owned, you mean,' said Mrs Damer sternly. 'I do hope Reform will do away with many of the pocket boroughs.'

'Well, yes, of course, that's a laudable aim,' he said rather defensively. 'But till that time, I can assure you I put in two good men in Lancashire.'

Interesting, thought Eliza, *she seems even more of a Whig in her principles than Derby is.*

A stir in the House; Sheridan had risen to his feet. Derby craned to one side to see past the ranks of visitors. Elegant in a brown jacket, Sheridan looked strong in the shoulders; he pushed his notes aside and didn't give them another glance. Beside him sat Fox, and that brilliant boy Windham, and Burke, the thin, sadmouthed sage of the Whig cause in his tiny spectacles. Funny, Eliza thought, how two Dublin nobodies like Burke and Sheridan had come to such prominence in a Party of English aristocrats. Personally, she'd always found it best to downplay her Hibernian connections, especially since her father had lived up to the joke by dying of drink.

The speech began, and Eliza soon had to admit that it was gripping. Sheridan surveyed the twenty-two high crimes and misdemeanours with which Warren Hastings was charged as former Governor-General of India, then he focused on the most serious.

The Begums of Oudh were the venerable princesses of a noble
family of Indian Muslims whose treasures had been seized by
Hastings on the false pretext that the ladies had been fomenting
rebellion. As Sheridan warmed to his theme, he shaped the mass of
petty details into a grand drama. His eyes were brilliant; they transformed his face, so you barely noticed that patch of itchy red on his
nose and cheeks that the government papers called his *mark of Cain*
and attributed to brandy. He spoke fluently, Eliza observed, never
rushing, never forgetting to face the Speaker; every figure and date
came as if it had been burnt on to his memory. His voice was lulling
and smooth—no trace of a brogue—but his words were fiery.

She had to grant him this: Sheridan might be an appalling proprietor of Drury Lane—the stack of new plays he left unread was
known as the Funeral Pile and it was clear he was really only in it
for the cash nowadays, to fund his elections—but he was a master-
ful politician. And something else, which she respected rather more:
a self-made gentleman. He'd started out in life no higher than
Eliza—his father an Irish actor like hers—and look at him now.
Without benefit of title, wealth, foreign travel or distinguished connections, he'd crafted himself into a man of the World. He moved,
dressed, rode and spoke better than his titled colleagues (well, she
supposed he had to); he'd even fought two duels over his beautiful
wife. And recently he'd yoked his fortune to the highest star, by
joining Fox in playing mentor and bottle friend to the Prince of
Wales—though Eliza sometimes wondered how they could bear
the whims of such a petulant young lord.

Some ladies to her right let out faint moans and Eliza paid attention to the speech again. Sheridan was describing the violation
of the sanctity of the Zenana, where the Begums had lived in female seclusion. Hastings's men, he revealed, had kidnapped and
tortured the family's loyal eunuchs to reveal the whereabouts of
the treasure. Really, the thing was like some fantastical Oriental
burletta; Eliza was on the verge of a giggle when she caught Mrs
Damer's eye and straightened her face.

'The attack on the Begums stands for a whole shameful history of corruption,' said Sheridan. 'It exemplifies all that is rotten at the heart of the British Empire.'

'Strong meat,' murmured Mrs Damer.

'Are the people of far-flung lands to be herded and trampled like beasts to fill the pockets of idle nabobs?' he demanded, glancing up at the corner of the End Gallery where a knot of flashily dressed East India Company men sat, scowling over their canes. 'Man', he declaimed, 'was never meant to be the property of man.'

Mrs Damer seized Eliza's hand. 'That's one in the eye for the slavers!'

As the afternoon wore on, the audience stirred and shifted, and some pushed their way out—Eliza was in a slightly desperate condition herself and wishing she hadn't drunk coffee this morning—but the crowd never lessened. Derby's footman shuffled along the row with a hamper of bread and cold meat for him and the ladies. 'Gad,' Eliza whispered, 'it's nearly six o'clock. The fellow has stamina. I'll never call him a layabout again.'

'And in all this time he's never once lost his memory, nor his temper,' marvelled Derby. 'Sherry's the best speaker we have.'

Finally, standing tall and very still, Sheridan urged the House to impeach Hastings as a way of ensuring such barbarities would never be committed in King George III's name again. 'Would not the omnipotence of Britain be demonstrated to the wonder of nations, by stretching its mighty arm across the deep'—here his arm shot out to its full reach—'and saving, by its fiat, millions from destruction?'

And Eliza, tired and uncomfortable, caught the fervour; she could almost see it, justice gliding across the surface of the earth like a dazzling white hand, transforming all it touched. Sheridan fell into his seat and mopped his face with a handkerchief. Burke crushed him in his arms; Fox ran over to kiss him and Windham patted his thigh. The House erupted like a firework display. Cheers rang out, howls and frantic applause. Men were on their feet, tears streaming down their faces; women flapped their fans like the wings of desperate birds. Down in the chamber the stiff-legged

Members surged on to the floor. Anne Damer's eyes were glittering with tears. Derby was shouting in Eliza's ear, 'I've never seen anything like it.'

No, it was gone now; she felt flat again.

Pitt was consulting with Dundas; he stood up to announce that he'd support the Honourable Member's motion after all. This caused a hum of surprise. 'What, is he convinced?' Eliza asked.

'Not a bit, but he can read the mood of the House,' Derby told her. 'The *ayes* will have it!'

For the vote, the End Gallery was cleared. 'Thank God that's over,' said Mrs Damer as they emerged from Westminster Palace. 'I don't know about you, Miss Farren, but my nerves couldn't take much more.'

'Nonsense,' said Derby, 'a stronger-nerved pair of ladies I've never known.'

They laughed like children, blinking in the orange sunset.

'He should publish today's speech,' remarked Mrs Damer, 'that would relieve some of his terrible debts, surely?'

'Ah, but Sherry can't abide publication; he claims the words wilt on the page.'

'Ironic, for such a magnificent writer,' complained Eliza.

'The way he put it to me once,' said Derby, beckoning to his driver and steering them towards the carriage, 'he said—if you'll pardon the language—he said, "History won't give a damn what we've said, only what we've done."'

APRIL 1787

Their beautiful little theatre at the side of Richmond House was finally ready. It made all the difference, gave all their movements more dignity; instead of edging from side to side of a reception room, they entered and exited like proper players at last. The scheme was blue and gold, borrowed from the Queen of France's stage in the Petit Trianon, according to Lady Mary, and there were comfortable chairs in raked rows, instead of the usual benches.

Right now the only audience was Mrs Farren, embroidering *E.F.* on a handkerchief in the third row from the back.

'Act One, Scene One, ladies and gentlemen, from the top, William and Sideboard playing cards,' repeated Eliza, not letting her voice carry a trace of irritation. 'And Sir Harry, do remember, it's "*A plague go with it!*"' she enunciated.

'That's what I say, isn't it?'

'Yes, but it comes out rather like *A play go with it.* You must pronounce the two gs quite distinctly.'

A sigh from the Baronet as he took up his pose.

'I'm sorry to be such a tyrant about this,' Eliza said charmingly, 'but it's the very first line of the play; we don't want the audience muttering to each other, "What did he say?", "What's the fellow on about?"'

The Players all tittered at her imitation of a crabby dowager.

Eliza suppressed a yawn; her jaw barely moved. She was always running these days: a hackney to Drury Lane for morning rehearsals (she'd slept through two, and had to pay a steep fine of 10s. 6d), stewed beef brought in from a tavern (Mrs Farren prided herself on never letting her daughter go without a hot dinner), a change into a better dress, the Derby carriage to Richmond House to oversee rehearsals, then home to Great Queen Street for an hour with her script for next month's new play, before Derby was at the door to take her to Drury Lane for that night's performance of whatever it was, in the hopes of making 2000 people laugh.

Muslin the saucy maid scattered the pack of cards. 'Ah, Mrs Bruce,' murmured Eliza, 'if you remember, it was decided that in rehearsal you should only *pretend* to throw the cards about, because they take so long to pick up again...'

'Oh, a thousand excuses, Miss Farren,' said Mrs Bruce, 'I was so busy thinking of my lines, the thing went right out of my head!'

They all waited, frozen in position, as the Richmonds' housemaid ran in to collect the cards, far more deftly than Mrs Bruce as the maid in the play could have done.

Sir Harry Englefield was relaxing into the kissing scene now, Eliza was glad to see. Where once he and Mrs Bruce had pecked the air stiffly, begging each other's pardon, now they were going at it like veterans, smacking each other on the lips between every line. With an odd pang, Eliza remembered herself at thirteen in Liverpool, nerving herself for her first stage kiss with a stubbled actor—and finding out that it was no more intimate than any other bit of business.

Dick Edgcumbe had got the knack of doing asides at last and the others were remembering not to look at him. *'By all that's soft, she listens to me!'* he hissed and leered.

'Splendid,' Eliza said, then wished she hadn't, because he dropped his part, the pages coming loose from their string. Would he never have his lines off by heart?

Derby, watching her, counted the twelve days they had left before the first performance of *The Way to Keep Him*. He would happily go on rehearsing under Eliza's direction for the next ten years. It was the perfect excuse to spend the day with her, drinking in the elegant lines of her neck, the light in her aquamarine eyes, the angle of her fingertips when she held her fan. The repetitiousness of rehearsals never bored him; he was beginning for the first time to understand the alchemy his beloved worked on the stage at Drury Lane, night after night.

'Now, enter the Widow Bellmour, reading—'

Mrs Hobart ran on, holding her book, then bent her face to it.

'Walk on *while* reading,' Eliza reminded her gently, 'as if lost in thought.'

Derby caught Mrs Damer's eye; they shared a little grimace of exasperation. How was a careless rake like Lovemore supposed to be passionately enamoured of a widow played by the stout, clumsy Albinia Hobart?

'The fault I mean', she boomed, *'is the want of due attention to the art of pleasing... To win a heart is easy; to keep it the difficulty.'*

'I do wish our manager could have played the Widow Bellmour herself,' he breathed in Mrs Damer's ear.

'Richmond asked her, you know.'

Derby hadn't.

'But she rejected the very idea of mixing amateurs with professionals.'

'She'd have made a great Lovemore, even,' he said, rueful, 'if she hadn't sworn off breeches parts years ago.'

Mrs Damer nodded. 'We'll never be ready in a fortnight,' she said grimly. 'We badly need a burnishing.'

'A polish?'

'Yes, but done with a certain violence,' she told him. 'When the clay's dried, one rubs it very hard all over with a smooth tool.'

Derby's mouth curled up in amusement.

'My Lord?' Eliza was crooking her finger; he'd missed his cue. Her tone was a little chilly. He never quite knew where he was with her these days. Sometimes she greeted him in the hall of Richmond House, her eyes sparkling, but other days he moved to greet her and she looked at him with the polite disdain of a stranger. He rushed to lounge on for his wooing of the bulky Widow, calling her '*a palace in need of a tenant*'.

Mrs Hobart answered with a ghastly girlishness: '*I will let it to none but a single gentleman . . . and it must be a lease for life.*'

Eliza corrected him again. 'When the lady says "*Heavens! what a dying swain you are*" it will be more plausible if we've seen you act the dying swain.'

'Ah. I thought I was to seem rakish?'

'Well, yes,' she told him, 'but with a touch of the desperate Romeo too.'

Was that what he was to the actress? Derby wondered suddenly. A *desperate Romeo*? Over the six years of their intimacy he'd tried to maintain a relaxed, aristocratic demeanour—but he knew that the *dying swain* popped out sometimes. Yes, perhaps that was it; the real reason Eliza had refused to play opposite him on the Richmond House stage was because it was all too exposing, too much like real life.

'That's right, cold and sprightly,' she was urging Mrs Hobart, 'toss your head.'

It occurred to Derby that Eliza was only following the advice of every comedy she had ever starred in: *Variety's the spice of love.* Did she turn brisk and distant in order to make him pursue her all the more doggishly? Or perhaps—this struck him like a light blow in the chest—perhaps her moods and megrims were nothing to do with him at all. She could have preoccupations he knew nothing of. For all that he and this woman moved through London society like an accredited couple, he'd never addressed her by her first name.

Richmond and Lady Mary popped into the theatre to say good afternoon to the company. Mrs Hobart happened to mention that a cousin of hers at Slough had written objecting in the strongest terms to her participation in these *theatrical experiments.*

'Whyever so?' asked Lady Mary. 'They're all the rage these days.'

'Among people of quality, yes,' said Mrs Hobart with a gratified inclusiveness, 'but the cousin in question has married a merchant, don't you know, and turned very evangelical.'

Nods all round. There was an epidemic of piety sweeping the middling orders.

'Richmond,' asked Derby, 'when you took part in your first play at Goodwood, did you find it a corrupting business?'

'Well, no,' said the Duke, deadpan, 'but then I was only five at the time and my leading lady was my sister Louisa, a circumstance which is generally not conducive to passion.'

This prompted gales of laughter. 'Though it has been known...' Dick Edgcumbe whispered in Derby's ear, too loudly.

'Acting's a more innocent amusement than gaming our fortunes away at any rate,' Sir Harry put in.

Mrs Hobart, known for her faro table, stiffened.

'More than all that,' said Mrs Damer hotly, 'it does us good. I consider it enlarging, elevating. To discover in oneself seeds of qualities that one never knew one had—to take on new qualities, speak in a different voice—it thrills me.'

Eliza turned and gave her a magnificent smile.

The arrival of Mrs Siddons, who was to advise on costumes, caused a stir among the company. Eliza went to greet her at the door of the theatre and Derby followed. 'My dear Miss Farren,' her colleague declaimed, 'I speak, I believe, for all your fellow players when I lament that we have seen too little of you this spring, but it is a willing sacrifice that Drury Lane pays to Richmond House.'

Derby hid a smile; the Empress of Tragedy had always been incapable of everyday speech. Her famous nose was looking longer than ever, despite the mass of soft curls.

Richmond had given Mrs Siddons carte blanche with a Parisian modiste on Mount Street and a gentleman's tailor round the corner. She prescribed four changes for Derby: a chintz nightgown, a brown morning frock coat, a dauphin jacket and a rich vest with a light-mushroom coat. 'What a relief,' he told her.

'A relief, My Lord?'

'I was afraid you'd put me in crimson and silver, like Edgcumbe. I mean to say,' he pushed on, 'I'm no treat for the eyes as it is.'

Mrs Siddons didn't flatter him by denying it; instead, she inclined her head like a nun. 'I have always thought the importance of personal appearance exaggerated,' she told him. 'What matters is to live the role, not to resemble it.'

The ladies were to wear their own jewels, which Eliza clearly thought rather odd, since at Drury Lane the pearls were always made of wax and the diamonds of glass. 'Paste might look the same.' Mrs Hobart sighed happily. 'But we'd know the difference.'

Richmond bustled up with his memorandum book to say that he'd devised an elaborate system of ticketing to ensure that the audience of 125 would be truly select. 'The last thing I want is for dubious types to worm their way in and spoil the atmosphere.'

Derby caught Mrs Damer's eye. Really, their host could be laughably pompous, like his whole Tory tribe. This was meant to be a comedy, not one of the military fortifications Richmond spent his days fretting over.

Each actress was to have twelve tickets to give away. 'It's rather unfair', Derby murmured in Eliza's ear, 'that we actors only get six each. Have gentlemen only half as many friends?'

'Count yourself lucky,' said Eliza with a smirk. 'Lady Mary's first thought was that the whole business should be left in the capable hands of the ladies.'

The Duchess of Richmond came up just then and pressed a ticket into Eliza's hand. 'For your mother, my dear. Unless you need any more?'

'No, no.'

When Lady Mary had gone Derby asked softly, 'Wouldn't you have liked to invite some of your colleagues from Drury Lane?'

'No,' she said after a moment, 'best not.'

He supposed she was right. If she was going to enter these elevated circles, she'd move more freely alone.

Mr Downman—another loan from Drury Lane—came in with the seven portraits commissioned for the scene of Mrs Lovemore's drawing room: Mrs Damer and Lady Mary, Mrs Siddons, the Devonshire House ladies (Georgiana, her sister Lady Duncannon and Lady Bess Foster) and Eliza herself. Seven was an awkward number to arrange, it soon became clear. 'What would you say, Miss Farren,' the painter suggested, 'if your own picture were leaning casually against a chair, as if it had been just brought home and not yet hung?'

'What a perfect symbol,' cried Mrs Damer.

'Of what?' asked Mrs Hobart, who clearly resented not being on the wall among the other eminences.

'Why, of Miss Farren's being such a...'

Outsider? thought Derby, stiffening. *Interloper?*

'...very *new* friend of ours,' said Mrs Damer with a grin.

Sir Harry puffed in just then, with a still-damp print of a caricature published that morning, called *The Way to Keep Him as Performed at the Richmond Theatre.* The Players all crowded round. The engraving showed the Richmonds watching a rehearsal from a theatre box with a crossed-cannons crest (a nod to Richmond's job). 'I look like a spider,' the Duke lamented.

'And I like some vast barrel of brandy,' said Mrs Hobart with an unconvincing titter.

'But I've no face, I'm all wig,' complained Dick Edgcumbe.

'Every one of us looks equally dreadful,' Mrs Damer assured him.

'No, Mrs Damer,' said Mrs Hobart coldly, 'you and your sister are fairly drawn, except that your hair and muffs are shown triple size.'

Derby, peering over her shoulder, let out a guffaw. 'Come, I think I win the prize.'

'It's true, man,' said Sir Harry, his eyes watering with laughter, 'you're shown half the size of Mrs Damer—'

'A third, a quarter! With the dour face of an elderly baby. I could be put on show at a fair. Oh, I must add a copy of this masterpiece to my portfolio.' Over the years since he'd met Eliza he'd built up quite a collection of prints called things like *Darby and Joan*, or *Miss Tittup and Lord Doodle*.

'You collect caricatures?' Mrs Damer asked him.

'Only of myself and my friends,' Derby told her. 'I like to know what's being invented about us.'

'How odd,' she said.

'You think it an unwholesome habit?'

'Rather,' said Mrs Damer with a little shudder. 'I prefer to close my eyes and ears to such stuff.'

'Miss Farren? Do you concur?'

Eliza's face was uneasy; she hadn't known about his collection either. 'Perhaps your sex take these attacks more lightly than ours can afford to do.'

Lady Mary struck a pose and obliged with the famous prologue to the *School for Scandal*.

So strong, so swift, the monster there's no gagging:
Cut Scandal's head off, still the tongue is wagging.

'But as a true Whig,' said Derby, 'I should hardly object to the famous freedom of our British press, should I? I always feel that what one laughs off can't hurt one, and any man desperate enough to earn a shilling by that trade, at my expense, is welcome to it.'

———

DERBY ALWAYS went to Brooks's if he had nothing better to do; he only tried Boodle's if he was looking for sportsmen. (He was a member of White's too, by virtue of his name, but he never went there any more, since it'd become such a Tory stronghold.) He greeted a few old acquaintances as he passed through the gambling rooms; he nodded warmly at Fox, who was deep in a game of faro, elbows planted on the edge of the glossy painted table. 'Derby,' muttered Fox, looking up with red-rimmed eyes. He took off the hat he wore to blinker himself when at play and scratched his rat's nest of greasy hair.

'How's the game?'

Fox sucked air through his teeth. 'Fast and furious. I've been here since noon and my bum is sore. I'll *paroli* for *quinze et le va*,' he called out to the dealer.

The frail, lanky Duke of Bedford, with his tangled waterfall of black hair, was staring down too intensely to notice Derby, who wished he knew the boy well enough to lend him his hairdresser and recommend a tailor, perhaps; how curious that one of the fabulously wealthy Bedfords of Woburn Abbey should wear such a shabby cloth coat. Young Whigs today seemed to think that dressing like stable boys proved their freedom of thought.

Derby watched Fox lose on three cards in a row, then patted his shoulder and left the room. He'd always thought faro a nonsense; the odds in favour of the banker were second only to the demon roulette. Really, his friend's love of gaming bordered on tragic. Fox had been deep in debt since he was sixteen, and if he ever by some disaster lost his seat in the House and the immunity it gave him, his creditors would clap him in gaol.

The fireside chairs in the coffee room were the best thing about Brooks's; they were more like beds, with writing desks, lights and padded footstools all attached. Derby leafed through the newspapers, trying to ignore the nervousness that gripped his stomach whenever he thought of going on stage at Richmond House, three nights from now.

Sheridan dropped into the chair beside him and helped himself to Derby's bottle of brandy. He was ranting about Wilberforce's Royal Proclamation against Vices. 'I told him we'll never bring in abolition or parliamentary reform as long as we dissipate our energy on moralistic trivia. A crusade to make beggars give up bear baiting and observe the sabbath—Christ!' Sheridan gripped his glass. The skin round his eyes was heavy and dark.

'I don't care if my tenants at Knowsley go to church,' said Derby, 'if only they'd pay their rent every quarter without whining.' After a minute he said, 'You're looking worn out.'

Sheridan smirked. 'Blame Mrs Crewe.'

'Ah, yes, she's one of the most hospitable of our Party's hostesses, I hear.'

'Not to everyone, my friend!'

Derby wagged his finger at him. 'I'm not surprised you succumb to temptation, Sherry, but I do marvel at your apparent indifference to the dazzling charms of your own wife, on whom you haven't sired a child for the past dozen years! May I just point out that were I privileged to share the bed of that nonpareil, Mrs Eliza Sheridan, I doubt I'd ever leave it?'

Sheridan's cheeks flushed purple. 'May I just suggest that when you know nothing about a subject you should shut your mouth.'

Derby gulped some brandy. This from a man whose conversation frequently plumbed the depths of vulgarity?

Sheridan spoke very low in his throat. 'I haven't shared that bed since Tom was born because my wife came within an inch of dying. She offers but I mustn't, I can't. The doctor said, "Keep your hands off her, because every time you touch her, you drive a nail in her coffin."'

'My dear Sherry.' Derby licked brandy off his lips. 'A thousand apologies; I had no idea.'

A nod. 'So where were you during today's debt debate?'

That was an unnerving habit of Sheridan's; he could change topic and mood in a blink. 'Ah, rehearsal, as it happens,' said Derby, defensive. The fact was, he had mixed feelings about Parliament settling the Prince's debts, which had run up to £300,000; just think how many roads and canals could be built for that vast sum.

Sheridan lowered his voice. 'Well, it was a fiasco. Some pawn of Pitt's from Devonshire drops a heavy hint about constitutional dangers if the Prince were hypothetically to wed a twice-widowed Catholic lady—naming no names, but he might as well have said *Maria Fitzherbert*—then he bleats on about the Royal Marriages Act giving the King sole power to arrange his children's matches, the Act of Settlement reserving the throne for Protestants, blah blah blah. So our bushy-tailed Fox leaps up and says'—Sheridan put on a valiant voice—'"I am at a loss to imagine what species of Party could have fabricated so base and scandalous an insinuation."'

Derby grinned at the mimicry.

'Then Fox splutters—listen to this, Derby—and he claims to be speaking on Prinny's authority; he says of the hypothetical wedding, "The thing not only never could have happened legally, but never did happen in any way whatsoever."'

'Very firm hair-splitting. Well, there wasn't any such wedding, was there?' added Derby after a minute.

Sheridan scratched the skin round his nose. It was red and raging, as always in times of strain.

'Oh, Sherry.' Derby drank more brandy. 'Tell me there wasn't a wedding. The Widow Fitz is only Prinny's mistress, surely? He may be a wild fellow but he's not stupid; he'd never have—he wouldn't do something that would debar him from the throne.'

'What's a wedding?' muttered Sheridan with a small shrug. 'If it's not legal, because of the various Acts aforementioned, is it a true wedding? Can anything really be said to have taken place, December before last, in the lady's house in Park Street?'

Derby dropped his face into his hands. When he looked up, Sheridan was drinking deep. 'Did you know at the time?'

'None of us knew except Georgiana, damn her. What kind of loyalty to the Party d'you call that? She claims to have been *ever so miz* about it, but she gave them her own ring, because Prinny had tried to run himself through with his sword!'

The heir to the throne threatened suicide at least once a year. 'When did you guess, then?'

'Oh, I can't tell. We all believed what we wanted to believe,' said Sheridan through his teeth. 'Now I've got Mrs Fitz on my back like some harpy, wanting to know how I could stand to hear Fox deny her wedding in the Commons and imply she's a whore. I've got Fox running to me, tears in his eyes, to say Mrs Fitz's uncle came up to him in this very club this afternoon and broke it to him that he'd been *misinformed.* How could I have kept it from him, how could our good-hearted Prince have betrayed him so? But the point is, Derby, you know as well as I do, our Party needs Prinny, because Old George hates our guts. The only way the Foxites are ever going to get into government is when our fat young friend succeeds to the throne of England and kicks Pitt off the top step.'

His voice had risen. Derby glanced around. Brooks's was a Whig haven, yes, but to speculate about the death of the King was to go rather far.

'So what I'm saying', Sheridan snarled, 'is that marriage or no marriage, Prinny's our man and we stand or fall with him. He can wed a five-year-old Eskimo for all I care; he can fuck a vixen. No offence to the Widow Fitz,' he added almost normally. 'She's a lady above criticism, as I shall explain to my fellow Honourable Members.'

He was reaching for the bottle, but Derby held on to it. 'You won't spell it out that they're married.'

'Of course not. I'll spell nothing out, not even my own name; I'll be the tongue-twisting Jesuit the papers call me. Prinny says I have to defend Mrs Fitz's honour somehow, without losing him the throne.'

'That'll take quite a speech.'

'Luckily I write well with a knife to my throat,' said Sheridan, draining his glass and standing up.

It was true; he'd only finished one of his plays when Tom King had locked him in a room overnight. 'When's the vote on paying Prinny's debts?' asked Derby.

'Thursday.'

'Oh, but that's the night of our performance at Richmond House.'

Sheridan rolled his eyes. Derby could tell he was thinking: *a damned play and not even a real one.* 'We commoners will just have to manage without you, My Lord.'

'No, what I mean is it might be the perfect pretext for a delay. Pitt and Fox are both on the guest list—as are you. Why don't I get Richmond to propose to the PM that the House should adjourn till next week, to allow everyone to attend our performance?'

'Which would give me and my pen another few days.'

'Exactly.'

Sheridan grinned. 'So the Smith-Stanley brains have survived a millennium of inbreeding.'

Over the years, Derby had learned never to gratify Sheridan by showing shock at an outrageous remark. 'You're too kind.'

'Oh,' Sheridan remarked over his shoulder, as he left, 'I see you're in the World.'

What an odd remark; Derby would have gone after him to ask what he meant, except these comfortable chairs were so difficult to get out of. In the World? Of course he was; he'd been born into it.

Only half an hour later, when he was idly trawling through a piece on the balance of trade in the *Gentleman's Magazine*, did Derby hear Sheridan's phrase in his ears again. He clicked his fingers for a footman. On the fifth page of *The World* he found himself in a column headed THEATRICAL INTELLIGENCE.

Some say Lord D–y acts the part of an unhappy husband so vastly well at R-ch—d H——se because of his own marital Estrangement.

Derby folded the paper and read on.

When the unhappy Countess of D——y was recently lying on her sickbed, it was whispered that the Earl in question made anxious enquiries every day and many believe that but for pride's sake he would grant her pardon for her criminal Elopement nine years ago with the Duke of D-rs-t. Her lovely Contrition may yet prove THE WAY TO KEEP HIM.

Derby found his fingers closed round the crumpled page. His throat was locked. How dared these money-grubbing journalists? He would have preferred to see himself linked in print with any female in Britain rather than his own wife. What if Eliza saw this item? Someone would be sure to show her. Please God she wouldn't believe it.

Contrition, my arse! Self-pity, that was as much as Betty could manage and it had no hold on him any more. In the privacy of his own head Derby could admit that he wished above all things that he were free. He'd had his chance when Lady Derby had run away from Knowsley, but he'd gone no further than a private separation. An Act of Divorce in the Lords would have been slow, costly and a source of great satire in the press, but by now it would have been long over. Other members of the World survived such exposure, didn't they, and no one thought the worse of them for it nowadays? Why had Derby, at twenty-five, been so rigid in the ways of his ancestors, so convinced that the best thing to do with this marital humiliation was to bury it in silence? The years had rolled by and it was too late; if he suddenly sued the Duke of Dorset for *criminal conversation* with a consumptive invalid he'd be laughed out of court.

By now Derby could have been a single man again. Which meant that at any time in the last six years, say, he could have taken his freedom and thrown it at Eliza's slim feet. He could have knelt and said—

No, don't think of it.

He wouldn't care what mockery it earned him; he'd be more than willing to defy his forebears for her sake. This time, if only he were free, he wouldn't let discretion or reserve be his guide. If Eliza would be his on no other terms but marriage the, by God, he would get down on his knees—

Stop. You've no right to think of it.

Derby lay there in his chair, looking into the flames, his throat burning.

———

THE NINETEENTH of April came at last and the World was arriving at Richmond House. Eliza stood in the wings and peered across the small dark stage, tried to think whether there was anything she'd forgotten. She could hear the band of musicians tuning up; Richmond had drafted them in from his own Sussex Militia, impressive but hot in their scarlet uniforms. (Apparently they weren't happy about their drink rations.) 'Such a delightful occasion,' a female voice in the audience carolled. 'All the fun of theatre without the squalor.'

Eliza listened hard.

'I couldn't agree more,' said a man. 'I rarely go to Drury Lane any more and Covent Garden is just as noisome. It takes an hour for one's carriage to get through the traffic and then one has to squeeze through the sweaty mob in the corridors. I lost my mother one night, not to mention my left shoe!'

A little rain of bright laughter. *They're in a good mood, they'll be indulgent,* Eliza thought. *They'll need to be.*

'Who's there?' Mrs Damer stood at her shoulder in her Act One costume, embroidered gauze on white festooned silk, with wheat-sheaves of diamonds in her hair and a girdle of diamond stars. 'My mother's,' she said a little sheepishly, seeing Eliza's eyes on the jewellery. Eliza herself was wearing a simple Indian muslin tonight, to distinguish herself from the Players. Mrs Damer put her face to the crack in the curtains. 'I see the Cumberlands—'

'What, the playwright?' asked Eliza.

Mrs Damer laughed. 'No, I ought to have said the Duke and Duchess of Cumberland.'

No, I ought to have understood it, thought Eliza.

'Here's Mrs Garrick, the Sheridans—I campaigned for the Foxites with Mrs Sheridan once, she's such a beauty, still—'

'Never mind her beauty,' said Eliza, 'it was her voice that was spectacular.'

Mrs Damer nodded. 'Such a shame that he made her retire from singing when they married. As if there were anything shameful about a woman using her God-given genius! Oh, so many people,' she wailed. 'Good, Walpole's been given a seat at the front. Though I mustn't meet his eye; he'll put me off.'

'Are you a trifle nervous?'

The eyes turned towards her were huge and dark.

'Don't think of that last rehearsal; one can't judge a performance till it's on the boards.'

'I am frightened, horribly so,' admitted Mrs Damer. 'And the French lady's arrival only makes me worse.'

'I didn't know you had a visitor.'

Mrs Damer let out a shriek of laughter. She covered her mouth. 'I keep getting things wrong and the performance hasn't even begun.' She leaned to whisper in Eliza's ear; 'We say *the French lady* for our monthlies.'

Eliza flushed in annoyance at herself.

Derby came up then, in Mr Lovemore's nightgown. Eliza had never seen him without breeches before; she looked away at once. With his little calves, he was like a child, only hairier.

'Prinny's just swanned in,' Mrs Damer told him, 'with Mrs Fitzherbert, of course.'

'I'm surprised she came, given how shamefully she's been treated in the press this week. There's the Duke of York with him,' said Derby, his eye to the crack in the curtains. 'I'm glad he only brought one little brother; seven princes and six princesses is more than England will ever need, even if an epidemic of cholera were to run through St James's Palace.'

'Treasonous talk.' Eliza giggled.

'Gad,' murmured Derby, 'here comes Fox, arm in arm with the Prime Minister. Now that's a gracious gesture.'

'Wouldn't you do the same yourself, for the occasion?'

'Well, I might, but I'd tempted to break Pitt's twig of an arm once I had it in my grasp.' Derby looked round with a grin, then seized each lady by a hand. Eliza let him, for once. His palm was hot. 'You know, we three...'

'Yes, Derby?' said Mrs Damer.

'I think we're alike, aren't we?' He looked from face to laughing face; he squeezed their fingers. 'We each know what it is to be pre-eminent in our field, whether it be sculpture, or acting, or sport—and we know the pressures that distinction brings too. Fame! As Milton dubs it, *the spur* that pricks us to labour in the cause of greatness, but also our weakness, *that last infirmity of noble mind.* We three understand each other.'

'Have you been drinking, My Lord?'

'Oh, not more than a couple of bottles over dinner,' Derby assured Eliza. 'Just enough to help my lines flow.'

Mrs Damer rolled her eyes.

The bell rang, to Eliza's relief. For a moment she found herself searching her mind for her first cue. How absurd: she'd forgotten she was the manager.

Mrs Hobart, in front of the curtain, began delivering Field Marshal Conway's prologue. 'Well, at least she's loud,' Eliza whispered in Mrs Damer's ear to make her laugh. They were on their own in the wings, Prompt Side, while on the Opposite Side, in the shadows, Sir Harry Englefield was giving them a manic wave. The band was playing a musical overture. Mrs Damer pressed her fingers to her mouth, then took them away; she looked at them to see if they were stained with rouge. 'Are you in pain?' Eliza whispered, remembering the *French lady.*

'Not much. I was up very late last night, reading over my lines; I'm so afraid I'll forget them and let you down.'

'Oh, but you won't,' she assured her, touched that the woman seemed to care less about acting well than about Eliza's approval.

'Did you suffer from stage fright, when you began your career?'

Eliza tried to cast her mind back to those crude pantomimes in Liverpool. 'Really, I can hardly remember a time before I was on the boards, one way or another. And when I advanced to Drury Lane, well, it was only a bigger house. I find acting strangely relaxing; to play a part gives me the confidence of always knowing what to say. No, I sometimes suffer from life fright, if anything,' she added quietly.

'Life fright?' Mrs Damer stared at her.

'The difficulty of being Miss Farren,' she said, 'and knowing my lines. Deciding what to wear, what to do, whom to see, what to say.'

The sculptor was nodding.

'But yes, of course,' said Eliza more lightly, 'there've been a few occasions when my heart's been in my mouth before curtain-up. I trust my own powers, but I don't trust the crowd.'

'But don't we—don't your audiences always love you?'

Eliza made a face. 'What I hate is a spirit of controversy and titillation; it's so distracting. Sometimes the newspapers have been so full of nonsensical talk about me—my character, my connections'—she didn't want to say Derby's name—'that nobody in the crowd is following the play.'

'I know. I know exactly. I suffered that way after my husband's death. And Derby,' she said bluntly, 'how does he bear it? Does he always laugh off publicity, as he claims?'

'He and I never speak of it.'

The bell went again and they both jumped. The music had ended without Eliza noticing. The stagehand came to lower the chandeliers and light the scores of tapers. Mrs Lovemore's drawing room flickered to life.

The green curtain was winched open. Everything was slower than at Drury Lane, but this was an audience of friends, Eliza reminded herself. They immediately recognised the six ladies hung up in gold-edged frames and there was a thunderclap of applause. Eliza's own portrait was leaning against a chair, in what she realised now was quite the most prominent position on the stage.

Sir Harry bounded on to the stage. He pronounced the opening line with such gulping clarity—'*A plague...go with it!*'—that he provoked another round of clapping. Eliza felt oddly moved. They were really trying to please her, all her Players. She gave Mrs Damer's shoulders a gentle push and she was off, crossing the stage and settling herself at the tea table. She stared into her cup with what Eliza almost mistook for an air of contemplation. The fixed gaze gave her away. Eliza began to panic. *Go on. You don't need a prompt, not for your first line. 'This trash of tea'*—

'*This trash of tea!*' declaimed Mrs Damer with such vehemence that the pent-up audience broke into another wave of laughter. She glanced up at them, startled. '*I don't know why I drink so much of it,*' she admitted. '*Heigho!*'

They roared, they shrieked, as if they were all tea addicts and had never heard a wittier sally. Eliza could see the colour warm Mrs Damer's cheeks, pinched by an invisible hand.

At the interval Richmond had ices served in bowls. Mrs Farren and Eliza stayed backstage to avoid the crowd. 'It's stifling hot,' observed her mother, fanning Eliza. 'Too much of a crowd for this tiny playhouse.'

'It's going well enough, isn't it, don't you think?'

'Splendidly,' said Mrs Farren.

In the second half Derby caused whoops of mirth when he fell asleep during dinner. The crowd even tittered on painful lines, such as when Mrs Lovemore cried out, '*I am lost beyond redemption.*' But they weren't mocking the actors—Eliza could always tell what kind of laugh she was hearing—they were just keyed up. Meeting her husband at Lady Constant's, Mrs Damer drew herself up to her full height. '*Do you come disguised under a mask of friendship?*'

As for Derby, he was quite the libertine. Did everyone contain their opposite, Eliza wondered, and did it only take some play-acting to let the demon out? '*Hell and destruction!*' he roared, when all his plots were exposed in the last act.

The curtain swung shut and the applause rang out like brass. Strange, thought Eliza. For one night only a few ladies and gentlemen put on an old play and it was an event worth interrupting Parliament for.

Mrs Damer came in front of the curtain for the epilogue her father had written for her. The point of the piece seemed to be that theatre thrilled her even more than chiselling marble.

Oh, could my humble skill, which often strove
In mimic stone to copy forms I love,
By soft gradation reach a higher art,
And bring to view a sculpture of the heart!

She took her bows and walked off, straight into Eliza's arms. 'Thank you,' she said, cheek to hot powdered cheek, 'thank you, thank you!'

The footmen were removing the chairs from the theatre, to let the crowd mill around, and bringing chilled champagne on trays. Eliza feared her face was scarlet from the heat; she tried to mingle unobtrusively, but people kept rushing up to congratulate her. John Philip Kemble, the gravely handsome rising star of Drury Lane, appeared at Eliza's side; he must have been invited by his sister Mrs Siddons. Somehow he always had the air of an ancient Roman wrapped in a cloak. 'A very creditable job, Miss Farren,' he murmured, 'considering what you had to work with.'

There was Horace Walpole, spindly as a spider, declaiming that his cousin Mrs Damer was the most wonderful actress ever to grace the boards. 'Well, who should act genteel comedy so perfectly but genteel people? The generality of actors and actresses—though I exclude the divine Miss Farren, of course'—catching sight of Eliza and making a stooped little bow—'have seen so little of high life that they can only guess at its tone, and put on second-hand airs.'

Smiling, Eliza thought his theory nonsensical. As if one needed to have killed a man to act Macbeth!

'How the nobility of the last century would have thought themselves degraded, though, to see their descendants play at being players.' The remark came from a plainly dressed woman Eliza recognised as an authoress who'd recently given up playwriting, because of the sinfulness of the stage.

'What old-fashioned views you hold, Miss More,' said Walpole, regarding her quizzically. 'You make me feel so young.' He waited for the round of laughter. 'What I say is, let each of us express our particular genius however we can, whether with speeches or songs or—a chisel,' he added, as Mrs Damer joined them. '*Ars longa, vita brevis,* as Seneca puts it.'

'Well, yes, of course,' said Miss More awkwardly, 'true talent never degrades.'

Sheridan had come up a moment before and given Eliza a casual nod for greeting. Now he remarked loudly, 'One might go further and say that there's a glory in the name of poet or painter, actor or politician, that will outlive any merely hereditary titles.'

'Hear, hear,' said Mrs Damer mischievously.

'One might, if one were a downright leveller,' said Walpole, squinting at the newcomer over his tiny glass of champagne.

Sheridan wandered off with the gaudy-suited Prince of Wales and Mrs Fitzherbert, telling them something that made them laugh uproariously. 'Do you notice how Fox keeps his distance?' murmured Mrs Damer in Eliza's ear.

'Hm?'

'From Prinny. Fox hasn't spoken to him all evening! Derby says Fox is still too furious about the secret wedding. It's caused a dreadful breach between the Prince and the Party.'

'You're so *au courant* when it comes to politics,' said Eliza, 'it's a shame you don't campaign any more.'

'Nonsense! All I pick up are scraps. Now for true insight into Foxite affairs there's no one like Georgiana,' said Mrs Damer, pronouncing it to rhyme with *saner,* as everyone did. 'Do you know her?'

'I haven't had the honour...' Eliza looked over at the swarm of guests around the red-haired Duchess of Devonshire, splendid in blue satin.

'Then come with me.'

It wasn't that the Duchess was so very beautiful, Eliza thought as they got closer, it was that she wore her clothes so naturally. That rather shocking novel, *The Sylph,* was said to be the Duchess's own story, but of course she couldn't admit to its authorship. On one side of her stood the long-limbed, sleepy-looking Duke, and on her other arm hung the tiny and coquettish Lady Bess Foster, in matching blue—beloved companion to the Devonshires for the last five years. Recently there'd been talk of Devonshire putting Georgiana aside—as punishment for her gambling away so much of his fortune—but they all looked perfectly happy tonight. The financial affairs of the Beau Monde were mysterious to Eliza; they could owe so much and be in such straits, yet never be seen in last year's fashions.

Georgiana embraced Mrs Damer as frankly as a child. 'Oo star, oo! We've decided to forgive you for hiding away at Richmond House all these months.' She and Lady Bess were wearing little jewelled miniatures on chains, Eliza saw—oh, yes, they must be portraits of each other—and the same flowery scent.

'Have you noticed our latest invention, by the way?' asked Lady Bess. She and Georgiana tossed their heads, showing off an unusual arrangement of ostrich feathers that stuck out sideways.

'It'll be copied all over Mayfair by Saturday,' Mrs Damer assured them.

'They nearly put my eye out a few times tonight,' grumbled the Duke of Devonshire. 'Delightfully acted, I must say, Mrs D., and delightfully managed too'—with a nod to Eliza.

Mrs Damer made the formal introductions.

'It was all simply *ravish*,' said Georgiana. 'We've only ever read aloud from Shakespeare. Why couldn't we put on some theatricals of our own at Chatsworth? Something with *childies* in, so our Little G. and Harry-o can play.'

Eliza remembered that the Duchess was much resented by her in-laws for having produced only daughters so far. 'I could supply you with some charming comedies featuring little girls,' she offered.

'Oh, yes,' said Lady Bess, clutching Georgiana. 'Let's us, Canis, *pwitty pweez*'—turning to the Duke.

'Well, perhaps, Racky,' he said, 'if you and Rat are *vewy dood.*'

Eliza kept her face pleasantly blank, but when she and Mrs Damer moved off she risked a grin. 'Do they always go on that way?'

'I'm afraid so,' said Mrs Damer. 'Vastly affected—but one can't help but love Georgiana for her warm heart.'

It was on the tip of Eliza's tongue to ask if it was true what people said, that Lady Bess went out riding alone with the Duke, betraying her friend behind her back. Could such an astute politician as Georgiana really be oblivious to what was going on at Devonshire House, or was it possible that she didn't mind? But no, she'd better not say any of this to Mrs Damer, for fear of offending; as a newcomer, Eliza was better off keeping her eyes and ears open and her lips sealed.

TONIGHT EVERYTHING had changed, Derby thought, with a light-headedness that didn't come from the champagne. The World was treating Miss Farren as the next Lady Derby. He'd introduced her to Prinny and Mrs Fitzherbert, to the Duke of York, to Field Marshal Conway and Lady Ailesbury, to a brace of other titles—and she'd been received by them all with rapturous respect. For Derby, it was like that moment in a cockfight when one's bird got the other by the throat.

He felt like laughing aloud. He was in a spin. In all the confusion he'd forgotten his cane. Could he have set it down in a dark corner of the stage after making his last exit? He ran up the steps and went in behind the flats.

There was Eliza. She must have retreated from the crowd of guests; she was picking up bits and pieces, a handkerchief, a folded page torn from somebody's part. For a moment there was no glamour to her, no brilliance; she was simply a young woman picking things up off the floor and Derby had never seen anything lovelier.

She must have heard his breathing; she turned.

'Ah, I was just hunting for my cane,' he said, aware that he sounded drunk. 'Have you seen it?'

Eliza shook her head.

It was the first time that they had ever been alone together. The thought struck Derby like a knife in the ribs. This was no accident, this was a stage set for the great scene. He took a step closer. 'I wonder,' he said, 'I wonder, Miss Farren, whether you saw that paragraph in the newspaper the other day? In *The World.*' His tone was uneven.

'Oh, I don't read such stuff,' she told him.

That was an equivocal answer. 'Perhaps some friend brought the item to your attention? It was a libel, about—' He had been going to say *my wife,* but he feared to pronounce the phrase and break the bubble. 'About me. I just wanted to tell you there's no truth in it.'

'I wouldn't credit anything said of you in a newspaper.'

He couldn't tell if she was lying. It didn't much matter. His destiny was the manager and Derby knew his lines by heart; hadn't he been practising them for years? He went close to her. 'How long are we to go on pretending?'

'Pretending, My Lord?'

'Six years is a long time.'

'I pretend nothing,' she said.

'Rehearsing, then, if you like. For six years I've paid you every possible attention, every homage of the most particular and striking kind.'

A lesser woman would have stepped back, but Eliza only narrowed her eyes. It was a tiny gesture, not one that would be visible from the gallery.

He rushed on. 'You can't be in any doubt about the nature of my feelings.'

'Feelings?' she retorted. 'I think I should call my mother.'

Derby seized her by the hand, astonished by his own gall. 'For once, just this once. Let's speak privately.'

She looked down at his knuckles till he lifted them. A more ordinary woman would have tugged her arm away, he thought; Eliza could do it with a single glance. 'I've nothing to say of feelings.'

'Let me speak, then.' Derby disliked the note of pleading. 'Just listen,' he said more firmly.

'What kind of speech am I to listen to?'

'Not a declaration of love—' he assured her.

'I'm glad to hear it.'

'Not that,' Derby pressed on, 'because after six years you can't need me to spell out what every look, every word's revealed to you and the whole World beside. Also because I'm not a boy of eighteen, to declaim starry-eyed speeches.'

She jumped in as soon as he paused for breath. 'Also because you're a married man.'

Derby was chewing his lip. 'Irrespective—'

'It's true.' Eliza's heart was banging. She'd never said those words to the Earl before, never thrown the fact in his face. She'd thought—hoped—it need never come to this. Why should he need reminding? Why did he have to wreck everything? The scene was all wrong, she thought. *Leave off, ladies and gentlemen, we'll try that again from the top.*

'I don't deny it, in a strictly legal sense,' Derby blustered. 'Though I've never laid eyes on the lady in question since she left Knowsley nine years ago, I swear it.'

Why didn't you divorce her then, and be done with it? Eliza wouldn't say it; she'd made herself that promise a long time ago. She'd never protest, never beg, never let him believe she was waiting for him.

'You know my peculiar situation as well as I do,' he pleaded, 'everyone knows it, despite those lies in the newspaper about a reconciliation.'

She stiffened. *What reconciliation?*

'But surely two sophisticated individuals—surely in these awkward and exceptional circumstances, it could still be possible for us to...to rise above our difficulties and come to some kind of discreet arrangement,' he said unhappily. He blinked twice, three times.

The word stuck in her craw. *Arrangement.* It was a petty, sneaking, shopkeeping sort of word. Had Eliza come so far and made so many sacrifices, won the nation's respect as a new kind of actress, kept her dignity, turned herself from a pauper into a lady, only to be accosted with an offer of an *arrangement*? 'Good night, Your Lordship,' she said loathingly and turned on her heel.

She was almost at the door, but Derby got there before her, surprisingly agile. He didn't touch her, but he barred her way. There was nothing *exceptional* about these circumstances, she saw now, sickened. It could be any run-of-the-mill comedy of manners: the predictable tos and fros of it, the crowing and clucking, like a cock and a hen in a barnyard.

'You misunderstand—'

'I understand you perfectly,' she told him. She wouldn't play the shrieking harridan. 'My profession has made me only too aware of the meaning of that soiled word, *arrangement*. Mrs Jordan has an *arrangement* with Mr Ford, the father of her child. The sums and conditions may vary; the nature of the bargain not at all. Whether in an Oxford Street emporium or a Spitalfields shack, a sale is a sale.' Her delivery was perfectly crisp. 'You're not the first to have asked me to stoop to this, only the wealthiest.'

Derby's narrow eyes were bruised. 'I mean my proposal in the most honourable spirit—'

'There is only one kind of honourable proposal.'

'—everything done very handsomely and quietly, with tact and discretion, so the World won't object—full contracts—I mean a marriage in all but name—'

She was aghast at his stupidity. 'Derby, you know my circumstances. My mother and I have no property, no rich relations, nothing to fall back on. I've only my talents and my energies, and I've bent them all on my profession. It's bad enough that half the scandal sheets in the country call me your *platonic inamorata*,' she said, her voice rising towards shrillness. 'A marriage in all but name? Tell me, what do I have but my name?'

'My dearest, if I could offer you your due', he groaned, 'I would. You know I would, the very moment I were free. If the Countess— when the Countess—her health—'

She flinched at that. He shouldn't have dropped so gross a hint; it sounded as if he were betting on his wife's death.

Derby's face had fallen; she could tell he knew he'd made a mistake. He drew himself up, though he was still so much shorter than her. 'Like it or not,' he said sternly, 'you have my love. You've had it for long enough to know its nature; it's no fleeting lust. And I don't believe your heart is coldly pious enough to think such love disgusting.'

'What do you know of my heart?' she barked. He was right, of course. This wasn't about piety. Dignity, if anything.

'All I ask is that you show me some mercy. Consider bending your principles so that we might both know some happiness in this uncertain world.'

She stood a little closer to him. She said, 'My happiness is none of your concern.'

Then she was gone, leaving the Earl standing there like a fool behind her. Like a bad actor who'd forgotten his exit line, Eliza thought, and hung on, shifting from foot to foot, while the crowd started to titter.

ANNE WAS trying to remember if she'd ever been happier. Such a night! As Mrs Lovemore, she'd made more than a hundred of her oldest friends and nearest relations laugh and cry out. For once she hadn't been the artist in the silence of her workshop, toiling over beauty in stone; she'd been the living statue. She looked for Eliza Farren to tell her how grateful she was—but she couldn't see her anywhere.

The First Gentleman of Europe enveloped her in a sweet-smelling embrace, one of his frizzed side curls poking her in the eye. 'Mrs Damer! You made me weep in your big scene.'

'I did?' she asked, foolishly gratified. The Prince's black velvet suit was lined with pink satin and ornamented with gold embroidery and pink spangles, which didn't make him look any thinner, and he was wobbling in pink shoes with high heels.

'Proof positive,' said Prinny, holding up a crumpled handkerchief with tiny letters embroidered all over it in gold; G. for George, she realised. 'Mrs Fitz had to poke me to silence my sobs.'

It was hard to think of the slow-moving woman by his side taking the liberty of poking anyone, least of all the heir to the British throne. The Widow Fitzherbert was older than her husband, but ageing well, with her smooth plumpness and golden hair. She wore a tiny jewelled cross at her throat, Anne noticed; you had to grant her that, she wasn't ashamed of being a Catholic. Her expression was oddly calm for a woman whose reputation was being fought over so bitterly in the Commons. She'd been through so much, she must be used to wearing a mask of serenity.

'But tell me,' Prinny said, seizing Anne by the fingertips, 'how's your *real* work going? When are you ever going to carve me something for Carlton House?'

She was touched. When people mocked the Prince of Wales as overdressed, overweight and oversexed, they forgot what a passionate patron of the arts he was—like Henry VIII, almost. His succession to the throne, bringing the Foxites to power with him, might usher in a new Golden Age for the arts, as well as all the liberalising reforms he promised.

Anne was about to say that she'd be honoured to carve a piece for him, but he rushed on happily. 'The renovations are such a *slog*, I have to choose everything myself: the colours, the lamps, the design of the pastry scullery, the maids' quarters...'

When he swept Mrs Fitz off to greet someone else, Lady Mary appeared at her sister's elbow. 'Apparently their son's being raised in Spain.'

'Why Spain?' murmured Anne. 'Isn't France the more usual for fostering?'

'It's too close to home—practically our back garden—and the newspapers would be sure to track the baby down.'

Anne winced, considering what it would be like for a mother to send her child to Spain and probably never see him again. She'd never had any maternal sentiment herself, unless she could count her feelings towards her sculptures, and she always made those in order to give away. 'What I can't understand is why they risked that secret wedding; they might have known it would all come out in the end.'

Lady Mary shrugged. 'You've such a cool spirit, sister, you forget how people can act in the heat of passion.'

Anne felt rather stung.

There was a crash of glass; it sounded as though all the champagne glasses had been flung down at once. Startled, she sensed a cool breeze and turned towards it. Ladies began to squeal. There was a gaping hole in the window nearest to Anne—a dark mouth that let in the night air.

'Good God,' a male voice roared.

Outside there was a confused music of voices and the banging of saucepans. Anne realised that she'd been hearing this faintly for some time without paying any attention. While she was staring at the smashed pane, she saw the one beside it break; this time she actually witnessed the explosion, noticed the stone thump on to the boards beside her. She felt no fear, only an acute curiosity. There was something tied round the stone; she bent to disentangle it.

'Quick, this way.' Fox's arms were round her; he was herding people out of the theatre. She went with him, still clutching the stone.

'My dear guests,' Richmond was calling hoarsely over the throng, 'don't be alarmed. I've sent for the constables. Just be so good as to move along the corridor into the main house and our festivity can continue.'

'Is it a riot?' Anne asked Fox. Her fingers scrabbled at the string that tied the paper round the stone. 'Look. This says—' She struggled to read while the chattering crowd pushed them along. 'What a curious little couplet.'

'Let's see.' Fox almost snatched the page from her.

> *God dam the Duke of Richmond and all his works.*
> *We'll put down Luxsury and Extravegance in high life.*

'They can't spell,' said Anne, facetious.

'Oh, dear,' murmured Fox, 'I feared as much. Your brother-in-law has become rather *persona non grata* with the lower orders.'

'But—you mean it's a political mob?'

He shrugged. 'Every mob has a bit of politics in it, and a bit of restlessness, and a lot of porter.'

'How dare they!' Anne's eyes were prickling. 'To attack our harmless theatricals...'

'I know, I know.' His voice was soothing and he held her elbow firmly as they climbed the stairs into the main house. 'But they have so little, they spend a third of their wages on bread—did you know that?—and when they gawked in the bright windows of the Richmond House Theatre tonight, what did they see? Lords and ladies dressing up and pretending to be what they aren't, at enormous expense.'

Anne felt rebuked. This stained, rumpled man was her conscience. She recognised Mrs Hobart's shrill voice behind her. 'For this, in Paris, they'd swing from the gallows.'

She turned. 'There's not much harm done, after all. Only a few panes of glass.'

Mrs Hobart, ten rows of pearls round her throat, goggled at her. 'To threaten the person of the heir to the throne—'

'For my part,' Anne told her, 'I delight in our British liberties, even if they lead to occasional abuses.'

'That's the spirit,' Fox told her jovially.

But she was still shaken. She wondered what the constables were doing outside. If one could be hanged for picking a pocket, or burned at the stake for coining like that poor woman last year, then what was the punishment for attacking a duke and his guests? The irony was that ten years ago Richmond had been a radical Reformer who'd gone so far as to argue for *one man, one vote*; how must he feel, to be so hated by the people now?

There was Derby in the corner, the unruffled aristocrat, his face as smooth as an egg. She looked for Eliza Farren, but couldn't see her anywhere.

ELIZA LAID her head back on the cracked padding of the hackney cab as it jolted along the Strand.

Her mother, after three glasses of Richmond's champagne, was voluble. 'Well, I call that very strange. My Lord never forgets lending us his carriage at night, unless he's got a prior engagement. Either he escorts us back to Great Queen Street himself or at the very least he lends us the carriage. It's understood, has been for years.'

Eliza's eyes were shut. The upholstery of the cab smelt of something faintly rancid; she tried not to wonder what it might be.

'You say he was fatigued,' Mrs Farren went on, 'but that can't be it. Why, you're fatigued too, after you oversaw the whole performance, with all your responsibilities—and seized with headache, or else you wouldn't have brought us away before the Duke's select supper,' she added a little resentfully. 'I'm fatigued too, come to that.'

Why couldn't her mother just say *tired*?

'Was Derby the worse for liquor, I wonder? I didn't notice. But I think he must have been such to have forgot our arrangement about the carriage.'

Eliza snapped into life. 'Since you insist on knowing—I told the driver we wouldn't be needing it tonight.'

Her mother gawked at her. 'Betsy Farren!'

She winced; the name made her fourteen again, with wrists too long for her frayed lace ruffles. 'Don't shriek, the cabman will hear you. I don't want to discuss it.'

'You won't talk to your own mother, who's spent her life watching over you?' Though Margaret Farren's career on the provincial stage had been undistinguished to the point of humiliation, she could still turn on the tragedy voice. 'You won't tell your own mother what shocking thing has happened?'

Eliza sighed loudly. She might as well get it over with, or there'd be no sleep tonight and she had a rehearsal at nine in the morning. 'I was backstage—I don't know where you'd got to,' she added with quiet spite, 'and Derby rushed in and made a proposition.'

'What kind of proposition?'

'Oh, Mother! A proposition to sail to Kathmandu, what do you think?'

The older woman absorbed this in silence and for a moment Eliza thought it was over. Then the real interrogation began. 'Did he lay hands on you, any?'

She shook her head.

'Did he speak obscenely?'

Eliza didn't dignify that one with a reply.

'Did he mention any figure?'

'Mother!' Eliza's head was tight with pain and she had a terrible thirst. The last thing she wanted was to work through the whole tawdry business again in the hackney cab, like a low afterpiece to the main drama.

'One must keep all facts in mind,' said Mrs Farren, knotting her fingers on her lap.

'The facts are these,' said her daughter, turning on her, 'item, the person in question is still married; item, I don't care to be any man's mistress; item, it's therefore irrelevant whether he was about to offer me a house in Hanover Square and £10,000 a year!'

'That's enough items for now,' said Mrs Farren, as if discussing laundry. Then, after a minute, 'Do you think it would be as high as £10,000?'

'Christ!' They both reeled back a little at the curse. 'I won't haggle. I won't sell out. I thought you understood that about me.'

Mrs Farren's eyes were watery. 'I do, I do. You've never been like other girls, you're a cut above. But, and I don't mean to anger you, but it's been years and years, Betsy—'

'Eliza.'

'Eliza, then, it's been near ten years since we came to London and where's your fine principles got us?'

She was watching out for their door on Great Queen Street; she rapped on the ceiling to make the cabman stop.

'You're twenty-four, my dear, and you won't get any younger,' said her mother, wheedling. 'Maybe now's the time to make the best settlement you can. His Lordship's friends all dote on you since these theatricals; they wouldn't drop you if there was gossip, or not all of them. The thing could be done decently enough. Just provisionally, like, till the Countess snuffs it and you're free to marry.'

Eliza was fumbling in her net purse.

'Don't forget, Derby's a man, for all he's an earl,' Mrs Farren warned. 'He won't wait for ever.'

She found the coin and looked up. 'We won't speak of this again.'

Struts

*Narrow pieces of stone, wood or ivory connecting
small, delicate elements or limbs of a statue to
prevent them from snapping off.*

⟶

THIS Paper has received a veritable deluge of letters on the
question of Immorality in high life. Our correspondents point
out that every vice known to man is presently practised on the
dark side of that little moon known as the World. Do we not
hear daily of disgusting episodes of Drunkenness, with
p-ssings under tables and v-m-tings in the street? Even our
P——e M——r himself has been seen to address the H—e of
C——ns in an intoxicated state. The Sporting realm, in particular, is known not only for excessive tippling, smoking and
blaspheming, but also Gambling, the greatest peril of our age.

As for the gentler sex, they are among the most addicted
practitioners of Faro and Roulette, but reserve much of their
energies for Tittle-tattle and Carnality. But we do not speak of
these matters to cast harsh judgement, as do some pious publications. It is said there is nothing new under the sun and,
since Adam was first corrupted by his blushing Eve, has not
our race struggled with its Appetites? And if the vices of the
great are so prominent, perhaps it is only because they live in
the glare of Celebrity, while lesser folk commit their misdeeds
behind closed doors.

Is the foremost young gentleman of the land, the P—e of
W—s himself, not first among sinners, whether we speak of
gluttony, drunkenness, prodigality, gambling, or fleshly passion? No wonder so many say to themselves, whatever our future Monarch does must be right!
— THE BEAU MONDE INQUIRER, *June 1787*

VISCOUNTESS MELBOURNE'S CONFINEMENT WAS ALMOST OVER
and Anne was taking her first look at the newcomer. The bedroom
was hot and musty, since the windows couldn't be opened till the
month was up; only faint rattlings of carriage wheels leaked across
the courtyard from Piccadilly. Lady Melbourne was in the great
pink bed with the floating tester. 'Emily's a good name,' Anne remarked, bending down to the carved rosewood cradle and putting
her finger into the tiny creature's grip.

'Isn't it *ravish,*' chimed Georgiana.

The mother shrugged and adjusted her satin wrapping robe
round her strong neck. 'It's in the family; Peniston likes it and I
picked the last three names, after all.'

Anne hadn't seen Lord Melbourne on this visit, or not that
she'd noticed; the Viscount was never more than a smiling ghost in
the corridors. He and his wife were so fashionable, they were hardly
ever seen together. The baby's cap had slipped sideways now, revealing a lick of dark-red hair. 'She doesn't look very like you,'
Anne remarked carefully.

'No. She's the spit of her father,' said Lady Melbourne.

Nothing ruffles her feathers, thought Anne in rueful admiration.

'And is Lord Melbourne...happy with the new arrival?' asked
Georgiana.

'Perfectly.'

'How well you manage things,' the Duchess murmured, widen-
ing her eyes at Anne.

Anne thought about the red-haired Lord Egremont, an intimate at Melbourne House for the last ten years; Lady Melbourne's little twins who'd died at birth had had the same colouring. Emily's brother William, at eight, had dark-red curls too, whereas George, the toddler, was named for his godfather, the Prince of Wales, and had the little pursed royal mouth. Only young Peniston, away at Oxford, had the indolent looks of Lady Melbourne's husband— but he was the heir and so the one that mattered, of course.

Anne found her friend's ménage rather extraordinary; she felt quite at sea when she tried to reconcile the principles of virtue and self-respect with the complexities of Lady Melbourne's private life. But she couldn't find it in herself to condemn it, as it was so evidently harmonious and the lady was never indiscriminate or obvious. Perhaps, Anne thought, Lady Melbourne's long and serene attachment to Lord Egremont should be considered a sort of marriage of the heart, with its own form of honour; it was significant that when he'd tried to form an engagement elsewhere (to Walpole's niece, unfortunately), he'd ended by breaking it off. Viscount Melbourne had his freedom and so did his wife, and the children were well loved; it was a strange arrangement, but it seemed to work.

'So,' said Lady Melbourne, setting down her cup of caudle, 'I heard about your marvellous show at Richmond House.' Anne was about to give her details, but the Viscountess was already listing the parties she'd missed during her confinement, including an assembly at Devonshire House. She'd been most amused to hear that several ladies had bribed Georgiana's seamstress for the secret of her latest design and they'd all turned up in exactly the same costume— which was nothing like what Georgiana was wearing.

'A vastly elegant assembly, but such a stifling crush,' Anne told her. 'I couldn't get near the supper room and I confess I came home early. You're just too popular,' she told the Duchess.

'You didn't miss much, the desserts were paltry,' said Georgiana with a little grimace. 'I've been trying to retrench my expenses, don't you know, since my last talk with Canis, when he was *so kindy* about my debts and agreed not to go through with the separation.'

'Splits and divorces are far too common these days,' said Lady Melbourne, smoothing her sheets. 'The art of marriage has been quite lost.'

Not in this house, Anne thought with dark amusement.

Lady Melbourne reached for their glasses. 'Have some more caudle while it's hot.'

Anne could never tell if she liked the drink or not; the spiced wine was good in itself, but the gruel and honey made it oddly cloying.

'*Delish,*' said Georgiana. 'Was the birth vastly gruelling?'

'No worse nor better than usual,' Lady Melbourne answered with a shrug. 'I know of no less perilous way of bringing the creatures into the world. I always ensure my Will is up to date and leave letters of advice for the children, just in case.'

'I've been starving myself for a fortnight,' said Georgiana, 'but I can't resist your plum cake.' Reaching for the plate again, she offered it to Anne, who shook her head.

'You run too much into extremes, my dear; if you weaken your constitution how will you ever do your duty by the Duke?' asked Lady Melbourne.

'Oh, I know, I know, that's what Bess says,' mumbled Georgiana through a mouthful of cake. 'Since the little girls I've miscarried time and time again—tried electric shocks and milk baths and Dr Graham's frictions—and still Canis's beastly family accuse me of deliberately thwarting their hopes for an heir, when it's all I wish for!'

'Poor darling—but you've only just turned thirty,' said Anne. Her eyes moved to the picture in the top left-hand corner of the bedroom: the whimsical painting of the three of them as witches that Daniel Gardner had painted in the '70s. Herself in black, with a pointed hat and a wand to echo her sharp features, guarding the steaming cauldron—and Georgiana and Lady Melbourne, in creamy satin draperies, descending from the sky with handfuls of herbs for the brew. How unmarked they all looked on the glossy canvas and how merry.

'I spent my birthday in self-examination,' Georgiana assured her. 'I'm sick of my wild and scrambling life—dress, gambling, admiration, gorging—and I'm giving up all my follies. My beloved Bess has promised to watch me like a strict but tender mother. I hardly buy any lottery tickets and I only play for shillings now.'

Lady Melbourne's eyebrows shot up. 'I thought you'd sworn off gaming.'

'Well, only whist, commerce, that kind of thing—no faro or roulette, no games of chance or at all,' Georgiana told her weakly.

'I simply can't understand why, with your financial embarrassments—'

'Oh, that's all very easy to say,' interrupted Georgiana, chewing her pretty lip. 'Canis and Racky and my mother and sister play; everyone plays. People expect one to play, and play high; they protest it looks eccentric or priggish if one doesn't and they never believe one isn't rich as Croesus's wife.'

'Gambling's a strange passion,' said Anne.

'A scourge, more like,' pronounced Lady Melbourne.

'It leaves me unmoved,' Anne told her, 'but I know a dozen people who need it like salt.'

'I don't *need* it, exactly,' protested Georgiana and Lady Melbourne rolled her eyes at Anne. Was the Viscountess one of the many friends who'd lent Georgiana money and would never see it again?

'How's the Duke of Dorset?' asked Lady Melbourne.

'Oh, perfectly well,' said Georgiana blandly.

'Isn't he our ambassador in Paris these days?' asked Anne.

'Well, yes, but he often comes to London; it's an easy journey.'

Was that an indirect admission? Anne wondered.

'I don't know why so many women find Dorset irresistible,' remarked Lady Melbourne.

'Don't chide me, darlingest,' said Georgiana, 'I hardly see the fellow except in company. He does have the most charming, almost melancholy manner.'

Lady Melbourne gave a tight-shouldered shrug. 'Be careful,

that's all I say. It was Dorset who ruined Lady Derby for one and a few years ago he did your dear Bess's reputation no good either.'

'Tish tush, there was nothing in that,' Georgiana protested. 'People are so mean about my lovely Racky. Her life's been such a difficult one and every time she so much as smiles at a fellow she's been abused for it.'

Lady Bess Foster's name had been linked with several other gentlemen's as well as the Duke of Devonshire's, Anne knew. It was rumoured that the real reason for her prolonged trip to Italy, two years ago, was the birth of one of Devonshire's by-blows. Some said the Duke and Lady Bess took shocking advantage of the naïve Duchess, but to Anne the triangle seemed another of those peculiar arrangements people made for their own happiness. No, what puzzled her was Georgiana's insistence on the innocence of her beloved. Perhaps all she meant was that Lady Bess was good at heart?

'You misunderstand me, my dear Georgiana,' Lady Melbourne was saying with a smile. 'I don't care in the least about Lady Bess's conscience—that's her private business. But the look of things—one's reputation—is in the hands of society. Discretion is the tax we pay the World, or suffer the consequences.'

'I know, I know.' Georgiana sighed. 'But sometimes I feel like declaiming that famous line of Mrs Freelove's from *The Jealous Wife*, do you remember?'

'Of course,' said the Viscountess. She quoted grandly, '*My rank places me above the scandal of little people, and I shall meet such petty insolence with the greatest ease and tranquillity.*' She leaned back against her pillows and suddenly changed tack. 'Now you, my dear Anne, with your ascetic disposition—'

Anne stiffened; what was Lady Melbourne going to say about her reputation?

'It's lucky you've avoided the whole business of breeding, so far at least.'

Anne preferred to think of herself as a woman of sensibility; *ascetic* seemed a rather unfeeling word. What had her sister called her that night at the Richmond House Theatre? *A cool spirit.* 'So far?' she echoed. 'I'm thirty-eight.'

The Viscountess shrugged. 'Lady Louisa Parchett dropped her first at forty-three.'

'My statues are my progeny.'

'Did you and Damer have no...near misses, even?' enquired Georgiana, taking a long swallow of caudle.

'None.' Anne was going to let it go at that, but the other two were looking at her with lazy anticipation. 'The truth is—there was really no question of any of that. After the honeymoon, well, John and I had so little in common,' she said awkwardly.

'Had he mistresses?'

Lady Melbourne's bluntness sometimes embarrassed Anne. 'I think so. The late Mrs Baddeley, the actress—'

'Oh, yes, Sophia Baddeley never could resist a hug and a bracelet.'

'Of course, that's what leads to dying of the pox at thirty-seven,' said Georgiana sympathetically. 'I was just reading her memoirs the other day, in the carriage coming down from Derbyshire; terrible trash, but amusing.'

'I don't know if I ever told you, Anne, but my husband had a lapse in taste and kept Baddeley himself for a while in the '70s.' The baby started to cry and Lady Melbourne reached for a bell-pull on the wall. 'It led to an amusing incident: once, a superb diamond necklace he'd bought her was delivered here by mistake. I put it on for dinner and thanked him kindly for the present.'

Georgiana whooped with laughter.

Anne had to admire her old friend's verve. 'Perhaps, if I'd been as pragmatic as you I'd have made John Damer a better wife.'

Lady Melbourne shrugged. 'One can't conquer one's nature. Could one of you pass the baby?'

Georgiana leapt to scoop up the wailing infant, whose skirt was folded over her feet to make a compact bundle. She gave her to the Viscountess in the high bed, who rocked the child and planted a kiss on the little red curl.

This reminded Anne, for some reason, of her eagle. 'At the Academy, I'm showing the osprey I saw your gamekeeper catch at Brocket Hall.'

'Mm,' said Georgiana, 'I hear your pieces are all marvellous, *oo cwever fing*! I long to see them myself, but I just haven't had a *mo*.'

'We must pop in as soon as I've got my figure back,' Lady Melbourne told the Duchess.

'How's the original?' asked Anne.

The wet-nurse hurried in just then, curtsied and took the screaming baby.

'Did His Lordship ever manage to tame it, or did he let it fly?'

'What? Oh, no,' said Lady Melbourne, calling up the details, 'the bird got a moult, I'm afraid, and died in a fortnight.'

Anne felt oddly shaken. Right through the cold spring she had lived in such intimate conjunction with the eagle—thought through its muscles, conjured up every feather out of curls of clay. It had seemed the epitome of strength, of furious ambition, despite the chains. And now, to think its bones had been fed to the dogs at Brocket Hall.

MORE THAN a month after the actress had told Derby what she thought of his proposition he was still rigid. No one had spoken to him that way since he'd been a puny new boy at Eton. These days he tried to concentrate on business—committee meetings about the Hodge Podge Bill for any unfinished matters at the end of the Session, his investment in Lancashire canals and a remarkable new flour mill powered by steam, improvements to his tenants' cottages at Knowsley, as well as the redecoration of his Surrey villa, the Oaks. That was what men did, they got on with things. They didn't crumble because one woman, out of all the women in England, had turned her back and said *My happiness is none of your concern*.

Some nights he lay awake and raw against his great carved headboard in Derby House. *Amo ergo sum. I love therefore I am*. He knew he'd trampled on the best thing in his life. But first thing, waking up between sweaty linen sheets, different words spoke themselves in his head: *chilly bitch*. Who did Eliza Farren think she was? A brewer's granddaughter and a drunkard's daughter, turning down an earl; how his ancestors would laugh in their marble vault.

Tonight Derby was sitting on the bottom row of the Royal Cockpit behind Buckingham Palace—the spot reserved for better-born cockmasters. This sporting establishment had outlived the houses of Tudor and Stuart, and looked set to last at least as long as the house of Hanover. Its octagonal walls were lined with men's bodies; the Babel of wagers and speculation filled the air. Derby leaned forward, elbows on knees, peering into the light the dangling chandelier spread on the twenty-foot circular stage, its yellowing grass. They should have put down some fresh sod; you could see the matting of old bloodstains.

A whack on his shoulder. Sir Charles Bunbury, whisky-breathed, leaned down precariously and shouted in his ear, 'You didn't keep me a place!'

'Beg your pardon,' mouthed Derby.

'Didn't you get my note saying I'd see you at the fight? Now I'm stuck up here between my former wife's third cousin and a shoemaker. Such a ghastly mob—the master should charge more than two shillings in, that's the problem.'

But that was one of the things Derby liked best about sports. *All men are equal on the turf and under the turf,* as the saying went and the same was true of cockpits as of racecourses. In this raffish atmosphere he could sit beside working men in trousers, fellows with chapped, black-nailed hands, and no one cared about anything but the game. He'd lost his purse to a butcher in his time and been bowled out by one of the Duke of Dorset's under-gardeners on another occasion; there was a refreshing equality among sportsmen. It allowed Derby a respite from the dignity and duties of his ancient name.

'How's your own birds these days—had any good mains?' called Bunbury from the row above.

Derby shook his head. His gaze was fixed on the platform of worn sods.

'May I just say, old man, that sometimes you're about as much fun to talk to as my deaf, blind, dumb and flatulent great-aunt?'

Derby's face cracked into a smile.

'I blame those theatricals of Richmond's. You haven't been yourself since.'

'That must be it,' said Derby over his shoulder. 'I've let fame go to my head.'

'Ah, fame,' cried Bunbury. 'That legendary hussy whose favours, like those of a pustulating whore, unfit us for ordinary life.'

Here came the cocks from the pens—Lord Peckinshaw's Red and Mr Foyton's Yellow, held tightly in the hands of their setters—and the spectators leapt to their feet. The law-teller, blank-faced, checked their marks against his identification list.

Bunbury roared down, 'Who's leading the main so far?'

'Peckinshaw,' said Derby. 'His birds have won seven out of ten, at £20 a battle. But the big stake's on this odd match.'

'I should say so. A lovely pair of five-pound champions. The Yellow's a famous warrior; killed three in a row in Newmarket at the autumn meet. I hope you put a hefty sum on him. How big's the bag?'

'£200.'

There were a few last shouted wagers—'forty shillings to one on the Red'—'Done and done!'—and then the law-teller waved everyone back from the grassy platform where he and the two setters stood.

Derby had eyes only for the narrow, close-cropped birds, each of them strapped into a pair of long curved silver spurs. Peckinshaw's scar-thumbed setter moistened the red's head with his own spit to flatten the feathers. The birds struggled as they were set down a yard apart on the wide chalk ring. The setters backed off, raised their hands to show they weren't interfering. The Yellow was the first to let out a shrill crow of defiance. He mantled fiercely, spreading each wing over each outstretched leg in turn, making himself look huge. The Red didn't make a sound, but ran straight at the other and seized him by the neck. The crowd let out a deep grunt.

It was rare for a fight to be a true battle from the start; often all the birds wanted to do was get away from each other. But these two were the right stuff, thought Derby with a quiver of pleasure. They broke apart in a flurry of colour, then closed in again. Every man in the cockpit leaned forward to see what was happening; the audience moved like one body. Foyton's Yellow was a hasty, hearty fighter, but he wasted too much of himself shrieking out his superiority; the silent Red was closer-heeled and deadly with his grip. Another hiss from the crowd; the Yellow had staggered backwards and might have fallen over the raised rim of the stage if the setter hadn't seized him and thrown him back in. Both birds were bleeding now, but not heavily. The Yellow had stopped crowing; neither of them let out a sound. They walked to and fro, toes gripping the worn grass, regarding each other.

The law-teller started the count. It was often like this. Derby could think of a hundred battles in which an initial show of valour settled down into this wounded sullenness, as if courage had leaked out of the birds with the first drops of blood. 'Nine and twenty, thirty, one and thirty.'

Derby found his fingers digging into the polished knob of his cane; he loosened them and rubbed them on his leather breeches.

'Five and thirty, six and thirty.'

At last the Yellow stirred into life; he ran at his adversary as if to peck him in the eye. A chaos of feathers and Lord Peckinshaw's Red struck. Screeching, dragging. He was hung in the Yellow's wing. Peckinshaw's setter jumped in bare-handed and disentangled the red bird's spur from the other's wing feathers with one twist.

Rumpled and outraged, the birds backed off again. 'Five, six,' chanted the law-teller. The setters stood over their cocks but didn't touch them, only hissed incitement. 'Nineteen, twenty, one and twenty.'

'Fight, by gad,' roared Derby, surprising himself.

As if obedient, the birds engaged. The Yellow's wing was ripped and dripping scarlet. He had the Red by the hackle feathers, he was heeling him hard but half the kicks went wide. Derby's eyes stung but he didn't blink; in this game you could miss the decisive moment if you so much as wiped your face. There was a lot of gore now, on grass and feathers, but it was hard to tell which bird had lost the most. A shame, Derby always thought, that blood couldn't be identified by colour as plumage was.

They shook each other loose and withdrew. 'Eight and twenty, nine and twenty.' The law-teller's face was unmoved as he chanted the numbers, his fingers marking them out. After forty counts between fighting, the rule said that the birds were to be set close to, because otherwise they'd never finish it.

'Chop 'em in hand,' shouted a spectator.

Each setter seized his bird in two hands; it was hard to get a tight grip when the blood was fresh and slippery. The silver spikes on the heels were muddy-looking now. The birds were set down beak to beak on the chalk mark at the very centre of the circle. Mr Foyton's Yellow was staggering; the Red broke away, but Lord Peckinshaw's setter had him back on the mark in half a second. The cockpit rang with shrieks now; the birds were silent but the men were crowing out their urgent fury. The Red drew himself up, clawed the Yellow to the floor and with one movement sliced open his throat.

Derby relaxed on to the bench. All around him men were whooping or cursing, arguing or slapping each other on the shoulder. Derby shut his eyes. All things considered, he preferred a battle to the death. Though a fight could be won by default—when one bird turned tail and refused to fight ten times—it always felt unsatisfying. And what was the point of saving the life of a broken-spirited cock, after all, when you'd never risk a penny on him again? No, it was better to let nature take her course.

Foyton's setter had picked up the Yellow by his torn neck to carry him off. Derby found himself thinking of Hector's body, dragged round the walls of Troy. Peckinshaw's man had the Red in his arms, as if embracing him, but of course he was checking his wounds; he put his lips to a deep cut and sucked out the dirt. Now he would pack up the bleeding bird in a warm crate and bring him back to the sheds, for a week of careful nursing, then a month or two of convalescence at His Lordship's estate in Shropshire. It occurred to Derby that the bird couldn't complain; this was better treatment than most army officers got after a battle.

The crowd was shuffling and pushing out. 'Can you drop me home? My carriage's got a broken wheel,' said Bunbury.

'If you help me find mine.'

It was a humid June night; Derby's shirt was sticking to his ribs. They stood on the corner, looking up and down the crowded street, till Derby's coachman managed to thread his way through the other carriages to his master.

'How much did you drop on the Yellow? I'm down by £50.'

'Nothing,' said Derby.

His old friend glared at him. 'I told you to put £100 on that bird.'

'Well, just as well I didn't, since it's coq-au-vin by now.'

Bunbury's bristling eyebrows met. 'Don't tell me you backed the Red,' he said.

'I didn't wager tonight.'

'What, at all?' Bunbury puzzled over this. 'Are you broke, M'Lord?' he asked satirically. 'Or ill?'

'I didn't care who won.'

Bunbury blinked twice. 'That's not like you. So why did you go, if you weren't meaning to stake so much as sixpence either way?'

'I wanted to see it,' said Derby through his teeth.

AFTER THE terrible scene at the Richmond House Theatre, Lord Derby hadn't sent a single note to Eliza, or even his footman to enquire after her health, but his carriage did continue to turn up outside her door every day, as always. Mrs Farren saw this as a hopeful sign—'*a mark of great* politesse,' she called it—but Eliza knew it for what it was: an outstretched claw. Derby was a stubborn man and he thought he could win her back by mute pressure. Well, she didn't need an armorial carriage (*Sans changer*, it nagged her, *Sans changer*) and she didn't need a maritally entangled aristocrat who had nothing better to do than hang around her like a noose. So every day she told the coachman, 'Please tell your master that we don't require his carriage.'

After a week it stopped showing up. Perversely, this made Eliza afraid. Her mother preserved a stiff silence on the matter. At first Eliza had felt that this hiatus was a punishment she was inflicting on Derby; now it occurred to her that he was punishing her. The afternoons were warm, so she walked down Drury Lane to the theatre, or hailed a hackney if it was raining; she was getting used to their scarred upholstery, the marks of other people's muddy boots. She was working very hard to memorise her last role at Drury Lane this season—the satirical spinster Beatrice in *Much Ado About Nothing*—as well as her new ones for the summer season at the Haymarket. She hadn't time to consider what it would be like to be an unmarried actress who was no longer being wooed by the richest man in England.

It was in a Mount Street hat shop that Eliza bumped into Mrs Damer. 'My dear,' said the sculptor, 'it seems for ever! I've been working so hard on a bust of my mother, I've barely been out.' She admired Eliza's green silk redingote with black buttons. 'You're always such a picture of elegance.' Eliza memorised the compliment for her mother, who had a sharp eye and helped her pick out her costumes every morning.

They ordered some raspberry ice to eat at one of the little tables. Mrs Damer was dithering between a slouch hat in felt and shirred silk, and a high-crowned beaver with tassels, for her daily ride. She went on and on about what a friendly fellow feeling the theatricals had produced among the Players, whose constant company she missed. 'Such a distressing sensation, when the mob broke the windows, though,' she murmured. 'I've always thought of myself as a friend to the people, a true follower of our dear Fox. But that night, with broken glass all over the floor, I must confess I shrank from my own countrymen as from wild beasts. So fortunate that you'd gone home early,' she added, patting Eliza's hand.

Conversations with Mrs Damer never stayed on the surface for long. So Derby mustn't have said a word to his old friend about the quarrel, Eliza realised. The ice was tasteless on her tongue. Had he told no one, then? Or was Eliza being discussed at this very minute, with coarse contempt, in the coffee room at Brooks's Club? She shook herself slightly. 'I've had a hard morning's shopping. Drapers, confectioners—I couldn't resist those new chocolate drops at Gunter's—and then three different hat shops, looking for the perfect *bergère*.'

'I think you've found it,' said Mrs Damer, nodding at the box between them, which held an immensely wide, shallow-crowned straw with ribbons to tie it on.

'But should I wear it with fresh flowers, or a lace valance?'

'Lace.'

'You're right. I'm no child of Nature,' said Eliza drolly.

'I'm surprised not to find Derby at your side today, carrying your purchases in his usual devoted-servant style,' said Mrs Damer, looking her in the eye.

'Ah,' said Eliza, her mind a blank. How to turn this conversation? The pause was already too long.

The brown eyes were very penetrating. 'Is he busy at the Lords? My father thinks it's dreadful for the country, the way Sessions stretch right into summer nowadays.'

It would be so easy to nod, but Eliza said, 'I've no idea where or how Derby is. The fact is I haven't seen him since that night at Richmond House.'

'Ah,' said Mrs Damer and spooned up the last of her raspberry ice.

Eliza never knew which way this woman was going to turn. On an impulse she asked, 'Was there anything at all you liked about being married?'

'Well, let me see.' Mrs Damer sucked her spoon. 'I was considerably richer than I am now—or at least I lived high. I refused no invitations and dressed well, though not as well as John did; he was such a dandy, he even rouged his mouth. Of course, I was very young, with a shallow taste for glamour and luxury; I didn't know my own nature,' she added. 'Lady Melbourne and Georgiana and I did a lot of gadding about to masquerades. We had our hair dressed three feet high—oh, how it hurt,' she said, touching her hand to her soft curls reminiscently—'ornamented with birds and fruit, or a ship in full sail. And we played silly tricks.'

'Such as?' asked Eliza.

'Oh, you know; we ran round Ranelagh Gardens popping our cheeks.' Mrs Damer demonstrated by puffing her cheeks up like balloons and bursting them with two fingers.

Eliza suddenly remembered doing the same thing as a child. She let out such a loud laugh that a couple at a nearby table stared at her. Wonderful, she thought irritably, now there'd be a paragraph in the papers about *a prominent Comedienne heard guffawing in a Mount Street hat shop.*

Their kettle arrived. 'This trash of tea!' said Mrs Damer with a languid sigh. 'I don't know why I drink so much of it.'

'Heigho!' Eliza finished the quote, grinning at her.

'In the end I sickened of all the high jinks,' confided Mrs Damer. 'After a few years John and I couldn't bear the sight of each other and he moved out. Then, when he came to me and said he and his brothers were so deep in debt with the Jews—'

'How much?' Eliza put in, unable to stop herself.

Mrs Damer blew on her tea. '£70,000,' she whispered with dark relish.

Eliza couldn't imagine quite how one could run up such a debt—enough to buy a dozen houses. She added another jagged lump of sugar to her cup. She and her mother had never bought sugar for their tea till Eliza had made her début at Drury Lane ten years ago and received her first London wage; for her it would always be the taste of the city.

'He told me to pack my trunks for France, before he could be arrested,' Mrs Damer went on. 'Then, when I'd said all my goodbyes, I got the news that John had wound up the comedy with a suicide.'

Eliza knew not to offer sympathy. 'That would never do on the stage.'

Mrs Damer gave her a rueful smile. 'No, because it's not a real ending, is it? It leaves everything hanging. All I felt was rage that the man had chosen the most shameful way of escaping from his cares—upstairs in a public tavern, at three o'clock in the morning,' she murmured in Eliza's ear, leaning across the table, 'after carousing with four harlots and a blind fiddler.'

'No!'

'Ladies, can I show you anything else today?' asked the shopkeeper.

Mrs Damer waved him away. 'Of course, he was declared lunatic, as suicides always are, but the truth is that John was a coward.' She spooned up some sugar from the bottom of her cup. 'He left me bankrupt at twenty-eight, and my vile father-in-law put all the blame on me and made me sell my jewels to set against John's debts.'

'Oh, my dear,' said Eliza, 'what a story!'

'It'd do for a cheap three-volume novel, I suppose. Other things happened too, as a consequence; appalling things I don't like to recall. Like a dirty thumbprint on my life.' Eliza waited, but Mrs Damer, fiddling with the knot of her lace apron, didn't elaborate. 'However,' she said finally, 'my husband's exit was the making of me, though I wouldn't say so to anyone less understanding. In fact, I've never spelled it out to anyone but you, Miss Farren.'

'I'm—I'm honoured,' said Eliza. When the Richmond House theatricals had ended she'd known she risked slipping out of that circle—Derby's circle. But today she thought perhaps she was going to retain Anne Damer's friendship after all, despite their differences in age and rank and education.

'These days, with my widow's jointure—£2500 a year,' Mrs Damer added frankly—'I have a comfortable sufficiency.'

It was actually less than Eliza had assumed; many ladies lived and dressed less well than Mrs Damer on twice that. Eliza and her mother, on the £1200 or so she made from wages and Bens, had to be very careful and resourceful; food was a terrible expense these days and lighting was worse.

'I can live and buy my marble blocks, and travel too,' Mrs Damer continued, 'because a widow may do what an unmarried woman mayn't. I've discovered what few women know: to live alone has its own pleasures. John gave me back my liberty before I was old, so I suppose I should thank him for that much. Also, the scandal parted the sheep from the goats,' Mrs Damer added grimly. 'Those who were fearful of taint by association simply melted away. Georgiana was splendid, of course, and Lady Melbourne too; she said *Good riddance to bad rubbish!* And I'll always be grateful to Fox, because it was he who broke the news of the suicide to me when no one else dared. He galloped to catch up with my carriage—his horse almost dead under him—and he took my hand in his hot paws and said, *My very dear friend, don't go home tonight.*' Mrs Damer's eyes were shining.

'Fox hung around me my first season at Drury Lane,' Eliza said lightly, 'till I was misguided enough to accept a breeches part and he swiftly came to the conclusion that I was far too skinny for him.'

Mrs Damer put her head back and laughed. 'Such strange tastes men have. Tell me, have you ever been in love?'

Eliza was staggered by the question.

'I beg your pardon, I don't know where that came from. I've no right to know.' But Mrs Damer's lips were curling into a smile. 'I only ask because I've never fallen into those dread thralls myself.'

The two of them had been speaking so freely in this cramped little shop—discussing money and marriage and other matters of life and death—that Eliza felt it would be childish to back off now. She spoke very low. 'Nor I. Unless a juvenile infatuation counts.'

'A fellow actor?' whispered Mrs Damer.

Eliza winced at her accuracy.

'Was it...Kemble?'

'Oh, no,' said Eliza, appalled at the thought of that saturnine jaw. 'This was years ago, before Kemble ever came to Drury Lane.'

Mrs Damer waited, her long arms crossed on the table.

'No, my preference has always been for comedy over tragedy,' murmured Eliza.

'Palmer? Plausible Jack!' Mrs Damer crowed quietly. 'I've guessed it, haven't I? And is he so very plausible?'

'Well,' said Eliza, embarrassed, 'he's certainly charming. But I don't think it counts as love; I was only a girl.'

'Like Juliet was, or Viola?'

Eliza chuckled, conceding the point. 'Oh, but it was no grand passion, I assure you; it was petty and miserable. The others used to mock me in the Green Room because I'd been unwise enough to mention that I could recognise the sound of his footsteps. They'd cry, *Here comes Jack, pit-a-pat!*—and pretend to swoon.'

'What humiliation.' Mrs Damer's brown eyes were eager. 'And did Palmer reciprocate your feelings?'

'Oh, I doubt he even noticed. Jack's so civil and obliging, he flirts equally with all the actresses and even the dressers. But then someone must have told him about the state of my poor juvenile heart because one night, after a performance, he came upon me in a corridor—he'd drunk rather a lot, I must say that in his defence—and he...insulted me,' said Eliza, hot-cheeked as she resorted to the hackneyed phrase.

'I don't see how drunkenness is any excuse.'

Eliza shrugged. 'He was under the impression that I'd welcome his embraces. I screamed like a banshee; he got such a fright.'

'Better than he deserved!'

'He's been a true friend to me since,' Eliza told her; 'it was only a momentary misunderstanding.'

Head on one side, Mrs Damer was considering her. 'I wonder if he's ever regretted the occasion. If he'd begun more respectfully—how strange to think you might have been Mrs Palmer.'

Eliza tingled with something like disdain. 'Oh, he was married already. I've met Mrs Palmer, as it happens, and her dozen children. He makes her very unhappy.'

'Ah.'

'I don't know what my fate may be,' Eliza added, 'but I know this much: I could never have been Mrs Palmer.' She pulled her watch out of her bodice. 'Which reminds me, I'm going to be late for a rehearsal of *The Way of the World*.'

She gathered up her parcels, but Mrs Damer offered to have them all sent on to Great Queen Street. 'You must come to dinner some time. Will you?'

'There's nothing I'd like more.'

THE UNDER-PROMPTER, William Powell, was overseeing the rehearsal in the Green Room. 'That's two of Millamant's scenes missed at two and six each, Miss Farren.'

'Yes, just note it down in the book,' said Eliza, trying to keep her patience.

'It's dreadfully hot in here, Powell. Can't we use the stage?' asked John Bannister pleasantly.

'They're setting up the flats for *Caractacus*,' said the underprompter, eyes on his curling script. 'Now, Act Two, Scene Five, if you please.'

Tall and plump, Palmer was lounging against the wall, the bags under his eyes showing he was well past forty. 'I've got a bloody demon of a headache. Haven't I said it before, Eliza?' He yawned. 'Group rehearsals of an old play only deaden it.'

'Come now, Jack, it's just the one, to refresh our memories; we haven't played *The Way of the World* in years,' said Eliza. She felt oddly awkward after her revelations in the hat shop. Palmer was the only colleague with whom she was on first-name terms; she and Tom King went back together as far as Garrick's day too, but somehow he was always Mr King, whereas Jack was Jack.

In the corner a wail went up; Mrs Jordan was rocking her enormous baby. She turned to Palmer, wide-eyed, and spoke in her lilting Irish accent. 'Perhaps we should simply trust you to turn up knowing your lines?'

The Bannisters, father and son, roared at the idea and so did Jack himself. 'Rather more than half the time,' he protested with a grin. 'And if I dried, Powell could feed me the words—or I could ad lib, or use my old trick of inserting that all-purpose speech from *The Earl of Essex.*'

'Please, spare us Essex,' begged Eliza. 'Well, for my part I rather welcome the chance to practise my cues and movements,' she added, crossing the playing area to be ready for her entrance.

'Very industrious of you, madam,' said Mrs Jordan, reaching into her muslin fichu and unlacing her bodice to pop the infant's head in. 'But some of us have other demands on our time.'

Eliza shot her a contemptuous glance. Really, it was no accident that the actress's assumed surname, Jordan, happened to mean *chamber pot.* Was the woman really boasting of having Ford's bastard latched to her bosom—and another on the way, to judge from her loose wrapper? The most irritating thing was that Dora Jordan, pink-cheeked, had never looked prettier.

'Now, I've spoken to you before about bringing the child,' said Powell gloomily, 'and you gave me your assurance—'

'Oh, don't fuss, dear Willy,' said Mrs Jordan, 'the mite will be quiet as cotton. I'm ready now. Enter Mrs Fainall, left of stage?' She strolled to her place, the baby's milky mouth working vigorously.

Jack, elbows against the wall, cradled his head. 'How', he whispered to Eliza, 'am I supposed to exchange sophisticated repartee with *that*?'

A tap at the door; Sarah Siddons and her brother Kemble. 'I wonder,' she began gravely, 'might we beg leave to intrude upon your patience and practise quietly in the corner?'

Palmer let out a groan.

'Plenty of room,' said Bannister the Elder, skipping sideways.

The room got hotter and stuffier. The *Way of the World* actors ran through the scenes at speed, muttering their lines but making sure to get every step, pose and traditional bit of business right; Powell was a stickler and cleared his throat to stop the action if they diverged in any way from his notations. During a long and particularly witty speech of Eliza's, the baby's head lolled and some milk dripped on to the floor before Dora Jordan got her damp fichu adjusted; Eliza averted her eyes. *Shameless creature!*

What made it even harder to concentrate was that in the corner Siddons and Kemble were doing the Knocking at the Gate from *Macbeth*. Even just running through the business without the words, they were riveting; Kemble's asthmatic cough only added to his air of panic and Eliza couldn't keep her eyes from following his sister's torturous hands. At one point Mrs Siddons bent in two as if she'd been stabbed in the stomach and then reared up, her face a mask of rage.

'Millamant's cue,' muttered Powell. '"*Some do say—*"'

Yes, pardon me. I know the line,' Eliza interrupted.

When they were finally released, she rushed off to the proprietor's office before anyone else could get hold of him. There was no answer to her knock—but after a few minutes he strode down the corridor, his arms full of rolled-up papers. 'Good day,' she began with a civil little curtsy.

'Is it?' Sheridan raised one eyebrow.

She ducked after him into his office before he could shut the door. 'Now, I hate to make a fuss—but really, you must have Cumberland rewrite my new part. I sent you a letter yesterday—'

'Come now, you know I don't open the post; it would take up too much of the day.'

She wasn't in the mood for bons mots.

'My dear Miss Farren,' said Sheridan with a flicker of his famous charm, 'pray excuse my surliness. You see, I haven't had so much as a glass of Madeira yet today and it's past noon.'

She found herself beginning to smile.

'You know, I have under me a company,' he went on, 'which consists of forty-eight actors, thirty-seven actresses, twenty dancers—two of them children, what's worse—thirty dressers, fourteen doorkeepers, seven box keepers, seven office keepers, four lobby keepers, three messengers, three box inspectors, two numberers, two pensioners, two prompters and one treasurer. That's not including the musicians, porters, scene builders, candle trimmers, fruit-sellers... Need I go on?'

'You may if you like, but it's not to the purpose'—and Eliza took the crisp manuscript out of her pocketbook.

He put up his hands like a shield. 'I give you my full endorse-
ment to talk to King about it.'

But the poor old manager had little power at Drury Lane.
'Couldn't you mention the matter to Cumberland, playwright to
playwright?' she asked flatteringly.

'Did you hear about the time he brought his children to see my
School for Scandal,' Sheridan asked, 'and when they laughed he called
them little dunces? It was rather unfair of him, for I'd just been to
see one of his tragedies and laughed from beginning to end.'

Eliza let out a giggle, despite herself. And Sheridan had his
hand in the small of her back, and she was outside the door and the
key was twisting in the lock.

By the time she met Cumberland in the Green Room for the
appointed private rehearsal, she'd decided to lose her temper. 'No, I
haven't *forgotten to learn my lines*, like some neophyte,' she told the
playwright, thrusting the script into his hands. 'I've informed
Sheridan that I have no intention of performing your Lady Rustic.'

Cumberland's sprouting eyebrows shot up. 'Do I need to remind
you, madam, how much glory has been showered on you for acting
in my other plays?' His voice was at its most chillingly refined and
she remembered that he was a Cambridge-trained scholar. 'Wasn't it
in my *West Indian* that you made your début nine years ago? And
didn't you shine as Lady Paragon in my *Natural Son*?'

'Lady Paragon was a shining part,' she snapped. She struck an
archly menacing pose and quoted, '"*When love holds the whip, reason
drops the reins!*"'

The playwright's mouth twitched with pleasure.

'Write me more good lines, sir, and I'll win you more glory.'

'You argue like a spoiled child, Miss Farren, if I may say so.' He
closed her hands over the script.

She slapped the air with the pages. 'Lady Rustic is a prudish
simpleton squiress. She's entirely devoid of wit and sparkle.'

Cumberland sighed. 'No character played by the famous Miss
Farren can ever lack those charms.'

'Flattery's a weak currency in this establishment,' she told him, letting her eyes scan the drab walls. 'We hear a lot of it and find it won't pay the rent. Why don't you ask Sheridan to give this part to Mrs Jordan?' she added cuttingly.

Cumberland snatched the pages back from her. 'All right, then,' he growled. 'What would you have me do to my poor play?'

'Move my introductory scene to Act Two, where it'll stand out more, and polish up my exchanges, that's all,' Eliza ordered, sweeter now. 'Write me an epilogue too, won't you? Give me some memorable sallies, a few tags I'll hear quoted at parties.'

'Oh, that's right, you move in exalted circles nowadays,' he said coldly. 'She-manager at the Richmond House Theatre, aren't you, and always hobnobbing with the Beau Monde?'

A cold thought struck Eliza on her way out of the room. Once Derby's friends knew that he was alienated from the actress, why would they take any further interest in her? *Mrs Damer will,* she comforted herself.

In the dressing room Sarah Siddons was sitting with her face in her cupped palms. 'What is it?' asked Eliza. Could one of the actress's children have died?

'I am perfectly well,' said Mrs Siddons, looking up owlishly, 'merely gathering my forces in preparation for performance.'

Eliza repressed a retort. She thought of herself as a serious, hard-working performer, but sometimes Siddons made her feel like a mere fan flutterer.

'There's a message for you,' said her mother eagerly, fishing an envelope out of her work-basket.

The paper was creamy, expensive, and the red wax was sealed with a strange blunt mark, like a nail. Eliza cracked it.

8 Grosvenor Square
My dear Miss Farren,
It was so delightful to meet you by happenstance this morning. Perhaps you might give your bergère *its first airing at my house on Wednesday at five? An intimate little dinner, just half a dozen of our mutual friends.*

Did that mean what Eliza thought it meant: Derby? How crafty Mrs Damer was. No, Eliza couldn't go, it was impossible. The awkward conjunction of it, the mortifying feelings on both sides...

>   *I remain always your admirer & obedient servt,*
>   *A.D.*

IN HER HOUSE on Grosvenor Square, the *sole Sculptress of Renown in this or any nation* (as a newspaper called her recently, not that Anne cared for flattery and she loathed the word *sculptress*) had been up since six, wearing a plain skirt and jacket like some washerwoman. She had to rise at such an unfashionable hour to get any work done, before the danger of unexpected calls. Not that visitors ever minded finding her in her filthy old dress and apron; indeed, they were usually charmed to come into her workshop and watch her *go to it with vigour,* so long as they could be accommodated with a dish of tea, *the dust being so very parching,* and might they trouble her to explain the mythological significance of the wreath, and the purpose of those little holes she was boring, and however did she manage to lift such heavy tools? Anne could always have Mrs Moll tell a mere acquaintance that the lady of the house wasn't at home, but friends and family (who knew her daily regime) were not so easily put off. She'd tried hinting that she worked best alone, but her intimates—one and all devoted connoisseurs of virtu and the *beaux arts*—took no notice.

Fidelle danced around the workshop like a butterfly in the form of a dog. 'No scrabbling in the wet clay,' Anne warned her. 'And I'm not modelling you today, so there's no use your curling up on the stool so becomingly.' She considered the half-blocked-out marble of the Countess of Ailesbury on the high table and compared it with the fired terracotta model. Her mother had been a famous beauty, but today, as Anne examined the lines of the jaw (simplified somewhat in the modelling, to bring out a timeless classicism) she was struck by a tough, steely quality. She'd have to be careful to soften the lines a little in the marble version; she didn't want to disturb her parents with a hatchet-faced bust for the stairwell at Park Place.

Anne always found it so distracting to have to worry about the feelings of her model, when she should be serving nothing but art. In some ways it would be easier to use strangers—hired paupers, even—as models, but she knew that she wouldn't be half so impassioned about doing a portrait if she didn't care about its subject. For instance, Richmond wanted her to model his favourite foxhound 'before he's obliged to cross the Styx', as he put it gruffly, but Anne meant to find some excuse, as she had in the case of Walpole's appalling Tonton, who was always leaving messes on sofas; she wasn't in the business of grinding out cats and dogs to order.

She checked a pointing mark and picked up a claw chisel. Now, what had she been trying to do with the angle of her mother's left eyebrow?

In the back of her mind, as her hammer tapped, Anne fretted over the preparations for today's dinner party; servants always forgot something if one didn't check every little detail oneself. She dearly hoped she was doing the right thing. When Eliza Farren had revealed her estrangement from Derby, Anne had shied away from interrogating her for details. As for Derby, old friend though he was, Anne had always found it difficult to persuade men to talk about their innermost feelings. (Even her beloved Walpole had a habit of leaping brilliantly from the personal to the general.) The actress's relation to the Earl was mysterious to Anne, but she knew she wished them—and whatever there was between them—well. So she'd decided to take action, in the form of a little dinner, which would bring them face to face. Though now she came to think about it, how could their dispute be cleared up over a noisy table? *Oh, dear.* Still, it was all she could think to try.

Concentrate, Anne rebuked herself as her chisel skidded on a thread of metal in the marble. *Strike for seven, rest for four.*

Many hours later Lady Mary picked her way through the workshop unannounced. 'Why, you've not even begun dressing yet,' she scolded smilingly.

Anne felt that surge of sullenness known by all younger sisters. 'It's not three yet, is it?'

'Five past! What astonishing filth,' said the Duchess, holding her Chinese silk skirts off the floor and revolving to show off her little bustle.

'Well, stay outside then,' muttered Anne.

'That reminds me, I've brought you a marvellous new goose grease and almond salve for your poor fingers; our Mrs Butchet cooked it up in the stillroom at Goodwood.'

As her sister dug the little pot out of her hanging pocket, Anne closed her roughened hands over each other. It was as if her half-sister and she were of different species. Everything Anne found a struggle came easy to Lady Mary: marriage, for instance, or the endless social round, or the running of a great house. Griefs and frustrations never seemed to stick to her sister; they glided right off.

'What are you wearing for dinner?'

'Just a white lustring chemise with a plain muslin fichu,' said Anne a little defensively, 'and a yellow sash.'

'Yellow, interesting,' said her sister neutrally. 'So who's coming? No bores, I hope.'

THEY WERE ten to dinner. Derby was one of them, to his own surprise, because despite the probable humiliation of seeing Eliza, he hadn't been able to resist the invitation. At a quarter to five, when he went round the corner of Grosvenor Square to the narrow town house at no. 8, his stomach was clenched like a fist. (It was rare for him to walk much these days, except in his own long gallery; quite apart from the filth of most streets, Londoners were so fiercely assertive of their liberties that the Earl had once had a sailor refuse to give him the wall.)

There was the actress in Mrs Damer's parlour, looking more beautiful than Derby remembered, in a straw milkmaid hat the width of a tea table, hung with lace. Less than two months since he'd seen her: it felt more like a year. Beside her sat her mother, gazing in satisfaction at the chandelier. Half the Richmond House Players were there: Mrs Hobart, Dick Edgcumbe, Sir Harry Englefield, with the Richmonds as Honorary Players, according to Mrs Damer, and her cousin Walpole to leaven the mix.

Derby handed Mrs Hobart in to dinner. Mrs Damer waved him to a seat on the same side of the table as Eliza—so that he wouldn't have to meet or avoid her eye? he wondered. The sculptor didn't entertain very often, but when she did she ordered a good dinner: never less than a dozen dishes to each cover and nothing cheap or paltry. Derby cast his eye over the entrées spread out for the first cover: he spotted a lobster au gratin, a sauté of mutton with gherkins arranged with elegant geometry, some fricassées decorated with flowers, a soupe-maigre, and three or four other side dishes, including baked tomatoes—a brave choice, since old-fashioned people still called them noxious to the health. Derby knew he was hungry, having ridden to Chiswick and back since breakfast, but the presence of the actress was causing a sort of blockage in his throat.

Mrs Damer, at the head of the table with the Richmonds (as the highest-ranking guests) on either side, let her manservant pour her a glass of claret—a good expensive château claret, Derby noticed, tasting it. He liked to see someone of her sex enjoying a fine wine; most ladies drank only light things like peach ratafia or almond orgeat.

The servants were carrying each dish round to offer it to the ladies. Derby picked up the one nearest him and peered at it. He had to say something to the actress, just to get it over with. 'Miss Farren, may I help you to what looks like a fricassée of duck?'

'Capon, I believe,' Mrs Damer corrected him, smiling. Her eyes flicked up and down the table as he passed the dish to the actress. 'So. Our little theatre, or I should say yours,' she addressed her brother-in-law.

'Without the Players,' said Lady Mary, 'what would it be but an empty building?'

Mrs Hobart simpered and fanned herself.

'I hear there's a play being written about you all,' remarked Walpole. 'No, no roast beef for me,' he told the whispering servant, 'my gout forbids it.'

'That's right,' Edgcumbe chipped in, 'a farce, to be called *Private Theatricals.*'

'Oh, yes, that's coming up at Covent Garden,' said Eliza, 'but I hadn't realised we were the butts of it.'

'The best riposte', suggested Anne Damer, spooning sauce on to her plate, 'might be for us to put on another show, even more successful than the last...'

She caught Derby's eye. 'Richmond,' he asked, on cue, 'would you consider letting us mount another play next year?' He spoke a little hoarsely, afraid that Eliza might think his request was a way of procuring her company.

'I don't see why not,' said Richmond, 'as the first was a success—'

'A glittering triumph,' Walpole corrected him.

'—apart from that pack of malcontent jackals outside, who cost me so much in plate glass.'

Murmurs of embarrassed sympathy. '*Belua multorum capitum,* as Horace would say,' contributed Edgcumbe.

Derby translated for the ladies' benefit: 'The mob is a many-headed monster. Is that boiled salmon, Sir Harry?' he added. It wasn't done to ask for a dish, but one could always throw out a hint.

'Mm and very good it is.'

One of the footmen scurried to bring it round to him. It was tasty but lukewarm, as always on these occasions; Derby had a fussy preference for hot food and when dining at home in Derby House he always had each dish carried up under a metal cover. (He'd given up the attempt at Knowsley, where the kitchen was ten minutes away from the dining room.)

'We'd need tighter security next time,' Richmond went on. 'I'll hire a team of private police to patrol the building.'

Lady Mary patted her husband on the cuff. 'Also, better ventilation.'

'Yes,' said Eliza, 'it was rather hot.' She shook her head at the pommes de terre au gratin Dick Edgcumbe was holding out.

'Stifling!'

'The fieriest circle in Dante's Inferno,' contributed Walpole.

'My paint melted into my eyes,' Mrs Hobart assured them.

'Ventilation, certainly,' said Richmond, nodding, 'and I think I'll have Wyatt design a special little box for our royal visitors. Next time, perhaps the King and Queen will grace us with their presence.'

Then Prinny couldn't be invited, Derby thought wryly; they could hardly coop Their Majesties up with their most rebellious child out of the whole thirteen, and his unlawfully wedded wife. He could just imagine the monarch muttering through the performance in his twitchy way, going *what what what? eh eh?*.

'What a tip-top plan,' cried Dick Edgcumbe. To his left, Mrs Margaret Farren produced a gappy smile.

'Of course, it all depends on our manager,' Richmond said, turning to the actress. 'We can hardly demand the gift of her time and energies again—'

'I do believe you can,' said the actress, laughing. Watching that perfect face, Derby felt slightly breathless. Did this mean he would have to do the gentlemanly thing and withdraw from the proceedings, claiming pressure of Party business? Or that she intended to treat him as any other of the Players? Or—could it be—that she had slightly softened towards him during their long parting?

'Dare we face the public again, and the critics?' wailed Mrs Hobart.

'Tish, tush,' said Lady Mary, 'you all loved it.'

'Oh,' said Mrs Damer, 'but that review that said I moved my face too much...'

'Nonsense, my child,' Walpole told her, 'you were as expressive as the role demanded.'

'Now you all know what it's like to be prey to the whims and megrims of the press,' said Eliza.

'I don't know how you bear it,' Derby told her. She looked back at him briefly, but her eyes were unreadable.

'Have any of you read Cumberland's nasty piece in the *European Magazine*?' asked Walpole.

'No, but I quarrelled with him only the other day,' said Eliza.

'He mocks people of breeding for their feeble attempts to play at being actors—'

Mrs Hobart let out a yelp of protest.

'—and he deplores the hiring of professionals as managers, which is clearly a hit at you, dear Miss Farren,' said Walpole regretfully. 'Cumberland claims that when a lady of fashion is coached in all the trickery and airs of an actress whose own job is to ape ladies of fashion, the result is only the facsimile of a facsimile.'

'I think we've heard quite enough of the playwright's malice,' said Mrs Damer, signalling to the servants to swap the first cover for the second.

Over a selection of savouries and sweets, somehow they got on to the old debate about whether Woman's intellectual properties were as different from Man's as her physical ones. 'I don't mean inferior, exactly,' Dick Edgcumbe insisted, 'only distinct.'

'In what ways?' asked the hostess.

'Well—'

Richmond stepped into the breach. 'She thinks, but he meditates. She improves, but he creates. She feels, but he acts.'

'What balderdash,' said Mrs Damer, which caused a little hiatus.

'Asparagus, madam?' Derby, not fancying the look of the pale peeled spears, limp on their bed of soaked toast, offered the dish to Mrs Hobart—and she accepted with enthusiasm. Mrs Damer could do with some more expert service, he thought; that was three times now that he'd been offered the same cod purée.

'I hear William Beckford is back in England,' remarked Sir Harry Englefield.

'The cheek of him!' Mrs Hobart fanned so hard that her front curls bobbed.

'He can't think the World has forgotten the Powderham Castle affair; it's only been, what, three years,' remarked Richmond.

Of all the ludicrous risks for Beckford to run, thought Derby, to molest a boy—Lord Loughborough's nephew, what's more—while the house was full of visitors. The sugar heir must have known he was courting ostracism and exile.

'Sir William Hamilton defends him and says there was never any proof,' mentioned Mrs Damer, her eyes on her plate.

'I never liked *Vathek*,' said Lady Mary with a little shudder.

'No, the tale reveals Beckford's propensities on every page,' agreed her husband. 'Didn't he cause his wife's death, too?'

'Childbirth kills many,' Mrs Damer pointed out.

'She must have been weakened by the mortification of the scandal, surely,' said Sir Harry.

'But your news of Beckford's return is out of date, Edgcumbe,' Walpole put in with his well-informed smirk. 'The family packed him off again to their estates in Jamaica—but the amusing thing is my correspondent at Lisbon reports the young man has hopped ship there.'

'I don't call that very amusing, I must say.' Mrs Hobart sniffed.

Walpole gave shrug. 'At my age, madam, most things are amusing.'

A servant muttered over Derby's shoulder, 'Roast fowl, M'Lord?'

'Oh, yes.' At last the fowl had made it to his plate and there was still one thigh left. Sometimes at these dinners one might watch a favourite dish wander back and forth in front of one's nose, without ever getting to taste it. Derby dowsed his plate in oyster sauce.

'Your cousin is British Minister at Lisbon, isn't he?' Mrs Damer asked Walpole.

'Yes, and he swears he won't receive the sinner, won't present him to Queen Maria—and Beckford's relatives won't send him any letters of introduction—so he remains excluded from all good society.'

'Need we talk of the nasty monster?' said Mrs Hobart, wriggling in her seat.

'Certainly not, if you don't like,' said Walpole, changing the subject smoothly. 'In Russia, so my diplomat nephew Mr Fawkener tells me, dinner is served one dish at a time.'

Lady Mary turned her long lashes on him. 'But that must take all night.'

'They don't have half so many dishes,' he explained, 'only one big one for each course. The servants bring it round and serve every guest in turn.'

'How very odd.'

'The food must stay hotter,' Derby suggested, 'if it doesn't sit on the table for an hour.'

'Yes, but it doesn't sound very varied or convivial,' Richmond protested.

'Relaxing, though,' said Mrs Damer. 'Without all the to-and-fro of serving each other, and the interruptions, one could concentrate on conversation.'

'Oh, I think we manage well enough already,' said Derby. 'More mutton, Miss Farren?'

The actress shook her head, but this time she met his eyes for half a second.

Derby rinsed his fingers in the water bowl by his plate, then leaned back as the servants removed all the dishes and pulled off the cloth to show the handsome mahogany table.

'Is this chestnut purée from Gunter's?' Eliza was asking her hostess.

'Where else?' said Mrs Damer. 'And the cornucopia of spiced biscuits, and those bergamot wafers.'

'Gunter's my neighbour in Berkeley Square,' Walpole boasted. 'Best ices in the city.'

Derby had a bowl of Parmesan cheese ice cream, but left half of it to melt. He watched Eliza out of the corner of his eye, passing her some burnt almond sorbet and a glass of orange wine from the cordial frame.

After the table had been cleared they drank toasts to the health of all the ladies present and to the excellence of the food. Derby would usually have proposed Fox and he guessed that Richmond would have named the King, but on this occasion they both refrained. Their hostess called for paper and pencils so they could have a game of verses. 'For theme, an old favourite,' she said with a grin, 'the war of the sexes.'

'Ha ha!'

'Come down, o muse,' murmured Derby.

'Of course,' said Richmond, 'we have one muse among us already—Thalia, muse of comedy.' He dipped his head towards the actress.

Scattered claps greeted the compliment and Derby felt a prickle of resentment.

'Richmond, your partner shall be...Mrs Hobart,' announced their hostess, 'and I'll pick Sir Harry. Let's pair Mrs Farren with Walpole—'

The actress's mother looked paralysed by fright and muttered something about her incapacity.

'No, you can't withdraw,' Eliza told her in a low voice, 'or we'll have odd numbers.'

'Fear not, good lady,' said Walpole merrily, 'just make a stab at it and I'll supply rhymes enough for both of us.'

'That leaves Edgcumbe and Lady Mary, and Derby and Miss Farren.'

She planned this, thought Derby, glancing gratefully at Mrs Damer. *She's giving me a chance.* But his mind was blank. Whatever he wrote would have to bear reading aloud, they were all sitting too close together for him to risk a secret note. He concentrated furiously and produced four halting lines, which he passed down the table with a sheepish smile. Eliza read the slip, but her face told him nothing. There was a little bead of moisture at her hairline, he noticed. The room was warm.

'Done,' cried Mrs Hobart, thrusting her page into the Duke's lap.

'A moment, I beg you,' said the actress. She wrote two lines, quickly, then folded the paper.

'Miss Farren,' said Mrs Damer, 'won't you give us courage by being the first to recite your partner's verse?'

Eliza's rich tones filled the dining room.

> *Poor Adam longed to open up his heart*
> *To his fair love, but alas, he lacked the art.*
> *Women are famous talkers one and all—*
> *Ever since Madam Eve brought on the Fall.*

'Good hit, Derby!' Dick Edgcumbe clapped.

Derby made a face. 'The metre's most irregular.'

'How our masters at Eton would have caned us for such a slip,' cried Richmond.

Derby accepted the page Eliza passed up the table to him and cleared his throat. 'Ladies and gentlemen, Thalia's eloquently terse reply:

> *Some say that ladies gossip worse than men—*
> *But every noisy cock drowns out his hen.'*

'You've topped him.' Mrs Damer beamed at the actress.

'A perfect analogy for the Master of British Cocking,' said Lady Mary.

'I wouldn't say your sex gossip worse than mine on the whole,' Walpole quipped to Eliza. 'I'd say *better*. Besides, gossip's only a nasty word for the thread that binds society together.'

When the verses had been read, Walpole suggested they all come up to Mrs Damer's drawing room to see his terracotta eagle.

'No doubt the less abstemious gentlemen would rather stay and drink,' she rebuked him gently.

'No, no, let's not divide our cosy party,' said Derby, leaping to his feet.

The bird stood furled in rage on his square pedestal. 'Charming,' cooed Lady Mary.

'That's a mild word for such a fierce bird,' said Derby.

'Oh,' cried Eliza, 'but it's transformed since I saw it last. Those eyes—'

How odd, thought Derby, *she's been in Mrs Damer's workshop.*

'It's got something of you about it,' Richmond told his sister-in-law.

'Hasn't it, though,' cried Walpole. 'Young Missy in a tantrum at Strawberry Hill, as on the occasion when I slapped her legs for stealing the heads off all my roses.'

The company roared with laughter. Derby grinned at Mrs Damer, whose cheeks were pink. 'You haven't signed it.'

She shrugged. 'My godfather knows who made it.'

'But after I'm gone—which could be any day now,' Walpole told the company dramatically, causing more titters—'the heedless World must be reminded; it's always so quick to call a lady's work the secret production of some gentleman. The pedestal must say, *Non me Praxiteles finxit, at Anna Damer, 1787.*'

The gentlemen all clapped. Watching Eliza's animated smile, Derby remembered that she knew no Latin. '*Not Praxiteles the famous sculptor, but Anne Damer, made me,*' he glossed it in a murmur.

'That's enough flattery,' said Mrs Damer; 'who'll take tea and who'll take brandy?'

The silver slider the brandy stood in bore their hostess's crest, Derby noticed as he helped himself; it was rather unorthodox for a lady to display her coat of arms, but then Mrs Damer was a very independent character.

Sir Harry was prevailing upon the actress to favour them with a song. She chose Handel's 'Chastity, Thou Cherub Bright', which Derby couldn't help taking rather personally. Then Mrs Damer, apologising for her voice, said she'd oblige with a piece of Dibdin's, because it alluded to her chosen art. '*We bipeds made up of frail clay,*' she sang merrily,

> *Alas are the children of sorrow,*
> *And though brisk and merry today,*
> *We all may be wretched tomorrow...*

Afterwards the talk drifted inevitably to the Prince of Wales, whose debts were to be cleared by the public purse at last. 'Isn't it strange', Mrs Damer murmured, 'how much sympathy this scandal has earned for Mrs Fitzherbert?'

'I think her a heroine,' said Eliza. 'People have abused her for the secret wedding, but doesn't it show strength of mind? Instead of succumbing to the predictable carnal intrigue with the Prince, she held out against all his pleas and threats until he married her.'

She was looking across the tea table, nowhere near Derby, but he knew she was talking to him and his face began to scald.

'If the reports of their sending a child abroad are true, she's had to make a terrible sacrifice. It's not her fault that her husband tried to disown her as a harlot for the sake of his debts,' she finished sharply.

There was a silence. Derby thought the guests were probably wondering what they'd stoop to for the sake of £300,000.

'She is very pious for a Catholic,' observed Mrs Hobart.

'She has self-respect,' Eliza said.

'Yes,' said Derby, the single syllable like a pill in his throat. Eliza glanced over at him. 'The Prince shouldn't have asked what she couldn't give,' he went on in a neutral tone, as if he weren't talking to the woman he adored. 'Since by the Royal Marriages Act he was prevented from offering Mrs Fitz a valid union, he should have respected her principles and bitten his tongue.'

'Given her up, you mean?' asked Richmond, confused.

'Or loved her, but at arm's length.' Derby cleared his throat.

'You're very high-minded tonight,' said Dick Edgcumbe with a snort.

Derby could tell that the group was puzzling over this stern condemnation of the Prince by a Foxite, since that Party had always been so indulgent to their royal patron. And amused by the very notion of Europe's most famous royal lecher attempting platonic love. *Be careful what you say,* he told himself, *or you'll end up a laughing stock.* This was absurd, this indirect communication with Eliza, but what if it was Derby's only chance? What if he waited and said nothing tonight, and didn't lay eyes on her for another two months?

Lady Mary helped herself to a pinch of scented snuff from an exquisite egg-shaped box with her husband's portrait on it and handed it on to her sister.

Derby had to drag in the theme of reconciliation somehow. 'Fox still hasn't forgiven Prinny for his lies. How sad', he said too vehemently, 'when people who care for each other let the cord of friendship snap.' He looked everywhere in the room but at the actress. 'One stupid little row to end so many years of intimacy!'

Another silence. Mrs Damer sneezed into her handkerchief. 'Mm. Marvellous stuff, this Bolongaro. Would anyone like some?'

'Is it violet-scented, like the Queen's?' asked Mrs Hobart.

'No, she takes Macouba, I believe; too flowery for me.'

As the tea kettle was filled up again by the footman, Mrs Damer turned to the silent chaperone. 'Are you and your daughter happy in your present lodgings, Mrs Farren?'

The sudden question threw the woman into a pop-eyed panic.

Her daughter came to the rescue. 'Great Queen Street is just a few minutes from the theatre and it suits us well enough.'

'I ask', said Mrs Damer, giving Derby a glance so brief that only he would notice, 'because I happen to know of a house just round the corner from here on Green Street'—she gestured through the wall—'which is falling vacant next month.'

'Which?' Eliza wanted to know, after a slight hesitation.

'The one with the bow window.'

'Oh, that's in a fine terrace,' said Walpole, who'd been born in Mayfair and knew every inch of it. 'But no mews for stabling, alas. I have trouble enough in Berkeley Square—'

'Miss Farren doesn't keep a carriage,' said Derby, before he could stop himself. Eliza looked over at him and he feared his remark had sounded proprietorial.

'Green Street would be an excellent address, wouldn't it?' she asked her mother. Mrs Farren looked back with a pent-up face.

Derby's heart was thudding. Was it possible? She'd be living in the heart of Mayfair, five minutes' walk from Derby House. They'd almost be neighbours. But could she afford it, on a salary of £17 a week not counting Bens? He resisted a mad impulse to send over to

Derby House for his pocketbook, so he could fling banknotes into his beloved's lap.

The conversation trailed off into other matters: fashions and the latest from Versailles (where the Princesse de Polignac was now the Queen's unrivalled favourite), and the weather. Derby heard none of it. At the end of the evening he stood beside Eliza in the hall. 'Might I have the honour to drop you and your mother home, Miss Farren?'

A tiny silence. 'Thank you, that would be kind.'

Joy started up between his ribs.

EVEN IF he wasn't running a horse on Derby Day at Epsom, the Earl always went down to Surrey to cast his blessing on the race that bore his name. This year the Farrens went with him, since Eliza had a few days' breathing space before the Haymarket's summer season, and Derby assured her that Epsom was much quieter and more respectable than Newmarket; nowadays it was very rare for disappointed bettors to horsewhip a jockey.

Though most gentlemen were watching from horseback or their carriages, strung along the edge of the course, Derby led his guests to reserved seating at the top of a small stand. Three rows below sat Prinny, beside Mrs Fitz; Eliza was glad that she wasn't the only lady attending this race. A breeze lifted the carefully shaped curls off her jaw. Down at the track a crowd was milling, held back only by a chain strung between posts.

'To be strictly fair,' said Derby, settling the tails of his buff coat under him, 'Bunbury and I invented the race together over a long night's drinking at Brooks's. At the time, you see, most runs were for four-year-olds or older—strong, heavy goers—over courses of at least four miles, with handicaps, which tested nothing but stamina.'

'A worthy quality,' said Eliza, straight-faced. Wasn't Derby that kind of horse himself? Stamina was his main advantage as a suitor; God knew, she could have had her pick of handsomer men.

His eyes registered the tease. 'Certainly, but what about sheer, glorious speed? Bunbury and I came up with the idea of setting younger horses over a shorter course, say, three-year-olds over a mile and a half with level weights. Speaking of novelties—' He pulled out a silver watch and flipped it open to show Mrs Farren a tiny spinning hand. 'What do you think that shows, madam?'

The older woman's eyes were a vacant blue when she stared up from her knotting. (Eliza had recently persuaded her mother that the making of decorative braids was a genteeler way of occupying her hands than needlework.)

'Fifths of a second,' he told her.

'How very...accurate, My Lord.'

Eliza let out a giggle. 'You must forgive me, Derby, but I really can't—I simply don't understand the appeal of sports.' Derby laughed. Oh, it was good to be on these pleasant terms again. There was so much about this man that Eliza liked: his intelligence, his humour. 'Of course I can see it's pleasant if one's own horse wins,' she corrected herself, 'or the horse one's put a guinea on. But I can't see its importance.'

'What if one stands to win 1000 guineas?' he suggested. 'The Derby's a sweepstake, not a cup; we each put in 150, the runner-up gets 100 and the winner all the rest.'

The figures staggered Eliza. 'Well, then the money would matter to me, I suppose,' she said carelessly, 'but not the race in itself. It's only animals running along a field, after all.'

'Best keep your voice down in this company,' Derby whispered theatrically.

'I'm sorry, I'm being very rude,' she said, giving him one of her slow-ripening smiles.

'No, no, I appreciate your candour, Miss Farren, and I take your point. These are just games. It's an English preoccupation, all this racing and football and prizefighting; French visitors think us obsessed with speed and violence. But then, isn't much of life composed of games? What do you do at Drury Lane but play dress-up, like my daughters did at five years old, with papier mâché trees and folding knives?'

Eliza looked away, pricked into resentment. Is that what he thought of her career? 'A game, perhaps, but a serious one.'

He shrugged. 'One can take any game seriously. The more one knows about a game and the more one spends on it—whether time, thought, or money—the more serious it becomes.'

'Well,' she said with a rueful nod at the racecourse, 'I certainly know very little about this one, so I'll shut my mouth.'

'Please don't,' Derby told her fondly. 'What would you like to know?'

Where to start? The jockeys were leading out the horses, with their stubby tails. 'Are these all... males?'

'No, no,' he assured her, 'colts and fillies together; we don't exclude the gentler sex from the turf! In fact, some of the great Derby winners have been fillies, many of them sired by Eclipse—the best stud horse I've ever seen, a chestnut stallion who won eighteen races in a row. Gunpowder, that chestnut colt of Colonel O'Kelly's'—pointing at a horse, but Eliza couldn't tell which one—'he's by Eclipse.'

'So... many of these horses are cousins, as it were?' she asked.

'Oh, all of them,' Derby assured her with a grin. 'It's worse than the House of Lords. There are really only three sure male lines: Eclipse, who was great-great-grandsired by the Darley Arabian—Herod, out of the Byerley Turk—and of course Matchem, from the Godophin Arabian. Then there were ten great foundation mares—'

'Oh, stop, I beg you, my head's in a spin already.' She pushed her curls out of her eyes. Derby was so forbearing, it was hard not to punish him sometimes.

'I know the pedigrees are bewildering, but talent's mostly in the blood,' he told her.

'Has training no part to play?' she asked drily.

'Oh, it's essential, but it can't add that spark of genius.' Derby scanned his programme. 'Ladbroke's entered a filly called Dora Jordan, I see. Seems thick-legged and skittish to me.'

Eliza hid a smile. 'Tell me about your horse; this is his first race, I believe?'

'Well, he was named for one of your husbands.'

Mrs Farren's head shot up.

'In the theatrical sense, I mean! Sir Peter Teazle: I chose the name after seeing *School for Scandal* for the fiftieth time.'

Eliza knew Derby came to almost all her performances, but she hadn't realised he counted them. 'Your colours are green with a white stripe, aren't they?—so that must be Sir Peter,' she said, staring down at the line of seven horses.

'Gad, no, that's a nasty biter of a filly, belongs to some City man who rides her himself, so as not to have to pay a jockey,' said Derby. 'Our colours were almost identical and the rogue wouldn't switch, so I did; *noblesse oblige* and all that. My man Sam Arnull's in black with a white peaked cap, at the end,' he said, waving to the rider.

'Oh, very tonish,' said Eliza, trying to make up for her mistake.

'Sir Peter's by Highflyer out of Papillon, he's got the true neat Arabian head and plenty of bottom.'

Mrs Farren was staring fixedly at the horse's rump. 'I believe *bottom* is sportsman jargon for pluck, Mother,' Eliza murmured in her ear.

'Ah, there's Lord Grosvenor,' said Derby, pointing out an ageing aristocrat who was leaning over the rail talking to a groom. 'He spends £7000 a year on his Newmarket stables. It'll ruin him in the end, though he owns most of Mayfair—'

Since Mrs Damer's dinner party Derby had made no reference to the vacant house on Green Street, but Eliza knew it was on his mind; she could hear it like an echo behind his words. She and her mother were still mulling over the figures, trying to decide whether they could afford not just the rent, but the extra servants the move would require.

'Here comes dear Bunbury, he's the president of our Jockey Club, you know. Our number have swelled past a hundred, which alarms the snobs. Really, the Derby might just as easily have been called the Bunbury,' he added with a laugh, 'except that he and I tossed a shilling for the honour of naming the race and I won.'

'You have a knack of winning.'

'Oh, it's no knack,' he said seriously, 'it's a habit of mine, as much as port or snuff.'

'And how exactly do you do it?'

'I have patience,' he said with a small shrug. 'I watch and I wait. I never gamble unless I'm sure I'll win. Though the irony is I haven't won my own race.'

She kept her gaze on her lace apron. Did he mean the Derby? Or did he mean her? Oh, their conversations had been littered with traps, ever since their terrible row at Richmond House. Sometimes it was as if the last six years had never happened and they were making their first tentative acquaintance—but there was a freshness to it, too.

'And I spend a lot of money,' he admitted. 'I breed 3000 cocks a year and keep a stable of horses; you can't buy victory, but you can certainly shorten the odds.'

'His Lordship plays very high,' she told her mother.

'When I bet at all, yes. Well, since I have so much it would seem ungracious to count pennies. But I never bet on chance.' Mrs Farren was looking confused. 'Well, not unless I'm begged to make up numbers at a card table. I get no thrill from the random throw of the dice,' Derby explained.

'Then—'

Eliza finished her mother's thought. 'What do you bet on?'

'Knowledge,' he told them. 'For instance, if I know my fighting cock is better than the other man's I back him. If I'm not sure about the matter I don't bet. Similarly, if I believe a certain bill will be rejected by the Lords I might lay a stake on that at the Club.'

'He rarely loses,' Eliza remarked.

'When you do, My Lord,' said Mrs Farren, 'it must smart.'

He let out a long laugh and his ugliness lifted like a mist, Eliza thought. 'How perceptive of you, madam. It hurts like the devil— if you'll excuse the phrase—because it proves me not unlucky but stupid.'

'Oh, hardly,' Eliza objected. 'Misinformed, perhaps. There must be so many unknowns.'

'That I grant you. I believe Sir Peter's a winner,' he said, his eyes besotted as he picked out his horse from the line, 'but I haven't staked the deeds to Knowsley on him!'

The pistol made her jump. They were off, galloping thunderously away from the line. The crowd was howling and Derby was on his feet, straining to see over taller men. She stood up, but the horses were a blur of brown. 'Where's Sir Peter?'

'In fourth, behind Lord Grosvenor's Bustler; that thug of a jockey's trying to cross him. Now they'll curve left down to Tattenham Corner. Oh, he's edging up, good boy.' Derby's fingernails were embedded in his palms. 'It's a nasty turn into the last four furlongs, then it's straight uphill to the post...'

One jockey broke away from the knot. He was in black with a white cap. 'That's not Sir Peter, is it?'

'It is.' Derby seized her hand in his and in the excitement Eliza let him; she didn't care if her mother saw. She gasped as two horses slithered off their feet at the turn. Sir Peter was still in front. How could anything move so fast? *Sir Peter.* The winning post. *Sir Peter.*

Derby leapt in the air like a boy. 'We've done it, by gad!' The crowd whooped and hats went up like bullets. Gentlemen turned to bow to Derby. 'Oh, it's a sweet day. Eliz—' He caught himself. 'Miss Farren, my dear ladies, you've brought me luck!'

She'd never seen him look so happy. She disengaged her hand, but gently. There was a stir in the stands, people backing out of the way. The Prince of Wales, a peacock in lilac and silver, thumped up the steps. 'Magnificent form, Derby. So you've won your own race at last.' Derby almost disappeared in the crushing royal embrace. Eliza could smell the sweet perfume from where she stood. Prinny cast an appreciative glance at Eliza over the Earl's shoulder. 'Miss Farren, always a pleasure,' he cooed.

She curtsied. *He likes us tall,* she thought apprehensively, *but surely I'm too thin for him?*

'Two thousand guineas,' he boomed, releasing Derby to arm's length, 'and that's my final offer.'

For one terrible second Eliza thought the Prince was trying to buy her favours from their presumed owner. Then she realised: *the horse.*

Derby was silent; confused, or considering the offer? But when he spoke, Eliza realised that he'd just been savouring the moment. 'I *am* sorry, Your Highness, but Sir Peter's not for sale.'

She thought then, with an inward sting: *He never gives up what he loves.*

JULY 1787

Eliza had done it: with shaking hands she had signed a lease on the Bow Window House, Green Street, Mayfair. Now she could climb into a cab and sing out that address like a challenge to enemies, a whistle in the dark. Instead of a set of rooms, the Farrens had a whole small house to themselves, with a handsome fanlight, and an iron extinguisher for torches by the door; a wainscoted parlour and narrow dining room on the ground floor; a kitchen and scullery in the basement; two bedrooms upstairs; and garret space for the manservant and newly hired maid above.

To get to Derby House or Mrs Damer's Eliza only had to turn right down North Audley Street and go two blocks to Grosvenor Square. Walpole's town house in Berkeley Square was just a few minutes by carriage; so were Devonshire House and Melbourne House on Piccadilly. Fox, Sheridan, Pitt, everyone who mattered in England seemed to live just a few streets from her door, now painted a brilliant green. Nor had Eliza muscled in like some dreadful parvenue; she'd changed her lodgings on the express invitation of some of the most distinguished residents of Mayfair. Her connections were formed; her circle was enlarged but still select. She had moved west.

The only problem was that nobody else was there. It was perverse, Eliza always thought, how little the social seasons matched nature's. As soon as Parliament was prorogued in June London life—or rather, high life—shut down. Just as the roses were blooming in Grosvenor Square the World scattered to the country-side: their estates, spa towns, or the newly fashionable seaside. The Richmonds were down in Goodwood and Walpole wouldn't stir from Strawberry Hill; Mrs Damer was with her parents at Park Place near Henley and, of course, Derby was up in Lancashire, see-ing to his estate and children.

Through the heat of July Eliza worked herself ragged. In the sticky evenings she sat in the parlour at Green Street beside her mother while insects veered around the lamp. Muttering under her breath, with her eyes on the ceiling (vines in plaster, a very genteel touch), she memorised the roles Tom King had sent her in a dog-eared bundle from Drury Lane. Twelve to play this autumn, four of them new, though they all sounded familiar somehow: *La, sir, you put me to the blush!*

At the Haymarket Colman had given her Beatrice in *Much Ado,* a host of small parts and the lead in a new play called *The Follies of a Day* by a promising shoemaker-turned-playwright called Holcroft. Eliza turned twenty-five, but marked the day only by sharing a bottle of cold hock with her mother after the show. The little Haymarket theatre was so *cabined, cribbed, confined,* as Jack Palmer put it, that Eliza was forced to share a dressing-room not only with foul-breathed old Mrs Hopkins but with Mrs Jordan too. Mrs Farren had to fold herself up in a corner like a newspaper, to be out of everyone's way.

One afternoon when Eliza was reading a satisfactorily apolo-getic letter from Cumberland, enclosing the rewritten part of Lady Rustic, Dora Jordan, baby on the breast, had the cheek to read the signature over her shoulder. 'Oh, Cumberland—when he's not in a brooding temper, he's always leering and nuzzling one's hand, don't you find?'

The playwright had never attempted to nuzzle any part of Eliza. 'No, I don't,' she said glacially.

'Methinks he protests too much! Bannister says the man's a fin-ger twirler.'

'Surely not,' said Eliza, startled into a response.

Mrs Jordan pursed her lips and applied red greasepaint with her finger. 'His plays are always very luscious in describing the heroes.'

Mrs Hopkins, clambering into a skirt held open by the squatting dresser, gave a snort. 'Cumberland's no woman hater, just proud and fussy. Is that cloak pressed yet?'

'I'll do it presently, madam, I assure you,' said the harried dresser, muffled beneath the expanse of old brocade.

'Shall I?' asked Eliza's mother.

'Oh, Mrs Farren, you're a living saint,' said Mrs Hopkins, tossing her the cloak. 'Tighten my tapes,' she ordered the dresser, sucking in her bulk. 'No, poor Bickerstaffe, now, there was one with it written all over his face.'

'I've been in four of Bickerstaffe's comedies,' said Eliza, 'but I've never met him.' She stepped out of the way to let her mother hurry off to the costume room.

'No, you wouldn't have, none of you girls; he lives abroad, and hasn't written a line since. Back in the early '70, I believe'—the ageing actress frowned, retrieving the memory—'Bickerstaffe got word halfway through a rehearsal at Drury and had to scarper off to France.'

'Got word of what?' asked Mrs Jordan.

'Imminent arrest.'

Mrs Jordan was grinning through her fingers. 'For unmentionables?'

'With a soldier!'

Eliza suddenly registered the vulgarity of the conversation and took herself off to the Green Room to go over her lines for the after piece, *What's to Do?*

The main piece was a melodrama, *Vordigus of Carthage,* and Eliza's part was only a minor one. 'Ghastly stinking summer, this one,' Palmer remarked when she met him in the wings.

'You say that every year, Jack. I like your hero's plumes, by the way.' He grinned and jerked his head like a charging bull. 'Your devotees will certainly be able to pick you out from the very back of the galleries.'

His face furled up again. 'I'm getting too old for these falderals.'

Eliza reached out to straighten up one of the purple ostrich feathers. 'Nonsense.'

'Forty-three, Eliza!' he said in a dreadful whisper.

'You don't look it, in paint. And the ladies wouldn't care anyway. You'll always be their Plausible Jack.'

He smiled again, stretched his muscular arms over his head, like an orang-utan in a cage. 'I need a change. I'm not coming back to Drury.'

She looked at him sharply. 'Where are you going—the South Seas?'

'I'm in deadly earnest. I've had enough of working for that Machiavelli. Sheridan gives every plum role to Kemble, with his grandiloquent manner and leaden pauses—why, the orchestra could play a tune between one word and the next! The plays are old and the costumes are mouldy. Tom King's a sweet man but his hands are tied; Sheridan couldn't delegate if the theatre were burning down around him, as well it might, for all he lets King spend on water buckets!'

'Well, but what choice—' Her cue, she'd nearly missed it. She sped on stage. '*I hear him!*' she screamed. '*He means to murder me!*' She fainted neatly into Mrs Hopkins's meaty arms and let herself be supported back into the wings. 'What choice to do you have, Jack?' she continued in an undertone. 'I doubt Harris would have you at Covent Garden, since Edwin does all the witty beaux and rogues there.'

Palmer spoke in her ear, his breath making her jump. 'I'm setting up my own theatre.'

'Don't talk silliness; you'll never get a patent for spoken drama,' she reminded him. Drury Lane and Covent Garden in the winter, the Haymarket in the summer, the King's Theatre for operas and ballets—those four had held the monopoly for fifty years. All the small premises were permitted to put on were musical burlettas, pantomimes and such trash. 'You might as well try to set up a new Parliament or Bank of England.'

'Aha, but what if I mean to open outside the city?'

'Where, in the middle of some field?'

'Tower Hill,' he whispered triumphantly, his eyes on the action on stage. 'Turns out it's got ancient liberties. I've drawn up a prospectus for investors.'

'But—'

He strode on stage, struck a few attitudes, drew his sword, threatened suicide.

'Jack, this scheme is pure fancy,' Eliza snapped on his next exit.

'Oh, you're a female attorney now, are you?' he mocked. 'So you won't be wanting to join us when we open in August? Even if you can have your choice of roles—Olivia, or Miss Tittup, or Lady Townley—whatever you fancy...'

Eliza thought of her shocking rent at Green Street. 'I have a position at Drury Lane—'

'An oppressed position.'

'—still, one I don't mean to lose.'

He shrugged magnificently. 'I'll ask you again at Christmas, since we're old friends.'

'You're an old fool, Jack.'

August 1787

Eliza lay in a wet winding-sheet. Her ears were buzzing, as if a fly had got trapped in her head. The air was too heavy to breathe; she tried to move her legs but they were tangled, knotted fast. *Bam, bam.* There it came again, that terrible noise. Had she heard it before, or only imagined it?

Voices on the stairs, one low, one sharp. 'If your young mistress is all alone, I insist—' The door squeaked open and the room was suddenly full. 'My dear Miss Farren.' A huge white hat; brown curls; a narrow, vital face. Eliza struggled to sit up. 'Don't move,' said Mrs Damer, sitting on the edge of the bed and taking Eliza's hand between her own cool, slightly rough palms. 'You must forgive me for bursting in like this. Won't you forgive me?'

Eliza cleared her throat to speak, but it was quite dry. Mrs Damer poured the last half-glass of wine from the bottle beside the bed and held it to Eliza's lips. She sipped and sank back.

'Here, you can't rest lying down, it's not healthy.' Mrs Damer helped Eliza to sit up against the pillows. 'I never thought you'd be here today; I only meant to have my driver enquire of the staff whether by any chance you were the new tenant of this house. You can imagine my shock when your maid revealed you were up here on your own, lying in a dreadful fever!'

'My mother—' said Eliza, hoarse. She knew Mrs Farren was haggling over chops at a market, but she couldn't bear to say so.

'Yes, the girl said her mistress is out and that's all very well, but what are we to do with you? Has your doctor called?'

'He says I'm mending.'

'You don't look it,' said Mrs Damer.

Suddenly Eliza's vision swam and a tear ran into the corner of her mouth. 'I do beg your pardon'—and she sobbed.

'Oh, my dear girl!' Mrs Damer whipped out a handkerchief and wiped Eliza's cheek. Dizzy, she closed her eyes. Mrs Damer laid her cool knuckles against Eliza's forehead. 'A bad summer fever.'

'Take care.'

'Oh, I never catch a fever; no, my weakness is for coughs and catarrhs and such wintry English nastiness. Whereas you—' She was looking down with stern fondness. 'This won't do!'

She came back to Green Street that afternoon with a hamper of ice and a peppermint throat syrup from Gunter's. The day after next, when Eliza was beginning to feel rather better, she brought some of the famous plums of Goodwood, 'with my sister's compliments. You must have your cook mash them up for our dear invalid,' she told Mrs Farren.

Eliza felt a surge of mortification, but luckily her mother only nodded. Mrs Farren was cook, housekeeper and general factotum; Eliza might have the right address nowadays, but she still couldn't

afford to live at the level of her neighbours. Her mother seemed a
little ruffled by the visitor at first, but Mrs Damer paid her some
very soothing compliments on the care she was taking of her
daughter. Soon Eliza knew all was well, because Mrs Farren had
fetched Mrs Damer the best chair from the parlour and put it beside the bed, before excusing herself and going downstairs to hound
the maid.

'Have you heard from Knowsley?' asked Mrs Damer.

'A kind note, yes.'

'I really should be at Goodwood myself,' said Mrs Damer, 'or
back in Park Place with my parents, or paying an overdue visit to
Strawberry Hill. But instead I'm living up here, quite incog. My
mother wailed, "What will your neighbours think if they hear you
were in town in July, like some pariah with nowhere else to go?"'

Eliza managed a faint chuckle.

'I promised her I'd be most discreet—keep all the shutters
closed on the Grosvenor Square side—toil in my workshop, have
dinner on a tray in the library, with only Seneca and Epictetus for
company.'

Authors, Eliza guessed, and nodded as if she knew them well.

'If I take Fidelle for a stroll or ride in Hyde Park I go darkly
veiled,' Mrs Damer added in Gothic tones.

'It would take more than a veil to disguise you.'

The sculptor grinned. 'Now, what can I offer to amuse you?'

'News,' said Eliza. 'I feel as if I've been lying at the bottom of a
well.'

'Let's see,' said Mrs Damer. 'The Devonshires have gone to
boring old Bath.'

'Lady Bess Foster with them?'

'Of course; that's a marriage of three souls. I assume you heard
about the disaster of the new Royalty Theatre, near Tower Hill?'

'Oh, Jack!' said Eliza, remembering his plans.

'You're on first-name terms with Mr Palmer, are you?' Mrs
Damer's tone was odd. 'Well, full-scale war broke out in the ranks
of Thespis. Sheridan, Harris and Colman made common cause

against your Jack; after a single performance of *As You Like It* the cast were clapped in gaol overnight as vagabonds.'

'He might have known!'

'A fool, but a brave one,' said Mrs Damer. 'He's switched to variety performances for the moment, to stay within the law, but he vows he won't shut down.'

Eliza ravelled the edge of the sheet.

'You mustn't fret, about this or anything,' Mrs Damer told her, leaning close. 'I fear you succumbed to this nasty fever because you were working too hard, and eating too little, quite cut off from your friends...'

'You're too good to me.'

'Nonsense,' said Mrs Damer. 'Some neighbour I've been so far! I was the one who encouraged you to move to Green Street, then since June I didn't so much as send a note to enquire about your whereabouts; somehow I assumed you were touring, or on some country estate. You could have died of this fever, two streets from my door! Will you forgive me?'

'Oh, Mrs Damer, don't talk so.'

She pressed Eliza's hand. 'I shouldn't take advantage of a convalescent's weakness—but I'm going to ask a favour.'

'Anything.'

'Despite the brevity of our friendship—will you call me Anne?'

SEPTEMBER 1787

Eliza had forgotten how exhausting a long carriage journey was, especially after an illness. The potholed roads into Oxfordshire shook her like a rattle, slurred the words in her mouth. They had to stop at every toll-pike to pay and overloaded stagecoaches clattered past them, going a dozen miles an hour.

'You'll feel the better for a cup of strong tea,' said Anne Damer as they crossed the bridge at Henley. With one hand she scratched Fidelle behind the crumpled ears, with the other she cooled Eliza with a large paper fan that bore an illustration of the ruins of Pompeii.

At the point where the horses turned through a pair of pillars inscribed *Park Place* and began to climb through dense woods, Eliza's stomach made a wasp's nest of itself. She caught herself thinking what great houses always made her think: *I'll be found out.* The footman would open the door of the carriage, then say there'd been some mistake; she'd be sent round to the trade entrance.

Anne touched her arm. 'You're not missing your mother, are you?'

'Now you're just being polite,' said Eliza. 'It's a treat to travel without my duenna for once.' Though Mrs Farren rather dreaded meeting new members of the aristocracy, it was with some difficulty that Eliza had persuaded her that her daughter would manage perfectly well on her own at Park Place. 'She's my ally and indispensable guard dog—but let's not pretend that it's a matter of kindred spirits.'

The sculptor was laughing. 'That would be too much to require of a mother; I certainly don't ask it of mine.'

'Mother's devoted to my success; she wants me to be the performer she never had the talent to be, in all her years in my father's troupe.' With a slight shock Eliza realised that she'd broken a private rule and mentioned George Farren. Since the day she'd gone to shake her father awake from his haze of gin and found him cold, she'd avoided his name. 'She wants success in *life* for me, too,' she added, not spelling out what that might mean: a countess's coronet. 'But I've never really experienced an intimate friendship; I imagine it as flourishing in idleness, on silk-upholstered sofas.'

'And on £10,000 a year?'

'At least,' said Eliza with a grin. The carriage was still climbing; this wasn't an avenue, it was a winding trail, several miles long. Through gaps in the trees, Eliza could see the soft Berkshire slopes fall away down to the Thames: grass and tangled undergrowth, sweeps of dark forestry. A slim branch smacked the open window; a bright green leaf shook in her face.

'Well, in my experience', said Anne with a little yawn, 'the ladies with that kind of money are often too busy spending it. Take

Lady Melbourne: she and I have been friends ever since we met as new brides, being presented at the same Queen's Drawing Room— but these days she can rarely spare me a private quarter of an hour. Friendship in the World's often kept on such short rations, I don't know how the creature clings to life.'

'So it's possible that busy females of moderate means have a chance of finding true friendship too?'

'I think it's a rare bird,' said Anne, her dark eyes fixed on Eliza's, 'and at the first glimpse of its feathers, the first note of its call, you must drop everything else and seize it. *The friends thou hast, and their adoption tried,*' she quoted, '*grapple them to thy soul with hoops of steel.*'

Eliza was picturing a tiny bright bird in hoops of steel.

'Your only obligation, on this visit, is to get well,' Anne remarked. 'Derby helped me persuade you to come down on the strict understanding that I'd bring you back to London in the pink of health.'

'By the end of the month, I hope, or Sheridan will start giving my plum roles to Mrs Jordan.'

'Ah, but those worries must be left behind in the outside world. You're in the forest now. Home at last,' she added, looking out of the window at Park Place and gathering Fidelle into her arms.

THE HOUSE was only ten windows across and three up, to Eliza's relief—not a fraction of the size of a mansion like Knowsley. (Though she'd never been to Lancashire, she'd memorised every detail of the Derby ancestral seat from an article in the *Gentleman's Magazine.*) The aged Field Marshal Conway hurried past his footmen to show Eliza to her room himself and there was a fire burning there, in August, 'as we mustn't take risks with your delicate constitution'.

'My room is just through that little door,' Anne told her when her father had gone downstairs. 'If you need anything, anything at all, in the night, you've only to call.'

'Maid!' cried Eliza with an imperious click of the fingers. The two of them giggled. 'On second thoughts, no, I shouldn't try that; half a dozen of them might come running.'

Since Conway had been Governor of Jersey for the past fifteen years, Eliza had prepared by flicking through a book on the geography and manufactures of that island—but it turned out he loathed the place. 'The subjects are loyal, Miss Farren, so I rarely need to show my face,' he assured her. 'On my last trip I whined so much in my letters to Horry that he said I was more like a boy crying for a sugar plum than a servant of His Majesty's government.'

'Horry's our cousin Walpole,' Anne explained.

'Yes,' said the Countess of Ailesbury with benign satire, looking up from her worsted frame, 'even when we're only up in town, at our house in Soho Square, my husband's always panting to be back at Park Place, undertaking his improvements.'

It was from her mother's Campbell family that Anne had inherited her chiselled, handsome features, but where had she got her artistic genius? Lady Ailesbury's copies of Rubens, Gainsborough and Cuyp in thick dull thread were all over the house and uniformly hideous. Anne's energy, however, clearly came from both sides. The elderly couple walked through the meadows and came home all over burrs, went on fishing trips, paid calls on neighbouring estates and delivered hams to the poor.

At first Eliza moved round Park Place like a frail old woman. She leaned on Anne's arm while walking in the gallery, where a painted host of the aristocratic Campbell connections outfaced a handful of the more low-born Conways. She sat in the kitchen garden and in the flower arcades, where gold and silver fish danced in ponds, and a fountain went up higher than her head. Anne wouldn't let her learn her parts for the autumn, or even write a letter: 'I've told all your friends that the doctor's forbidden you to lift a pen.' Eliza was growing fat and stupid and childishly happy. Well, not the kind of fat that showed—she'd always been considered regrettably thin—but she felt plumped up, somehow; her skin moved slowly and comfortably over her limbs. She rinsed her face twice a day in strawberry water, to clear it of the pallor of illness. Such luxury, to be looked after and waited on, like a real lady of leisure. What a curious life.

Field Marshal Conway took her south of Park Place to see what he called the Druids' Temple. When the forty-five granite stones had been discovered on Jersey the inhabitants had presented them to their Governor 'as a testimonial of gratitude', then had the cheek to object when he'd had them all shipped back to Berkshire.

The stone circle on the hill was tiny and incongruously neat; it reminded Eliza of one of the flaky stock scenes at Drury Lane, known as the Old Ruins. 'Magnificent,' she murmured.

'I've had a French verse about human sacrifice inscribed on the biggest megalith, which is fully eight foot by seven,' said Conway with satisfaction and out of the corner of her eye Eliza was sure she saw Anne suck in a giggle.

'I'll never get stronger if I don't go further,' Eliza told Anne the next day. They went into the woods in simple walking dresses, saw pale deer among the beeches and the oaks, and small, preoccupied rabbits that Fidelle chased in vain. Anne showed Eliza all her father's follies: the Rustic Arch (made from blocks pillaged from the ruins of Reading Abbey), the Pyramid, the Chinese Cottage where they took tea. 'What's that ravishing scent?' she asked.

'The lavender stillhouse,' Anne told her. 'He had a notion to use the spare heat from his coke ovens for distilling lavender oil; ours is the only plantation in the country. It hasn't paid for itself yet, but it smells like heaven.'

They lay back against the trunk of the first Lombardy poplar in England (a very ordinary-looking tree, which some marquis had brought from Paris as a gift for the Countess), idly discussing the progress of the Hastings impeachment. Since she'd come to know the sculptor, Eliza had begun to find politics more engrossing. Not being embroiled in the details of Party business, as Derby was, Anne could pierce to the heart of a controversy and explain why it mattered. 'You'll make a marvellous Whig hostess some day,' Anne remarked, 'perhaps Georgiana's successor.'

Eliza bristled. 'Lord Derby and I don't speak of the future.'

'Oh, come now,' Anne told her, 'this isn't one of your brittle comedies! You can speak freely here, Fidelle doesn't spy for the newspapers.' She scratched the dog's white barrel of a ribcage. 'When he's free, you'll marry him, won't you?'

Eliza gave a short sigh. 'Assuming that when the time comes the question is put to me...I'll decide then.'

Anne was staring at her. 'You mean you really don't know?'

Eliza spoke too sharply. 'Oh, I suppose you think, with the rest of England, that a nobody like me should collapse with humble gratitude at the very idea of such a proposal from an earl?'

'Not at all,' said Anne, shaking her head, 'quite the contrary. Any man would feel exalted to be your choice.'

Eliza softened into a smile.

'But I've always thought—from the terms you and Derby have seemed to be on all these years—he's your constant escort and you have no other—'

She made a face. 'I tell you this in confidence—'

'Of course,' said Anne, leaning closer.

'I can never quite make up my mind about Derby. He's a man of integrity, of course, a diligent politician; a marvellous friend, a dutiful father. He's very polished and his sports are a harmless amusement; he hasn't gambled away his fortune or bred up a nursery of bastards. He's been the most polite and patient of suitors,' Eliza conceded. 'I like him very much indeed.'

'Only like?'

Eliza fanned herself crossly. 'It's hard to tell. Since my juvenile infatuation with Jack Palmer, perhaps I've been too busy, or I might have a defective heart. Some days, Derby hops down from his carriage to give me his hand and I find myself thinking, in spite of myself...'

'Yes?'

'What a silly little man.'

She met Anne's eyes. Their peals of laughter went up like birds.

They ate well at Park Place: guinea fowl and fresh peas, and so many eggs that Lady Ailesbury sent boxes of them up to Twickenham for Walpole. Conway was trying his hand at a play—well, adapting it from an old French one—and hoped it wouldn't be too much trouble for dear Miss Farren to cast an eye over it? Now Eliza was stronger, they took her on excursions and introduced her to select neighbours; she'd been afraid the local gentry might look askance at an actress, but in fact they all seemed dazzled by her famous name.

The family walked all the way down to Henley one day, to show her the bridge. 'I had the honour to be a commissioner for its erection,' Conway boasted, 'and it cost £100,000. The workmen were shocking drinkers; after one of them got himself drowned, we made a rule that if the foreman saw a fellow the worse for drink he was to tie him to a tree.'

'So much for the liberties of the individual,' said Anne with a smile.

'Better shackled and alive than free and drowned, surely; even dear Fox couldn't dispute that,' put in Lady Ailesbury.

Eliza picked her way down the bank to examine the carved stone masks on each side of the bridge: Thames, a stern old man, and Isis, a beautiful, sober girl. 'Oh, my dear, what unforgettable faces,' she said to Anne. 'To think of them there, gazing down on the boatmen, while the centuries flow by...'

Anne gave a little shrug. 'Yes, I suppose my art will last—but sometimes it seems so sluggish of growth, so static.'

'Well, my talent dies as soon as it's seen, like a sunset,' said Eliza.

Anne shook her head. 'The play may be fleeting,' she said, 'but the memory of your performance lingers on in our hearts.'

Eliza laughed and turned away.

On the way back up the grassy hill her breath began to rasp, but she pressed on; she was almost fourteen years younger than Anne Damer, she reminded herself. Anne stopped and gave her an arm to lean on. 'Our guests have always complained that a visit to Park Place involves a great deal of scrambling. But it gives a good stomach for dinner.'

It was an indelicate remark, by the World's standards. Eliza grinned back at her friend. Down here in the country many things no longer mattered; London seemed a thousand miles away instead of thirty.

Dinner was at four, then the Field Marshal and *the girls* played bowls on the lawn. Eliza tried to remember if she'd ever taken part in a game outdoors on a summer's evening. At nine years old, perhaps? She lost, badly, and didn't mind. The air smelt darkly green. When they came in Eliza insisted she wasn't tired, not at all, so she and Anne and Lady Ailesbury played Pope Joan till ten.

Anne and she went up the stairs to their rooms, with a candlestick apiece. 'Your father called you Missy this evening,' said Eliza.

'Did he?' Anne laughed. 'When I was about four years old Walpole used to address me with superb formality as *Miss Seymour-Conway*, which degenerated into Miss, then Missy.'

'I was Betsy,' she offered.

'You weren't!'

'*Wee Betsy Farren, Darling of the Liverpool Pantomime.*' She pronounced the phrase with grim relish.

'But you're such an Eliza! The very definition of an Eliza.'

'What's an Eliza?'

'You are,' said Anne. And she leaned over to kiss her good night.

'YOU'RE TRANSFORMED,' Derby told Eliza on the terrace. 'Park Place has been the making of you.'

Anne readjusted the sleeping dog in her arms and watched her friends with an anxious sort of pleasure. Under her parasol the actress now had pink cheeks against her golden hair, but more than that—a new ease, a nonchalance. It struck Anne that this was probably the only time Derby had ever met his beloved without her mute, awkward mother. It was a mystery how a woman who looked every inch the brewer's daughter had given birth to such an exquisite. 'I think she should come to Park Place every summer, for the good of her health.'

'A capital idea! I used to visit as a child, you know,' Derby told

Eliza. 'I remember once my visit overlapped with Monsieur Rousseau's. I wept my eyes sore over his *Julie*.'

'Didn't we all,' said Anne. 'I think I read it five times.' The devoted triangle of the two beautiful cousins and their tutor still lingered in her mind, when she'd forgotten so many other plots.

'I do wish I could stay more than two days,' said Derby, turning to take in the whole sweep of forest and valley, 'but Fox insists we all get together at Devonshire House to make plans, even though the Session's still six weeks off. He's rather upset about these riots in Glasgow.'

'I'm afraid we've been so cut off here...' Anne began.

'Oh, I beg your pardon. It's the cotton weavers, they've been on strike all summer, you see.' He paused. 'When they started throwing stones at the blacklegs it seems the troops opened fire and killed half a dozen.'

Anne was shaken. 'Guns against stones?'

'They must have been starving to try it; the strikers, I mean,' said Eliza.

A silence. It occurred to Anne that while she and Derby had never gone to bed hungry in their lives, the same couldn't be true of a child among strolling players. When Anne tried to imagine the lives of the poor in detail she always got a kind of vertigo. What sort of squalid lodgings might a Glasgow cotton weaver live in? Surely, in a country so prosperous and peaceful, something could be done to relieve such miseries? But no, the government simply sent in the troops; how typical of Pitt and all his hatchet-faced henchmen. If only Britain were governed by a man with a conscience—with some sympathy and imagination. 'Derby,' she said suddenly, 'if you were to make a wager—will Fox come to power in the next five years?'

The look that came over his face was very like embarrassment. He glanced at Eliza, then back at Anne. 'Well, there's reason to hope. Our Party has all the best speech makers—and Fox attracts the pick of the new MPs, youngsters you wouldn't know, like Charles Grey.'

Anne pressed the point. 'But our chances of toppling Pitt?'

'Under the present King?' Derby's voice automatically lowered, even though they were outdoors, Anne noticed. 'Nil. To be candid—when Fox got into office five years ago he was toppled by a royal plot.' He sounded gruff with rage. 'Old George let it be known that he'd consider any MP who supported reform in India as his personal enemy—so the Bill was lost, the government fell and the King's new pet Pitt seized the reins.'

'What an outrage!' said Eliza.

Anne, watching her, thought with a private thrill, *She's changing, maturing. She's coming to care about the things that really matter.* 'Oh, royal influence can make a farce of politics. Old George squats in the way of progress, like a warty toad.'

'He's not fifty yet,' said Eliza, 'so why does he seem so old?'

'I suppose because he's ruled us for nearly thirty years already,' said Derby. 'And God knows how long he'll drag on! Unfortunately for Prinny and our Party, there's no chance of the King being carried off by a binge at a banquet, in the royal tradition,' he added satirically. 'He's so very clean-living—gruel and lemonade, early nights and no game more exciting than backgammon. He and Pitt are the true father and son: two skinny, abstemious, heartless icicles!'

When their laughter had died away a silence hung on the air. Anne tilted back her parasol to look up at the sun, wondering if the August afternoon would ever lose its burning sheen. Fidelle stirred in her arms, so she put her down on the grass.

'But enough nasty politics,' said Derby, pulling a folded paper out of his pocket, 'here's something that will amuse you both. It's a long and execrable verse in your honour, Miss Farren, from this month's *Town and Country.* Here's the very worst rhyme, I believe.

> *In Teazle, the springs of mild elegance move her,*
> *But the sightless sweet Emmeline, that's her chef d'oeuvre.'*

The women shrieked. 'Wait, wait, here's another gem of erudition.

> *To copy her frame, where divinity's seal is,*
> *Would beggar the talents of famed Praxiteles.*

'Oh, dear,' said Anne, hand to her mouth, 'it's a warning to me; I was thinking only yesterday of attempting to capture our friend's beauty in marble.'

'Nonsense,' Derby told her. 'It would clearly be easier than trying to capture it in verse!'

'Pliny tells a good story about Praxiteles,' she remarked to Eliza. 'His mistress wanted to find out which of his works he valued most highly, so she ran up to him and told him that his house was burning down. "Save the Satyr and the Cupid," said Praxiteles.'

'But why did she need to trick him?' Eliza wondered. 'Why not just ask?'

'Oh, he might have been unwilling to praise his own work,' Anne told her.

'Yes,' said Derby, 'artists are queer folk.'

'What would you save?' asked Eliza, turning to Anne with her gauzy blue eyes.

'Fidelle and my tools,' Anne answered, before she'd time to think. 'I carve almost all my sculptures as gifts for friends, so they wouldn't be in my burning house. If I could go back in again, I'd—'

'No going back,' said Eliza. 'Derby?'

'If I may ask, which of my three houses is hypothetically on fire?'

'Oh, dear,' mocked Anne, 'the complexities of wealth!'

'Derby House,' Eliza told him. 'London's so combustible.'

'Ah, but at least there, the Sun Fire Insurance Company would rush round with their pumps and their hoses,' Derby told her. 'Whereas if the ancestral pile of the Smith-Stanleys were to burst into flames it would be *Farewell Knowsley*.'

'Very well, what would you save if Knowsley were on fire?' Anne asked.

He screwed up his face. 'Sir Peter Teazle—my prize breeding birds—and young Edward, Charlotte and Elizabeth, I suppose.'

'Oh, you shocking man, to list your children last!' Anne went to smack him with her fan, but he dodged it. 'What are they like?' she asked.

'My children?'

She glanced at Eliza, who was looking up into the canopy of an oak tree. *I'd lay a bet she's never asked about them; she never mentions Knowsley, or his past, or anything that even touches on his marriage.* 'Yes,' she said lightly, 'what sort of temperaments have they?'

'Rather too early to tell, I'd have thought.'

'Oh, nonsense! Lady Melbourne says hers pop out of the womb with characters fully formed.'

Derby made a helpless grimace. 'Perhaps I haven't spent enough time with my lot. Edward's a bright fellow, bookish—a trifle earnest. Charlotte—she's named for her godmother, the Queen—well, she's quite the proper lady at eleven. And Elizabeth, well, she's just as pretty as the others, but with fairer hair and skin.' He was looking hard at the horizon, as if he'd spotted a rider. 'To be perfectly frank—if I may—I doubt she's mine.'

'Ah,' said Anne. She was aware of Eliza beside her, listening hard.

'Not just the colouring, but the timing of her birth.'

He must mean that the Duke of Dorset had put a cuckoo in the nest before running off with Lady Derby.

The long silence was becoming awkward. Anne had an idea. 'Come with me,' she said, leading her friends between the trees. 'This way.' Fidelle raced after them. Round a corner what looked like the mouth of a cave opened in the ground. The walls were white and smoothly rounded; the floor squeaked underfoot. 'Solid chalk,' she told them.

'Is it safe for Miss Farren?' said Derby.

'Oh, yes,' said Anne impatiently.

'It's so cool,' Eliza marvelled. 'What luck to find a cave in the woods.'

'Luck had nothing to do with it,' Anne told her. 'Father had it dug out one summer, to provide labour for idle workmen.'

A lantern stood on a ledge near the entrance, with a tinderbox beside it. She lit the flame. 'Fidelle,' she called and listened for the pattering paws. 'I think she's gone on ahead. She knows the way well. Here'—touching Eliza's humid hand—'mind your footing.'

They followed the passage as it sloped down. Derby, she noticed, had taken Eliza's other hand, muttering something about not wanting her to slip. They were like dancers in some strange figure for three. Soon the lantern swinging from Anne's hand was the only splash of light in this artificial night. Their shadows rocked against the shining walls. The little greyhound came back and leapt round them, barking to make an echo; her eyes glittered. Trying to see all this through Eliza's eyes, Anne thought, *We gentry are a strange breed, to play at work like children—shipping giant stones from one country to another, boring through hillsides.* This tunnel was like a pure white mine, a mine as imagined by someone who'd never seen miners come back from work at the end of the day, blackened and gasping.

The passage ran for several hundred yards. Eliza shivered slightly in the chill. 'Are you all right?' said Anne and Derby at the same time and laughed.

'It's wonderful,' said Eliza.

Then the air began to brighten and Anne could see daylight. She blew out her lantern. They emerged into the dazzling light; the sun sparkled in her eyelashes, touched her neck. Derby was blinking; Eliza was shading her eyes. They were standing at the lip of a bowl of infinite green.

III

Life Mask

An image made by taking a plaster mould of the
face of a living human subject.

⁓

READERS of this publication will have noticed that a certain Family, whose chief residence is not a thousand miles from Windsor, is becoming notorious for its internal discord. Old George Hun-over, or Farmer George, the paterfamilias, is the epitome of a Miser. Lotty, his fair wife, has given him no less than fifteen progeny, thirteen still living and now aged between twenty-six and five: seven boys, namely Georgy, Freddy, Willy, Neddy, Erny, Gussy and Dolphy, and six girls, to wit Little Lotty, Aggy, Lizzy, Sophy, Meely and Mary. But instead of being grateful to his tireless helpmeet, Old George complains of the Expense of the family and grudges her snuff (the poor woman's only indulgence). Since the children can't marry without the father's permission, they hang miserably around the farm, where formality, dullness and ennui reign eternal, and the corridors are the coldest in England.

The eldest son and heir to the Property is known from his girth as Georgy Porgy, the Prince of Whales, or the Great Whale. Two greater opposites could not be imagined than this tight-pursed father, whose favourite dish is milk gruel, and this prodigal (but unrepentant) son, who has no less than twenty dishes to every dinner. As well as extravagance and irreligion, he is a lecher of unparalleled energy and is also be-

lieved to have entered into an illicit Marriage—which adds filial defiance to the list of charges.

To his credit, it must be noted that the Whale is an ener-
getic promoter of art, sport, cuisine, literature and architecture—all foreign words to Farmer George—and that his
outlay on fashion would keep a hundred tailors from penury,
if only he'd pay his bills. Until last year the Whale's dearest
friend and tutor in libertinage was none other than a filthy,
bushy-tailed Fox, but now he clings more nearly to a bottle of
Irish Sherry, rumoured to be poisonous...

— THE BEAU MONDE INQUIRER, *October 1788*

THREE DAYS AFTER ANNE'S RETURN FROM FRANCE, ELIZA SAT
for her in the workshop at Grosvenor Square. Anne was slapping
wet handfuls of reddish clay on to a wooden armature to make an
egg-shaped head. She narrowed her eyes at Eliza, as she used both
hands to shape two rudimentary ears. 'I can't believe we've been
friends almost two years and I'm only now attempting to immor-
talise you. Your proportions are mathematically perfect,' she muttered, 'but I can tell you're going to be the most difficult of models.'

'Oh, dear. Have I been moving already?' asked Eliza, barely
parting her lips.

'Not at all, it's just that your beauty has a sort of live, unpin-
downable quality.'

'No flattery,' she scolded.

'It's nothing of the sort,' the sculptor defended herself. 'When
gentlemen pour out their homage, you may accuse them of flattering, but from a member of your own sex, with the cold eye of an
artist, you must accept it as the truth.'

'Well,' said Eliza, 'I'm relieved to hear I'm sitting still at least.'

'Oh, your experience of the stage gives you a marvellous freedom from self-consciousness.'

Eliza frowned. 'But it seems to me that I'm always conscious of
myself.'

Anne's hands kept scraping away at the jaw. 'I suppose I mean awkwardness, then. Some of my models are so dreadfully aware of my looking at them, they're always flinching; even Lady Melbourne lost her insouciance when she sat for me.'

'Practice,' said Eliza with a little shrug, then froze in position again. 'Since childhood I've held so many poses on so many stages—with managers and authors and dressers viewing and poking and discussing me from every angle—that I've grown accustomed to considering myself as a sort of puppet. A movable statue, perhaps.'

'Didn't you once play Hermione in *The Winter's Tale*?'

'Years ago, when I was far too young for it,' said Eliza, smiling at the memory. 'That scene in which I had to pretend to be a statue and listen to my husband lament—how the audience wept!'

'I know I did.'

'Ah, you were there?'

'I don't think I've missed more than one or two of your roles over the years,' said Anne.

Eliza was a little disconcerted; she hadn't realised that she had any viewer as faithful as Derby. 'I rehearse stage business in the mirror, you know.'

'Do you really?'

'I watch myself form every expression, every gesture, every movement; I inherited most of my roles from Mrs Abington, but I've tinkered with the business of them over time. After so many years in front of the mirror, you can imagine that my looks hold no surprises for me.' She watched Anne's fingers digging to form the left eye socket. 'Except for the little lines that say twenty-six.'

The sculptor looked up with a smile. Eliza wondered why she'd revealed her age, when popular report called her several years younger than that. 'There are no lines, except in your imagination,' Anne told her.

'I must be realistic; I live by my face.'

'And when you're as old as I am it will still be dazzling 2000 people a night, because true beauty is a weapon that strikes every-

one, and doesn't rust! Unless, of course,' Mrs Damer added in a
rush, as if she'd been tactless, 'fate has provided another sphere for
you to shine in.'

Eliza changed the subject. 'Such a pity Richmond's decided
against mounting any more theatricals.'

'Oh, don't remind me, I'm quite put out with him for his mean-
ness! That's one reason I needed this trip to Paris to lift my spirits.
I do love to escape from England at least once a year, I have a
sailor's soul. I wish you could try the same cure, my dearest; you still
seem weakened by last year's fever.'

'I'd feel perfectly well,' Eliza told her, 'if you and Derby didn't
keep harping on my delicate constitution.'

Anne grinned at the rebuke. 'Of course, I don't have the entrée
to glittering circles any more—not like my honeymoon visit when
I was received so charmingly by Marie Antoinette,' she reminisced.
'She's so unpopular these days, they call her Madame Deficit and
accuse her of drunken orgies, though I know for a fact she drinks
nothing stronger than mineral water!'

'Well, my mother and I voyaged as far as York,' said Eliza, 'so I
could play in my sister Peggy's Ben and see her married to an actor.
I missed the great excitement of the Season so far, when some vil-
lain in a crowd came at Fox with a knife!'

'I believe it was a black who ran between them?'

'Yes, and got a shocking cut on the head; Mrs Sheridan's getting up a collection to reward him.'

'Further proof that nobility exists in all races.' Anne sighed,
rolling some clay between her fingers. 'D'you know, Georgiana
wants a black footman like my Sam, but Devonshire forbids it out
of sheer prejudice! I've been agonising over whether to give up
sugar; the anti-saccharite campaign does seem a powerful blow to
the slave-holding planters.'

'Oh, I know.' Eliza sighed. 'Rum I never touch, but to gulp
down sugarless tea and coffee and chocolate, that's hard—'

'And then what would one serve for desserts, apart from oranges and walnuts?'

They lapsed into guilty silence. 'Tell me,' asked Eliza, 'how does the work go?' The clay head still looked to her much like the ostrich egg Derby kept in his cabinet of curiosities.

'Very badly,' said Anne, 'my fingers are talentless today.' She seized a damp cloth and threw it over the armature.

'Are we finished?' Eliza was disappointed.

'Unless...I wonder, my dear, might I try a different technique? I've never done it before, except on my own hand. If I could take a mask of your face—'

'As with a corpse?' Eliza stared at her.

'Oh, don't be alarmed. Not a death mask but a life mask.'

'You mean to cover me with clay?'

'No, no,' said Anne, laughing, 'plaster of Paris; much lighter, finer stuff. It sets fast, too; it should only feel a little disconcerting.'

Eliza was nervous, but felt it would be feeble to refuse. Anne began by tying the hair back from Eliza's face with one of her own broad scarves. Then she mixed up a little bowl of oil and applied it with a sable paintbrush, so the plaster wouldn't stick to her skin.

'Oh, it tickles—I can't bear it.' Eliza laughed, twitching away from the brush as it touched the corner of her mouth.

'Then I'll use my fingers, if I may.' The sculptor stroked the oil on with firm fingertips, reaching every little crevice.

Eliza held still, absorbing the peculiar sensation. 'I must look like a glazed ham.'

'Not strikingly.' Anne turned away to grind up a block of Paris plaster. She mixed the dust with water in a basin, testing the texture with her fingers; it flowed like cream. She scooped some up in her fingers and began to apply it to Eliza's cheeks. 'Now don't be alarmed, I'll leave a space round your nostrils so you'll be able to breathe. I can leave out your eyes too, if you like—though I would have liked to capture the angle of your upper lid...'

Eliza shut her eyes tight. 'Don't let my timidity stand in the way of art,' she said with an odd merriment. Her eyes watered a little; she hoped it wouldn't ruin the plaster.

'Thank you, that's wonderful.'

Eyes pasted shut, Eliza found herself thinking of the Gospel passage she'd heard last Sunday in the Derby pew at the Grosvenor Chapel—the one about Christ putting mud on the blind man's eyes to cure him. How long was this going to take? A flutter of panic, an urge to open her eyes, but she told herself not to be silly.

A finger, soft on her lip. 'If you were to let me cover your mouth too, I'd be able to record one of your finest features—the deep cleft in the middle of your upper lip. But perhaps it would be too frightening?'

'Go on,' muttered Eliza through leaden cheeks.

'You're breathing through your nose perfectly well?'

She made a little inarticulate sound.

Anne sounded guiltily delighted. 'I'll work fast. If you don't like it, just reach out with your hand and I'll make a hole for your lips.'

Eliza inhaled slowly as the sculptor covered her mouth in cold, heavy paste. She felt the plaster hardening rapidly, stiffening on her forehead, now, her eyelids. She felt something itch in her cheek, but she forced herself to stay still. She thought of that time she'd been playing Lady Teazle, hidden behind the screen, when some crawling insect had bitten her on the knee and she hadn't let herself cry out, or scratch it, or move a muscle.

'I've finished now; I'll let it sit,' said Anne, very close to her ear. 'Are you feeling quite comfortable? Well, hardly. But you're not scared.' She held Eliza's hand in her own sticky fingers and stroked it. 'I'll consider this an early birthday present.'

'Mm?'

'I turn forty in a fortnight.'

It sounded terribly old; Anne seemed nothing like a widow of forty. But Eliza could say nothing, only sit frozen, eyes pressed shut, waiting.

'You've been very patient,' said Anne at last, 'and now the mask is quite dry.' She started prising it off.

At first it felt horrible, as if part of Eliza's face were being wrenched away, but then the mask popped free. Eliza blinked, rubbed crumbs from her eyelashes. She found herself looking into a white hollow shape, held in Anne's hands. It made no sense to her. Then she turned her head a little and all of a sudden she saw it: herself. Or rather, the ghost of herself, the space where she'd been a moment ago. Not a flat image, like a mirror, but the exact shape of the air around her face. 'It's me,' she whispered.

Anne smiled at her, then looked back at the image—no, stared into it as if it were a pool or a cloud. 'I thought you told me that you were used to seeing yourself—that the sight could never surprise?'

'But this is like a skin I've shed,' said Eliza, 'myself turned inside out.'

As USUAL Derby had joined his Whig friends at Holkham, Thomas Coke's Norfolk estate, for the autumn shoot. They always tried to stay off Party matters; instead they joked about women and compared fowling pieces. After five days the bag was pretty good: 835 pheasants, 645 hares, 59 rabbits, 10 partridges and 4 woodchucks. Derby had come back to Knowsley with so much game that he'd had to present most of it to his neighbours before it could rot.

This was his last moment of peace before the two-day journey down to London for the Session. His agent had come in this morning while Derby was having his nails cut, to give a full report on how well his stocks and holdings in land, canals, mines and mills were doing. Derby's money gave him a feeling of great solidity, as if he stood on a mountain high about the scrabbling crowds of ordinary men. He'd been rather a frantic spender in his youth, but since he'd come under Eliza's influence he'd reformed and now he husbanded the Derby fortune to pass on to his son's sons, so the Smith-Stanley name would never tarnish. He couldn't help feeling a little smug that, almost alone among his peers, he hadn't loaded his estate with debts and never had to refuse a friend who asked for money.

His cocks and horses cost a lot, of course, but they won a good deal of it back. Every day he spent at Knowsley he went riding with his dogs and there was nothing he enjoyed as much as stepping into his cock sheds, despite the acrid air. This afternoon Busley, his chief feeder, was showing him a one-year-old with a rich-red back, deep-orange feathers on his hackle and saddle, maroon wings and an iron-black breast and tail. 'He's of the true Knowsley strain of Black-Breasted Reds all right, M'Lord. We should put the hen to her sire again this year.'

Derby had once made the faux pas of giving a detailed answer to a marchioness who'd expressed curiosity about the line breeding of pedigree game fowl. Before that he'd never considered that mating cocks with their own dams or daughters was an indelicate idea; after all, it was the only way to keep the blood really pure, to fix and preserve good qualities from generation to generation.

The cockerel lay tensely in the old man's hand; his neck was long and flexible, his wary eyes wide awake. 'Such strong feet,' marvelled Derby, fingering their rough surface. 'I'd almost be tempted to break my own rule and let him have a trial before he's two.'

'Ah, now, mustn't hurry them,' said Busley. 'It's all in the thighs; no point flashing your spurs and crowing up a tempest if your legs aren't thick enough to hold you right through the fight.'

'Well, that's true. Fools rush in, eh?' Derby twisted the bird's head, checking the shape of the comb, the delicate frilled wattles. He'd always liked the look of young cocks, whole in all their parts, the natural princes of the barnyard; it was a shame that, to fit them for the pit, they had to be cropped and clipped, whittled down. 'This one reminds me of that game warrior we had a few years back, with the white feather on his throat.'

Busley smiled, hard and reminiscent. 'He was perfect otherwise, but that spray of white on his breast stood out like the mark of Cain, so I had to bring him home for the pot. The missus was grateful.'

'I sometimes regretted not even giving him a trial.'

The feeder frowned. 'Ah, come now, M'Lord. Breed's all in the colour. Why else would folk say that a coward shows the white feather?'

'Sheer superstition and dyed-in-the-wool ignorance, that's why, man. This is the era of scientific advancement, haven't you heard?'

Busley dumped the bird back in the pen—sliding the slatted front down after it—and folded his arms. 'Now you're only trying to rile me.'

'What about Sir Francis Boynton's champion Dun?'

'That was a fluke. Markam says the grey, the yellow and the red fight best, and dun is even worse than pied or white.'

'Markham's been dead since Queen Anne's day.'

Busley sniffed, whether disputing this fact, or simply loyal to his favourite authority on game fowl, Derby couldn't tell. The Earl was always amazed by the firm prejudices of the lower orders.

'The darks may be hardier and more tenacious,' he told the Feeder, 'but you must grant that some pale cocks are intelligent players and deadly with their heels. I like a bird that has some subtlety to it and knows how to play the waiting game, instead of just wading in and kicking his rival to pieces.'

'Subtlety'll get you nowhere unless you can kick too.'

Derby let out a chuckle. 'I'll repeat that epigram to my friend Walpole and he'll put it down in a book.'

'Who's that? I never heard of him.'

'Ah, no, I fear Walpole's extensive erudition doesn't stretch to fowl.'

'Well, then, I'll never buy his book,' said the feeder. 'I've only three books and they're all about cocking.'

'I envy you, Busley.' Derby sighed. 'I have upwards of 10,000 volumes and I'll never have time to read them all if I live to be a hundred.'

The feeder rolled his eyes, whether at the thought of such an overwhelming library, or the dubious likelihood of the twelfth Earl holding the title that long, Derby couldn't tell.

'Good morning, Father,' came a chorus.

Derby jumped slightly and turned to see Lord Edward Smith-Stanley, slim-legged in long pantaloons and a short jacket. He thanked the gods, and not for the first time, that the children had all taken after their handsome mother rather than their father. Edward's fringe had a charming natural curl to it this morning; his serious face gave Derby a rush of paternal sentiment. The boy was shadowed by his sister Lady Charlotte in a white muslin sashed gown. 'My dear children. Did you sleep well?'

'Yes, Father.' Their voices chimed together; Edward's hadn't shown any signs of dropping yet.

Derby clapped his son on his narrow back. 'You know, since you're here, Edward, it's high time I introduced you to the mysteries of cocking.'

Charlotte was wrinkling up her aquiline nose. 'Pugh, what a stench.'

'Good healthy bird smell, that,' Busley rebuked her.

'Where's your sister Elizabeth?' Derby asked her.

She shrugged.

'You two mustn't leave her alone all day.'

'Yes, Father.'

'Off you go and play a game with her, Charlotte.'

At twelve, she had an almost womanly hauteur; her protruding bottom lip suddenly reminded him of her mother's. 'Neddy,' she hissed at her brother, 'are you coming?'

'In a minute.'

Derby gave the boy a tour of the vast sheds, pointing out the famous Black-Breasted Reds, the White-Legged Duckwings and the Lancashire Piles. 'This fellow here,' said Derby, pointing through the wooden bars at a bristling bird, 'he's a tip-top specimen.'

'We've received no less than thirty applications for breeding him,' Busley mentioned. 'Sketchley at Loughborough just wrote to say would M'Lord put his cock to Sketchley's hen and M'Lord could name his price!'

Edward's small forehead was furrowed. 'But Father, why do you need to charge for it?'

Derby smiled thinly. 'There won't be much wealth by the time you succeed me if I start giving everything away for free. Besides, Sketchley's not a gentleman, he's in trade; that sort would rather keep it businesslike.'

'What about this cock here, is he valuable?' asked Edward, peering through the bars at a straw-coloured bird with a bright yellow hackle.

'Yes, she is,' said Derby, laughing. 'Though the hens never leave the yard, they're just as important. This one's bred three marvellous fighters. I must take you to a main some time, come to think of it; thirteen's quite old enough. That would be splendid fun.' Derby often found himself adopting a falsely jovial tone with his children. He'd never puzzled out quite how to play the role of father without a mother at his side. They could hardly be missing Lady Derby; he doubted they remembered her face. But Derby didn't feel like a widower, that was the thing; to be honest, he felt more like a bachelor. His long and chaste courtship of the actress kept him yearning, ever young.

'We Smith-Stanleys are heirs to a glorious tradition,' he said now, too bombastic. 'The Knowsley Black-Breasted Reds are known the length and breadth of this island. How would you like to grow up to be a famous cock master like your father and his forefathers before him?'

The boy's face was shut up like a book. 'I don't know, Father. Why—'

'Yes? Speak up, boy.'

'When I grow up,' Edward confided, 'I should very much like to have a menagerie here, with creatures from the four corners of the globe.'

It gave Derby an odd shiver to think of himself in the tomb and his son as master of Knowsley, playing with tiger cubs and parrots.

'But I was wondering, why must you make the cocks fight?'

Derby let out a stunned laugh. 'Fighting's the whole point, Edward. Don't you understand that much? Why else would I spend thousands a year on the biggest breeding yards in England if I wasn't going to make most of it back in prize bags?'

'But surely the birds would rather just...live.'

Derby rubbed his forehead hard. What were they teaching them at Eton these days? Rousseau's softening influence had clearly

gone too far. 'On the contrary. They love to fight,' he said heavily.
'They live to fight. It's natural to males. If you'd ever spent a morning in the farmyard—' He decided not to explain about winning a
harem of females. 'Why, in the menagerie of your dreams, when
I'm dead and gone,' he said cuttingly, 'would the animals all be
wrapped up in cotton?'

'No, Father.'

'Well, then. They'd have to *do* something; they couldn't just
sleep all day.'

'I expect not.'

'Though I dare say you'd like that, given how late you come
down to breakfast!'

Edward gave a small, obedient laugh and Derby was plunged
into gloom. For some reason he found himself thinking back to August and that fight between Tyne and Earl he'd attended with
Prinny down in Brighton. The two men fought bare-knuckled (because mufflers spoiled the fun), their fists weighted with lead, and a
blow to the kidney had felled Earl, who'd died that night. Of course
it had been a sad accident, but Prinny had gone into fits, called in
Dr Warren to bleed him and sworn that was the last prizefight he'd
organise or attend. Some sportsmen had weak stomachs, Derby
concluded, and it looked like his son was going to be one of them.

NOVEMBER 1788

'Derby! You've missed half the banquet.'

'Traffic on the Strand.' He sighed, with his hand in Fox's sticky
grip. 'But it's not midnight yet—still the glorious fifth of November.' The Crown and Anchor's enormous ballroom was packed with
tables and men. 'Have I missed your speech?'

'No such luck.' Fox chuckled. 'There might even be some turtle
soup left; two tons of the beasts were boiled up this morning.' He
pulled Derby down to whisper in his ear with brandy breath, 'You
know my terrible creditors?'

Derby nodded. Was he going to be fleeced indecorously before
he'd even sat down?

'Well, good old Coutts has offered to pay them off with annuities to the tune of £10,000,' hissed Fox.

Derby grinned and rubbed his friend's shoulder. He took it as a good sign of the Party's prospects if Coutts, a notorious social climber and a banker to much of the government and the royal family, was willing to take such a gamble on Charles James Fox's future.

He squeezed on to a bench—'Evening, Devonshire. Windham, how d'you do?' He noticed that young Charles Grey was gazing at the Duchess of Devonshire with worshipful, melancholy eyes. Some of the old Whigs called Grey a brash hothead, too eager for the spotlight to serve his political apprenticeship like the rest of them, but Derby was rather impressed by such vaulting ambition.

He helped himself to a glass of cold hock and his eyes slid back to Georgiana's plumped-up, pigeony gauze bosom. 'Your wife's looking particularly lovely in honour of the great centenary,' he remarked to Devonshire.

'Mm,' said Devonshire through a faceful of lobster.

Derby wondered if the oblivious Duke knew how many men here envied his situation, even if they disapproved of it. To live like the sultan of some seraglio, with one's beautiful tall wife and her petitely ravishing friend (Lady Bess had recently returned from a discreet six months in France, slim-waisted again); to have a choice of company in bed (or even, rumour had it, both ladies at once, tangled up in the sheets...). That was one solution to the problem of marital disharmony—invite a newcomer in!

He felt a stirring in his groin and tried to concentrate on the dish in front of him, which appeared to be stewed tongue. He called down the table for a soup tureen to be passed, but he couldn't make himself heard. Some men had two women and some men had one, or none, that was how it was. And it wasn't as if anything was forcing Derby to sleep alone. He was one of the richest men in England, for God's sake; what woman couldn't he tackle if he pleased, by one means or another? If he lay awake at night in the cold state bed at Derby House, whose perverse choice, whose fault was that but his own?

Across the table the Duke of Portland pushed his little spectacles on to the dome of his forehead and asked Derby how he did.

'Excellently, Your Grace, and you?'

Portland put his glasses back on his nose and looked at his fingernails, and up and down the table, before replying, 'A little liverish, I believe, as a consequence of yesterday's dinner.' He'd hosted Derby, Burke and that brilliant American, Paine, whose pamphlet had done so much to inspire the colonists to throw off Old George's yoke. 'But on the whole, well.'

Derby had to repress a smile. Portland couldn't give a quick answer if a highwayman were holding a pistol to his head. The Duke's defenders said he was marvellously diligent, tactful, prudent, took the long view; the youngsters called him a feeble ditherer. Portland held the strange position of nominal head of the Whigs, since—as Fox put it cheerfully—a party founded by great families could hardly be led by a plain Mr, a second son. But Fox was their real leader, *primus inter pares*. Portland was devoted to him, of course; sometimes Derby thought their whole Party was held together not by a set of principles but by love of one man. And, obviously—he thought of the frigid face of young Pitt—hatred of another.

The clamorous chatter was dying down; there were cries of 'Hush'.

Fox was on his feet with a skewed flourish, leaning his belly on the table. 'My Lords, gentlemen, friends all,' he began, 'we are gathered here to celebrate the birthday of King William of Orange and of England, and the centenary of our most Glorious and Bloodless Revolution of 1688.'

Wild cheers all round, a few beaver hats and canes shot into the air. One of them landed on the table and broke a china dish, which caused much hilarity.

'Our grandsires' grandsires, and I mean that quite literally'— Fox nodded at representatives of the great Whig families who'd taken part in that coup—'they did a greater thing than they knew when they cast out one corrupt absolute monarch and replaced him with two excellent constitutional ones, William and Mary. They established the principle that the people of England should have some say in who's to rule them.'

'Huzza!'

'Three cheers!'

It was a stirring speech, on the need to renew the independence of Parliament, the Bill of Rights and the spirit of liberty and Reform, but Derby had heard it all before, so he happened to notice a boy pushing his way through the crowd to put a paper into Fox's hand. The leader scanned it and his sentence trailed off.

'Lost his thread, has he?' wondered Devonshire. 'Pass the hock, Derby.'

Fox looked up and thumped the table with his glass till the base broke off. The laughter and chatter died away. 'This statement is to be made to the Cabinet tomorrow,' he said in a shaking voice. He read the note: '*His Royal Majesty George III is gravely ill and his doctors fear for his life.*'

And in the silence, which was more potent, more prickling, more thrilling than any huzza, Derby thought: *This is it. Our cue.*

SEVEN OF them met the next morning at Devonshire House on Piccadilly: Fox, Portland, Sheridan, Derby, Grey, their eminent attorney the Earl of Loughborough and, of course, Georgiana, very crisp in blue and white stripes. Once her footmen had served strong coffee and tea, as well as steaming cups of sassafras saloop for those still poisoned with brandy, Georgiana gave orders that they weren't to be disturbed till she rang.

Fox mimed the tolling of a bell. 'Out with the old, in with the new!'

'It's hardly come to that yet,' protested Portland.

Sheridan ignored the Duke. 'Here's a plan of action,' he began, taking a page out of his pocketbook.

'I beg your pardon, Sherry?' said Fox pleasantly. 'At what meeting was this plan drawn up?'

'I saw Prinny earlier at Carlton House.'

Derby could see the tension flickering across faces. They all knew Sheridan had taken advantage of Fox's damaged friendship with the royal heir to strengthen his own position as intimate adviser to the Great Whale. Now he'd evidently begun private negotiations. 'Earlier than this?' Derby put in, trying to ease the atmosphere. 'Gad, I didn't know you were capable of such feats of early rising.'

Sheridan shook his head. 'I never went to bed.'

This raised a laugh. Sheridan grinned, scratching a red patch on his nose.

'Now, first of all,' said Fox, taking quiet control of the meeting, 'what do we know about His Majesty's illness?'

'Eh...in brief, that's to say...not enough,' said Portland.

'His symptoms, at least?'

The Duke consulted his notes, fingering the lines. 'The patient is sleepless, giddy, no thirst, no appetite. The veins in his face and feet are swollen, the whites of his eyes are yellow; cramps in his legs, a rash on his arms.'

'Some say it was brought on by overwork, or by sitting all day in wet stockings and eating too many pears,' Grey put in, flippant.

'Very unwise,' remarked Portland. 'I myself was reckless enough to consume a vast peach once—'

'But the key point, surely, is that His Majesty's mind is now said to be entirely alienated,' Loughborough interrupted in his deep Scottish voice. 'He slurs and muddles his words, babbles, rants about America.'

'I heard a rumour this morning at the coffee house,' said Grey, 'something the King said.' The young man quoted it with relish, like a line from a melodrama. '*I fear I'm mad, and I wish I might die quickly.*'

They absorbed this in silence for a moment, then Georgiana made one of her rare, blunt contributions. 'A week?'

Grey turned, smoothing a curl out of his handsome eyes, and grinned at her.

'Your Ladyship,' stammered Portland, 'I find it a...a rather inappropriate, or should I say, I don't believe speculation about the possible date of the unhappy event to be in the best of taste.'

Georgiana put her head on one side, wide-eyed. 'If I were in as melancholy a situation as His Majesty's, Your Grace, I assure you I'd pray to be released from it.'

'He's nearly fifty,' said Grey with the scorn of the young.

'A fortnight, perhaps, if he's not eating,' mused Georgiana. 'I'm sorry to offend anyone's sensibilities,' she added with a winning smile all round, 'but we must be ready for action, because our opponents certainly are.'

'Fox,' said Sheridan, 'you should drop Prinny a note—utmost sympathy, unqualified support, that kind of thing. I can draft it.'

'Thanks, but I'm sure I'll manage.'

There was a silence like an itch.

Suddenly the Prince was no mere buffoon but their imminent ruler. At Brooks's, recently, Derby had been among the members who'd blackballed two of the Prince's more disreputable candidates—from the new generation of cocky, underbred rakes who were clamouring to get into the Club—so Prinny and his brother the Duke of York had left in a huff and organised their own private gaming parties instead. How could the Foxites have been so careless of the heir apparent's favour?

'Portland—' began Fox without looking up.

'Yes,' said the Duke leadenly, 'I'm quite aware that the Prince's severe dislike of me, ah, ever since I protested against his robbing the public coffers of £300,000 to clear his debts, may constitute a problem.'

Derby could imagine the public uproar if the Great Whale demanded, not the safe candidate Portland as his Prime Minister but someone like Sheridan.

'I'll talk to him,' murmured Sheridan.

'Can we be quite sure of the Prince?' Derby asked, a little hoarse.

Six faces stared at him.

'If he wakes up King of England tomorrow, can we trust that he'll dismiss Pitt and call our Party to form a government?'

'We're his friends,' snapped Sheridan.

'We'll ride him to power like a thoroughbred', Grey suggested, 'that needs the barest tug on the reins.'

Georgiana was smiling through her fingers, like a child. But Fox was silent. Was he thinking about thoroughbreds, Derby wondered, the most temperamental horses in the world?

A HARD frost had set in and the stocks were still plummeting. The nation could talk of nothing else but the King's mysterious malady; wild stories flew from soirée to breakfast party, from snuff seller's to opera box. Old George was said to foam at the mouth, swear obscenely and howl like a dog; he'd thrown the Prince against a wall and hailed an oak tree as the Emperor of Prussia. For the convenience of his London physicians he was lodged at Kew, a summer palace with no carpets, where draughts whistled down the corridors. His doctors had blistered his scalp and his legs, leeched his face; they were using purges, emetics and ice to calm his frenzies, when he wasn't tied to his bed.

Eliza wished the poor man would die and be done with it.

Everyone was jumpy. Derby had the preoccupied, twitchy air of a conspirator and was always at Devonshire House or the Lords; Fox had fallen ill with a bloody flux. Her colleagues forgot the lines of parts they'd played all their lives. Dora Jordan (*the breeding sow of Drury Lane*, as Palmer called her) had a third child by her Mr Ford, but this one died and Eliza resented having to sympathise.

Sheridan—who, Eliza knew from Derby, was lurching headlong into an affair with Georgiana's lovely and unhappily married sister Harriet, Lady Duncannon—rushed through the theatre one afternoon, handing out satirical couplets alluding to madness and government, to be inserted into epilogues wherever they could be made to fit. 'Isn't this a dangerous game?' Eliza asked quietly, stepping into his path.

He stared back with bloodshot eyes.

'Do you really mean to cast Drury Lane as a Foxite theatre and lose us half our audience?'

'Miss Farren,' said Sheridan, 'the only stage I give a fig for is the British Empire. Now get out of my way and learn those lines.'

Tom King, a pillar of promptitude for all these years as actor and manager, didn't turn up the next morning. In the Green Room Eliza found a knot of people gathered round *The Times*. John Bannister was reading in a rapid but clear voice: '…*having been called to account by authors for the non-performance of works I never before heard of*—'

'What is it?' she asked.

Charles Bannister, at his son's shoulder, looked up sorrowfully. 'King's resignation.'

'No!'

'Who'd deny poor Tom his freedom?' asked Jack Palmer. 'Sheridan's been a lunatic.'

'There's a lot of it about,' quipped Mrs Jordan.

Eliza gave her a cold look.

'But to abandon us so publicly, in the middle of the season—' lamented Mrs Hopkins. 'Who on earth can replace him?'

'You could, Jack,' said Eliza after a moment.

He snorted.

'Miss Farren's right,' said Mrs Jordan suddenly. 'After all, you set up your own theatre, summer before last.'

'Don't remind me! That's exactly why our proprietor wouldn't trust me with the running of a nose—begging the ladies' pardon,' he added with a grin. 'I had to grovel long enough to be taken back into the company. Besides, it'd be the most thankless job in London, being manager under Sheridan.'

'Yes, look at this bit,' said Roaring Bob Bensley, reading over Bannister's shoulder, 'poor Tom complains he lacked authority to *command the purchase of a yard of ribbon, or the cleaning of a coat, which was often much needed.*'

'That's a good hit,' said Mrs Jordan. 'My dress for *Follies of a*

Day stinks to heaven and there's a rip all up the back from when I stood on the train.'

Eliza ignored this vulgarity. 'Kemble, then?'

John Bannister made a face at his father. Jack Palmer laughed. 'Kemble, with his finicky pretensions and his *Pray halt this rehearsal, let us consult Dr Johnson's Dictionary?*' His mimicry of the actor's hoarse solemnity was perfect.

'Between him and Siddons, it'd be a family takeover,' said Roaring Bob glumly. 'Since Gentleman Smith retired and poor Brereton died in the asylum, and with you in the doghouse, Jack, hasn't Kemble snuffed up every half-decent role?'

'Then the more fool he to turn to squabbles over lace and laundry,' Jack went on. 'Manager? He'd find it easier to fish corpses from the Thames with a banana skin!'

'Gentlemen. Ladies.' John Philip Kemble stood just inside the door, as grave as ever. Eliza's head snapped round. The fellow was tall and well-built, but his ability to slip in silently was unnerving. 'I came to acquaint you with my new position, but I gather you've surmised it.'

There was a painful pause, before Dora Jordan ran to his side. 'Oh, Mr Kemble, Johnny, dear.' He stiffened at the informality as she clutched his arm. 'You're not taking it on, truly? Such a fag it'll be!'

'I've never feared hard work in the service of Thespis, Mrs Jordan,' he assured her.

Another silence. 'Well, good luck to you, that's all I can say,' said Jack, striding over to shake his hand. 'If any man can stand up to our esteemed proprietor...'

'The fact is, Mr Sheridan and I have come to terms and I am to have a free hand,' said Kemble, the corners of his chiselled mouth twitching with pleasure.

Eliza and Jack exchanged a dubious look. 'My congratulations,' she said, dipping into a curtsy. 'Are we to have some new plays? Comedies?'

'Perhaps, in the fullness of time,' Kemble said, which sounded like *no* to her. Dora Jordan crossed her arms. Little liking as Eliza had for the woman, they had a common cause.

'But above all,' he went on in the ringing tones of a prepared speech, 'we will dedicate ourselves to raising standards of acting, a new authenticity in costumes and scenery, a scholarly rigour in interpretation.'

Roaring Bob let out a faint groan.

DECEMBER 1788

The cold didn't break for a single day; Britain was in the unremitting grip of ice. There was a prophecy that showed up on walls and in letters to newspapers: *fourteen weeks frost, a bloody riot and a dead king*. If only it were that simple, Derby thought tiredly. After yet another meeting of the Privy Council to interrogate the doctors, he concluded that Old Satan hadn't shown any signs of dying in weeks. (Derby always felt like a fraud in that august advisory body; he knew he owed his place to his ancient title, vast landholdings and influence in the North, rather than to any desire His Majesty had ever had to hear the views of a Foxite troublemaker.) He went straight on to Devonshire House to report every word spoken in the Council— he was a useful spy, at least—and stayed for a five-hour meeting to hammer out the arguments for Prinny to become sole regent.

He left the Lords late the next afternoon to wind his way through the corridors and cloisters to the Commons for the big debate on the Regency Bill. 'Fox looks...well, not thin, but distinctly thinner,' he muttered in Sheridan's ear in the lobby. The bloody flux must have come back.

'He told me he thought he might be dying,' said Sheridan with an unreadable expression.

'Wouldn't that be hard luck,' said Grey with a nervous smirk, 'with the apple about to fall into his mouth?'

Derby stared at the young man, who he knew was devoted to Fox.

'Have you ever had an apple fall into your mouth, Grey?' barked Sheridan. 'You'd lose a few teeth, I can tell you.'

'It was only a figure of speech.'

They were all short-tempered with excitement. Derby found himself wondering whether Sheridan had ganged up with him against Grey, just now, in order to mask his own hostility to their sick leader. *Frontis nulla fides,* as Juvenal put it; never trust a face.

From the End Gallery, Derby looked down at his colleagues on the Opposition benches. He watched the pale Prime Minister rise to his feet and propose that the House appoint a committee to consider all possible candidates for a temporary regency.

Fox lurched to his feet, sallow and sweating, with swollen eyes. 'We need no committee, Mr Speaker, to tell us that there exists in this kingdom an ideal regent, an heir apparent of full age, discretion and capacity.'

'Capacity for quim and brandy!' roared some Tory wit, setting off a wave of laughter.

'It behoves us, therefore, to waste not a moment but proceed with all diligence to restore royal authority in the person of that heir. It is not for the people or Parliament to choose their sovereign ruler. For us to deliberate on the *merits* of that Prince,' Fox fumed, 'who has sole and unfettered prerogative to lead this nation by hereditary right, would be improper and a waste of time.'

'Order! Order!' bawled Pitt's men.

A beatific smile spread over the Prime Minister's face. Derby groaned inwardly; in his urgency, Fox had gone too far. For the celebrated Man of the People to tell Parliament that its deliberations were irrelevant—Sheridan was gazing upwards, as if waiting for a deus ex machina. Derby pressed his lips against the crystal top of his cane.

As the Whig leader flopped into his seat and mopped his forehead, Pitt rose like a wraith. 'Mr Speaker, sir, the Prince of Wales has no more *right* to take up the reins of power than has any other individual in this country.'

'Such as yourself?' shouted out someone on the Opposition bench. Derby craned to see; it was Burke.

'Order!'

'Yes, or my under-gardener,' said Pitt, two red lamps flaming in his white cheeks.

'So the Honourable Member would set up himself or his servant as rivals to his Royal Highness,' roared Burke.

'Order! Order!'

'Sit down!'

'For the Honourable Members across the floor from whom we have just heard to assert such an inherent hereditary right in the Prince, disregarding the views of the people as expressed in Parliament,' continued Pitt gently, 'verges on treason to the Constitution.'

A roar of excitement and horror. Derby suddenly wanted to laugh. Were they all mad today, had the House turned inside out? Here was Fox, the hero of Parliament, trumpeting about the divine right of princes, and Pitt, the tyrant's mouthpiece, the royal eunuch, posing as the people's champion!

'I venture to make two predictions, Mr Speaker,' Pitt added, 'that the manager of Drury Lane Theatre will never be manager of the House of Commons—' He paused to allow a plume of laughter to go up.

Gad, thought Derby, *that's the first joke I've ever heard him make.*

The bony finger moved from Sheridan to Fox. '...and that none of us here will live to see the reign of *Charles III.*'

'So MY life mask was another false start?' asked Eliza.

'No! Not at all,' cried Anne, laughing. She wasn't usually like this; she prided herself on a clarity of vision about her work. 'The life mask is wonderful; I mean to hang it up on the wall, to keep me company in my long labours. But I've decided I can't use it as a basis for your bust, it's too distractingly lifelike. For instance, it captures this tiny mole here—' Anne walked over and touched her fingertip to the small brown dot above the actress's lip.

'Oh, yes,' said Eliza, 'I usually paint that out.'

'It's lovely. But too private. I wouldn't include that in a bust for all the Exhibition visitors to gawk at. No, I've begun again from scratch; what I want my sculpture to be is you, but also the very type of mysterious womanhood, with a beauty that the Greeks would have recognised.'

'Then you'll have to keep bringing me back to this freezing workshop for sittings all winter,' said Eliza, amused.

'Perhaps so,' Anne admitted grinning as she pulled a damp sheet off the half-roughed-out clay head, 'like Scheherazade in the Arabian Nights. This way I have the pleasure of your company at least once a week, no matter how hard Sheridan drives you at Drury Lane!' She worked in silence on the delicate right ear. 'Have you heard the latest? The King tried to run a race against a horse.'

'I seem to remember Derby telling me that he attempted the same thing as a boy. Out of high spirits, presumably, not insanity,' Eliza added.

'Oh, these are strange times,' Anne murmured. She felt oddly constrained when talking about Old George; indecently excited at the prospect of a new Whig regime, and ashamed.

'I can barely read the papers,' Eliza complained, 'they're so full of the most disgusting medical details—*heavy sweats, tube feedings* and *profuse stools.*'

Mrs Moll, the housekeeper, came in to announce the Earl of Derby, to Anne's surprise.

'Your mother said I'd find you at our mutual friend's,' he told Eliza, kissing her hand, 'but I'd no idea I'd be privileged enough to witness a sitting. How long has this been going on, Mrs D.?' he scolded.

'Didn't I mention it?' That was odd. Perhaps she'd felt shy because of the peculiarities of this case; she hadn't wanted the Earl to think she was asking his permission. He came close, now, and stared at the contours. 'I'm still roughing it out,' she told him.

'A marvellous start, though. Will you leave the eyes unincised?'

'Yes; the effect's more antique.'

Derby was very animated today; there was an odd shine in his little eyes, but tired lines round them. He made one of his rare bad jokes, when they got to talking about Drury Lane: 'I only wish our

King would retire as fast as your *King* did! Has Miss Farren been singing the praises of her new manager?' he asked Anne.

He often did that, she noticed with a hint of amusement—demonstrated that he knew all about his inamorata's life.

'Yes, Kemble's surprised us all with his energy,' Eliza told them; 'he's somehow found the funds to pension off ancient players and to give the poor old theatre a new face with gold and white paint.' As she spoke she leaned forward a little; Anne always found it hard to get a model to sit still when there was a visitor in the workshop. 'He's all for equality, keeps calling us *professionals*—says we leading lights should be willing to take small roles on occasion and come to every rehearsal to be drilled as if we were beginners. He tells of going behind the scenes at the Comédie Française and seeing an actor earnestly try out ten different tones and attitudes. Kemble asked him what famous role he was preparing—Hyppolytus, or perhaps Tartuffe?—and the actor said no, he had only one line: "*Madame, votre voiture est prête.*"'

Anne and Derby laughed in chorus.

'Well,' Derby jested, 'Reform is the spirit of the age. Perhaps Kemble's new regime should be called Thespian Whiggery.'

'Speaking of which—what news of the Regency Bill?' Eliza asked and Anne realised they'd been avoiding the inevitable subject.

Derby let out a long sigh. 'Pitt keeps blocking us, insisting that the King's illness is temporary. When, you know, the truth is if I had a dog half so mad I'd drown it in the river.'

'That's high treason,' Anne pointed out.

'No, just kindness to animals.'

The three of them laughed again, a little wildly. *How cruel this long wait is making us,* Anne thought. 'If the Bill goes through—' she hesitated.

'When, not if.' Derby grinned at her. 'Georgiana will whip our votes in, Pitt will topple like an obelisk and we'll toboggan into power on Prinny's spangled coat-tails.'

Of course, it wasn't quite that simple; as Anne worked on the slim eyebrows of the bust, Derby started describing the squabbles the Foxites were having about the place each would hold in their new government. When Eliza had to rush off to a rehearsal he stayed on, watching Anne's fingers shape the clay throat. 'What we really need are allies, great lords who can bring a swathe of votes with them; someone like Richmond, for instance.'

Anne stiffened.

'He's never been a real Tory, you know, just a lapsed Whig. I wonder,' Derby murmured, 'once Prinny is Regent, would there be any chance of your brother-in-law...crossing the floor?'

Anne decided to pretend the question was rhetorical.

Derby laughed a little, as if at his own cheek. 'I can tell you in confidence that Lord Chancellor Thurlow knows which way the wind's blowing, he might well come over to our side. But only on condition of keeping his office—which is causing fury in our own ranks. It's always been this way among the Whigs, I'm afraid; like that terrible summer at Coxheath.'

'When was that?'

'Oh, didn't you come down? This was in '78, when it looked like the French would invade England in support of the Americans,' he said. 'There was a huge military camp, it was all very jolly at first; lots of us went to Kent to drill our battalions. That was the summer Coleraine sold Lady Melbourne to Egremont, and Lady Clermont took up with a local apothecary. And, of course, there was my own wife and Dorset,' he added grimly.

Anne's head was whirling. It was very rare for him to refer to Lady Derby, but that was not the detail that had shaken her. 'What can you mean, *sold*? I'm aware, of course, that Baron Coleraine was...linked with Lady Melbourne at the time.'

'I'm terribly sorry, didn't you know?' asked Derby sheepishly. 'I oughtn't to be raising these matters with a lady at all, of course.'

'Oh, Derby, don't *lady* me.'

'Well, since you insist. Coleraine and your friend were...a little tired of each other, but there'd been no breach. Then Egremont comes along that summer, mad for her, rich as Croesus, that sort of thing. A deal is struck and Egremont agrees to pay a certain sum.'

'How much?' Anne couldn't stop herself.

After a second's hesitation Derby said, '13,000.'

'*Pounds?*'

'Oh, guineas, of course.'

Yes, she thought, *gentlemen always pay each other in guineas, an extra shilling on the pound.* 'Did Lady Melbourne have any idea?' she asked huskily.

Derby blinked at her.

'Or did these dreadful machinations take place behind her back?'

'Mrs D.,' said Derby fondly, 'you're too unworldly. Why, your friend brokered the deal; she and her husband were full parties to the contract and they split the fee.'

Anne put her hand over her mouth.

'I do truly apologise for shocking you,' he told her, nibbling his thumb. 'The point I was trying to make', he went on after a minute, 'is that Fox has to rule a team of flamboyant, mettlesome characters—whereas Pitt has only a set of dull clerks to manage. But, of course, just as our Party's been damaged by quarrels over women, it's been strengthened by the efforts of your sex, too, and I don't just mean Georgiana,' he went on more cheerfully. 'For creatures without a vote, you have an immense power; I've always thought my fellow politicians underestimate it. Do you go to Goodwood this Christmas as usual?' he asked, as if changing the subject.

'Probably.'

Derby's eyes were fiery little marbles. 'Perhaps you might... sound out the Duke?'

'Oh, Derby,' she wailed.

'You're practically Richmond's sister. He has an enormous respect for you. I'm only asking you to probe him gently,' Derby pushed on. 'You might hint that we'd let him stay on as Master-General of the Ordnance, since he finds sandbags so absorbing and it's the one job none of our lot want. Just dip a toe in the waters.'

'They're full of pike,' she snapped. 'You put me in a very delicate position.'

His grin had something unbalanced about it. 'And aren't we all in a very delicate position? Isn't the whole country adrift in dangerous waters?'

'Very well, very well, but only for your friendship's sake, and Fox's,' she said, scrubbing her hands on her apron.

FOX'S ILLNESS was pure pleasure to the Tories. They kept him on his feet as much as possible, entangled in legal complexities; several times he had to excuse himself and rush out of the Chamber, clutching his belly. The government-funded papers quipped that the lining of Fox's stomach had been eaten away by the regular necessity of eating his own words.

When he was too weak to leave his dear Liz's country house at St Anne's Hill, his followers drove down there. Georgiana wasn't with them, of course; the Duchess could hardly call on a former courtesan. Derby remembered his last visit to St Anne's Hill in September, before this regency crisis had ever been dreamed of. He and Fox had played battledore and composed epitaphs for Dick Fitzpatrick's terrier in six languages. (Derby was only able to help in English, Latin and French.)

Today was gunmetal grey and the avenue was hard with packed snow. In Mrs Armistead's neat parlour the Foxites talked in low voices, as if at a funeral. Sheridan was in the process of extracting a bank draft for £500 from Derby to buy up the whole print run of an obscene pamphlet about the Prince's secret marriage, when the door opened and Fox staggered in on Mrs Armistead's arm. She was still marvellously voluptuous, Derby thought, and her face showed no sign of being nearly forty. Her lover was black with bristles and his shaggy, matted chest showed through the limp opening of his shirt. 'Huzza,' cried Derby, and the others joined in.

Fox dropped into a chair and begged for a cup of tea.

'Now, Charlie, I think some wine'd fortify you better,' said Mrs Armistead, pouring him a glass; her voice still had a strong Cockney slant to it.

'Good of you all to come. Sherry, how's our royal friend?'

'Very steady,' Sheridan said. 'He's quietly promising offices, pensions and peerages all over the place, and our support is growing.'

'I want numbers. I've promised Liz we'll be in power by New Year, haven't I, dearest?' He patted her plump knuckles. 'Who's false, who's staunch, who may be deceiving us about their plans to vote? Oh, and any fresh word of the King?'

Loughborough shrugged. 'He's said to be *in a comfortable state*, meaning, not quite violent in his lunacy.'

'Apparently he's now convinced that London lies underwater,' said Charles Grey.

'Solid ice, more like it,' said Fox with a shuddering glance out of the window.

'The only, ah, complication', said Portland, 'is a new physician. Named Willis, I believe; a certain Doctor Willis. He hails from, ah, from Lincolnshire.'

Sometimes Derby couldn't stand the Duke's tentative delivery. 'His methods are rough, but they call him a miracle worker,' he broke in. 'Lord Harcourt says Willis cured his wife's mother, the way you might break a horse; whenever she threw her food at the wall, or spoke obscenely, Willis brought out the straitjacket and it calmed her down at once.'

They all considered the revolting image.

'Can we settle this matter of places, once and for all?' Grey broke in. 'I won't take a Lordship of the Treasury, it's beneath my capacities. If you won't give me the Exchequer, I'll accept Secretary at War.'

Fox frowned sadly at him. 'My young friend—'

'I'll surrender the Exchequer to you, sir, or Lord John Cavendish, if I must, but not to lesser Pelhams or Norfolks or Windhams.'

'Lesser, you cocksure puppy?' barked Sheridan.

'Windham is a, ah, most brilliant Greek scholar and mathematician,' Portland pointed out.

'So?' asked Grey.

Fox spoke hoarsely. 'The good of the Party, of the country—'

'Oh, so other men may have their eyes on the prize they fight for, but not me?' asked Grey. 'We know Sherry will be Treasurer of the Navy and Head of the Board of Trade, with £4000 a year!'

Derby caught Liz Armistead's eye and wished they were outside, walking along the frozen terrace. Oh, the wearisome ambition of landless men.

'For my own part,' said Loughborough, 'I demand an assurance that the Chancellorship will go to me, not to Thurlow or any other rat from Pitt's sinking ship.'

Fox clapped his hands with surprising vigour. 'Listen to yourselves, you squabbling vultures! Do you consider yourselves fit to take up the reins of power? After fretting in opposition for fifteen of the past eighteen years we Whigs are going to have our day at last! Don't you see a new England on the horizon?' He pointed out of the window like a mystic.

In the leaden silence Derby spoke. 'Did you ever hear of Lord Thomond's Irish feeder?'

'Is this a joke?' snapped Sheridan.

'A fable, rather. The feeder was entrusted with some cocks that were to be matched with another lord's for a considerable purse. Thinking that Lord Thomond's birds were all on the same side and so wouldn't disagree, the feeder shut them up together in one shed. The next morning...' He looked at Fox for the punch line.

The leader didn't smile. 'All dead.'

'Quite so. We must drop these petty feuds, we can't afford them,' said Derby, sweeping his eyes over the whole group. 'The readiness is all.'

'Well said, quite so,' murmured Portland.

'More tea, gentlemen?' asked Mrs Armistead.

Fox's eyes were pained. 'Excuse me, m'bowels,' he said, lurching towards the door, his stockings sagging like an old man's skin.

And it occurred to Derby for the first time: *We're going to lose him.*

CHRISTMAS AT Goodwood was as elegant as ever, with the addition of a candlelit fir tree, a fashion that Queen Charlotte had imported from her German principality. The topic of the nation's parlous state was banned. Despite his fatigue and toothache, Richmond took his many guests hunting. Anne always hung back from the kill; she knew it was absurd, but she preferred it when the fox got away. In the saloon she stood absorbed in an early Stubbs of the Duke riding to hounds; really, no painter had ever made dogs look more alive than Stubbs, though she had no rivals in sculpture.

Walpole arrived from Strawberry Hill enveloped in furs; 'quite the Canadian trapper,' he said with a giggle. To everyone's relief he had left Tonton at home. Ensconced in the seat closest to the fire in the gallery, he murmured politics to Anne. 'Inasmuch as George III is the despotic monarch who waged war on America—and incidentally, threw your dear father out of office for standing up to him back in '65, or was it '64?—I loathe and execrate him. But inasmuch as His Majesty's a feeble and feeble-minded man in his declining years, subjected to brutal treatments in the name of medicine, whose wastrel of a son is openly plotting against him—how can I but pity him and wish him a swift recovery?'

'Do you really think there's any chance of that?' she asked uneasily.

Walpole tapped his bulging nose. 'I have my sources at Kew.'

Anne discounted all such rumours as Pittite lies.

There was a great celebration for the sixteenth birthday of Henriette Le Clerc, an orphan ward of the Richmonds' who was generally assumed to be the product of the Duke's liaison with some French lady. Lady Mary, who had no children of her own, called her *our darling fosterling.* Either her sister was a singularly tolerant wife, Anne thought, or a consummate actress. And if one acted a role for the length of one's days, in all company, who could say the role was untrue?

The girl was a sweet thing, if rather spoiled; she sang often (somewhat out of tune) and chattered constantly in her French way. Lady Mary was teaching Henriette the embroidery stitches she'd learned from her own mother. 'My sister Anne's never had any skill with the needle,' she said, laughing; 'I suspect she despises it, as the pastime of ordinary women.'

'That's not true,' Anne protested, 'it's just that my hands are more accustomed to hammers and chisels.'

Walpole piped up from the fireside, 'Mrs Damer was no older than you are now, Henriette, when she discovered her vocation.'

'Oh, not that old story—'

'Old men must be let tell their old stories,' he informed her, 'for what else is left to us? It happened like this. Conway had for his secretary a wise Scot of the name of Hume; Philosopher Hume, many called him. This chit of a girl was tagging along with him on a walk through the woods of Park Place when they met an Italian urchin.'

'He was selling little manikins he'd made out of mud,' Anne supplied and Henriette made a face. 'Hume bought one as an act of charity and I'm sorry to admit that I sneered at the beggar's work. So Hume dared me to do better.'

Walpole broke in gleefully, 'She took some wax, locked herself up in her room for a week—'

Anne shook her head at his exaggeration.

'—and came out with the most charming little *ébauche* of her cat!'

'I wasn't cured of my arrogance, I'm afraid.'

'But at least now it was grounded on skill and effort, rather than sheer snobbery.'

'I'd like to be an artist, or maybe an actress,' Henriette said suddenly.

Lady Mary blinked at her. 'Oh, I don't think so, not an actress.'

Anne looked away. Really, the prejudice against Eliza's profession was ineradicable.

'You won't need to be anything, darling,' said Lady Mary, 'because you'll be some lucky man's wife and have dozens of little Henriettes to look after.'

Anne's mind was still on the past. 'Hume was a shocking sceptic, poor fellow; he wouldn't believe anything without the evidence of his eyes. He once said to me, "The sun may not rise tomorrow."'

'Whatever did he mean?' asked Lady Mary.

'That we'd no firm reason to believe it would rise, it was just an assumption. When the next day I saw him and pointed out that the sun had indeed risen, he smiled gloomily and said, "Ah, but what about tomorrow?"'

Henriette whooped with laughter.

In the Duchess's room later that day, Anne was looking through some family jewels her sister wanted to give her—a thick choker of pearls on black velvet and a ruby parure. She took the opportunity of their being alone and murmured, 'Don't you mind at all about Henriette?'

'Mind?' Lady Mary stared at her. 'I dote on the girl. If the Duke's ever under the influence of the blue devils I send in Henriette. He lets her sit beside him while he's working and he helps her with her spelling; she's made quite the nurse of him.'

'Not so much her, then, as Richmond's...straying.' She held her breath.

Lady Mary was smiling oddly. 'How does it threaten my position? He's always genteel and discreet about it, for I couldn't abide scenes. Oh, and the party must be of good birth; I wouldn't like it if he entangled himself with anyone vulgar.'

Anne shrugged in bemusement. 'If I had a husband—a husband I loved,' she corrected herself—'I think I'd be just as hurt whether it was a kitchen maid or an empress who made me feel I wasn't...the dearest object of his heart.'

The Duchess's handsome throat caught the light. 'That should be a speech in a play. You're such a creature of sensibility, Anne; I think I inherited all our mother's sense. I *am* the dearest object; Richmond treasures me, consults me on everything, from Pitt's orders to the enclosure of a field. Since I hold his prime affection, why should I mind his lifting his spirits with little flirtings and the occasional scrape?'

The morning after Christmas Anne was in the library, reading Sophocles, only two tables away from the Duke of Richmond. Her eyes rested on his shiny, smooth head.

A woman's role in life was often to play go-between. Tact, suggestion, encouragement, delving—Anne was not ignorant of these feminine arts. But this was politics, where women had to tread carefully. *Damn Derby for asking this.* This was harder than chanting slogans on a hustings; this was private, tricky, embarrassing. She was being used. No, she was being useful to Fox and to the cause of Reform, and a bright future for Britain. She cleared her throat.

Richmond looked up from a volume of parliamentary precedents, owlish.

All Anne's prepared lines fled away and she spoke simply. 'What's going to happen to us?'

'Our family?'

She smiled; what a paterfamilias he was, for a man with no acknowledged heirs. 'No. Our nation.'

'Ah.' Richmond let out a long breath. 'I suppose you mean, will the greatest rake in the kingdom become regent, and your friend Fox and his motley crew shoo us out of Cabinet?'

She winced. 'You were once in the vanguard of the Whigs, the champion of Reform,' she reminded him.

'Reform's a dead duck,' he said flatly. 'And besides, it's not the issue at stake now. Your precious Foxites are behaving with a shocking hurry and lust for power; they're even trying to poach some of our key men.'

This at least raised the topic for Anne. 'Perhaps Fox is trying to extend the olive branch—form a coalition of talents, you know, for the good of the nation.'

Richmond snorted. 'Form a ladder of bodies, you mean, and climb up it.'

'Are there no possible circumstances under which you'd join in the new government?' she asked, trembling at her own nerve.

Her brother-in-law looked at her hard. 'Don't meddle, Anne.'

A blush began to rise from her throat. She looked down and pretended to be engrossed in her Sophocles.

JANUARY 1789

When Derby turned up at Fox's lodgings in South Street at half past one the table was awash with papers. He bowed to the Prince, who was curled up on the sofa in an uncharacteristically sober brown coat, then shook Fox's hand. His friend looked pale and sweaty, but no longer dying. 'I came as soon as I received your note.'

'Thank God somebody knows the meaning of punctuality!'

Derby's eyebrows went up. Fox wasn't known for this virtue himself. 'What's the matter?'

Fox was a hungry bear woken out of hibernation. 'Pitt's been good enough to supply the Prince with a list of the proposed *restrictions* on the regent's power and Sheridan's got it. He promised me he'd bring it over at nine this morning.' Fox stabbed his finger at a note propped against the mirrored mantelpiece.

'Pitt's to wait on me at Carlton House at three,' said Prinny, 'and the devil of the thing is I can't remember more than one or two points.'

'Didn't you think to read it before you gave it to Sherry?' barked Fox.

'Oh, I did, I protest, I skimmed it through, but now the details have gone clear out of my mind. The cheek of Pitt, to draw up any such nasty list! What sort of a noodle will he think me?' he wailed, punching the upholstery.

Just don't threaten to slit your throat again, thought Derby, watching his future king. 'Well, gentlemen,' he said, sitting down without being asked, 'why don't we pass the time profitably by reviewing our Cabinet?'

Fox brightened and rummaged through his notes. 'Portland for PM, myself for Secretary of State. Loughborough for Lord Chancellor—'

'Since when?' asked Derby.

A frown. 'It turns out Thurlow won't switch sides after all; he believes these nonsensical reports of an improvement in the patient's health.'

Prinny stroked his chin unhappily.

'I've persuaded Grey to accept a Lordship of the Treasury for now,' Fox went on.

They were building a government out of the air, a castle in the

sky, thought Derby. They played with the names like a frantic game
of chess.

'Oh, I offered Lord Sandwich the Admiralty,' remarked Prinny.

'You did what?' asked Derby.

'It seemed, you know, it seemed the thing; persuasive.'

Fox was biting both his lips in a clear effort not to howl. 'That's
a plum job, Your Royal Highness. If you don't discuss these things
with us, your advisers—'

'But I'm sure I mentioned it to Sherry.'

'Speaking of the devil, greetings.' Sheridan strolled into the
room, pulling off a new fur-lined coat. A gift from the Prince,
wondered Derby? 'It's bitter out there.'

Fox snatched the note from the mirror and brandished it.
'Where in all the hells have you been? I have here your *word* that
you'd bring me the list at nine. Do you just happen to be five hours
late, I wonder, or could you be deliberately trying to leave me out of
the most crucial stage of negotiations?'

Derby swallowed painfully. How had it come to this? A
stranger would think these two men hated each other.

'Pooh, pooh,' said Sheridan, 'be as cross as you will.'

Fox's eyes bulged and Derby looked at the wall for the nearest
bell-pull; was their leader going to fall into an apoplexy? Fox
opened his mouth and Derby stiffened. But what came out was a
roar of laughter.

Sheridan smirked.

Fox's face was wet with mirth. 'Damn your eyes, Sherry,' he
said, whacking him on the back. 'Is that all you can say to me?
Pooh, pooh, like a schoolboy? Where's the famed silver tongue now?'

Sheridan stuck it out.

'Ha ha,' the Prince joined in a little nervously. 'Very good, ha
ha ha.'

Sheridan really should have been an actor, like his father; he had
a remarkable ability to charm his audience at moments of crisis.
'Derby, cast your eyes over Pitt's restrictions with us,' said Sheridan,
sitting down.

It was worse than they'd thought. The regent wasn't to be allowed to grant remunerative offices or pensions, create new peers,
dispose of the King's property, or interfere in any way with the care
of the King or the royal household, which was to be in the Queen's
sole control. Prinny would be like a swaddled child, propped up on
the throne.

'Now, old Fox,' Sheridan began soothingly, 'I've drafted an answer for Prinny to give Pitt, but of course it's subject to your approval. What delayed me today, in fact, was that I had to find my
wife to copy it out, her hand's so much clearer than mine. I realise
you're opposed on principle to a restricted regency, but I beg you to
be pragmatic; consider that, once in power, we could—'

'I've changed my mind, I give it up,' Fox interrupted, tossing
the list back on the table.

They all stared at him. 'I say, I protest,' said Prinny.

Fox kept his eyes on Sheridan. 'Oh, I'll move amendments and
fight these restrictions all the way, but I expect the vote to go
against us. You might as well knuckle down, Prinny,' he threw over
his shoulder; 'the Virgin Boy can't stop you choosing your own
ministers at least. But if this circus drags on much longer I fear the
Queen may seize the regency herself.'

The Prince blanched.

Sheridan's eyes were narrowed. 'So...we're in agreement?'

'Amazingly so,' murmured Derby. He should have been glad,
but all he could feel was a grudging bewilderment.

FEBRUARY 1789

The Great Frost had broken at last. Was it a sign, Eliza wondered
superstitiously, that their hopes were about to come to fruition?
Still, it was a damp thaw. She shuddered slightly and pulled her
cloak round her more tightly as she left Anne's workshop, where
she'd had the curious experience of watching the sculptor slice off
the back of Eliza's clay head and scoop out the insides, so it wouldn't
crack while baking. Her cloak was buff satin with blue-dyed fur
trim; Georgiana wouldn't let Whig ladies be seen in any other

colours at the moment; it was as if she meant to usher in the new regime by sheer chic.

Eliza wished she didn't have to play in *All in the Wrong* at Drury Lane tonight; the Regency Bill was receiving its third and final reading in the Lords and she couldn't think of anything else. In a matter of days Pitt was going to fall; change was so close, she could taste it on the air like a cut lemon. In the dressing room her mother fussed around her, putting her paint on too thick; Eliza wiped half of it off as soon as she was alone. The bell rang and she made her way through the corridors to the wings. When the orchestra played the last note of the overture she glided on stage to begin her comic prologue.

She heard an indistinct roar from the pit, then other voices took it up. 'God save the King!'

She nodded at the sentiment and gave a flat smile—well, she had to—and curtsied again.

'God save the King!'

She narrowed her eyes to see past the glaring oil lamps. All the voices were from the same part of the pit; a sure sign of a government clique who'd planned this, or been hired to cause trouble. Kemble stepped on from the Prompt Side. In his fastidious diction he pronounced, 'God save the King, indeed.' She knew he just wanted the play to go on.

But it wasn't enough for the crowd. 'Play it,' roared a Scottish voice.

'Play it!'

And an apple soared into the orchestra, hitting a cello player in the back of the head. He let out a bark of annoyance. A long *oo* of excitement went up.

'Play it!'

'*God Save the King!*'

The fervour was spreading through the theatre; this wasn't just a small knot of men now. How these things caught like fire. *They're all so keyed up, the whole city's wound tight like a watch.* Eliza, observing from behind her painted-on smile, thought there might very well be a riot. She'd never lived through a riot herself; there hadn't been any at Drury Lane since '76, two years before her début. Her nearest exit was behind the back flat that showed a view of St Paul's.

Kemble raised his hand for a moment's silence, as Julius Caesar might have done. 'Gentlemen, ladies,' he called, 'as it so pleases you, the orchestra will now play "God Save the King".'

'Huzza!'

This was most irregular; Eliza had never heard this anthem played unless the monarch was attending a performance. Her face tightened. When the orchestra launched into the opening notes the crowd's hysterical delight almost drowned out the words. People in the audience started roaring along.

> Send him victorious,
> Happy and glorious,
> Long to reign over us...

Eliza's eyes swivelled over to Kemble; he appeared to be joining in and his dark eyes caught hers. She opened her mouth and mimed along prettily, but her throat refused to make any noise. What, God save that slobbering lunatic who'd kept a stranglehold on the forces of freedom for so long? Save Fox's nemesis and Pitt's puppeteer, that old tyrant who'd never given a fig for the bony paupers outside his golden gates?

When the verse reached the line about *Scatter his enemies* there were shrieks and war cries.

> ...and make them fall.
> Confound their politics,
> Frustrate their knavish tricks,
> On him our hopes are fixed,
> O save us all!

After she'd rushed through her Prologue Eliza stood in the empty dressing room and stripped off her faux-pearl ear clips with shaking hands. To be dictated to by a bunch of footmen parroting their Tory lords—to have to mouth sentiments she didn't feel—

well, of course, she did that every night when she played a role, but
this was different, this turned her stomach. Was half the country in
a delirium with its King? The sooner Old George was in his coffin
the better. It was time for the coming generation and for Reform.

A soft knock at the door; probably Kemble. He was always
scrupulous about the possibility of walking in on a half-naked actress. 'Come in,' she called.

It was Derby.

Eliza blinked at him, disconcerted. 'My mother's fetching me
some soup' was all she could think to say.

'I do beg you pardon for bursting in like this.' He hovered on
the threshold.

'Come in, have a seat.' She beckoned, suddenly impatient with
herself for being afraid to be in a room alone with this man she'd
known for so many years. 'I didn't see you in your box.'

'What?' He advanced a few steps and put his hand on the back
of a chair, his face taut with some hidden emotion. 'Oh, no, I
haven't been—I only just arrived from the Lords. I wanted to be
the first to tell you.'

Her shoulders eased as if a burden had fallen away; her face
began to light up. 'What, the vote passed so early?'

The door swung open and Mrs Farren, two hands clutching a
dish with a tin lid, walked into the Earl's back. 'Oh, My Lord!'

Derby jumped out of the way, but there was a dribble of brown
down his pale-blue silk coat.

'Oh, sir, Your Lordship, I could chop off my clumsy hands!'
Mrs Farren was rubbing at the soup mark with her apron, spreading the stain.

'Leave it, Mother,' said Eliza. 'Lord Derby's only just come,
with great news from the Lords,' she added defensively.

'No,' he said, 'you mistook me. It's the worst.'

Eliza stared at him. His face was grey, now he was nearer the
lamp; how could she not have noticed? Her mother knotted her
hands in her apron.

'Before the debate could begin,' said Derby, 'Chancellor Thurlow stood up and said—I doubt I'll ever forget the words—*I wish to inform my honourable peers that His Majesty King George III has made a full and perfect recovery.'*

'No.' Eliza's voice came out as gruff as a man's.

'Thurlow read detailed reports from Doctor Willis. Today the King was allowed to shave himself and he made a good job of it.'

She turned her head away, she couldn't bear it. She caught her eye in the mirror. Had the last five months been an almighty waste of time, a gruelling and chaotic rehearsal for a performance that would never take place?

'You must despise us,' Derby said suddenly. He threw up his hands, then let them fall; it was a curiously schoolboyish gesture. 'At Park Place, last summer, Mrs Damer asked me what chance we had of toppling Pitt, remember? Well, we got our chance at last— and let it slip.'

'Oh, Derby,' said Eliza, as if to a child. 'It was in the hands of the gods.'

'They help those who help themselves, don't they?' He was almost snarling. 'If we'd worked as one and not wasted time bickering, we could have swept into power before Christmas.'

'But the King would have got better and thrown you Foxites out again,' she reminded him gently.

'Perhaps,' he said, very low. 'Or perhaps Prinny could have held on to the throne, once he had it. It might have been too late to turn back history's clock and Old Satan would have crawled off to retirement in Hanover.'

She felt the urge to take his hand, but of course it was impossible. Not just because her mother was sitting there, but because it was one of her own rules. Apart from kissing her hand as a greeting, Eliza allowed him no other favours; it was the least she could do, to be consistent.

MARCH 1789

London was lit up at night: at least six candles in every window, little oil lamps forming the shape of a crown or *Rejoice,* or *GR,* for the King who'd never been so popular in all his long reign. People drove around in coaches for no reason but merriment, throwing squibs and crackers out of the windows. Queen Charlotte, whose hair had gone snow-white during the crisis, pointedly cut the Foxites at a thanksgiving ceremony in St Paul's and handed out fans that said *Health Restored to One, and Happiness to Millions*. To slight Drury Lane, the King made his first appearance at Covent Garden, in a long coat to hide his emaciated legs. Addresses of gratitude to the Prime Minister for safeguarding the nation flowed in from towns across the country. Shops came up with the most satirical window decorations; several included very dead-looking stuffed foxes.

Derby felt strange, these days, as shaky as a convalescent. First thing in the morning, an immense lassitude seemed to press him back against his pillows. What was the point of meetings and strategies now? Old Satan and his Eunuch—whose standing in Parliament had never been higher—would rule for ever.

After seeing the King up close at a meeting of the Privy Council—a spare, calm man of fifty—it struck Derby that it was as if the whole thing had never happened. A phantasmagoria. Was it the Foxites who'd been mad, caught in coils of self-deception, a straitjacket of ambition? If they hadn't been able to behave like a band of brothers when faced with the greatest opportunity they'd ever had, what chance had they of holding together in hard times? Was Derby staking his whole career on a bad card, a lost cause?

AT NEWMARKET Derby stood by a huge grave in the rainy dusk. Bunbury's hand lay heavy on his shoulder. 'He was one of a kind,' said the Baronet.

'He was.'

'Good to see such a big turnout. I think half London's come down for the funeral.'

There was no coffin, obviously, but the deceased was draped in his master's colours, for which he'd won so much glory. With enormous strain, twenty men lowered him into the hole. When Derby's turn came, he accepted the shovel and heaved a clod of wet earth into the grave.

Afterwards they all packed into the biggest tavern and still it couldn't hold them; Derby estimated there were 200 gentlemen of the turf there. 'Eclipse,' said Bunbury solemnly, glass in the air.

'Eclipse.'

'Eclipse!'

'Eighteen wins in a row.'

They drank.

There were boasts of the number of mares Eclipse had covered in his splendid quarter-century of life, how he never needed prodding but always went to it with a will. His name would never be forgotten; *King of the Turf,* someone called him and the title caused a quiver to go through the crowd.

'Long live King George,' someone shouted automatically and others took up the cheer, but not everyone.

Derby found Sheridan in a corner and slumped into a chair beside him. 'How's Prinny these days?'

Sheridan's smile was dark. 'He's staying in a perpetual state of blind drunkenness, the better to feign delight. He's shitting his breeches with fear that Papa might cut him out of the line of succession and make the Duke of York his heir. He went to throw himself at the royal feet and beg forgiveness, but the Queen wouldn't let him in the door.'

'Is it true he tried to run down a mob last night?'

Sheridan shrugged wearily. 'The street was crowded, so his coach got stuck. The people recognised the crest and started shouting *King and Pitt for ever!* So what does Prinny do? He lets down his window and shouts, *Fox for ever!*'

'Did he really?' asked Fox, joining them. 'How sweet.'

'A fellow pulls the door open, Prinny slaps him across the head—and the crowd might very well have torn the heir apparent asunder if the coachman hadn't had the sense to drive off at top speed, with the door flapping like an orange skin.'

'I'm sure they wouldn't have done any real harm,' said Fox uneasily.

'Oh, but wouldn't they!'

'Not Englishmen, Sherry. Not their Prince. I'm sure they only meant a bit of sport.'

Derby put an arm round his friend. 'My dear Fox, for a Man of the People you're terribly sentimental about them.'

'I suppose I am.'

'How's your health?' asked Sheridan.

'Recovered, I suppose,' said Fox grimly, 'my bowels at least. But I feel fat, foolish and a failure. I'm cut or laughed at whenever I appear in company and I find it hard to take an interest in anything but good brandy.'

Sheridan handed over his bottle.

'What I want to know is'—Derby spoke quietly but didn't whisper—'the question I put to providence is a simple one: why couldn't the horse have lived and the King have died?'

AFTER THE funeral Derby wanted to drive home to bed, but Sheridan insisted on dragging him off to a masked ball the Duke of York was throwing as an irreverent celebration of the royal recovery. The company was select: the two Princes, their best friends of the *buff and blue,* together with twenty of London's loveliest women of no character.

'The Venetians go masked almost all year,' remarked Sheridan as he and Derby walked down a long corridor. His voice echoed oddly from behind the china. 'Doesn't it feel marvellous to take a break from our much-caricatured faces?'

'It does, rather,' said Derby, adjusting his black domino and cloak.

In the saloon they found a tight huddle of veiled women, costumed as in a Turkish harem, entirely swaddled round with gauzes. In front of them a card on a silver music stand. Derby went close enough to read it through the slits in his mask.

Gentlemen, we've 'guised us all the same—
We are mysterious females of the East—
You'll never tell our persons at a glance!
He who can rightly guess a lady's name,
Shall win the right to lead her to the feast—
She'll sweetly be his partner in the dance.

Derby could imagine what was meant by *partner in the dance.*

Prinny, masked but obvious in pink stripes, let out a howl of laughter as he seized a woman by the shoulder. 'You must be Mrs James. You simply must be!'

The woman shook her head.

'I believe I have Mrs James over here,' his brother called.

'Not a bit of it, she's too short by a foot.'

Sheridan identified a certain woman as the famously expensive Mrs Merchant and ran off with her outermost veil; she chased him round the room.

Fox had declined to come tonight. Derby thought of him at home in St Anne's Hill, his face buried in Liz's lap. In her day she'd been the belle of just this kind of party; strange how people changed. Derby strolled around the outside of the cluster of ladies, thinking how convenient a mask was, because you didn't have to smile all the time.

When at least half a dozen gentlemen had claimed to be certain about their captives and were demanding that the veils be lifted, the doors burst open. In filed the ladies they knew, barefaced: Mrs James, Mrs Merchant and the others. The gentlemen reeled back. Sheridan pulled the veil off the woman he'd picked out as Mrs Merchant and a broad stranger's face grinned back at him.

'They're our maids,' shrieked Mrs James, helpless with laughter. 'It was Mrs Debralle's idea. They're all common servant girls and none of you idiots knew the difference. Ha ha!'

In all the hilarity Derby slunk away through the corridors. It had been a clever trick and it left him oddly uneasy. If he could only find a footman and get his greatcoat, hat and cane, he could go home to Derby House.

There was a shape ahead of him, moving fast. Something about the tall silhouette struck him; a fluid grace of moment. 'You,' he called, mannerless. 'Come here a moment.'

The girl stopped and moved towards him cautiously. Not yet a woman, he thought; something indefinably young about her, though he could see nothing of her face through the Turkish draperies. He took her by one gloved hand.

'Sir—' The voice came out high-pitched. He couldn't tell much from one syllable. With her other hand she reached up to pull off her veils.

'No,' he said in a hiss, 'leave them, leave them. Please.' She was tall and moved gracefully, those were the only similarities. He knew that if she lifted her veil she would prove to be no more like Eliza Farren than ash was like wax. But she wouldn't lift her veil, she wouldn't do that to him, not tonight, not when he was so tired and confused and swollen and desperate for a little sweetness.

The girl who was not Eliza let him lead her into an empty room, and sat down on a divan. When she was still she could be anyone; she smelt like young women did. Derby knelt down, like King Cophetua proposing to the beggar maid in the story. He turned her over, this girl who was not, could not, could never be Eliza, and kept his eyes on the fabric that covered her thick hair. He lifted all the layers of silk skirts in one bunch and took her hard. He worked fast; he wanted it to be over.

IV

Cire Perdue

From the French, meaning lost wax, *a technique
for casting by means of a wax model dissolved
away by molten bronze.*

⟨ornament⟩

OUR forebears sang paeans to religion, to honour or to patriotism, but our softer generation knows no higher title than that of Friend. Even Love is not so highly rated by this paper's many correspondents, viz., love is cruel but friendship kind, love is quick but friendship lasting, love is a sharp arrow and friendship a caressing plume, love humiliates and friendship exalts, et cetera. However, of all that has been said in the praise of Friendship—that smokeless flame, that rose without a thorn—we respectfully submit that nine tenths is nothing more than HUMBUG.

In the World today true friendship is as rare as a black swan. Among gentlemen, it is generally mere bottle friendship, a jesting, back-slapping sort of intimacy in which the parties spur each other on to new heights of profane filthiness. Among the female sex, where friendship has reached its zenith of romantic idolatry, it is all too often hypocritical and fleeting. That lady who boasts that she would sacrifice her life for her *alter ipse,* her other self, proves unwilling to give her a favourite fan, let alone surrender a lover. Even that much-vaunted quality of the fair sex, Sensibility, is friendship's enemy, as when Mrs Whatsit falls into illness, grief, or financial embarrassment, and her *soi-disant* friend Lady Who sends a note to say, *My dearest, I would fly instantly to your side, were I not too prostrated by sympathetic distress to rise from my bed.*

As for claims of platonic friendship between the sexes, they are chimerical; in such cases friendship is but a mask that passion wears to delude the World and sometimes even itself.

—THE BEAU MONDE INQUIRER, *May 1789*

ANNE RODE EVERY DAY IN HYDE PARK, BUT LIKED TO VARY her route there and back. Today she headed up North Audley Street; this north-west corner of Mayfair had only been developed in the last few years, since the government had ended indecorous public executions at Tyburn. Walpole was always marvelling at the speed with which a village in the middle of green fields (as he remembered his childhood Mayfair) had been transformed into a chessboard of mushrooming mansions and shining terraces; he declared there'd soon be one continuous street from London to Oxford.

With a touch of her heel Anne turned her horse down Green Street and when she came to the Bow Window House she looked up at the parlour window. The sunlight was white, obscuring the glass, but she gave a little bow, just in case; sometimes Eliza would be sitting by the window, learning her lines. On Park Lane Anne followed the wall that blocked off Hyde Park; some of the more discerning residents were beginning to replace their sections with railings, she noticed, so they could admire the view. She rode in through the dilapidated Grosvenor Gate. 'Come,' she said to the stallion with a kick.

She loved a canter; the jolt and flying of it, the air in her face. She'd go as far as Bugden Hill today, then sweep round by the Reservoir. The skies were clear; to the west she could glimpse a village that must be Kensington and Hampstead stood on its prominence to the north. Anne knew she was a creature of the city, it was the hub of everything that mattered (art, politics and theatre, her friends, her independence), but sometimes she itched for real countryside. Not just some pretty green prospect, but a river without scum or dead cats floating in it; a mountain that took a day to climb; a wood large enough to get lost in.

She was sweaty and breathless, in her tight cotton riding habit, as she brought the horse back to a trot. *Turn home now,* she rebuked herself, *you've work to do.* She went through the day in her mind: wash, breakfast, at least two hours of carving, then have her hair done and dress for an early dinner; afterwards she'd read or study one of her languages.

An hour later, in her workshop, she was lining up her gleaming tools. The three kinds of chisel—the pointed punches, the claws with their fine teeth, the flats—and a gouge and a rounded bullnose for tricky details. The lump hammers, the rasps, the tiny files for crevices. Because stone dust got everywhere she wore a shabby wrapping gown, a big apron, soft boots and a huge mob cap that enclosed her hair. Fidelle was snoozing under an old blanket at her feet.

On her left was the fired terracotta head of Eliza Farren as *Thalia,* finished in Roman style, with the draped and rounded-off bosom on a square socle over a waisted pedestal. Below the title the inscription was simple: *Anna.Damer.Lond.f.1789.* On her right, clamped to a small, heavy table, was the marble block. One could find coloured marbles, but Anne disliked the distraction. This block was pure white statuary marble from Carrara, the quarry Michelangelo had used and the great ancients before him. Her old acquaintance John Flaxman in Rome had picked it out to her specifications; when she tapped it with her hammer she heard the clear bell tones that proved it sound. Flaxman was a fine sculptor; Anne thought it such a shame that he had to earn his living by overseeing the team who adapted ancient friezes for Wedgwood's china factory. She'd always been grateful that her own talent was untrammelled by commerce.

In the early days of Anne's career she'd limited herself to modelling in wax and clay. Even that was considered downright unfeminine; she'd lost count of the number of dowagers who'd told her it was messy, heavy work and wouldn't she be better off doing portraits in pastels (using holders so as not to dirty the hands), or painting flowers on ivory? She thought of her tutor Ceracchi, a Roman in London, and the day he told her she was ready to pick up a chisel. How she'd shaken all over at the thought of wrecking that expensive, translucent cube of stone, though she'd paid for it herself with her widow's jointure. 'I can't,' she'd told him; 'I'm not strong enough.'

She smiled now at the memory of her timidity. 'The great Michelangelo', her tutor had told her, 'was no taller than this'— and he marked a line on his own chest, barely five feet off the floor. Then he'd put the chisel in her hand and closed her fingers round it. 'It's not a matter of the strength of the blow,' he went on, 'but the right way of holding the chisel.' He'd shown her how to place the edge and hit it decisively with her hammer, going with the grain, so the stone flaked off like butter, as if it wanted to fall.

Anne closed her eyes for a moment, now, and told herself she could do this. Perhaps it was the deadline that was making her stomach so tight; she'd promised Agostino at the Royal Academy that she'd send Miss Farren's bust for the Exhibition by the middle of June. She played for time, now, giving her flats an extra sharpening by wetting the York stone and pushing them along its length.

She stared at the lovely milky mass of the marble, covered in faint black lines and pocked with holes. She'd already done the trimming with a wide pitcher chisel, and the pointing too. The terracotta model bore the black pointing marks at all the crucial places: temples, brows, corners of eyes, bridge and tip of nose, top and bottom of ears, jaws and chin. She always enjoyed the task of transferring the proportions to the marble, using a measuring frame and callipers and drilling to the exact depth needed. (Sam the footman came in to hold the cord drill steady while she pulled on the straps.) Then she'd done detailed charcoal drawings on every side of the block to guide her hand. Now it was only a matter of letting the chisels cut away the extraneous stone to reveal the goddess hidden inside.

Today she'd start the blocking out—a satisfying, deep, cutting motion. Many sculptors found this task tedious and called in professional statuaries to do it. But Walpole had warned his goddaughter early on that she'd better do all the work herself, or risk accusations that she relied on male *ghosts*. She'd taken his advice; in her early years she'd sometimes used a fellow called Smith, but only for the menial tasks of lifting heavy things, wedging clay to get the air out and cleaning tools. No, she was better off quite alone.

It had been many years now since she'd ruined a marble—breaking off Fidelle's slim, quivering paw—and had to start all over again. Stone was brittle and unforgiving. This was ridiculous, was Anne trying to scare herself? She'd learned anatomy as well as carving; she wasn't some untrained dabbler like the women one heard of, every now and then, for their minor achievements in wax or plaster; *your Imitatrixes*, as Walpole called them. She'd exhibited at the Royal Academy on four previous occasions. There was no reason for her spirit to quail.

She set her punch to the spot that would become the crown of the head. *Strike for seven, rest for four*, that was the tradition; it saved one from having to think. She struck.

ELIZA WAS being wooed in a rather overwhelming fashion. At first meeting Mrs Hester Thrale Piozzi had determined that they should be bosom friends. It was not a gradual sinking into intimacy, as with Anne, Eliza found; it was more like being tugged into a rapid gavotte. Short and plump, her face still handsome at almost fifty, Mrs Piozzi was a whirlwind. Despite having no advantages of birth, connections or fortune, she'd achieved a measure of fame as a lady of letters. She knew things about people. 'I write everything down in my commonplace book, that's the trick,' she boasted. 'I defy even your dear Mr Walpole to out-remember me.'

She and Eliza were sitting in the Piozzis' comfortable three-storey brick farmhouse at Streatham, looking out across Tooting Common. Behind them her young second husband, Signor Piozzi, her *caro sposo*, played some delicate Gluck on the pianoforte. They were talking—as everyone was these days—about France, where the furious professional men of the Third Estate had renamed themselves the Assemblée Nationale. 'When the deputies found themselves shut out of their meeting place on the King's orders,' reported Eliza, 'they held their meeting in a tennis court and vowed not to disperse until their work's done.'

Mrs Piozzi's lips twisted. 'The French nation was never a favourite of mine; the lower ranks are ignorant and the higher arrogant. As for selling them the 20,000 sacks of flour that Monsieur Necker's demanding—why, we may need it ourselves. Already this summer my own countrymen in Wales have been driven to riot over the price of bread!'

Eliza was taken aback. 'But don't you think the starving, subjugated masses in France are worse off, having none of our British liberties?'

'On the topic of liberty, I remember Doctor Johnson once said to me...' Sooner or later Mrs Piozzi always circled back to her late lamented friend. Eliza let her mind wander. 'Oh, yes, the wits of today seem a shabby race to one who was privileged to know Johnson and Garrick,' murmured Mrs Piozzi. 'But now the time has come, I feel, for the women to shine,' she added, brightening. 'Here we have you, Miss Farren and Madame Kauffmann, of course, the only woman painter who's dared to tackle monumental historical subjects. Mrs Inchbald's witty plays, and Mrs Cowley's—'

'Your own books,' suggested Eliza.

The old woman flapped her fan at her coyly. 'Some critics may sneer, but how can the exhibition of a God-given talent be unfeminine?'

'How indeed?' said Eliza. 'My dear Mrs Damer often comes under fire for her high ambitions in sculpture—as if the shaping and polishing of marble weren't a perfect womanly art.'

'But you, my dear, now you really are the most fascinating creature in London,' gushed Mrs Piozzi, seizing her hands.

Eliza had to deflect many of her new friend's questions, for instance, about her childhood; she didn't fancy having the whole shameful narrative recorded for posterity in the commonplace book. But above all, Mrs Piozzi was enthralled by the Derby connection. 'Only you, in this tarnished age of scandal, seem capable of inspiring such a pure devotion...'

Eliza thought of the Earl, backstage at Richmond House two years ago, pebble eyes bulging, stuttering out his hopes of *some kind of arrangement.* 'Speaking of scandal,' she said to change the subject, 'could it possibly be true about Lord Bolingbroke?'

'I believe so,' hissed Mrs Piozzi, unable to resist the bait. 'Fled to Paris—with his half-sister, who's in a certain condition—and not for the first or second time, either!'

'No!'

Mrs Piozzi sucked in her lips to form a tight seal. *'Female punctuation forbids me to say more,* as Mrs Malaprop would say.'

Eliza tried to imagine what it would be like to stagger outside the magic circle of the World; to make yourself an outlaw, or worse, a monster.

But Mrs Piozzi had the mind of a terrier. 'What a repellent contrast with your own platonic friendship with Lord Derby,' she murmured. 'You are all man desires in woman, but of a type so refined that the desire itself becomes ethereal.' With a modest expression she mentioned that she'd written a poem on the subject of her new friend's charms. It was in Italian, the language of the heart. 'Oh, but don't you read Italian? What a shame; do you hear that, *caro sposo?'* she threw in Gabriel Piozzi's direction. 'I suppose Miss Farren's never had the leisure for concentrated study, but you must converse with her sometimes in your beautiful tongue.'

The English translation arrived at Green Street before supper; Eliza marvelled at the energy of Mrs Piozzi, who managed to run a household, write books, quarrel with her daughters and still find time for fripperies. She read it aloud to her mother.

> *Lines on 'La Farren'. From the Italian.*
> *In that roguish face one sees*
> *All her sex's witcheries;*

Playful sweetness, cold disdain
Everything to turn one's brain,
Sparkling from expressive eyes…

'Why, it rhymes as good as if it was English in the first place,' mar-velled Mrs Farren. 'But she does gush on, rather.'

Eliza resumed, satirically.

Sure destruction still we find,
Still we lose our peace of mind,
Touched by her half-trembling hand,
Can the coldest heart withstand?

Her mother's forehead was wrinkled. 'One would think it from a gentleman, it's so very ardent.'

'Oh, that's just what poems are like, Mother. It's far smoother than the ones I've ever received from men, I must grant Mrs Piozzi that. I suppose the polite thing would be to reply in verse,' Eliza added grimly.

'Very true, but don't look for any help from me,' said Mrs Far-ren, ringing for the maid to clear away the game pie.

Eliza groaned. 'I find anything more than a couplet a strain. I'll have to pop over to Grosvenor Square and throw myself on Anne's mercies; she can improvise in iambic pentameter.'

'Between all your fine friends,' said her mother, 'no wonder you can't find an evening to sit down with me and learn your lines.'

Something sharp in the tone made Eliza look up, but Mrs Far-ren was gazing out of the window at the late afternoon sun.

JUNE 1789

The Damer carriage rattled down the Strand and stopped at the great pillars of Somerset House. Sam the footman got down and opened the door of the Royal Academy. Anne told him to wait with the driver; she needed no escort here.

The square entrance hall was guarded by plaster casts of Apollo, Hercules, the Centaurs and Minerva with her spear entwined with

snakes. Anne nodded to the porters and walked past the Life School;
she'd never been let in there, of course, because of the nude models.
She gathered her skirts at the bottom of the elliptical staircase. Men
tramped past her, carrying vast canvases, or hauling them up through
the stairwell on ropes. 'Stand back, madam, if you please.'

'Mind the lady!'

She met the head keeper on the second floor. 'Mrs Damer, always a pleasure,' he said, inclining his pointed head. 'May I offer a
catalogue?'

'Are the preparations for the Exhibition going smoothly, Signor
Agostino?'

The Italian let out a chuckle. 'Always some surprises, shall we
say? A gentleman in Kent sends in a picture made of hair.'

She shuddered.

Behind Agostino Anne caught a glimpse of the students in the
Antique Room hunched over their easels, drawing from a gigantic
cast of the Medici Venus, her nervous arms failing to hide her
shame. She felt a prickle of envy; she was grateful for her own private tutoring, of course, but it had been solitary and sporadic.
These Royal Academy boys were luckier than they knew, being
forced to give art their whole attention at such an early age.

Upstairs, over the double doors of the Great Room was an inscription in rather bad Greek, which Anne translated as *Let no
stranger to the Muses enter here.* She might not be a Member of the
Academy—they'd elected no more women since that first burst of
enthusiasm at their founding—but she was hardly a stranger to the
Muses. The vast space of the Great Room and its four curved sky-
lights made it the perfect place to show sculpture, but this wealth of
natural light was always kept for the paintings; besides, she told
herself, any statue set up here would be toppled by the jostling
crowds. Only half the paintings were up, there were still many gaps.
Sir Joshua Reynolds—an old family friend of hers—was showing
twelve canvases this year and the centrepiece was his huge flattering portrait (commissioned by Georgiana) of Sheridan making his
last stand on the Regency Bill.

Anne's own work was in the little room for sculpture and drawings at the back. She made herself look at the animal piece first, because it mattered less. The ink in the catalogue was still a little smeary. *The Hon. Mrs Seymour Conway Damer. Two Kittens in Marble.* This was for Walpole; the kittens were muscular bird hunters at Strawberry Hill by now, but he'd wanted them immortalised in all their luxuriant curled-up youth.

Only now did she let herself turn and—as objectively as she could—regard her *Thalia.* That was all the pedestal said, but there wasn't a man, woman or child in London who wouldn't recognise it as Eliza Farren. The porters had set it at an odd angle, looking slightly away from the viewer, but she could have a word with Agostino about that. The light was good enough and there were no chips or cracks, thank God; marbles stood up better to the crating and moving than terracottas did. She'd given the bust a low, almost matte finish on the hair, but a sheen on the cheeks and bosom. The face was tilted down, gracious, Grecian, slightly sombre; the gaze was blank, inward. The marble looked like packed snow. Yes, it had been worth the endless hours with rasps and files and glass paper, the washings and dryings, the final going over with pumice to bring up the sparkle. *This might well be my masterpiece,* Anne thought nervously.

There were raised voices in the Great Room; she went to the doorway. There was John Downman of Drury Lane, adding a dot of delicate red to a lip. She recognised it as a larger version of his watercolour from the set of *The Way to Keep Him* at Richmond House. How appropriate, she thought with rueful pleasure, that out of the whole collection of seven ladies he'd chosen to exhibit Eliza.

Beside him a man she didn't know, clutching a palette, some paint bladders and a bunch of brushes, was barking, 'I shall demand to speak to a member of the Hanging Committee. I was personally assured that my *Suicide of Brutus* would be hung on the line—' punching his finger at the wooden moulding that ran round the chamber, seven feet up—'but it's been skied up there in a cobwebbed corner, where anyone who hopes to see it will have to climb a ladder! While you, sir—'

'My watercolour's a small piece,' Downman murmured, 'so it must hang here, at eye level. You know the rule, big canvases go above the line.'

'Daubing it with extra carmine, are you, in the hope someone will notice it?' asked the man. 'What have we come to, when the game is won by mere flashy colour and famous faces? When important contributions to the noblest form, to history painting, are shunted out of sight, so that silly sketches of actresses can hog the view!'

Anne felt the blood rush into her face. 'It could be said, sir'— her voice coming out like a gunshot—'that Miss Farren's career represents the triumph of merit over birth. Through genius alone she has won herself a place as great as any duchess in this gallery.'

The furious painter had whitened. 'I beg your pardon, madam.'

'Mrs Damer,' said Mr Downman with a bow.

The other man blustered. 'I meant no disrespect to any friend of yours...'

'Oh, come, I'm a friend to merit in any form, in art as in theatre,' Anne told him in what she hoped was a more relaxed tone. 'Speaking of which,' she said, strolling over, 'I'm greatly taken by your Brutus, especially the elegant line of his sword arm.'

'You can see it, all the way up there?'

'Perfectly, sir; fear not. It dominates the room.' Anne had placated him without even knowing his name; all it took was a compliment. At times like these she was glad to be a mere Honorary Exhibitor who didn't have to earn her bread, or entangle herself in the vicious politics of the Royal Academy. The Members thought her rather a freak, she knew, but better that than one of their snarling pack.

ELIZA WAS just back from a trip to her cousins in Dublin, where her Bens (Miss Tittup, Beatrice and Kitty Hardcastle) had cleared her a startling £492. Derby hadn't been sure he'd get back from Newmarket on time to bring her to the Exhibition, so after consulting with her mother she'd decided to let Walpole be her escort, thus offending neither the Richmonds nor the Devonshires; Eliza had almost too many friends of rank these days.

'Such a shocking mob,' said Walpole happily, 'but it's always the way on Opening Day. This vertiginous staircase, did you know, is said to represent the arduous climb of the artist to Olympus.' Eliza placed her arm on Walpole's as if to lean on him, but actually she was supporting his brittle wrist between her fingers. 'Gad, my gouty foot will burst at the seams,' he groaned, as they were pressed up the stairs.

'Perhaps you should be at home in Berkeley Square.'

'Oh, better than that, my dear, I should be in a little boat gliding down to Twickenham, amid sweet June breezes and the chime of blackbirds, far away from this noxious city. And I've much to do at Strawberry Hill; have you heard of the opening of the tomb of Edward IV?' The antiquary spoke as if this were the most exciting news of the summer. 'I'm in hourly negotiations to buy a lock of the miraculously intact royal beard.'

'You might come again another day,' she suggested, 'when the crowd is less overwhelming.'

'But my dear, it's the crowd I'm here for,' said Walpole. 'I didn't pay my shilling to look at art under such ghastly conditions; I'll consider these pictures' pretensions to immortality at my leisure, some other time. No, today I'm here to watch the World lining up to look at themselves in oil and watercolour, like monkeys hee-heeing at a looking-glass!'

Eliza laughed behind her ivory fan.

They had to move slowly with the crowd; it was like wading through mud. They edged into the Great Room. 'Modelled on the Salon Carrée in the Louvre. You notice the resemblance?'

'I'm afraid I've never seen the Louvre,' Eliza told him, trying not to sound pathetic.

He blinked at her. 'What could have possessed you to bypass that sacred portal?'

'I've never crossed the Channel; my education didn't include a Grand Tour,' she reminded him with a smile.

'Of course not, but my dear Miss Farren, this won't do!'

'My time isn't my own. I'm answerable to the public,' she explained, hiding her impatience. 'When do I ever have the time to go off on a pleasure trip?'

'Dreadful,' said Walpole, shaking his desiccated head. 'Something must be done. I'm past all hope of travels myself, I'm afraid, but perhaps Mrs Damer—' The crowd swirled them apart for a moment. 'Nothing here worth looking at,' he reassured her, when she had hold of his twig of a wrist again, 'except Georgiana in that corner, with her spaniel.'

Eliza scanned the portraits.

'No, no, my dear, the person herself, there.'

She laughed at her mistake, recognising the Duchess through a crack in the crowd, beaming up at her sister's portrait. It was an indifferent painting, but the crowd was thick around it, because the word was that the beautiful Harriet and Sheridan had been caught in flagrante last week and Harriet's husband, Lord Duncannon, meant to institute divorce proceedings.

'Any canvases of you this year, my dear?' asked Walpole.

She led him to Downman's watercolour.

'Charming; that'll sell well in engravings. *Portrait of a Lady*, a very suitable title,' he read in the catalogue. 'Do you notice all the ladies in the big oils look identical this year? Gad, how they leer down at one! The same vast hat, fluffy grey powdered curls and winsome expression.'

'We're slaves to fashion.'

'Whereas an old lizard like me is immune to its siren call. I've had this waistcoat since 1765,' he boasted.

Passing a small oil of Dora Jordan in breeches, Eliza managed to feel a moment's sympathy because her rival was said to be having a dreadful summer; first she'd fallen out with an Edinburgh manager over money and had resorted to the desperate, undignified tactic of writing to the papers to justify herself—then her mother had died in her arms. Eliza couldn't imagine daily life without her mother by her side.

She and Walpole finally managed to squeeze into the little sculpture room. 'Ah, my beloved child,' he said, seizing Anne's gauzy ribboned sleeve, 'if I may address a genius so improperly!'

She gave her hand into his, then kissed Eliza. 'It's been weeks,' Anne murmured. 'I heard the most thrilling accounts of your conquest of Dublin from the Duchess of Leinster. Here, come and meet yourself'—tucking one arm into Eliza's.

Eliza hadn't yet seen the *Thalia* finished. Besides, it made all the difference to have it posed on its pedestal, as if floating above the crowd. The lustre of the white marble startled her. 'It's astonishing,' she said in Anne's ear. 'People will think me a poor, fleshly copy of the stone original.'

Walpole found his tongue at last. 'I can hardly imagine', he murmured, 'how sweet it must be to see all those long months of labour transmuted into beauty.'

'Oh, but you write books, sir,' Eliza protested.

'Not the kind that transfix their readers with ecstasy,' he said, rueful.

'Are you enjoying yourself, despite the crush?' she asked Anne.

The sculptor loosened into a smile. 'I am, I confess. It does me good, once a year, to feel my chosen art matters so violently to so many people. I always half expect someone will be trampled to death on the stairs!'

'Perhaps the Muses would appreciate the sacrifice,' Walpole said merrily, then caught sight of one of his many nieces and excused himself to greet her.

'I can't take my eyes off my own marble face,' Eliza said, then turned to look at Anne. 'I don't think I've ever thanked you, have I?'

'Why should you?'

'Thank you,' said Eliza simply. But even as she said it she was aware of performing the phrase, of delivering it in as modest and charming a way as she could. That was the problem with her profession: it made it impossible to stand, sit or speak without some aura of self-consciousness.

'It's I who should be thanking my model,' Anne protested. 'In fact, I have a little gift—nothing that need embarrass you, just to mark the happy occasion.' She took a tiny package out of the pocket that dangled in the seam of her gauze-covered skirt.

Eliza peeled open the paper, wishing the two of them were in the workshop at Grosvenor Square, instead of amid the humid flurry of Opening Day. The final layer of paper tore and a ring fell into Eliza's cupped hand; she almost dropped it. 'Oh, my dear,' she whispered. The ring was tiny and gold, in the shape of an aquiline eye; it seemed to wink at her. The eye was an insert of painted ivory, with a tiny black pupil. She turned it over and read, in minute italic engraving, *Preuve de mon amitié.*

'Proof—'

'Of your friendship. Yes, I know enough French for that,' said Eliza, laughing to ease the moment.

'Friendship, or affection, or love; the two languages don't quite correspond,' said Anne, laughing too.

'Well, whatever it says, it's beautiful,' said Eliza. It fitted perfectly on the little finger of her left hand. 'However did you guess the size? Did you put me into one of Monsieur Mesmer's trances without my knowing and measure my finger with a thread?'

'No need,' said Anne. 'I have a trained eye.'

'So do I, now,' Eliza joked, holding up the ring.

'Do you know why I chose that device?'

'Could it mean...that you're always watching?'

'Looking at you, yes. Watching over you. I knew you'd understand,' said Anne.

'Excuse me, Miss Farren.' It was Mrs Piozzi, tugging at Eliza's sleeve. 'Might I speak with you?'

Eliza gave her a puzzled glance. The older woman's manner was urgent; this was a strange way to force an introduction. 'Mrs Piozzi, how delightful. Mrs Damer,' she said, turning, 'I wonder, might I present—'

'So sorry to interrupt, but really I must presume on your kindness,' said Mrs Piozzi rapidly.

Had the Honourable Mrs Damer just been cut by a person from Streatham? Time to go. Eliza pressed Anne's hand. 'I'll leave you to your worshipful throng.'

'Write to me tonight?'

'I promise.'

IN THE sculpture room Derby's eye was pulled straight to the glowing marble face; he stood still and let the mass of people swirl around him. 'My very dear old friend,' he said, pressing through the crowd to clasp Anne Damer's hand, 'it's a triumph.'

'I'm so glad you think so. You've just missed the original, I'm afraid.'

He felt drunk with excitement. 'It's the lady to the life, yet the Muse of Comedy in all her Grecian purity too. You have this knack—no, that sounds too easy—you have this power to see into the hearts of women. You've never sculpted one of us poor men-folk, have you?' he asked, tearing his eyes away to focus on Mrs Damer.

'Not yet, no,' she said, 'only boys and the occasional god. I tried some clay sketches of my father once, but he complained he looked like a frog. No, it seems women alone stir my imagination. Women and animals.'

Derby's eyes had slid back to the *Thalia*. He licked his lip. 'I simply must have it. No, I mean it, truly, I absolutely insist. I'll pay any price.'

Mrs Damer lowered her voice. 'Derby, I don't think you understand. I don't *sell* my work.'

'I beg your pardon,' he said, chastened, 'I only meant—to recompense you for the costly materials—or perhaps you'd rather an exchange? I have some splendid Old Masters in my collection at Knowsley; you must come up for a visit one of these days and take your pick.'

'You've many fine things,' said Mrs Damer, a little tight-lipped, 'but I'm afraid the bust is not for sale or exchange.'

'Don't tell me you've promised it to Richmond already? Or Walpole? What engrossers of the market those fellows are!'

'No,' she said, 'I've intended from the beginning to present it to Miss Farren herself.'

Derby was taken aback. 'But...our friend has herself to look at, in the mirror,' he said with a laugh.

'Oh, come, think how often she's been drawn and painted, yet she owns none of the results,' said Mrs Damer. 'Her image is pawed over in a dozen print shops and hung over fireplaces across the country, but she doesn't own a single representation of her own beauty. Is that just?'

Something occurred to him and he brightened. 'What about the terracotta version?'

There was a moment's pause. 'That will have to go to Walpole, I'm afraid.'

There was something curious about her phrasing. He'd almost have thought that Mrs Damer was lying—except that she'd no reason to lie. Walpole did have a particular fondness for terracottas, Derby knew that. So why did he have the impression that she'd only just decided to offer it to her godfather? 'Well, I resign myself, then, but not with good grace,' he said with a little bow, before he turned away.

No, he must be imagining things. His old friend had always been so encouraging of his quiet pursuit of Eliza Farren. He was simply unsettled because it was so rare—almost unprecedented— to find something that the Derby fortune couldn't buy.

OUTSIDE Somerset House, on the noisy Strand, Eliza was sitting in Mrs Piozzi's slightly shabby carriage, staring at her. 'I have no idea what you're hinting at.'

Mrs Piozzi sighed theatrically. 'I don't mean to hint, dear girl, but it's impossible to be explicit on these dreadful matters.'

'*What* dreadful matters?'

'The ones I've mentioned.'

'You've mentioned nothing,' snapped Eliza, 'you've only muttered darkly about *notorieties* and *criminalities*. Why was it exactly that you dragged me so rudely out of the Exhibition?'

The lady of letters, her lips pursed, put her hand on Eliza's knee for a moment. 'You may have heard the appalling rumours about the Queen of France and the Princesses of Lamballe and Polignac, in that sink of iniquity known as Versailles?'

'Which rumours?' asked Eliza. 'Marie Antoinette's enemies have accused her of every vice in the encyclopedia.'

Mrs Piozzi's eyes were beady. 'An example closer to home, then: you know the Devonshire House ménage?'

'I know Lady Bess is said to have had two children by the Duke—'

'Not just that!' Mrs Piozzi sighed like a bellows.

If she were an actress at Drury Lane, Eliza found herself thinking, *she'd be told to pull herself together and stop hamming it up.*

'Your innocence appals me, my dear,' said the older woman. 'Don't you know what sort of times we're living in? There's an unnatural, fantastical vice spreading across Europe, from Italy to France and now to our own shores. Haven't you ever heard of those monsters who haunt their own sex?'

'Ah,' said Eliza, on surer ground. 'You mean sodomites. Why are you telling me this?'

'Because you may be in danger,' hissed Mrs Piozzi.

'From a sodomite?'

Mrs Piozzi folded her arms. 'Are you being deliberately obtuse?'

'No, no, indeed.' Eliza suppressed a yelp of hysterical laughter.

Mrs Piozzi spoke in a rapid whisper. 'I'm speaking of man-hating *females*. Monsters in the guise of women. They go by a Greek name, *Sapphists,* after the criminal passions of Sappho, don't you know.'

Eliza's head was swimming. 'I thought she was a poet.'

'That and worse,' said Mrs Piozzi darkly. 'They're known as Tommies too.'

'Tommies?'

'Like beastly tom-cats.'

Eliza ignored that strange reference. 'I still don't understand—'

'Your so-called friend, Mrs Damer, was that a ring I saw her give you?' She took hold of Eliza's fingers and peered at them in the dark carriage.

Eliza snatched her hand away and covered it with the other. 'Mrs Piozzi, you forget yourself.'

'I beg your pardon, but—'

'You're babbling as if you have a fever. Or as if you're intoxicated. I don't know what you're talking about—'

'I have proof.'

'—and I don't wish to know.' Eliza was breathing heavily. She rapped on the side of the carriage for the coachman to come round and help her down.

'Oh, my dear,' said Mrs Piozzi, holding on to Eliza's lace apron, 'I'm only trying to warn you. Already there's a dreadful epigram going the rounds—'

Eliza stopped, her foot on the top step. She leaned back into the darkness. 'What epigram?'

'I was afraid you might have heard it already. I so wanted to be the first to prepare you against the shock. I thought of writing, but I couldn't wait, not when I saw her flaunt her sculpture of you in there and make a public show of your intimacy. How does it go? Yes, I have it.' Mrs Piozzi declaimed in a theatrical whisper:

> *'Her little stock of private fame*
> *Will fall a wreck to public clamour,*
> *If Farren leagues with one whose name*
> *Comes near—aye, very near—to DAMN HER.*

Damn her, Damer, d'you see?'

Eliza stared at her, then stepped down into the street.

JULY 1789

Derby had come to town for a few days, to escape the monotony of Knowsley, where his girls Charlotte and Elizabeth had developed a genius for reporting each other's petty misdeeds with the precision of law clerks. He dropped into the Farrens' with Fox and Grey one evening, to make up a rubber at whist. Mrs Farren was always relieved if there were three guests, so she didn't have to play. She had to ring for the tea kettle to be refilled twice and the gentlemen used up half a cone of sugar. Derby thought Eliza was looking rather pale; for years now he'd wished she could give up the arduous summer season at the Haymarket, but he knew better than to offer his opinion. She seemed preoccupied tonight and took little part in the conversation. Fox and Grey were having a heated debate about the importance of the Germanic, as compared with Latinate, contributions to the English language. Derby had never been much of a scholar; in Cambridge it hadn't been necessary to follow any particular course of studies or, heaven forbid, undergo any examinations. He edged the conversation towards politics, which somehow led to money, and whether it was possible to live in Mayfair on less than £3000 a year.

A low laugh from Eliza, eyes on her cards. 'I assure you, gentlemen, that my mother and I survive on less than half that, and put savings aside too.'

'What, you've got money in the bank?' asked Fox, aghast. 'What's it doing there?'

'On first coming to this metropolis Miss Farren adopted an extraordinary procedure,' Derby told them; 'she pays for things the day she buys, or she doesn't buy.'

'I never heard of such a prodigy of thrift,' said Fox.

'Doesn't your conscience prick you', she asked him, smiling, 'if you ignore a tradesman's bill for years on end?'

'Not a bit of it,' cried Grey. 'It's all part of their business, that's why they reward themselves with such shocking rates of interest.'

'To quote our friend Sherry,' said Fox, *'paying creditors only encourages them!* I should, of course, cough up for a debt of honour, mind you—'

'I've always thought that a rather hollow phrase for gambling losses,' Derby offered in the direction of Mrs Farren, who smiled over her knotting work.

'Tell your Lade story,' said Grey.

Fox beamed, reminiscent. 'At Newmarket once I was writing out a promissory note for Sir John Lade and I noticed he was doing some sums on the back of a playbill. Turned out he was calculating the interest he planned to charge me! "Are you, by gad?" says I. "I thought this a debt of honour, but as you seem to have turned Hebrew, Lade, I must tell you I make it a rule to pay tradesmen last!" And I ripped up the note on the spot.'

Grey clapped.

'Not that a promissory note from you would have meant much,' Derby pointed out.

'Oh, no, it was a promise that my good friend Lord Derby would pay him,' said Fox, deadpan, and Grey giggled into his tea.

Derby grinned; the joke was on him. It was well known in the Party that Derby was a soft touch, though Sheridan was by far the worst for sponging off him.

'But really, it won't do, Miss Farren, this secret saving habit of yours,' said Fox, shaking his ursine head and holding out his cup to be refilled. 'What would the World come to if everyone behaved so timidly?'

'There'd be no debtors pining away in the King's Bench, for one thing,' Eliza suggested.

'No prosperity either, no growth!' He blew on his tea, sloshing some over the brim. 'Money's a liquid commodity, it mustn't be hoarded or it'll stagnate. It must be given, borrowed, lent, lost, without embarrassment—circulating like the very blood in our veins!'

A knock at the door downstairs and Mrs Farren put her knotting down. 'Whomsoever could it be, at this time?'

Derby saw a flicker of pain cross his beloved's face at her mother's bad grammar.

The manservant announced the Duchess of Devonshire and they all leapt to their feet. Mrs Farren wore a frozen grimace.

Georgiana swept into the little parlour and kissed Eliza on both cheeks. '*Pweez* forgive my frightful rudeness in barging in on this cosy scene,' she said, 'but I'm just back from Paris—and such news!'

She had a gift for setting people at ease, Derby thought; they all sat down again at once, and Mrs Farren poured the Duchess a cup of tea without asking.

'It's about the Bastille—that grim symbol of tyranny, that dark dungeon from which none returns!' Georgiana held the pose of a Gothic heroine. 'Well, *mes amis,* they've gone and knocked it down.'

'Who have?' asked Derby.

'*Le peuple.*'

Mrs Farren was looking bewildered.

'Canis and Racky and I had already determined to go on to Brussels, as things were hotting up—riots and so forth—the theatres were closed, which seemed a bad sign,' said Georgiana, relishing her story. 'There were rumours going round that the King's brother was plotting to dissolve the Assembly and arrest the deputies. So a crowd went to seize weapons and powder from the Bastille and release the political prisoners. Picture it: on one side a trained army of 30,000 soldiers—on the other a few hundred desperate Parisians, shouting "*Aux armes! Aux armes!*".'

Grey was watching the Duchess like a star-struck schoolboy.

'Some of them had raided the Opéra for axes,' Georgiana added merrily, 'not realising the weapons used on stage were cardboard. So all they had were stones and pitchforks, hammers and spits, but they tore down the fortress and triumphed. Isn't it simply *ravish*?'

'That'll give Louis a poke in the eye,' said Derby, grinning.

Fox put his hand over his mouth. 'Imagine if it happened here,' he stage-whispered. 'Say half London stormed the walls of Newgate roaring, "Crawl off the throne, mad Old George. It's time for Prinny's reign!"'

'Technically that's high treason,' remarked Grey.

'And you'd have got two dozen stripes for that back in Eton,' Derby told Fox. They were being very giddy, considering all they'd drunk was tea; the news was acting on them like champagne.

'Were there any deaths?' It was Eliza who asked.

'A few on each side, yes, including the governor of the Bastille,' said Georgiana, sobering. 'In fact, the rumours are rather disgusting—apparently the mob tore him apart with their hands.'

Derby was taken aback. 'I'd have believed that of a gang of hardened Cockneys more easily than of some cowed Frogs.'

'Such violence does rather tarnish the cause of Reform,' said Fox sadly.

'Oh, come now,' Derby told him, 'you haven't sat through enough cocking mains. No fight's glorious without some bloodshed.'

'This isn't sport, man,' Fox reproved him. 'The best thing for France is a thoughtful, peaceful progress towards liberty.'

'Were you frightened?' Grey was asking Georgiana, leaning in close.

'Oh, not for myself; a Parisian mob is nothing to the Westminster Election of '84!'

Fox grinned round at his old comrades.

'But Bess and I are rather *fret* for dear Marie Antoinette and Little Po and other friends at Versailles. Still,' Georgiana said, brightening, 'these are only the birthing pangs of Reform and I'm sure the worst is over. *Vive la France!*'

'*Vive* indeed,' said Derby, raising his cup of cold tea. He tried to catch Eliza's eye, to share the joyful toast, but her gaze was unfocused, as if her mind were miles away.

THROUGH THE sweaty days of July Eliza played at the Haymarket, ate half of whatever her mother put in front of her, slept badly. She avoided Mrs Piozzi and answered about one in three of Anne's letters from Park Place, Goodwood and Strawberry Hill. When she looked on the post tray in the hall and saw the familiar wax seal marked with a little chisel, her stomach always went into a spasm.

My dearest A.D., she wrote,
Yes, yes, yes, to what you write so eloquently of Lafayette's Declaration of the Rights of Man. For the French to set down in

law for the first time that all are born free and equal—having the right to liberty, to property, to security & to resist oppression—it stirs my heart.

To be strolling through your father's lavender plantation, or chasing little Fidelle through the famous oaks of Goodwood— these are visions of bliss to one who must stay in London all summer & scarce can find a moment to pick up the pen, let alone think of a fortnight's holiday, so must regretfully decline your kind invitation. How I wish...but in vain.

Ever your servant and chère amie,
E.F.

It had a forced, gushing tone to it, she knew; did it sound like a tissue of lies?

Eliza's feelings for her friend weren't gone, they'd just been frozen up, iced over with panic, ever since that day at the Exhibition. In the long hours of the night she stared at the dark ceiling and Anne Damer's handsome, angular face seemed to float there. What Mrs Piozzi had said couldn't be true. It was impossible, absurd, obscene, laughable, terrible.

Had the sculptor's brown eyes ever revealed any emotion that was warmer than other women felt for their friends? Or no, not warmer; *darker*, rather? Was that smile suspect, that burning look on Anne's face as she'd given Eliza the ring? Was that what a *Sapphist* looked like, Eliza asked herself, squirming at the word? The band of gold was warm on her little finger; it felt like part of her body. Did Anne look at Eliza more lovingly—or no, less lovingly, but more peculiarly, more greedily, more carnally than other women did? Eliza didn't think so—but then, what experience of friendship had she for comparison?

It wasn't as if there were anything wrong with passionate bonds between women; they were praised to the heights in almost every novel Eliza picked up nowadays. Ladies in the World exchanged portrait miniatures and sat embracing on sofas; the more sensibility a woman had, the more overwhelmingly devoted she was to her female friends. How could something so respectable, so fashionable, be a mask for unnatural vice?

Of course, Eliza'd heard of such things; sodomy was a dirty whisper on everybody's lips these days and, now she came to think about it, she was sure she'd come across the word Sapphism before, though she couldn't remember where. In a book translated from the French, perhaps? But Eliza had never heard of any Englishwoman being accused of such exotic perversities.

Insomniac, she replayed fragments of conversation between herself and Anne over the last two and a half years; brief kisses, easy embraces. She felt her face heat up now, but not with guilt, only confusion. Did the sculptor's strong hands press Eliza's fingers any harder than those of other friends did? No harder than the small, slightly wrinkled hands of Mrs Piozzi, it occurred to her. Why, Anne had never given any evidence of besotted infatuation like Mrs Piozzi's Italian verses.

Could the authoress be mad? Jealous, perhaps, of Eliza's admission to a glittering circle which she herself, with no birth or wealth, a low-born foreigner for a husband and a Streatham address, could never hope to enter?

How could one look into the human heart and tell the sheep from the goats, the shining feelings from the stained ones? *Amitié means friendship, affection, love,* she remembered Anne saying as she gave her the ring; *the languages don't correspond.*

'My dear?' Her mother tapped at the door in the middle of the night.

Eliza jerked awake. No, there was yellow light coming through a gap in the curtains; it was another day. She cleared her throat.

'Will you take a bowl of chocolate?'

'No,' she called, heaving herself upright.

Mrs Farren's face came round the door. 'You worry me, daughter,' she remarked. 'You've been queer and unsettled all summer.'

'I'm perfectly well.' Eliza splashed her face with cold water.

Shopping for a light set of whalebone stays on Pall Mall, she found herself popping into Alderman Boydell's new Shakespeare Gallery, which was filled with illustrations of the Bard's plays by all the best artists of the day. One of Anne Damer's contributions was a bas relief of Cleopatra with a lady-in-waiting stretched out dead at her feet. Eliza went up very close and stared at the curved draperies of the blank-faced queen, how they blended into the body of the bare-armed attendant, who knelt behind her, her hand on the Queen's limp wrist, her mouth pressed to the Queen's shoulder in a kiss of grief. There was nothing that unusual, nothing obscene here—so why did it make Eliza's heart thump? And would others see what she saw? How many people had heard that epigram so far? What if the Queen of Comedy were observed here, on a Tuesday afternoon, staring at her friend's sculpture, biting her lips?

'That's a charming little ring,' remarked Derby over a game of piquet in his smaller drawing room, with her mother keeping score.

'Thank you,' said Eliza, shuffling the slim set of cards.

He took up her hand for a moment on the pretext of examining the gold and ivory eye on her little finger. Her heart began to thump. 'Wherever did it come from?'

'Gray's, on Sackville Street,' she said, deliberately misunderstanding.

His tone was light. 'A tribute to your genius from some gentleman whose heart you've conquered?'

'Oh, hardly,' she said with a little laugh.

In the carriage taking them round the corner to Green Street, Mrs Farren brought it up. 'Surely there was no need for obscurity when the thing only came from Mrs Damer?'

'Really, Mother, it's none of His Lordship's business where I get my jewels.'

'But now you've roused his suspicion—'

'He knows he has no rival,' said Eliza sharply, laying her head back against the cushion. 'I packed off the last cow-eyed suitor a good four years ago, didn't I?'

Her mother sat silent in the dark of the carriage, but only for the time it took them to reach their house. 'Still, a dash of jealousy never spoils a dish, only sharpens the appetite,' she concluded more happily.

Eliza resented being the *dish*, but held her tongue.

The next day she took a hackney to Streatham, to get it over with. Mrs Piozzi, surprised in a shabby yellow wrapping gown at her desk, begged her caller to excuse the disarray. 'I've had so many visitors recently, fleeing the heat and dust of London, and this morning I've been writing down everything I've garnered about the shocking violences in Paris.'

Eliza couldn't spare any energy for arguing that the rapid pace of change in France struck her as utterly thrilling. 'May I ask, what did you mean when you said that you had proof?' She spoke very low, though she knew the door was shut tight.

Mrs Piozzi blinked at her.

She's going to make me repeat it, thought Eliza. 'Of the lady in question being...what you alleged.'

Mrs Piozzi settled herself comfortably in her chair. 'I knew you'd be ready to hear me, once you'd got over the shock,' she confided. 'I didn't take offence, when you slammed the door of my carriage without so much as a good day.'

'I'm sorry about that,' said Eliza haltingly.

'Quite understandable, my dear. Did you manage to get home that afternoon without coming over all faint? It's your long experience of the stage, I suppose; such stamina! Dear Sally Siddons tells me that when she's got through a tragedy, she feels wrung out like a rag. You recall she once passed out cold during the sleepwalking scene in the *Scottish play*?'

Eliza pressed her teeth together.

'I mention Mrs Siddons for a particular reason,' murmured Mrs Piozzi. 'I've discovered that it was none other than her husband who composed that nasty epigram.'

Eliza stared. She barely knew Williams Siddons; he was a failed actor, a man who lived in his wife's shadow and did little but spend her money. 'But what did he mean by it?' asked Eliza, anger like a bit of gristle in her throat. What motive could he possibly have? Did he resent Eliza's fame for encroaching on his wife's, even though they never competed for the same parts? The man was a nobody, a nonentity. How dare he go around making up libels on ladies whose boots he wasn't fit to polish?

'Well, my dear,' said Mrs Piozzi, 'I went straight to our dear Sally Siddons, and asked her where William had got such a wicked idea.'

'I wish you hadn't spoken to her,' said Eliza, flinching.

'Oh, no, she was perfectly nice about it,' Mrs Piozzi assured her. 'All her husband could say in his defence, she reports, was that it's a well-known fact that John Damer killed himself because of his cold, unnatural wife!'

'To call a woman unnatural', said Eliza, 'because her husband runs into debt and proves his cowardice by suicide—why, it's ridiculous! It would be like calling you a...a pickpocket because your husband is Italian.'

Mrs Piozzi squinted slightly. Eliza regretted the remark; her friend was very sensitive on the subject of her husband's nationality, for which she'd endured so much censure. 'I only mean the two traits are entirely unconnected,' she stumbled on.

A nod. 'Now, I have a very good bookseller I go to off the Strand who supplies me with anything I need, he's a gem,' said Mrs Piozzi, as if changing the subject. 'I was sure I remembered hearing about some old broadsides about Mrs Damer and it took him a week or two, but he found them.'

Them?

'They all came out after she was widowed in '77 or '78—that's just before you came to London, I believe? Vulgar, disgusting stuff, of course—I can let you study the publications at your leisure, I have them locked up in my drawer here.' Already Mrs Piozzi was fiddling with the key of her cherry *secrétaire.* Now she had the things in her hand; thin paper, yellowing with age.

Eliza found herself rising to her feet. *Old lies,* she thought, *stupid, cruel old lies.*

'The worst of them's called "A Sapphick Epistle",' said Mrs Piozzi with relish, 'it's addressed to *Mrs D—dash—r,* well who else can that signify? It says she was delighted when her husband killed himself, because she was already a man-hating Tommy.'

Eliza was at the door. 'I'm afraid I have a rehearsal.'

'Won't you see for yourself?' asked the older woman. 'I warn you, there's one very obscene line about her relations with Italian girls—'

'No. That won't be necessary.'

'Well. You did say you wanted proof,' said Mrs Piozzi, her voice a little hurt. 'Not that such scurrilous stuff proves anything for a certainty, of course, and it was more than ten years ago, but one does have to wonder—no smoke without fire, as they say—'

'I've heard enough,' said Eliza. 'Thank you,' she added, delivering it like an insult.

'You know where they are, if you want them,' said Mrs Piozzi, locking the drawer again and patting the high polish of the desk. 'I had my suspicions about a friend of mine, a Miss Weston, until she overcame her reluctance to marry,' she confided, turning. 'The vice is on the rise, I do believe; Bath is said to be a cage of unclean birds.' Her voice had gone down to a hiss. 'Every week I hear some new evidence that we're living in the End Times...'

As the hackney took Eliza out of Streatham, through the villages of Brixton, Stockwell and Kennington, she breathed in fresh air. She must have been delirious these last few weeks. Clearly Anne was the victim of a tasteless hoax that had begun ten years ago as a way of cutting an independent, artistic widow down to size. Eliza didn't need to read the pamphlets; they looked so flimsy and greasy, with their curling edges, so much like every bit of journalistic trash she'd ever flicked through to find out what was being said of *Miss Tittup* and *Lord Doodle*. Who knew better than she did that nine-tenths of what was committed to print was lies, damnable lies? Didn't she know from bitter experience that a woman of distinction had a million enemies; that the men of the press hated no one more than a famous woman with an income of her own? And if a feeble wit like William Siddons could hit two targets with the same poisoned arrow, by linking *Damer* to *Farren* in a punning epigram, then all it meant was that this was a wicked little world.

Eliza resolved to trust her senses, and her instincts, and the best friend she'd ever had.

SEPTEMBER 1789

The schedule at Goodwood was sensibly early, in Anne's view, but Richmond invited his guests to join him in so many activities—badminton, boating, chemistry demonstrations and riding over the South Downs—that she had little time to herself, whether for writing or taking solitary walks in the woods.

When she and Lady Melbourne were sitting up to their chins in cold water in the bathhouse, she remembered to ask, 'How's Lord Egremont?'

'Oh, perfectly well.' Lady Melbourne yawned. 'He popped in just the other day and sported delightfully with little Emily on the rug. But we don't see so very much of His Lordship these days, as it happens.'

The *we* was a fiction, Anne knew; if the Viscount ever met his wife's guests in the hall or on the stairs, all he did was smile in his vacant way and shake their hands. Did this mean the long Egremont affair was over? She watched her friend's blue-tipped nose. 'I hope there's been no...falling-out?'

The Viscountess laughed as if Anne had said something silly. 'It's just that we're so busy. I do envy you the untrammelled simplicity of a single life!'

Anne splashed her face to hide her irritation.

'But as it happens we have been seeing rather a lot of newer friends, since the regency hoo-ha, especially those whose views chime with our own,' Lady Melbourne murmured.

Anne felt weary, almost repelled. How many intrigues could one woman fit into a lifetime? It had to be one of the Foxite hotheads. 'There are so many of the younger members of the Opposition whom I barely know,' she ventured.

Lady Melbourne rewarded her guess with a smile. 'The Duke of Bedford calls, for one.'

That strange, long-haired grandee who dressed like a clerk? The Viscountess was old enough to be his mother.

'Bedford's awkward, but vastly eager and ardent', murmured the Viscountess, 'when it comes to the cause of Reform. And he shares my passion for irrigation and enclosure, sheep breeding, that sort of thing. I've persuaded him to invest in the new chaff cutter we've been using at Brocket Hall.'

'Fascinating,' said Anne, standing up in the bath and waving her arms to increase the flow of blood. She'd had enough of coded confidences. 'I always enjoy my visits to Goodwood, don't you? My sister invited Miss Farren, but they're such tyrants, her managers, they'll work her into an early grave.'

A shrug. 'Oh, the girl seems tough enough to me. It's her job and she's well paid for it, I understand. Besides, she's so pampered by her well-born friends.'

'Pampered?' Anne repeated, sinking back into the cold water.

Lady Melbourne climbed up to sit on the edge of the bath. 'To be perfectly honest, my dear, I've never understood this sentimental friendship of yours.'

'What is there to understand?' asked Anne, the consonants hard in her mouth. Surely she couldn't mean what Anne feared she meant?

The Viscountess shrugged and the soaked canvas clung to her bony shoulders; water ran off it in glacial streams. 'She's an actress.'

'Miss Farren has genius—she's earned herself a place in the World—'

'But she'll never be *of* it, not if she'd sprung from the loins of Jupiter himself,' said Lady Melbourne. 'For all her fine dresses and matching manners, she's the child of a strolling troupe and she works for her bread. You might as well have picked a grocer's wife for a pet, or started doting on my milliner.'

A pet; the phrase choked Anne, who reared up in the icy water with a great splash. 'You astonish me,' she said. 'My sister, my mother, Georgiana, Lady Bess, Walpole—they all adore her.'

One wet aristocratic eyebrow went up. 'Tolerate, rather; they invite her to parties, yes; she's a colourful adornment and popular with the Whig men. But only you, my dear, exchange loving notes with the girl twice a day. Only you go to Drury Lane every night she plays, and drag her into every conversation, and spend the best part of a year sculpting her nose.'

Anne clambered out of the bath. 'Do I understand you?' she asked, shaking. 'Do you dare to throw in my face—'

'I never said anything before,' the Viscountess interrupted, 'because I assumed this little misbegotten intimacy would run its course. But really, Anne, to see you at the Exhibition, proclaiming to the world your attachment to that sly little *arriviste*—'

'I don't remember asking you for your opinion of Miss Farren—a young lady, may I add, of unimpeachable virtue.'

The Viscountess folded her clammy arms. 'Oh, don't say you've been taken in on that score? Prig and prude the girl may be, but not virgin.'

'You filthy liar!' The walls of the bathhouse rang. 'How dare you drag her down to your own level? Not every woman counts her lovers on two hands and bears a bastard to each of them. Not every woman lets a new keeper buy her from the last for 13,000 guineas!'

And at that moment, seeing Lady Melbourne's pupils contract to tiny black points, Anne knew the friendship was broken; she could almost hear it, like the tinkle of glass.

OCTOBER 1789

To launch the Season the Earl had decided to hold a masquerade. Though public masquerades at Ranelagh or Vauxhall were frowned on these days for their improper mixing, a select gathering was quite a different matter. After long deliberations Derby had chosen the authentic, imported costume of a Chinese mandarin; he could have rented it, but he liked the heavy silk sleeves so much that he bought it outright. It spoke of power and ceremony, and it suited a short man, too. The mask came with a long moustache of real hair.

Derby House was looking magnificent. Robert Adam had designed the sequence of rooms for just such an occasion; the contrasting geometric shapes of hall, ante-room, parlour, dining room and library formed a delightfully surprising sequence. Derby ordered every alcove and cubicle lit up with wax candles, he didn't mind what the evening cost. The great staircase was hung with red, white and blue silk banners as an homage to the brave French, and in its dome hung coloured glass lanterns. In the hall a little band in uniforms and feathered caps played serpents and clarinets. There was a supper—including a roast swan—laid out in the rectangular dining room that looked oval because of the plaster curves on the walls. Upstairs the vast saloon, with its fantastically stuccoed vaulted ceiling and its mythological panels by Madame Kauffmann, had been emptied for dancing. (The room was really too big, he knew, ever since he'd impulsively ordered a wall ripped down to make space for a bigger orchestra. That was in his wild and high-living days, before he'd come under Miss Farren's influence.) The chimney pieces were draped in red, white and blue velvet, and candles in gilt vases stood between tall arbours of flowers. Derby had rented most of the orange trees in London for the night, as well as some huge mirrors to supplement his own; dancers loved to watch themselves. He'd banned card tables—the enemies of conversation—but in the other drawing rooms there were sofas and teams of maids dressed as Vestals to brew constant supplies of tea. As a finishing touch he'd ordered boxes of Wedgwood's new cameos—France holding hands with Athene, goddess of wisdom—to present to all the ladies.

When the masquerade was in full swing, Derby stood by the door of the saloon and watched through the slits in his Chinaman mask. The orchestra looked splendid in their red robes. He saw a fat nun talking to a tiny Spanish Maja whose seams were laced together with ribbons—Lady Bess Foster?—and here came the Duke of Bedford, who'd made no further effort than to tie a black

eye mask over his lank long hair; a splendid shepherdess on his arm
was surely his new *déesse*, Lady Melbourne. Derby bowed warmly
to a tall Diana in a white and gold tunic and sandals, with a chap-
let of flowers, who had to be Mrs Damer, but he wasn't sure she
recognised him. He counted three Quakers, another Chinese mandarin in vastly inferior robes, a pirate, several pairs of Rubens and
Rubens's Wife (the mid-seventeenth-century look was still unaccountably popular), a Turkish sultan with a female attendant
muffled in black, a Good Queen Bess and various vaguely pastoral
costumes. The question was, where was Eliza? Derby couldn't believe that any mask could hide her from his eyes. He examined the
pairs walking through a minuet: no, none of the women was tall
enough to be the actress. It was getting late; surely she'd have sent
him word if something had prevented her from coming?

The Turk was at his side. Derby didn't recognise the fellow
under that long flowing caftan with the ermine trim—unless it was
Windham, who was tall enough. He turned and raised his glass.
'Your health, o great Sultan. How do these maidens compare with
those in your harem?'

The tinkling laugh gave her away. Beside her, her mother in
black wrappings gave a curtsy.

'Miss Farren!' He seized her by one gloved hand.

'You mistake my name and my sex, o mysterious Mandarin,'
she reproved him huskily, adjusting her turban. 'I have come with a
message for you from your restless peasants. Let there be no more
tedious quadrilles, minuets and gavottes. The people demand
country dances!'

Derby made what he hoped was a Far Eastern obeisance. 'I
submit to the Majesty of the People.' He beckoned to the master of
the orchestra.

When he and Eliza were opposite each other, hand in hand, in
the long double line of men and women, he whispered in her ear, 'I
thought you vowed after your first year at Drury Lane that you'd
never wear men's clothes again?' The critics had humiliated her by

calling her *skinny* and complaining that you'd hardly know her for a woman.

Her eyes were on the first quartet as they led off with a skip. 'I believe my words were, *no breeches parts.* I hope I can point out, without immodesty, that these aren't breeches.'

Her caftan was kilted up by a jewelled girdle, showing loose red silk pantaloons, gathered above her shoes, which had curled-up points. Derby was about to make some flirtatious response when the hussar in tasselled boots ahead of him, with the bulk and flowery scent of the Prince of Wales, leaned back and said, 'Splendid party, mine host.'

'Thanks—' Derby stopped himself from saying *Your Royal Highness* just in time. If the Prince couldn't taste anonymity at a masquerade, when could he? Suddenly it was their turn and Derby was off, whirling in and out, tripping on the hem of his robe.

On a sofa, he and Eliza shared a pear ice, with her mother opposite them on a stool. He feasted his eyes on the glimpse of his beloved's cheekbone between mask and jewelled turban. 'I've been tormenting myself', he remarked, 'by wondering, if I were a French *aristocrate,* in Paris on that night in August, would I too have stood up to renounce my ancient feudal privileges, asking no compensation?' Some said the *comtes* and *marquises* had been afraid of the mob's noose, but Derby could well believe that they'd acted in a spirit of grand enthusiasm.

'I doubt it,' Eliza teased him. She couldn't see his expression behind his moustachioed mask. It occurred to her that he might be asking himself whether she only tolerated him for his title and estates—for her hopes of one day sharing them. She dropped the flippancy from her tone. 'But there'd be no need for such a sacrifice, as the British nobility has always had its country's welfare at heart,' she said, laying it on thick. 'Those cottages you've built at Knowsley, for instance,' she added, scrambling for examples. 'Whereas the French system was so oppressive, with all those fees and the free labour the lords extracted from the peasants, it needed to be demolished.'

'I was a rebel once,' said Derby fondly.

Mrs Farren stared at him. Eliza savoured the melting ice in her mouth.

'It was at school, in my second-last year. Now I never resented being punished if I deserved it—Grandfather was scrupulously fair—but the Master of Eton, in those years, was addicted to the whip. What happened was a Praeposter—that's a sort of prefect—was pursuing some youngsters who were out of bounds and so happened to be caught out of bounds himself. The Master wouldn't listen to the boy's arguments; he flogged half the skin off his back.'

Eliza flinched.

'Well, we older boys got all fired up about it, we'd never heard of such flagrant injustice!' Derby's voice came mockingly from behind his Chinese mask. 'I think it was the first time we realised what authority is, when it drops all disguises: a master doesn't have to obey the rules, it's as simple as that. Well, we burst out of the gates, about ten dozen of us, and marched off to Maidenhead. We demanded wine and punch at an inn called Marsh's, and there were so many of us they didn't dare refuse. Oh, it was glorious fun! I'd had beer before, but never been truly drunk. The next day we woke up all over the floor, feeling vile, of course.'

Eliza laughed at the image. 'What did you do?'

'Drifted back to Eton en masse, hoping to negotiate terms. But the Master said the only terms were unconditional capitulation and a dozen of the best all round.'

'He must have had a tireless arm,' said Eliza. She was remembering one of the few times her father had ever beaten her, when she'd left a wagon of cardboard props out in the rain.

'Many of us ran away. I sold my watch and caught a coach to Liverpool,' said Derby, reminiscent. 'When I turned up at Knowsley my father and grandfather had already had a letter from the Master.'

'What did they say?'

'They didn't need to say anything. They took it in turns to flog me, then they sent me back to school.'

'My dear!'

Eliza jumped away from the hands on her shoulders.

'Oh, I gave you a fright, I'm so sorry.' Anne, a tall Diana in tunic and sandals, pulled the ribbons of her mask loose. Eliza threw herself into the embrace, but kept her mask on; she kissed the air beside her friend's hot cheeks.

'Did you have prior knowledge of Miss Farren's Turkish disguise?' asked the Earl.

'Derby! Is that really you behind that frightening moustache? No, I didn't know what our friend would be wearing,' said Anne, curling up beside Eliza on the sofa, 'but I recognised the line of that throat at a glance, even though we haven't met in the flesh all summer.'

The Mandarin mask nodded benignly. 'The artist's eye. Myself, I mistook her for a man.'

Anne carolled with laughter at the idea.

Stop looking at me, Eliza thought, *stop speaking about me.*

Anne leaned so close her breath stirred Eliza's ear. 'I've sent something to your house—something long overdue.'

She was grateful for the mask that covered her burning face.

When the Farrens got home to Green Street, in the colourless dawn light, they found a large packing case in the hall. Her mother, who'd had too much champagne, grinned from ear to ear. 'May I? May I?'

'If you like,' said Eliza exhaustedly. 'But the manservant could do it in the morning—'

The wood squealed and nails popped as Mrs Farren wrenched back the lid, and there was the face. Soft, creamy, female beauty turned to stone: *Thalia.* Eliza thought she might burst into tears.

'How vastly kind of Mrs Damer to make you a present of it!'

'Yes.' Eliza's voice was almost inaudible.

'We might put it on the sideboard in the dining room, where it'll catch the light. Or perhaps in the window, so it can be glimpsed from outside? I always say there's nothing more *tonish* than a piece of original statuary.'

'D'you know, Mother, I've got a splitting headache,' she said, lurching towards the stairs.

Eliza stripped off her turban and robes, leaving them on the floor like some rich lady with a dozen servants. She lay awake, listening to the early traffic.

She was nine-tenths sure the old rumours weren't true: Anne had never once laid a hand on her in an improper way. When the sculptor looked at Eliza it was warmly, but without any peculiar insinuation. It wasn't how a man looked when he desired a woman; surely, Eliza thought, a Sapphist would ogle the way a man would, or worse?

But to say the rumours were lies was no comfort. Eliza still strained over every scribbled note, flinched when she heard the name of Mrs Damer and tonight she'd recoiled from her touch.

There'd be no point in embarking on a mortifying confrontation. (*Did you—are you—I know you're not, but they say—*) What mattered was the story. Perhaps only some people had heard it, but it'd circulated, it would no doubt continue to circulate, in conversation and in print; it had the slippery longevity of all good scandals. What if a guest saw the *Thalia* in Eliza's house and sneered knowingly? What if she walked into the Green Room at Drury Lane and heard giggles die away at her entrance? Why, what if she were on stage some night and a wit in the pit sang out that damned epigram? Her face went fiery at the thought.

> *Her little stock of private fame*
> *will fall a wreck to public clamour*
> *If Farren leagues with one whose name—*

The hard fact was that Eliza couldn't afford this friendship. It was all right for the Honourable Mrs Damer, who'd survive any amount of petty malice; she had the inextinguishable confidence of the gentry, as well as her own money, her own house, her own work; she didn't rely on the favour of the public. Whereas Eliza couldn't risk spitting in the face of the wind. To end her days on the provincial circuit, dragging her reproachful mother behind her, fleeing rumours of *unnatural vice* . . .

She lay very still and waited till her breath was steady again. She formed her policy. She'd tuck the bust into that dark niche on the third-floor stairs, where no guests would ever see it. There'd be no sudden noticeable breach between the two women; that would draw down too much attention. (It might even be interpreted as a lovers' tiff, it occurred to her with horror.) But Eliza was going gradually, smoothly, firmly to end the friendship.

Oh, God, how cold I am. But what else was she to do?

Eliza sat up, slightly dizzy, and tugged at her little gold ring, but it resisted; her fingers were still swollen from the warmth of the dancing. Oh, well, she might as well leave that on, to spare Anne's feelings; the woman had never meant her any harm. Besides, no one else knew what it meant, that unblinking little ivory eye.

FEBRUARY 1790

Outside the windows of Brooks's a rocket went off with an enormous bang and Derby twitched slightly. It was after midnight on the anniversary of the King's recovery. He and Fox were doing their best to ignore the occasion and chasing their umpteenth bottle of sherry with some fine brandy. 'My dear friend,' said Derby, his arm slung round Fox's shoulders, 'has anyone ever remarked on the fact that you stink?'

Fox let out a giggle and a small fart. 'Funnily enough, Your Lordship, the matter has come up once or twice, over the years.'

'Is it a kind of hydrophobia, d'you think? D'you fear that, on the application of water, your coating of black fur will peel away?'

Fox coughed with laughter. 'I do realise, believe me, I am quite cognis—cog—cognisant of the fact that for a dapper beau such as yourself, Derby, to embrace me is to run a risk hardly less than if you were to walk along the Cheapside gutter. And I'm grateful, I assure you—fervently, aromatically grateful.'

'The funny thing is, I remember you as quite the sleek dandy, in the '70s.'

Fox grinned. 'And I remember you, in the same period, as quite the Tory.'

'You put me to the blush,' said Derby, covering his face stagily.

'I don't know what I was thinking. But I wasn't a Crown supporter for long, not once my uncle Burgoyne came back from defeat at Saratoga and persuaded me that peace with America was the only just solution.'

'Justice be damned,' crowed Fox. 'It was me who flipped you. You became my friend first and then joined my Party!'

Well, that was probably true, Derby thought ruefully. His life had experienced a sort of earthquake in the year 1778, when he'd become a fervent Foxite and lost his wife. It was hard to disentangle principles from personalities and God knew, he loved this sweaty, black-nailed fellow.

'And just as it took you a while to find the right Party, I discovered only gradually that I don't give a damn about being elegant, or clean for that matter,' said Fox. 'It's a matter of finding one's true nature,' he said, only slurring a little.

'But I should logically have stayed a Tory, considering how cruel to me you were at Eton.'

'Come now, hardly cruel,' protested Fox. 'We seniors always despised you runtish little fags, by tradition.'

'You weren't just any senior, you were the star in our firmament—six languages and all that. I'll never forget the first thing you said to me,' said Derby. 'You were lounging around arm in arm with Lords Carlisle and Fitzwilliam. "Come here, ugly boy," you said, beckoning with one finger. "Fellows, I do believe this is the ugliest little boy in Christendom."'

Fox let out a whoop. 'Did I? I'm sure I was drunk; the remark has an alcoholic timbre to it. Did it crush you?'

'I'm still a broken man today.' Derby, pretended to wipe his eye.

'You can blame my father for my insolence; he raised me on the principle that discipline stifles genius, so it never occurred to me not to say what came to mind.'

'Oh, I've heard the stories,' Derby assured him. 'The infant Fox smashing Papa's watch to see how it worked, demanding to paddle in the cream tureen, pissing on the roast pig…'

'Cease, for shame!'

'Considering your eccentric upbringing, you've turned out quite a decent fellow,' said Derby, squeezing his shoulder.

'Well, still, I heartily apologise for calling you *ugly boy*.'

He shrugged. 'It was true.'

'I was no Adonis myself,' said Fox, 'and my ugliness caught up with yours about five years ago by my reckoning and overtook it! Lucky for us it turns out that men don't need beauty to get on in life and women don't require it of us.'

Derby grinned back at him.

Sheridan and their old friend Dick Fitzpatrick came over with full bottles of sherry, and soon after that Derby spotted Bunbury and waved him over to join them. 'Oh, I forgot to tell you,' Derby remarked, moving his finger between Fox and Sheridan, 'Mrs Damer says Lord Bristol's looking for a sculptor to take on a colossal *Hercules Slaying the Hydra*; Hercules will be modelled on Pitt, and the monster a triple-headed likeness of you two and Burke.'

Sheridan snorted. 'That won't please Grey.'

'No,' Fox agreed, 'the lad hates to be left out of anything.'

The Club quietened down as members drifted off and most of the waiters went to bed. Alone by the dying fire, Derby and his friends started playing a favourite drinking game, Connection. 'We'll commence with my lovely Mrs A.,' said Fox, 'so there need be no beating about the bush in deference to my feelings. We've none of us any secrets here. To the beauteous Liz Armistead and long may she bless me with her presence!'

They drank deep.

'Who connects to the Right Honourable Member C. J. Fox,' said Bunbury.

'A masterly statement of the obvious from the sporting Baronet. Now it's your go, Dick,' said Sheridan.

The handsome Colonel pulled at his moustache. 'Our foxy friend connects to…the enigmatic former actress, Mrs Robinson.'

'Mm, yes,' said Fox, reminiscent.

'Who, before that, granted free ingress, egress and regress to her Privy Chamber to…the Prince of Wales,' Derby put in.

'Now that really is too obvious,' Fitzpatrick protested with a belch.

'Ah, but we couldn't leave out such a famous intrigue,' said Derby. 'Now Prinny connects to...Sherry?'

'He does not,' protested Sheridan. 'Slippery devil I may be, but no bumboy.' They fell about laughing. 'No, I leave such obscure pursuits to our beardless Prime Minister to investigate,' he said virtuously.

'Sh,' howled Bunbury. 'That's a foul libel.'

'Forgive me, Sherry, I only meant it was your go,' Derby told him, sniggering. 'Prinny connects to...'

'Oh, gad, how to choose?' Sheridan groaned. 'The field's too wide. Let's plump for the plump-bosomed Lady Melbourne.'

'Interesting choice,' said Fox, nodding like a judge, 'and a great supporter of our Party. Really, women of a certain age, women of experience, have so much more to offer than green girls.'

'You don't fancy virgins, then?' asked Sheridan.

'I had one once, for the novelty,' Bunbury put in.

'I like them, myself,' said Sheridan, 'but I like them all the more ten minutes later, when they're not virgins any more!'

This discussion was making Derby uneasy, in case Sheridan might be on the brink of making some crack about Eliza Farren.

'But we're wandering from the game,' Fitpatrick objected.

Sheridan said, 'The invaluable Viscountess Melbourne connects us to...Lord Egremont.'

'Whoa, it's my go,' said Fox. 'You took two.'

Sheridan slapped his forehead. 'May the gods strike me dead for it. Go on, then.'

Fox brooded for a long moment. He cleared his throat and hawked into the fire. 'You rascal, Sherry! You knew I'd get stuck on Egremont.'

'What, can't you think of a single name?' asked Fitzpatrick.

Fox chewed his lip. 'Well, till Bedford ousted him, Egremont was devoted to the Viscountess for so many years—what about that niece of Walpole's he nearly married, till Lady M. put a stop to it, does she count?'

'Only unless they're generally agreed to have achieved *connection*,' said Sheridan, legalistic.

'I can think of three or four of Egremont's previous dalliances,' said Fitzpatrick and winked at Derby.

'By Jove, yes, five or six,' said Derby, to torture Fox.

'Twenty or thirty,' yelped Bunbury and Derby winced; Bunbury sometimes ruined a joke by pushing it.

'No, my mind's a blank, I forfeit,' said Fox. 'Give me the bottle.' As was his duty, he drained it, choking a little on the final inch.

'Good man.' Derby thumped him on the back. 'Now you have to start again, with the lovely Mrs A.'

'Who connects to...' began Fox blearily. 'You, Derby!'

Derby held up his glass. 'Happy memories, though brief.'

'Gad, you fellows spread your nets wide, in your youth,' grumbled Bunbury. 'My name never comes up in this game. All right, Derby here connects to...' He wrinkled his brows. There was a long moment.

'Go on. Wives can count at a pinch, as well as mistresses,' Derby told him drily.

'Lady Derby, then,' said Bunbury.

'Who connects to Lord Dorset,' said Fitzpatrick, unembarrassed, 'who connects to...'

'Hm. All roads lead back to the lovely Mrs A.,' said Derby, remembering that strange year in which Dorset had taken Derby's wife from him and he himself had taken up with Dorset's mistress, Liz Armistead. 'But no, I'll choose another name. Dorset leads to...Georgiana, for one.'

'I've never understood the fellow's pull,' groaned Fitzpatrick. 'Your go, Sherry.'

'As I took an extra turn before, I'm willing to surrender mine to Fox now,' said Sheridan, innocent.

They waited. 'Sherry,' Fox complained, 'you put me in a delicate position here.'

'Oh, go on, tell us,' Sheridan urged. 'Georgiana, Queen of our Party, connects to...your Right Honourable Foxiness?'

'I'm not saying either way,' maintained Fox, rather red in the face.

'It's a bit late in the evening for such delicacy,' Derby put in. 'I propose that the meeting assumes it to be so, but unproven—and on to you, Bunbury.'

'Fox connects to... damn it, sir, give me some ideas,' begged the Baronet.

'Mrs A. again?' suggested Sheridan.

'All right. Poor dear Mrs A., we're using her as the universal crossroads,' said Bunbury.

They were all staying carefully away from Sheridan's own history, Derby noticed, as the Harriet Duncannon matter was so fresh and painful.

Fitzpatrick spoke: 'Mrs A. connects to... Lord Bolingbroke.'

'Good choice,' Derby approved. 'Who connects to... his own sister.'

They shrieked with laughter. 'Bit of a dead end, there, though,' said Sheridan.

'Worth it. I'll stand the forfeit.' Derby drained the bottle into his throat. It took longer than he thought and by the end he was feeling rather shaky.

Sheridan proposed a toast to the spirit of fellowship, 'For when this Honourable Member's member'—here he clutched his groin—'makes his entrance into any particular House, he does so in the knowledge that it is a Commons where he's among friends and that he's making a contribution to the General Fund!'

Derby leaned over the side of the chair and threw up the entire contents of his stomach.

ELIZA WAS in the wings at Drury Lane, waiting to go on in Mrs Centlivre's old comedy *The Wonder*; her role was the lovely Lisbon aristocrat, Violante, who risked everything to protect her friend's secret. She adjusted the bow of her sash in the small of her back, where it was tied too loosely; the Drury Lane dressers never took as much care as her mother did. On stage, Frederick and Don Lopez were discussing the English. Eliza heard what sounded like shrieks of approval from the pit, and she straightened up and listened properly to Jack Palmer's speech.

> ... *the English are by nature what the ancient Romans were by discipline: courageous, bold, hardy and in love with liberty. Liberty is the idol of the English, under whose banner all the nation lists.*

Jack had a good strong voice, but it was almost drowned out by the hullabaloo in the theatre. Such howls, such cheers! 'Liberty!' Eliza heard them chant. 'Hurrah for Liberty!'

When the speech finished she listened for Charles Bannister's answer, but he was a true veteran; he waited till the cheers had died down and there was something approximating silence. Then he gave Don Lopez's reply: *'I like their principles. Who does not wish for freedom in all degrees of life?'*

More clapping and chanting broke out. 'Huzza! Huzza! Freedom!'

Eliza grinned to herself. The spirit of French insurgency seemed to be contagious this year. *Freedom in all degrees of life*; the old line had a splendid ring to it.

After the performance, when she and her mother emerged from the side entrance of Drury Lane, the carriage with the crest was waiting as usual. Derby jumped down. The little man always looked at her as if she were the only woman in England; it was certainly comforting at the end of a long day. 'Take care, madam,' he told her mother, 'the stones are icy.' Mrs Farren heaved in beside Eliza and gave sigh of satisfaction.

'Were you in the house?' Eliza asked Derby as soon as he'd rapped on the roof to tell the coachman to go.

'Marvellous, wasn't it?—that hullabaloo in honour of liberty! By the way, I'd a note from Mrs Damer inviting me to pop in for a bite of supper tonight after the play.'

'Yes,' said Eliza warily, 'I had one too.'

In the four months since the masquerade at Derby House she'd held to her resolution of curtailing the friendship, but it was harder than she could have imagined. She refused most of Anne's invitations on various pretexts; she dashed off notes in reply to long letters and the letters soon stopped coming. She'd thought Anne might send some wounded, angry accusation—but she hadn't. When they met in company Eliza couldn't bear to cut her, so she greeted her in a friendly way, apologising for being so busy, then edged away and spoke to someone else, her heart contracting with guilt.

Her mother had put the question bluntly as early as last November: 'Don't you care for Mrs Damer any more?'

The truth was too mortifying to explain. 'Oh, she and I were chalk and cheese, Mother. In upbringing, temperament, everything.'

Mrs Farren nodded. 'I always thought it a little odd that a widow of her age should cultivate a friendship with a girl of yours, though she was so kind. In my experience great beauties like you have no friends!'

Her mother meant it as a compliment, Eliza knew, but it made her shiver. She did need friends, she knew that now; she felt what she was missing. She didn't want to be cruel, but it was a matter of survival; she couldn't be seen to be attached to Anne Damer. The wretched subject was very much in the air this year for some reason; Marie Antoinette's Court was now said to have been riddled with Sapphists and some German tourist was claiming in his book on England that London had several secret societies for the obscene rites of *Anandrynes,* meaning *manless females.*

A long pause had developed as the carriage rattled down Long Acre. 'I don't think you see as much of our mutual friend as you used,' Derby remarked.

Had Anne been complaining to him, Eliza wondered? It seemed unlikely she'd stoop to that. Probably he'd noticed it himself. 'It's been such a gruelling season,' Eliza murmured, 'I've neglected all my acquaintance.'

The Earl didn't answer immediately. When he did, the lightness of his tone showed that he'd decided not to probe further. 'Shall we show our faces at no. 8, then?'

'I am rather tired tonight,' she said with a yawn.

He nodded.

She suddenly thought of herself and Anne and Derby, in the wings at the Richmond House Theatre, gripping each other's hands. How keen and sweet that threefold friendship had been, before anything had come between them.

ANNE WAS sitting on a Roman-style leather stool in her cousin Walpole's tribune at Strawberry Hill. The room was a tiny treasury shaped like a flower, with stone-coloured walls ornamented with gilt and a barred door. He was doing the dusting himself, with a tuft of feathers, because once, twenty years ago, his housekeeper Margaret had cracked a Delft vase. His hand shook a little, but his grip was sure. Every niche held a little bronze or china statuette (a bull, a goddess, an angel; a hermaphrodite with two satyrs); every inch of wall was covered with miniatures in elaborate frames. Over their heads, the gold ribs of the fan vaulting met in a star. Walpole was so unselective in his enthusiasms, Anne thought; he had some real treasures here, like a small bronze of the mad Caligula with silver eyes, but he kept them alongside dubious oddities like Cardinal Wolsey's hat, or an ivory box containing two dates from Herculaneum.

Their conversation had somehow strayed on to the one subject that they fought about: France. 'I don't approve of *all* the changes,' Anne admitted, 'but I applaud the daring spirit of enlightened reformers such as the Marquis de Lafayette and the Comte de Mirabeau. It's a real revolution, a renewal! This must be the first time in the history of our race that a nation has set out to forge itself anew, according to the highest principles of liberty, equality and fraternity.'

Walpole looked as if he'd bitten into something sour. 'Nothing is good except in moderation, says Horace—not even Reform, say I. Those frantic fools in the Assembly have acted like a man with frost-bitten fingers, who thinks to thaw them by setting his house on fire! In half a year they've pulled down their monarchy, church, nobility, law, army, commerce and manufactures,' he listed. 'What was it Burke called them the other day in the Commons? *The architects of ruin!*'

It did worry Anne that Fox and his old mentor Burke had had such a public quarrel on the subject of France. 'Come now, he exaggerates and you do too. They're drafting a model constitution, aren't they?'

'While Paris transforms from a theatre of good-humoured gaiety into a scene of squalid bloodshed! Didn't a pack of fishwives slaughter the guards at Versailles? I assure you I love liberty as much as the next man,' Walpole fumed, 'but this is not the way to win it. Too much, too fast, too bloodily.'

'Teething troubles,' Anne soothed him, 'and there's been nothing half as bad as our own anti-popery riots of ten years ago.' She shuddered to remember the week of nightly fire attacks that had left more than eight hundred Londoners dead. 'For France, the worst is over and Madame de Staël in her last letter tells me that one can breathe more freely somehow.'

'Unless one happens to be sentenced to hang for selling a rosette in any other colours than white, blue and red,' Walpole pointed out. 'Cousin, I can't believe I'm speaking to a friend—or should I say a former friend—of Marie Antoinette.'

Anne flushed, but stared him down. 'I wish her no ill; I believe Louis will survive this storm and become a gentler, fairer ruler of a better France. Why, he's proud to be seen in the tricolour cockade—'

'My dear, what a political *naïf* you are!' Walpole's fingers closed round the neck of a Meissen shepherdess. 'The émigré nobles arriving at Twickenham tell of riots, murdered priests and burning châteaux all over the country, and the poor are still starving, because *natural rights* don't fill bellies. Louis and his family are hostages and he's wearing the mask of a tame bear for the moment. It wouldn't surprise me if they banish him and set up an American-style republic!'

'Oh, cousin, don't be silly; no one wants that.'

'Or else Louis will throw down the mask, shake off his chains, turn into the despot of their worst nightmares and it'll come to civil war.'

'You're such a Cassandra!'

He snatched up her fan to cool his cheeks. 'If you'd lived as long as I, my dear Anne, you'd have a nose for such things.'

A faraway gong. On their way down to the dining room he mentioned, 'I invited our dear Miss Farren to join us, as she's not to perform tonight, but apparently she has a touch of headache.'

Anne spoke before she could stop herself. 'Try asking her when I'm not of the party.'

Walpole stopped and turned on the dim staircase, so she almost ran into him. 'Is there some cause of alienation?'

'None that I'm aware of.' Her voice came out rather strangled. 'No quarrel, only a sort of withering away of the friendship on Eliza's side. It's rather mortifying.'

'I should say so!'

'I don't give my affection so easily that I can be blasé when it's thrown back in my face.'

Walpole took her hand in his warm paw. 'My dear! I always thought Miss Farren aware of the honour you did her by befriending her.'

'Oh'—Anne shrugged—'I never considered I was doing her a favour. I thought she liked me. I know she did; she can't have kept up a pretence for so long. And I'm not aware of anything I did to hurt or insult her, so what is it?' She wiped one eye hastily with the back of her hand. 'I know I can be candid to the point of bluntness—and I'm sometimes so wrapped up in my work that I forget the social niceties. Perhaps I was tactless or insensitive?'

'On the contrary, you're the soul of sensitivity,' said her godfather. 'Could it be that you're brooding unnecessarily, in fact? Perhaps Miss Farren really is snowed under with work. A woman who labours for her bread, if I may spell it out so tastelessly—'

'She had time for me before, no matter how busy she was,' Anne interrupted, her throat tight. 'She spent all those afternoons sitting for her portrait bust and now she can't find the time to pop round the corner for a dish of tea.' That prompted another painful thought: when Anne had last made the mistake of paying a spontaneous visit to the house on Green Street she hadn't seen the *Thalia* displayed in the parlour or the dining room and Eliza had muttered something about keeping it upstairs to prevent accidents. As if marble would shatter at a touch! All that beauty, hidden away from view. *I could have kept it for myself,* she thought.

MARCH 1790

'Mr Lawrence,' said Eliza, rushing into the studio on Jermyn Street, a little breathless from the damp cold. *'Enchantée.'*

The young painter kissed her hand; he had a soft, effeminate look, but his pink lips were very firm on the back of her gloved fingers. People said Tom Lawrence was a better portraitist than even Sir Joshua had been at his age.

'Will you be so very good as to excuse my lateness?' asked Eliza, as he bowed to her mother. 'Piccadilly's all slush and two coaches have smashed into each other at the corner.'

'There's nothing to excuse,' said the boy with a succulent grin. He had long curls at the sides of his face. The studio reeked of paint; Eliza rather liked it. She pulled off her muff to hand to her mother; she tugged off one glove and reached to unclasp her fur-lined pelisse. Lawrence raised one finger. 'Don't do that.'

'I beg your pardon?'

'Stay as you are.' He was holding his hand up as a frame.

How commanding he was, the young pup. 'Mr Lawrence, if I might just take my heavy things off—I've worn the plain white muslin you asked for—'

'Lord Derby said he'd leave all the details of the picture up to me,' said the painter, snatching up a stick of charcoal and using his foot in its red-heeled shoe to pull his easel nearer. 'So it strikes me that I'll paint you just as I see you now, Miss Farren.'

Eliza smiled through her irritation. 'I haven't even tidied my hair.'

'All the better,' he told her, engrossed in his sketching.

'Well, where should I sit?'

'Stay standing, if you please.'

'Should I lean on something?' She looked around for a plinth or some other bit of scenery to drape herself against, but saw nothing suitable. 'Where should I put my hands—either end of my fan, or crossed over at my waist?'

'No, no, just stand like that, sideways on to me,' he muttered. 'Don't pose.'

She gave him a sharp glance, but his eyes were on the paper. 'You're to paint me, sir, so it follows I must pose.'

He looked up and grinned. 'Granted, but I don't want it to look like a pose. Do what you did when you came in—your right hand bare, at your throat, opening your cloak, with a bit of fur showing inside the white satin. Your glove and muff in your left hand, dangling. But don't stiffen, I beg you; you must look as if you've only paused for an instant and you're about to rush away.'

That was exactly what Eliza felt like doing. Mrs Farren had found a stool in the corner and tucked herself away, her eyes roaming across the studio in fascination.

'Do you know why Lord Derby sought me out, Miss Farren?' Lawrence asked suddenly.

'No, but I suppose he likes to encourage the young.' That should put him in his place. 'And you've been much talked of since you burst on the scene in the autumn when Queen Charlotte sat to you,' she added more kindly. 'Was Her Majesty an entertaining model?'

He gave her a glum look. 'I think you can imagine the answer. As soon as I'd sketched her face, she sent a lady-in-waiting with quite a different figure to pose as a replacement. Then the King refused to buy the picture, because I'd left off the cap the Queen always wears!'

'They're calling you a sort of infant prodigy, you know.'

Lawrence drew himself up. 'I am twenty years old, madam.'

'Exactly.'

'If I say so myself, I do have a knack for catching a likeness,' he murmured. 'Especially the eyes. Lord Derby said to me, "Sir, you paint eyes better than Titian."'

'I'm delighted to see you don't suffer from underconfidence.'

'Nor do you, Miss Farren, judging from your air as you strut on stage.'

Eliza choked. 'Strut, sir? I've never strutted in my life. You must be thinking of a fighting cock.'

'One of the famous Knowsley Black-Breasted Reds, perhaps?'

She turned her head and looked him straight between the eyes. What was she thinking of, sparring like this with a young man she'd only just met? 'I'm sitting for this portrait as a favour to His Lordship, but that won't induce me to put up with any impudence.'

'Oh, there'll be no *sitting* involved,' Lawrence muttered, sketching rapidly. 'I intend to keep you on your toes.'

Eliza thought of several possible replies to that. The minutes went by. The painter's girlish curls and rounded lips might suggest a certain *propensity,* as Mrs Piozzi would no doubt call it; Eliza didn't like to follow that train of thought. But then again, if she wasn't mistaken he'd been flirting with her just now.

In the corner, her mother yawned covertly. 'Are you quite comfortable, Mrs Farren?' murmured the painter.

'Oh, yes, sir.' She blinked. 'Don't mind me, it's an honour to be here.'

After a while he remarked to Eliza, 'You don't twitch. That's a help.'

'Well, I have been much painted,' she pointed out, playing the woman of the world.

'Oh, I know. Dreadfully.'

She stared at him.

'Eyebrows back in their places, please, while I'm sketching them,' he murmured. 'Yes, I thought Zoffany's recent effort was particularly poor.'

'That canvas was found universally pleasing.'

Lawrence nodded. 'A sure sign of mediocrity.'

'What—'

'That's why old Zoffany specialises in theatrical scenes,' he interrupted, 'because all he can do are costumes and props. Oh, he got your green satin dress and your black Spanish hat well enough—he's a sound drapery man—but where was the woman inside them?'

The cheek of this plump-faced Ganymede took her breath away.

'I always wanted to be an actor,' Lawrence remarked, 'but my father thwarted my ambitions.'

'Did he mean you to follow him in his own profession, then?'

Lawrence snorted. 'He has none. He failed as a lawyer and ended up as a publican.'

She felt a strange pang of sympathy for the boy. Her mother's father had been a Liverpool publican; she might have mentioned it, if Mrs Farren hadn't been sitting there. 'Well, the theatre has its *longueurs* too; rehearsals can be a bore.'

'I imagine they must be much like sessions with a sitter,' he said. 'Frequent and arduous, but necessary if the work's to be brought to perfection. Oh, and you'll have to leave your muff with me,' he mentioned without looking up, 'for closer study.'

THE PORTRAIT sittings at Jermyn Street were frequent, but not particularly arduous, Eliza found. Tom Lawrence was a good listener and had a fund of gossip, especially about the art world. Poor Sir Joshua Reynolds was going blind, he told her as he pricked and squeezed a little bladder of paint, and Romney was a soft-hearted fool who never asked for cash up front.

She couldn't resist asking. 'Has Lord Derby paid you in advance, then?'

'Only half.'

How much was that? she wondered. Reynolds charged 200 guineas for a whole-length, but surely this newcomer couldn't ask a fraction of that—50 guineas perhaps?

'For a man of such infinite riches,' he murmured, 'the Earl's tight with his purse.'

She wondered whether to protest. 'No doubt that's how the riches stay infinite.'

'Did he give you that little ring, Miss Farren, the one with the ivory eye?'

Lawrence was unnervingly observant; she supposed it came with his trade. 'Sir, you overstep your mark.'

'Not again,' the boy cried. 'I seem to do that every time we meet.' He smirked a little, wet the tip of a brush in his stained mouth and dabbed at the canvas.

Eliza found herself gossiping shamelessly about her colleagues. 'I hear the Duke of Devonshire's managed to persuade his brother-in-law to call off his *crim con* action against Sheridan.'

'Isn't Mrs Sheridan seeking a separation, though?'

'Well, she's said to have forgiven his affair with the lovely Harriet—but last week at Crewe Hall he was caught in a bedchamber with the governess! Mrs Sheridan has all my pity,' said Eliza, shaking her head. 'I suppose she knows it's not in his nature to reform.'

'Nor in any man's,' joked Lawrence.

She gave him a severe look. 'Your sex boasts of its weakness, but I'd call it self-indulgence.' She was rather surprised at herself to be discussing such indecencies with a young man she hardly knew, but there was a strange intimacy about sitting for a portrait for hours on end at such proximity. She slid one eye towards her mother, to gauge her disapproval, but Margaret Farren was fast asleep on her stool in the corner.

Lawrence scrubbed some paint off the canvas with a rag and began to hum a tune under his breath.

'Please,' said Eliza, 'if you want this sitting to continue a moment longer don't hum that wretched song.'

He stopped, then laughed. 'Oh, yes, it's Little Pickle's, isn't it?'

'How Mrs Jordan has won such unconscionable fame by portraying a small boy who ties people's clothes together for a trick', she said, 'I can't imagine.'

A little later, to her consternation, Eliza found herself dropping the name of Anne Damer into the conversation like a baited hook. She put it all in the past tense; she was talking about the Richmond theatricals.

Lawrence didn't look up from the gaudy palette round his thumb. 'She turns all you ladies to stone,' he remarked. 'That bust of you she showed last year? Rather beautiful in a cold kind of way, but it wasn't *you*. Some anonymous goddess who'd taken possession of your skin.'

So what am I like? she wanted to ask him. She thought of the *Thalia*, which stood in the shadowy niche on her upper staircase at Green Street and reproached her silently whenever she went past. *Am I sillier than that? Plainer? Less like a goddess?* 'I scarcely see her these days,' she put in, a little hoarse, and then she felt a stab of guilt.

'Gorgeous animals, though, so furry and alive,' he conceded. 'I've a spaniel at home, I'd like to see what Mrs Damer could make of him. Not that she ever takes commissions, of course; these genteel amateurs wouldn't soil their hands with cash,' he said satirically. 'Actually, you might know, Miss Farren, is it true she uses ghosts?'

Eliza blinked at him. 'You mean...spectres?'

Lawrence let out a roar of laughter. 'No, I mean men to help her on the sly. At the Academy, some of my teachers called her a fraud—swore a woman couldn't carve marble all by herself.'

'I've watched her do it,' said Eliza frostily. 'If there are ghosts, they're invisible.'

'Oh ho,' he said, 'what an eloquent defender of your sex! A man must watch his tongue, in these days of *égalité*, or female tempers will run as high as French ones.'

Let it drop, Eliza told herself, *let it drop*. It looked bad that she got so fired up in defence of a woman who wasn't a close friend of hers any more. The important thing was that Tom Lawrence hadn't said a word against Mrs Damer's personal reputation.

But then, would he, considering that Eliza herself was implicated by that dreadful epigram?

DERBY BROUGHT the painter into the Club. He always found this helpful when negotiating with men of business; the severe architecture and atmosphere of exclusivity intimidated them. After the beefsteaks he faced his guest squarely. 'Now, what's all this about the price?'

'It's gone up,' said the boy, sipping the excellent claret.

'Has it, indeed,' Derby scoffed. 'If my memory serves, I commissioned the picture at 60 guineas—a very good rate indeed for such an untried talent.'

'Well, I'd been thinking of painting Miss Farren before that, Your Lordship,' said Lawrence, 'so I don't know that I'd call it your *commission,* exactly.'

What strange times these were. Derby was all for Reform and a more equal society, but really, had it come to this, that a young commoner could defy an earl?

'Besides, as I said in my note,' said Lawrence, 'these two other gentlemen dropped into my studio, and offered me a hundred for the picture.'

'Which gentlemen?'

'Oh, I don't think I ought to mention their names without permission,' murmured the painter, bashful.

Derby's teeth were clamped. *He reads me like a book, this sinister, ringletted pup. He sees my weakness. He hopes, by his talk of imaginary gentlemen, to make me pay a ludicrous sum for a picture of the woman I adore.* He relaxed his jaw and took a sip of claret. 'Well, in that case,' he said lightly, 'I won't stoop to squabbling.'

'You mean—' Lawrence's long lashes batted with excitement.

He thinks I'll pay a hundred or more. Time to call his bluff. 'Since you choose to break your word as a gentleman,' said Derby, 'far be it from me to prevent your turning a profit from these *other gentlemen.*'

The painter sat back, registering the insult. But it was safe enough, Derby knew. If he'd said the same thing to a man of birth, or even a fiery fellow from the professional classes, a challenge to a duel might have followed (and Derby preferred to let his birds fight for him). But it would probably never occur to the son of a tavern keeper.

Sure enough, Lawrence took on a conciliatory tone. 'Come, My Lord, you misunderstand me.'

'I do?'

'I only meant to say that the interest of these...other parties makes me hope that this will be rather an exceptional portrait. Miss Farren's ravishing beauty and expressive charms', Lawrence murmured, 'have inspired me to new heights, if I say so myself. So I thought, if perhaps you came to see the picture—I've done the face and half the body—you might wish to reward me to the tune of, say, 85 guineas?'

Derby repressed a smile. *My card.* 'I've seen it already. I called this morning and in your absence your housekeeper was good enough to show me the canvas.'

The boy's face contracted.

'I like the brushwork well enough and the originality of the composition,' Derby went on, 'but there's one thing that won't do: Miss Farren looks far too thin.'

'I paint her as she is,' said Lawrence, almost growling. 'She is of unusually tall and slender dimensions.'

'Oh, I know—there's not a woman in England like her,' said Derby, beginning to relax as the game turned his way. 'But the vagaries of fashion are currently against her special charms on this point, so you might plump her up a trifle.'

This gambit was received in silence. Derby wondered whether he'd pushed things too far; to refuse to raise the price, to criticise the painting and to imply the painter was no gentleman, all in one conversation...If these *other gentlemen* were real they might secure, for a mere 100 guineas, what was looking to be one of the strangest, loveliest portraits ever painted. His stomach began to knot. 'But of course you must do as you think proper in these matters. Ah, Bunbury!' he hailed his passing friend to create an interruption.

The Baronet turned, startled.

'How was Newmarket?'

'Rained out, shocking muddy,' said Bunbury, coming over.

The painter remembered his manners and jumped up. 'I shouldn't keep you any longer, Your Lordship.'

'Have you met young Lawrence here?' Derby asked Bunbury, deliberately avuncular. 'Only twenty years old, and a rising talent.'

'Oh, yes? Talent at what?' asked Bunbury, oblivious, and Derby bit down on a smile; it was as if they'd rehearsed the insult.

'Phiz-mongering,' said the young man drily and took his leave.

Weakening at the last minute, Derby thought of agreeing to 85 guineas. But no, that would be capitulation.

ON HER WAY out of the theatre Eliza glanced at the new playbills pasted to the door. Then she stopped and looked more closely. She ripped one off the door and went back into the building. When she swept into the manager's office Kemble was alone, looking over the accounts. He'd recently surprised them all by marrying Pop Hopkins (widow of the poor lunatic actor Brereton), the most prim and undistinguished member of the company. 'Excuse me, Kemble—' Eliza laid the bill on the desk and tapped it at the relevant spot— 'but I'm afraid there's been a printing error.'

The manager scratched his hairline. 'I believe I made an announcement on Monday that players' names will from now on be displayed in order of the *characters'* ranks, with gentry roles first.'

'Oh, I don't mind that,' she said graciously; 'my role of Miss Tittup is now listed after Mrs Hopkins playing Lady Toss, I see the logic there. But it should say, "*and*, Miss Tittup, *dot dot dot*, Miss Farren". Or, "*and* Miss Farren *as* Miss Tittup".'

Kemble cleared his throat. 'There's been a decision to remove the *ands*.'

Eliza drew herself up. 'But the *and* in italics has always been used to mark out a player of particularly distinguished reputation.'

'Not any longer. It's been agreed that—'

'Agreed by whom, you and Sheridan?'

'All Drury Lane Players will now be listed the same way on a bill, as colleagues and as equals.'

'Ridiculous,' Eliza spat. She wasn't behaving like a lady, but she couldn't help it. 'I draw the crowds, not old Mrs Hopkins or Mrs Powell. I'm better known than anyone else in this cast—' Her finger jabbed the playbill.

'Is this privilege of *ands* written in your Articles of Bond?' asked Kemble rhetorically.

'It is a matter of custom,' said Eliza through her teeth, 'and of justice.'

He looked back at her like a gloomy emperor.

'Mrs Siddons has always been indulged with the *and*,' she said, 'a lead soprano like Mrs Crouch has, Mrs Jordan has, and I have and I will. It's a simple thing to ask; a few letters, that's all. Unless Sheridan would rather mark my special status by raising my salary from £18 to, say, £20 a week?'

Kemble pretended he hadn't heard that. 'My dear Miss Farren, you know I have an infinite respect for your talents. To shield myself from the tempest of your displeasure'—oh, how he liked his metaphors, she thought—'I would have been happy to give way on this point if it were only a matter of my own whim. But this is now the policy of His Majesty's Theatre and must be applied fairly to one and all. Including, may I add, myself and my sister.'

She gave him a long, frigid look.

'And remember, Miss Farren, you're so very celebrated, so graven on the heart of every member of the audience', he added, 'that you hardly need italics to mark out your name.'

She wasn't going to win this one, she knew it in her bones. Better to keep her dignity. 'You're too kind,' she said and turned on her heel.

The Bow Window House, Green Street
My dear Mr L.,
You'll think me the most troublesome of beings I dare say, but my friends who've seen the painting (of which you've not yet allowed me a glimpse) tease me to death about looking so narrow as to seem likely to crack in two & insist on my writing to beg you to make me somewhat more substantial. For that pound of flesh I will be eternally
your grateful servant,
E. F.

When she arrived at Lawrence's studio he wasn't there; his housekeeper showed Eliza in to wait, and offered to bring some wine and cake.

'No, nothing just now.'

Only after the woman had left did Eliza realise something: she never thanked servants any more. In her early years in London she'd done it all the time—partly because she couldn't get used to being waited on by strangers, but also as a sort of superstition. She'd feared, in some crevice at the back of her mind, that if she proved arrogant and ungrateful all this luxury would be snatched away like a carpet from under her feet. Whereas now...Eliza was changed, but when had it happened? she wondered. That was the kind of detail left out of the silly verses and pamphlets that memorialised her rise to fame. Little by little, Eliza had come to feel entitled to a life of ease. Or habituated, at least. The only person she still thanked for small services was her mother—when she remembered. Mrs Farren wasn't with her today, for once, being bedridden with an inflamed toenail. How astonished the lanky Betsy banging the troupe's drum would have been if a fortune teller could have shown her this future in a cloudy glass ball: a celebrated lady, flattered and fêted on all sides, with little to worry about except whether she seemed too thin in a portrait...

'Have you seen yourself?'

She spun around. Tom Lawrence was at her shoulder; how had she not heard him? 'Good morning,' she said prettily. 'You didn't answer my note.'

'I've spent the last three days doing the landscape. People think me a careless dandy, but the truth is I work like a dog; I'm as much a slave to each painting as if I were chained to it.' He seemed in a strange humour today; could he be drunk? 'I think you're ready to face your audience.' Lawrence turned the easel round and whisked off the dust cloth.

Under brooding aquamarine clouds and low dark trees spread a carpet of moist grass and summer flowers; the effect was both blooming and menacing. There stood Eliza, pale in muslin under

her furs, shrinking back as if the warm air were her enemy. With her
bare hand she clutched her white satin cloak round her neck, its fur
edge and ties hanging; in her other hand, gloved in reddish leather,
dangled a huge fur muff. Lawrence had added a limp blue ribbon
to the muff, Eliza noticed; it picked up the sky and her eyes. This
wasn't Miss Farren of Drury Lane, this was a private person, rushing across a summer landscape in winter clothes. How had Tom
Lawrence seen such tentativeness in Eliza's eyes as she posed for
him in his studio with a worldly confidence? How had he glimpsed
the fears that she carried around like tiny pebbles in her mouth?

'Well, Eliza?'

'I look so...vulnerable,' she said, realising a second too late that
he'd had the cheek to use her first name.

'Mm,' he said, standing close to her, drinking in the picture.

For once, she wished her mother were here; she felt oddly unchaperoned. 'And where's my extra pound of flesh?' she asked, trying for flippancy.

Lawrence turned and looked into her eyes. 'I won't change a
thing. You couldn't be more beautiful,' he said fiercely and she
didn't know whether he meant her or the Eliza in the picture. 'This
image will unnerve its viewers, grab England by the throat and
make me nearly as famous as you. It'll be copied in watercolours
and engravings within a week of the Exhibition. In every drawing
room in the land your beauty will make other women tremble.'

'Mr Lawrence,' she began, stepping away.

His mouth was a pale red pout. 'And that fabulously wealthy
Whig grandee who poses as your *sincere admirer*, informs me that
60 guineas is high enough, he won't go up to 85!'

'The price is nothing to do with me.' Eliza's pulse was thumping in her neck. She couldn't bear this haggling. *Eighty-five, that's
not so very much, for Derby, she thought, why would he balk at paying
eighty-five?*

Tom Lawrence's mouth was on hers before she knew it. His
breath, his tongue burnt her. His hands were under her cloak, his
legs seized hers. He was wrenching away her muslin fichu; only

when his fingers plunged into her bodice did she manage to move. She shoved him away so hard that he staggered into his easel and the portrait fell face down on the smeared floor.

They stared at each other. *Not so frail and brittle now,* she thought. *Not a poor lost girl shuddering in the breeze.*

'I beg your pardon,' said Lawrence.

'I don't grant it.'

His eyes were full of wonder now. 'You're not cold, like they say. Not cold at all.'

Eliza shook out her cloak and put her hands in her muff, before she walked out through the door.

She was feverish with fury as she sat back in the Derby carriage and let it carry her up Dover Street towards home. The naïveté of the fellow, to think that she'd preserved her virtue for so many years, through all trials, only to give it up to a nobody like him! She examined the tear in the neck of her dress and her cheeks scalded. She couldn't remember how to be indifferent. She found a smear of green paint on her left nipple, drying to a scab.

MAY 1790

Anne woke at dawn and pulled back the curtains of her blue tester bed. On the pale-green wall opposite hung the plaster life mask of Eliza Farren. She'd put it concave side out, so it showed the smoother shadow face. It hurt her to look at it. *One of these days,* she thought, *I shall really have to have it taken down.*

Today was Opening Day at the Royal Academy Exhibition. She'd come up from Park Place to show the marble version of the bust of her mother; she was glad of the excuse to get away, since Lady Ailesbury was going through a period of *nerves.* Anne had never been clear whether her father was really oblivious of his wife's depressions—could that be true of a man so interested in the arts, so respected for his military and political achievements?—or merely pretended to be. And Lady Mary, despite her endless fund of good nature, was neglectful; she sent their mother occasional notes from Richmond House and threw out hints of visits to Park

Place, which put the Countess into a flurry of anticipation, then
never turned up. It was up to Anne to step in as Lady Ailesbury's
younger and unmarried daughter, she knew that without being
told. But her own nerves were so unreliable these days that she
found her mother's company unendurable.

Anne had been sleeping badly for months now. She blamed the
weather; her constitution needed winter sun and if it weren't for the
troubled state of France she might have thought of going on one of
her trips. Mayfair was too small. A week couldn't go by without
Anne either riding past the Bow Window House on Green Street,
or seeing Derby's open phaeton skim along Grosvenor Square, with
the two Farrens clearly visible opposite the Earl. She'd glimpsed
the party recently at the Grosvenor Chapel, one of the many private chapels in Mayfair with celebrated visiting preachers, where
the pew rents were a shocking £15 per year. The actress, entering on
Lord Derby's arm, with her mother hovering behind her, had appeared not to see Anne's face in the crowd, at first, and then had offered her the pleasant nod of an acquaintance. It was a strange
performance and it gave Anne the giddy, nauseous feeling that the
whole friendship had been a figment of her imagination.

Derby had nodded to her very warmly, but that wasn't much
comfort. On the rare occasions when she encountered him on his
own they talked of politics, or art, or philosophy. She didn't know
how to raise the topic of Eliza; though she was very fond of the
Earl, she wasn't used to speaking to him of matters of the heart.
He mentioned the actress, of course, but in his usual rattling manner—how well she'd played some new role, or looked in the latest
style of hat.

By now, all Anne's intimates knew that the friendship was at an
end. Walpole had quietly cut Miss Farren from his list. Some, like
Lady Mary, assumed that it was Anne who had tired of the actress's
company. The idea wounded her, but it was too humiliating to explain the truth. *Non finito,* she thought, remembering the old
phrase: *a sculpture interrupted, left unfinished.*

Anne couldn't stomach any breakfast today. She got to the

Royal Academy early to beat the crowds. For several minutes she
stood staring up at a canvas in the Great Saloon. The brilliant newcomer, Tom Lawrence, was showing no less than thirteen portraits,
as if to make a point of outdoing poor old Reynolds, and this one
was the best. The pose was startlingly spontaneous; there stood
Eliza Farren with one glove off, as if interrupted in the middle of a
rapid journey. She was as thin as a silver birch sapling; Lawrence
had caught all her serpentine grace. The sun was shining through
turquoise clouds and the colours sang, but she shivered in her en-
veloping cloak; it made one want to take her in one's arms and
comfort her. The brushwork was dazzling; Anne knew enough of
painting to judge that. She stood there rigid with jealousy.

At this Exhibition, only a year ago, she'd given the actress the
little gold ring with the ever-watching eye. Now she could hardly
imagine calling her by her first name. Somehow the most rich and
confiding friendship of Anne's life had slipped through her fingers.
Only dignity had prevented her from walking up to the house on
Green Street, banging on the door and demanding an explanation.
She'd searched her conscience, over the long months of their estrangement, and could only conclude that she'd been found dispos-
able. Her memory conjured up a line from *The Way to Keep Him*:
*Surely never was an unhappy woman treated with such cruel indiffer-
ence*. And another, even more pointed: *To win a heart is easy; to keep
it the difficulty*. Strange that such a lovely face as Eliza Farren's
could veil such a dark and tricky heart.

'What an engaging expression,' said a man to a woman behind
her. 'So arch, so spirited. It's the Farren to a tee!'

Anne moved off to one side as fast as she could without drawing attention to herself. She glanced down at her catalogue: *Mr
Lawrence. Portrait of an Actress*, it said.

'Signor Agostino,' she addressed the keeper, spotting him a few
minutes later, 'did Lawrence choose the title for his picture of Miss
Farren?'

Covertly he bent to her ear. 'On the contrary, Mrs Damer. The
young man has made a dreadful fuss. The title he submitted was

Portrait of a Lady, but a gentleman on the Hanging Committee said that wouldn't do, because she is a woman of no birth.'

'How dare they?' snapped Anne. '*Portrait of an Actress* sounds as if she's no better than any other strumpet who ever walked the stage. They might at least have added an adjective: *Distinguished*, or *Celebrated*. Look,' she said, tapping the page with her finger, 'even Sir Joshua's picture of Mrs Billington is called *Portrait of a Celebrated Singer*.'

'I know, it's a shocking business,' the Italian assured her, 'but nothing can be done until the catalogue goes to be reprinted. Ah, here's the lady herself,' he said, smiling past Anne's head.

She turned and there was Eliza, dressed to echo her portrait; the same gloves, the same dress and a lighter summer version of the same fur-edged pelisse. There was a little storm of applause; the actress scattered smiles and curtsies in all directions. Beside her, dwarfed by her as always but holding his right arm high to support her hand, walked Derby. His face was inscrutable, but Anne could read its private pride.

She couldn't bear it, couldn't steel herself to go and greet the happy pair as if she were yet another acquaintance. They were hemmed in by admirers and she was bone-tired. She slipped off to the little sculpture room, which held only a few stragglers, and they soon drifted off without paying much attention to the *Marble Bust of the Countess of Ailesbury*. Anne stood looking at her mother's severely handsome features; she clasped her hands and tried to calm herself. She fingered the little chip of stone from the Bastille that she wore on a chain round her neck under her fichu.

'My dear!'

She spun round. Eliza, with her doll smile painted on. *She didn't know I would be here so early in the day,* Anne thought. *She doesn't know what to call me.* 'Why do you say that?' she asked in a low voice.

The actress blinked.

'Does that word *dear* signify anything to you? Do I? If not, why say it?'

Eliza had her hand against her mouth. 'I don't know what you mean.'

'You know too well.' Anne's voice surprised her by its rage. 'I no longer claim any right to your company, or your affection, God knows'—she swallowed a sob—'but it's the inconsistency that I find outrageous. You spurn my invitations, leave my letters unanswered, cut me in the street—and then sidle up and call me *dear*!'

The younger woman's cheeks were scarlet. 'Must I remind you we're in a public place?'

'I'd have been glad to speak in private,' snarled Anne, 'but I haven't seen you in months.'

Someone came into the room, then, and both women froze. Anne turned her head and pretended to be examining a wax relief of a baby. When the intruder had gone and the room was silent again, she spoke as calmly as she could. 'All I need, all I demand to know, is what came between us?'

There was no answer from Eliza and Anne felt a moment's relief. Instead of protests and denials, was the young woman going to tell her the truth at last? What unspoken quarrel, what stupid misunderstanding had come between them? Could Eliza bring herself to open her heart to Anne and treat her as a true friend again? Perhaps she was crying. *Oh, the darling girl—*

But when Anne spun round, she found herself alone.

V

Multiple View

*A term applied to a sculpture that is meant to
be seen from various points; the viewer must
walk around it to appreciate its meaning or beauty.*

⎯⎯⎯⎯⏝⎯⎯

ONE subject, it seems, of which our readers can never have
enough to sate them is Travel. Curiosity about the manners
and *moeurs* of other lands is combined with a relish for the
surprising accidental events that befall the traveller.

Nor is mere reading of these adventures enough to please
the World. Every day the packet boats from Dover or Fal-
mouth are heavy with eager voyagers and their trunks and
carriages. An Englishman's house may be his castle, but he is
just as happy in some foreign inn, cabin, or even tent. In high
life it is not done to profess oneself content to linger on one's
estate all summer; instead, one visits friends in the Highlands,
calls in on acquaintances in Vienna or Cologne, takes the waters at Spa or climbs the rumbling slopes of Etna. The peri-
patetic life is the only truly fashionable one these days. And
one must not come back empty-handed; it's as necessary to
display a vase unearthed from Pompeii or a new dress from
Madame Bertin in Paris as to litter one's speech with *caris-
sima mia* and *enchanté*.

So far from last year's Gallic metamorphoses having put
off English visitors, they have only whetted curiosity. Even as
the French increase their fleet to be ready to offer aid to their

ally Spain against us if the Nootka Sound dispute provokes a
war, it remains a curious fact that one of the most à la mode
activities for English travellers is to visit the Revolution.

—THE BEAU MONDE INQUIRER, *July 1790*

THE STONE WAS PASSED UP THE LONG TABLE. IT WAS AN
ordinary-looking lump of grey granite, but on all sides men pressed
nearer to touch it. Sheridan, sitting across from Derby, grinned and
tossed it high in the air. It very nearly fell into a silver platter of
greasy bones; Derby snatched at it, stinging his fingers. The stone
was heavier than it looked. He relished the heft of it in his palm. A
piece of the Bastille!

He passed it up the line to Earl Stanhope, chairman of this anniversary banquet. The size of tonight's crowd was astonishing, considering it was July; the members of the World, like Derby, must
have come up to town specially for it. He hadn't seen most of his
friends since the depressing election, when despite their most passionate efforts—Georgiana had paid fifty calls a day—the Whigs
had lost a further three seats to the Tories.

There were calls for a hush. Stanhope rose to his full height, his
balding head shining like a billiard ball. 'Men of Britain,' he roared.

It was a rather odd opening, Derby thought. Perhaps the Earl
didn't want to address the crowd as *gentlemen* in the usual way?
Derby supposed there were men of trade and business among the
throng of about 700, as well as the Dissenting Ministers who were
the mainstay of the Reform movement; certainly there was a lot of
bad tailoring, and some greasy old wigs and tricorne hats. Stanhope
himself wore his hair lank and uncombed, and his cravat was askew,
as if to show that his mind was on higher things than elegance.
How mortified William Pitt must feel, Derby thought pleasurably,
that his own brother-in-law was turning into such a firebrand,
more Whiggish than the Whigs; the latest story was that Stanhope
had even renounced his carriage, among other trappings of aristocratic privilege! Derby was all for liberating and bettering the lot of

the people himself, but he didn't see why that meant he had to walk through streets as filthy as London's.

Stanhope banged his glass on the table for silence. 'I welcome all you friends of liberty to this most noble Crown and Anchor tavern—particularly the many parliamentary Members I see and even some of my colleagues from the Lords—' a warm nod each to Derby, Lauderdale and Bedford. 'Despite our differences, we're gathered here tonight to celebrate the fact that one year ago, by the honest hands of the people of Paris, was levelled the most iniquitous of dungeons, a symbol of stifling secrecy and oppression!'

'Huzza! Huzza!' Clapping and whistling.

It saddened Derby that Fox had decided it would be more politic to stay with his lovely Liz in St Anne's Hill tonight, so as not to be named in the papers as an uncritical admirer of all the startling changes France had seen over the past year; he knew the leader had to bear the nagging of colleagues like Portland who'd become persuaded by Burke's dire views on the subject.

'We lay down this Bastille stone'—Stanhope set it on the cleared tablecloth—'to invoke the Supreme Being and the spirit of Liberty. The French Revolution is complete,' he proclaimed. 'Let us drink to its high, hard-won achievements.'

The men, 700 or so, drained their glasses; it produced a curious gurgling sound, thought Derby, like the noise a school of fish might make underwater.

'In every land', Stanhope was intoning, 'men are turning to their neighbours and asking, *Where is Justice? What has happened to the universal, eternal Rights of Man?* Here in Britain, we lovers of Reform sense that the hopeful hour is at hand. It is time to light the fire of burning patriotism in every breast—to prune and renew our moribund government. Lo, the millennium approaches,' Stanhope sang out, 'and all things will be made new!'

There was a thunder of applause.

'He sounds like he's escaped from Bedlam,' Derby mouthed at Sheridan over the table.

Sheridan grinned. 'But there's no better stirrer-up. If young Willie Cherry-Pitt could hear this crowd he'd choke on his own tongue!' As soon as the clapping had subsided Sheridan was on his feet, his voice effortlessly carrying across the huge saloon. 'My Lords, gentlemen, I believe I speak for many in proposing the following resolution: *That this meeting does most cordially rejoice in the establishment of liberty in France.* All those in favour?'

'*Aye*,' came a ragged chorus.

'Anyone against?' Sheridan asked, scanning the crowd. Only a few voices muttered '*No*'. 'Then I'll send the news to my correspondents in Paris tonight.'

Derby, watching this piece of showmanship, felt slightly uneasy.

'May I add', said Stanhope, 'that I'm sure our resolution will be read to the Assembly as evidence that Englishmen will soon follow the French example and love each other as equals, friends, brothers and free men!'

'Derby.' The veteran Reformer, Horne Tooke, was tugging on his sleeve while scribbling on the margin of a letter with his other hand. 'We can't let the papers mistake our zeal for sedition. If I come up with something tactful, will you back me?'

'Very well,' he said, amused at the novelty of the Reverend being tactful.

'While sharing fully in my friends' fervour,' said Horne Tooke loudly, rising to his feet, 'might I propose a clarification, vis-à-vis our own country, as follows? *That we feel satisfaction that the subjects of England have not so arduous a task to perform as the French; but have only to maintain and improve our excellent Constitution.*'

Sheridan rolled his eyes and Stanhope frowned. There were loud hisses from several parts of the room, which caused Derby a spasm of irritation; really, some self-styled advocates of freedom didn't extend it to anyone who disagreed with them. 'I'd like to second the motion, if I may,' he said, only half rising from his seat.

Hours later, the vast crowd was dispersing, and he and Sheridan were having a last bottle in a corner, as the menservants cleared away the ruins of the banquet bit by bit, like ants. 'Oh, come on,' Derby protested, 'I had to back Tooke or the papers would call us revolutionaries and tear us to rags.'

'What do you care what's printed about you?' barked Sheridan. 'You'd still hold your seat in the Lords if you were proved to have cooked and eaten your own children.'

With his friend in such a wild mood, Derby knew it was time to change the subject. 'So how have you been amusing yourself this summer?'

'I've been trapped in the city by business,' said Sheridan. 'But I went to the trial of the Monster last week—you know, the dancing master who slashes skirts? Claimed to be mad but couldn't prove it, so they gave him six years.'

'That's rather mild,' said Derby, 'considering mere children hang for the theft of a spool of thread.'

Sheridan shrugged. 'Six years in Newgate, that's as good as a death sentence. Oh, another piquant detail: he's a member of one of those sods' clubs, where they drink tea and call each other *Molly*, that kind of thing.'

'Well, I suppose it makes sense that someone who stabs women in the thighs would be a woman hater,' murmured Derby.

'If his tastes were more in the regular line, he'd have used his own tool.' Sheridan cackled.

'Ugh! What strange times we live in.'

'Though I wouldn't hang sods myself, if I were in charge,' remarked Sheridan. 'Take my countryman, Bickerstaffe. One of Garrick's best writers—but our theatre lost him overnight when he fled to France for fear of his life, and all for poking a soldier.'

'I'd keep your voice down if I were you,' Derby told him. 'Look what trouble Burke got into for arguing against the pillory for sods. You don't want to be tarred with that brush.'

'Unlike Burke'—Sheridan grinned—'I've fucked enough women to safeguard my honour!' Now he was scanning the emptying room restlessly. 'There are faces that should have been here tonight that weren't and I don't just mean Fox's.'

'I sometimes think it must be very difficult for men who aren't rich to maintain their freedom of thought,' mused Derby. 'After all, they're constantly looking out for patronage or preferment; they depend so much on the goodwill of their superiors.'

Sheridan was wearing an odd smirk. 'Whereas an earl, for example, is above all influence?'

'Well, I suppose so. After all, he's nothing to fear, nothing he needs from anyone,' said Derby, rather regretting having brought this up.

'But mightn't his thoughts be limited to the traditional thoughts of earls?' suggested Sheridan. 'Mightn't he seek protection for his whole class and fear any attack on its position?'

Derby didn't know what to say.

'In my view the best guarantee of freedom of thought isn't wealth,' said Sheridan flatly, 'it's having known what it is to be poor and consequently being unafraid of it. Oh, good night, Bedford,' he called, waving to the young Duke, who'd contributed a staggering £3000 to their election fund, for all the good it had done them.

'Did you hear he won the Oaks for the fourth time?' asked Derby. 'It put me in the blue devils, rather, as the race is one of my own inventions, after all, and named for my villa at Epsom. Of course, Sam Chifney was Bedford's rider; I'd hire the genius myself if Prinny hadn't just put him on a retainer.'

'Surely you of all men could afford to outbid him.'

Derby snorted. 'If I wanted to alienate someone who's going to be my king, any year now!'

'Listen to us. *Any year now,*' repeated Sheridan gloomily. 'We've been saying that ever since Pitt came to power. And at the rate Prinny stuffs and soaks himself, he'll drop dead long before his father.'

Derby took out his snuffbox—painted with a miniature of Sir Peter Teazle winning the Derby—and put a good pinch on the back of his hand. Sheridan took some, without a word, and gave a convulsive sneeze.

'Say, who brought the Bastille stone, I wonder?' Derby sniffed,

enjoying the tingle in his nose; his eyes watered. 'I know Mrs
Damer has a little fragment she wears on a silver chain—several of
the ladies do—but I didn't think there were any more complete
stones to be had.'

Sheridan snorted. 'You're very gullible, old sport.'

'You mean—'

'I picked it up in my back yard this morning. Thought it would
go down well.'

'It's not real?' Derby feared that his face looked like a tricked
child's.

Sheridan shrugged. 'It's a prop; the sentiments it inspired
tonight are quite real. That's what matters, not the provenance of
some lump of rock.'

'Well, if it comes to that, Britain itself is a lump of rock, and
one to which I and my ancestors have been rather attached,' said
Derby drily.

Sheridan rolled his eyes. 'You peers of the realm. You're so
literal.'

AUGUST 1790

Anne had made the necessary changes. In her bedroom at no. 8
Grosvenor Square, for instance, there was a round mark on the
leaf-green paper, which was slightly less faded by the sun that crept
through the curtains. The life mask was in a box, in a trunk, in the
back of Anne's workshop, along with other discarded studies.

These days she avoided Drury Lane, unless it was a tragedy
with the incomparable Siddons in it. Sometimes if Anne glimpsed
Miss Farren at an assembly she went home early, pleading a
headache. If she managed to find out in advance that Miss Farren
was on the invitation list she simply sent her excuses. She took a
certain pride in not stooping to say a word against the actress; Walpole was the only friend in whom she'd let herself confide. When
others asked, *Weren't you and she once rather great confidantes?* Anne
shrugged and said that the friendship had faded, *as often happens between persons of different position, don't you find?*

Once, glimpsing the Farrens descending from the Derby carriage on Green Street, Anne went rigid with rage. Why had she ever risked befriending a young woman whose birth, education and principles were so utterly unlike her own? Above all, in what reckless moment had she encouraged that person and her gargoyle of a mother to move to Mayfair, and set up house around the corner?

Park Place was somnolent in August. Anne read her mother Bruce's *Travels to Discover the Source of the Nile*. She hadn't gone abroad in almost two years. Her health was pretty sound, considering, but there was always the danger that if she stayed in England right through another winter her lungs might succumb. Perhaps she should consult Dr Fordyce?

Gazing out through the rain-striped window, she let her eyes unfocus. Later she should stir herself and go for a walk. She would have to stop avoiding the routes she had taken with Eliza Farren on that visit to Park Place three summers ago. It was one thing to be a woman of sensibility and another to be prey to every passing emotion, every upsetting memory.

She slept in her old room. The familiar walls, hung with faded prints on ribbons, linked by stencilled outlines, gave her the vertiginous feeling that the last thirty years hadn't happened. She'd never been married, never widowed, never set up housekeeping on her own, made her own friends, carved out a place in the world. Anne was the Countess's girl again, a maker of light conversation, a holder of coloured worsteds, a fourth at cribbage.

Her note must have sounded rather desperate, because it brought Walpole down within the week. 'I'm so very grateful,' she told him again, under parasols on the terrace. 'The other day I was telling the maid how to clean the bust I brought down after the Exhibition and you know what Mother said? *It will do nicely for my tomb.*'

Walpole grimaced. 'It's a strange thing that solitude and reflection—which are often the best medicines for strong characters like yours and mine—only make Lady Ailesbury worse.'

'Yes, she starves for congenial company. And Father's overjoyed you're here too, of course,' Anne added. 'He says it's too long since

Horry and Harry rambled through the woods together.' Here she was exaggerating, because the Field Marshal, busy with improvements to his lavender still, had greeted his cousin with an absent-minded handshake.

Walpole considered his swollen foot. 'I'm not sure I'm up to *rambling...*'

'Oh, I meant it figuratively. The footmen could carry you in your chair.'

'It's been a melancholy summer, then?'

She knew he was thinking of the actress; his pouched eyes rested on her tenderly. 'Well. *Sweet are the uses of adversity,* as the saying goes.'

'Now I myself have had the great good fortune, in my seventy-third year, to make the friendship of a whole family,' said Walpole.

Anne arranged her face pleasantly, but she could tell what was to come: gloating about the Berrys. They were his latest craze, more preoccupying—but mercifully cheaper—than china, painted glass, or the hair of dead kings.

Mr Robert Berry, a widower in humble circumstances with two daughters, had taken a house on Twickenham Common. 'They come to me every Sunday evening for conversation. They're not of the World, to be sure, but Mr Berry is indubitably a gentleman. It's a tragic story, stop me if I've told you before...'

What a shock he'd get if I did, Anne thought.

'Berry's a smiling fellow, never says a word—but must be counted a hero in his own way; he met a woman with no fortune and married her for love. Well, the uncle was incensed, cut him off without a penny,' said Walpole with a storyteller's relish. 'The impoverished beauty died, as an evil fate would have it; the widower cherished her memory and nobly refused his uncle's command to make a second marriage. So the brother got the uncle's whole fortune instead, and grudgingly tossed Berry and his girls an allowance of a mere £800 a year, only to avoid the censure of the neighbours!'

Anne felt a small pang of sympathy at this point; that was less than a sixth of her own income and she had no dependants.

He was on to the Misses Berry now. 'Such sensibility and such wit,' he crowed. 'Miss Mary has the face of a heroine in a sentimental novel, but none of the foolishness. I've found out, quite by chance, that she's a perfect Frenchwoman and a Latinist besides, with a very penetrating intelligence for one so young. In fact, she reminds me of no one so much as you, Anne.'

She gave the appropriate smile. Was she being replaced?

'Miss Agnes is clever too, in a milder style, and works wonders with her pencil. Really, they're the most accomplished and agreeable young creatures I ever met. Entirely natural and unaffected, too. They're two pearls, don't you see, that I found in my path.'

'You're a born collector,' she teased him. They sounded like pert little horrors to her. It was the story of those milkmaid poetesses all over again; would the Berrys' talents earn so much praise if the girls weren't so poor? 'Tell me,' she went on slyly, 'if Miss Berry—the elder—is so very beautiful, how is she still unmarried past twenty-five?'

Walpole's little eyes blinked. 'Why, my dear, she's devoted to her family.'

'Mightn't she have served them better by finding a rich husband who could offer them all a home?'

'I—now you ask, I hardly know how to answer you. I don't know whether she's had proposals; they live very quietly. Perhaps her brilliance intimidates young men,' he suggested uneasily.

Stop it, Anne told herself. Poor Miss Berry was probably a harmless country spinster with a mole on her nose. Anne was behaving like some jealous widow. All this gushing on Walpole's part was reminding her of the era when every letter of his had contained some high-pitched reference to his goddaughter's *extraordinary talents* and *luminous graces*. But she could hardly expect to be anybody's protégée any more; she was past forty.

His trembling fingers were shuffling through his watered silk pocketbook. 'Here's one of her verses in response to mine, I had Kirgate print it up on the press at Strawberry Hill.'

Anne accepted the paper.

Far in a wood, not much exposed to view,
With other forest fruit two Berries grew…

Her eyes skipped down the lines. Here came *a wandering sage*—
Walpole, of course—who tasted the fruit and sang its glories.

The Berries, conscious all this sudden Name
Proved not their value, but their Patron's fame—
Conscious they only could aspire to please
Some simple Palates satisfied with ease…

'Isn't that charming, the final couplet?' asked Walpole, tapping the
paper with a knob-knuckled finger.

…No greater honours anxious to obtain,
But still your favourite Berries to remain.

'Charming,' she echoed, but privately she thought *coy stuff.*
He struck. 'So may I introduce them, when you come at the
end of the month?'
'Am I coming at the end of the month?'
'Evidently, my dear, since that's when you're to meet the Berrys.'
Anne laughed in capitulation.

THE HOUSEKEEPER at Strawberry Hill, Margaret Young, led her
through the star chamber to the long gallery, wheezing a little.
Anne hadn't been in the gallery for some time; the crimson damask
walls, mirrored recesses and tables of ancient busts made her smile.
Faustina, Julia Maesa, Zenocrates, Domitilla, Antonia Claudii
Mater…These inscriptions had been her nursery rhymes.
'We spied your carriage through the windows,' cried Walpole,
beckoning her over to his chaise to be kissed. 'Oh, splendid, you've
brought Fidelle; Tonton's been so looking forward to playing with
her.'
'Hunting her like a rabbit, you mean,' she said, keeping the
little greyhound safe in her arms as the black spaniel ran and
yapped at Anne's silk skirts.

Walpole let out a titter and the middle-aged man beside him joined in. The girls were wearing white chemise gowns with broad matching hats and blue ribbons; they were clearly aiming for a rural look, with no pretensions to elegance, Anne thought during the introductions and handshakes.

'I was just explaining about the ceiling,' said Walpole, craning up so his Adam's apple bulged in the folds of his throat. 'It's an exact copy of the fan vaulting from Henry VII's chapel, Miss Agnes, except not in heavy stone or plaster, but in papier mâché— to my mind the most marvellous of modern discoveries.'

'What about electricity, or balloon flight,' Anne teased him, 'or false teeth?'

'The first two are mere games,' he scoffed, 'and a man who cleans his teeth will never lose them'—baring his own in a grin.

Miss Agnes mentioned that she should like to draw the vaulting. 'My sister is learning perspective,' Miss Berry told Anne. She was a little bird of a thing, with dark eyes and a surprisingly deep voice with a trace of Yorkshire in it.

'And a marvellous thing too,' cried Walpole, 'since young ladies can never have too many inner resources.'

'They're more necessary to our sex than weapons to yours,' said Miss Berry.

'But so many of our ranks seem to get by on cards and scandal,' Anne remarked lightly.

'Two things my sister and I despise.'

Anne felt rather rebuffed. She hoped the Misses Berry wouldn't prove to be stern Evangelicals, like that ghastly Hannah More; Walpole's taste for female company was sometimes really too broad.

Mrs Young came in with a footman staggering under the weight of a great tea kettle and she lit the spirit lamp. While they were waiting for the water to boil, Anne decided that the father was a mute, round-faced puppet. He'd been trained to the law but never practised it, she learned, and she could see why. Agnes Berry had a sensible, composed face and dainty movements, but less conversation than her sister.

After tea they went walking in the grounds, which were looking rather overgrown and shabby, but still charming; Walpole had a
passion for trees and let them spread wherever they liked. Wild
strawberries poked up through the grass. Anne went in pursuit of
Fidelle, through the avenue of lime trees by the Thames. She heard
steps behind her and the elder girl caught her up. 'You must loathe
us, Mrs Damer,' she said rather breathlessly.

Anne stared.

The little creature wasn't scared off. 'Mr Walpole has been kind
enough to praise us so excessively—both to our faces and, I know,
in his correspondence—that you must wonder what he sees in a
very ordinary family.'

'Fidelle,' cried Anne, clapping her hands, playing for time. 'Are
you fishing for a compliment, Miss Berry?'

'Not at all.' The fine brown eyes met Anne's.

*The same colour as mine, but several shades darker. A much neater
face; symmetry, that's the first principle of beauty. Pallor; has she a
bronchial constitution? It undercuts the sweetness of the features, makes
them more interesting.* 'Wouldn't you agree, then,' she went on,
deadpan, 'that as my cousin devotes the greatest part of his praises
to your beauty in particular, and your brilliance, that most of my
putative loathing for your family should be yours too?'

'I suppose it should.'

Anne dissolved into a soft laugh. 'I'm glad we've settled that.'
The tiny dog raced out of a bush, yipping with excitement, and
stood on two legs to claw at Miss Berry's white skirts. 'Fidelle, stop
it—' Oh, no, the dog had attached herself to the girl's shin and was
humping it unmistakably. Anne ran over. 'Miss Berry, I'm truly
mortified. She almost never—Fidelle!'

The girl had already bent and wrapped the dog up in her arms.
'No need to apologise. They crave affection; don't we all?'

Well, not so Evangelical after all. 'You're very kind,' said Anne
foolishly.

The dog twisted and whimpered with pleasure. 'What a lean
little dancer! She's all muscle, isn't she,' said Miss Berry, her cheek

against Fidelle's coat, 'and such an elegant, cool little nose. I've never seen an Italian greyhound this silvery colour. Is that a break in her tail, where it curls up?'

Observant, too. 'Yes, they're often damaged during birth. Fidelle's usually shy with strangers, but she's taken to you at once.'

'We used to have a dog,' said Mary Berry, her voice painful.

They were walking side by side now, along the river bank. 'Are you interested in horticulture?'

'I expect I would be, if I'd ever had a settled home,' said the young woman, setting Fidelle down and picking up a fat acorn. 'Some of the houses we've rented have had gardens, but it hardly seems worthwhile planting a tree if you don't expect to taste its fruit.'

'Well put,' said Anne. 'I grow some vegetables at the back of my house in Grosvenor Square, but I don't take any trouble with flowers.'

'You have your art,' the girl reminded her. 'Why cultivate a transient bloom when you can carve an immortal one?'

Anne's mouth twisted with amusement. 'I'm not sure I've ever carved a flower, now I come to think of it. Some laurel wreaths, that's all. You'd be surprised to learn what a filthy, tiring pastime sculpture is.'

'More than a pastime, surely?'

'Well, yes, I think of it as my profession, but I'm not sure the members of the Royal Academy would agree. My status there is *Honorary Exhibitor.*'

'I should have thought what mattered was your status not in their eyes but in posterity's,' said Mary Berry.

Anne smiled again. 'The young are always so idealistic.'

'Rather, I've so little opinion of this life that I take a longer view, trusting to posterity to make up some losses,' said the girl darkly. Anne looked at her sideways. 'I've never felt young. I consider this existence—what's Hobbes's phrase?—nasty, brutish and short. Are you appalled?'

'Intrigued, rather,' Anne told her. 'My cousin Walpole said nothing about your saturnine philosophy.'

'I don't believe I've ever shared it with him.'

Anne was aware of a small surge of pleasure. 'Why not?'

The girl shrugged. 'It's not a matter of hypocrisy, but of adapting the conversation to the listener. Mr Walpole likes me to sparkle, so I do my best; he says glumness is only suited to old curmudgeons. Whereas you, Mrs Damer—'

'Yes, what of me? As you don't know me yet, how can you guess how you should please me?'

'I know you've suffered.'

Anne narrowed her eyes at her. How could the girl have any idea—

'Being widowed so young.'

'Ah, yes.' She ducked under a low branch and turned to hold it up for Miss Berry. 'Candid. That's how you should be with me.'

The young woman nodded, as if making a note of it.

'And what's your chief pastime, as we've discussed mine already?'

'I have none. None that are meant to pass the time, that is; the time passes too quickly already,' said Miss Berry. 'Self-education is all that interests me. I'm still trying, at the advanced age of twenty-seven, to fill the dreadful gaps in knowledge left by my sporadic schooling.'

She seemed younger than that, thought Anne; there was a clean, unworldly air about her. But also wiser than her years. 'An admirable aim. So it wasn't at a tutor's knee that you read Hobbes?'

'No, it was in your cousin's library, not a fortnight ago.'

Anne laughed. 'Strawberry Hill's a treasure chest, isn't it?'

'A small but perfect paradise!'

'I'm delighted that you and your sister have the run of the place, now poor Horry is so often confined to his chair.'

'Horry?'

'My father and Mr Walpole were always great friends, they used to call each other not Horace and Henry, but Horry and Harry.'

'*Were* great friends?' Miss Berry had a penetrating way of repeating a word, as if nothing could slip past her. 'But I believe your father's still alive.'

'Well, you know what advancing age does.'

'You think all friendships fade, Mrs Damer?'

The blunt question was unsettling. Could the girl read her mind? That was exactly what she'd been wondering this summer, every time she'd woken up and remembered the friend she'd so inexplicably lost; every time she'd driven past the Bow Window House on Green Street. Could affection last, could it bear one's weight, or was one better off relying entirely on one's own strength? 'In my experience,' she said a little hoarsely, 'many intimacies shrivel like daisies because of some inherent weakness, rather than the passage of time. But in the case of my father and Walpole, I'd call it a strong devotion that has lost some of its brightness. They rarely meet, these days, you see, and meeting is the lifeblood of friendship.'

'What about correspondence?' asked the girl. 'Can't two people become almost closer through a frank exchange of letters than in the shallowness of social intercourse?'

Anne looked at her hard. 'I suppose so. But my father and Walpole don't write to each other much either; I think their friendship lives on in their heads like a memory of youth. Sometimes I feel they've carried on their great intimacy through me.'

'Quite a responsibility,' said Miss Berry, nodding. 'For my poor father I think sometimes I'm my mother come back to life, to soothe and organise him. Each generation is the page on which the last one writes.'

'Whom are you quoting now?'

'No one,' said the girl, a little pink.

When the Berrys had gone home, Anne stayed on by an evening fire in the library. '*Now* you understand,' said Walpole triumphantly.

'Oh, I do, I do,' said Anne. 'I renounce all my prejudice. I should have let you introduce me the day after you'd met them.'

'My dear,' he said, seizing her hands in his. 'It's like discovering a mutual taste for some obscure branch of art.'

'Miniature still lives, on ivory,' she suggested.

'Yes, something with fruit in it!'

'Is Miss Berry—Miss Mary Berry—your favourite?' she asked, sure she knew the answer.

'Oh, I have no favourite,' he protested with a fey expression. 'The girls are equally meritorious.'

Walpole was deluding himself, Anne thought, but that was a common activity of humankind.

He leaned forward. 'I sometimes address them as my *daughters*, or even my *Rachel* and *Leah*. I'd hate to be suspected, at my age, of the affectation of playing the gallant.' He tittered. 'But I believe I'm safe from that charge, since I divide my devotion so evenly between the two. I assure you, if there were but one Berry girl I should be ashamed to be so strongly attached, but being quite in love with both my *little wives* I glory in my passion!'

Anne smiled, unsettled. She'd known his feelings for the Berrys were warm, but not that they were so flirtatious. It seemed rather bizarre, in a septuagenarian gentleman, to fix on two impoverished girls in such a besotted way. Something else was troubling her: she'd never thought of her cousin as a woman's man exactly. Womanish in some ways, yes, with his fussy habits and shrill laugh, and a great friend to women, of course. But hadn't the finest feelings of his heart been expended on friends of his own sex? Gray, the poet, for one, in their youth; and of course Anne's father. There'd never been any question of marriage for Walpole, or none that she knew of. Surely he wasn't thinking of it now, with his jokes about *little wives*? The other day he'd seemed troubled at the idea of Miss Berry having suitors; could it possibly be jealousy? Had Walpole's heart, so long wrapped up in cotton wool in his miniature castle, been won by a woman at last?

'You know,' she remarked, looking up at the painted crusaders on the ceiling, 'when I was very small and came here for summers while my parents were abroad I used to think you were my father.'

He yelped with laughter. 'Nothing is certain in this life—except that I've never begotten a child.'

'Well, I felt more yours than theirs. I had the impression that you'd given me to them to raise—'

'What lurid storybooks had you been reading?'

'—and it was a secret between us all. Every now and then you'd wink at me, or put your finger to your lips, and I'd *know*.'

Making her way to the red bedchamber that night, through the succession of narrow rooms crammed with *objets de virtu*, Anne thought that in some ways this was her true home—far dearer to her from her earliest childhood, far more magical, than Park Place. She tried to imagine Strawberry Hill run by a mistress, a young Mrs Walpole with brown eyes. Surely her cousin wouldn't be so defiant of the World, so reckless of propriety, as to try to marry his Elderberry? The thought choked her, somehow.

SEPTEMBER 1790

> *26 North Audley Street*
> *Being eager to leave our names at your door, Mrs Damer, I took the liberty of asking Mr Walpole where you lived. This card will tell you where you may find the undersigned, your humble servts,*
>   *Miss Berry*
>   *Miss Agnes Berry*
>   *Robert Berry, Esq.*

Every few days, now, Anne had herself driven or rowed up the Thames to Strawberry Hill. Walpole remarked teasingly that he hadn't seen so much of her since she was three years old.

Though the Berrys had moved back to town at the end of the summer, when Miss Berry found them some lodgings on North Audley Street, Anne preferred to see them in the countryside where they were all more at ease. At Strawberry, Mr Berry seemed less intimidated by the Honourable Mrs Damer and Miss Agnes didn't risk being frightened into silence by a swooping visit from the Duchess of Richmond. They all spent many afternoons together strolling in the meadows that sloped down from the terrace to the river, or (if the skies darkened) looking through Walpole's collections of prints, drawings and curiosities. Anne kept a covert eye on her cousin, wondering how this new hobby of his twilight years would play itself out. Her initial alarm had calmed; she was fairly sure now that he wouldn't joke about Miss Mary being his *amour* or his *rib* if he had any serious intentions.

Anne hadn't yet had what she'd call a conversation with Mr Berry, but she didn't take it personally. He preferred to sit on the edge of the group, buried in Gothic novels from a circulating library, looking up occasionally to nod at a joke he hadn't quite heard. In private, Anne and Walpole laughed over the fellow's tastes; a more harmless connoisseur of the morbid and macabre could not be imagined. His tragic history of disinheritance and widowhood didn't seem to have subdued his spirits at all, but there was a certain smiling fatalism about him that suggested he was incapable of being the real head of the family.

Miss Agnes didn't speak very much either, but what she did say was intelligent enough; she deferred to her sister Mary on any knotty point. Anne encouraged her in her sketching and offered some small suggestions about the framing of a composition, which Agnes accepted immediately.

'If it came to it,' Miss Berry told Anne one day when they were alone in the orchard, 'my sister could go to work for an engraver, colouring in prints.'

Anne was startled. 'If it came to what, may I ask?'

'A visit by the bailiffs to carry away the sofa and writing desk and beds. All we have is our £800 a year,' the girl said bluntly.

'Couldn't Mr Berry...' Her voice trailed off.

'Mrs Damer, my father is the best of men, but providence hasn't granted him any connections, nor marketable talents. No, Agnes will have to use up her sight in an engraver's studio and I—perhaps I'll be a governess.'

A bubble of laughter escaped from Anne's lips. 'I do beg your pardon,' she said through her fingers, 'it was just the tone of intense bitterness with which you said that word! I suddenly pictured you *growling* at some viscount's children.'

Miss Berry's face broke into a smile. 'You're right. I'd certainly hate them and might prove a tyrant. Perhaps I should think of another job.'

'Perhaps', Anne suggested, tossing her a little scarlet windfall, 'you shouldn't think so much.'

'Impossible, I'm afraid.' Miss Berry polished the apple on her linen sleeve. 'It's the only real talent I seem to possess. I can fret in English, French, Italian, Latin and somewhat in Greek.'

'Why borrow trouble?' asked Anne. 'Unless there are terrible debts? You mentioned the bailiffs—'

'They're hypothetical. I'm just fearful for the future; we've bought nothing we can't afford, yet.'

'What a refreshingly honest attitude! And all too rare, I'm afraid. Though Eliza—' Anne stopped herself just in time. Miss Berry was looking at her. 'A former friend used to say the same thing,' she went on awkwardly. 'I'm not quite so scrupulous myself, but I pay all my bills in the end. In the Beau Monde, you know, money's a sparkling liquor that's poured from cup to cup, with a great deal of spillage. Why, the Duchess of Devonshire once asked me for £50 at an assembly, lost it on the faro table and never remembered the matter afterwards!'

Mary Berry's eyes were round. The sum had actually been £100, but Anne had halved it to shock the girl less. After a minute she bit into the apple. 'My sister Agnes doesn't brood as I do; her mind is more cushioned. She doesn't even dread thunderstorms!'

'I love them,' Anne told her.

'No!' The girl was pale.

'It's nature's concerto and all performed free,' Anne told her. 'In fact, don't those dark clouds in the west look promising?'

Mary spun round to examine the afternoon sky, which was quite clear. 'Mrs Damer,' she said, turning back, 'that was a lie.'

Anne laughed. 'And not the last you'll ever hear from my lips.'

Later on, when Agnes was drawing some cows—her father by her side, armed with a sharp stick—Walpole hobbled out to join Anne and Miss Mary on the terrace in the shade of his great oak. 'The slaves of Martinique are engaged in a bloody uprising,' he announced with grim relish, waving a letter. 'I blame this *levelling* infection that's spreading from France. For instance, one of my Paris correspondents tells me that the Assembly has decreed women are to testify in court, just like men, and inherit equally from their fathers!'

'Now that sounds eminently sensible,' murmured Anne, to make trouble.

Walpole goggled at her. 'If you cast aside distinction between the sexes, Frenchwomen will lose all the protection, all the special status their English sisters enjoy.'

'I don't see why I shouldn't testify in court,' she remarked. 'After all, I'm better educated than nine-tenths of the men who presently do. So is Miss Berry, for that matter,' she said, to draw her in, but the girl kept her eyes on the grass.

Walpole looked uneasily between them. 'As for the Marquis de Condorcet, with his call for the suffrage to be extended to women—now, that's an assault on nature!'

'Well, yes, there Condorcet exceeds himself a little.' anne laughed. 'But his theory of the equality of the sexes is a refreshing one. Miss Berry, are you aware of the Marquis's writings? He says that if we suppose human beings to have natural rights, we must grant them to *all* human beings.'

'Rights to eat and sleep, perhaps,' cried Walpole, 'but would he extend the franchise to savages and make naked Hottentots line up to elect their own Member?'

'You've chosen the most absurd example you can find,' Anne protested. 'But with regard to women, Mrs Macaulay argues that we've no proof of any real difference between the sexes except the physical, and we should try the experiment of educating boys and girls the same way.'

A snort from Walpole. 'The historian you cite is best known for eloping with a man twenty-six years her junior!'

'Perhaps,' said Anne, nettled, 'but her point stands. For instance, Miss Berry and I both care more for Latin than for needlework; that's an assault on tradition, perhaps, but hardly on nature. What do you say?' she asked the young woman.

'Nothing, till I'm better informed on the subject.'

Anne felt unaccountably irritated. 'Condorcet asks why exclude women from politics for their liability to...to feminine indispositions,' she said, hoping the phrase was discreet enough, 'when men aren't barred by their tendency to gout, say.'

'Oo, you touch me in a sore point there!'

She laughed with him.

'But my dear Anne, we wouldn't dream of excluding the ladies from politics,' Walpole went on. 'Why, your friend Georgiana, or Lady Gordon in Pitt's camp, are at the heart of everything political in this country, without ever needing such a lowly tool as a vote.'

When he'd gone in—insisting that he'd send shawls out to protect the ladies from the evening air—Anne said, 'You never dispute with him, do you?'

'I wouldn't dream of it.'

'But why swallow your true views? Walpole doesn't mind arguing with me, as you can see; he takes pleasure in the sport and doesn't try to exclude our sex from *that* realm.'

Mary Berry was examining her knuckles. 'You're his cousin. His equal.'

'Come now, none of that. Condorcet would say you have the intrinsic human right to an opinion.'

'Not to express it, though, when it's barely formed. Not when I've got it out of one of Mr Walpole's own books, half a day before!'

'Oh, this is nonsense,' said Anne, seizing her hand. 'You're a thoughtful young woman. Tell me honestly, what do you think of the Revolution?'

There was a pause. Mary Berry was staring at something; Anne turned to see the tiny figures of Agnes and Robert Berry walking up the meadows, arm in arm. The girl spoke almost painfully. 'I consider it the most thrilling event in human history.'

Anne let out a long laugh.

Miss Berry squeezed her hand. 'I feel just what you were saying the other night at dinner, Mrs Damer: that the world is being hammered out afresh in some extraordinary forge.'

'There, I knew it!' She shivered a little; the evening was turning damp. 'So why didn't you say a word in my defence?'

'You needed no defending. Besides, Mr Walpole's been so very good to my family. He's...more than a friend.'

Anne's heart thudded. Surely not. The girl couldn't mean there'd been a proposal?

'He's our constant benefactor. He sends a brace of pheasants up to North Audley Street one day, a crate of French wines the next,' said Mary Berry almost angrily. 'We roam at will through his library and print room. Out of sheer kindness he acts as tutor, guide and mentor. I believe he means to pull us up above our present rank into the World, by his efforts alone! He introduces us to the best of acquaintance and speaks more highly of us that we can deserve.'

'You're too modest,' Anne told her. 'I don't think he acts out of sheer kindness.'

Miss Berry glanced at her, eagle-eyed.

'My cousin is a passionate lover of merit, wherever it lies, and in you he finds intelligence, integrity and beauty fused.'

The girl blushed so purple that Anne was about to apologise, but Miss Berry spoke. 'When I was an infant, someone said to my mother that I looked set to be handsome. My mother said, "All I pray heaven is for her to have a vigorous understanding." Isn't that a remarkable prayer from a mother who was only eighteen?'

Anne nodded. 'Did she tell you that?'

'No, my father did. I was only three when Mother died in giving birth to our sister—as the baby would have been,' she finished awkwardly.

'Do you remember anything of her?'

Mary Berry stared into the distance. 'I can see a thin woman in a green gown—pea-green—and I wanted to go to her, but she was ill and I was sent to play outside.'

'My dear girl!'

Then the other Berrys were on them and all the talk was of cows, and cross-hatching, and the warming effects of tea.

LETTERS, crusted with sealing-wax, piled high on their desks.

M., I shall be at home the whole day, so come if you can, either soon, or late, or when you please.

You left your Mount Etna fan here at Audley Street last night, dear A., have you missed it yet? I don't enclose it, because it must be collected in person.

M., tell your naughty sister from me that she mustn't break in on your Italian studies with her talk of 'shopping', or she'll be visited with some dire vengeance out of Dante!

A., were I not confined with one of my dreadful stomachaches I'd be tucked into a corner of your workshop at this moment, watching you finish your father's retriever. I do hope he passes uncracked through the kiln. I'd give anything for a vocation like yours—some vessel to contain my brimming thoughts and feelings.

Oh, dearest M., you're not near thirty yet! I can imagine you maturing into a woman of letters, what do you say to that? Come and discuss it over cherry cake.

It was all very strange and quite simple. They were thirteen years apart, not to mention the difference in wealth, but their minds were hand and glove. This was wholly different from the Farren affair, Anne assured herself. This time she was standing on solid ground; this time there weren't the complications of celebrity and (she could admit it now) infatuation. Mary Berry had the most candid eyes Anne had ever seen; brown and clear like bog water. Fidelle adored her, had done from their first meeting and dogs always knew. This young woman cared nothing for her own face and everything for knowledge. Instead of the silky, glittering charms of an actress, Mary had intellect and wit, a tender heart and a black-edged

melancholy that was startling in one so young. And here was another sign: Anne couldn't remember when they'd slipped into the
use of first names without either of them ever having asked or offered permission. *This time,* she thought, *there are no masks.*

Agnes and Robert Berry were delighted by the intimacy that
had sprung up between their Mary and the famous sculptor—and
as for Walpole, he was in ecstasies. It was more than he'd dreamed
for two of his favourite ladies to become so devoted to each
other—like Claire and Julie in Rousseau's novel, he suggested, with
himself as the aged Wolmar.

Anne was in her library, puzzling over a passage from the
Odyssey, when Mary burst in. 'I had to see you.'

'I'm glad to hear it,' said Anne, putting a ribbon in the book
and rising to take her hands.

'There's something you don't know. We—my sister and father
and I—have for some months been thinking of going abroad.'

'Marvellous,' said Anne automatically. 'Italy?' The girl's face lit
up at the magic word. 'A month or two?'

'No,' said Mary. There was a pause. 'Perhaps a year.'

Anne's heart sank. Of all the cruel accidents of timing. Was this
friendship to end as soon as it had begun?

'We mean to go through France,' said Mary excitedly, 'and then
winter in Florence, or perhaps Pisa. The climate will do my constitution good and Agnes's too.'

It was true, neither of the Berry girls could be described as
sturdy; Mary had weak lungs as well as her sensitive stomach, and
Agnes's skin and mood both suffered in the cold. And travel was the
universal panacea. But a whole year... 'The South might offer a
more beneficial air than Tuscany,' she said dully, 'but then Tuscan art
is sovereign for the spirits. I know Florence has always lifted mine.'

'My family took a long trip to Italy when I was twenty,' said
Mary, 'and I date my real life from that point.'

Ann nodded. 'One feels freer there, somehow.'

'I knew you'd understand. And also the matter of expense,' said
Mary awkwardly. 'Our rent in North Audley Street is really too

much for us. Our little subsistence will stretch much further on the Continent; even with the costs of travel we should be more comfortably off than in England.'

Anne had to bite her tongue. Of course she'd be glad to help in the case of any financial embarrassment, and Walpole would too. But the Berrys would never be able to bear that; Mr Berry had the dignity of the nephew of a rich man and Mary had such stern views on debt.

'Mr Walpole will be anxious, of course,' said Mary, looking into her lap. 'That's why Agnes and I have agreed not to mention it to him till the very end of the month—to put off the evil hour.'

The end of the month. So soon.

'I must tell you', said Mary rapidly, 'half my heart refuses to go. My greatest regret will be the loss of your company.'

Anne's eyes were wet; she blinked.

'If I didn't think it for the good of my family in every way—' Mary broke off. 'May I trust you'll be my chief correspondent?'

'Oh, I don't know,' said Anne with a theatrical frown, 'what with the price of paper these days...'

Mary's laugh emerged like a flower.

But Anne's heart was loud in her throat. She was wondering *why not?*. What was there to stop her from travelling with the Berrys? Why not leave England behind for a year and see her beloved Tuscany again, but this time showing each arch, each canvas, each hill to Mary?

THAT AFTERNOON, washing the dried clay off her hands, Anne found herself making wonderful plans. Her parents would complain of her absence, but they knew Italy had always been good for her and she was sure Dr Fordyce would agree.

Mrs Moll brought up the post on a silver salver. There was a letter from one of Walpole's distant relatives asking for her support for a Society for Bettering the Conditions of the Poor—its main aim was to teach them how to make soup—and a second cover, in an odd, convoluted hand Anne didn't recognise. The blob of red wax had no imprint. The page, opened out, bore some kind of verse, just four short lines.

> *Her little stock of private fame*
> *Will fall a wreck to public clamour,*
> *If Farren leagues with one whose name*
> *Comes near—aye, very near—to DAMN HER.*

Anne sat down in a high-backed chair and read it again. Then one more time. She didn't understand. Or rather, she recognised what was hinted at all too well, like a nightmare come back in broad daylight—but hadn't those obscene rumours been banished long ago? That was all part of the bizarre aftermath of John's suicide; it had been a dozen years at least since the publication of those filthy pamphlets. Anne had lived through the whole ludicrous episode and lived it down; she believed she'd retained the respect of everyone who mattered. She hadn't thought of this dreadful subject—or rather, let herself think of it—in years. But *a word published can't be recalled,* as Horace put it. Why now, though? Why was this coming back to haunt her at forty-one? What could she have done to provoke this malice?

Anne read the nasty verse again, trying to be rational. It didn't say much in itself; it only gestured at the old rumours. To say that her company might *damn* the actress only meant something to those who knew what it meant already. But that was small consolation; a story this peculiar spread very easily. Oh, the foul injustice of the thing!

Who could have written it? Possibly her old enemy, William Combe, the hack with the grudge against her whole family. As far as Anne knew, he'd been the first to call her such names. But whyever would he start up his mad campaign again so many years later? It mightn't be Combe at all; there was no scarcity of scurrilous wits in London, God knew. Some of them maintained that carnal knowledge between females was impossible—but they kept on writing about these *impossibilities* nonetheless. Anne couldn't say whether it was possible or not; she had no information on such topics and no curiosity. She suspected the whole thing was an obscene fantasy of newspaper men, merely a novel way of attacking famous women. Lady Eleanor Butler and Miss Ponsonby, for instance, two Irish cousins living in famously hermitic quietude in the Vale of Llangollen, had recently been made the subject of a sneering attack in the *Evening Post*.

But the fact that Anne wasn't the only victim of such abuse was little comfort. She read the horrible epigram again. It struck her that it sounded more like a warning to Miss Farren than a denunciation of Mrs Damer. If so, it was puzzlingly belated; for this verse to have been composed over a year ago, when she and the actress had been visibly devoted to each other, now that would have made some kind of sense—but what could have provoked it now, when all friendship between them was over? This was salt in an old wound.

And then she thought of something. Had Eliza Farren heard this verse already, or received an anonymous copy in the post? As early as last summer, even? If she'd guessed what it meant—or had it explained to her, God forbid—that could account for her having turned so cold and pulled away from Anne. Yes, it was all coming clear. It was even some kind of paltry relief to Anne to find a plausible reason for the collapse of that friendship. Instead of blaming herself, or Eliza, Anne could blame the enemy—the man (or even woman, she supposed) who'd cut through their bond with one slash of a wanton pen.

But still she puzzled over something: why had the mysterious enemy sent this verse to her now? She and the actress hadn't met in many months; there was no need to warn Anne to stay away from her. Was it simply meant to hurt?

Or did it refer, obliquely, to a newer friendship? Her heart leapt into her throat nearly choking her. *Not Mary*. Miss Berry was an innocent newcomer on the outer fringes of the World. What did anyone care whether Mrs Damer befriended her? How could such a private, harmless friendship bring down disaster?

But perhaps it had. Anne steeled herself. She thought, *the Berrys will be better off out of England right now. And I mustn't dream of going with them.*

ROUND THE corner, in the smaller parlour at Derby House, Eliza studied her cards. The theatres had been closed for six weeks, by order of the Lord Chamberlain, to mark the death of the King's brother, the old Duke of Cumberland. Sheridan was convinced that this act of slavish royalty worship had the sole purpose of bankrupting him. Kemble was drinking to kill the time; brandy turned their manager from the most ceremonious and gentlemanly of men into a bad-tempered lout. For Eliza, unemployed, the days were hanging heavy on her hands for the first time since she could remember.

'Hearts are trumps, dear,' murmured her mother.

'Yes,' said Eliza, meaning *I know.*

'I've never seen Miss Farren forget the trump,' joked Fox. 'After all, she can hold so many thousands of lines in her memory.'

He was scratching inside his collar; Eliza felt a moment's anxiety that the Man of the People might have fleas. 'Pass,' she said, folding her cards together with a tight smile.

Derby slid in another shilling, and gazed up at the Lawrence portrait of Eliza, which—she happened to know—he'd finally had to pay £100 to secure. Still, he didn't seem to consider himself the loser. He'd got the thing he wanted, as he always did.

'The game would be so much livelier if we were playing for real money,' Fox complained as he flicked through his cards.

Their host snorted. 'No doubt it would make Mrs Farren's fortune if you were to be allowed to play for high stakes—' this prompted a shocked giggle from Eliza's mother—'but as your friend I can't allow it. Derby House shall remain the only premises in London from which you escape unfleeced.'

'I do sometimes win, you know,' Fox protested.

'Of course you do,' murmured Eliza, 'just as you sometimes wash.'

The little foursome fell about laughing. 'Oh, *la belle Farren*, she has stabbed me to the heart!'

'During the closure of the theatres she's taken on a new job as one of Pitt's secret agents,' Derby told Fox in a stage whisper. 'It's the Boy Eunuch's latest plot: the fair sex are to be the Whigs' downfall.'

'Then we'll die happy,' said Fox, tossing two shillings into the middle of the table.

Eliza smiled, but she was preoccupied. Anne Damer must have received the epigram by now, unless she was out all day. What would she do when she read it? Nothing, Eliza hoped. She'd written it out unrecognisably with her left hand. The last thing she wanted was any kind of confrontation; if Anne Damer rushed round the corner to Green Street to rail against the unknown enemy who'd composed the epigram—well, Eliza would just have to instruct the manservant to say she wasn't at home.

On the whole she was glad she'd sent it. Ever since last April's Exhibition, when she'd seen Anne Damer's wrecked face and been unable to offer her any explanation, she'd been brooding. Finally it seemed only fair to her to let the sculptor know—anonymously— why a respectable woman might suddenly drop her like an infected handkerchief. Eliza meant the sending of the epigram as a sort of warning, but also as an act of kindness to a woman who was in all probability innocent. It gave a reason for the death of friendship, after all; it made some dark sense of it. *I must hurt you now, one last time, for your own good*, she said in her head. She met the eye of the gold ring on her little finger and looked away, her guts knotted with guilt.

'Eliza, my dear,' whispered Mrs Farren.

She put down a card pretty much at random and Fox's furry eyebrows shot up. 'You're full of surprises, Miss Farren.'

She smiled as if she had some cunning strategy.

'So how were they all at Devonshire House?' Derby asked.

'Oh, well enough,' said Fox. 'The long-longed-for heir's a jolly little thing, already nicknamed Hart, short for the Marquis of

Hartington. Georgiana nearly died of the birth in Brussels, but she's come home rather fatter—which is all to the good,' he added with relish. 'Grey was there, hanging around like a puppy and picking quarrels...'

Significant nods all round.

'Oh, and they've brought back an orphan of the French troubles, one Mademoiselle St Jules, about whose parentage there's...some mystery.'

Eliza met her mother's eye; this must be one of the Duke's children that Lady Bess was rumoured to have had abroad.

'Lady Spencer's launching one of her periodic campaigns to root out her daughter's companion,' Fox went on, his eyes flickering over his cards before he threw two down.

'A foolish policy,' murmured Eliza, 'because it's Lady Bess who's saved that marriage.'

Derby nodded, taking up a card. 'People invent all sorts of arrangements for their happiness.'

Eliza kept her eyes on her hand. Well, she supposed this was one of those arrangements. How domestic she and Derby were, with their daily greetings and their card games—like a husband and wife who'd never so much as kissed.

October 1790

For a full fortnight Walpole raged and wept. He wrote daily to Anne in a script so trembling she could hardly make it out. He railed against the fever-breeding miasmas of Tuscany and the even greater risks posed by a journey across a continent where riot and anarchy kept breaking out—not just at Paris, but in Flanders, at Florence itself—like a forest fire.

'You can't keep two such girls cocooned in your little Arcadia for ever,' Anne told him gently at his house in Berkeley Square. 'You know they'll travel sensibly. As for France, the Assembly and the King are now said to be working peaceably together; Miss Crawford and Miss Lockart met with no disturbances on their recent tour.'

He snorted. 'The radicals of the Jacobin Club could unleash chaos at any moment.'

Anne sighed. 'And the house in North Audley Street could be carried off in a tornado, or the girls die of getting their feet wet after a London ball!'

His hand was over his mouth. 'Why do you torture me with these dreadful possibilities?'

'Because if we love the Berrys we must let them go,' she said, as much to herself as to him.

'But why now, of all ill-starred times?'

'These times are the most exciting,' said Anne with a shrug. 'History's in the making.'

Walpole goggled at her. 'You mean this wild, uncomfortable plan is all due to a roving humour? A volatile itch to see *sights*? I've been a witness to history,' he protested, 'three reigns, countless changes of government, the Jacobite Rising of '45, the Seven Years War, the American War...and I've done it all from the comfort and privacy of my own library.'

'I've never regretted a day of my own travels,' she told him, 'and I don't believe you have either.' She smiled, thinking of the time at Spa she'd woken up livid with flea bites, or her packet boat to Jersey, ten years ago, that had been temporarily captured by a charming French *capitaine*.

He turned his head away, like a moping dog, and mentioned that he'd sent the girls to a Miss Foldstone to have their portraits taken in miniature.

'For you to gaze upon, in case they die during their trip?'

Walpole gave her an injured look. 'In case *I* do.'

'Oh, coz—'

'You toy with my feelings.'

'Only to lighten their load.' But was that true? To lighten her own more like.

'The friendship of these girls has become the great solace of my declining life,' Walpole said stiffly. 'If, as seems all too likely, I find myself on my deathbed this winter I would like to have their sweet faces to hand.'

Anne had to restrain herself from snorting. Yes, he'd just turned seventy-three, and his fingers were knotty with chalk stones, but he'd all the vital energy of a man who would live for ever. 'Let's have no more sad songs. They'll go and come back rich in health and experience, and we'll all spend countless happy days together at Strawberry Hill.'

He shuddered, eyes on the ceiling, as if the spiteful gods were listening.

'So, my dear Strawberries, my precious Both,' he began his lament on the day of departure, standing outside the narrow house on North Audley Street, 'since you persist in your determination to throw your friends into fretful agonies—'

'Dear Mr Walpole—' Mary's voice was constricted.

'Cousin,' whispered Anne in his ear, 'the horses are restless.'

Harnessed to the hired carriage that would take them as far as Brighton, the bays snorted in the cooling autumn air. The sisters were looking very smart in their travelling costumes, with their hair curled and a little line of pearls round each throat. They were more of the World every day, Anne thought, with a twinge of absurd regret. 'You'll remember not to wear scent in Italy?' she asked Agnes.

'Oh, yes, they don't like it, do they?'

'I'll remind her,' said Mary, her dark eyes burning through the veil of her bonnet. 'Thanks for the loan of your Bet and Mrs Moll; we'd never have finished packing otherwise.'

'And don't be shocked to see Parisian ladies riding astride, in breeches.'

Mr Berry let out a giggle.

'Mes chères fraises! You must watch over each other tenderly,' said Walpole, weeping now like a biblical patriarch, and squeezing Mary's right hand and Agnes's left together with one of Mr Berry's into a sort of bouquet of fingers.

'We will, we promise,' cried Agnes.

Two gentlemen walked by arm in arm and gave the group a curious glance.

The command performance was winding up. 'You know I wouldn't love any one of you so much did you not love each other so well. Wife the First, and Wife the Second, and Papa Berry! No, I mustn't call you my wives any more, my Rachel and my Leah,' Walpole said, tears dropping from his nose. 'Gone are those playful days. Now I can only think of you as darling children of whom I am bereaved.'

Agnes let out a ragged sob and her father had his face in his handkerchief. But Mary, Anne noticed, was watching Walpole with a pale, strained expression, more like a mother's than a child's. The girl leaned forward and spoke a few words in his ear.

He kissed them all again. Anne, feeling peculiarly upstaged, did the same. 'Cara anima,' she murmured in Mary's ear, but the endearment was swallowed up in the clatter of a passing hackney.

'Don't change in your feelings to us, Mr Walpole,' cried Agnes from the window.

'If I live to see you again,' he pronounced with tragic amplitude, 'you will then judge whether I have changed!'

ANNE WALKED straight home to Grosvenor Square and sharpened half a dozen quills. *My dear M.*—

She stared at the words. She'd been about to write a cheering letter of good wishes for a safe sea crossing. But her hand wouldn't move that way; her brain refused to form those harmless words. Truth was knocking in her head like the beak of a chick, cracking the egg from the inside.

If not now, when? If she and Mary weren't to speak the truth to each other, to fling open the doors of their hearts, then what was the point of this abstraction called friendship? If Anne seized the moment—if she took the risk and unburdened herself—then she might lose, but wasn't a rapid loss better than a postponed one? She couldn't bear to watch another friendship strangled by degrees.

And after all, the chance to explain might be taken from her; Mary might learn the terrible secret from someone else, in an envelope from England, a whisper at a party in Florence...

The draft took her three hours; she sweated over every line. Mrs Moll came to ask whether to serve supper in the parlour or bring it up on a tray, but Anne rubbed her forehead with inky fingers and said she wasn't hungry.

My dear—if I may use that phrase?

I hardly know how to begin this letter. How to broach this dreadful subject? That's how I think of it, on the rare occasions when my guard is down & I find myself admitting it to consciousness: my dreadful subject. Though how it ever came to be called mine I still can't tell.

I'm writing to let you know that my virtue is what you believe it, but my reputation is not. (Would that the two were the same, or that only the former mattered.) You think me unimpeachable & unassailable, a widow of scholarly tastes who lives for her art. I am these things, but I am also the subject—the unwitting object, rather—of a terrible libel.

After my husband's rash self-murder in '76 I went to Italy for my health, just as you're doing. On my return I learned that the most appalling rumours were circulating about me: not only that my frigid character was to blame for my husband's act of despair, but that in Italy I had indulged in—consoled myself with—intrigues of the most unnatural nature. Oh dear, that phrase sounds like a contradiction. Perhaps if you were more of the World I wouldn't need to spell this out, my dear M., but at the risk of embarrassing you I will explain that I was, in several scurrilous doggerel pamphlets, accused of liking my own sex in a vile way.

I was too stunned to take this seriously. My friends responded with perfect loyalty by laughing off all such fantastical inventions. It turned out that the lies could be traced back to one William Combe (I won't grant him the veil of initials). His is a curious and instructive story of intelligence sold to the D—l. Though educated like a gentleman, Combe soon ran into such dreadful debts that he had to turn to miscellaneous writing & calumny to earn his bread; dear G—g—a was frequently his target. At Eton he'd known my father's nephew, Viscount B—ch—p, & he now took a violent grudge against him for a squalid reason: Combe decided to marry a common woman who'd been kept by Lord B—ch—p, & got it into his head that His Lordship would reward him for taking her off his hands by an annuity. When no money proved forthcoming Combe felt that his friends in high life had taken advantage of him & decided to wreak vengeance by inventing obscenities about the Viscount's sisters, aunt and cousins (who happen to include W. & my unfortunate self).

Dear W. shrugged off the abuse & I, following his lead, ignored it as best I could. Perhaps that was reckless of me. But I assure you, it seemed as if the evil shadow was easily shaken off; the rumours soon forgotten; no one of my acquaintance has ever mentioned them in the past dozen years.

I'd almost scrubbed this dreadful subject from my mind until just a few weeks ago, when I was sent an anonymous epigram that called my friendship dangerous to ladies (how it burns me to write that). So it seems as if the baneful seed hasn't withered away after all but flourishes in secret.

But I wouldn't have you too alarmed, my dear M. It's only a matter of a scribbled rhyme, which may not have circulated at all; nothing (as far as I know) has appeared in print, and I have no reason to believe Combe involved this time.

Anne paused, puzzled by how to go on. Why did she feel guilt hang around her neck like an albatross?

If I've been at fault—and somehow, for the first time, as I unburden my heart on paper, I dread that I have—it was only in responding too carelessly to that first malice all those years ago, too lightly, or rather, too squeamishly, too disdainfully. It's possible that the judicious payment of £50 or so might have killed off the many-headed dragon in its infancy; should I not have paid that tax to the World? Perhaps I was too confident, too proud.

You & I are now to be parted for so long, dear M., you may well ask, why haven't I told you as a true friend would, face to face? To which I can only reply that my courage failed me; these things are more easily committed to paper. Though I know this letter will frighten and mortify you.

Oh, God. Anne didn't want to beg. What should she say now, what could she ask for?

I only hope, when you've reflected on the matter, that the goodness of your heart & the valour of your spirit will still let you count among your correspondents & friends
your servant,
(I need not risk signing; you know my hand well)

THE POST brought her notes twice a day, but they were all from Walpole, and irritating. *I long for a line from Dieppe & then Rouen, Paris, Lyons & Turin, he scribbled. Not till the family are settled in Italy & I have confirmation of the fact will my anxiety subside into steady, selfish sorrow.* When two days had passed without word, he became convinced that the little sloop had foundered in the Channel. Finally he wrote to let Anne know the joyful news that he'd got a brief note from Agnes announcing their safe arrival in Dieppe after a twenty-four-hour crossing that had been only slightly rough. Anne, who'd heard nothing, had other terrors. Why didn't Mary reply to her letter? Put another way, why had she written of such terrible things to a young woman with eyes as stern as a hawk's?

She was so shaken that afternoon that she took four drops of laudanum. She hadn't touched the stuff since a very bad headache a year before; she'd almost forgotten what a magic elixir it was. It

only sent her to sleep if she was tired already; on a restless day like
this one it lifted her spirits and smoothed them out like a hot iron.
She didn't feel drunk, only blissfully at ease; for hours on end she
read Dante. That night, though, she was pulled back into turgid
nightmares; she walked through gigantic pagan temples, looking
for something, she couldn't remember what.

The next morning the letter arrived. It was postmarked Paris.

Oh, my dear A.—

*How very honoured I feel that you've trusted me—as a friend of
such recent date, though boundless affection—with your dreadful
subject, as you call it. I'd never heard a word of this appalling
libel, but that's not surprising, considering what restricted circles
I've moved in until recently. The ways of the Beau Monde are
still strange to me & its language a harsh one.*

*I can assure you, you still have my friendship, for as long as
you want it.*

*You don't ask for my advice in this matter of the recent re-
vival of the rumours, but somehow I feel inspired to offer it; forgive me this forwardness. Perhaps you were at fault, as you say,
in taking the first battle too lightly instead of forcing a retraction
from Combe. (Though I know, of course, that for rumours to be
publicly denied is for them to be repeated.) It's as a friend that I
say, now, don't let your reputation go undefended; it (I mean
any woman's) is a frail fortress. Though you can't fight an invisible enemy (this latest epigram), you can keep watch.*

*I suspect it wasn't only the circumstances of your widowhood
that left you open to the first dreadful accusation, but your splendid and enviable prominence in the masculine field of sculpture.
My own unhappy circumstances in life, which have made me
dependent on the kindness of my superiors, have impressed on me
the necessity of holding on to people's approval. Perhaps you, too,
should err on the side of pleasing the World rather than always
following your own inner guide?*

But enough of this & perhaps too much already.

We three Berrys are all well & enjoying Paris. The strangest things have changed since our last visit; the carriages of the nobility all have their coats of arms painted over, for instance. We purchased tickets to the Assembly at a very high price & heard a lively debate on the draft Constitution, during which the President had to ring his bell to try to hush the Comte de Mirabeau—a vast, shaggy bear of a man. Don't tell W., but Ag. and I have bought ourselves some tricolour bodices & iron bracelets, which are somewhat like light shackles. Things made of poor stuff like iron and cotton are all the rage here, it's the Democratic look.

Remember your promise, cara anima *(yes, I carried your words away from North Audley Street, hidden in my ear) & write to me often. Write to me always candidly upon the subjects uppermost in your mind, be they what they may. It may bring you some relief to express yourself to one who, though she may sometimes reprove, will always sympathise. I hardly need to assure you that despite all the slings & arrows of outrageous fortune, I'm honoured to count myself*

   your friend,
   M.

Anne read it through three times, her face flushed with relief. This was more than she had hoped for. How bravely Mary was grasping the nettle! And how mature she sounded—no trace of the humble protégée about her.

The rain began to spatter on the parlour windows. Anne wished she were in France herself, where everything seemed new-made. Or in Italy. If she stayed here all winter she'd go as pale as a maggot.

She flicked through the post on the salver. Various invitations to musical soirées and routs to launch the Season. She really had to say yes to three of them—her sister's, Georgiana's and Lady Melbourne's. (Though the two of them were no longer intimates, Anne was still on the invitation list for large events.) She thought of what she might wear—who else might be there—the acceptance cards she had to send as well as the polite refusals. An enormous weariness was creeping over her. To live in the World was a full-time activity; how did anyone find time to do anything but socialise? Coming out at seventeen, hundreds of wedding visits, the elaborate protocol of mourning clothes—each stage of life brought new obligations. So many things one had to remember, and do, and buy, and say, and not say: a tiny universe of rules and whispers.

NOVEMBER 1790

'Aha,' said Derby when the black footman showed him into the parlour at no. 8, Grosvenor Square, 'I can tell by the trunks in the hall and the rolled-up carpets that I've caught you just in time.'

Anne grinned as she shook his hand. She was looking well; her mouth had lost that melancholy line it had worn on the last few occasions he'd glimpsed her. 'You know what it's like, trying to pack in the middle of farewell visits. I was meaning to call on you, if I found a moment.'

He wasn't sure he believed her. 'I won't keep you long,' he said, accepting the chair the footman brought to his side. 'Actually, I *don't* know what it's like, though. I haven't been abroad since I was a boy.'

'Derby!' She moved from her paper-choked *secrétaire* to a plump silk chair beside his.

'Oh, I admit it's a scandal, especially for a man of my political sympathies. I haven't the least prejudice against foreigners—I pride myself on being cosmopolitan—but I prefer to meet them in Mayfair.' She laughed. 'It's Lisbon you're off to, I hear? "*O Portugal,*" he quoted the famous tag from *The Wonder,* "*thou dear garden of Pleasure*—"'

She capped it. '...*where Love drops down his mellow fruit, and every bough bends to our hands and seems to cry, "Come, pull and eat."*'

The line sounded mildly licentious. 'Do you know anyone there?'

'No,' said Anne, 'which is one of its attractions.'

He grinned at her. 'Well, if you really want to strike off from the familiar route, you could cross into Spain—explore the whole peninsula.'

'Oh, I'd like nothing more,' she said, 'but my parents are fretting about the risk of war over this Nootka Sound business—'

Derby shook his head a little smugly. 'I've just come from the Privy Council and I can tell you in confidence that's quite blown over; the Spanish have submitted to British terms.'

'How marvellous! Well, maybe I'll see the Alhambra at last.' Her eye fell on the long strip of paper in her hand. 'If I ever get through my list, that is. *Letters of introduction, bankers' instructions,*' she read at random, '*portable writing desk, mouse-proof hamper, bedding, dictionaries, hot-water bottle, chess set, cushions for Fidelle, stick and gun...*'

'Oh, yes, where is the clever creature?'

'Under your chair.'

He fished out the tiny greyhound and inspected her paws before lifting her on to his grey silk breeches.

'I'm determined to manage with only two servants. I've dreamed of going alone—just myself and dog,' said Anne with a touch of self-mockery. 'Has any lady ever travelled without servants, I wonder? I imagine it would be exhilarating to be driven along through the mountains, quite solitary and undisturbed...'

'Ah, but who'd lay out dinner when you were hungry?'

'And even more to the point,' she said ruefully, 'what if I needed a man to go into a tavern on my behalf and I couldn't find one who spoke English? That wouldn't be freedom but its opposite.'

'Well, I'm sure you'll have a memorable winter. You'll be much missed by your many friends.' The pause stretched. *That wasn't the best-chosen phrase,* Derby thought.

'Well,' said Anne. 'I wouldn't say they're *many,* but the ones I do claim are loyal.'

'And I hope I'll always be counted among their number,' said Derby, ridiculously awkward. What he really wanted to ask was, *What in all the hells happened between you and Eliza?* He'd raised the matter with the actress once or twice now, in a tactful way, and she'd pretended not to understand his questions. He didn't like to go asking a third party behind their backs. No, really the only person Derby could dream of asking was his old friend Anne. *Come on,* he told himself, *she's about to leave the country.*

'While—'

'I think—'

They both stopped short. Derby apologised and urged her to go on; Anne insisted it had only been the most trivial of observations.

'Well, then,' said Derby, 'what I was going to say was, while we're on the subject of friendship—I must just say, I'm heartily sorry that you and, ah, Thalia aren't on the terms you once were.' There was a heavy silence. He groaned inwardly. Plain statements were so much easier in male company. Sometimes he felt as if the sexes spoke different languages; a fellow could so easily commit the equivalent of double entendre. Like the story of the English débutante at the end of a Parisian banquet who loudly claimed to be *pleine*; she meant *full* but what the other guests understood was *pregnant*. Derby rushed on, now. 'I know it's not my place, and I wouldn't dream of intruding on your privacy'—wouldn't he? What else was he doing at this minute?—'but I must admit the thing mystifies me.'

Her face was closed.

'Was there some...misunderstanding?' he asked feebly. 'Or a quarrel? A political matter, even?'

Her mouth twitched, perhaps in derision. 'No, no quarrel.'

'Anything a mutual friend could help with at all?'

'I don't think so,' said Anne at last.

Was she in the grip of anger? he wondered. It looked almost like embarrassment, but what had she to be embarrassed about? It was Derby who was blundering crassly, ripping open old wounds. He'd never have made a diplomat. 'It's just that I have the greatest of respect and...and liking for both of you.'

'Thank you. These things happen,' she said bleakly.

'Oh, yes,' he assured her.

'Friendship isn't always a hardy plant. But there are no hard feelings,' she added after a second, 'at least on my side.'

'Excellent,' he said foolishly.

'I really do appreciate your visit, Derby,' said Anne, getting to her feet, which told him it was over.

FEBRUARY 1791

Eliza was in the dressing room, eating a hot veal pie her mother had brought in and glancing through her lines for *The Country Wife*. Sarah Siddons entered and sank into a chair. 'How was your tour?' asked Eliza politely.

'It is not for nothing', said Mrs Siddons sepulchrally, 'that Leeds is known as the actor's Botany Bay.'

She was still looking pale and swollen after her long absence from Drury Lane. According to Mrs Piozzi—whom Eliza continued to see from time to time, but without enthusiasm—the horrid husband had infected Mrs Siddons with an unmentionable disease and the cure was almost worse; the actress's mouth was one mass of sores. But last night as Isabella in *The Fatal Marriage*—a favourite part she'd refused to play again till Sheridan handed over her arrears—she'd moved Eliza, and several thousand other Londoners, to tears.

'Didn't the Northerners like the Scottish play, then?' Eliza wasn't superstitious herself, but she knew what a fuss it would cause to say the word *Macbeth* within these walls.

The tragedienne laid the back of her hand against her forehead. 'The theatre was so crammed and overheated, Miss Farren, I began to suffer from a dreadful thirst, and between the third and fourth acts I entreated my dresser to send a boy in haste to fetch me some beer.'

It was remarkable, thought Eliza, how grandiloquently the Kemble family could pronounce a word like *beer*.

'The fellow failed to return before I had gone on stage again. It was the celebrated sleepwalking scene; I was, as always, so immersed, so caught up, so transported by my role, that I knew not who I was if I were not Lady—' She stopped herself. 'I need not say the ill-omened name.'

Eliza repressed a sigh of impatience and set down the remains of her pie.

'Well. As I thrust out my hands before me, straining to scrub from them all trace of murderous gore, on comes the creature.'

'No!'

Mrs Siddons nodded. 'He may have been slow-witted; his instructions had been to deliver the drink to me and he followed them to the letter. He trotted up and offered me the foaming mug. At first the audience were confused and thought it an addition to the play. Grandly and darkly—in the very manner of the Scottish usurpress herself—I waved him away, as if to signify that I was so steeped in crime that no mere human beverage could pass my lips.'

Eliza started giggling; she could just see it.

'Thrice the lad offered the mug and thrice I waved him away, till the whole house was hooting with laughter.' Mrs Siddons's neck was flushed with remembered shame. 'Finally I roared, "*Leave my presence, churl,*" whereupon the demon ran off, slopping beer on the stage. And that', she concluded, 'is why I will never, never, never return to Leeds.'

'Well. At least', Eliza told her, 'you can be sure that your career has passed its nadir.'

'Somehow, I don't feel consoled.' After a moment Mrs Siddons added, 'What about you, my dear Miss Farren, have you experienced a performance of which you can say *this is the worst of my life?*'

A boy ran in then, to tell Eliza she was wanted for a words-and-business rehearsal of *The Rivals* on stage.

'No,' she said drily, getting up, 'I suspect my darkest hour is yet to come.'

Mrs Siddons gave her a meaningful, sympathetic nod.

Dora Jordan too had bounded back to Drury Lane this week, after giving Mr Ford a third bastard. She seemed bolder as well as fatter; she'd somehow talked Kemble into taking on her useless brother to play Sebastian to her Viola and by waving a rival offer from Covent Garden, it was said, she'd forced Sheridan to raise her salary to an undisclosed but much guessed-at sum. All this Eliza could have borne if the management had followed the usual practice of casting the two Queens of Comedy in different plays, so each could shine alone. But Sheridan had decided to get up his old comedy *The Rivals* again, as a sure-fire earner that would keep his creditors at bay—and he insisted that Eliza play the elegant, drooping Julia opposite Dora Jordan's scatterbrained Lydia.

Considering that the action of the play covered only five hours in Bath, this rehearsal of the first scene felt as if it was lasting for ever, mostly due to Kemble's fusses over pronunciation and gesture. Eliza finally made her Scene Two entrance and Mrs Jordan rushed at her. '*How unexpected was this happiness!*' she cried, engulfing Eliza.

'If Julia could respond to her cousin a little more warmly?' suggested Kemble.

'She would, sir, if I had any room,' Eliza said sharply. 'Mrs Jordan so smothers me in her fichu...'

'I beg your pardon, Miss Farren, I'm sure,' said Mrs Jordan, now holding Eliza by the shoulders as one would a naughty child. '*How unexpected was this happiness!*' she repeated with a look of shock.

'*True, Lydia—and our pleasure is the greater.*' Eliza smiled past her glassily.

She knew they were being ridiculous, and predictable. Sheridan was already capitalising on their mutual dislike; paragraphs in his trademark style had started to appear in the more vulgar newspapers, announcing a deadly feud between two actresses known only as *the Rivals*. Eliza would have liked to confound his off-stage choreography by maintaining the most amicable relations with Mrs Jordan—but the woman's vulgarity made that impossible.

The role of Julia, to make matters worse, was the only unfunny one in the play; Eliza had to keep coming on in anxiety, suffering in silence through painful misunderstandings with her fiancé, then exiting in tears. And as for the dress—

'My costume's so *démodé* they'll howl with laughter,' she told Kemble in his office.

'You exaggerate, Miss Farren.'

'I don't. When you began your tenure as manager of this theatre two years ago you vowed to improve the stock.'

'Great strides have been made—'

'Oh, yes, I've noticed some marvellous new things,' Eliza said furiously. 'Mrs Jordan, as Lydia Languish, will be gorgeous in a white satin wrapping gown caught up with pink bows, while I as Julia must drag myself across the stage in a hooped sack-gown with filthy grey ribbons from the play's first production sixteen years ago—an *eternity* in fashion.'

Kemble chewed his thumb. 'It could be worn without a hoop, perhaps, like a chemise gown?'

She gave a sharp sigh to let him know how little he understood female underclothes. 'That would look even worse.'

'It's more silver than grey, I believe,' he offered. 'You look delightful in it.'

'If so,' she barked, 'then the credit is all mine, because it's a rag! A scullery maid wouldn't use it to scrub a floor.'

'Perhaps one of the dressmakers could freshen it up for you.'

'That would be to throw good thread after bad.'

'Mr Sheridan has vetoed all additional expense,' said Kemble grimly. 'The whole point of this production is to earn money, not spend it.'

'So he'd have us make an omelette without breaking eggs?'

The manager's eyes lit up. 'Perhaps you'd like to choose something of your own?' he suggested. 'You're widely celebrated for your fashionable wardrobe...'

'I don't wear my own clothes on the public stage,' she told him coldly. Some actresses liked to receive an allowance as part of their salary and buy their own costumes, but to Eliza that seemed unprofessional; it smacked of the days of Nelly Gwyn, when women turned to the stage to display their wares to the highest bidder.

'What's the matter, dear?' asked Mrs Farren as the carriage bumped and skidded through the icy ruts on Long Acre.

'I fought with Kemble over my costume,' said Eliza through her teeth. 'I'm not going to give in, not this time. I've had enough of being treated like the dirt under Dora Jordan's heels.'

'Oh, I know, I know. But—'

'It's the only thing for it. I'll announce I've been taken ill.'

Mrs Farren made a little sound of shock and covered her smile so her missing tooth wouldn't show.

My dear Miss Farren, came Kemble's civil reply the next afternoon,

> *I am so sorry you feel indisposed. No doubt it will take an effort of heroic proportions for you to be at the theatre at six o'clock to play your part, but given the importance of the occasion, & the full house we expect, I am sure you'll feel amply rewarded, not least by the gratitude of*
> *your humble servant,*
> *J. P. Kemble*

She consulted her mother on the wording of the reply. 'Should I tell him I've discovered from Jack Palmer that Jordan now gets a full £5 a week more than I do?'

'No, no, don't muddy the issue with money,' said her mother. 'But dear, now you've given Kemble a fright, don't you think you'd better play tonight after all? He does speak of his *gratitude*; he'll owe you a favour.'

'He owes me a new dress.'

Her mother was nibbling a thumbnail. 'It's always risky to defy management.'

Risky for a fourth-tier actress like you were, Eliza was tempted to say, *but for a self-respecting Queen of Comedy, it's sometimes the only thing to do.*

She got her mother to take down the next letter.

My dear Mr Kemble,
Would that it were, indeed, possible for me to struggle up from
my sickbed & take part in tonight's performance! Left to myself,
I would make that extraordinary effort, no matter how injuri-
ous the consequences to my constitution, for the sake of the The-
atre—but my physician forbids it & my dear mother (who is
writing this note at my dictation) prevents it.
    Yours sorrowfully,
    E. Farren

Kemble's reply came back at ten past five.

Miss Farren,
I have announced The Rivals *on today's playbills & it's too late*
to change. If I may say so, your sickness bears all the hallmarks of
whim & spleen. I won't be dictated to any further: forgive the
unaccustomed coarseness if I say that you'll act Julia in your shift,
if you don't like your gown, & I won't hear another word on the
subject.
    Your Manager,
    J. P. K.

'You'll have to go in now,' said Mrs Farren, tutting over the
scribbled lines. 'Shall I have the manservant call a hackney?'

Eliza shook her head and took another slice of cold beef.
'Kemble's borrowed Sheridan's tough talk, but he doesn't have the
charm to pull it off. If he thinks to achieve by thuggishness what he
failed to do with flattery and whining—'

'Oh, but Betsy!'

Eliza ignored the old name. 'This is no time for capitulation,
Mother. I must hold to my dignity.' She chewed the beef, though it
was hard to swallow.

She barely slept that night. As she lay flat on her back, staring
at the ceiling, she wondered what the next morning would bring. A
note from Sheridan, telling her that her services were no longer

required at Drury Lane? Well, then, she could drive over to Covent Garden and tell Harris it was his lucky day. This fight was worth it, Eliza told herself. If one let people walk all over one—

And suddenly, oddly, she found herself missing Anne Damer. Mrs Farren was a stout ally, but she still thought like a provincial small-timer; the height of her ambition was for her daughter to please everyone. This was the kind of crisis that had to be mulled over with a friend and what real friends did Eliza have these days? Her colleagues were too involved themselves; they might consider that on £18 a week she'd no reason to complain. As for Derby, she couldn't talk about the crises of her profession to him because he'd wax gallant and lose his temper. He might threaten to call on Kemble himself as her agent—which could end up with Sheridan challenging the Peer to a duel in Hyde Park. Or, almost worse, Derby might tell her it was beneath her dignity to work for such masters and offer to pay her a yearly stipend himself. Yes, what Eliza needed was an intelligent woman friend, who knew the pros and cons of wrath and civility—but somehow her life didn't include any. There was something about being a famously beautiful actress that discouraged female friendship. Were all women rivals, then, in the end?

The next morning brought a brief note from Palmer—*Cheeky lass! We had to do* The Beggar's Opera *instead and I fluffed my lines in the last act*—and another with the Derby crest on it that asked for assurance that she was not seriously ill. There was also a surprisingly mollifying note from Kemble, with a parcel that turned out to contain a new dress. He must have bought it ready made. It was blue lustring, cut in the latest slim style with quite a high waist, a white sash tied in a bow behind, and an overskirt of spangled gauze.

Miss Farren,
I trust you've fully recovered from your indisposition & that it's
not a lingering or recurring disease? I enclose your new costume
& hope to see you in it tonight.
    With respect,
    J. P. Kemble

'So you won!'

'This battle, yes, Mother, I suppose so,' said Eliza, examining the rough edge of the sash.

'Well, I never. I take my hat off to you, daughter, I really do. A good strengthening ragout for your dinner, I think...' And Mrs Farren bustled off downstairs to the kitchen.

Eliza didn't feel as triumphant as she expected. Until now she'd been known for being ladylike, unlike Dora Jordan, who relied on outrageousness and charm. But really, sometimes only gutter tactics worked.

The Derby carriage was already waiting outside when a slim packet arrived from Mrs Piozzi. *My dear,* said the note, *this is most distressing, but I thought you'd appreciate seeing a copy before anyone mentions it to you.* Eliza steeled herself. It was a strange friend who relished nothing better than to be a bearer of bad news.

A Peep Behind the Curtain at Widow Bellmour, the cheap print was called, alluding to the role she most often played in *The Way to Keep Him.* Its ink was still smeary. It showed her naked in the Green Room, trying to cover herself with her hands like a statue. Words bubbled out of her mouth.

> *Here I stand a fresh proof of the Manager's meanness,*
> *Not a rag to my back like the Medici's Venus!*
> *At their second-hand wardrobe I turn up my nose,*
> *By the Lord I won't act till they find me new clothes.*

And there, ogling sympathetically through a parted curtain, was Lord Derby. Not that he really looked like a swollen-headed goblin boy, but over the years Eliza had become familiar with these cartoon distortions. *Oh, fie you, Sheridan, curse your niggard heart,* he was crying,

> *Why won't you let Miss Farren dress her parts?*
> *Were I of Drury's property the sovereign,*
> *I'd give the lovely maiden choice of covering!*

She had to read it twice before she understood the lewd puns: *parts* and *covering,* like the mating of dogs or horses.

Eliza wouldn't cry; she wouldn't get angry, even. It could have been worse; imagine if the print had shown Anne Damer peering through the curtain? She tore it neatly in two. She'd won the battle with management and that was what mattered, wasn't it?

At Julia's entrance in Scene Two that night Eliza's admirers sent up a burst of applause, but there were some catcalls too. She knew an apology was expected, so she walked to the edge of the stage and made a deep curtsy. Derby, in his box, gave her a fervent smile. 'Ladies and gentlemen,' she said, seeming to wipe a tear from the corner of her eye, 'you see that even the slightest mark of your disapproval touches me to the quick. I beg leave to assure you that I'd never have absented myself from the duties of my profession but out of *grave* indisposition.' She pressed her hand to her chest as if she was having difficulty breathing. 'In light of the many years I've had the honour and happiness to serve you, I can only appeal to the gallant protection of the British public.'

The cacophony of clapping drowned out the few lingering hisses. *Well, at least that's done with,* thought Eliza as she turned and launched into her opening lines.

But she was wrong. Dora Jordan, halfway through her speech about her poor cousin's endless engagement, suddenly deviated from the usual gestures. '*This ungrateful Faulkland,*' she said, jerking her head unmistakably in the direction of the box where Derby sat, arms on the railing, watching the action. The quicker members of the audience began to giggle and Mrs Jordan went on meaningfully, '...*who will ever delay assuming the right of a husband, while you suffer him to be equally imperious as a lover!*'

By now the joke was spreading among the audience; laughter pooled and flowed. Mrs Jordan stood, grinning broadly; she gave another little jerk of the head in Derby's direction, in case anyone had missed her meaning, and the laughter built to a crescendo. Eliza was rigid with rage. Was this the hussy's own idea, to give the lines an extra piquancy at her rival's expense, or was she following Sheridan's instructions? Not Kemble's, surely; he hated to mar a play with contemporary references—but perhaps he'd do it for the sake of punishing her. She allowed herself a tiny glance at Derby, who'd sat back and folded his arms like a calm sportsman. Didn't he care that she was being laughed at by several thousand Londoners? *No,* she scolded herself, *he's just refusing to be ruffled. If I were a true lady I'd do the same.*

Eliza opened her mouth to say her next line, but nothing came. Her cheeks began to scald under their coat of paint. *'Nay—'* she began. For the first time in many years she'd forgotten her part. *'Nay—'*

'Neighhhhhh!' A wit in the pit reared up like a horse and hilarity filled the house.

AFTER MORE than three months in Lisbon, Anne was thriving. The language wasn't difficult for a woman who already knew French, Italian, Latin, Greek and some Spanish. After the terrible earthquake thirty-five years ago, which had left 60,000 dead, the streets of Lisbon's Lower Town had been laid out with a classical grace—but they were full of skinny, howling dogs. The innkeeper's children laughed to see Miladi Damer with her miniature greyhound tucked into the crook of her elbow like a baby and they crowded round when she fed Fidelle from her own plate.

But Anne passed most of each day quite alone, in her cabinet, as she called it: a tiny whitewashed room at the back of the inn, half filled by a farmhouse chimney in rough stone, with a table, two chairs, and a shelf for her books and writing things. (Bet and Sam slept in the maids' and men's attics.) Why, she wondered, had she ever felt she needed more? What did she do with all that space, back in Grosvenor Square, except stuff it with possessions?

The Portuguese intrigued her; the women hid their faces behind a fine black mantilla called a *velo,* and the poor of both sexes enclosed their hair in a mesh with a bow over the forehead and a long tassel behind; Anne drew Mary a little sketch of it in a letter. The labourers she saw in the fields seemed to work sporadically and sleep long in the same coarse cloak and slouch hat. When she'd first arrived the November wind had rushed into her cabinet through a broken pane of glass, because although she sent Sam after the workmen a dozen times a day, with his ten words of Portuguese, neither entreaty nor money would bring them in till it suited their convenience. Now she knew never to expect immediate service; she was learning the local rhythm. She modelled a little in clay, but nothing strenuous; Portuguese indolence was evidently catching.

In bed at night, with Fidelle coiled at her feet, she took strong Masulipatam snuff and reread letters, especially Mary's. The Berrys were passing the winter at Pisa, rather than Florence, because some Englishwomen in the Florentine colony had proved decidedly demi-rep and Mary hadn't wanted either to offend them by refusing their acquaintance, or risk her and her sister's reputations by contamination. *Would that I'd been so sensible, when I was your age,* Anne answered ruefully, alluding to her subject, as they called it. *What a luxury it is, all this 'thinking together' on paper,* she added.

> *You need hardly have told me—tho' I liked to hear it—that your soul when unconfined flies to my side, for I've felt it hovering about me on a hundred occasions—in all my walks to Roman aqueducts or Gothic churches or olive groves, whenever contemplating the sea & even in the midst of tiresome company. What is distance to two sincere hearts?*

The Portuguese aristocracy, their clothes encrusted with jewels from their South American colonies, kept to themselves in superb dignity; unlike their British equivalents, they had no gambling clubs or racecourses. Really, Anne would have been happy enough to live like a hermit in her cabinet, but Lisbon had an English population of considerable self-importance, so sometimes she felt obliged to accept invitations, which meant getting into one of her silk costumes and having Bet do her hair. (The girl wasn't a patch on a French hairdresser, but it was better than nothing.) All Anne had ever found available for hire was an awkward two-wheeled chaise, which let in the rain on her skirts as the mules strained up and down the vertiginous shattered pavements of the city.

On Saturday one had to go to the French ambassadress's; on Sunday to the opera or theatre. The players were all male, and watching a swarthy boy in powder and hoops play Viola in Portuguese was not Anne's idea of entertainment. She could still conjure up the image of Eliza Farren in the role. Was it because she'd shaped that face with her fingers and cut it out of a block of stone? *So far from England, I seem to be shedding painful memories as easily as hair, or nail parings,* she wrote to Mary, *only my few real affections bind me to my homeland.*

Thursday afternoons were Mrs Walpole's—wife to the British Minister, Robert Walpole, who was one of Horry's cousins. The Minister took to his distant relation immediately, invited her to dinners and sat her at his right hand, boasting of her artistic reputation. His guests were the kind of English who always drifted to foreign towns, Anne observed: fat, husband-hunting girls and their scowling fathers, most of them merchants from the English factory.

By the third course, on one such evening, the Minister had had too much *porto* and began boasting of how he had rid Lisbon of the notorious William Beckford. 'Little did the cur realise,' he trumpeted, 'that one moment of vile self-indulgence had toppled him from his fashionable pedestal for ever and all his money couldn't buy it back!'

'Excuse me,' interrupted the French ambassadress, 'but what was this Beckford's crime?'

There was an awkward pause. 'The worst, madame,' blurted Robert Walpole, before anyone could change the subject. 'At Powderham Castle in '83 he was discovered in a bedchamber—with a *boy.*'

'Not to excuse the crime, just as a point of interest,' remarked a visiting baronet, 'young Viscount Courtenay doesn't seem to have been quite the innocent his uncle claimed at the time. Now he's grown up, he's so effeminate in his manner his fellow peers call him Kitty!'

'Which to my mind proves, sir, that Beckford corrupted him fully,' barked the Minister.

The ambassadress spoke up mildly. 'But in France, you know, since last year this is no longer a crime.'

Several pairs of eyes bulged, including those of the Minister's wife. Anne kept her head down. The subject—too like her own—made her nervous. Gossip travelled by water as fast as by land; could anyone here have heard the rumours that stuck like burrs to the name of Mrs Damer?

'Well, madame, whatever the dangerous innovations of your nation,' said Robert Walpole, 'I'm proud to report that my own is pre-eminent in the punishment of sodomites. We won't have such monsters on British soil; we never let a year go by without hanging one or two, or stoning them in the pillory, which is what would have happened to Beckford if he'd been a shoemaker instead of the heir to a sugar empire!'

The Frenchwoman gave a graceful shrug. 'As a lady, I must resign all such unpleasant questions for the gentlemen to adjudicate.'

This sentiment met with general approval; then the ladies withdrew and left the gentlemen to their toasts.

Anne couldn't sleep that night. Such vengeful fury in Robert Walpole's eyes! She knew what sodomites did was wrong and against the natural order—but so were other things she read about in the newspapers, like unwanted babies being thrown into drains; she didn't know why sodomy was the *worst of crimes*. So many of the great Ancients appeared to have indulged in it, judging by their writings—so why was Beckford a monster? Besides, he'd never been proven guilty; he was said to have loved his poor wife dearly. Who better than Anne to know that shocking rumours could be built on foundations of air? Not that her case was the same as Beckford's, of course. What she stood accused of by those awful pamphlets was a shameful matter, but she'd never heard of it being prosecuted as a crime. Perhaps it was so rare, so bizarrely obscure a female vice, that it had never been put on the statute books. She shuddered and rolled over in bed, raising a yip of protest from Fidelle.

How I wish you were here in Italy, my dear A.! The idea of our travelling together in some future time keeps returning to my mind—my narrow, irritable mind, which has made my life (tho' lacking in incident) one of constant agitation & which on melancholy days is not sufficiently uplifted by the incomparable art of the Quattrocento.

She heard from Mary every day or two and from Walpole more irregularly, since the posts from England might bring her nothing for a fortnight, then three packets all at once. He had a horror of his writings falling into strangers' hands; although he was careful not to talk French politics (and this was a great relief to Anne), he was haunted by the possibility that his letters would end up being read aloud in the Assembly.

I do apologise for my illegibility; the gout & rheumatism have formed a coalition against me. You ask about my sleep & I can assure you that it is excellent, in that I do little but sleep, or walk three steps leaning on the shoulder of my sulky Swiss valet. In this vegetative state I scarce see anybody, nor can have anything to talk of but my suffering, helpless self. I let you know these de-tails, my dear Anne, so that, should the conclusion prove fatal, you might not be wholly unprepared.

She knew half of it must be hyperbole, but she wept anyway. She even thought of going home early—but then she might never see Spain. And besides, she knew hers wasn't the face Walpole longed for.

Yes, he misses you & his other Berries sorely, she wrote to Mary, *but I can't believe he'd want you to curtail this Grand Tour of yours; he only needs to relieve his woes on paper. Those of us who pine for you, know there are good reasons to bear it.*

The strange thing was she felt even closer to Mary than when she'd been round the corner in Mayfair. By now there was no subject their correspondence hadn't covered, from their notions of the afterlife to their failure to love their families enough, to their hopes of Reform (Anne wanted MPs elected annually to make them more accountable and houses of refuge for impoverished spinsters; Mary wondered if the death penalty could be lifted from petty crimes of theft). Each knew the other's income, hat size, digestive troubles and bad habits. (Mary wrote in the margins of books she didn't agree with; Anne picked her teeth with her thumb.) Anne's writing was tighter than Mary's and heavier. She sealed her folded pages with a rectangular mark like a chisel bite, on red wax; Mary with a circle on black wax.

In Walpole's next letter he seemed somewhat revived by having so much bad news to communicate. Not only had a hurricane burst the Thames's banks and smashed chimneys (including Anne's at Grosvenor Square), but the collapse of a share syndicate had rocked the Stock Exchange. Georgiana was said to have lost the unimaginable sum of £50,000 and her Devonshire relatives were so furious they'd taken to cutting her in public.

> *Your friend F-x calls every budget, treaty or amendment Pitt proposes 'untimely, ill-advised, ill-begotten or unconstitutional'—which achieves little, but provides entertainment, & keeps everyone on their toes. Of your sister's husband I must say that R——m—d seems ever more unhappy in the Cabinet. His latest hobby-horse is an Ordnance Survey for the better defence of the realm, which he claims will map out the whole island at the minute scale of one inch to one mile!*

Anne put the page down, half read. Fidelle wasn't herself, hadn't been for several days now. She'd stopped running, jumping and eating; she lay listlessly under her mistress's skirts, her tail between her legs. Her eyes seemed cloudy, her pointed nose too dry. Anne stroked the warm silvery throat, felt for the irregular pulse. Was it the change of climate, or could she have eaten poison? The dog was only nine; she should have another half-dozen years ahead of her.

The next day Fidelle was no better and barely lapped at a saucer of water. *Not here,* Anne said in her head, *not now, not while I'm away from everyone and everything I know.* She wrote to no one but Mary. *You'd hardly credit what a desperate state I'm in; I sent a note to the Minister, but all he told me was that lapdogs don't thrive out here. Fidelle is entirely dependent on me, & I can do nothing for her.*

That night she lay down on her bed fully dressed and curled round the tiny dog. She stayed very still. She didn't expect to sleep, but fatigue caught up with her and pulled her down into the dark.

A little before dawn the screeching cocks woke her and Fidelle was cold.

Anne didn't cry. She swaddled the corpse in her best Kashmir shawl and considered what to do. She couldn't bear the idea that the dog's grave would be here in Portugal, where Anne might never come again. She knew the words for *fire* and *burn*; she consulted her dictionary for *ashes.*

Against the fierce morning light of the cabinet's doorway a dark bear. Anne jumped with fright.

'Have I the right house for Mrs Damer?'

It was the voice that brought him back to her—a rough, amused tone from long ago. 'O'Hara!'

'The very man.' The General stepped in, stooping a little so as not to hit his head on the door frame.

She sprang up. 'My dear old friend. What on earth are you doing here?'

'I've been three years posted at the fortress of Gibraltar,' he said, 'just been made colonel of the 74th Regiment of Foot, quite a promising bunch—but now I'm on my way home for a spell of leave. The ship was passing Lisbon and I'd heard from your father that you planned to be here till February, so I gave the captain a barrel of brandy to stop in for half a day.'

'I can't imagine a better surprise.' Anne seized his hands in hers; the skin was warm, scored leather. General O'Hara had to be fifty by now, but he was looking well. 'It's been years. How many years?'

He grinned. His teeth were as startlingly white as ever, or was it only that his face was bronzed? 'I've been knocking around the world so long I can't keep track. And you, you're here for your health?'

'Oh, the southern sun has done me good already,' she said, waving him to a chair. 'I'm an idle tourist, really.'

'I can't believe that the Muse of Sculpture is ever idle. Have you your scrapers and gougers with you?'

'Always,' she said, smiling back at him.

'And little Fidelle, I assume. Where is she, have I scared her under the table?'

Anne put up her hand but not in time to catch the tears.

'My dear Mrs Damer.' His hand touched her sleeve.

'I do beg your pardon. She...she happened to die this very morning, I don't know of what, there was no one to consult and it happened so fast.'

'Oh, gad, I'm fearfully sorry.'

'That's quite all right,' she said, wiping her face with her handkerchief. 'I mean to have her cremated and put her ashes in a little japanned box to take home with me.'

'Splendid notion,' said O'Hara.

Anne cleared her throat and tried to remember how to play the hostess. 'Shall we have some wine on the terrace, with the local marzipan cakes?'

Under the shady trees he told her about being Lieutenant-Governor of Gibraltar, a tiny and chaotic peninsula that was home to 4000 people. Though Charles O'Hara was a natural son of Lord Tyrawley (or so Anne's father had always said), there was nothing of the aristocrat about the man and somehow Anne liked him better for it. He'd served in Germany, Portugal, Africa and India; underneath that military uniform, just above his heart, she knew he carried the pitted scar of an American bullet from Yorktown. She was remembering what she liked best about O'Hara: he never made her feel as if her femininity was a distracting mosquito—not even when she burst into tears. Walpole had the same knack, it struck her now, and Derby too—though her favourite men were all so different as to seem as if they belonged to distinct species.

'Is there much art to look at here?'

Anne made a little face. 'More architecture. The best pictures were swallowed up in the earthquake, or stolen or sold off long ago. At the home of a marquis I was shown a Raphael, but it'd been wretchedly painted over. I gained much credit for finding this out and cleaning off the overpainting—and I a mere woman,' she added ironically. She was about to pour herself some more wine, when she remembered her English manners and let O'Hara do it.

'So you've made friends among the Portuguese gentry?'

'Oh, I wouldn't claim that; it's difficult for foreigners. Such strange tribes! The ladies are round as barrels by twenty-five, and live strictly separate from the gentlemen among herds of servants, foundlings and dwarfs. They aren't supposed to talk to their own brothers, even.'

'So your hosts will think you scandalous for entertaining me tête-à-tête?' he asked, jerking his head towards the inn.

'We English are known for eccentricity,' Anne said with a shrug, 'and at least we're outdoors, not shut up in my cabinet together! Oh, and a girl must never so much as look at her *futur*—her intended,' she glossed. 'I heard a story about a young man who'd courted his cousin with all due form at a respectful distance. One evening she looked him in the eye and asked him how he did, from which the distraught suitor knew that the match had been broken off!'

'Imagine how that would go down in Mayfair, where both sexes casually discuss the latest adulterous intrigues,' he said with a guffaw. 'It just proves that all rules of behaviour are arbitrary conventions, whether ours or the Redskins'.'

'Oh, don't you think you go rather too far there?' Anne asked, uneasy. 'Surely the values of civilisation—'

'Yes, but which civilisation? The Hindu one is far more ancient than ours and they'd be shocked to see me butcher a cow! I tell you frankly, Mrs Damer, the more I see of different nations, the less sure I feel about the pre-eminence of my own.'

'Well,' she said, rather overwhelmed, 'why else travel, I suppose? If our journeys aren't going to change us we might as well stay at home.'

'You understand me,' said the General, draining his wine.

The pause was oddly intimate. 'Speaking of other nations,' said Anne briskly, 'Walpole's sent me Burke's remarkable *Reflections on the Revolution in France*.'

'I must be the only Englishman or woman who hasn't read it yet.' O'Hara laughed. 'But didn't your father tell me you were quite the democrat?'

She flinched from the word. 'Oh, General, not a *democrat*! But as a Whig, my sympathies are naturally with the cause of liberty and I wish the French well. I must admit, though, that Burke's eloquence has shaken me somewhat. He goes too far—he has these exaggerated fears of a tide of revolution sweeping across Christendom, even to our own shores!—but his catalogue of the mistakes and crimes of the French leaders is rather damning.'

She waited for O'Hara to reveal his own views, but he only nodded and said, 'You must have a great deal of correspondence to keep you busy, too.'

'Oh, yes, my parents, of course, and Walpole—and a newer friend, a Miss Berry.'

'Which one?'

She blinked at him.

'The sketcher, or the beauty? I met them in Italy many years ago when I was travelling with your father, as it happens—unless there are other Berrys in the world?'

'The beauty,' she told him, disconcerted. Conway had mentioned something about encountering the Berrys long before Walpole had discovered them, now she came to think of it. 'Though Miss Berry would rather be known for her intellect.'

He grinned and she was suddenly afraid. In all his travels, in rough company, could the rumours of her dreadful subject have reached O'Hara? 'I'd no idea you were acquainted with that family.'

'Oh, the girls may not remember me; one brute of a soldier among many,' he said with a roar of laughter.

But looking into his sparkling eyes, Anne doubted that the Berrys could have forgotten him.

MARCH 1791

At Elvas she crossed the Spanish frontier and presented a letter of introduction to the governor from his brother (an old friend of her father's), so her baggage would be let through. He mortified her by insisting that the Honourable Miladi Damer should be received with full honours of war, including an escort of thirty horsemen, drums, trumpets, cannons firing and a vast banquet to follow. Anne made a private vow that from now on she wouldn't use her letters, she'd take her chances as an ordinary traveller. Lying awake with heartburn that night, she realised how much she'd changed with the years; as a newlywed of nineteen, she'd been delighted by ostentation and all-night balls. Now she'd much rather be lodging in one of the quiet villages that looked to have been crumbling into the landscape since before Columbus set sail.

From now on Anne spent fifteen hours a day in the carriage. She bumped along through sandy plains, pine woods, craggy gorges riddled with streams, spring flowers, cork trees and ilex groves. *For shame, sir, the Iberian peninsula is more than 'backward governments & primitive economies'*, she wrote to Walpole, the potholes making her words jerk along the paper. *Spain is indeed wild— no route for mere tourists—but sublimely picturesque & I have complete trust that my* calessiere *(who combines Spanish dexterity with almost English caution) & his seven skinny mules will bring me safe through the mountains.*

The carriage was a little world of its own; it smelt of food and musty clothes. Anne and Bet relieved themselves in the pot, averting their gaze. For breakfast they dipped their stale rolls in oil, tostadas con aceite, or had a cold egg tortilla from the hamper. When they stopped for dinner Anne never could tell what was in the paella, but sometimes suspected it was rabbit; she preferred the fishy zarzuela. She couldn't help but notice that Bet and Sam seemed on more intimate terms, these days. The footman sat up top with the driver, and he and the maid never touched each other in front of their mistress, but their eyes rested on each other during meals and the two of them tended to wander off during the long midday siesta, while Anne sat under a tree and read *Don Quixote* to brush up her Spanish. *The private lives of servants are a mystery,* she wrote to Mary. And Bet had seemed such a sensible, stolid girl. Anne eventually decided that, unless this affair produced some disaster such as a mulatto baby, she'd pretend she hadn't noticed.

For a country steeped in ancient tradition, untouched by what Walpole called the *French infection,* Spain had an oddly democratic spirit. Everybody Anne encountered, high or low, had an air of languid dignity and seemed to expect to be spoken to, rather than being satisfied with a mere nod. *Condeos,* the labourers resting among their stony terraces blessed her as she was driven by and Anne, who would have been shocked at such cheek in her native Berkshire, called back, *Condeos, Condeos!* This always made them grin, though whether out of a sense of being honoured or in derision of her accent she couldn't tell.

At inns—or what passed by that name—Bet always smoked the room with thyme to chase out the fleas. Anne slept on the straw pallet from her own carriage, wrapped up in the vast cloak she'd bought in Lisbon, or shared a bed with a female stranger, exchanging no more than a few civil words. The sagging bed might be the only piece of furniture in the room. There were always small yipping dogs that were nothing like Fidelle but reminded her painfully of the box of ashes at the bottom of her dressing case.

I am somewhat of a freak to these people, she told Mary,

> *an English Miladi with no husband or family, often forgetting to wear her mantilla, driving through the wilderness for no good reason at all! I feel young all over again. I'm surprised to find that I can put up with more discomfort than I'd ever bear at*

*home in Mayfair, & gratified to think of the two of us travel-
ling simultaneously, tho' through different parts of the Continent—both at the mercy of the next angry storm or pestilent,
damp-sheeted inn. It's almost like being together.*

*Once settled in Seville, I mean to begin the small self-
portrait in terracotta you asked for in your last. Why should you
call it a favour, my dear M., with the original at your entire
disposal?*

The last stretch across the Santa Morena was so rough that
Anne thought the carriage might crack apart. Bet and Sam chose
to stay inside and take their chances, but Anne put on her veil and
trudged alongside the gasping mules. To distract herself from the
grit in her boots she kept her eyes on the mountaintops. She spoke
to Mary in her head, preparing that night's letter.

*It's here, drinking in Nature's most grand & awful draughts,
that I breathe more freely than I ever have. Painful recollections
fall away & the World is nothing to me; the things & persons I
love, everything.*

She was worn to the bone, but by twilight there was the silver
Guadalquivir and Seville, with its Gothic buttresses, twelve-sided
citadel, and minaret, standing up against the purple sky.

APRIL 1791

Anne sensed the difference as soon as she crossed the Pyrenees:
France had become a country where travellers had to justify their
presence. In Bayonne she was called on by a ridiculous frog-voiced
mayor who wanted to present her with a tricolour cockade. She
pinned it on her hat promptly; she needed to please him to get
French money, a *passeport,* fresh horses and permission to leave
town. He apologised for not having any *ponche,* the English
favourite; she assured him she never drank punch and would be
glad of some tea instead.

In Paris, glittering in a superbly hot spring, the blue, white and red rosette was everywhere—on buildings, in gentlemen's lapels, on ladies' bonnets; even the Queen's Easter gown, ordered from Madame Bertin as always, was garnished with tricolour ribbon. Fashionable women were wearing the most extraordinary costume: a thin chemise gown of a startling simplicity, in white muslin, worn without stays: long unadorned sleeves, a drawstring neck without ruffles, a high waist just under the bosom and a skirt hanging straight down with no padding at all. Why, even Anne's night-gowns were of a more complicated design! The delicate, almost transparent drapery was a kind of legitimated nakedness. It was if Grecian statues had come to life and were drifting through the streets of Paris. Some ladies wore their hair caught back in loose, unpowdered waves, and others had taken the boldest step of all and cut it short, letting it curl round their faces. Anne had never seen women with cropped hair before, but the effect enchanted her; they looked like playful boys.

The Champs-Elysées were full of strolling couples; the Bois de Boulogne was thronged with horse-riders taking their exercise *à l'Anglaise*. There were no less than twelve theatres open every eve-ning. Anne went to a rather silly piece about a nobleman who'd spent the Revolution in a coma; now convalescent, he was shocked to find his servants out of livery, addressing him as plain *Monsieur* and his creditors banging on the door with presumptuous demands for him to pay his debts. He reached the nadir of gloom when he discovered that a bourgeois was trying to marry his daughter, and that he could no longer procure a royal *lettre de cachet* to imprison the upstart in the Bastille; that was a very amusing scene. But the lord-turned-citizen was finally educated and enlightened, of course, and it all ended happily. The audience seemed very merry and be-tween the acts they clapped and sang 'Ça ira'; Anne thought one of the lines referred to hanging aristocrats, but she assumed it wasn't to be taken literally.

She'd come prepared to pay her obligatory calls, but the Parisian manservant she'd hired returned to say that almost everyone she'd known was gone, many of them to London, where little colonies of émigrés were forming in Richmond and Belgravia. There were lots of English visitors in Paris, including Romney, the once-fashionable painter, and the notorious William Beckford. Anne did call on Madame de Staël, who was at her toilette with a host of visitors and her delightful baby. Everything was perfectly quiet at present, the *salonnière* assured her English friend, 'except for some demonstrations and effigy burnings, and we've learned not to mind them. How do you like our new fashions?'

'Very much,' Anne told her. 'So simple and natural!'

'Yes.' Madame de Staël laughed. 'Though ruinously expensive. We have to send our muslins back to Santa Domingo to be laundered, you see; that dazzling whiteness can only be restored by the tropical sun. Now I must carry you to the Assembly tomorrow, *ma chère*, as I know you're a political animal; you'll find it most stimulating. Shabby coats, but great flourishes. Though you've missed your chance to hear our great Comte de Mirabeau,' she said, her face sobering; 'he's just died of a putrid fever.'

Anne was shocked by that bit of news. That afternoon at the Louvre, the best thing she saw was a vast canvas by the celebrated Monsieur David, representing three young brothers of Ancient Rome pledging their lives in combat. It was of a pristine simplicity, almost brutal in its effect. The men swore on their bunched swords, the womenfolk and children sank down in grief, and behind were only two primitive columns and a yawning space, representing the abyss of history into which the Horatii meant to throw their lives. It was like marble sculpture, but on a canvas.

The next morning she was still in her dressing gown, having her hair put in loose curls in the Antique style—since she couldn't bring herself to cut it—when she heard vociferous voices and bustle in the ante-room. Bet came in, red in the face, and said it was a mob of women and she couldn't understand them, except that they were insisting on seeing Miladi Damer, whether she was dressed or not.

'What kind of women?' asked Anne.

'I'm sure I don't know, a low sort,' said Bet, looking over her shoulder as if the strangers might understand her English.

'*Ce sont les Poissardes,*' murmured Anne's hairdresser into his collar.

Sure enough, the miscellaneous reek when they swarmed in confirmed to Anne that these were half a dozen of the famous fish-wives and street traders of Paris, the ones who'd forced the royal family to march back from Versailles with them. A few had mar-vellous features that Anne would have liked to model—broad cheekbones, strong jaws. One of them marched up and presented her with a bouquet of white lilac. The exquisite scent startled Anne. What had she done, what did her name mean to these women that they should bring her flowers?

They stared back at her, as if waiting for something. Ah, they wanted more than thanks. In a murmur, Anne consulted the hair-dresser, who suggested she should offer some francs, as nobody cared for the new worthless *assignats*.

'*Merci, merci, jolie Citoyenne,*' they chorused.

Citizeness, she translated mentally; what an odd form of ad-dress! Of course, all titles had been abolished, she kept forgetting.

The leader emptied the six francs into her pocket and held her hand out again with a rather sinister smile. '*Merci, merci, s'il vous plaît.*'

Anne bit her lip. Really, she couldn't be dictated to by this odorous gang. But Sam was out at the market, buying wine with the hired manservant, and the hairdresser didn't seem inclined to offer any protection. And from the sounds of it, there was a larger body of women in the court below. Anne took another six francs from her purse and dropped it into the outstretched hand. '*C'est tout,*' she said with all the British firmness she could muster.

This seemed to cheer them up; they spoke of the Citizeness's *amabilité* and her *bonté,* and one of the women seized her in a vio-lent embrace. Anne smelt sweat and fish and something else she didn't recognise. She kept her spine rigid and waited to be released. '*Vive la nation!*' one of them roared.

'*Vive la nation,*' Anne repeated and another women kissed her on the cheek with a wet smack. *Oh, God,* she thought, *must I run the gauntlet and be caressed by them all?* But at this point they trooped off downstairs.

Anne sank back into her chair. She would have to have these night clothes washed before she left Paris. In the mirror her hair, half curled, looked a shambles. The hairdresser set to work again, tutting about the interruption. No one dared to stop the *Poissardes* from marching around with their bouquets, extorting money, he told her; next time, she could save herself time and inconvenience by sending cash down as soon as they knocked on the door. '*Visiter la Revolution,*' he teased her, '*ça coute cher!*'

VI

Tool Marks

*Marks left on a surface by the sculptor's tools,
often best preserved in hidden areas.*

⌒

THERE is a curious aspect of the British character, not often remarked on, viz. a positive fascination with the French. If the Emperor of China were to change magically into a Woman, or if the Russian serfs were to take to walking backwards, it would merit only a paragraph in a London newspaper. But when it comes to matters Gallic, no investigation is sufficiently exhaustive, no report long enough, to please the English.

In the days of the *Ancien Régime,* when the French lived in subjection to their Monarch, our preoccupation with them was mostly a matter of High Life. Given the close bonds of friendship and even sometimes kinship between the British aristocracy and the French, it is not surprising that this publication's readers have always taken an interest in the goings-on of the Comte de Poo, the Princesse de Pshaw, their furniture, amusements and cuisine. A certain *on ne sais quoi* in the atmosphere of Paris lends an air of chic to every bodice or jacket cut out in that city. Since the Revolution, the styles have altered radically, and cropped heads and transparent dresses are all the rage. Nonetheless, we continue in our slavish imitation—and not only in matters of Fashion but in Politics, too.

Many Englishmen have taken to crying like jealous children for Liberty, merely because the French have it, and to demanding a further dangerous toy, Equality, of which their Grandsires never dreamed. But others take Mr B—ke's tack and abuse France as a sort of volcano, which spews out Anarchy in all directions. This disagreement between this esteemed Hibernian and his colleague Mr Sh-r—n threatens to cause a Schism in a certain parliamentary Party. But both sides err in granting one nation such pre-eminence. As our Prime Minister recently put it, France should be considered neither as Heaven nor Hell, but as a country in a state of some Chaos, which should be left to its own devices.

—THE BEAU MONDE INQUIRER, *May 1791*

ELIZA LOOKED OUT PAST THE KNOT OF ACTORS ON THE stage, past the proscenium, to the ranks of stalls and boxes. When it was empty, Wren's theatre looked like such a strange thing, she thought; the dried-out inside of a honeycomb.

'So tell us, Manager, how's the Old Dame to be primped and patched?' It was Jack Palmer who threw out the question. Eliza smiled at her old friend, leaning stoop-shouldered against a flat. He was wearing a large grubby bandage, because in last night's *Siege of Belgrade* he'd sung his way through a scimitar fight with Michael Kelly and managed to thrust his forehead so violently against Kelly's wooden blade that blood had spurted all over the stage.

Kemble's hands were pressed together in front of his face, in a priestly way. When he spoke it was in his quoting voice. '*And behold, the veil of the Temple was rent in twain from the top to the bottom.* If you'll excuse the blasphemy,' he added.

Eliza stared at him and then at Mrs Siddons, who looked as bewildered as anyone; clearly he hadn't told his sister what was coming.

'Come now—' began the elder Bannister.

'For some time you have all have been aware that this celebrated theatre is in a parlous state.'

'Shabby and in need of repairs, but hardly *parlous*, surely,' protested Mrs Hopkins.

'Am I ever imprecise?' he asked his mother-in-law. She didn't answer.

'But she's stood up all right since the reign of merry King Charles,' protested Dora Jordan, still wearing her bright smile as she jogged her pudding-faced baby on her hip.

'In the opinion of all the architects Sheridan has consulted,' Kemble told them, 'this venerable edifice, this oft-patched, much-renovated monument to British genius—'

'All right, we're with you,' Palmer interrupted, helping himself to a finger of snuff from his Bastille souvenir box. 'When's she coming down?'

'Our last performance between these hallowed walls will be June the fourth, the king's Birthday. Complete demolition will follow.'

It seemed like a nasty joke. Eliza met the pouched, sad eyes of Tom King, their former manager. '*Our revels now are ended...*' he quoted glumly,

> *The cloud-capped towers, the gorgeous palaces,*
> *The solemn temples, the great globe itself,*
> *Yea, all which it inherit, shall dissolve...*

Eliza waited for him to trail off. 'But Kemble,' she asked, 'can it be rebuilt by September?'

Kemble shook his heavy head. 'Perspicacious as always, Miss Farren. It's not a question of mere rebuilding. The new Theatre Royal, Drury Lane, will rise lofty and awful, like some phoenix, full twice the size of its extinguished parent.'

There were murmurs of shock. 'What the hell's Sheridan up to this time?' asked young Bannister.

Jack Palmer straightened up and grinned, showing his stained teeth. 'Sherry's got a nose for the future, you must grant him that.'

Eliza turned on him. 'What do you mean?'

'Giant playhouses. The city's bulging and it's mad for entertainment. Why, look at the crowds turned away from our doors on

a Siddons night—or a Jordan, or a Farren,' he added quickly with
a sweeping bow that took in the three ladies.

Smooth, she thought.

'I wonder is it true', asked Pop Kemble timidly, 'that Covent
Garden's expanding too?'

So the manager didn't even confide in his own wife, it seemed.
That wasn't Eliza's idea of a real marriage.

Kemble nodded. 'Mr Holland is supervising the remodelling of
the rival theatre as well—but for us he will be creating something
entirely new and magnificent.'

'How?' asked Eliza too sharply. Henry Holland usually worked
for great lords like the Prince of Wales. 'Has Sheridan found a
backer with a bottomless purse?'

Dora Jordan raised one saucy eyebrow and Eliza felt a flush on
her throat. It couldn't be—surely—Derby wouldn't be fool enough
to let Sheridan wind him into his schemes?

'The whole is to be achieved by public subscription,' Kemble
explained. 'Debentures will be issued—'

'Deben whats?' asked Roaring Bob Bensley from the papier
mâché stump he was sitting on.

Mrs Siddons spoke up. 'The vital question, as it seems to me,
brother, is wherever shall we play in the meantime?'

'We have been offered a temporary home for next season at the
King's Theatre in the Haymarket,' said Kemble.

Eliza had heard enough; she muttered her excuses and walked
into the wings. The King's was a vast barn of a place, used for operas and ballets, all wrong as a *temporary home* for spoken drama.
She'd worked at Drury Lane for thirteen years and the thought of
its walls being pounded into dust was more than disconcerting.

Alone in the dressing room, she reread the invitation she'd received that morning. *Come, o Thalia, I beg of you a boon,* it read in
Horace Walpole's spidery hand, *lend your sparkling presence to a little
gathering at Strawberry Hill next Wednesday, to celebrate our dear Mrs
Damer's return from Iberian wastes. Dinner at four,* it ended more
practically.

Her mother popped her mob cap in the door. 'Are you at home, my dear?' *Fully dressed,* she meant.

Our dear Mrs Damer. Eliza would have to send a polite refusal. Could the whimsical antiquary really not know that she and his cousin hadn't been on speaking terms for more than a year? 'What is it, Mother?' she asked without turning her head.

'Lord Derby begs the favour of being perhaps permitted to pay his compliments.'

Sometimes Margaret Farren's borrowed speech set her daughter's teeth on edge. 'By all means.'

Derby picked his way past the open costume trunks to take a seat in the corner; there was no room for his footman, who waited in the corridor. Mrs Farren took her usual stool and picked up the stocking she was darning. (Years ago Eliza had tried to make her resign these duties to the dressers, but the only concession her mother had made was to swap her darning for a more genteel knotting bag when they were out in company.) Derby had come straight from the Commons and he seemed very agitated about a showdown over the French question, which had concluded with Burke denouncing his former protégé Sheridan as *a gull of the Jacobins.* 'They're two of our strongest pillars,' he groaned. 'This could very well split the Party.'

'Surely not,' murmured Eliza, her mind still on Walpole's invitation.

Derby leaned his chin on the knob of his cane. 'When the Bastille fell, I never anticipated it would cause such aftershocks in this country. Oh, I passed Citizen Stanhope's carriage on the Strand,' he added more cheerfully after a pause.

'I thought he didn't keep one?'

'Well, that's the joke of the thing; the radical Earl still won't answer to *Your Lordship,* but he evidently found he couldn't manage without a carriage—so the compromise he's hit on is the coat of arms has been painted over, like in France!'

Eliza laughed, but her eyes were on Walpole's invitation. She moved to fold it up.

'Ah, yes,' said Derby, recognising it, 'this Strawberry Hill dinner sounds rather fun, doesn't it? I haven't been rowed up to Twickenham in years.'

'I don't believe...I may not be free on Wednesday.'

The Earl sighed. 'Your objection is to Mrs D., I assume?'

Eliza stiffened.

'I must confess—I didn't mean to pry—I asked her about the
puzzling breach in your friendship.'

Her voice came out like a bullet. 'When?'

'Oh, before her departure for Lisbon. She said little, but she
seemed mortified.'

'Yes,' said Eliza, very low.

'Ah, so she does have something to reproach herself with, then!'
Derby sounded as if he'd solved a puzzle. 'It's a shame; during our
wonderful theatricals at Richmond House Mrs Damer seemed to
like you so much—took to you like a long-lost sister, in fact—and
I'm sadly disappointed that she let some old scruple of birth or rank
get in the way in the end.'

Eliza winced.

'Why, she talks so Whiggishly, parading her liberal views—'

'You misunderstand, My Lord,' she said. *Oh, God, will this subject never stay buried?* What if he accosted Anne Damer about her
snobbish views on Wednesday? 'It wasn't she but circumstances
that curtailed our friendship.' Eliza flicked a look at her mother,
who was examining her needle as if she were alone in the dressing
room. She felt a weary impulse to get this over with, since Derby,
for once, was refusing to drop the subject. 'There was...well, a
scandal. This is really very painful for me to speak of, particularly
to you.'

Margaret Farren's head had shot up; it was the first she'd heard
of any scandal. She met Eliza's eyes in the mirror for a moment,
then dipped to her darning again.

Eliza cleared her throat, the way inexperienced actresses did.
'Almost two years ago I was told—I was made to understand—that
Mrs Damer's...amiability, her warmth of friendship, was being

looked askance at in some quarters. Sneered at, maligned, you know. Libelled.' She could feel the blood creeping up her neck. She decided not to mention the fact that she herself had been named; that would only distress the Earl further. 'I was shown a lewd verse about Mrs Damer—'

Derby's face cleared. 'Oh, not that old Sapphist stuff.'

Eliza stared at him. It wasn't relief that she felt; she wanted to slap him.

'Forgive my flippancy, my dear. It's only, don't you know, *that* silly story must date back a dozen years or more.'

'I am aware of that,' she said, almost growling.

He was wearing a broad smile. 'And none of us—no one with any sense—credited it then, nor wouldn't now either. Less, in fact, since the lady in question is now past forty! Why, the very idea that a scholarly widow would indulge in such Oriental vices...' He let out a yelp of laughter.

Put like that, it did sound ridiculous. Eliza stared at her buffed fingernails.

'It's tommyrot, if you'll forgive the pun,' Derby went on, not even lowering his voice. 'The pamphleteers say the same thing of the poor Queen of France and half her friends, just for fantastical malice. I probably shouldn't mention this in female company,' he added, 'but I met a real Sapphist once, a German countess. She was an extraordinary creature—leering at all the maids and mannish in the extreme, with a hairy mole on her chin.'

She felt dizzy with embarrassment. 'These indecencies may be funny to you, My Lord—'

'Oh, come now, Miss Farren,' said Derby, rushing over to seize her hand in his, 'I didn't mean to offend your sensibilities. I do apologise. I've been rather a boor.'

Margaret Farren was staring at their joined fingers as if an alarm were going off in her head. Eliza took back her hand, but traded a small tight smile for it.

'I simply can't bear that two delightful ladies like you and Mrs Damer should be alienated from each other by such nonsense.'

'I never said I believed it,' said Eliza incoherently. 'I knew there couldn't be any truth in it. Not that I know anything about these things, but Mrs Damer isn't a bit like...the female you describe.'

'Well, then,' said Derby, resuming his seat.

'It's not as simple as that,' she said through her teeth. 'Oh, no doubt it's different for men of the World, at Newmarket, or in the dining room at Brooks's; the Prince has some intimates with the most appalling reputations. But men seem to have a firm foothold on the height where they stand, whereas we women—how we totter and wobble, and the least tug at our skirts can bring us crashing down!'

'You put it very eloquently,' he murmured.

'Reputation's a harsh goddess. In my position—' Eliza waved at the narrow walls of the dressing room, and hoped to God that neither Mrs Siddons nor Mrs Hopkins was about to walk into the middle of this scene—'I can't afford to rouse her wrath by allowing myself to be associated with such an unspeakable vice. I'm no great lady, I'm plain Miss Farren, soon to be an actress without a theatre'—Derby looked puzzled by that, but she hadn't the patience to explain—'and I can't weather what you call *nonsense*.'

After a moment he said, 'I can see I've angered you.'

'No, no,' she said unconvincingly. Her heart was hammering.

'Again, forgive me. But I have to dispute one point: you're no mere *Miss*. You're the idol of the English nation and your position on Olympus is unassailable.' Derby's voice was smooth as cream. 'I only wish you'd confided your fears two years back and I could have said what I say now: this bizarre rumour withered away long ago.'

'It sprang up again, then,' she snapped. 'Mr Siddons wrote this epigram—'

'William Siddons?' asked Derby, incredulous. 'I never heard a thing about it. But in any case he's a nobody. All these scandalmongers are nobodies: jealous gossips, petty poetasters, newspaper hacks. They don't matter. They're just the scum that floats on society's river; the hungry curs snapping at our heels. An age of liberty is coming, my dear; the old proprieties and timidities won't matter any more.' His beady eyes were gleaming. 'Why, your daughters will laugh to hear how rule-bound and hedged-in your sex used to be in back in 1791!'

Your daughters. It came to Eliza then that the Earl expected to be widowed in time to marry and get children on her. For all his respectful gallantry, he never seemed to doubt that it would happen. His confidence staggered her.

Derby had remembered his point. 'And I can assure you that the true members of the Beau Monde—men and women alike—have the greatest respect for Mrs Damer. Speaking for myself, I'm honoured to count her as my friend.'

'I was too,' said Eliza, hoarse, avoiding her mother's eyes. 'But I'm afraid it's too late.'

'Surely not.'

'I treated her coldly,' said Eliza, wanting to cry. 'I dropped her and I wouldn't give an explanation. I didn't know what to say. I still don't.'

'But do come along on Wednesday. Won't you?' he asked, rising to take his leave.

'Perhaps,' she said, miserable.

When he'd gone Eliza turned to face Margaret Farren, who was clearly in a sulk. 'Mother, I know you're wondering why I never told you this before.'

A loud sniff. 'No, no. Such filthy things are better not spoken of.'

Eliza wasn't sure how to take that. After a minute she asked, 'What do you advise, in view of what Derby said—should I go to Strawberry Hill or not?'

But Mrs Siddons and Mrs Hopkins came in together just then, discussing their mutual dislike of Gothic melodrama and the best shade of greasepaint for scars.

ANNE ARRIVED at Strawberry Hill at half past three. Walpole, encased in an old-fashioned but finely cut grey silk coat, told her she was looking marvellously Spanish. 'Not tanned, of course, but there's a warm glow about you; it suits your eyes and your dark hair.'

'Who's coming to this dinner?'

'Your sister, Richmond, your parents, Derby, Miss Farren and her mother, and Sir Charles Bunbury to even up the sexes.'

She looked at him hard. 'You invited Miss Farren?'

'I did,' said Walpole, fingers at his lips. 'I thought it a suitable occasion.'

'For what?' Anne asked almost rudely.

He gave a little shrug. 'Rapprochement.'

She let out a sharp sigh. 'There's no chance of that, I assure you.' He didn't know about the epigram—the real reason for the broken friendship. Anne had no intention of upsetting her god-father in his twilight years by revealing that William Combe's cruel and fantastical invention was dogging her again. 'Miss Farren will send her excuses.'

'No, I have a pretty note from her saying she and her mother will come,' said Walpole sleekly. 'And another acceptance from her *unalterable Earl,* as I've taken to calling him.'

Sometimes her cousin's fondness for his own phrases made Anne's hackles rise.

But his face had fallen. 'I keep thinking how perfect it would be if the Berrys could be here with us—but for that we must drag out perhaps six more endless months.'

To distract him from that topic she asked him about the recent theft of silver from his house in Berkeley Square.

'Oh, it wasn't much—just a strainer and a spoon.' Walpole low-ered his voice. 'Philip looked into the matter and found the shop where they were pawned; the culprit's description sounded dread-fully like my footman John. I had no stomach to accuse the boy, so I let him ride behind the carriage to Twickenham just as usual—but Philip and Kirgate privately urged him to confess it to me. Instead, the boy ran away on Friday night; the housekeeper had locked all the doors as usual, so he seems to have dropped from the library window and gone off across the meadows, without his hat, even!'

Anne's mouth twitched at Walpole's concern for the hat. 'That is upsetting.'

'Poor fellow, he might have confided in me; I wouldn't have turned him off, only docked his salary somewhat for a lesson,' lamented Walpole. 'I should have kept my silver locked up and not put temptation in his way.'

Affection surged through her.

Now I'll have to hire another footman; do you know of anyone reliable?'

Anne shook her head. 'Good ones like my Sam are diamonds at the moment.'

Her parents arrived with the Richmonds at ten to four and shortly afterwards Derby came up the drive on horseback with his friend Bunbury. But no Farrens, *fille* or *mère*. Walpole put off dinner by half an hour. Anne answered questions about her travels a little distractedly. 'Yes, via the plains of Andalusia to the kingdom of Granada.'

'Such stamina, through all privations,' marvelled Lady Ailesbury.

'Did you see the Alhambra?' asked Sir Charles Bunbury.

'Of course. I adore Moorish style,' Anne said, 'but the palace is miserably ruined and daubed with whitewash.'

'Ah, if only the thing could be shipped wholesale to England, we'd know how to preserve its glories,' said Derby.

He glanced over at the door. Was he thinking what Anne was thinking—that the actress wasn't going to show up?

The gentlemen were standing up. Anne leapt to her feet. There was dumpy Mrs Farren, lifting off her daughter's pleat-edged pelisse and passing it to the footman. Anne felt a blush mark her cheeks like a slap. *It's all right,* she thought, no one's looking at me. She was dizzy; she feared she might faint. It was simply the shock of such an encounter after all this time. The mortification of it. Eliza was making her apologies to Walpole: a rehearsal had run late, the hackney driver had been unwilling to go as far as Twickenham, then the cab had cracked a wheel.

'Why, how very à la mode you are, Miss Farren,' murmured Lady Mary.

'And how you carry it off!' said Lady Ailesbury.

The actress was in the new French look from head to toe. Sheer
white muslin with tinsel spots, shirred at the neck, which was very
décolleté, showing creamy breasts; the dress was bound just below
the bosom and hung down as straight as a candle, except where it
touched the delicate curves of hipbones and belly and thigh; little
slippers with no heels; short fair hair, curling round her ears like
a baby's, with a single feather dancing from a headband above it.
'Oh, it's an easy style,' the young woman murmured, 'it flatters any
wearer.'

'Not so,' said Anne, too loudly, and Eliza's eyes flicked up to
hers. They hadn't greeted each other yet. 'Only the tall and slim can
really achieve such a Grecian impression,' Anne went on as imper-
sonally as she could. 'Last month in Paris I saw a terrible old dowager in one of these dresses, like a pudding forced into its bag.'

Sir Charles Bunbury brayed with laughter.

Eliza, who was wearing barely a hint of rouge, gave her a remarkable smile. It had amusement in it and a shadow, too, Anne
thought. 'They're so comfortable, and freeing. One seems to float
along.' They had evidently decided not to be afraid to speak to each
other.

Derby was watching his beloved, *like he watches a winning horse*,
Anne thought. 'Was it a wrench to sacrifice your wonderful hair,
Miss Farren?' The title sounded strangely formal in her mouth.

'No, no,' said Eliza. 'I'm so used to altering my looks on stage,
you know—brunette one evening, silver-wigged the next—that I
never mind a change. It's not that I'm not vain, but my vanity per-
tains to the whole, not the parts.'

'You look exquisite, of course,' Walpole fretted, 'but mightn't
you take cold in these delicate draperies?'

'It is almost June,' she reminded him sweetly, 'and I have a
shawl.' It looked like kashmir to Anne; the actress had draped it
over one shoulder in the antique style.

'Oh, that reminds me,' cried Lady Ailesbury, 'our dear Sir
William Hamilton's coming to England this summer, with Miss
Emma Hart, whom he means to marry—you know, the lady who's

won such fame for acting all the famous classical statues in an Indian shawl; people rave about her expressiveness.'

The girl was also famous for being Hamilton's nephew's cast-off. Anne shuddered with relief that she hadn't accepted the diplomat's proposal if his tastes were so low. 'I should have thought classical statues were known for their serene *lack* of expression,' she murmured.

'Let me take you in to dinner now, Miss Farren,' said Walpole, offering his left arm, as the right was swollen with gout. Bunbury, with a show of enthusiasm, asked Mrs Farren to do him the honour. Walpole had planned that well, Anne thought; Mrs Farren would be less embarrassed by a baronet than by a duke or an earl.

The dishes were laid out in neat patterns all along the table in the dim refectory. Walpole found Eliza a seat near the fire that was blazing within the arches of one of the villa's elaborate carved hearths. He drew everyone's attention to the fire screen—one of Lady Ailesbury's worsted pictures depicting a vase of flowers, inlaid in mahogany and ivory. Anne happened to know that he kept the thing in here because he only used this room about once a year.

Anne was describing to Richmond the swathings of black lace she'd had to wear in Spain. 'I beg your pardon?' she said, turning towards the actress.

'I only asked were you happy there?'

It occurred to Anne to say, *What concern of yours is my happiness?* 'Yes,' she said defiantly, 'immensely happy. The climate—and such antiquity and grace in everything I saw, I was almost inclined to settle there.' Cries of protest from several of the guests. 'Really, to be reincarnated as a fine orange tree in a Moorish garden at Seville, with cooling fountains playing around one's roots, would be a fine fate.'

This bit of Oriental whimsy caused considerable amusement.

Anne had little appetite; she fiddled with some stewed lamb. Walpole was describing his consultations with mad-doctors on behalf of the young Lord Orford. 'My nephew's financial affairs are of a singularly chaotic nature and he's taking to harnessing his phaeton to four red deer.'

'Oh, dear,' said Lady Ailesbury.

'That's what I said,' he joked, 'oh, *deer!*'

The Richmonds started describing the new fashionable dance from Vienna, the *ländler*. Bunbury, on Anne's left, was pestering the actress for information about her colleagues at Drury Lane. 'Is it true that Mrs Crouch and her husband live in a harmonious threesome with Mr Kelly?'

'It was,' Eliza said coolly, 'but the singers have recently sent Lieutenant Crouch packing with a good allowance.'

'And Dora Jordan—can you reveal what terms she's come to with the Duke of Clarence?'

Eliza's lips pursed. 'The papers have been so full of the royal negotiations, I don't see what I can add.'

'I read that her friends are asking an annuity of £12,000 a year and an equipage for her,' contributed Field Marshal Conway, 'with her children by all parties to be provided for.'

'Miss Farren is an expert on the arts of theatre,' Anne found herself commenting, 'not on the scandalous lives of other players.'

'Well said,' murmured Derby. There was a slightly awkward pause. 'Did any of you see Kemble play Cato the other night? When he fell on his sword rather than submit to the dictator Caesar, I wept like a babe.'

'Stupendous, isn't he?' said Conway.

'I've been reading Mrs Inchbald's *Simple Story*,' said Lady Ailesbury. 'Apparently she based the priest hero on Kemble; he was schooled in a seminary, did you know?'

So they were back to gossip about actors' private lives again; Anne sighed inwardly. Well, the one thing she was determined not to let the conversation sink to was political strife; too many dinners ended in a quarrel nowadays. There was a bad moment after dessert, when someone rashly mentioned Mirabeau's death. 'Yes, My Lord, I *do* call it good news,' Walpole said to Derby.

'The cause of liberty—' the Earl began.

'Liberty!' Walpole interrupted. 'No one's more devoted to true liberty than I am. That's why I abhor the Assembly, which has marred a good cause by the most outrageous extremism. A lion attacks only when hungry or provoked, but who can live in a desert full of hyenas?'

Walpole had a knack, Anne thought, for making his own hyperbole sound like the King James Version. 'No contention at table, gentlemen,' she said a little crisply. 'Might I suggest a game? Twenty Questions, perhaps?'

Walpole, a little sheepish, nominated Anne—as the guest of honour—to take on herself the responsibility of choosing a subject.

'It must be something generally known, though,' said Bunbury; 'none of your obscure Greek things.'

'Very well,' said Anne. 'Give me a moment...'

Richmond asked the standard opening question. 'Does what you've thought of belong to the animal, vegetable or mineral kingdom?'

'The animal.'

'Is it living or dead?' asked Walpole.

Anne made a little face. 'Living, I suppose.'

'You suppose?' repeated Walpole severely.

'Well, I suppose it's not quite dead.'

'My coz is toying with us,' he told the group. 'Trying to throw us off the scent. May I remind you that your father and I have been playing Twenty Questions for the last half-century?'

Eliza giggled, showing her pearly teeth.

'Third question?' asked Anne.

'Is the thing entire in itself, or in parts?' said the Duchess of Richmond, covering a tiny yawn with her hand.

'Entire in itself.'

'Is it private or public?' asked Eliza after a second's pause.

'Private,' said Anne with some significance. She let herself look at the actress.

'Does it exist in England or abroad?' said her father craftily.

'In England.'

'Oh,' said Conway, 'I was sure it would prove to be something foreign.'

'It could be foreign, but presently in England,' said Walpole, tapping the side of his nose.

'It could indeed,' said Anne.

'Is that a hint?' asked Mrs Farren.

'Not a bit of it,' said Derby. 'Mrs Damer would never give a hint. Is it unique or are there others of the same kind?'

She hesitated. 'I would have to say...unique.'

He fixed her with his eyes. 'Meaning there are things that are similar to it but not identical?'

'Is that question seven?' she asked innocently.

'No, it's a clarification of question six.'

'Perhaps you should have clarified question six before you asked it.'

Derby chuckled and had a long draught of claret.

'Ah! You're a hard player, my dear,' said her father, shaking his head.

She smiled like a sphinx.

Gently elbowed by her daughter, Mrs Farren ventured a question. 'May I ask, what is its shape?'

'The question's too particular!' came a chorus and she shrank back.

'Ask something else,' Eliza whispered.

'Is it large? I mean to say,' Mrs Farren corrected herself hastily, 'is it larger than, say...this apricot?' Her hand held the fruit up nervously.

'It is,' said Mrs Damer, giving her a reassuring nod.

'Larger than this table?' asked Bunbury.

'No.'

'That leaves us with quite a range,' complained Richmond to his wife.

'Question nine, I believe,' said Lady Ailesbury. 'Has it any connection with the person of the King?'

'Oh, Caroline,' complained Conway, 'you always ask that.'

'None,' Anne told her parents.

'Is it generally stationary or movable?' asked Walpole.

'Movable. Moving, in fact,' she added.

He furrowed his brows. 'I'll get it, you know. You've never beaten me yet.'

'There's always a first time.'

'Question eleven—' began Richmond.

But Derby was there before him. 'Is it historical or does it exist at present?'

'Both,' she said.

Mrs Farren looked puzzled.

'Meaning it's existed for some time?'

'Yes, if that's question twelve,' she said.

Walpole folded his skinny arms. 'No, your first answer was obscure. *This* is question twelve. What—'

'I hate to interrupt you,' drawled Richmond, 'but Derby here stole my go. My question is: is it for ornament or for use?'

'Neither,' she said, smiling to herself. *They'll never guess it.*

This caused some consternation.

'If it provides neither ornament nor use, neither beauty nor utility, what's it for?' complained Walpole.

'Is that a rhetorical question?'

'Not a bit of it.'

'Of course I'm not going to tell you what it's for,' Anne answered. 'Besides, I don't believe I know the answer.'

'You won't weasel out of it that way,' said Bunbury.

'To know a thing's name is not fully to understand it, sir.'

'Question thirteen: is it a bottle of brandy?' asked Walpole, which raised a laugh. His cheeks were scarlet. She shook her head at him fondly. 'Question fourteen—'

Derby wagged his finger at him. 'You, sir, must hold your tongue, even if you are the host. Mrs Damer, has the thing in question any connection with any person here present?'

'It has.'

A stir of interest. 'Which person?' wondered Eliza.

'Too particular!' they all shouted and she laughed.

'Has it any connection with...the Duke, say?' asked Lady Mary, putting her hand over her husband's.

'None,' said her sister.

'You'll use up all our questions that way; the company numbers ten,' objected Walpole. 'Question fifteen—'

'Sixteen,' she corrected him.

'Is it?' he asked suspiciously.

Conway, counting on his fingers, nodded.

'Sixteen, then. Has it any connection with any gentleman here present?'

'None,' she said demurely.

'Ah, that narrows the field,' said Lady Ailesbury. 'So we know it's to do with a female guest.'

'Unless she's not counting one of us as a gentleman,' Derby told Bunbury with a chuckle.

'Question seventeen,' Walpole rattled out before anyone could stop him, 'has it any connection with yourself?'

She rewarded him with a long smile.

'Well hit, Walpole,' said Derby.

'I know how the little demon's mind works,' he told the company. 'After all, I've had to put up with her since she was in swaddling clothes.'

'I never swaddled either of my daughters,' objected Lady Ailesbury. 'Even before I read Rousseau I was all for liberty.'

'Well, I suppose I mean those tiny dresses Missy used to run about in when you'd leave her with me at Strawberry for the summers.'

'That's quite enough reminiscence,' said Anne, mortified at the image.

'We need an eighteenth question,' Derby pointed out. 'Mrs Farren, would you be so good?'

'Oh. Oh, dear, my turn again. Is it, is the thing green?' the old woman ventured.

The company couldn't help but laugh.

'How could an animal thing be green, Mother?' asked the actress with a hint of irritation.

'Oh, I'm sorry, I'd forgotten, I thought she said vegetable.'

'Were you thinking of the asparagus soup, Mrs Farren?' asked Conway merrily.

'A bird could be green,' objected Bunbury, 'or an insect, or a frog.'

'They're not classed as animals,' Richmond put in.

'Never mind,' said Mrs Farren, sucking in her lips, 'somebody else ask something.'

'No, no, your question is perfectly valid,' Anne told her. 'The thing is sometimes...metaphorically green, yes. And that's a vital clue.'

'Oh, thank you,' said the older woman, but her face was more confused than ever.

'Only two left, and just about all we've established is that it's something that's occasionally green, to do with my sister,' said the Duchess with mild despair.

'No,' said Derby, 'we know that it's something entire and more or less unique, which has existed in relation to Mrs Damer for some time and still does. It moves, it's of an animal nature, for private use—' That sounded somehow obscene, Anne thought, and Derby must have thought so too because he hurried on. 'Or rather, a private thing, of no clear use nor ornamental value. It's currently in England and has no connection with any gentleman here, nor with the King. In size it's something between an apricot and a table.'

Several of them laughed. 'Clearly put, Derby,' murmured Richmond. 'We could do with a mind like yours in the Cabinet.'

Anne gave him a startled look; was this a joke or a bait thrown out in full view of the company?

Derby smiled blandly.

'It's her dog!' roared Conway. Bunbury laughed and so did Mrs Farren. 'I've hit it. That charming little greyhound, what's her name?'

His wife gave him a glare.

'Fidelle,' said Anne into the silence. 'She was of a highly ornamental and useful nature,' she added as lightly as she could, 'but I'm
afraid she died in Lisbon.'

'Oh, terribly sorry, of course, my dear,' mumbled her father, 'I
don't know how it slipped my mind.'

'Question nineteen,' said Walpole, wiping one eye. 'Is the thing
hot or cold?'

'Sometimes the one, sometimes the other,' she told him.

'Oh, you equivocating chop-logical female!'

She grinned at him. 'Last question, anyone?'

'Does it beat?' asked Eliza.

Anne looked her in the eye. She laughed softly and started
clapping.

'What?'

'Has Miss Farren hit it?'

'What's the answer?'

'Oh. Poor show. We should have guessed,' said Derby ruefully.

'What?'

'I don't understand,' wailed Mrs Farren.

'It's her heart,' her daughter told her.

'What?'

'Mrs Damer's heart.'

'Oh, I call that a very hard one,' said Lady Ailesbury re-
proachfully.

'I'm fairly vanquished,' said Anne, giving the actress a little
bow. Philip came in just then and whispered in his master's ear. It
was probably time for Anne to lead the ladies off to the drawing
room so the gentlemen could get on with the serious drinking. She
was about to suggest this, but then she noticed Walpole's stricken
face. 'What? What is it?' she asked him.

His fingers were pressed to his shaking lips.

'Bad news, Horry?' asked the Field Marshal.

Walpole cleared his throat. 'The worst.'

'France?' asked Derby.

Their host shook his head. 'John.'

For one ridiculous second Anne thought of her husband. *Don't be absurd.* Which John could Walpole mean?

'My footman,' he said brokenly. 'The poor creature's hanged himself. One of the gardener's men just found him in a tree near the chapel.'

There was a terrible silence. 'He'd stolen some silver,' Anne told the company. She meant it as an explanation but it sounded like a judgement. She wished she could take the words back.

'I suppose he feared he'd hang for it anyway,' said Walpole, 'but I never would have sent him to the magistrate for the sake of a spoon! I have more spoons than I'll ever need. I meant to pardon him as soon as he confessed to the theft; I'm not a harsh master.'

'Of course you aren't,' Lady Ailesbury told him.

'Oh, but I should have called him in and forgiven him; I should have set the boy's mind at rest. Why did I wait? He couldn't have been more than eighteen,' sobbed their host.

The company were looking at each other uncomfortably.

'He's already half putrid—oh, excuse me, ladies!—which means he's been hanging there since Friday!'

Anne thought she might be sick.

'Don't blame yourself, Horry, my dear,' said Conway hoarsely. '*Felo de se* is getting shockingly common these days; there's always one or two in the papers.'

'That's true,' said Richmond, glancing at Anne despite himself. She knew they were thinking of her husband. 'It's said that the English temperament, by its tendency to melancholy, is more prone to it. When *The Sorrows of Young Werther* came out there was a rash of imitations.'

'Perhaps people don't fear God as they used to,' suggested Lady Ailesbury.

'Or they're lonely,' said Eliza.

A tear fell on Walpole's dessert plate.

Bunbury spoke up suddenly. 'Too much sitting around and dwelling on things, that's the problem. More hunting and horse riding would clear out the cobwebs.'

Anne looked at the Baronet coldly.

'But Hume—the philosopher, you know, he was my secretary once,' said the Field Marshal. 'Hume had a theory that every rational man is free to kill himself if he wants to.'

The party broke up fast after that.

JUNE 1791

Eliza chattered over the tea table. 'So Lord Derby and I mean to go to see the wreckers start next week. His theory is that if we observe the destruction of Old Drury as a grand spectacle we won't find it upsetting. Audiences are all for spectacle, these days, you know.'

'Miss Farren—' said Anne Damer.

'Why, just last week some workers at the Albion Mills Company, across Blackfriars Bridge, they'd been laid off because of new machinery, so they went in a mob and burnt the place down—and a huge crowd gathered to watch the fun!'

The visitor set down her cup. 'Shall we speak frankly?'

Eliza's pulse was pounding in her throat. She nodded.

'I must confess I was surprised when you asked me to call here at Green Street.'

She couldn't speak. A sort of paralysis gripped her. She hoped her mother wouldn't come back early from shopping for lace.

'You and I were once on close terms,' said the sculptor, almost businesslike, 'till something happened to alienate us. Forgive me for venturing on this mortifying subject, but am I right in thinking that you'd heard something—were told something—which reflected on my reputation?'

Eliza nodded again, like a scolded child.

'May I simply ask, was it in the form of... a verse?'

'It was.' Oh, the relief; she didn't need to spell it out.

This time it was Anne Damer who nodded. 'The very same bit of filthy doggerel was sent anonymously to me, before I left for Lisbon.'

She doesn't know it was I who sent it, thought Eliza. *She has no idea.*

'I don't mean to dwell on this ridiculous calumny, but may I just say…might I just clarify—' The older woman spoke almost sternly, but with hesitation. 'I've been puzzling over what to say to you since I got your note.'

'No need,' said Eliza, frantic. It was enough that they understood each other. She'd been right to give way to the overwhelming temptation to meet. 'No need to speak of it. I simply—'

'But I must tell you, Miss Farren—since you've given me this unexpected opportunity—I want to assure you, to give you my word, that there's no truth in the slander. No truth at all.' She spoke so plainly that no one could have disbelieved her.

It was a curious thing, Eliza thought, that the sculptor had never looked handsomer. 'No, I never thought so,' she answered, her throat raw.

'That vice is unknown to me. I've never committed—'

Eliza rushed in. 'It wasn't that I believed it, I assure you.'

A nod. 'In the case of our sex, private virtue is almost irrelevant.' The words came out bitterly. 'Shame doesn't depend on guilt. Why else did Richardson's Clarissa have to die after the rape, though her soul was still pristine?'

Eliza stared at her. 'I'm so very sorry.'

'Some might say that you had no choice but to cut off our connection,' said Anne Damer.

Eliza's eyes were wet. *Some might say.* But of course she'd had a choice. A choice, at least, to speak or stay mute; to be a friend or an enemy.

'In your position—dependent as you are on the continued approval of the public…' The older woman trailed off. 'Do you think I don't know how fortunate I am', she added vehemently, 'to be able to dedicate myself to art without having to sell my work? To keep my skirts lifted above the mud of the market place? We both enjoy fame, Miss Farren, but in your case it exacts a higher price. While I was abroad, I realised how free I am: I can come and go from England, sculpt what I like, live as I choose, no matter what some pamphlet readers may think of me. Whereas you are the public's servant.'

Eliza screwed up her courage and seized one of those thin, strong hands. 'Your words bring me such relief.'

The other woman squeezed back. '*Tout comprendre, c'est tout pardonner.*'

'I should have confided in you, when I first heard those dreadful rumours. I should have trusted you more. I can't explain what a terror gripped me—the dread of being suspected, of being associated, with...'

'...a Sapphist.'

Once the dreadful syllables were out, the air in the parlour seemed lighter. Eliza nodded; it was only a word, after all. How she'd missed this woman's frank rigour. She picked up her cup and half drained it before realising it was cold. 'My situation's so peculiar, you see. Not just in regard to my profession, but... Lord Derby as well. Some would say I've kept him at arm's length for so many years I must be cold. Unnatural.'

'Just what they said of me when my husband killed himself,' said Anne Damer. 'How quick they are to blame us for behaving with dignity in situations that are none of our making! We are women who have some power'—with a graceful shrug—'and so the favourite prey of the many-headed hydra.'

Eliza blinked at her.

'Scandal.'

'Of course,' said Eliza, pretending she'd caught the allusion.

'I found myself arguing with Fox about this recently at a picnic in Richmond,' said Anne Damer. 'In the debates on his Libel Bill he spoke so eloquently in defence of the freedom of the press—despite the fact that his character has been subjected to constant flaying at the hands of the printers.'

'How admirable.'

'Yes, it is—but my point is that only a man can afford to take that attitude when portrayed as a grossly debauched sot and Jacobin traitor. No woman who'd been so abused could show her face in public.'

Eliza nodded miserably.

'Now, as I say,' Anne Damer went on, 'I bear no grudge against you. I've not been lonely,' she added, 'especially since I've been honoured by the close friendship of Miss Berry.'

Eliza felt a surge of something absurdly like jealousy. Had she been so easily replaced, and by a nobody from Yorkshire? 'I've not had the pleasure of making her acquaintance, but I hear great things of her.'

'All deserved, I assure you. But I feel it only fair to myself to tell you that the danger seems to have passed.'

'The danger?'

'Of further scandal,' explained Anne Damer. 'None of my friends has mentioned seeing anything in print. Whoever penned that nasty epigram seems to have held his peace since—or *her* peace, I suppose,' with a small shudder.

She doesn't know it was Siddons's husband. And she must never learn it was I who sent it to her.

'Really, I think libels erected on a foundation of complete fantasy do tend to crumble away.'

That was exactly what Derby had said; he'd laughed at Eliza's fears. Had she panicked because she was only a parvenue, lacking the inborn confidence of birthright members of the World? 'You and I could be friends again,' she said, her head suddenly clear.

The older woman's smile was wary. 'If you were willing to take that risk.'

Eliza swallowed her fear. She held out her hand to seal the bargain. 'Anne.'

The angular face seemed to tremble. 'Eliza.' And their hands came together like magnets.

I took tea with Thalia—you know who I mean, Anne wrote to Mary in Italy. *This will surprise you. But we had a very frank discussion & have cleared up our difficulties—or our difficulty, for there was only ever one. I'm rather pleased that the friendship seems to be reviving.*

The pen paused in mid-air. *Rather pleased* had a pallid ring to it. *Very pleased,* she added conscientiously, *tho' it's still provisional &*

I'll find it hard to trust again where my trust was betrayed before—for which I don't blame the party in question now, she added confusedly. How hard it was to explain this resurrection of a dead friendship. Anne feared she sounded both petty and naïve. *I must hope that Scandal has turned her pestilent tongue away from me for good, not only for my own sake but for the sake of those whose affection for me has been unwavering.* That sounded too vague and plural. *You'll recognise your portrait here,* she added awkwardly. She couldn't get the tone of this letter right. Of course, there should be no monopoly in affection, but still she couldn't help thinking that Mary would be less than delighted by Anne's reconciliation with the actress.

> *On Fordyce's instructions I've spent the last week at Felpham, sea bathing, walking & sitting solitary like King Canute while the waves plash my feet. It seems to be improving my circulation & easing the cough brought on by my return to England. The sun was so sparkling & the water so smooth, I couldn't help wishing some good spirit would gently transport you to me,* per aërum, *for one half-hour.*
>
> *By the way, I smiled at your excuses for the two-page letter that cost me double to receive. Do you imagine I'd grudge paying twelve pence to hear more of you & your proceedings than a single sheet can contain?*

Anne was about to scatter sand on the letter to dry the ink when Sam came into the library to ask if she was at home to Mr Walpole and General O'Hara.

'O'Hara!' Anne gave him her hand to kiss in the Continental manner. He was looking as ruddy and black-haired as ever. 'Cousin, you couldn't have brought me a more welcome visitor.'

Walpole smirked. 'The General's only just out of quarantine and his leave is almost up, you know.'

'I asked if I might be lucky enough to catch a glimpse of you before heading back to Gibraltar,' said O'Hara. 'It was such a great pleasure to drink a glass of wine with you in Lisbon.'

His eyes flashed, almost flirtatiously, Anne thought. 'A glass? I think you finished the bottle. Will you take some now?'

Once Walpole was ensconced with his swollen foot on a cushioned stool, he asked had she heard the news from Paris.

'The entire royal family of France have disappeared,' O'Hara explained. 'It seems they've made a dash for the border to escape into Austria.'

'Oh, but this is dreadful,' cried Anne. 'For Louis to conspire with the Queen's relatives and flee—after he wore the tricolour—after all those vows to stand by his people and the Revolution! That's the worst kind of perjury.'

Walpole snorted. 'I wouldn't term it a flight but an escape from captivity. Vows to gaolers don't count.'

'I didn't know Louis had so much courage in him,' said O'Hara.

'You call it courage to betray his country?' Anne protested.

'On the contrary, my dear,' said Walpole, 'I'm sure he means to save it by returning from Austria with an army of liberation. The rebels may cry *Vive la Nation* as loud as they please, but they've lost their puppet. Now we may see the Revolution put down at last.'

Anne was too upset to carry on the argument.

Pretty soon, Walpole make his excuses; he really had to get home to Berkeley Square and take to his bed. But the General settled back comfortably into the red silk armchair.

'Have you been fêted on all sides during your stay?' she teased as she passed him a tray of cinnamon biscuits. 'Breakfast parties, routs, balls, boating excursions...'

'That sort of thing,' he said with a grin.

'War heroes must tire of such treatment.'

O'Hara snorted with laughter and opened a button on his waistcoat. Anne stared, startled. He pulled his shirt a little to one side and showed her a red pockmark, almost hidden in black fur. 'My American scar's ten years old now. I'll need some fresh wounds if I'm to pose as a hero. And of course England will have to go to war again first.'

As he buttoned himself up again Anne thought, *What's happening here?* No man had ever unbuttoned his shirt in her library before. 'It's a shame you haven't been able to renew your acquaintance with the Misses Berry,' she said distractedly, 'but we don't expect them till the autumn.'

'You must give them my warmest respects.'

'I will,' she said, still seeing in her mind's eye that hairy inch of muscular chest. 'Do you look forward to Gibraltar with pleasure?'

'Oh, the Rock's a handsome sight, rearing up out of the ocean. You'd love the place,' he told her, leaning forward suddenly. 'That dry Spanish climate, the light—wonderful for sketching or carving—'

It couldn't be, Anne thought. *I must be imagining this.* She was forty-two. *But then, O'Hara's past fifty.* She decided to pretend she'd no idea what he was hinting. 'Oh, London suits me well enough.'

The General was shaking his big, piratical head. 'Your father says you suffer with your lungs.'

'I can still out-walk him on every hill in Oxfordshire,' she said with a small laugh.

'I'll bet. You always did have more than your share of vigour,' he told her, lounging back in his chair and fixing his eyes on her. 'You're made of stronger stuff than the mass of your sex.'

'I'll take that as a compliment, though an odd one,' said Anne.

'Oh, do. You know I've never met a woman I liked so well.'

O'Hara, O'Hara, what are you doing? What absurd scene are we playing out, here in the soft candlelight of my library, in our middle age?

'You know that, don't you, my dear Mrs D.?'

What am I supposed to say now? Anne opened her mouth and covered it with her hand. *I am no one's Mrs D.* 'Your glass is empty.' She got to her feet in one movement. 'What a churlish hostess—'

'No, I'm the boorish guest who forgets to make his exit,' said O'Hara, on his feet.

'Well, I'm afraid I am expected at my sister's,' she improvised. 'You've been very kind.'

'I'm...I'm truly sorry I couldn't ask you to stay longer. I wish you every success in Gibraltar,' she said, forcing herself to look into his black eyes.

'You could wish for another war, with another wound to make me famous!'

'Never that,' she said, shivering. 'Don't even joke about it.'

'Till next time, whenever or wherever that may be.'

'Till then,' she told him.

She slept wretchedly that night. She dreamed of the old Moorish town of Gibraltar, with its clogged streets; she was chasing a woman who turned out to be Marie Antoinette. Not the creamy-skinned Dauphine whom Anne had known in the '60s, but an old hag with cynical eyes.

She woke and stared at the ceiling. O'Hara's hinted proposal had been bizarrely sudden; whatever was happening to courtship in this hasty modern age? Should she have asked him for a little time to consider the offer he'd been about to make? Several of her friends and relations would think it a marvellous prospect for her to spend the rest of her days in a hot climate with a cheerful, handsome general, even if it would mean a step down in rank from the Honourable Mrs Damer to a mere Mrs O'Hara. But no, Anne didn't want to leave her native land. On the other hand he was an old friend of the family; she knew him better than she'd known John Damer on the day she'd married him. At least O'Hara was sturdy; Anne couldn't see him shooting himself in the head over money.

Oh, this was pointless, why was she arguing the pros and cons when she knew in her bones that she could never marry Charles O'Hara? The idea was laughable, somehow. There was nothing wrong with him, but she liked not being married, she realised now. She liked being answerable to no master, coming and going as she chose, picking her own friends and working as hard as she liked. She wasn't so much a widow as a spinster reborn. She suddenly found herself thinking of Piranesini, said to be the last of the great castrati, whom she'd recently heard sing at the Hanover Square Rooms. His voice had such an unearthly sweetness that it had made her cry. Was this because Anne too had unsexed herself for her art?

Besides, it hadn't come to a proposal; she'd steered O'Hara away in time. Nothing had happened. She wouldn't tell Mary, even; she'd bury the incident too deep for recollection.

The next morning word reached London that the escaping French royals had been arrested by a grocer at a village called Varennes.

OCTOBER 1791

One Friday at Newmarket Heath, Derby and Bunbury sat side by side in a light autumn rain, looking down at a field of six. Really, there was no better way to spend a morning than watching horses run, Derby thought. He was in a good mood and so was the country, because the wheat harvest had been splendid. Despite Burke's frothing speeches, the Cabinet had declined all pleas from the émigré princes for a joint invasion of France to restore an absolute monarchy; instead, they'd sent congratulations to the Assembly on Louis's signing the new Constitution. Finally, after ten years of unbroken peace, Pitt had agreed to reduce Britain's armed forces and cut unnecessary taxes. The tight-jawed Eunuch was still the enemy, of course, Derby thought, but every now and then he couldn't help but do something right.

'Who do you fancy, Derby? Barrymore's Chanticleer is the favourite, but at seven to four it's hardly worth the stake. I've put a bit on Lord Grosvenor's Skylark at eleven to five,' said Bunbury. 'Have you got yourself a *General Stud Book,* by the way? Splendid new publication; you can check a pedigree in half a minute.'

'Yes, but there's more to a horse than his lineage,' Derby pointed out. 'I was going to back Escape today, but he did so poorly yesterday that I lost 50 guineas on him. The other horses were practically rubbed down by the time he limped in.'

'Past his best,' said Bunbury, nodding sorrowfully. They watched Escape's jockey, the dandified Sam Chifney in ribboned boots and love-locks, whisper in his ear. 'Very odd the Prince is still running him, when he's so much good horseflesh in his stables.'

'Well, he's always been a chancy creature—'

'Who, Prinny?' This made Derby laugh. 'Actually, I'm surprised he hasn't withdrawn Escape from today's course, as it's a full four-miler,' Bunbury pointed out.

'Well,' said Derby with a shrug, 'Escape's a stuffy horse who needs a good gallop to warm him up. And if Sam Chifney's feather-light hands can't coax some speed out of him...'

'Yes, the Prince's pet has invented a new species of riding, hasn't he?' said Bunbury enviously. 'Ever so subtle in his pacing, doesn't push till the final stretch and never beats a horse, or cuts his mouth, even.'

The noisy flash of a pistol and they were off, Chanticleer leading, with Skylark behind him. The gap narrowed; the horses clumped together, all running well despite the wet ground. Derby used the spyglass in the top of his cane to examine the field. Skylark, now, then Chanticleer, with All for Nought in third. Babylon, Mother of Pearl, Little Pickle, Escape. Skylark still had it; Bunbury must be counting his winnings. Derby looked away from the course to grin at his old friend. But Bunbury was pointing with a frown. Derby looked back as the horses came into the final furlong and scrubbed the rain off his spyglass with his handkerchief. Escape was speeding past the others as if he had wings; Chifney, bottom in the air, perched on him like a monkey. Escape, Chanticleer, Skylark. *Surely not.* Escape, it was Escape, past the line.

A few scattered cheers soon died away. There was a strange kind of silence. Derby looked at his friend, who was going purple. 'Bunbury—'

No answer.

'What just happened?'

'It smells like rat, that's all I'll say. It smells damnably like rat.' The Baronet stamped down the steps of the stand. Derby rushed after him.

The betting room was pandemonium. A herd of men who'd backed Chanticleer were protesting. 'We've been done—bilked and bubbled,' howled one.

'You took your chances,' snapped the man opposite him.

'Pox on that! There's been some skullduggery.'

Bunbury and the Prince of Wales were standing less than a foot apart when Derby caught up with his friend. 'All I'm saying, Your Royal Highness,' said Bunbury with pointed deference, 'is that the matter needs to be looked into. As President of the Jockey Club, I feel it my duty—'

'What *matter*? What *matter*?' Prinny interrupted him, staccato, sounding oddly like his father. 'The race was run and the race was won.'

'It's very curious, that's all,' insisted Bunbury. 'Very strange that a horse from your stable, that crawled along like cold sausage yesterday should suddenly get such a spring in his heels today.'

'What are you insinuating?' barked the Prince, standing very tall in his striped silk jacket; his stomach bulged from under it. 'That Sam Chifney deliberately and maliciously held Escape back yesterday to get a long price today? I don't believe you're making that accusation!'

'I'm making no accusation.'

The Earl of Barrymore threw his arm carelessly over the round royal shoulder. 'Well, as Chanticleer's owner and the loser, surely it's up to me to cry foul? My horse was beaten by my honourable friend's here and that's all there is to it.'

Bunbury looked between the two aristocrats. 'All I'm saying is that a full investigation's called for, if the Jockey Club's to retain the faith and goodwill of its members. I propose that Chifney be questioned by myself and my fellow stewards, Mr Panton and Mr Dutton—'

The heir to the throne turned on his heel and walked away, Barrymore hurrying after him.

The next few hours were a whirlwind of rumour. Later in the

afternoon, after some cold beef in an inn, Derby glimpsed Bunbury in the crowd and pulled him aside. 'What did you get out of Chifney?'

Bunbury made a rude noise. 'Claims the horse just needed a good warm-up and that he only made 20 guineas off the race.'

'So will you be leaving it at that?'

'I will in my hole,' said Bunbury. 'Chifney may ride like the Archangel Michael, but he's a cocky little lying dilberry.'

'How far up does the cheat go, then?' Derby murmured in his ear. 'Just Chifney? Or the stable manager? Or Prinny himself?'

'I don't know,' said Bunbury, 'but I know my duty. Fudging a horse's height by making him duck an inch, or calling a young four-year-old three, or claiming a false start, those aren't worth a fight with royalty—but this is an outrage. Come on.' Arm in arm with Derby, he marched back into the betting room.

There was Prinny in the corner with a glass of champagne. Derby felt Bunbury quail slightly beside him. 'Are you sure about this?' the Earl asked his friend.

'I am.'

'Even though you'll be making an enemy of the next ruler of England?'

'Are you telling me not to? The Jockey Club mustn't be a respecter of persons. If we suspect sharp practice we must name it, in commoner or king.'

'I wouldn't dream of stopping you,' said Derby, grinning at his friend.

'Well, then.' Bunbury walked forward and stood at the perimeter of the little circle. The Prince was finishing a joke, something about the new look in ladies' clothing, how high-waisted dresses made them all look *enceinte*, so the guilty were camouflaged among the innocent.

'Ha ha!'

'Splendidly put, Prinny!'

Finally he turned and said with crisp rudeness, 'Well?'

Bunbury began a little hoarsely, but didn't clear his throat. 'I've

been deputed by my fellow stewards, Your Royal Highness, to inform you that no proof has been found of the guilt of Sam Chifney
but there remains a strong suspicion.'

The Prince of Wales looked at the Baronet with a kind of attentive disgust, as if memorising his face.

Derby found himself moving forward. He didn't push; he just
positioned himself gracefully by his friend's side. They were on the
edge of the cloud of perfume the heir to the throne always carried
with him.

The Prince's eyes flicked over him. 'Derby,' he said without a
nod. 'Don't tell me you're mixed up in this business?'

Derby threw up his hands. 'Only as an observer. I wouldn't
dream of interfering in a Jockey Club inquiry; after all, that's what
we elect the stewards for.'

This gentle reminder made the royal eyes bulge.

Bunbury spoke up again. 'Our decision has been a painful one
but necessary. We wish to tell you that if Sam Chifney ever rides
one of your horses again, no gentleman will enter the race against
you.'

'Oh, you *gentlemen* need have no fear of that,' said the Prince
after a long moment. 'This was my last race. I shall retire from the
Turf.' He turned aside and held out his champagne glass for a refill.

That night, at the noisy inn, Derby and Fox sat sucking the
bones of a very tasty duck. 'Don't you think there's a kind of glorious independence in what the stewards did, though?' Derby asked.
'Isn't it a sign of the times, a mark of our confidence as a generation
whose task is to root out corruption and reform Britain? Our fathers would never have stood up to a Prince of the Blood Royal like
that.'

Fox started to laugh. He wheezed and then he coughed, and
Derby thought his friend might be choking on a small bone.

'What is it?' He thumped Fox's back.

'When you put it like that, Derby, there's something peculiarly
English about the whole affair. Trust us to have our own Revolution, but on a miniature scale on a racetrack! No, but I think it's a

sad misunderstanding,' added Fox, sobering. 'I'm convinced the Prince's people pulled a cheat but he knew nothing of it.'

Fox never liked to believe any ill of his friends, thought Derby. 'The Prince may be near thirty, but he's as temperamental as a child,' he pointed out. 'I suspect he was rather glad of an excuse to sell up his stable and clear some of his debts; they say it'll save him £30,000 a year.'

'We simply must stay on good terms with him if we're ever to get into government,' said Fox in a low voice. 'He's been vastly twitchy about *Frenchified ideas,* especially since Louis's botched flight to Varennes; he called me and Sherry in to Carlton House in July and showed us that outrageous Gillray cartoon with myself as executioner holding an axe over King George's head! He pretty much ordered us to stay away from the Bastille celebrations.'

Ah, so that was why they'd been conspicuously missing from the Whig party for the second anniversary; Derby felt irritated that neither of them had told him at the time.

'So Sherry and I went to Ascot with the Prince instead and I lost a shocking lot of money. Mrs A. wasn't pleased. She'd be just as happy if I gave up horseflesh, especially after a scandal like today's. To tell you the truth, I've been thinking of selling my own stable.'

'Gad, the market will flood if you all desert the Turf at once,' complained Derby. He put his hand over Fox's and said more seriously, 'My friend, you're doing a marvellous job of tightrope-dancing.'

Fox's doggish eyes brightened as he laughed at the image.

'No, really. You're holding to the middle ground on these divisive French questions and keeping the Party together, focused on what matters—Reform and British liberties and resisting Pitt,' he finished rather incoherently. 'Posterity will thank you for it.'

Fox gave his hand a hot squeeze. 'Loyallest of hounds!' Then the Duke of Devonshire walked past their table and Fox sang out, 'Pull up a chair and crack the marrow from a bone with us.'

He stood between them, unsmiling. 'Can't do. I've just been given a message.'

'Bad news?' asked Derby.

'No idea.' Devonshire lowered his voice. 'I don't know the fellow who spoke to me. All he said was he'd been asked to tell me I should visit my wife immediately.'

Derby and Fox exchanged a blank glance, trying not to let their thoughts show. 'When did you see dear Georgiana last?' asked Derby.

'Oh, not for six or seven weeks; she's been in Bath for her health.'

'Well. The message probably got muddled,' Derby murmured.

'Yes. Do give her our warmest regards, though, won't you?' said Fox.

They waited till the husband was well out of hearing. 'Could it be what it sounds like?' Derby asked.

'All too easily, I'm afraid,' said Fox, his jowled cheek falling on to his fist. 'Grey's been up and down to Bath a lot this autumn; he's missed more committee meetings than I can count. And I've heard him bandy her name about when he's drinking.'

'Grey may be a hothead, but Devonshire's a cold fish,' pronounced Derby. 'He must be the only man in England who's never been even slightly in love with Georgiana.' That got a rueful laugh out of Fox, who'd always been more than *slightly*. 'If he'd only treated his wife with a bit of respect and tenderness, she might never have got into this sort of trouble,' Derby went on. Of course Georgiana had had her little *affaires de coeur* over the years, with Dorset as well as Fox, if rumour could be believed, but she'd never behaved with such a wild disregard for appearances before.

ANNE WAS writing a letter of some delicacy to her mother.

> *You say that your kinswoman the Comtesse d'Albany has delayed her visit to Park Place, with the consequence that it will now overlap with Miss Farren's &, as you put it 'Miss Farren does not speak French well, it may not be the thing & de plus the house would be very full.' Am I to understand by this that you wish me to put off my friend's visit? Her French is certainly*

*adequate for group conversation. Would it not be 'the thing' be-
cause she's not of high birth? I confess I can't see why a young
lady of unimpeachable reputation, whose rank is based on her
own talents, should have to give way to the Comtesse—a* soi-
disant *queen only in being widow to the Young Pretender—
who's accompanied on all her travels, moreover, by an Italian
poet to whom she's not married!*

Then Anne took a long breath and screwed up the page. What was
the point of fighting her mother on this occasion and insulting the
pseudo-royal guest? Eliza would hardly enjoy a visit to Park Place
if her hostess were nervous or hostile. It would be better to put her
off with some excuse to another time. If it had been Mary, Anne
could have poured out the whole story, but the actress was a different matter. Though they were friends again, to Anne's great pleasure, there was always some reserve, some veil between them now.

Dearest M., *cara anima,* she began on a fresh page,

*As you asked I broke the news of your fall down the river bank
as gently as possible, but you know W.'s magnifying mind—he
received it like a bomb thrown under his chaise longue!*

*You say Ag. is far less willing to come home than you are, but
for once, my dear, I urge you to think of yourself; you're too fond
of making sacrifices. I now count the weeks, & soon the days, till
your return to London. Though how can meeting in the flesh
satisfy me any more deeply than our meeting of minds on paper
has, these twelve months? Travel safely; apply for your* passe-
ports *early; be sure to burn all letters, however harmless, before
you cross into France.*

'The Duchess of Devonshire, madam,' said Sam at the door of
the library.

'Oh! Have you shown her into the parlour?' Anne asked. 'Then
tell Mrs Moll to brew us some tea.'

Georgiana was sitting on a yellow sofa, examining the seams of her gloves.

'My dear! This is a rare pleasure.'

'*Darlingest* Anne.' A kiss on each cheek in the French manner. But the lovely Duchess's eyes were rimmed with red.

Chit-chat lasted till halfway through the first cup, then Georgiana's spoon clattered in the saucer. 'How lucky you've been to avoid all the dreadful complications of existence,' she remarked.

Anne felt insulted and smiled to hide it.

'Such a hurrying life we married women lead! Husbands, and friends, and *childies*, and everything—'

And lovers, Anne understood.

'—it's all too much, sometimes—and I've lost some letters of great value to me,' Georgiana went on. 'I thought I locked them up safe but I can't recall where they might be, in Chatsworth, maybe, or Devonshire House, or Chiswick—it's bewildering, having seven houses, or is it eight? What a freak my scullery maids must think me, with my elaborate problems and my astronomical debts!'

Anne took her hand to calm her. She couldn't help noticing that Georgiana's wrapping gown was tied rather loose. 'How's your health?'

Georgiana gave a little shrug.

'Are you by any chance...to be congratulated?'

A violent sob. 'No. No. Oh, Anne, I'm *miz*, I'm sorely entangled! I'm making my round of farewell visits.'

'Where are you going?'

'The town of Nice, if we can reach it.' Tears welled up beneath those beautiful long lashes. 'Pay no attention, I'm a leaky bucket,' said Georgiana, 'it's only my...' She waved vaguely over her bodice.

Anne nodded. So: *in an interesting condition* and leaving the country without delay, that could only mean that it wasn't the Duke's, it was Grey's. 'Let me lend you a handkerchief.'

'You're very kind, but I've got one,' said Georgiana, fumbling in her reticule. 'These tiny bags are all the rage since dresses have become too slim for pockets,' she said almost normally. 'I've got five, I must give you one. Derby calls them *ridicules*.' Her face was buried in the lace-edged handkerchief.

Anne wondered how to approach the delicate subject. Ten years ago it would have been easier—but Anne didn't feel on such close terms with Georgiana these days. No one in London judged the Duchess harshly for taking a lover, since in young Hart she'd already provided a legitimate heir for the Cavendish estates, and especially since she'd been so tolerant of her husband and Lady Bess. But a pregnancy did make the whole business trickier. 'Won't the Duke...guess the reason for your departure?'

'You don't understand, it's he who's ordered it.' Georgiana burst into loud tears. 'He rode into Bath at midnight and marched into my room, demanded to see my...my *figure*.'

Behind her back Mrs Moll came in with a plate of little cakes; Anne gave an infinitesimal shake of the head and the housekeeper disappeared.

'Oh, how he roared! And he denounced darling Bess and my sister Harriet as *conspirators*!'

Well, they were, Anne thought uneasily.

'Canis has made me choose: if I don't go to France to save his shame and quite give up the...the person in question,' said Georgiana with automatic euphemism, 'I'll never see my *childies* again. So I've agreed to go into a sort of exile—myself and Bess and the Duncannons and my mother. He's packing us off without a guinea between us. We couldn't pay for the passage if dear Lady Melbourne hadn't raised the sum for us—and God only knows when Canis will let us come home. Or if.'

Anne stroked the Duchess's arm through her thin silk sleeve. 'It seems strange of a man of liberal views to turn so judgemental,' she murmured.

'One slip—one *méchanceté*—and how we women are punished,' Georgiana wailed. 'He—not my husband, you know the very dear person I mean—he begs me to let myself be divorced, he swears he'll marry me—but I couldn't give up Hart and the girls.

He's furious, he writes such brutal letters...But the worst of it is the Duke won't let me bring the little ones abroad with me, nor say farewell to them, even.'

Anne, her arm round the shaking Duchess, had a moment of clarity. These were the powers men had. Charles Grey could destroy this woman's life by his indiscretion, then write her *brutal letters* because she wouldn't choose him over her own children. As for the Duke of Devonshire, he could let his wife and mistress and relations starve, or be captured by bandits, perhaps, as they made their way through the chaotic South of France. A husband might be the best of men, or the worst, but that was not the point: his rights were unlimited. She thought of O'Hara, and shivered at the idea that her life could ever have been in his soldier's hands.

NOVEMBER 1791

'Do my old eyes deceive me, am I dreaming? Is it really you?' Walpole held out two trembling, swollen-jointed hands to Mary Berry.

Even on this longed-for day irritation pricked Anne. Really, it was like a burlesque of Lear's reunion with Cordelia, performed on a crimson damask sofa at Strawberry Hill.

'And darling Agnes! And Father Berry! How astoundingly well you look, after all your perilous voyages and travails.'

'Oh, you too, sir, very much so,' said Agnes, who was wearing a chic small bonnet.

'You flatter me, *chère fraise*,' said Walpole, wiping one eye. 'Oh, there it is, the fatal scar,' he cried, one shaking finger extended towards Mary's nose.

It was a tiny pink line, under its dusting of powder; her hand shot up to cover it.

'Didn't one of Fielding's heroines have a broken nose and wasn't she all the more charming for it?' said Anne to lighten the moment.

Mary gave her a covert smile. They hadn't had a moment to themselves yet. Anne had brought the little terracotta head of herself, but she didn't want to present the gift in front of the whole company. 'Oh, when I was eighteen I would have been cruelly anxious about such a scar, but I've achieved philosophic indifference,' said Mary, not quite convincingly. 'The days of my vanity are over and heaven knows they weren't happy enough to regret.'

The guests had to be dined, and led all over the house to admire this new piece of china and that arrangement of Holbein prints, and given tea, and wept over again, and shown the latest products of the Strawberry Hill press. They all crowded into the tiny tribune, where Walpole sparkled as he told the story of his own recent fall. 'At ten past four, Tuesday fortnight, my foot caught in this carpet and I crashed down against the marble altar.' He patted it with satisfaction.

Agnes covered her mouth with a gasp.

'I bruised the muscles of my side so badly that for two days, I assure you, I couldn't move without screaming. The lucky stroke was I should surely have broken a rib, but that I fell on the cavity whence two of my ribs were removed ten years ago!'

'You're very noble to call that *lucky*, sir,' suggested Mr Berry.

'Well, I mended and lived to see this happy day.' Walpole clapped his hands. 'Now that my *wives* have returned, not another complaint shall ever pass my lips; I'm ready to dance at my own wedding!'

Mary gazed at him like a doting mother, Anne thought.

Over cordials in the small parlour he claimed that the Beau Monde had transmogrified into a nocturnal species since the Berrys had left England. 'They go about like ghosts. It's entirely out of fashion for a woman to be at home before eleven, so they invite you to drop in at midnight—which is rather too late to begin the day, unless one's twenty years old.'

They laughed in chorus.

In the evening he led the party across his estate, into the woods, to the slightly ramshackle house that was to be the Berrys' new country home. It had once been known as Cliveden, when his old friend the actress Kitty Clive had lived there, but now it was to be renamed Little Strawberry Hill. 'Don't thank me for fulfilling my own dearest wish, ' he protested in the sunny hall.

'As if we could know where to begin,' said Mary. 'But the fact that it's impossible to thank you sufficiently for your kindness— your burning interest in us, your matchless affection—shouldn't be taken to mean that we forget it.'

'Pooh,' he said pinkly. 'When two witty young beauties, who might have their pick of distinguished company, choose to throw away so much time on a forlorn antique...'

Anne couldn't listen to much more of this. Of course, she delighted in her cousin's devotion to the Berrys, but somehow she'd lost her tolerance for his high flights.

Walpole was wringing Mary's hands like a washerwoman. 'My sole ambition is to live long enough to pass an unbroken summer with my little wives here at Twickenham.'

'What, only one?' Anne teased him.

'Oh, I shan't spurn twenty more summers if they're granted to me,' he laughed. 'But one mustn't be presumptuous at seventy-four. And though my eyes, ears, teeth and motion have lasted this long, I don't know that I should care to survive any of them.'

'You forget to number your mind among your assets, sir,' Mary told him.

'Ah, my dear girl, how precise of you. I should thank the gods I'm not yet quite a vegetable...'

'What do you think?' Mary murmured to Anne, tucking her arm into hers as they walked up the second flight of stairs.

Anne could feel the small fingers against her ribs. After a full year apart, it was strange and delightful. 'Of Little Strawberry? It's quite charming.'

'No, but...of us living here. My family. It was all arranged so fast, I still don't know quite what I feel about it.'

Anne smiled at her. 'He won't accept any rent, I assume?' She knew Walpole had sent the family letters of credit to bankers in every city they were to pass through, just in case they ran short.

Mary sucked in her lips. 'I've argued the point, but his logic hammers me down. I worry that we'll be seen as taking the most dreadful advantage of him.'

'Oh, Mary, you're making an old man very happy.'

'Mrs Damer, should we have these pale-green walls painted cream for a more classical effect?' Agnes called up from the hall.

'I don't advise it,' said Anne. 'The green suits the pastoral atmosphere.'

'Will you come and stay here?' Mary asked softly.

'Try to stop me.' Anne laughed. 'Perhaps you and I could work on our Greek together this year?'

'Oh, *yes*. You know,' she said very seriously, 'my body may have only just arrived, but my mind and attention have been with you for months already.' She was flicking through her tiny memorandum book. 'I must go up to town on Tuesday on a business matter.'

'Then you'll come to dinner at Grosvenor Square,' Anne told her. 'I have that little terracotta of myself to give you.'

Mary's eyes lit up like dark candles.

'What are you two in such a huddle about?' called Walpole.

Anne looked down at him; she was tempted to say *none of your business.*

'Little Strawberry Hill, of course,' said Mary, going down the stairs. 'How could we speak or think of anything else but this extraordinary gift of yours?'

DECEMBER 1791

Eliza avoided going near the hole in Russell Street where the wreckers had reduced Old Drury to dust. She still wasn't used to performing in the cavernous auditorium of the King's Theatre, which rumour said was costing Sheridan far more than he could afford; on its vast stage she'd had to learn to walk more imposingly and throw her voice. Familiar faces were missing; Mrs Siddons, for instance, was taking the waters at Harrogate after a miscarriage caused by the unmentionable ailment passed on by her husband. (It gave Eliza some small pleasure that William Siddons, the source of that hideous epigram, was now the target of malicious talk in his turn.) And who could tell how long the Drury Lane company would be stuck here?

Today she'd got hold of Mr Holcroft in the Green Room. 'Call me Tom,' he said, grinning at her. 'I may dub myself a playwright these days, but it's not so long since I was an actor, and a shoemaker and stable boy before that, so I'm certainly no gentleman.'

She gave a tight smile. He was wrong if he thought she'd swear friendship with him because they'd both come from up from the gutter. Eliza had become a lady though her own efforts—and this *Tom* had better not forget it. He might be an old friend of King's and the Kembles', but he was getting a name for radical ideas. 'I fear Sheridan's political sympathies have blinded him to the risks of staging your *School for Arrogance*,' she said, tapping her script. 'My role, for instance—'

'Oh, Lucy Peckham's an eloquent Whiggish damsel, rather like yourself, Miss Farren—not an Amazon. You'd never catch her storming a Bastille!'

'But she might send men out to do it.'

Holcroft shrugged cheerfully. 'That's their lookout.'

The man was an outspoken atheist, too. Two years ago this comedy might have prompted cheers, Eliza thought regretfully, but nowadays it could just as easily be denounced as *Jacobinical* and *democratical*.

The boy rapped on the open door. 'Lord Derby outside, ma'am, says to say whenever you're ready—'

'Yes, yes,' she said. 'If you'll excuse me, Mr Holcroft?' She left him with one of her dazzling smiles, before he had time to object, and collected her mother from the dressing room.

'Apparently,' murmured Mrs Farren in the draught-whipped corridor, 'Mrs Jordan got horribly hissed last night.'

'For her acting?'

Her mother slapped Eliza's hand merrily. 'For her influence over the Duke of Clarence, of course.'

Eliza smiled like a cat. Gillray's latest cartoon had shown the

actress as a chamber pot or *Public Jordan, Open to All Parties.* Some
papers attacked Mrs Jordan for milking the King's third son of a
large allowance without even having the decency to retire from the
stage, while others jeered at Clarence for living off her salary. She'd
been accused of everything from abandoning her children by Ford,
to plotting to be a duchess. Eliza was usually sympathetic when her
colleagues came under fire in the press, but really, this time she
could only rejoice. 'Proof, if any were needed,' she murmured to her
mother now, 'that an actress who goes into keeping loses every last
shred of dignity...'

She waited for a smart answer, but Mrs Farren only pursed her
lips.

In the carriage Eliza sank back against the plump upholstery,
enveloped in her fur pelisse. 'A long day, my dear?' asked Derby.

'Too long,' she said. Really, the Earl was like an ideal husband:
all the compliments, and none of the demands; all the solicitude
and none of the orders. 'And you?'

He gave a concise and witty report on the company at Melbourne House; since poor Georgiana's hasty departure Lady Melbourne had become the reigning Foxite hostess. There'd been hosts
of émigrés, of course, the royalists glaring furiously at the more recently expelled moderates like Madame de Genlis and a 'rather
striking' protégée of hers who went by the name of Pamela Égalité.

Could Derby possibly be trying to arouse her jealousy by mentioning this girl, Eliza wondered?

The carriage had slowed to a crawl. Derby rapped on the ceiling and his coachman's head appeared, dangling sideways in the
window. 'Sorry about this, M'Lord. There's a fire on Whitehall.
They say it might be Richmond House.'

Eliza had clutched Derby's arm before she knew it. She took
her hand away again before her mother noticed.

'Bring us there, and quickly,' he called.

'But it's such a crush—'

'Take the side streets. Use your whip.'

'Make way!' Eliza heard the man roar, overhead. 'Earl of Derby's carriage, make way!' The whip cracked. A wagon lurched out of the way. Mrs Farren was craning out of the window. Eliza shut her eyes; she felt slightly sick.

'My dear ladies,' said Derby, 'I'll jump out at the corner of Whitehall and the driver can bring you straight home to Green Street.'

'I wouldn't dream of it,' said Eliza, injured. Sometimes the man could be *too* uxorious.

'Hm, well, I suppose if you stay well back—'

'Mother,' she said, 'you go on home; I'll come after you in a hackney.'

'If you promise to be careful,' said Margaret Farren dubiously.

It appeared to be snowing, but it was ash, falling heavy through the winter air. Richmond House had curtains of flame and it was sending up a black tongue of smoke. Oh, the crackle and the terrible howl of it!

By the time the driver helped Eliza down from the carriage, Derby had flung off his jacket and sprinted over to the burning building. Eliza felt unaccountably angry. What did he think he was playing at? The Sun Fire Insurance Company wagons were here already and the watermen were passing buckets from hand to hand. Three of them were trying to throw a hose in one window, while another three worked the handpump.

'Miss Farren! Eliza!'

She spun round, and there was Anne, with her sister, waving from the other side of the road. She ran to meet them. Anne's eyes were red from the smoke. 'Oh, Lady Mary, I'm so terribly sorry,' said Eliza. 'Has anyone—' She broke off, uncertain how to frame the dreadful question.

'We're all out, safe and sound,' said the Duchess of Richmond, calm as ever.

'That looks very like the Duke of York,' said Eliza, staring at the knot of men across the road. It was strange to see them in their shirtsleeves, especially in the middle of winter; indecent, almost. The backs of their waistcoats were much plainer and shorter than the fronts.

'Mm,' said Lady Mary, 'York's been marvellous, I must say; he brought his regiment in to help with the engines and keep back the crowd. And the Duke of Clarence has been up to his knees in water!'

'Well, that's a comfort,' said Anne wryly, 'to have two Princes of the Blood acting as your watermen. By the way, I heard York's to get another £18,000 a year on his wedding.'

'Yes, Derby says Prinny's sick with envy,' confided Eliza. 'Envy only of the money a legitimate marriage brings, of course—not the plain Prussian bride!'

'Was that Derby I saw plunging into the fray?' Anne asked.

Eliza nodded. 'He's covered in soot already. Look, he and Bunbury seem to be carrying statues out.'

'They're the antique casts from his sculpture academy, remember?' said Anne.

'Oh, yes,' said Eliza, suddenly taken back to that day in Richmond House; that foolish mistake she'd made, thinking all the statues thousands of years old. 'But isn't that one of yours?' she asked, shading her eyes.

'So it is! A pair of puppies, the first I ever carved,' said Anne, looking relieved.

'Luckily the fire started slowly,' said Lady Mary, 'so we were able to get the real valuables out hours ago.' She seemed unconscious of the insult to her sister. 'I have my jewels and most of my clothes. The high point of the drama was when Henriette spotted Délice at the window. My husband offered a reward of 10 guineas to whoever could rescue her and a fellow passing in the street lashed three ladders together, climbed up and brought the spaniel down!'

'Yes, and she bit his arm for his pains,' said Anne.

'Who's that young man?' asked Eliza, tucking her hands into her fox muff to warm them.

'Oh, Charles Lennox, our nephew,' answered Lady Mary, 'and heir, of course.'

Eliza's eyes met Anne's briefly. How strange to know that, because of your barrenness, your husband would have to leave everything to a relation.

Just then there was a crash and the gentlemen leapt back; something in the great house must have crumbled. 'Oh, our little theatre,' she said, startled by the memory.

'Charred beams by now.' Anne sounded so bleak that Eliza slid her hand into the crook of her elbow. Anne glanced at her with a ghost of a smile. It was rare for them to be seen to touch, since their renewal of friendship. 'Well, young Lennox's inheritance won't include Richmond House, not unless the insurance pays enough to rebuild it.'

'I'm afraid there's no question of insurance,' murmured the Duchess.

'Mary! What do you mean? To let it lapse—'

'Goodwood's cost such a great deal; we were cutting our expenses, or trying to,' said the Duchess, tight-lipped.

'But the risk of fires in London—' protested her sister.

'Oh, it was a gamble, that's all there is to say. At one time or another we all risk more than we should.' Lady Mary wiped ash out of her eyelashes.

Derby came over, his white shirt daubed with black. His ugliness had taken on a certain grandeur, Eliza thought, like a goblin of the underworld. 'Ladies. Do stand back a little, won't you?'

'Don't worry about us,' Anne told him. 'I've been thinking of Praxiteles, when he was told his house was on fire.'

He laughed. 'Trust you to come up with a relevant classical allusion.' A servant brought him a tumbler of beer and he raised it. 'To the passing of the Richmond House Theatre,' he said. 'What times we had!'

'Almost five years go,' Eliza murmured. Her throat was itching from the fire. She thought she might cry.

'It feels much longer,' said Anne, her eyes on the burning shell of the house.

'The scenery was carried out safely, you know,' Lady Mary pointed out.

'Was it?' said the Earl. 'Well, perhaps we should put on another play, but at Derby House.' Eliza gave him a radiant smile. He seized her and Anne by the hands. 'What do you say, my lovely leading ladies? Shakespeare, perhaps? *It is the East, and Juliet is the sun.* When shall we thespians meet again, in thunder, lightning, or in rain?'

They were laughing, now, though the air was bitter with smoke.

ANNE AND MARY were reading in the tiny, plain-panelled library at North Audley Street. They liked to sit opposite each other, so that either of them could look up at any time and tell the other some stray thought. Anne's eyes were resting on Mary, who glanced up. Her hand went to the bridge of her nose. 'Is it very red, today?'

'Not at all, it's fading,' Anne assured her. 'But all damage leaves its tool mark.'

'Like a chisel?'

'Exactly! Time's signature,' Anne suggested. They grinned at each other. 'By the way, I got four subscriptions for myself and you Berrys for the Haydn concerts.'

Mary clasped her hands in excitement. 'You shouldn't have. Oh, but I can't wait. To hear the great man conducting his own new symphonies—'

'Where's Agnes this morning?' Anne asked.

'Father took her shopping on Mount Street. She fancies a turban for evening wear, with one of those aigrettes with paste jewels bobbing on tiny wires.'

'Since your tour I believe I notice in your sister a desire to shine.'

Mary nodded, smiling. 'At Pisa she was quite the queen of our little circle—especially when I smashed my nose—and she discovered she rather liked it.'

'Don't we all? According to my father, even Walpole primped

and preened in the glass in his day. By the way, I believe you've persuaded him to start writing his memoirs?'

'Well, only by demanding tales of bygone days, till he decided it would be easier to write them down. He has some notion of making me his literary executrix,' Mary mentioned.

'He couldn't choose better,' said Anne, feeling only a slight pang of jealousy. 'You're a discerning, diligent, literary lady: you'll be his ambassador to posterity.'

'Oh, tush. I may do it, but behind the cover of my father's name.'

Anne frowned; she didn't approve of women hiding their lights under bushels. 'I called at Berkeley Square this morning, but I was refused. Walpole had shut himself up in his study with the post and told his footmen he wasn't to be disturbed. No doubt he's getting into one of his grand fusses.'

'Over what?'

'Who knows? When you were away, I noticed a rather comical peculiarity in him,' said Anne.

'Only one?'

She chuckled at that. 'He was always perfectly communicative with regard to your letters, or Agnes's—he'd read me parts of them, or let me read them myself—and he'd boast, with the insolence of a lover, of having received three letters in as many days. But if ever I tried to tell him anything you'd written to me he turned deaf— despised any information I had to offer—could never suppose I might know your date of return before he did, for instance.'

'How diverting,' said Mary a little uneasily.

'Isn't it? The child has a tendency to being fretful when you're not here to keep him in order...'

The library door flew open and they jumped. There stood Walpole, his face a mask of tragedy.

'What is it, sir?' Mary rushed to take his arm. 'No one came to announce you.'

'You mustn't call me that. It's no longer my name.'

She glanced at Anne, her eyes wide.

Was he losing his wits, all at once, as the King did? 'What is it, coz?' asked Anne soothingly.

'From plain Mister,' he said, 'I am elevated to *His Lordship.*'

They blinked at him. 'Your nephew?' said Anne.

'The poor young lunatic has died,' he spelled out, 'and I stand before you now, fourth Earl of Orford.'

Anne couldn't help giggling.

'It's hardly a laughing matter,' he protested, while she and Mary were leading him over to the comfortable chair by the fire and lifting his bad foot on to a stool. 'I'll be the poorest earl in England; Houghton Hall brings nothing but debts and draughts.'

'Congratulations,' said Mary, with a little curtsy, 'and commiserations too, if you like, Your Lordship.' Then even Walpole cracked a mournful smile.

ANNE AND ELIZA were at the nuts-and-oranges stage of a post-theatre supper at Green Street. The parlour was freshly hung with a stylish striped paper, Anne noticed; the actress had an eye for these details. It amused her to note all the differences between this smart town house and the plainer, calmer décor of the Berrys round the corner on North Audley Street. A nagging thought struck her: her two closest female friends hadn't met yet. She hadn't deliberately kept them apart, but nor had she brought them together since the Berrys' return. The occasion had to be right; she feared they mightn't take to each other at once.

'My *Thalia* looks very well in her new position,' she remarked, gesturing at the bust on the column in the corner.

'Doesn't she?' said Eliza, grinning back at her.

'I'm worried about my cousin Walpole,' said Anne, cracking a hazelnut, 'his new earldom's proving nothing but grief to him.'

'I've noticed you don't call him *Orford.*'

'Oh, it would seem unnatural. He complains it's the worst of times to come into a title; breeding's all gone out since the French had their Revolution and nobody asks *Who are his people?* any more but, *What is he worth?*'

Eliza laughed at the exaggeration.

'Also, after twenty years away from Parliament, he hasn't the slightest desire to take his seat in the Lords. Though he tells me that some of his bluestocking ladies are pleading with him to sponsor a bill to put down faro and roulette!'

'That would never pass,' said Eliza.

'Really, the thing's destroyed the tranquillity of his old age; he has packets of papers to read and answer every morning, consultations with lawyers and creditors, threatening letters from envious relations...'

'Tom Paine says aristocracy is intrinsically absurd,' said the actress.

'However can he claim that?' Anne asked. She hadn't yet nerved herself to buy the American author's *Rights of Man,* which Walpole kept denouncing as the most seditious of all the pamphlets published to rebut Burke's *Reflections.*

Eliza shrugged prettily. 'Well, he begins by asserting that all men were created equal and free when Adam and Eve walked in the Garden. He says titles are only meaningless nicknames, worn like shiny ribbons. Being born an aristocrat is no achievement or guarantee of merit; after all, haven't we all met wicked marquesses and stupid dukes? To see the silliness of choosing our lawmakers by their surnames we've only to imagine selecting authors, artists or actors the same way.'

Anne was taken aback. This philosophy was unsettlingly extreme. 'But history—the weight of tradition—'

'Paine says we should shake it off. The living matter more than the dead; every generation, every nation should be allowed to choose for itself.'

'Eliza, can you really believe all this?'

The actress fanned herself a little coyly. 'I don't know. His originality's refreshing.'

'But does it mean nothing, then, that my mother is Countess of Ailesbury? Am I no more *Honourable* than Bet my maid? Should Bet dine off my bone china, and should I mend hems in her place?' Anne heard herself beginning to whine.

'You've no talent for needlework,' said Eliza flippantly. 'Paine's main point is that kings are not necessarily wiser than other men—and our own George costs his people more than a million pounds a year to maintain in royal state. Paine says the best kind of government is one based on the public good—'

'The *res publica*, yes, I know the origin of *republic*,' said Anne a little sharply. She remembered, all those years ago, preaching to Eliza about the importance of Whig principles. Now her pupil had gone beyond anything she'd ever taught.

Mrs Farren came in just then. 'Very sorry to disturb, but there's a note for Mrs Damer, sent on from Grosvenor Square.'

Anne recognised Mary's hand. *Come to me*, was all it said.

She stood up. 'I'm so sorry, Eliza, it's been a fascinating discussion, but something urgent—'

'Not illness in the family, I hope?'

'No, no.'

'Do take our manservant with a torch, madam, to light your way home,' said Mrs Farren stiffly.

Not for the first time, Anne had the distinct impression that the mother was not particularly pleased that the friendship had been renewed. Strange how much it bothered her that she might be considered a less than welcome visitor by this former strolling actress! 'Thank you, Mrs Farren, that's very kind.'

She was at the house on North Audley Street in two minutes. Mary was waiting for her, pacing in the narrow hall. She seized Anne's gloved fingers in her own and helped her off with her greatcoat. 'Oh, my dear. The most appalling thing. I had to see you.'

'Calm yourself. What is it?'

'I've been noticed in a *newspaper!*'

Anne unfolded the page from Mary's reticule. She sucked in her breath as she read the paragraph, under the small caption, 'News of the World'.

Some would have it that a certain young lady's friendship with the new Earl of O-f—d is not Disinterested. We have learned

that she and her family have recently received a gift of a hand-
some three-storeyed residence on his estate at T—k——m.
When the Earl was asked by a female relation if he had any
view to marrying the person in question, or perhaps her younger
sister, his answer was, 'That's as Miss B——y pleases!'

'You see!' Mary burst out when Anne set the paper down on the
hall table.

Anne put her arm round her and chose her words carefully. 'I
see that you've become a true member of the World at last.'

'What do you mean?'

'Mary?' That must be Agnes in the shadows at the top of the
stairs.

'It's all right, go to bed; I'm talking to Anne,' Mary called back.

'What I mean', said Anne when they were alone again, 'is that
being a victim of scandalmongering could be considered the quali-
fication for membership in the World. It happens to almost all of
us at some point in our lives; it's the price of being distinguished.
Besides, the venom on this arrow is feeble. You know what infi-
nitely worse things have been said of me!' Mary let out a wild sob
and Anne thought perhaps she shouldn't have brought up that
comparison. 'Be rational, my dear. You're accused of no heinous
crime—merely of accepting the generosity of a septuagenarian,
who may or may not be intending to propose.'

Mary wiped her eyes. 'That's what Agnes said. She laughed it
off. But I can't stand the suggestion that I've been laying siege to
Mr Walpole, when my feelings have never been anything but filial.
Perhaps we shouldn't have let him use those foolish nicknames. But
I never thought—he's never behaved in the slightest way—' The
tears ran down her face again.

Anne embraced her tightly. 'As to that part of the libel,' she
said into Mary's dark curls, more certainly than she felt, 'I don't
believe it either. Walpole's the very definition of a bachelor. Mind
you, the line they quote does sound like him—as a piece of gallant
repartee—'

'But what could he have meant by it?'

'Well, perhaps one of his nosy old nieces asked if he admired you and he didn't want to be so churlish as to say *absolutely not*!'

Mary's voice shook. 'The blow to my reputation—I'll have to write to him—but I can't bear it. Anne, would you do this for me, would you tell him?'

'Tell him what?'

'That my family must move out of Little Strawberry at once.'

'Oh, Mary.' Anne let go of her for a moment. 'Why don't you come to bed and we'll talk again in the morning?'

'I won't be able to sleep, not a wink,' said Mary, letting herself be led upstairs.

But an hour later she was breathing in the shallow, regular pattern of those who were dead to the world. It was Anne who lay awake beside her, thinking with hatred of journalists and the havoc they caused. She'd have to play the diplomat, now, with all her skill. She wished she could protect Mary from all this, the vulgarity of it. The young woman's profile, a dim white in the darkness, was as clean as a child's.

It took Anne right through Christmas to reconcile Mary and Walpole. 'You must give her time,' she told him over a glass of sherry at Berkeley Square.

He swung the poker limply into the logs. 'How she hurts and punishes me! It comes near to breaking my heart.'

'But cousin, your fortune—your fame as an author and collector—your new title—all these things are like a harsh light reflected on Mary.' Anne knew she was repeating herself. 'She tortures herself with having profited from your generosity in Italy and now in the matter of the house.'

'What, would she only condescend to be my friend if I were a beggar?'

Anne sighed. 'The article was very mortifying to her feelings.'

'So will she let us be judged in the vilest of tribunals—the papers? Low, anonymous scribblers should simply be ignored,' declared Walpole.

'Oh, that's all very well for you to say!'

His bushy eyebrows went up.

'You're a man, and a rich one, who can defy the world if you want to. Mary has no such security. You're putting her happiness in peril,' Anne warned him. 'And Agnes's too,' she added as an afterthought.

Had she gone too far? His face seemed to fall in. His eyes were watering. 'Oh, Anne. I never meant her any harm!'

This would be the time to ask whether he'd really made the remark the newspaper had attributed to him—but somehow Anne didn't want to know. Even if he had, journalists distorted everything. The thought of him and Mary as a married couple was incongruous, and not just because of his age and ill health; it would be a sort of incest, now they were all such a family. It would unbalance everything, bring on chaos.

Walpole was plucking at his high starched stock as if it were compressing his windpipe. 'The World is so very harsh. I thought my years would allow me to enjoy this friendship in peace—but no. Please, my dear Anne, I beg you—for the sake of your old crippled godfather, but above all for hers—I beg you to use all your tact and wisdom to persuade her to stay at Little Strawberry! Don't let her chimerical scruples poison the end of a life which she, and only she, can sweeten.'

Anne very much wanted to shake him till the eyes popped out of his head. She nodded and patted his leathery hand. She remembered something Walpole himself had said once: *One should never be cruel to the old, because any day might be their last.* For some reason she thought of poor Sir Joshua Reynolds, king of British art, who was lying on his deathbed now, his body vastly swollen; they called him *tranquil,* but that was only the laudanum.

A week later she was able to report that the Berrys would not be leaving Little Strawberry Hill. In reply, Walpole sent his thanks and a verse which suggested he'd found his sense of humour again.

An estate and an earldom at seventy-four!
Had I sought them or wished them, 'twould add one fear more,
That of making a Countess when almost fourscore.
But Fortune, who scatters her gifts out of season,
Though unkind to my limbs, has still left me my reason…

MAY 1792

After one of their hard games of tennis—which Derby won on this occasion—he and Fox drank fresh milk from a bored-looking cow in Hyde Park. They waved to Mrs Damer as she went by on her stallion and caught a glimpse of Earl Spencer in his newly famous hip-length coat. The story was that he'd cut the tails off for a bet; it looked like a jacket a three-year-old would wear.

'Mrs A. protests she hasn't seen you since before Christmas, Derby,' said Fox, supine on the grass. 'You might dine with us at Maidenhead Bridge on Saturday, then come out rowing.'

'That sounds delightful.'

'How're the children?'

'Very well, I believe,' said Derby, searching his memory for any recent news. 'Edward's leaving Eton this summer; he'll go to Trinity, Cambridge, as I did.'

'Can the boy really be that old?' Fox laughed.

'Even little Elizabeth's turned fourteen. I let her spend most of last winter with her mother in Marylebone,' Derby mentioned, breaking his rule of never referring to Lady Derby.

'Ah, good of you. I imagine she's the invalid's sole consolation in life,' said Fox gently.

Well, it was partly kindness, but partly his secret conviction that she was Dorset's daughter, Derby admitted to himself; she'd always seemed out of place at Knowsley.

'And the other two…'

He wouldn't let anyone but Fox or Bunbury probe like this. 'Oh, they haven't seen the Countess or heard me speak her name since they were in leading strings,' he said more confidently than he felt. He wondered if Elizabeth told them much about Marylebone.

Who knew what went on in the shadowy minds of the young? 'Also, I've got four wards up at Knowsley, since my poor uncle's death,' he said to change the subject. General Burgoyne, the veteran of Saratoga, had not only been a fond uncle but had made a Whig of him.

'By-blows of the great man?' asked Fox.

'Yes, their mother was an opera singer,' said Derby.

'It's always jolly having youngsters about.'

'Yes,' said Derby, 'they take the bleak look off a place.' He knew that Fox had two children of his own by former mistresses. The boy was deaf and dumb, and the girl a little slow too; Mrs A. was very good to them and let them visit St Anne's Hill often. It was a great pity, Derby thought, that the happy couple had none of their own—but the *Impure* (as the papers called courtesans) generally ended up barren.

Sheridan threw himself down in the grass beside them, only an hour late, and refused a beaker of milk. 'Have you read Paine's latest?' he asked abruptly, waving a pamphlet. 'Brilliant ideas on every page. Payments to help with birth—marriage—funerals—allowances for every child and free schooling—pensions for the old and crippled—'

'And how would we pay for all this?' Fox teased him.

'Simple: an income tax.'

'Ouch!' cried Derby, clutching his pocket.

Sheridan grinned at him. 'Oh, you'd still have enough for your birds and horses.'

Fox rolled on to his stomach. 'No, but seriously, Sherry, you mustn't go round brandishing that thing; the author and publisher have already been charged under the new Proclamation against Seditious Writings.'

The Irishman's handsome features went hard. 'Paine has proved our so-called *representative Parliament* is rotten to the core. Only one man in a hundred has a vote, for God's sake, after all these years of Whig campaigning! Did you know that Old Sarum, with three houses in it, returns two Members, and so does all of Yorkshire with a population of over a million? Besides, the Commons is bought and sold daily—clogged with placemen who dread the PM will take away their pensions, snorers who can't stay awake through the debates and graspers who shove their way in by treating each village to a barrel of whisky!'

'I was giving speeches on these topics when you were still parsing sentences at Harrow,' said Fox quietly.

'Sherry, you sound like you'd rather move to France,' joked Derby to lighten the mood.

His friend stared at him. 'I'm not the revolutionary they call me; I just want liberty and justice. You should pull off those aristocratic blinkers for a moment. Last year, even when we stooped to accept the Eunuch's support, we couldn't pass Abolition—the most shining of causes—because of old farts who were afraid that if we freed the blacks they'd turn Jacobin, and up and slaughter us all!'

'Many of us feel as you do,' Derby assured him, 'but the state of France is causing jitters. No man will repair his roof in the hurricane season.'

'He must,' said Sheridan, 'or the whole thing may blow off.'

The silence stretched. 'This was such a pleasant day', murmured Fox with his eyes closed, 'until you turned up.'

'I've brought good news, actually, old Foxy,' said Sheridan, leaning up on his elbow. The rapidity of his moods had always unnerved Derby; too much like a virtuoso performance of Garrick's. 'Grey and Fitzgerald and I have just founded a new Reform society—not a populist one, but for gentlemen—we're calling it the Friends of the People. Has a good ring to it, hasn't it?'

A long pause. 'Mm,' said Derby.

'We mean to table a Reform motion in the next session.'

'*The time is out of joint,*' Fox quoted grimly. 'That riot of footmen, that fire at the House of Commons last week—'

'To be fair, it was found to be a pair of breeches smouldering in a cupboard,' Derby pointed out, 'hardly evidence of insurrection.'

'Oh, I know.' Fox sighed. 'But it all looks like anarchy—*Lib-*

erty's demon child, as Pitt's pamphleteers call it. The Prince is convinced there's a Jacobin agent under every bed.'

'I'm still his best friend,' Sheridan said cockily.

'A friend can be betrayed as easily as a mistress,' Derby pointed
out.

'Yes,' Fox agreed, 'I fear we're losing our grip on the Great
Whale. If Old George popped his clogs in the night, I very much
doubt Prinny would call us in to make up a Reformist government.
Pitt might even manage to change masters and rule on.'

'What a hideous thought,' said Sheridan.

'*O put not your trust in princes, nor in any child of man,*' Derby
quoted from the psalm.

Sheridan's voice was steely. 'So. You won't lend the Friends of
the People the support of your name?'

'I'd have to think about it,' said Derby. He knew he was one of
the last Whig peers whose appetite for change was still sharp,
but...Then he realised that the question hadn't included him.

Fox shook his heavy head. 'I mustn't, dear fellow. It'll drive a
wedge into the Party.'

'Fuck the Party,' said Sheridan with glittering eyes.

When their friend had cantered away Fox murmured, 'He's not
himself, of course. His wife's coughing up blood.'

What everyone knew and no one said was that the new baby
wasn't Sheridan's but Lord Edward Fitzgerald's—the most handsome and spirited of Fox's Irish cousins and an outright republican,
despite his title and the fact that he was the great-great-grandson
of Charles I. 'Isn't it strange that Sherry doesn't blame either of
them—his wife or his friend?' muttered Derby.

Fox shrugged. 'Unusual, perhaps; not strange in itself.'

'But look at Devonshire, say. The minute he heard about Georgiana and Grey, he banished her to the most dangerous region in
Europe.'

'Ha! For all his famous *ménage à trois,*' said Fox, 'Devonshire's a
conventional man—the sultan of a small harem. Whereas our

Sherry is a genuine original. He reasons that it's entirely due to his flagrant neglect of his lovely wife, in favour of Harriet Duncannon and other females, that Mrs S. finally succumbed to a more ardent lover.'

'You'd probably behave just as generously,' Derby teased.

'I hope I would, since I've never suffered from the disease of jealousy. Not carnally, that is,' Fox corrected himself, 'only in politics!'

Not even much there, Derby thought. Apart from the occasional storm, such as the regency crisis, Fox was as warm-spirited to his colleagues as to his *woman of no reputation*.

Derby knew himself to be a much more ordinary man—as stern as the Duke of Devonshire, when it came to being cuckolded. When he'd learned of Lady Derby's affair with Dorset, after all, he hadn't split any hairs or examined his conscience; he'd simply ordered her abroad for several years, and refused to see her face again. It wasn't that Derby had been convinced it was the right thing to do, but he hadn't been capable of anything else. He wondered now whether Devonshire would really be rigid enough to banish Georgiana and Bess from him—and England—for ever. It was said that the assorted progeny had been dumped at Devonshire House for half a year, now, and the Duke never went to see them. *At least I didn't abandon my children*, Derby reminded himself, uneasy.

AUGUST 1792

On the way to Strawberry Hill, rain rang like spears on the roof of the carriage. It had barely stopped in six weeks. Anne spared a thought for the driver up top—like a Roman fountain with water bouncing off his shoulders and knees. She shivered a little; she still felt half naked with nothing but a cotton tube under the straight muslin dress to replace her stays. Mary had assured her that this wasn't too young a costume for her; *timelessly classical, rather.* But the fact was that the new French look had made a chasm between those Englishwomen brave enough to embrace such novelty and freedom, and stuffy matrons who preferred to cling to their heavy silks, hoops and pads—and Anne knew which side she belonged to, even if she was forty-three. She and Mary had first tried out the look together this summer, to give each other courage, and had walked along the Mall giggling like schoolgirls, avoiding the glares of the dowagers.

She had her portable writing desk on her knees.

I'm so very pleased that you've been showing your comedy to se-lected friends. You're so perversely modest, dear M., you seem to be looking for the one person who won't like the play, so you can pin your faith on them, I suppose, and burn the manuscript!

I imagine the date hasn't escaped your notice. I won't at-tempt to put down on paper all I feel on the second anniversary of our meeting, but may I just say thank you?

She lay back against the cushioned seat and thought of something Mary had hinted the other day, about *never having had the pleasure of making Miss Farren's acquaintance.* Somehow Anne still felt an awkward sort of disinclination to introduce them. She knew that Eliza was no shallow fashion plate and Mary was no earnest blue-stocking—but each could seem so, just a little, in company at first, so she feared that was the conclusion each would jump to about the other. But even if she was wrong, Anne somehow couldn't quite imagine sitting between the two women, talking to them at the same time.

In his star chamber—all green with gold mosaic stars—Wal-pole was bent over a folio of engravings with a stranger. 'Ah, my dear Anne,' he said, straightening up. 'I didn't expect the pleasure of your arrival so soon; were the roads turgid with mud? Allow me to present Mr Fawkener, my nephew and neighbour in Berkeley Square.'

'You do me too much honour,' said the stranger amusedly.

'Well, your poor mother was half-sister to my brother-in-law, so I reckon you as a quarter-nephew at least.'

William Fawkener kissed Anne's hand. His name made her

think of a hawk, somehow, or perhaps it was the face—that sharp
curve of the nose. She guessed the diplomat was about her own age;
his black jacket was very tight about the shoulders. Hadn't he been
through a noisy divorce many years ago? Terrible how scandal
clung to a name. That's right, the runaway wife was a cousin of
Georgiana's called—of all Newmarket appellations—Jockey Poyntz.
Anne tried to think of something else to ask Fawkener about and
the word *Russia* floated into her mind just in time. 'We heard much
about you during your trip to Catherine's Court, sir.'

'For all it achieved!'

They talked a little about St Petersburg, where the ladies still
rouged very high, he told her, but at least they didn't dye their teeth
black as their grandmothers had.

'It must be difficult to represent one's superiors at such a remove,' she hazarded.

'You've hit it.' He laughed. 'I've never yet received a dispatch
from home that was up to date enough to be worth reading.'

The man seemed clever and oddly veiled; he spoke smoothly,
but lacked that frankness she found so attractive in men and
women. At one point she used the phrase *Pittites like yourself* and
Fawkener gave a little shrug. 'Well, I'm a servant of the present
government and Clerk in Ordinary to His Majesty's Privy Council;
that much is true.'

'But your own beliefs?'

Fawkener's neat eyebrows shot up at the word. 'I'm a Christian,'
he said, deadpan.

Was he not willing to argue politics with a woman? Walpole let
out a yelp of laughter. 'You must know my godchild is an out-and-
out Foxite.'

'Oh, I do. At Mrs Sheridan's funeral in June, when the topic
turned to exceptional women,' he told her, 'Fox was boasting of
your friendship.'

She blushed slightly. So Fawkener was on good terms with Fox;
perhaps he wasn't such an out-and-out Pittite after all. Then she

realised he'd suavely turned the conversation away from politics to personalities.

The old man excused himself so he could fetch some rather rare engravings from his library; they were too precious to trust to the servants.

'Since I've had the great good fortune of meeting you here, Mrs Damer,' Fawkener began, 'I must confess that on this occasion too I'm an emissary on a sort of diplomatic mission.'

'How so?' she asked, startled.

'You may be familiar with a certain Mr Combe.'

No one had spoken that name in her hearing in a dozen years. So this meeting wasn't an accident; Fawkener had come to Strawberry Hill in the hopes of an introduction. She felt slightly sick. 'To my cost, I am.'

'I know I risk offending you by mentioning him,' Fawkener apologised. 'I should begin by explaining that Combe's not what he was. He's a real recluse these days and lives under the rules of the King's Bench gaol, because of his debts; he drinks nothing stronger than water. He's given up all scurrilous scandalmongering and he only writes on serious matters.'

'Such as?'

'He's been very valuable to the government.'

Anne's mouth twisted. 'You mean he's one of Pitt's pamphleteers?'

Fawkener didn't wince. 'Well, call it what you like. The point is I've been asked—by a person I'm not at liberty to name—to intercede with you on Combe's behalf.'

Could he mean that Pitt himself had asked it? She swallowed. 'But what does Combe want with me? Didn't he get his pound of flesh from me long years ago and turn it to gold?' she said, almost spitting.

'He wants to bring out a purified version of his previous works, with the nasty passages excised and a properly apologetic preface.'

'But that's ridiculous,' said Anne shrilly. 'Clean up a cesspit and what's left but a hole?' She knew the analogy was coarse, but she didn't care. That was the worst thing about vulgarity; it dragged you in, even as you fought it.

'You see, Combe bitterly regrets that back in the late '70s he repeated a libel about you, with no foundation—'

Her cheeks scalded. 'Invented it, you mean.'

'No, no, he merely heard and took up idle slurs on your reputation—'

'Heard from whom?' she interrupted.

'Combe can't recall, now,' said Fawkener. 'At the time he was incensed with your whole family because of how shabbily your cousin Viscount Beauchamp had treated him—so he foolishly believed the exotic impossibilities he heard of you, Mrs Damer. His conscience pangs him on your account; he assures me he'd give a limb to redress the injury he did you.'

She sniffed.

'So, now,' he went on more cheerfully, 'Combe wants nothing more than to put this calumny to rest for once and for all in this new edition.'

Anne took a long breath. 'These matters are already at rest,' she told him. 'How can they be put to rest by being dug up again? And his repentance would be more touching if this new edition weren't intended to make him money.'

'Well, that's the life of a writer for you,' said Fawkener with a smile, 'whatever they do, for evil or good, must pay their rent.'

She found herself half smiling back in spite of herself. She'd been rather enjoying the battle. 'I'll be sure to consider the matter when I have some time, Mr Fawkener,' she told him, a little sweetness mixed with the hauteur. 'Now shall I play hostess in my cousin's absence and ring for tea?'

She couldn't bear to raise the matter with Walpole and she knew she mustn't dream of confiding in Eliza, who'd only consented to be her friend again on the understanding that the old scandal was quite extinguished. No, there was only one person she could ask, so she wrote to Mary that evening.

My stomach's unsettled, as it always is when this dreadful sub-
ject of my being abused in the press arises. Could Combe be sin-
cere in wishing to make up for his persecution of me? For all my
Oppositional sensibilities, I wouldn't wish to offend the PM, if
it is he who's commissioned F——r. Of course my heart revolts
from the idea of stooping to any negotiation with Combe, but
perhaps through this skilful intermediary the thing could be done
decently enough? The prospect of being acquitted in the court of
public opinion is a tempting one...

I confess my whirling head isn't competent to judge in this
case. What say you?

Mary's answer came back before bedtime, the ink smeared with
haste.

Oh, my dear, beware! I know I've urged you to combat these li-
bels, but how can this Combe be trusted now, when he proved so
malign before & how can the delicate fabric of a lady's reputa-
tion be mended with such crude tools? F——r I'm sure (as a rela-
tion of Mr W.'s) is sincere in his attempts to make peace—but as
for Combe, what good can it do you to have such a man (mon-
ster, rather) say anything further about you in print?

Believe me, dearest, I only regret that a friendship as ra-
tional & affectionate as mine for you can do so little to make up
for the vile injustice of an ungenerous World.

When, after a week, she hadn't seen anything of Fawkener she sent
a note inviting him to call at Grosvenor Square. They sat sipping
Madeira at eleven in the morning in her parlour and argued about
politics with a guarded civility. 'Doesn't it seem', Anne suggested,
'as if they were *provoked* into dethroning Louis by the Duke of
Brunswick's rash manifesto, urging the French to topple their own
Assembly and threatening to destroy Paris if any harm came to the
royal family?'

Fawkener shrugged. 'Brunswick's a firm commander of the Austrian and Prussian forces in their war with France; he knows what he's doing.'

'But mightn't he have done better to appeal to the love of the French for their King?'

'What love would that be?' asked Fawkener.

Anne subsided.

'Mrs Damer,' he went on in a flirtatious drawl, 'I confess I don't know whether to hope that you've an answer for me on the Combe matter or that you invited me here for the pleasure of my conversation alone.'

Anne gave him a sharp look. 'The former,' she said. 'Please tell Combe that I'm glad he's changed his opinion of me on the evidence of my irreproachable conduct over the last dozen years, but that I have less reason to change mine of him. Also, were he to fawn on me in print, ten to one it would be said that I'd bought the man. Therefore, I'd prefer him simply to omit my name or initials from his publications.'

'Well,' said Fawkener, sitting back in his chair, 'that's certainly clear.'

'Thank you,' said Anne.

He let out a short laugh and so did she, surprising herself. 'Mrs Damer, are you quite sure you won't regret letting slip this one chance to control what the press says about you?'

'Quite,' said Anne, though uncertainty suddenly gripped her.

'I do understand your position,' said Fawkener ruefully. 'Six years ago the papers named me as a cuckold when I fought a duel with Lord John Townshend.'

She blushed; she hadn't had any intention of bringing up his marriage to Georgiana's reckless cousin, Jockey Poyntz.

'No printed apologies or denials would have done me any good—since it happened to be true—so I went ahead and sued Townshend for Criminal Conversation with my wife as a means to divorce,' said Fawkener neutrally. 'I know exactly how mortifying such publicity is. But, of course, in your case the accusations were chimerical.'

'All the more reason not to give them another airing now,' she told him more firmly than she felt.

As Fawkener made his compliments and took his hat and cane from the servant, Anne wondered if she'd ever see him again.

SEPTEMBER 1792

'So is it a good thing that the French have declared a republic?' fretted Mrs Farren.

Eliza sighed. In the small dining room at Green Street the two of them were finishing a leg of lamb. 'I suppose so, Mother. Louis had to be deposed; he was vetoing their new laws, standing in the Assembly's way.' She tried not to think about the mob that had butchered the royal guards. 'And I'm certainly glad their General Dumouriez's beaten back the Prussians at Valmy. What right have the kings of Europe to make war on a nation because they happen to disapprove of its choice of government?'

'But they're calling Louis plain *Monsieur Capet*, now, and the whole family's said to be imprisoned in the Temple.'

Eliza nodded uneasily. The Revolution's latest twist left a bad taste in one's mouth. But it was so hard to know which wild rumours to believe, or how much weight to give a single anecdote; the newspaper reports all contradicted each other, or were out of date, and everyone she met seemed to have a different correspondent in a different part of France who, of course, saw events through his or her own slanted peephole. It was like trying to put together the plot of a five-act tragedy by eavesdropping on the crowd as it surged out of a theatre.

Here in London, the founding of the French Republic was being claimed by Pitt's Tories as proof of what they'd always told the Whigs—that giving more power to the people was incompatible with a monarchical government like Britain's. This had been a disastrous summer, what with the rained-out harvest and so many hungry and bewildered émigrés flooding into England. Up at Knowsley Derby had been disturbed by wage protests among Liverpool workers; he blamed the new cheap edition of Paine's *Rights of Man,* which he said could be found in every cottage and coal pit. And there was a strange new phenomenon: Loyalist Societies, thousands of them springing up across the country, to intimidate anyone who expressed any *Frenchified opinions.*

'Would you care for some gooseberry pudding?' Mrs Farren asked now, as if they'd settled the political question.

'No, thank you, Mother.' If she were perfectly honest with herself Eliza knew she was less troubled by the affairs of France than by those of the Drury Lane company, facing into a second season in exile at the King's Theatre. Fed up, Jack Palmer had gone down to Brighton to shake off his creditors and try to set up a provincial troupe of his own. Sheridan had been a wreck ever since his poor wife's death from consumption; he spent all his time with his son Tom and the motherless baby. (According to Derby, Sheridan and Lord Edward Fitzgerald had agonised drunkenly over which of them should raise the girl, before Fitzgerald had decided to *make atonement* by letting Sheridan give her the protection of his name.) The proprietor had failed to come to terms with Mrs Siddons about her salary—the press were calling her *mercenary*—so she was staying away, on an arduous tour of Ireland. And her brother Kemble was threatening to resign as manager, maddened, just as Tom King had been, by having his hands tied and no prospect of the new Drury getting a roof this year.

To top it all the unquashable Mrs Jordan was back, as popular as ever now her partnership with the Duke of Clarence was old news, with sparkling new roles written just for her: a daring comedy about the 'rights of women' by Joseph Richardson and one by Mrs Inchbald with a romantic song for Dora that Eliza just knew would be all round town in a week.

'I'd swear you've lost a stone this summer,' her mother rebuked her through a mouthful of pudding.

Eliza glanced at herself in the mirror over the fireplace. 'I believe not,' she said coldly. Ever since she'd turned thirty, in July—a date she hadn't spoken of to anyone except her mother—she'd been asking herself, *Does it show?* For over a year, now, she'd been using lemon juice to hide the grey in her golden hair.

Mrs Farren was saying something about a secret wedding. 'Whose?'

'Why Mr Fox's to Mrs Armistead.'

'I never heard anything of that,' said Eliza incredulously.

'He dotes on his Mrs A., all the World knows that,' said Margaret Farren, 'and if anything were to happen to him all of a sudden he'd wish her to be provided for, wouldn't he?'

'I don't believe Fox has anything to bequeath but debts.'

'Well, I think it's lovely, if the story should happen to be true. It just proves', said Mrs Farren sententiously, 'that when someone takes someone into keeping in a nice and regular way he doesn't necessarily grow sated of her. So faithful to his Liz, he's been, and vice versa, since they first set up housekeeping together ten years back! And now she's got her reward at last, maybe.'

The moral was obvious. Eliza took a long breath. 'Fox might have married Liz Armistead any time he chose,' she pointed out, 'but he's never chosen to, because you know why, Mother? She's his whore.'

Mrs Farren winced at the word but kept her eyes fixed coyly on her needle.

'She's been had by every wealthy gentleman in England at one time or another and that happens to include Lord Derby, by the way,' she added. '*Dear Liz* has been tossed from hand to hand like a ball. And you want me to model myself on this piece of used goods?'

'She's a very amiable woman, I hear.'

'She may be more charming than the Queen, but I'll never sit down in a room with her,' said Eliza, shaking slightly. 'If this absurd rumour turns out to be true I wish the couple all happiness, but I still won't be paying a call.'

'I never meant you should call on them—'

'No, Mother, what you meant was that I should have let Lord Derby take me into keeping while I was still the right side of thirty.'

'I never said so!' The old woman's eyes were spangled with righteous tears. 'I'm only concerned for my dear girl's future.'

'And your own.'

That was a low blow; Mrs Farren's lips trembled.

'Oh, Mother, I'm sorry,' said Eliza suddenly. 'Of course you want to see me settled. And you're right to wonder how long our savings would last if the World decided it fancied a younger face for its Queen of Comedy. But trust me, it would do no good for me suddenly to abandon all my principles at this stage in the game!'

A rap at the door below; they waited for the manservant to come upstairs.

'Lord Derby, miss, madam,' he announced.

Eliza stood and gave the Earl her hand. Derby had turned forty a fortnight ago, with a little supper for his intimates, but of course men's years were shorter than women's. He looked oddly haggard today. 'A hard afternoon's riding, My Lord? Or a long night at Brooks's?'

He shook his head and sat down before a chair was offered, which was unlike him. 'Ghastly news from Paris.'

Eliza steeled herself. 'More trials and executions?'

'Worse.'

Her mother sucked in her lips.

'The mob thought the Prussians were at the city gates,' he said in a ragged voice, 'and they panicked and broke into the gaols. With pikes and axes, clubs, shovels even. Some say they're drunk, or egged on by thugs hired by the Jacobins; I don't know what to believe. The thing is they're butchering everyone.'

'Aristocrats?'

'Yes—the Princesse de Lamballe refused to denounce the Queen and she was ripped—literally ripped—to pieces. The killers paraded parts of her—' He broke off, swallowing, his eyes shifting between the two women.

'Tell us,' said Eliza.

'They speared her head on a pike,' he said, 'and held it up out-side the Queen's window, shouting *Viens baiser ton amie!*'

'*Come kiss your friend,*' Eliza muttered to her mother, though she suspected it could mean something worse.

'The Duc de La Rochefoucauld...his mother, aged ninety-three, had her son's brains rubbed in her face,' said Derby hoarsely. Mrs Farren made a choking sound and rushed from the room. Derby didn't seem to notice. His eyes burned into Eliza's. 'They threw the heads of the Queen's ladies-in-waiting into the flames. But it's not just aristos they're killing, it's all the prisoners. Farmers, priests, maids, peasants, beggars, children—' His voice cracked. 'I've heard rumours of cannibalism. They say the gutters are run-ning, literally running over, with blood. And the French govern-ment stands by and does nothing!'

'Oh, Derby,' Eliza said inadequately. She hadn't taken it in yet. She couldn't feel anything for the victims he was talking about; it was all too sudden, too bizarre, a freak show of corpses. She'd seen some unpleasant sights in her childhood, as her father's troupe had worked its way back and forth across England, but she'd never seen a gutter filled with human blood. All she could feel right now was an appalled pity for the Earl, whose face was a papery colour, whose fingers twitched. And an absurd little bell was going off in her head, reminding her that they were alone together, since her mother had run out of the room. *Ridiculous,* she told herself, *he's hardly going to plunge his hand in my bosom right now.*

'Christ! It's all wrong,' he said. 'Soiled. They've taken the best of causes, the Great Experiment of our age, and shat all over it!'

It was this extraordinary vulgarity, more than anything else, that made her realise how upset Derby was.

ANNE AND MARY sat in the library at Little Strawberry Hill, hands locked together. 'They say Paris stinks of vinegar,' muttered Anne. 'Vinegar's the only thing that scrubs off bloodstains.'

Mary was as white as paper. 'The ones I blame are the leaders like Robespierre and Danton, who shrug and call it the will of the People to purge itself of enemies! I heard poor Lafayette tried to sail for America—but the Austrians captured him.'

'Our old friend Madame du Barry has just arrived safely via Calais,' Anne told her, 'she's staying at Park Place. She says dear Madame de Staël got out somehow, thank heaven. No one in Paris expects to live more than another day, but they all keep going out to restaurants and theatres, as if nothing's amiss! Apparently the Duchesse de Noilles landed at Brighton dressed as a boy—despite being *enceinte*—after spending fourteen hours on board hidden in a coil of rope, while her poor maid was locked in a trunk.'

The story didn't bring a flicker of a smile to Mary's face. 'There can't be any sane people left in France now,' she said; 'they're all either fled or dead. Liberty's not worth this price.'

'Liberty?' echoed Anne. 'The French have done what I thought no one could do, they've made me sick of the very word.'

'We once thought the Revolution so glorious—'

'Yes, and when there were outrages we blamed them on the work of lone maniacs or outside agents,' said Anne bitterly.

'But this massacre'—Mary's voice rose to a sob—'they say more than a thousand people were hacked apart in a day, quite systematically—children of seven years old—'

'I know, I know,' said Anne, reaching up with one hand to stop a tear halfway down the young woman's face. 'I hate to admit it but Walpole's right.'

Mary nodded. 'The French aren't fit for self-government. He says one might as well establish a republic of tigers in some forest in India!'

'And women are at the forefront of the violence, that's what appals me most,' confided Anne. 'They say Madame de Méricourt rides ahead of the mob in red with tricolour plumes, waving pistols and a sabre, urging on the slaughter...'

The maid came in to say Miss Agnes and Mr Berry were playing whist in the parlour, if the ladies cared to join them. They both shook their heads.

'At times like these,' said Mary, holding tightly to Anne's hand, 'I wonder how I can be made of the same stuff as my relations.'

Anne nodded. 'Despite their many merits, your father and sister don't understand you.'

'I confess', murmured Mary, 'to sometimes resenting that I must play the protecting mother, instead of the carefree companion, to my sister—and as for my father, I must be the guide, instead of finding in him a wise tutor…'

'Well, shall we say', suggested Anne with a slight laugh to lighten her tone, 'that if you had no other duties, no other connections in the world, I might persuade you to take up residence at 8 Grosvenor Square?'

Mary flushed with pleasure. 'Oh, my dear.'

'The thing's impossible, of course—'

'Quite. But thank you,' said Mary, eyes wet, 'thank you for mentioning it.'

Anne cleared her throat and put her hands back in her lap. 'You know,' she said, 'I've had a curious sort of…commission I suppose you'd call it.'

'But you never sell your work.'

'Oh, it's not a monetary matter. My uncle, Lord Frederick Campbell—I don't think you've met him—has a notion to offer the nation a life-size statue of the King, to be erected in the Scottish Register Office, and he insists that no one but myself is up to the task.'

'How odd.'

'At first I brushed it aside; after all, I never do whole-lengths. And men aren't my forte; I haven't tried one since my mask of Thames for the bridge at Henley. As for King George—well, I think I can say without treason that he's never been the object of any personal devotion on my part.'

Mary nodded.

'But now it occurs to me that his merits aren't the point,' said Anne, struggling to find the right words without sounding sentimental. 'He's our king. Last night I was lying awake, worrying about the spread of violent insurrection across Europe. Is it beyond the reach of possibility that it might erupt here? There was that riot of footmen in May, and so many strikes, and bread protests...Could a Cockney mob break into Newgate and hack the prisoners to bits?'

'Oh, surely not.'

'Well, *surely not* is what we'd have said about Paris a few years ago. Look, I found this on the floor of my carriage the other day and it's not the first—' Anne reached into her pocketbook and smoothed out a folded handbill. She'd read it over and over last night; the blurred print seemed to haunt her.

> PROCLAMATION *by the People, to the People.*
>
> *The peace of Slavery is worse than the war of Freedom. Our Ministers are oppressive, our Clergy parasitical, our Royals profligate, our Taxes outrageous. Let Tyrants beware! The time is at hand when the sovereign People of Great Britain will no long suffer themselves to be duped by the lukewarm apostasy of their sham Representatives, but will depend on their own exertions to produce a truly Reformed Parliament.*
>
> GOD SAVE THE PEOPLE!

'You're right,' said Mary with a shudder, 'that has more than a whiff of sedition about it. Their *truly Reformed Parliament* must mean a revolutionary assembly.'

'Imagine if our sovereign were to be reduced to *Georgie Hanover* at the tip of a pike!' said Anne. She remembered her point. 'So in the middle of the night it occurred to me that perhaps I ought to take on this statue after all.' She folded up the handbill and put it away, so the servants wouldn't see it. 'At times like these, one should overcome personal prejudice. Whatever my political views may be, I'm a loyal subject; I'm no republican. Perhaps my uncle's request is a sort of sign that I should take up this mighty task and see what I can do with it?'

OCTOBER 1792

Walpole didn't just approve of the proposed statue, when Anne mentioned it to him after a blackberry breakfast he held at Strawberry Hill for his seventy-fifth birthday. He took it as proof that his goddaughter had seen sense at last, like the Prodigal Son. 'What a splendid idea of your uncle Campbell's,' he crowed. 'What better moment to thank providence for the tranquillity we enjoy in this kingdom, in spite of the republican serpents we harbour in our bosom—the demon Paines, horned Tookes and harpy Barbaulds and Macaulays and Wollstonecrafts!'

'Is Miss Wollstonecraft a harpy?' put in Mary.

'Well, consider her title: *A Vindication of the Rights of Woman* indeed! What's next, the rights of mice?'

Anne kept her expression neutral. She'd lent Mary the book and they'd both found much in it that stirred them, especially the protest against the mire of triviality in which most women were caught. 'Vis-à-vis this statue,' she said, 'I'm inclined to think that catching a likeness of the King is unnecessary.'

'Quite so; unhelpful, even,' said Walpole, leafing through his engravings and tapping a print of George III's face with one horny fingernail. 'The man doesn't matter; the Crown's the thing. And what better time for such a project, now the rabid French are swarming over their borders—annexing Savoy and Nice, the Rhineland and the Netherlands, and calling it *reunion*! I expect to hear they've seized Rome and Madrid any day now.'

Though Anne's opinions had been altered by the horrors of September, she still found Walpole irrational on the subject of France. 'I plan to make the King rather young, slim, upright,' she said, 'but not an Adonis, more like Saint George the dragon killer.'

'Excellent,' he crowed.

'I wish there were any other topic of discourse than politics,' put in Robert Berry from the corner.

'Oh, I know, Papa Berry, I know,' cried Walpole, 'but who can hear, talk or think of anything else?'

Anne went home early, dropping the Berrys off at North Audley Street, and began some sketches for her statue. She knew that old friends would be amused, at best, and at worst appalled, by her sudden display of loyalty to the Crown, but she didn't care—at least, not enough to be put off. It was time to test her talents; otherwise she'd carve dogs and ladies' faces till the day she died and never know whether she could have done anything more.

She made a series of little maquettes on a little wire doll-man, trying out the pose, the balance of forms. Her King would hold his arm across his body, with a lance in his hand, she decided. He would wear long, heavy robes; every line would say *mastery*. The next day she started constructing the armature. Life-size wasn't enough; she wanted her creation to tower, to awe. The armature turned out to be eight feet high; she had to use a stepladder, and take Sam away from his duties for two days to hand rods and tools up to her. The clay model, on which the marble would be based, would be a few inches more than that.

Anne thought of that shabby fellow called Smith whom she'd made occasional use of at the start of her career. When he kept offering to mend cracks and finish polishing for her she'd mistaken it for gallantry—thought Smith remarkably mannerly for a member of the middling-to-lower orders, with little education except in pot making—but gradually, as she became more sure of herself and her vocation, she realised that the fellow was hungry for power. She could see it was humiliating for a man approaching middle age, who would have liked his own workshop, to be general factotum to a lady artist. Smith was always loitering and offering to rough out sections of the model for her: *Save you the labour, madam.* As if Anne had ever been afraid of hard work! When, after a few years of terracottas, she'd gathered her nerve and taken up marble carving, Smith had fretted over the weight of the hammer and muttered about her doing herself an injury…but by then Anne didn't care what he thought and she'd forbidden him to so much as move her tools except to scrape and wash them at the end of the day. In the end she'd let the man go and had never taken on a replacement.

Smith's revenge had come a few years later, when a snide article on the state of British art had referred to *a certain Sculptress whose best busts owe much to the skills of a Subordinate*. This from a rogue who used to leave blocks out in the yard to be streaked by rain or shattered by frost, and would excuse himself with *It's only stone, madam, what harm?*. The memory of Smith's lies filled Anne with rage even now. She looked down at Sam, who stood below the stepladder, his dark face expressionless, and never said a word, which allowed her to forget he was there until she needed a section of pipe or a length of wire.

NOVEMBER 1792

Eliza sat watching the sculptor high on her scaffold, at work on her *King*'s left ear. The clay figure was still primitive, except for the head and sober face, which was emerging slowly from the gigantic armature of wires and rods. There was a smear of grey clay on Anne's left cheekbone. Such patience the woman had, such tireless hands. Eliza remembered sitting in this workshop four years ago, having her eyelids pasted with plaster.

'Funnily enough,' remarked Derby, snapping his snuffbox shut, 'I thought you loathed the man. Don't we all?'

'It's not about the man,' said Anne, looking down owlishly. 'It's an abstraction.'

'Of what?' He paused for a pleasurable sneeze. 'The power of the Crown?'

'Oh, Derby, not in that sense, not the undue influence of King and PM on Parliament; we've always opposed that.'

She's still saying we, meaning Whigs, noted Eliza.

The sculptor folded her arms, holding a small muddy hook. 'What I want to express, I suppose, is that we English change and reform ourselves by degrees, not by pikes and gunpowder. I want to carve a symbol of…firmness.'

Eliza felt slightly embarrassed for her friend and looked away.

'Couldn't you call it *Albion,* then?' suggested Derby. 'Or do a lovely *Britannia* on a chariot?'

Anne chuckled. 'I doubt I could carve a chariot.'

'Well, an armchair, then.'

'For all your flippancy, Derby,' said Anne, 'don't you think the idea of kingship is a sacred tradition, something to cling to in these strange times? Why, your own noble title derives from it, as a stream from a river!'

Instead of answering he asked Eliza, 'Have you told her about Louis?'

Her stomach sank. 'He's to be put on trial for treason,' she told Anne, who stared. 'A strongbox was found in the Tuileries, full of his secret correspondence with foreign powers.'

'How very convenient,' said the sculptor, gouging at the clay. 'Just when they want an excuse to put their lawful king in the dock, they happen to come across a strongbox full of evidence.'

'It's a sad business,' Derby conceded.

'It's not some necessity of fate, Derby, it's an appalling crime.'

'Well. The French are making dire mistakes, but one wouldn't wish them the cowed serfs of Versailles again.'

'Oh, please. I *knew* Versailles.' Anne's head snapped round. 'You never go any farther than Liverpool.'

'As I was saying to Fox the other day,' he continued, unruffled, 'we must stand by the new Republic, because when it comes down to it we're on the same side. It's a crusade against the unchained power of kings'—and his eyes flicked upwards to Anne's clay model.

Eliza shifted uneasily in her seat.

The sculptor glowered down at the Earl. 'Perhaps you wouldn't speak so casually and naïvely about bloodshed if you'd ever been to war yourself.'

His eyebrows soared up.

Eliza had to speak. 'But my dear Anne,' she began as winningly as she could, 'while one deplores tragedies like the September massacres, one can still applaud the founding principles of the Revolution, can't one? Remember that day we read the *Declaration of the Rights of Man* together?'

'Barely,' said Anne, her face blank. 'So many more distressing memories have overlaid it.'

Was the older woman talking about politics, Eliza wondered, or the hiatus in their friendship? Her pulse began to throb in her throat.

'Tom Paine's arguing that Louis should be allowed to retire to America,' remarked Derby to Eliza, as if they were alone, 'since Louis helped the Americans win their war of independence—but I can't quite imagine the Capets settling down as good citizen farmers! Sherry heard that from Lord Edward, who's in Paris, staying with Paine. Only I shouldn't call His Lordship that—since he's solemnly renounced his title and now goes by *le Citoyen Edouard Fitzgerald.*'

'You'd never go that far, would you?' Eliza asked. 'I can't imagine you as plain *Mr Ned Derby.*'

'I'd rather fall on my own sword, frankly. Oh, another funny thing: Fitzgerald's married that girl Pamela, what's her name, Pamela Égalité.'

'But I thought she was engaged to Sheridan?'

Derby shrugged. 'There's a certain neatness to it, a poetic justice on Sheridan for his rakish years. Fitzgerald seduces Sherry's wife, then weds his fiancée and they're still the best of friends.'

'People are running quite mad these days,' said Anne from her scaffold.

'Yes,' said Derby, with a hard look at the formless statue.

'There's been a terrible run on the banks, Walpole tells me. Unrest all over the British Isles, reports of cargoes of arms smuggled in, not to mention the 3000 daggers ordered in Birmingham. And what of last month's declaration by the French that they'll aid any revolutionaries in *any land* who long for liberty?'

Eliza fanned herself. She'd witnessed a very comical scene in the Commons, when Burke had produced one of the famous daggers from his pocket and hurled it down, and Sheridan had hopped up and asked politely for the fork to go with it. She was beginning to wish she and Derby had taken their leave half an hour ago; they might have been on the Strand looking at prints of thoroughbreds and fashions by now.

Derby's lips twisted. 'That was a bit of Gallic hyperbole. And as for *arms* and *unrest,* that's all puffed up by the ten scaremongering papers Pitt finances. *Fama nihil est celerius,* as Livy would say. Nothing's faster than rumour,' he glossed for Eliza, apologetically. 'Take it from me, Mrs Damer: there are no English revolutionaries.'

Anne came to the edge of the scaffold and her jaw was sharp. 'I heard that one of these Societies tried to set up a Tree of Liberty on Kennington Common.'

'Yes, and the 15th Dragoons were marched all the way from Maidenhead to stop them,' drawled Eliza, 'which seems an excessive reaction to a tree planting!'

Her delivery would have raised a great laugh at the King's Theatre, but it was wasted here. 'I tell you,' said Derby in the urbane voice that told Eliza he was struggling to hold on to his temper, 'I know the kind of earnest, bespectacled tradesmen who fill the Reform Societies, and all they do is make speeches and draft petitions. Yes, there's occasional ranting by maverick preachers, or window smashing by the out-of-work, but on the whole this is a prosperous nation, run by a responsible aristocracy—and nothing like France.'

'Then why, when I ride to Hyde Park,' said Anne in a shaking voice, 'do I pass scribbles on walls that say *Damn Richmond, Damn Pitt, Damn the rich, Damn the King?*'

Derby spoke with deceptive lightness. 'You've turned quite the royalist these days, haven't you, with your symbolical giant'—one finger flicked up at the armature—'and your fresh-minted Tory sentiments.'

Eliza winced. 'Derby,' she murmured, 'perhaps—'

Anne had drawn herself up. 'I've been a firm Whig as long as you, My Lord—longer, in fact—and I'm devoted to Charles Fox.'

'Oh, really? I hear Nollekens is sculpting a marble bust of our dear leader these days, while you're raising a monument to Old Satan!'

The door opened and they all jumped. It was only the maid with the tray of wine and cake. Derby knocked back half a glass of Madeira without a word and announced he was due at the Lords for a committee meeting.

Alone, the two women avoided each other's eyes. 'You were harsh with him,' said Eliza, putting down her cake, 'particularly when you threw in his face that he's never been to war.'

'Perhaps. But then he called me a Tory.'

'Don't take it personally. Under normal circumstances—'

'Circumstances haven't been normal for some years now,' said Anne bleakly.

'Yes, but at this very moment', Eliza explained, 'the Party looks set to break up like an ice floe.'

Anne's head shot up. 'You really think Portland's anti-French faction would split away?'

'Not if, but when. If Fox ums and ers much longer, he'll lose the respect of both sides,' Eliza told her. 'Derby says it's time for him to show his true colours and lead all those, in Parliament and outside it, who're resisting Pitt.'

'Resisting Pitt,' Anne echoed mournfully. 'That's what we've talked of since '84, but I don't know what it means any more. Perhaps there are more important aims, like resisting anarchy?'

'Oh, my dear, don't be ridiculous,' Eliza snapped. 'Our poor aren't half as oppressed and starving as the French were; I know it, I was one of them myself! And even our radicals—take a man I know personally, Holcroft the playwright—they're high-minded, idealistic men with no taste for violence. The English hate to go to extremes; they'll never revolt.'

Anne's eyes were huge. 'I pray you're right.'

DECEMBER 1792

Derby stood in his hall. He had to decide whether to give orders for his trunks to be packed for Knowsley. His mind jumped around like a hare fleeing from the guns.

Tom Paine had been tried and found guilty of sedition *in*

absentia. Things were shaky in the City; the 3 per cent consols had fallen to ninety and a half. Pitt's spies were everywhere and there was a sinister new Loyalist organisation with hundreds of branches in London alone, whose main purpose was to watch their neighbours and servants for signs of *mutinousness* and send all reports to the Home Office. After months of being accused of weakness and procrastination by the hard-line Tories, the Prime Minister had struck hard. He'd just announced, via the King's Speech, that the country was at risk of riot and insurrection by Englishmen working in league with foreigners—but he hadn't given any hard proof. Pitt had called out the militia in ten counties to preserve order and summoned Parliament early, two things which were only legal in times of invasion or civil war. As Lord-Lieutenant of Lancashire, Derby should really have been at Knowsley already, ordering drills for his militia regiments. But the last thing he wanted to do was leave the capital.

A loud knock at the door startled him. On impulse he opened it himself; it was surprisingly heavy.

'Derby!' Fox's swarthy face goggled at him through the sleety rain. 'Don't tell me your servants have run away?'

'I just happened to be in the hall,' he explained with a little laugh and waved away the footman who was standing behind him, aghast at the sight of the Earl opening his own door. 'Come into my study, you must be freezing.'

Fox knocked back a glass of brandy in one. 'Pitt means to truss the country up in a straitjacket,' he began, like some breathless messenger out of Shakespeare. 'Troops are marching into London to guard the Tower and the Bank. There's going to be a bill to increase the army and navy, and another to round up and eject *undesirable aliens,*' he said witheringly.

'And Portland?'

'Oh, our putative leader appears to have lost his mind,' Fox reported. 'He dithers and nibbles his nails, and polishes his spectacles, and says perhaps we should maintain national unity by supporting the government's emergency measures at this time of crisis. I said to him, I said, "Portland, this *crisis* is Pitt's invention and there's no bill the evil Eunuch could propose that I wouldn't feel honour bound to oppose!"'

Derby grinned and patted his friend's knee. 'Have you prepared your speech for the opening of Parliament?'

'Mm, it's very simple; I'm going to ask where this hypothetical *insurrection* is happening. It's a wicked falsehood, a libel on the British people,' growled Fox, 'and a French noose is too good for the man who invented it. Let it be on Pitt's conscience, if his crying wolf comes true and he brings on civil war!'

'Calm down, man.' Derby refilled their brandy glasses. Fox was the Members' Garrick, their eloquent conscience, he thought, and the speech would inspire them to tears and rapturous applause— before they gave their votes to Pitt.

'But it's a nonsensical charade; the kingdom's not in danger! No, I'm going to propose that we should formally acknowledge the French Republic instead of getting dragged by Continental tyrants into hounding it, and ease what tensions do exist in Britain and Ireland by bringing down the price of bread and coal.' Fox's voice dropped. 'What kills me, Derby, is the suspicion that Pitt's staging this whole tempest-in-a-teacup in order to split the Whig Party. And they call *me* irresponsible!'

'All right, let's tally the names,' said Derby briskly, as if rousing an invalid. 'With Portland will go Fitzwilliam, Windham, Loughborough—' he was counting on his fingers—'Malmesbury, Porchester, Eliott, Sheffield...' He could think of dozens more.

The black bear's face cracked. 'These men are my friends. Or were.'

'We've seen this coming,' Derby said gently. 'It's not just France. Many of your most cherished views—on Catholics, Unitarians, blacks, free speech—are too strong for most of the Party. Your passion for liberty, which makes some of us love you, scares others off, especially now Pitt's spreading panic with his talk of bayonets and bombs.'

Fox had buried his cheeks in his hands. 'I wish Liz were here.

She doesn't like to be in London when I'm busy, but I miss her sorely.'

Derby was counting up devoted Foxites in his head. Sheridan, Grey, Whitbread, Francis, Lauderdale, Erskine, Fitzpatrick... maybe Devonshire...The young Duke of Bedford was made of sterling stuff. Last week he'd been invited to Portland's mansion on Piccadilly for what turned out to be a meeting of the cabal; on learning that Fox wasn't there, he'd picked up his hat and left. These loyal men had influence over a puny total of about sixty votes, perhaps, but they could also drum up protests among fellow Reformers outside Parliament.

Derby found he'd decided what instructions to send to Knowsley: the Lancashire militia would have to train without their leader. His place was by his friend's side.

VII

Écorché

From the French, meaning flayed *or* peeled.
*A sculpture representing a human or
animal figure in which the skin has
been stripped off to reveal the
muscles, tendons, arteries
and veins.*

SINCE February last, when the regicide French declared war on Britain, Spain and Holland, the letters of our Correspondents have taken on a not unsurprisingly military tone. We have received numerous communications from Loyalist Associations about the seditious symptoms displayed by their neighbours, such as the using of a Froggish word like *Enchanté*, or for that matter, *Beau Monde*. Some write seeking information on the Duke of R-ch—d's plan for Homeland Security, others to enquire how a Coalition of eight nations can be taking so long to subdue the ragtag Citizen Army of France, or how many Englishmen have been arrested under the Traitorous Correspondence Act for the crime of buying Burgundy wine. That the various new laws have not proved wholly successful in keeping down Discontent was evinced by the late riot at Bristol, where troops sent in to quell the crowd killed ten of them; whether this should be considered an example of the People attacking the Authorities, or vice versa, we leave to the discernment of our readers.

It is a curious fact that social relations of all kind have taken on a martial tenor. The Proprietor and Manager of the homeless troupe formerly resident on D——y L——e are said to be at Battle Royal. And that same Sh——d-n is not the only gentleman who's obliged to change his lodgings from month to month to avoid a swarm of Creditors. Because of the war, the rate of Bankruptcies is now full twice as high as last year and a certain Foxy Politician who plays deep may soon be among the unfortunates. The outbreak of war has caused a Schism in his W——g Party, which is now two, viz. the Duke of P——t—d's followers, who have washed their hands of all Reform, but cannot bring themselves to go over to their old Enemy P——t, and Mr F-x's stalwarts, who break out daily in more outrageous levelling and Jacobinical language.

Whether the war can be blamed for the startling increase in the number of Bills of Divorce is a moot point.

—THE BEAU MONDE INQUIRER, *October 1793*

SHE WAS TAKING HER DAILY RIDE IN HYDE PARK WHEN William Fawkener came up. 'Good day, Mrs Damer. That's a handsome mount.'

'Oh, I only hire him, I'm afraid,' said Anne, trying to think of some excuse to prevent him from riding beside her. Her mind was still full of something that Mary had told her the other evening: that there was a comedy of Mrs Cowley's on at Covent Garden called *The Town Before You,* which featured an eccentric ageing sculptress who in the last act threw away her chisels and vowed to make the hero a good wife. As satire it sounded mild enough—it didn't touch on her dreadful subject, at least—but Anne was uneasy. Could the author possibly have been inspired by gossip about the regular appearances of a certain handsome diplomat in Mrs Damer's workshop?

'Exercise becomes you,' said Fawkener.

It was a trite compliment—didn't pink cheeks suit every woman?—but she threw him a sharp glance. 'Any news, sir?'

'Yes, there always is these days, I'm afraid. Marie Antoinette is on trial.'

Anne's horse slowed to a walk. Fawkener reined in to keep pace with her. Now there was another woman who'd been accused of the most unnatural behaviour with her own sex—and probably without any foundation but envy. It was said the widowed Queen was grey-haired and crippled already. Anne tried to picture her in a damp cell with stains on the floor. 'Why can't they just let her leave the country?'

He shrugged, his face suave as ever. 'They've kept her from her lawyers and accused her of every possible crime against the Republic and against morality. They even plan to claim she took indecent liberties with young Louis!'

Anne covered her face with her gloved hand. 'They must hate women. Her own son? He's eight years old!'

Her horse stopped; Fawkener was holding two sets of reins bunched in his fist and offering her his handkerchief with the other hand. 'My dear Mrs Damer, I do beg your pardon. I'm afraid wartime presents so many horrors that I take refuge in flippancy.'

'I knew Marie Antoinette, you see,' she said, drying her eyes on the handkerchief. 'At Versailles, in the '60s.'

'Ah. How very thoughtless of me.'

That'll remind him how old I am, Anne thought vindictively, rubbing her eyes. She glanced around. It might be all over town by dinner: *Mrs Damer and Mr Fawkener riding together in Hyde Park, yes, and he made her cry—that's a sure sign!* 'Thank you,' she said, almost grabbing her reins from him, and she rode on.

When he caught up, she felt obliged to clear her throat and make conversation. 'I suppose they might banish her.'

'Except that they're not banishing anyone,' said Fawkener. 'There's only one verdict, these days and seven thousand prisoners awaiting it.'

'Seven thousand? That's mass murder. The whole French race has gone mad!'

'And they've banned Christianity, did you hear? Notre-Dame's become a Temple of Reason. They say Paris is silent these days, as if the plague's abroad; the loudest sound is the *chop, chop, chop* of the Guillotine.' Fawkener spoke as if telling a terrible fairy tale.

Anne blinked furiously, so she wouldn't have to use the borrowed handkerchief tucked into her cuff.

IN BOND STREET, Eliza was staring into a window at a small clockwork device in shining brass. The blade was drawn up and then fell, over and over, a little more slowly every time. A shopman picked it up to wind the toy and gave Eliza a civil nod through the glass—then beamed and bowed properly.

'He recognises you,' said Mrs Farren with satisfaction.

Eliza reread the neatly printed sign in front of the machine: *To satisfy curiosity, an ingenious and perfect Model of Dr Guillotine's swift and humane Invention, £2.* She thought for a moment she might be sick. Was there nothing the World couldn't turn into a game?

But then, look at her: was she any better? In these strange times, foreign news was as involving—but ultimately unreal—as a play. Like everyone else, she read of horrors, then turned the page to learn whether the Prince of Wales had been seen in the latest mad fashion, pantaloons; while prisoners slipped in each other's blood in Paris, Eliza searched for the most elegant headband in London.

She'd adopted a policy of refusing to discuss France with Anne, since it always made them quarrel—but she could hear it, like a high-pitched hum, behind their and every other conversation these days. What she would have liked to say, if it wouldn't have plunged them into deep water, was that the daily litany of atrocities appalled her as much as anyone, but it couldn't change her mind. She had to trust that this Terror would end, and the French would remember who they were and what their Revolution was for. In the meantime she was still for liberty and against this damnable war.

The real reason Eliza was shopping today was boredom. Kemble had finally lost his temper and resigned as manager, so the company-in-exile had given up their lease of the King's Theatre. What could they do until the new colossus rising on Drury Lane was ready to house them? Drowning in debt, Sheridan had discharged more than forty second- and third-rate players to save on salaries—including Jack Palmer, who'd taken offence and sailed to America in hopes of founding a company there. Eliza missed her colleagues, and her work, more than she could have imagined. Is this what it would feel like, she wondered, to be a *former actress*?

The Derby carriage was waiting at the corner and the driver jumped down to lower the steps. Eliza sometimes suspected Derby of riding his horse around town so that the carriage would be available for the Farrens all day. Well, never mind, it was good for his health; she'd been alarmed by his recent attack of gout.

On their way home, on impulse, she dropped into Mrs Damer's to see how the *King* was coming along. When Eliza and her mother came in, Anne looked down from her vast scaffold, her features lit up with a smile. She was looking unusually respectable today; she'd swapped her stained smock for a draped jacket pinned loosely on her bosom, and a white apron, and tied up her hair with a Grecian-looking bandeau. Her guests were so numerous these days that it appeared she'd founded a sort of salon despite herself. 'Lady Ailesbury, Lady Mary, Field Marshal Conway, how nice to see you all,' said Eliza, making her curtsies. Anne's mother was knotting, just as Eliza's mother did but in finer silk, and her father was reading a newspaper. Eliza was always amused at how little interest the visitors took in the techniques of Anne's work. They liked the idea of watching art in the making, but they were incurious. It was the same with theatregoers, she supposed; they wanted to be dazzled by a performance, rather than learn about the dogged preparations that lay behind it.

Eliza accepted a glass of wine and Mrs Farren was persuaded to her usual half-glass of ratafia. (To Eliza's relief, her mother appeared to have got over her silent grudge against Mrs Damer, since the actress's reputation was clearly no longer in any danger from the connection.) 'Mr Fawkener,' murmured Eliza, nodding to the Clerk of the Privy Council. He was here so often, he really must be courting the sculptor, despite her denials. Eliza found the prospect of her friend making such a late second marriage rather incongruous.

'How His Majesty grows,' Fawkener remarked, walking round the gigantic scaffold. The face and upper robes of the slim young man were emerging from the creamy marble and Eliza recognised the faint pointing marks with which the sculptor was transferring the proportions from the plaster model.

The monkey-faced dandy Dick Cosway was bent over his sketch pad. (Eliza had let him paint her several times, before realising that he made all his fluffy-haired ladies look exactly the same; according to Derby, the fellow made his real money from obscene snuffboxes.) 'Mr Cosway, how's your delightful wife, and may I peek?'

'I'd be honoured, Miss Farren.'

So far he'd only done Anne's face, she saw; he'd shortened the nose and shrunk the cloud of curls in line with fashion. 'Mrs Damer,' he called now, 'I wonder could I trouble you—just to catch the pose—'

'Oh, yes, Mr Cosway, where do you want me?' Anne looked down, wiping some stone dust off her face.

'Hm, I usually like to have a lady leaning on something, but you can hardly put your elbow on our sovereign,' he said, raising a little laugh from the group. 'Chisel in one hand, I suppose, and hammer dangling from the other.'

'But this is a rasp; I'm smoothing the cheek.'

Her right arm must be hurting again if she's not chiselling today, thought Eliza.

Cosway nodded eagerly. 'The thing is, the public understands hammers and chisels to be the insignia of your trade.'

Anne exchanged a tiny, impatient smile with Eliza. 'Sam,' she called to the footman standing against the wall, 'if you'd be so good as to hand me up the big hammer and a flat.'

If you'd be so good; that amused Eliza. She'd noticed that people of liberal sympathies sometimes spoke more politely to their black servants than their white ones—though they didn't pay them more.

'My dear girl, it just strikes me, you've forgotten the crown,' said the Field Marshal, blinking in dismay.

'The crown and the sceptre can't be of marble,' she explained, 'cut that thin it would snap. I've found a Monsieur Vulliamy to forge them for me.'

'His workmanship is exquisite,' her mother commented, 'and it's good to give the pathetic émigrés some work when one can.'

Her husband snorted. 'We stumble over too many of them in Soho. Could be Jacobin spies for all we know.'

'Oh, Father,' protested Anne, holding her pose.

'Nonsense, Conway,' Lady Ailesbury told her husband, 'spies would look better fed.'

'My mother and I were just at Ackermann's Repository of Arts,' Eliza put in.

'Yes, we bought some card racks and a fire screen,' ventured Mrs Farren.

'Made up on the spot by several *vicomtesses*,' Eliza added. She didn't actually know the rank of the haggard red-eyed French-women she'd seen there, but she thought that would hit home. 'And Lord Derby has sent a former *abbesse* and a widowed *marquise* up to Knowsley to educate his wards.'

'Splendid,' said Lady Ailesbury, yawning behind her fan.

'Many think the French should all be deported, even the ones who arrived before the Revolution,' remarked William Fawkener.

Eliza stared at him. *He likes to stir things up.*

'Oh, but how would we do without them?' protested Lady Mary, stirring. 'Think of the loss of lady's maids, milliners, hair-dressers and pastry chefs. The Beau Monde would fall into chaos!'

The talk turned to some family friend called General O'Hara, who seemed to have been involved in the British claiming of Toulon in the name of the Dauphin. 'Or young Louis XVII, we should say,' Conway put in heavily.

Eliza said nothing. The execution of the last Louis had been indefensible—he should have been merely exiled—but she found it hard to weep for one bloodletting among so many tens of thousands. 'Is it true that the Duke of York has had to give up the siege of Dunkirk?' she asked, just to keep the conversational shuttlecock in the air.

There was a strained silence and she knew at once that she'd said the wrong thing.

Lady Mary spoke up in a drawl. 'I'm afraid Richmond's been made the scapegoat of the matter, Miss Farren, as Master-General of the Ordnance. The guns never arrived at Dunkirk, you see, and York's had the gall to blame it on the neglect—or even malice—of my husband.'

There was much shocked tut-tutting. Eliza's mother gave her a private scowl for her faux pas.

'We were away shooting partridge at the time, as it happened, but Richmond had given the orders,' Lady Mary assured the group, 'so it's hardly his fault if the guns were accidentally packed on to a different vessel and never turned up.'

'I had a most eloquent visitor yesterday, let's dub him Dumby,' said Anne, smoothly changing the subject to Eliza's relief. '"Lord! what a charming, clever scaffold," he remarked, paying no attention to the statue itself. "What a delightfully constructed contrivance, and so sturdy and high!"'

There was much laughter. 'My dear girl, you're being harsh,' Lady Ailesbury objected. 'I know the party in question, because I brought him, and he's simply too shy to comment on matters artistic.'

'Is he a carpenter, since he's such an expert on scaffolds?' asked Fawkener.

'He must be French,' quipped the Field Marshal.

'That's right, Mrs Damer,' Dick Cosway chipped in, 'it's one of the *rights of woman* to mount a scaffold, but be sure you don't *lose your head*!'

That raised a general groan and Anne gave the painter a cold look.

Strange, thought Eliza, what tasteless jokes were going the rounds these days. It was as if the news from France was so lurid, so excessive, that satire was the only possible response.

WHEN DERBY arrived at St Anne's Hill, on a warm afternoon, he found Fox recumbent on the lawn, 'trying to fool the birds into thinking me dead'.

'Any luck?' He held out his hand to pull up his bulky friend.

'I believe so, till you roused me, and now they think I'm Jesus Christ.' Fox squeezed Derby's hand between his two paws. '*Ravished* you could come down. I thought of Italy this summer, but Liz persuaded me we wouldn't be safe on the Continent, because I'm known to be such a friend of the French—and I must confess, it's been so Arcadian here that I'm glad we stayed at home.'

They tracked Sheridan to a stump in the woods, where he sat grinning over a pamphlet by some clever radical called Pigott who was charged with toasting the French Republic in a coffee house. 'You're rather merry,' Derby pointed out.

'Because my manager's come back,' explained Sheridan. 'I smoothed Kemble's ruffled pinions by reminding him that we're brothers in the ranks of Thespis, promising to reform my ways—oh, and a roof on the new Drury by Christmas.'

'Christmas?' asked Fox, brightening.

'That bit was a lie,' Derby guessed. 'Our Sherry's a monster of deceit.'

'One has to be to run a theatre,' Sheridan pointed out.

The three of them played battledore, not to win but to keep the shuttlecock in the air; they got up to 1239 strokes before Mrs Armistead had them called in for a delicious dinner. (For a former courtesan, Derby noted, Liz was remarkably good at housekeeping on little or no money.) Then the men lounged on the terrace, filling the little pipes that were all the rage. Smoking was considered much manlier than snuff these days—probably because of the war-time atmosphere, Derby thought, but privately he still preferred a pinch of good Masulipatam.

Fox reported on Devonshire House, where the blind windows had finally brightened again on the return of Georgiana, Bess and the other ladies.

'And Grey's child?' asked Derby. 'Left abroad in fosterage, I assume?'

Sheridan supplied the information. 'She's been sent to his parents in Northumberland to raise under the fiction of being his little sister.'

'How bizarre!'

'Georgiana's distraught about it, obviously. But she's quite changed by her exile,' said Fox. 'Penitent, and grateful to the Duke for having forgiven her and allowed her to leave war-torn France after a full year! Altogether cowed.'

'Oh, *dear.*' A chill breeze flapped their neckerchiefs. 'It's almost November, isn't it?' said Derby. 'Time to screw our courage to the sticking place for another Session.' He spoke energetically, but all he could think of was *forty-one to two hundred and eighty-two.* That had been the division on Sheridan's and Grey's Reform bill back in May: forty-one Foxite Members, fifty on a good day, with only a leaderless handful in the Lords since Portland's desertion; did that still count as a Whig Party? There was a silence, and he almost wished he'd stuck to gossip.

'Yes, I must begin, like some fat, wheezing Sisyphus, to roll the stone up the hill again,' murmured Fox. 'Though weak, we are right and that must be our comfort.'

'I think most people are sickened by the war, even if they daren't say so,' Sheridan argued, 'and Pitt's repression is doing a better job of making the country hate him than we could do. Those Scottish judges are more rabid than any Jacobin committee; imagine, fourteen years in Botany Bay for advising a man to read a book! Remember Holt?'

Fox nodded.

'He was sent to Newgate in July for reprinting a harmless old article about Reform from '83. I just heard he died there.'

Fox shuddered. Derby wished Sheridan hadn't mentioned such a depressing thing—then told himself not to be ridiculous; they couldn't treat their leader like a child.

'But it's hard to sail on when half the crew have mutinied and rowed off the other way,' said Fox with a pained grin. 'There's Loughborough gone over to Pitt, to be Lord Chancellor, and Porchester bribed with an earldom, Carlisle with a Garter...'

'Better this way,' barked Sheridan. 'Now you know who your friends are and we know what you stand for.'

'We may be few,' Derby said huskily, 'but every one of us would go to the gallows for you, old Fox. And I'm quite convinced the tide will turn.'

'Tell him about your bets,' said Sheridan.

Derby grinned. 'At Brooks's the other night, I staked 500 guineas that some measure of Reform will be passed by March '95—that gives us a year and a half—and another 1000 that by the same date Pitt will be toppled and you'll be Prime Minister.'

'If he hasn't—Pitt, I mean,' said Sheridan, deadpan, 'we'll have to assassinate him.'

'Oh, my dear fellow,' said Fox, shaking his head at Derby, 'you used to be such a cautious guardian of the family fortune! *Bet on knowledge, not chance,* that's what you used to preach.'

'But I do know this, in my bones,' said Derby, trying to convince himself.

'We're not meant to reveal this before the ceremony,' said Sheridan suddenly, 'but—'

Derby nodded.

'To hell with it, this is as good a time as any. The fact is, old Reynard, we all know you're on the brink of bankruptcy.'

'You'll end up in debtor's gaol before me, Sherry,' said Fox, trying for flippancy.

'Undoubtedly,' said Sheridan, 'but it seems your friends love you more than mine do me. All this summer a committee at the

Crown and Anchor has been collecting funds from your well-wishers.'

'Let me tell you, it couldn't have been easier,' Derby broke in. 'Not just gentlemen but shopkeepers, farmers, country clergymen have all sent in their mites—even many of Portland's followers have subscribed, out of old affection.'

Sheridan was businesslike. 'It amounts to £61,000—which we calculate should defray your debts and give you and Liz an annuity of £2000 a year for the rest of your life.'

'My dear friends! I—' Fox's ripe face seemed about to burst. He crushed Sheridan to him and then seized Derby.

'You're wetting my lapel,' Derby joked after a minute, but his eyes were brimming too.

I won't pretend to you, Anne wrote to Mary,

> *that this intense effort of carving my* King *doesn't fatigue me— but moderation is impossible, from my nature & that of the work. Besides, seven hours in my bed cures me & when I think of the sleepless nights I constantly passed, in the misspent years before I took up sculpture seriously, I realise I owe much composure of body & mind to this very occupation.*

High on her scaffold, she set her flat to the stone robes again. *Strike for seven, rest for four.* Her right hand ached as it took the hammer's impact. *Strike for seven, rest for four.* She was trying not to think about the news of the execution. Marie Antoinette had gone to her death without a single friend to comfort her, and with dignity. Would Anne have that much strength in her?

The important thing in such times, she told herself, was to concentrate on one's own duty. And hers was to finish this huge statue this year. She felt a little faint; she'd lost count of her blows. The blade of the flat slid, gouging a line; she made a little growling sound and bent to correct it. Her back ached. She'd have to get the carpenters in to lower the scaffold so she could finish the hem of the robes.

'Madam?'—Sam, with a note on a silver salver, picking his way through the carpet of white dust.

'The post can wait,' she said a little impatiently.

'But this came by messenger from Mr Walpole.'

She put down her heavy tools and her hands felt curiously floating. She knelt and stretched down to pluck the note from the tray. It was probably another five-page eulogy of the late Queen of France. The footman slapped the dust from his shoes at the door on his way out.

> *My dear,*
> *I hate to impart such news, but I must. Toulon not having re-*
> *ceived the Allied reinforcements it asked for, has been besieged by*
> *French artillery encamped on the surrounding hills, & our old*
> *friend General O'Hara is reported to have been wounded &*
> *captured in a gallant attack on a battery. The enemy forces by*
> *the guile of an officer called Bonaparte have seized the fort &*
> *Admiral Hood has withdrawn the fleet—which leaves O'Hara*
> *in the brute claws of the French without hope of ransom or*
> *rescue.*

Anne stopped reading at that point. She had a choking feeling. Strange how horror wasn't quite real until it happened to someone one knew well. How was the General hurt, she wondered, and how badly? His legs, his chest, his massive shoulders or black-bristled face? Would his captors even bandage him, let alone find him a doctor? More traditional armies made prompt exchanges of prisoners; the raw volunteers of the Republic scorned the practice.

Anne remembered O'Hara in her parlour upstairs three summers ago, so warm and vigorous, pulling open his shirt to show her his old bullet hole. *Wish for another war,* that was what he'd joked, it came back to her now; *wish for another war, with another wound to make me famous.* He'd been on the point of a generous proposal, and Anne had turned chilly and spinsterish, pretended not to understand him. And now the man was face down in the fetid straw of a French gaol, bleeding his life away, or in a wagon on his way to the Guillotine.

She must have reached out blindly, or stepped the wrong way, because suddenly she was slipping through space. She grabbed a pole of the scaffold, she swung heavily and felt a terrible jolt. She was on the floor in a heap, but she couldn't remember exactly how she'd got there. When she tried to stand up her right leg wouldn't support her. She sat very still for a few minutes, breathing in the dust that covered the floor. It seemed as if death was in the room with her. She found herself thinking of a distant cousin who'd somehow got a splinter in his hand while foxhunting; the wound had festered and he'd died of it.

This was ludicrous. Anne gave a heave and clambered to her feet. Everything seemed to work. She was only bruised and shaken. She wiped her mouth with her hand. She tried walking round the workshop; she brushed herself down as she went.

Voices in the yard; the door swung open. 'I assure you,' her mother was saying, 'visitors delight Mrs Damer, she works even better with the eager eyes of posterity upon her! Isn't that so, my dear?' Lady Ailesbury bestowed a kiss on her daughter, who tried to smile. 'This is Madame Duvalle, of whose exquisite beadwork you've heard me speak.'

Anne knew she must look appallingly dishevelled. She shook hands with the bony, nervous Frenchwoman and found her voice, offering her visitors a seat.

'Are you granting yourself a little respite from your labours, dear?' asked Lady Ailesbury.

Anne nodded. Her right leg was throbbing so loudly she could hear it. 'I think perhaps—' She backed away unevenly.

'Darling girl, are you ill? You look shocking ill.'

She mustn't admit to the fall. 'Just a little faint.'

Lady Ailesbury had already picked up the bell and was clanging it. 'You must go upstairs directly and take some hartshorn and water. Or James's Powders—isn't Walpole always raving about James's Powders? Where are those idle servants of yours? They really do take advantage.'

Sam came into the workshop, slightly out of breath.

'If you could fetch Mrs Moll—' began Anne.

'Your mistress is ill,' butted in the Countess, 'you must carry her upstairs, and ask the housekeeper for a good big glass of hartshorn and water.'

NOVEMBER 1793

Anne's thigh swelled up like a balloon. There was a navy-blue bruise the size of a fist that turned purple, green and dirty yellow. Doctor Fordyce thought it might be nothing worse than an inflamed tendon. When he felt the leg for splinters of bone, she didn't weep but she bit her lip hard. He bled her, a procedure that had always filled her with ridiculous dread; although she knew it was for her good, she couldn't stand the sensation of her life draining away into a basin.

Only alone at night did she let herself cry. The poultice on her leg smelt foul and her whole body seemed to pulse with pain. She thought of gangrene. A female sculptor was freakish enough; imagine how the caricaturists would go to town on a one-legged female sculptor!

Now, now, there was no excuse for such morbid thoughts. Anne had to rest, that was all; she had to take a break from her marble *King* and recuperate in peace. Except that she wasn't in peace, she was tormented. A lifetime of riding and she'd never fallen off a horse. What a fool she'd been to lose her balance on that wretched scaffold. Was this how an independent life drew to an end—with one episode of low comedy? Was she always to be a feeble widow from now on, hobbling on a stick, or wheeled in a Bath chair, even?

Mary Berry came round from North Audley Street every morning and sat like a small forest creature beside the bed. Instead of calling in Bet, she changed Anne's poultice herself with light hands. 'You're such a comfort,' Anne said, 'I can't tell you how much.'

'No need,' said Mary. 'I must confess I'm taking a sort of pleasure from looking after you. Not that I like to see you in pain—but it thrills me to be useful, especially to one I owe so much.'

'It's quite the other way round,' said Anne, her eyes welling.

'Now, now. Don't fall prey to sentiment or I will too.' Mary's finger was held up like a teacher's. 'Shall we take up where we left off yesterday?' she asked, flicking through Herodotus.

Eliza, still unemployed in the absence of a theatre, dropped in some afternoons to entertain and amuse. They stayed well away from political controversy, except for one afternoon when Eliza produced a print from her pocketbook and laid it on the blanket that covered Anne's leg. 'You know you complain half your friends now call you a Tory? Well, I picked this up at Ackermann's.' It was a gaudily tinted caricature that showed a fallen sculptress abased at the feet of her unfinished marble monarch: *Behold Whiggery laid low*, it said.

Startled laughter pealed from Anne's mouth.

'I wasn't sure whether you'd laugh or fume. That's a very good sign,' said Eliza, smiling at her.

When Walpole dropped in he was naturally understanding of an invalid state, but his fretfulness tired Anne. 'Oh, such a shocking accident, it makes me shiver just to think of it. That damnable scaffold, pardon my language! And this, on top of the lacerating news of O'Hara's capture—oh, the cruel twists and turns of Fate. Are you in shocking pain, my dear?'

It wasn't so much the pain, Anne realised. It wasn't even fear of a crippled future—a fear which receded as the swelling on her leg went down. It was a kind of humiliation. She'd always prided herself on her vigour: walks, rides, carving marble, these weren't just ways of passing the time but aspects of herself. Means of escape from the corsetted etiquette of the World.

The eighth of November was her forty-fifth birthday. Mary came round with a carved ivory fan. 'Oh, my dear, I was sure I'd passed my prime, as nobody's given me a fan for more than a year; I thought I'd have to stoop to buying one myself,' Anne joked.

'Not while I've breath in my body,' said Mary, bending to kiss her forehead.

The next morning William Fawkener was announced. Anne thought of sending down her apologies—but it happened that Mary had been kept at home by one of her sister's weepy fits and Anne was desperate for some conversation. She had Bet wrap her up well, and Sam carried her down to the parlour and laid her out on a chaise longue, with rolled blankets supporting her leg.

'My dear Mrs Damer,' said the diplomat, more hawkish than ever in a fashionably high-cut coat, sitting down and resting his chin on the ivory ball of his cane. His tone had a curious warmth to it.

'I hope to be on my feet again in a fortnight,' she told him.

Fawkener shook his head. 'This won't do, it really won't.'

'What won't do?'

His hand circled elegantly, as if conjuring up the words 'This... this life of yours. So solitary and independent. So dedicated and stern.'

'I wouldn't say *stern*—'

'I've admired you vastly for it,' he butted in, 'but really, you must begin to consider your friends. What are we to think', he asked, pacing the room, 'when we see you laid out like this, a broken victim of art?'

Anne laughed shortly at the hyperbole. 'Nothing's broken, only bruised.'

'Toppling from such a height—you might have died! Forgive my solicitude,' he added, 'but you've been very much on my mind.'

This was really very curious, she thought. The Privy Council couldn't be keeping its Clerk very busy these days if he had time to brood over the health of every lady he knew.

Fawkener suddenly sat down again, three chairs nearer. 'Mrs Damer, I believe you know in what exceedingly high estimation—'

'No compliments, I beg you,' she interrupted.

'Very well, then. I'll be quite frank and hope you take that as a compliment in itself.'

She stared at him. *Surely*—

'I wish to remarry.'

The words seemed to expand; they filled up the room. Anne's breath came shallow. William Fawkener wished to remarry. He had divorced Jockey Poyntz for cuckolding him half a dozen years ago and now he wished to be married again. What was this to do with her? 'Of all the ladies of my acquaintance...' he was saying. Anne wasn't listening. *Solitude,* that was one word that came up, *the long years, esteem, devotion, duties, graces, companions, compatibility.* No doubt the diplomat was talking eloquently, but her pulse was so loud she couldn't hear him. Her leg was beginning to throb.

'Do you understand me?'

'I believe so,' she said, hoarse, 'but I hardly think—'

'Please,' he said, 'allow me to marshal a few arguments. My feelings aren't merely romantic, Mrs Damer, they're quite sensible. I believe you and I would make a good team.'

She saw them as two horses, trotting down Oxford Street in harness.

'Though your birth is higher than mine, I look to my career to raise me; after all, my father earned a knighthood as a diplomat.'

'Believe me, rank is not a consideration,' Anne managed to say. 'I feel—'

'Please,' Fawkener interrupted, 'do me the kindness of taking some time to consider my proposal. I wouldn't dream of demanding an immediate answer, especially in your current state of health.'

Anne resented that. 'It's just an inflamed tendon.'

'Widowed so young, you've done splendidly—you've impressed the whole World with your pluck,' he assured her, 'but haven't you struggled through life alone long enough? Isn't it time you had a protector?'

Her teeth met with a little click.

'You know my history, everyone does, and I won't pretend that

I was a good husband, on the first occasion—I neglected my wife for my work,' he said ruefully, 'but I believe I'd do considerably better this time.'

'Your candour is admirable, Mr Fawkener.'

'We've both sailed on the rough seas of matrimony, Mrs Damer.' He spoke in a comradely way and she almost smiled. 'We're both wiser than we were and we deserve some happiness.'

'I...have not been unhappy, on the whole,' she insisted. 'My work—my friends—friendship has supplied so much of what my heart—'

'And it does you honour,' he cut in, 'I assure you I delight in the contemplation of intimacy, especially female intimacy. I'd never interfere with that.'

She found herself bristling. Who did he think he was to interfere or not interfere?

'All I ask is that you think about what I've said.' Fawkener had her hand in his grasp and he was pressing his lips to it. They were cooler than she'd have expected.

'I will,' she assured him, 'thank you, I will.'

He'd made his bows and gone out through the door before she could think of anything to add.

ANNE FOUND herself wide awake at four in the morning. The room was dark and she couldn't reach the tinderbox to light the lamp without dragging her leg out of bed. *I'm forty-five years old,* she said; she moved her lips but no sound came out. *Struggling,* Fawkener had said. *Splendid. Struggling splendidly.*

After forty-five years spent in this empty yet bustling World, she wrote to Mary in Twickenham, *I find myself the object—I almost said the victim—of courtship once more. I need your counsel now more than I ever have. Come up for supper?*

With O'Hara it had been different, he'd only given the impression that a proposal had been on his mind; really, nothing had happened, Anne hadn't allowed anything to happen. She'd never told anyone and had barely remembered it till the news came that the soldier was in a French gaol. The same went for Sir William Hamilton in Naples; the ageing antiquary had only dropped some hints, sounded her out. But this Fawkener business was official and deadly serious.

Mary arrived with a parcel of books and a framed sketch from Agnes, and wrapped Anne in her arms. She felt better at once.

'Mr Fawkener, I expect?' Mary said the name in a brisk, almost sprightly way.

'You told me so months ago, but I wouldn't listen. For some reason', Anne told her, 'proposals of marriage make me feel dizzy and sick.'

'That's very natural. At least, I'd imagine so—never having received one in my life,' said Mary.

'How strange. Here you are, a beauty in the bloom of your youth—'

Mary rolled her eyes.

'—while I, with all my faults and oddities, have received or warded off a good handful. I shouldn't say from whom,' Anne added, 'since at the very least I owe those gentlemen discretion. But I can't see why—apart from monetary interests—they should fix their ambitions on a woman who seems expressly designed for a single life.'

'Mr Fawkener clearly doesn't think so,' Mary pointed out.

She's not happy about this, Anne registered, which lit a little glow in her chest.

'And quite apart from your personal charms and merits, which I needn't number—'

'No, my dear, please don't.' Anne laughed.

'There's your birth.'

'You're right about that,' said Anne soberly. 'I'm sure Fawkener likes the idea of a countess for his mother-in-law.'

'He has a respectable position,' said Mary in a tone of strict fairness, 'and—I assume—funds to go with it. There was no issue from his first marriage?'

'No,' said Anne uncomfortably, 'but there was talk about him and Lady Jersey, years ago—a child, possibly—'

'Ah.'

They sat in silence. This wasn't good, but it wasn't unusual for a gentleman in his forties to have some entanglements. The Countess of Jersey had little reputation left, anyway; it wasn't as if he'd debauched some virtuous wife.

'Mrs William Fawkener,' said Mary, trying out the phrase with forced cheer.

Anne gave an involuntary shiver. 'Not to you; I'll always be Anne, I hope.'

Mary grabbed her hand for an answer. 'Are you inclining to accept him?'

'Oh, my dear!' Anne was silent for a minute. 'I like the fellow well enough, but I barely know his character.'

'Given time, that would change.'

'Well, yes, but by then it might be too late. I don't know whether we have much in common; he works for Pitt,' she protested. 'He's lively and pleasant, with a down-to-earth, man-of-the-world air; there's nothing dull or priggish about him. But sometimes he's very modern and cynical. The man's a puzzle to me; I can tell he likes my company, but it doesn't have the ring of passionate affection.'

'Well, as a husband Fawkener might occupy your feelings, whether or not he'd satisfy them,' said Mary uncertainly. 'If you were married, at least the powers of your heart would be...called into action. If you don't think him absolutely unworthy, why not risk it?'

'But my heart's not inactive,' Anne cut in, defensive. 'Friendship is the most perfect good I know. No, really, all my instincts say no,' she said, suddenly decisive. 'My liberty's precious to me—'

'Oh, Anne!'

'What? What is it, my darling girl?' Anne kept hold of the small hand. 'You think I'm wrong.'

Mary nodded slowly.

'You want me to marry this man whom I barely know and whom you haven't even met except in a crowd?'

'I want you to be happy.'

She saw tears glittering in the deep-brown eyes. 'But I like my life; I have all that I need. Why would I change my condition?'

Mary seemed to be having some difficulty speaking. 'It's your chance.'

'My chance of what?'

'Your last chance, perhaps, to clear up all the vile mistakes and misapprehensions about you.'

'Ah,' said Anne, sitting back and letting go of Mary's hand. The dreadful subject; she might have known it would come up again.

'The day after your wedding', said Mary eagerly, 'such a bizarre idea would never more be thought of and you'd become as respectable in the eyes of the World as you've always been in your own—and mine.'

Anne sighed. She got to her feet carefully; she still couldn't put any weight on her right leg. Mary jumped up to support her, but Anne waved her away. She made it to the window by leaning on the furniture and looked down on the vast oval of Grosvenor Square, the grass browned with dead leaves. 'With regard to the World,' she said, 'even were I inclined to buy its uncertain favour, I very much doubt if marriage would have the cure-all effect you imagine. In the past I've been attacked by malicious invention, not because of the sober opinion of any living creature.'

'Isn't it worth trying? I just know I'll regret it', said Mary, wiping her eyes, 'if I don't use all my influence to persuade you not to give a hasty answer to Fawkener. For God's sake, Anne, don't let false ideas of personal *liberty* prevent you from entering into a partnership which might keep you safe!'

A partnership, thought Anne. She tried to see herself and William Fawkener at the breakfast table together, discussing their plans. *Do you require Sam for your errands, my dear? I don't believe so, not today.*

'Think what your heart has suffered and how much it deserves to be repaid,' said Mary.

'But not with false coin,' said Anne under her breath.

WHEN FAWKENER called again it was a mild day, for November, and Anne was well enough to go out for a ride in Hyde Park in his sporty two-wheeled phaeton. 'I'm a careful driver I assure you,' he said, tucking the furs round her, and she wondered if he was being metaphorical.

Perhaps it would be easier to do this outdoors, she thought, watching the last yellow leaves quiver on their branches. It was wonderful to be out again, with the air rushing past her face; she'd been missing her rides.

When he slowed the horses to a walk, Anne thought she'd better get it over with. 'Mr Fawkener,' she said in a low voice, 'I've been considering whether a union—such as you've paid me the great compliment of proposing—would be likely to contribute to my future peace and happiness. And on the whole, I regret to tell you that I think...not. Believe me, I'm sorry.'

Fawkener didn't say a word.

'Are you surprised?' she said at last.

'No. Irked, if anything.'

'Irked?' Anne repeated.

'You're making a mistake,' Fawkener told her. He had the reins bunched in one hand, like weeds, she noticed. 'We'd live handsomely, and with our joint means and connections we could be a highly successful couple. You might prove a good hostess, appealing to Whigs and Tories alike.'

He really doesn't understand me at all, she thought, shaking her head.

'But instead, you'd rather live and die alone and eccentric,' he said, his voice hardening. 'And what do you think the World will say when it hears that you've turned down an eligible husband?'

First came nervousness—*there's going to be a scene, another scene in the Park, why didn't I wait until we were back in my parlour?* Then anger slid into place. 'How should it hear it, sir, unless from you?'

He ignored the question. 'Really, Mrs Damer, how long d'you think you can drag on in your present style?'

'Drag on?'

'Swinging sledgehammers and parsing Greek, I mean. It's no life for a woman of your age, with a crippled leg.'

Anne pulled herself to the very edge of the seat. 'It's my life,' she said between her teeth, 'and I have dedicated it to the Muses.'

Fawkener snorted. 'For God's sake! Don't you think the art of sculpture will survive without more of your clay doggies or blank-faced marble belles?'

She was speechless. The man had lost his temper, or his mind. 'I've given you my answer, sir, and you can hardly hope to change my mind by such abuse.'

'Oh, you call this abuse? I've read a lot worse of you. When it comes to the fair sex,' Fawkener added sneeringly, 'scandal haunts you and you'll never outrun it as long as you defy the World.'

Anne couldn't breathe under her tight striped riding habit. 'This is outrageous,' was all she managed before she was interrupted.

'I could have saved you from all that, by the way. I don't happen to care what truth there may be in the stories; you'd have found me a most tolerant husband,' Fawkener added with a half-smile of peculiar nastiness. 'So long as you fulfilled all the duties of a wife, I wouldn't enquire further into your business, or burst in on you and a lady friend—the actress, say—'

Anne found her voice. 'Silence!'

His eyes refused to drop. 'Does the thought of a husband appal you, is that it? Can't you stand my sex at all?'

'There are men in this world whom I esteem greatly, men of whom I'm very fond,' she snarled, 'but by your behaviour these last five minutes you've barred yourself from their company. Now stop the horses and let me down.'

Fawkener rode on, wordless; he made no attempt to rein in.

'Please'—and her voice broke in a way that made her ashamed.

'I'll leave you to your door,' he said. After a long minute he added, 'I know I spoke in heat, but really, you drive a man to it. *Dedicated to the Muses* indeed!'

Anne was peering over her shoulder to see if she knew anyone in the passing carriages whom she could hail. 'I asked to be set down.'

'Don't be silly, you can barely walk and I'd hardly be so uncivil as to watch a lady foot it home.'

She narrowed her eyes. 'Apparently your incivility knows no bounds. Set me down!'

With a theatrical sigh Fawkener reined in the horses. He came round and opened the low door for her with a mocking bow. If she could have avoided leaning on his arm as she got down she would have.

Anne set off along the path. Her right leg was beginning to cramp and she knew she was limping jerkily. From behind came the sound of the horses walking and a leisurely voice. 'This is a poor farce, Mrs Damer. Why don't you let me drive you home where you can sulk in peace?'

She turned off the path and went across the uneven grass where Fawkener's phaeton couldn't follow. These shoes weren't made for walking; she could feel every pebble or old acorn. She could tell her beaver hat was askew and there was a damp curl dangling in her face.

FEBRUARY 1794

Derby sat in the coffee room at Westminster Palace, which lay in the maze of passages and chambers between the Lords and the Commons. He was drawing up a list of technicalities on which the Duke of Bedford could denounce the transportation of the leaders of the Reform Convention. It would do no good, of course; the poor men were already lying in the hulk at Greenwich and the next fair wind would take them across the world to Botany Bay. Little that Derby undertook these days came to much, whether he was calling the handful of remaining Foxite peers to strategy meetings or trying to persuade 'Citizen' Stanhope to sound less like the bloodstained zealot Robespierre.

'Derby, my dear fellow.' The Duke of Richmond sat down in the next chair and motioned to the waiter for coffee.

The greeting was unusually effusive, Derby thought. 'How's the Duchess?' he responded. 'And Mrs Damer?'

'The first is only so-so, I'm afraid, and the second is much improved; she's been convalescing with us at Goodwood and at the sea nearby in Felpham.' The Duke covered a yawn with the back of his hand. 'As for me, this war will be the death of me!'

As the only military man in Pitt's wartime Cabinet, Richmond was known to be worked off his feet. Derby probed warily. 'Any news of Lord Moira's expedition to aid the royalists in Brittany?'

The Duke waved his hand. 'Complete disaster, I'm afraid. It'll be in the papers tomorrow.'

'What a shame,' said Derby, careful to keep his tone grave.

Richmond sipped at his coffee, then blew on it. He leaned on his knees so he was nearer Derby. 'My wife's very perspicacious; she said from the start that this war would be an unpopular measure,' he said in a low voice. 'And it doesn't help that some of the highest gentleman in the land like playing at soldiers.'

Derby grinned. Richmond meant Prinny—who'd squeezed his bulk into the magnificent blue and gold of the 10th Light Dragoons and was loudly whining to be promoted to major-general— and also Prinny's brother the Duke of York, whose campaign in the Low Countries was proving so disastrous.

'But the thing is, and forgive me if I come straight to the point—'

'Please do,' said Derby, curious.

'It's a necessary war.' Richmond spoke flatly. 'I suspect you know that, deep down, beneath all your talk of the *rights of the people* and your loyalty to Fox. This is our civilisation's stand against an enemy of a kind we've never encountered before. The French revolutionaries have an infinite thirst for blood. Our sources tell us that they're massing at Brest with a view to invading England or

Ireland, by the way,' he added quietly. 'They want to extinguish religion, erase not just monarchy and aristocracy but all tradition;
they aim to spread their infection of anarchy till all Europe is one
howling furnace.'

Derby's back was as stiff as a poker. 'Your Grace, if I want to hear
speeches—' He gestured in the direction of the House of Lords.

'I don't mean to speechify; bear with me.' Richmond scratched
his eyebrow and spoke so low that no one in the coffee room could
possibly hear him. 'My point is that you're wasted in Opposition,
Derby. Your intellectual abilities, your powers of conciliation, your
influence—'

Meaning your voting bloc. Derby stared into his cooling coffee,
almost embarrassed for the Duke. He wished for a moment that
Sheridan were here to hear this. Were the Pittites approaching
every one of Fox's apostles, to tempt them one by one, or should
Derby consider himself particularly honoured?

'You and I are rather alike, it seems to me,' murmured Richmond, crossing his legs. 'We're not intransigent factionalists, are
we? As aristocrats with ancient names, our deepest loyalties are to
the land and to England, not to any Party. The real crusade of our
time is the war against the mob, Derby, and I don't believe an earl
in his right mind can be a true democrat.'

Derby stared back at him.

'Don't you see that the rolling acres of Knowsley are a downright insult to a landless man who reads Paine? Come a British revolution, you'd lose your title one day, your houses the next and
finally your head. Why, a Jacobin aristocrat's like an ox fawning on
the butcher who's sharpening the knife!'

'I am not a Jacobin,' said Derby in a controlled voice, 'just a
lover of liberty. And there won't be a revolution in this country.'

'Why, we had one a mere century and a half ago, and the regi-
cides killed King Charles,' Richmond pointed out. 'Aren't you
afraid it might happen again?'

Sometimes, yes, thought Derby with a twinge of shame. He
leaned in, till he and the Duke were eye to eye. 'I'll tell you this: I'm

more afraid that Pitt and the King, on the pretext of *national security*, will destroy everything I love about England.'

Richmond let out an impatient sigh. 'What I wanted to say was that I've been authorised to extend the hand of friendship.'

Derby's eyebrow sailed up. 'It looks suspiciously like the claw of conspiracy. For the last two years your master Pitt's been driving a wedge into our Party, and now he's managed to split it in two he's poaching many of our best men.'

'It's hardly poaching when the creatures come willingly.'

'To the bait! The Prime Minister has so many places and pensions in his gift, after all.'

'Such men as the Duke of Portland haven't been bribed; they're as independent and principled as yourself, Derby,' Richmond scolded. 'What I'm talking about is a possible coalition, a union of the greatest talents of both Houses—

'Led by one William Pitt?'

'It's not about Whigs and Tories any more, it's revolutionaries versus the rest of us,' said Richmond wearily. 'Pitt has to remain PM, because you know the King will never consider Fox.'

Derby spoke very clearly 'I'll never betray him.'

'You're on history's losing side.'

He shrugged. 'I've picked my cock and I'll back him to the end.'

Richmond got to his feet and made a curt bow. Left behind in the coffee room, Derby saw that his hands were shaking.

APRIL 1794

'Yes, I did mean to send it in for the Exhibition at the Royal Academy as usual, before it takes up residence in the Scottish Register Office,' Anne was telling Agnes Berry, 'but then Walpole took it into his hoary head that this statue needed a showing all of its own.' She smiled sideways at Mary. The little party was gathered in the Leverian Museum on the Surrey side of Blackfriars Bridge. Anne had never been there before—she wasn't sure if it still counted as London—but it had a splendid rotunda and her *King*, polished to an angelic glow, with one hand ready on his sword hilt and the other brandishing his sceptre, looked magnificent on his plinth in the middle of the gallery.

'To think', Agnes marvelled, 'that for the next three months crowds will flock into this building to pay homage!'

Anne felt a surge of pure sweetness—even though she'd never have admitted to caring what people in general thought of her work.

'Will there be an admission fee?' asked Mr Berry.

'Well, at first I thought not,' Anne told him. 'But then Sir Ashton—the museum's owner—pointed out that charging a shilling is really the only way to weed out undesirables and reduce the crowd to manageable proportions.'

'Child of my heart!' cried Walpole, limping back from his close contemplation of the statue. 'Your *King* is a triumph at the level of pure aesthetics and also as an act of patriotism.' He kissed her on both cheeks; his lips were chapped and warm. 'How proud I am to know you—to be your close relation, and your godfather too. *Fama semper vivat,*' he crowed, 'may her fame live for ever!'

'Oh, hush now,' said Anne.

'I won't, indeed it's very cruel of you to try to hush me at my time of life. When each sentence could be my last, my words should be treasured like rubies.'

'Ah, but there are so many of them, sir,' Mary told him, 'and that always depresses the price of a commodity.'

He giggled, pink-cheeked, and rested his clamped hands on his cane.

Anne had welcomed a stream of visitors all morning, but there were two conspicuously missing faces: Derby and Eliza. She'd sent them invitations—after all, they'd both been to see her carve her *King*—but of course today's gala opening was different, a matter not merely of looking and admiring but of being seen to look at and admire an artwork that had already been hailed by one Pittite newspaper as *a grand rebuke to democratical sedition.* Sedition: that was one of those words that had changed its meaning in a handful of years. Anne used to think it signified terrible deeds, threats to the life of the monarch—but nowadays it seemed as if any song, any speech, any casual conversation in a tavern could land a man in the dock.

'My old friends will really think me an out-and-out Pittite now,' she said to Mary grimly.

'Not those who really know you, surely.'

Anne's smile twisted. 'Well, there's little room for subtleties of opinion these days. The World seems divided into two camps, each shouting abuse at the other, *Tory warmonger* or *Jacobin anarchist*.' Mary nodded. 'It's like some strange light that turns all shades to black and white.'

'The other day at Mr Jerningham's,' Agnes chipped in, 'a young miss who looked about thirteen demanded to know whether I was a *democrate* or an *aristocrate*.'

They are shared a rueful laugh.

'Sometimes I wonder how people remain friends at all in these tumultuous times,' said Anne in Mary's ear.

There, between the columns of the entrance, was the unmistakable ursine silhouette of Charles James Fox. Anne rushed over to him—her limp barely noticeable now—and took both his hands in hers.

'Well, my dear Mrs Damer,' said Fox, staring up at the statue of his old enemy, '*what a piece of work is a man*.'

She laughed, recognising the quote from *Hamlet* and capped it. '*And yet, to me, what is this quintessence of dust?*'

'It's a triumph, that's what it is,' he told her. 'The lines flow magnificently, especially that slim leg, revealed where the robes fall open. And the firm, boyish face. Doesn't look a bit like Old Satan!' The insult came out like a fond nickname. 'I see what you're after: it's a symbolic representation of all the best elements of leadership.'

Her heart pounded with gratitude. 'Yes, it's not about the man himself. I felt somehow...as if it were my duty to carve this statue as a gift to the nation.'

'Well,' said Fox, 'there's no better reason.'

She wanted to throw her arms round him and kiss his hairy, quivering jowls. He seemed tidier than he used to be, it struck her, and his linen was, if not crisp, then fairly white; evidently his Mrs Armistead was taking good care of him. Perhaps it was true about their secret marriage. 'You and I haven't seen as much of each other lately as we used to,' she found herself saying, as if picking at a scab.

'No; I've been shockingly busy,' said Fox, 'and it's clear you have too.'

'One's always in such a hurry nowadays,' she said.

It was a meaningless remark, but Fox nodded as if she had produced some pearl of wisdom. 'Shall I tell you a little secret, Mrs Damer?'

'Do.'

He whispered it in her ear, like in the old days. 'I'd like nothing better than to retire.'

Anne stared at him. *Impossible.* Fox was only in his mid forties; though he'd entered the Commons in his teens, he hadn't yet had his time in the sun. She always used to say that the day he became Prime Minister would be the happiest day of her life. She felt a terrible impulse to tell him that, this minute—except it wasn't exactly true any more. It struck her now that she dreaded to think what might happen to England with Fox and his more radical friends at the helm. Her throat hurt. She realised that she preferred to picture him as always waiting, always full of fine ideals and righteous indignation.

'Oh, I know I mustn't, it would be a gross dereliction of duty.' Fox sighed. 'But I must admit the thought of living year-round in the country is a sweet fantasy to me. Grey could keep up the good fight better than I in the Commons, and Bedford in the Lords.'

Anne knew that people were looking at them and speculating about their conversation. She felt a sort of raging affection. 'Dear old Fox. Our opinions may have diverged, but I revere your character as much as ever,' she told him. 'I've never thought so well of you in all my life as when I've seen you reduced in your followers and embattled on all sides, but persisting heroically.'

He laughed. 'I don't think I'm a natural martyr; I rather liked popularity, if memory serves. But you're very kind, Mrs Damer. Now, any chance of a glass of wine?'

THE COLOSSUS at Drury Lane was open for business at last. Its roof, topped with a statue of Apollo, stuck up on the London skyline as if it were a temple, but the building looked more like a vast barracks. Eliza counted its windows: twenty-seven wide, five high. The interior was like a gigantic, airy birdcage. When Eliza walked on to the vast stage, the first day the actors were let in, she felt slightly giddy. The proscenium arch towered above her; it was over a hundred feet high, to allow for the lifting of flats. 'Dizzying, isn't it?' said a voice behind her.

'Jack! I didn't know you were back from America.'

Palmer put his hands round her waist and stole a kiss on the cheek so quickly that she hadn't time to get offended. 'Oh, you can't keep a mole from circling back to his old burrow. Even if it has been polished up a bit,' he added, his eyes taking in all the cut-glass candelabra.

'So you've talked your way into Kemble's good graces?'

'Indeed, though my salary's lower than what it was in my heyday—just to keep my head from swelling,' he said, scratching his democratical crop.

Eliza tucked her arm into his. 'Oh, it's good to be a real company again.'

Since the old stock scenes were now too small, Kemble had hired Mr Capon to paint exquisite flats and wings, many in the Gothic style which Walpole's toy house at Twickenham had helped to make so fashionable. 'This is the finest theatre in Europe,' Sheridan kept saying with a shark's smile that defied anyone to disagree with him. He claimed it would take in £700 at every performance; he referred to it as his Grand National Theatre, but everyone else simply called it New Drury.

Since its official opening had the bad luck to fall during Lent, it was celebrated with a concert of Handel's sacred music rather than a play. The real opening was the first performance of *Macbeth* on Easter Monday, with fifteen new pieces of scenery that dropped down on rollers as if by magic. For the first time the weird sisters really would be seen flying through *the fog and filthy air*. As an innovation Banquo's ghost was going to be invisible; Kemble's horrified gaze alone would persuade the audience that there was something there, or so he claimed.

Eliza wasn't in the play herself, but Sheridan—with a touch of malice—had written her a speech to introduce the new fire curtain. She shivered with cold as she applied her paint. 'I must say these new dressing rooms are no improvement on the old; narrower, if anything.'

'Oh, they can't be, Miss Farren,' said Pop Kemble with mild reproach.

'Half the size,' cried Dora Jordan. She had no role tonight, but much to Eliza's irritation had come to *pay a call* and was sitting in a corner suckling the latest boy she'd presented to the Duke of Clarence. 'Your memory deceives you, Mrs Kemble; it's been three years since poor Old Drury got knocked down.'

Mrs Siddons, darkening her eyelids with kohl, spoke up gravely. 'Whatever about our backstage conditions, to my mind the theatre itself is entirely beautiful.'

Despite Lady Macbeth's classical draperies she looked huge; could she be carrying twins this time, Eliza wondered? Mrs Siddons was known to need the money too much to withdraw from the role, but her *I have given suck* line would be sure to raise some titters tonight.

'First call, Miss Farren,' said the boy, his head in the door.

Eliza's mother hurried after her down the corridor. 'You've forgotten your hammer.'

'Oh! Thanks.' Mrs Farren tugged at her daughter's ringlets to lengthen them. 'Don't fuss,' Eliza told her, 'I'll only be on a few minutes.'

'Oh, but your speech will be the highlight of the night,' Mrs Farren assured her. 'People can't but take an interest in whatever'll stop them being burnt to cinders!'

Jack Palmer had a curious philosophy about that, she remembered; he said all theatres were doomed to burn to the ground in the end, being as mortal as men. But Sheridan insisted that modern progress had finally solved this problem and that the new Drury Lane was spark-proof. Eliza remembered the terrible night in February when the King's arrival at the Haymarket had triggered a crush and a dozen members of the audience had been trampled to death. 'I wonder if Old Satan felt responsible at all when they told him what happened,' she said, not needing to explain her thought.

'Oh, I doubt it,' said her mother, shaking out Eliza's skirt like a bridesmaid. 'Bringing such vast crowds under one roof will always have its hazards. Theatregoers are great excitable children, always ready for riot and tumult; they couldn't form an orderly line if their lives depended on it—which they did, that night, I suppose,' she added with a shiver.

New Drury held 3600, almost double the capacity of its predecessor, but the moment Eliza stepped on stage—passing Kemble in Highland dress, with a huge bonnet trimmed with black ostrich feathers—she could tell the house was packed like a barrel of fish. She gave a sweeping curtsy to her friends in the boxes.

The conceit of Sheridan's speech was that Eliza, in apron and mob cap, was a housekeeper giving the public a tour of the treasures of some titled collector. (She'd borrowed the mannerisms of Walpole's Margaret.) With her long feather duster she pointed gracefully to the walls of the theatre, which she happened to know were only wood, behind a thin facing of stone, but never mind.

Our pile is rock, more durable than brass,
Our decorations gossamer and gas—

She had the uneasy feeling that her words weren't reaching the fifth gallery, where the crowd seemed restless. Could they all see her from that height, even? She felt dwarfed, muted, overshadowed by the racks of stacked faces. She threw out her voice as she swirled round, her arms soaring.

> *Blow wind—come wreck—mages yet unborn,*
> *Our castle's strength shall laugh a siege to scorn.*
> *The very ravages of fire we scout,*
> *For we have wherewithal to put it out!*

Here the curtain was drawn up—*come on*, Eliza thought, *speed it up*—and she ran to the edge of the stage. In response to her feathered wand, a great iron shutter was lowered. There was a storm of clapping.

She drew the hammer out of her apron—thank goodness her mother had remembered it—and gave the iron curtain a bang. This produced the heartiest applause so far, especially in the top gallery; *well, at least they heard that.* What a silly spectacle this was—but Eliza couldn't help enjoying herself. She waited for a hush and held up one finger to let the audience know there was more to come. She waved her wand to raise the iron curtain, revealing a shallow artificial lake, which brought on much more applause.

> *In ample reservoirs our firm reliance,*
> *Whose streams set conflagration at defiance.*
> *Panic alone avoid—let none begin it.*

She wagged her finger scoldingly at her friends in the boxes, one by one: Anne, Derby, Bunbury, Fox, Richmond...

> *Should the flame spread, sit still—there's nothing in it—*
> *We'll undertake to drown you all in half a minute!*

This raised the first great laugh of the evening. It was followed by *oos* and *ahs* as a huge tank was revealed and tipped forward; water plunged into the lake. Eliza had to raise her voice to be heard.

> *The hottest flame shan't singe a single feather,*
> *No! I assure their generous benefactors,*
> *'Twould only burn the scenery and actors!*

How the audience howled at that. A tiny boat floated on to the lake, with Bannister Senior and Junior in it back to back, trying to row different ways, and the band struck up 'The Jolly Waterman'.

MAY 1794

Derby left Newmarket after barely three days. His horses had come to nothing. Familiar faces were missing from the stands; bets were down. 'With the economy so uncertain,' Bunbury complained, 'no one's risking their money.' But it was more than that, Derby thought. There was an unease in the crowd; it reminded him of birds before a storm, hunkering down in the branches.

Brooks's was a madhouse; everyone seemed to be eating bloody steaks. Sheridan collared Derby. 'Horne Tooke's been arrested,' he said without preamble, 'and Hardy, and Holcroft, and a dozen others.'

'Whatever for?' asked Derby, blinking. He knew that Hardy's London Corresponding Society had held some large public meetings recently—drawing up to 4000, on one occasion at Chalk Farm—but that wasn't against the law.

'Sedition,' said Sheridan, 'that commodious portmanteau of a word which covers anything and everything Pitt dislikes! He's set up a Secret Committee—our former friends Portland and Lough-borough are on it—which has seized the papers of the LCS for ex-amination.' He knocked back his brandy like medicine. 'Holcroft, Jesus Christ, little Tom Holcroft! The tribe of playwrights have committed many crimes against the British public—implausibili-ties, tediosities, hideous rhymes—but nothing that deserves the gallows, a spell in Newgate, or Botany Bay.'

'But what's Pitt after?' asked Derby.

'A complete stranglehold on the nation,' growled Sheridan. 'He means to suspend habeas corpus for a year, to allow for arrests and detentions at will. His spies claim the Reform Societies are plotting to call a pan-British Convention as a rival to Parliament, and si-multaneously inviting the French to invade.'

'Oh, what fantastical notions.' Derby could feel a headache starting up behind his eyebrows.

'We'll fight the Bill on the second reading but I don't know…' Sheridan scratched the flaming patch of skin on his nose. 'Did you hear about the judge who calls it an act of treason to speak the word *republic*?' He kicked the table leg like a child.

'Now, now, none of that, sir,' said the manager of the Club, hurrying over.

'And how many of us will be left to buy your mangy steaks and urinous wines', roared Sheridan, 'when the King's Eunuch has arrested every man who dares to disagree with him?'

Derby covered his jaw with his hand. He had a sudden vertiginous vision of being called into court in defence of Sheridan. *Yes, Your Honour, I did hear him say those words in Brooks's Club, but only as it were in jest*…He put an arm round Sheridan and bent to his ear. 'Mind what you say. Spies are everywhere.'

Sheridan rolled his eyes. 'You think I'm blind, Derby? My letters arrive ripped open, or not at all.'

'Then you must take more care.'

'That same prominent judge has bet 120 guineas at White's that I'll be in the Tower in two months. It's too late to be *careful*, my friend. *Lucky* will have to do.'

Derby suspected Sheridan of enjoying himself in some strange way.

The next week had a nightmarish quality. Events followed each other without logic or pause. He couldn't wake up in the mornings; he'd have liked to stay asleep behind the tight shutters of Derby House. He didn't have time to visit the Farrens, or send more than a quick note. Soldiers marched along Oxford Street like some surreal procession, the gentle May sun glinting on their bayonets; they were part of a new army called the Volunteers.

News was on every tongue, but one didn't know what to believe. Some organisation called the United Irishmen had been outlawed. Radicals were said to have gone into hiding, retreated to the provinces, or slipped abroad. The Secret Committee reported to the Commons that it had learned of orders for the manufacture of thousands of pikes, to be used in simultaneous uprisings in Dublin, Edinburgh and London; the Duke of Richmond spoke of a conspiracy to seize the Tower of London. Absurd details trickled out, or they seemed absurd to Derby. On the day the Revolution began, one spy claimed, farmers would be ordered to bring all their grain to market and all gentlemen would be confined to within three miles of their homes. At the Privy Council it was decided to call in several Foxite MPs for questioning about their meetings with enemy agents; one of the names was Richard Brinsley Sheridan's. Derby tried to protest, but his throat felt knotted tight.

In the Commons Burke spoke in dark riddles; he said it was necessary to withhold British liberties for a while in order to preserve them for ever. Fox and his men forced fourteen separate divisions on the Habeas Corpus Bill and lost them all. Some of the Whigs tired and went home to their estates; in the final vote they mustered barely a dozen. By the time the Bill came to the Lords, Derby knew it was hopeless.

He woke up that morning, sweaty and hot, and thought: *I must speak.* There were so few Foxites left in the Upper House that his diffidence was no longer a good enough excuse. Sitting in his study in his silk dressing gown, he wrote notes till noon, then sweated to memorise them. *It doesn't matter how I speak,* he told himself, *only that I do.* 'Make haste, man,' Derby snapped at his valet as he struggled into a narrow black silk frock coat to wear under his scarlet robes; he puffed out all his breath so the hooks and eyes would meet over his hammering heart.

The Lords wasn't even half full. Derby's eyes scanned the ranks of red-robed peers, counted the bishops and the judges. The Pittites knew they'd win, so they hadn't bothered with a whipping-in. He felt insulted, but also slightly relieved that his first speech in many years wouldn't be to a vast crowd.

The Lords, as always, behaved more calmly than the Commons; not having a Speaker to run the show, they'd learned centuries ago how to take turns. Bedford spoke against the Bill, then Lansdowne, Lauderdale, Stanhope (sounding rabid as ever) and Norfolk, each of them followed by one of Pitt's men, who spoke in the most loathing terms of *the lower orders*, of *enemies to all those of us distinguished by worth and wealth*, of *conspiracies to deprive us of our God-given property, dignity, and even our lives*.

Derby was trying to remember when it had happened, this turning of lords against men. His father and grandfather had raised him to think of the tenants of Knowsley as his children, his pupils, his people. When did the rot set in, he wondered, when had peers begun to see laxity in every magistrate, treason in every tavern, evil in every labourer's muddy face?

Finally it was Derby's turn, and he rose and wished he were taller. 'My Lords,' he said, too faintly, 'I am unaccustomed to address you, but on this occasion of grave importance I feel called to do so.'

A loud yawn from the opposite side.

He clasped his sweaty hands and pressed on. 'Are we a nation of terrified boys, so to deceive ourselves about the dangers we face? The government has reported on meetings and plans for a Reform Convention; well, conventions have met in this country before, without so much as a window being smashed as a consequence.'

'Jacobin!'

These insults had become so familiar that they were losing their power to hurt. In fact, this was the perfect prompt for Derby's next paragraph. 'No, rather,' he said, his voice too high and reedy, 'it is the government's Secret Committee that strongly resembles the sinister Jacobins. It is the spider's web of spies and informers that stretches across our islands—men who invent conspiracies to earn their pay—it is these spider's webs', said Derby, losing control of his grammar, 'that adopt the abominable techniques of the French!'

He took a breath and desperately tried to remember his next point. He scanned the rows of blank faces above the scarlet robes. Who were these men? He used to think he knew them; he used to feel one of their ancient, dignified company.

'We've been told of the discovery of paltry caches of pikes and a few rusty muskets—but *no weapons of mass destruction*,' he spelled out, a word at a time. 'Ours is a populace that has neither guns nor the skill to use them—thanks to our ancestors, who framed the Game Laws that give us landowners the sole privilege of hunting on our own estates.' He threw that in as a sop to aristocratic pride. 'I don't deny that in a population generally loyal there may exist a handful of Britons with dangerous views—but I'm convinced that all they do is sing the "Marseillaise" and make fiery speeches. My lords, if you pass this Habeas Corpus Bill in a spirit of panic, you'll be suspending that sacred liberty, won by our forefathers, that until this year has defined us as Englishmen.'

He sat down rather abruptly, his face hot, to a few desultory *hear hears*. He shut his eyes. *Well, at least that's over.*

AT NIGHT in her canopied bed on Grosvenor Square, Anne lay puzzling, as if over a page of mathematical problems. Some of the men arrested in the recent swoop might be innocent, but could they all be? What percentage of rumours could be discounted; did ten rumours amount to one fact? The poor rate had tripled this year; did this mean that three times as much was being done to help the poor, or that three times as many of them were starving, because of press-ganged husbands and other effects of the war? How many pikes added up to a conspiracy? How many French ships did an invasion require?

After church she walked in the Mall with Eliza. 'Mrs Siddons?' the actress repeated.

'Yes, she's agreed to sit for me; I thought I'd do her in marble as Melpomene, the Tragic Muse.' Anne was too queasy with fatigue to stay off the subject on everyone's mind. 'But Eliza, suspending habeas corpus must have been necessary to preserve national security,' she said, taking up their argument again, 'because almost the whole of the Commons and Lords voted for it.'

'That only proves that Pitt has bought extensive flocks of sheep,' said Eliza.

'Well, perhaps if *you* thought for yourself like a rational being,' said Anne, dropping her arm and turning on her, 'instead of following your man like an obedient spaniel—'

The actress's gaze was ice. '*My man?*'

Anne knew she'd got in too deep. But for years now these words had been lodging like grit under her tongue. 'Your words, your arguments, your very tone parrot Derby's.'

'I happen to agree with His Lordship,' said Eliza, 'and with Fox and the fearless few who stand with them.'

'How convenient! Because you can hardly afford to quarrel with the Earl, given the delicacy of your arrangement.'

Eliza folded her arms. 'To what arrangement do you refer?'

Anne was shaking now. 'I simply think it's revealing, the fact that you're still spouting the glories of *liberty* when the French fleet may be at the mouth of the Thames! You must have made up your mind to accept Derby when he's finally widowed. Your political views declare that you mean to be his.'

'My views are my own. And I'm nobody's.' Eliza walked away, her parasol like a shield between them.

Anne had to hurry to catch up with her. 'I don't blame you for your choice,' she said unconvincingly. After a moment she added, 'I spoke too harshly.'

Eliza turned and looked her in the eye. 'You're in a very trying mood today, I must say.'

She chewed her lip.

'What can I tell you, Anne?' said Eliza with a shrug. 'Of course Derby's views have influenced mine—as yours did, years ago, when you taught me to think like a Whig,' she added pointedly. 'But I must tell you, as to the future, there's no more clarity between myself and Derby than when you first asked me this question.'

'But that was what, seven years ago?' Anne remembered that shining afternoon at Park Place. How fresh they'd been back then, how unhardened. 'The quantity of time you've spent together since then, the whole tenor of your behaviour...'

'Oh, I'm well aware that I seem like a Whig countess-in-waiting, grooming myself to be Georgiana's successor,' said Eliza sharply. 'None of which alters the fact that my own mind is not made up.'

'But if you don't mean to marry him—'

'What am I doing?' Eliza looked at Anne almost guiltily. 'I hardly know. I certainly don't mean to marry anyone else.'

'Then—'

'I've no fear of single life; it suits me perfectly well. If I build up my savings until I retire at, say, fifty, I should have a comfortable sufficiency to support myself and my mother.'

Anne narrowed her eyes. *Miss Farren, an ageing spinster, formerly of Theatre Royal, Drury Lane?* 'That's a touching little vision, but it doesn't ring true.'

'Well, harass my mother with your questions, then! She's had it all mapped out since I was nineteen,' said Eliza sullenly. 'The Countess will kick the bucket, Derby will go down on his knees, I'll give him another half-dozen brats and we'll all live happily ever after at Knowsley.'

Anne's chest felt tight when she considered the image.

'But many an invalid dies of old age,' Eliza went on, 'and Lady Derby's not forty yet. Now that really would be tragic, if I fixed my heart on a future that never came to pass!'

'So have you fixed your heart on it? We want what we want,' Anne persisted. 'Which of us ever managed to give up a strong desire merely because it mightn't be gratified?'

'Well, perhaps it's not a strong desire,' said Eliza.

'Don't you love Derby?' No answer. 'How can you bear to live so cheek-by-jowl if you don't?'

Eliza shook her curls off her face. 'How can I tell if I love him? It's not like the ecstasies in the plays, I know that much.'

'What you felt for Mr Palmer, when you were young—'

'Oh, that was just childish infatuation. Derby seems more like a husband, from what I've heard of them, than a lover,' said Eliza, looking down the tunnel of leafy trees that marked out the Mall. 'Part of daily life. I've never had occasion to miss or long for him.'

Anne nodded. 'Perhaps we only know we love when we lose.'

Her eyes were burning; for some reason she found her mind going off at a tangent, to that awful day in the Royal Academy when she'd demanded an explanation from her former friend and turned to find herself in an empty room. *If she asks me what I can possibly know of love, what shall I say?*

Anne hadn't told Eliza about William Fawkener's proposal; the scene in Hyde Park had been so ghastly that she'd spilled out every detail to Mary, then tried to forget it had ever happened. She'd never been what they called *in love*; perhaps John Damer had snuffed out that possibility in her. But she did feel strongly about things. Her heart moved like a bird in its cage.

JUNE 1794

In the interval between the musical burletta and the main play, which was Mrs Centlivre's old favourite *The Wonder*, Eliza was in the dressing room running through her lines for Act Four.

> *She who for years protracts her lover's pain,*
> *And makes him wish, and wait, and sigh in vain,*
> *To be his wife, when late she gives consent*
> *Finds half his passion was in courtship spent...*

She paused, struck by the lines, though she must have spoken them twenty times before. Was the observation true, she wondered, or merely cynical? Could Derby possibly be as zealous in marriage as in courtship?

Mrs Siddons, huger than ever, came in to collect a fan she'd left in her paintbox. 'I do hope you're not reading that dangerous book, Miss Farren,' she murmured.

Eliza glanced up and saw that *The Adventures of Caleb Williams* had slipped out of her bag. 'Dangerous?'

Mrs Siddons blinked owlishly. 'Full of subversive doctrines, I mean.'

'Have you read it?' asked Eliza with a fixed smile.

'I wouldn't touch such stuff—'

'Oh, do you get all your views second hand?'

'My dear—'

But there was a tap at the door. Her brother Kemble came in looking grave as ever. 'I must warn you, Miss Farren, Frederick's opening speech—the liberty one—I've had to change it, against my better judgement.'

'Why don't you follow your judgement, then?'

'Have a little appreciation for my position,' the manager pleaded. 'That line in Holcroft's comedy gave extreme offence to the crowd the other night. Do you care to see our fine new theatre ripped up in a riot?'

Eliza shook her head, wrestling her temper into submission. She'd rather liked the Holcroft line: *I was bred to the most useless, and often most worthless of all professions: that of a gentleman.* Derby'd found it hilarious. Surely not every witticism counted as an attack on the established order? But then, poor Holcroft was still in gaol, awaiting trial, which rendered every word of his suspect.

'I fear to provoke the crowd, it's so strangely excited,' Kemble added.

'Brother,' said Mrs Siddons mildly, 'don't you know that the city's in fits of joy over that naval victory off Brittany? Mrs Jordan wants to play *The Country Girl* for a Ben for the widows and orphans of the men who perished.'

'Ah, yes.'

'Earl Stanhope's windows got smashed the night before last, for not being lit up in celebration. Don't you ever read a newspaper, sir?' asked Eliza flippantly.

'Never,' he assured her, half smiling. 'My reading hours are devoted, like the rest of my life, to the theatre.'

Eliza, standing in the wings during Palmer's opening speech, realised that Kemble—that famous purist, that t-crossing quibbler—had simply changed *liberty* to *loyalty* all the way through it. She couldn't tell whether she was more irritated or amused. '*My Lord,*' Jack Palmer roared out, very clear so the potential troublemakers in the upper gallery would be sure not to miss, or mishear, the lines,

'*My Lord, the English are by nature what the ancient Romans were by discipline: courageous, bold, hardy and in love with LOYALTY.*'

A long ragged cheer went up from the crowd.

Politics got in everywhere, like dust, Eliza realised. Even the stage, the last refuge for irreverent and daring speech, had come under Pitt's chill shadow. She watched Jack's cheerful face. Did he remember doing this play with her in '89, did he remember shouting out *in love with LIBERTY*? Was she the only one who recalled the bissful grins that word produced? '*LOYALTY is the idol of the English, under whose banner all the nation lists,*' Palmer went on now, '*give but the word for LOYALTY, and straight more armed legions would appear than France and Philip keep in common pay.*'

Most of this crowd could have no idea who King Philip had been—the play was eighty years old, after all—but they howled their delight like wolves, so Palmer could barely be heard. 'Huzza!'

'Hurrah for loyalty!'

'King George and England!'

Some fellows in the pit began singing the latest catch. '*With soldiers and sailors and ships heart of oak,*' they chorused,

> *we'll pay those French dogs for their barbarous work.*
> *With spirits like fire we'll make them to dance,*
> *and we'll baffle the pride and the glory of France...*

Eliza, watching at the edge of the curtain, despised them. Had they no guiding principle except fashion, whim and mob rule? If they'd only hold their tongues, she could run on stage now as Violante, the same way actresses had been playing Violante since the beginning of the century; she could charm them and amuse them and transport them to long-gone Lisbon. Instead, it seemed, they wanted to stay here with *King George and England*!

Her cue: she stepped out, smiling like an angel.

ANNE WAS in her room at Park Place, with curtains drawn against the blinding sunshine, scribbling furiously. Her parents had insisted on her coming down, as London was in such turmoil and the streets full of soldiers. 'And if those French dogs were to invade,' said her father, 'Park Place has a good hilltop position for defence.' She'd smiled at that, but hidden it.

A radical journalist, a man called Charles Pigott, had just brought out a rash of pamphlets that insulted almost everyone Anne knew, Whig and Tory alike. Someone—she suspected William Fawkener—had sent her a batch of them, tied up with string, before she'd left London. Pigott, who boasted of writing this doggerel from his cell in Newgate, sneered at Miss Farren of Drury Lane and the Duchess of Richmond, among others, for their *mannered affectations* and at the Duchess of Devonshire for her *spendthrift ways*. The Misses Berry were named among the *bluestocking prudes* whose charms were beginning to wither on the vine; that was the bit that enraged Anne most, until she read the sneering reference to the girlish ways of *Lady Horace Walpole*. Pigott called all aristocrats brutes and offered as proof an old story about the Earl of Darlington, who'd ridden his horse sixty miles in six hours, whereupon it dropped dead.

Then came the bit about Anne's statue.

> *Lord! what a lumpish senseless thing*
> *And yet 'tis very like the King!*
> *Why strive to animate the marble rock?*
> *His sacred Majesty's more like the block!*

Poor stuff, but not funny, not at all. It might be mild by comparison with what Anne had endured before, but it was a perfect example of the kind of thing she'd promised Mary to be on the watch for nowadays. In the past she'd been negligent, but this nasty little seed would have to be rooted up at once.

If Pigott had been a man of any position in the world—a proprietor of a newspaper, say—Anne might have asked a gentleman friend to communicate her displeasure, but since the creature was in prison already she decided to take a direct approach. The rat, holed up in his stinking cell but still spewing out contagious bile! *Pigott,* her letter began (since she didn't want to call him *sir*),

> *your scurrilous productions have been brought to my attention. I give you warning that I, for one, won't stand for such treatment. If you ever hope to be a free Englishman again, I advise you to cease your libellous & foul vituperations. It is godless, subversive men like you who have brought this country to its present pitch of crisis.*
>
> *Yours,*
>
> The Honourable Mrs Damer.

THERE WAS a paragraph in the *Morning Post*; Mrs Piozzi sent it to Eliza, with a circle of ink round it.

> *The Countess of D—y, long an invalid, is said to be at Death's door. Should Fate so decree, we must wonder whether a happy event will follow swiftly upon a sad one and Hymen, who once fled wounded from Kn——y Hall, return there in wreaths of fresh blossom!*

The coy tone set Eliza's teeth on edge. She heard the same tone, too, in vague well-wishing notes from friends and acquaintances: hints that virtue was always rewarded in the end.

She needed to stay calm and find out whether it was true. Was Lady Derby really going to die and when? There'd been false alarms before, though never this dramatic. Eliza couldn't concentrate on memorising her part for *A Wife, or No Wife*; she had to know whether the whirlwind was going to descend upon her. But Derby hadn't mentioned his wife's illness, of course, and to ask anyone for information would be intolerably vulgar.

One morning someone left a print lying around in the dressing room—Eliza suspected Dora Jordan. She recognised her own silhouette instantly; tall, nip-waisted, with a cropped head of curls. It showed her visiting an old fortune teller in a workhouse and the bubble coming out of the fortune teller's mouth said *Miss Tittup, I see a Coronet suspended over your head*!

Anne's carriage carried them up Bond Street towards Marylebone. 'I know it sounds outrageous,' Eliza told her friend, 'but I'm convinced I must make the attempt. By accident my life has been connected so tightly to this woman's—and I've never laid eyes on her.'

'But my dear, even if Lady Derby's well enough to receive us and on some strange whim allows me to make the introduction,' said Anne, 'what can you hope for from such an encounter?'

Eliza shrugged and fanned the sticky air in front of her face. 'To clarify my mind.'

'You don't mean to triumph over the poor Countess as her possible successor?'

'How could you think that?'

'Very well. Because I must tell you I've always had a certain sympathy for Lady Derby. She and I were both married off without much consulting of our feelings,' Anne added, 'and both of us found ourselves unhappy in our mates.'

'But you behaved quite differently,' Eliza reminded her. 'You were faithful to John Damer till his death released you.'

Anne pursed her lips. 'It's true, but it doesn't make me a saint; it was more a matter of temperament than morality.'

'I realise now that I've always wanted to meet her—and time is running out,' said Eliza.

'I assume you didn't tell Derby what you were up to this afternoon?'

Eliza shook her head. 'My mother will tell his man I'm indisposed.'

'He'll be worried,' said Anne, amused. 'Hasn't he enough on his plate, with the Portland Whigs on the brink of a coalition with Pitt and Lady Derby on her deathbed?'

'I won't have him take me for granted,' said Eliza. 'Not now, not ever.'

Anne let out a dry chuckle. 'Every wife remembers that line. We've all said it on the way to the altar.'

'But I'm not—'

'You'll have to renounce such airs if you marry him.'

The carriage turned off Oxford Street and rattled up Baker Street. Eliza had a strange thought. 'I don't believe you like the notion of us marrying, Derby and me.'

'Nonsense.' Anne stared at her.

Eliza grinned back. 'You're rather prickly on the subject, despite the fact that you're a close friend to both parties.'

'Well, perhaps that's it,' said Anne after a minute examining her fingers. 'The idea of such a change...unsettles me, I admit. I'd rather we all stayed the same.'

'But nothing does, does it?' Eliza asked. 'I've a new wrinkle every month.'

'Oh, my *dear*—'

'No, I'm not looking for compliments. What I mean is— what's the tag?

At my back I always hear
Time's wingèd chariot hurrying near—'

The carriage went into a pothole, throwing them against each other. 'These Marylebone streets! We could do with a *wingèd chariot* right now,' said Anne, straightening up.

'No, but really,' Eliza persisted. 'I'm getting to that age when I can't expect my career to go on for ever—'

'You're only thirty-one. Mrs Hopkins must be twice that,' Anne protested.

Eliza gave her a cold look. 'I'm not going to hang about Drury Lane in my dotage, doing aged crones. The day Kemble asks me to be Juliet's nurse I'm off.'

Anne was suddenly helpless with mirth.

'What? What is it?'

'I'm sorry. Only the idea—the very *idea*—of you as the Nurse. All those padded skirts—"*What, lamb! What, ladybird!*"' she quoted.

On Gloucester Place, Anne sent her footman to the door with an inscribed card. He came back almost at once; that must mean a refusal, thought Eliza grimly. Or perhaps Lady Derby was too ill to be disturbed. Or already dead? Something leapt up in her throat at the thought and it didn't taste like hope.

'Her Ladyship would be delighted to receive you,' said the footman.

Anne turned to Eliza, her eyebrows up. 'Either she misheard our names,' she murmured, 'or she's in a very Christian mood.'

But neither was the case, Eliza thought a quarter of an hour later as they sat sipping tea by the bedside of Derby's wife.

The Countess was a most alarming yellowish-brownish colour about the eyes. Her features were good—wide and aristocratic, thought Eliza—but her face had fallen away from them. She looked more like sixty than forty; one could tell that she'd been ill for many years. But she still had a spark to her.

'I've been besieged by visitors,' Lady Derby croaked. 'There's nothing like an advertisement for one's demise in the *Morning Post* to bring down the hordes. I don't think we've seen each other in twenty years, Mrs Damer. Are you well? You look very well indeed, you must be quite recovered from your famous plummet from the scaffold. How widowhood suits some people!'

'I'm very sorry to see you like this,' said Anne awkwardly.

'Ah, yes, you'd probably like a full report, how remiss of me. I believe the precise phrase is *ravaged by consumption*—ravaged, as if by a hyena.' The Countess coughed wetly. 'In the same month as the fall of the Bastille I lost the use of my legs. Now, whether the consumption brought on the paralysis or the paralysis had some separate origin is a fascinating question on which I dwell in my many leisure hours. Then for a while last year I had a most irksome symptom: I began to speak so slowly that you could have recited the Lord's Prayer in the time I took to say Jack Robinson.' She began a ghastly parody. 'J-J-J- a-a-a-a-a-a-k R-o-o—'

Eliza couldn't bear it; she had to interrupt her. 'I've wanted to make your acquaintance for a very long time, Your Ladyship.'

'Have you, Miss Farren?' Lady Derby put her head on one side.

'You're not much like the caricatures, I must say; they always draw you so hideously thin.'

'Yes,' said Eliza.

'And it's really not true that you're twice the height of my husband,' she added with a scientific eye. 'One and a half times at most.'

Eliza felt her cheeks scald.

'I'm being rather rude, aren't I? It's a deathbed privilege,' said Lady Derby, cackling.

Eliza felt Anne take her hand; she clung to it.

The invalid's eyes missed nothing. 'Mrs Damer,' she asked hoarsely, 'did Derby send you here by any chance?'

'By no means!'

'You're not a sort of spy, the kind they used to keep around the poor King when he was mad? No, I suppose not; you'd have come alone in that case. Then what's your role in this touching scene?' asked the Countess.

Anne was looking guilty. 'I'm a friend.'

'To which party?'

'To...all parties.'

Lady Derby shook her head, tutting. 'Can't be done.'

Eliza felt the conversation was circling away from her. She had a feeling there was some question she ought to ask—had come to ask—but she couldn't think of it.

A girl came in with a medicine tray. 'Mrs Damer, Miss Farren, allow me to present my daughter, Lady Elizabeth,' drawled the invalid.

Eliza recognised Derby's forehead in the young face. She almost jumped out of her chair; it rocked on its spindly legs. She'd never met any of Derby's children. What was Elizabeth now: fifteen, sixteen?

'She doles out my drops herself, not trusting the maids,' explained Lady Derby. 'I used to have three offspring, you know, but by accident I mislaid two of them.'

Only now did Eliza feel a stab of something she recognised as pity. How curious.

An awful gasping laugh brought on a fit of coughing. When she'd recovered, Lady Derby whispered, 'My husband lets me have this girl with me because he's never been quite sure if she's his or the other party's. To an unbiased observer, Elizabeth's the spit of him, isn't she? But of course the scales of jealousy have blinded his eyes. And I never like to point out the resemblance in case he snatches her away!'

The young woman seemed inured to all this; through the discussion of her parentage she was measuring out her mother's drops. She never met the eye of either of the visitors. *Oh, poor Derby,* thought Eliza, *why did you convince yourself that this wasn't your daughter?* As soon as the girl had administered the medicine she excused herself.

They'd stayed too long already, but Eliza didn't want to leave this weird, stuffy room with its whiff of dissolution. On an impulse she moved her chair a little closer to the bed. 'Lady Derby,' she began in the lowest, most winning voice she could manage, 'you must wonder why I asked Mrs Damer to bring me here.'

'Not at all.' Relaxed by her laudanum, the invalid wore a ghastly little smile. 'The wife may turn a blind eye to the mistress, but the mistress is invariably curious to meet the wife.'

Eliza flinched and almost as quickly Anne was on her feet. 'I didn't bring Miss Farren here to insult you—nor to be insulted.'

'Sit down, Mrs Damer, and don't make me squint up at you,' drawled Lady Derby.

'My friend's reputation is impeccable. She has never spent a moment unchaperoned with Lord Derby in her life,' Anne insisted.

Eliza blinked. This scene was turning stranger and she herself seemed to have no lines in it.

'Oh, you take me up too literally,' said the invalid in a bored voice. 'There's a lot more to being a mistress than *rutting*.'

Eliza flinched at the word.

'I hear from every newspaper and pamphlet that my husband's relations with Miss Farren are platonic. So much so that I wonder if he's still capable of anything more.' The Countess grinned. 'All I meant by the word *mistress* was the beloved companion of a married man. Granted that Miss Farren's as pure as the most prudish of nuns, yet still the fact remains that for the last dozen years she's allowed my husband that daily conversation, charm and domestic comfort for which, as much as for anything else, men go to mistresses.'

Eliza considered which bit of that was worth denying. The dying woman made her flesh creep, but what she said was true. 'Lady Derby,' she said on impulse, 'have you any advice for me?'

There was a heavy silence. Then the Countess's sallow mask broke into a smile. 'As it happens, I do.'

Anne broke in. 'I really don't think—'

Eliza threw up one hand to hush her.

'You probably think Lord Derby very gallant, don't you?' began his wife.

Eliza blinked, disconcerted.

'Not in the sense of being a devoted wooer—though he can be; we've both experienced that—but honourable, decent, fine. After all, though he's a friend to rakes, he's courted you in the most high-minded spirit.'

That was true, Eliza supposed, as far as his actions went. But she'd never thought of the pent-up hunger in the Earl's eyes as *high-minded*.

'And on the occasion of my fall,' Lady Derby drawled on, 'didn't he veil my shame by continuing to extend to me the protection of his noble name—by only separating privately and making me a generous settlement, when most of his friends were advising him to divorce me in the harsh glare of the House of Lords? Isn't that the behaviour of a perfect English gentleman?'

'I suppose,' said Eliza haltingly. To her, his refusal to obtain a divorce had always seemed more obstinate than anything else.

Lady Derby giggled; that was the only word for it. It was a wet, indecent sound, like something from the mouth of a baby. 'Don't be fooled. Edward's the epitome of the dog in the manger.'

What shocked Eliza was the informality of the name. If she married Derby, she realised, she'd have to call him that: *Edward.*

'He's got a rare stamina; he'll breed his precious horses for twenty years in order to win a single race. And he has an infinite greed to hold on to the thing he once set his heart on—even if he doesn't desire it any more. That's why he didn't divorce me. I begged him for a divorce; you never heard that, did you?'

Now this was something new. Eliza glanced at Anne, who looked at a loss.

'Yes, I didn't mind the shame of it,' the bitter voice continued. 'I wanted the Duke of Dorset and he'd have married me like a shot. It was sheer pride and grudge on my husband's part. He left me in limbo; he waited, while most of my friends dropped me; he hung on till Dorset got tired of waiting and moved on to the next conquest.' The Countess was beginning to wheeze.

Could that be true, Eliza wondered? *How simple, how cruel.* Could Derby really have kept himself and this woman horribly yoked together all these years out of sheer perversity?

'You know what he said to me?' Lady Derby's claw-hand jumped closer to Eliza's skirts. 'He said, "I'll be damned if I let you ruin another man's life." But what he really feared was that I might be happy.' She slumped back on her pillows.

'Should we call in her daughter?' Anne whispered. But Eliza couldn't take her eyes off the Countess. In her head, she was trying to hear that brutal line in Derby's voice. *I'll be damned if I let you ruin another man's life.* Yes, Eliza could picture his damp forehead, his narrow eyes, his cramped little features trembling as he said the words. Although Lady Derby had every reason to lie, somehow this rang true.

'So the actress wants coaching on her next role, does she?' came a feeble mutter.

'We should go,' said Anne, standing up.

'Wait. I'll be dead in a week,' said Lady Derby. 'You want my advice, you say, Miss Farren?'

Eliza had to nod.

'Here it is. I don't say refuse him.' A laugh like a gasp of pain. 'I only say know what you're doing if you agree to be his next Countess.'

At that moment Eliza was revolted by the prospect.

'Go in open-eyed.' She sucked in a breath between each phrase. 'And expect no mercy!'

JULY 1794

At two in the morning Derby lay in a chair at Brooks's, dazed with port. The Hastings trial was drawing to its dreary close at last, after sucking up Whig energies for six long years, and no one expected anything but an acquittal; the Empire's crimes in India would go unpunished after all. It was only a matter of time before Portland and his followers entered the government of their old enemy, Pitt; *for the nation's good,* they said, the hypocrites!

But, to Derby's shame, he could barely think about politics, or anything but the prospect of his wife's death. He'd got so accustomed to living in this limbo—a married man without a wife—that he was almost shaken at the thought of emerging from it. (He'd already put in a discreet order for a dozen suits of mourning, though; good tailoring couldn't be done overnight.) He'd written to Eliza, only hinting at the situation, but he longed to speak to her. She'd been rather elusive recently, it occurred to him now; he wondered if he'd offended her somehow, or perhaps it was just the tension of waiting. He knew he mustn't make a move until Lady Derby was in her coffin, for the sake of Eliza's reputation; the papers would be sure to have posted spies on Green Street to watch for a visiting earl. Even afterwards, how long would he have to wait before she'd find it acceptable to hear his proposal? And—the real question—what would her answer be?

He'd been foolishly complacent over the years. He should have been preparing for this moment; he ought to have courted the actress more intensely. What if Eliza decided that she was very well content with her life as it was: her success on the stage, her many friends, her perfectly adequate income? She knew the art of living well on little and had no debts to escape from; she wasn't a young girl whose head could be turned by a coronet, if she'd ever been. Did she long to be married to one of the richest men in England— or did she perhaps not much care? How little he knew her, it struck him now. Her aims were as dark and changeable as any politician's.

All Derby could do was sip his port and wait. Wait for his old comrades to go over to the devil; wait for his wife to go over the Styx; wait for the moment to ask Eliza the question; wait for an answer. Derby was a small, still, helpless dot and the world spun round him.

'It's over,' said Fox grimly, clapping him on the shoulder.

Derby leapt up in his seat. He had a vision of Lady Derby stretched out on her deathbed, her beautiful mouth stiffening. 'When did it happen?'

'I suspect the deal was struck a week ago, but Portland's only just had the decency to write to me.'

Derby, recovering from his mistake, tried to concentrate. 'How many Cabinet places?'

'Five out of the thirteen, with pensions and Garters aplenty. Spencer will be Lord Privy Seal—Georgiana's own *brother* in this coalition, she'll be sickened—Windham is Secretary of War, the bloodhound!—and of course Fitzwilliam for Lord President. That's what kills me the most: my old friend Fitzwilliam. I happen to know that he held out the longest, for love of me.' Fox wiped his inky sleeve across his eyes.

Derby reached for the port decanter and poured Fox a glass. He could think of nothing to say, now this day had come at last.

'The entire Opposition could fit into a hackney coach now.'

'I deny that,' said Derby sternly. 'Two coaches would be called for at least.'

That won a tiny chuckle. After a minute Fox said, 'I can't remember why I ever wanted to enter Parliament.'

Derby nodded, his head as heavy as a cannon ball.

'Did you see the *Morning Post* today? There was a mention of Lady Derby,' said Fox with an odd gentleness.

Derby's heart leapt. 'Is she worse?'

His friend shook his head. 'Her doctors are astonished. She's on the mend.'

THE FACE was small-featured, pure, serious, dark. The eyes looked down and into space. The curling hair was held back by a fillet and a diadem; the effect was of some early Roman Diana. The drapery round the neck was in the antique style, but also had a contemporary air. How different this bust of Mary was from the one of Eliza, Anne thought. Firmer, unsmiling, with strength behind the prettiness. It stood on a blunt squared herm; it was more truly classical. Anne looked hard at her completed work and felt at rest. She had an odd impulse to keep this piece for herself instead of giving it to Walpole, as she'd intended.

Your bust is come home from the oven, she wrote to Mary, who was staying with her grandmother in Yorkshire,

> *but the fire was too violent & there are some small cracks—also a blemish on the right cheek which, in the case of a face without a blemish, detracts from the likeness! But I'll make these small repairs as soon as I have a spare moment.*
>
> *Do thank Agnes from me for her charming Bookplate. I like the conceit of my soul pointing at my tombstone, with hammers, chisels & two dogs among my coat of arms—a perfect summary of my affiliations.*
>
> *Tonight I go to the summer theatre at the Haymarket to see La Farren play in* The Mountaineers & All in Good Humour.

Alone in the Richmonds' box at the Haymarket, Anne settled in comfortably to watch the performance. She noticed a few people nudging their fellows and pointing up at her, in the pit as well as in the galleries, and she felt a small glow of satisfaction; since her *King* had gone on show her reputation as a sculptor had grown rapidly. Clearly her face was beginning to be recognised, even by the middling and lower sort of Londoners.

The curtain rose for *The Mountaineers* and here came Eliza, looking very lovely in yellow satin. One would never know that she had worries; that ever since that unfortunate visit to Lady Derby's, Eliza had been caught in a quicksand. Loathing of Derby for refusing his wife a divorce and rage at Lady Derby for refusing to die; unease as to the years gone by and confusion as to those to come. Since old Mrs Farren had a closed mind on these matters, having staked her all on becoming an earl's mother-in-law, Anne was Eliza's only confidante; in the last few weeks, she'd been in such demand at Green Street that she'd quite neglected Mary. She settled back in her chair now, smiling down at the actress. How delicious it was to know someone privately, but to watch them repeatedly transformed into someone else...

Eliza was in sparkling voice tonight. But five lines into her opening speech things started to go wrong. There was a shout from the pit: 'Tommy!'

Anne didn't quite catch the word at first. The actress faltered visibly, then went on with her speech.

But now there were two men standing on a bench, roaring it: 'Tommies! Tommies!'

Something flew past Eliza's head; a fruit, or a stone? She backed gracefully towards the wings. There was confused laughter and hissing. Anne was gripping the edge of the box. She registered that some of the troublemakers were facing into the auditorium, looking in the direction of the Richmonds' box. One of them was pointing. Could he possibly be pointing at Anne? His arm jerked like a gun.

Below her, above her, the hissing of snakes. 'Filthy Sapphists!' Now the crowd was laughing as if at some particularly clever couplet. Anne looked into a boiling cauldron of faces. The stage was empty; Eliza must have run off. Anne lurched from her seat like a wounded hare; but her bad leg kept shaking, refusing to bear her weight. Such laughter, such yowls, such terrible hissing. She wrenched the door open and fell into the corridor.

In the carriage she stared up at the black silk roof. *This can't be happening.*

At home in her library, Anne kept a tight grip on her feelings. She wouldn't give way, not yet. She busied herself writing notes. The first was to Derby House, just round the corner.

> *I don't know where to turn. I didn't see you at the Haymarket tonight, but you may have heard by now from Miss F. herself of what happened there. My spirits are entirely bewildered. As my old Friend, and one so interested in all that concerns Miss F., I wonder might I ask you to investigate this outbreak of libellous Malice?*

The second was to Mary, in Yorkshire.

> *I need you. Some disaster has come upon me, connected to my dreadful subject. Do, I pray you, ask leave of your family to come down to me at Park Place where I'll go tomorrow or the day after.*

She thought of writing to Eliza, but didn't know what to say, not yet. She took some drops, but they didn't help her sleep, not peacefully at least; bad dreams kept her tossing all night.

The dawn came pale and yellow over the rooftops of Mayfair. Anne woke up with the sensation of having her head encased in lead. She took no breakfast. She waited for an answer from Derby, but it didn't come. She asked Sam if the Earl had been away when he'd delivered her note last night; was he up in Knowsley, perhaps?

'No, madam, he was at home, but you said not to stay for a reply as it was late.'

That's right, she'd forgotten that. 'Well, go over there now and ask.'

Five minutes later the footman was back. 'They say there's no reply.'

'No reply?' She stared at Sam stupidly. How could Derby have said *No reply?* Then she looked away. It suddenly occurred to her to wonder what Sam knew. If things were being shouted aloud about his employer in a public theatre, if she was being called *Filthy Sapphist,* how could he not hear of it? Her cheeks were burning. It had never really troubled her what her staff might think of her before. 'That'll do,' she said and didn't look back till the footman had gone.

Anne cried a little, then. But self-pity would get her nowhere; she needed information. She rang for Sam again and told him to drive to Twickenham with a note for Walpole.

His reply came back before noon.

My dear child, my poor darling!
Since you ask for it (for on no other account would I show you such a vile thing) I enclose a broadside entitled The Whig Club *published I believe on Monday last, in which among others you & Miss Farren are calumniated. My sources tell me it was written by one Pigott, a radical. Do you know the name?*

Anne fumbled for a chair and let herself down on to it. Her heart was a hard knot. *So I did it,* she thought. *I brought this on myself. I picked up my reckless pen and I wrote to Pigott.* A desperate man, in gaol; she'd threatened him with all the haughtiness of her rank. And he'd hit back. Was there any weapon in England more powerful than a pen?

She made herself flick through the limp, inky pages of the pamphlet Walpole had sent, till she found the relevant section. It began with speculation about how soon Lady Derby would die, freeing her husband to propose to *a well-known fashionable Actress.*

But though the Actress's Vanity must be interested in the event, her amorous Passions are far from being awakened by the idea.

*Superior to the influence of Men, she is supposed to feel more ex-
quisite Delight from the touch of the cheek of Mrs D——r, than
from the fancy of any Novelties which the wedding night can
promise with such a partner as His Lordship.*

Reading the words, Anne thought she might faint. She forced herself to go on. The actress was also entangled, claimed Pigott, with a
certain *Lady M——r*, the cold wife of a drunken husband and *a for-
midable rival to Mrs D——r for the affections of Miss F—n.* Anne
blinked rapidly. Lady Milner, that was the only name she knew that
fitted. But the Milners weren't real intimates of Eliza's at all, were
they? Only friends with whom she occasionally stayed when in Yorkshire. Where in all the hells had Pigott got this story? Did these evil-
minded scribblers pluck names at random out of the ether?

There was a loud knock on the door. *Mary,* she thought with
dizzying gratitude, before she remembered that it couldn't be, not
so soon.

WHAT FILLED Eliza with dread was that her mother hadn't said
anything yet. She'd packed up Eliza's things in the dressing room
without a murmur and, when they'd reached Green Street—three
hours earlier than usual, with the sun still shining—all she'd done
was lay out some cold beef and greens. Eliza had thought of
broaching the topic—*Mother, I don't know why, I've no idea what
could possibly have brought on this storm*—but her nerve failed her;
she'd never been so tired in her life. After two bites of beef she'd
gone to bed, though evening light pricked through the shutters.

This morning silence had filled up the narrow house on Green
Street like dirty water. Something occurred to Eliza: *our contract is
broken.* She'd nothing to confess, God knew, but that she'd kept her
mother at a distance, failed to confide. She'd let another friendship
supplant the oldest one and look what disaster had come of it.

Over the breakfast table she listened to the sound of toast
crunching in their jaws. Across the parlour the impossibly perfect

face of *Thalia* watched over them; Eliza avoided its blank eyes. Mrs Farren suddenly said something about a *crudité*.

Eliza stared. 'I beg you pardon?'

'A *coup d'état*, they call it,' her mother pronounced awkwardly. 'In France, don't you know.'

'Oh.'

'Some moderates have upped and toppled the awful rulers—executed Robespierre and all—and they're letting the prisoners out.'

Eliza put down her piece of toast. The bite in her mouth tasted like wood, she could feel its hard, tooth-marked edges. She chewed twice and forced it down. She didn't care about the good news from France, that was the strange thing; today it really made no difference to her one way or another.

Mrs Farren carried on in the same cool, conversational tone. 'You should go and speak to her.'

'Her?'

A jerk of the head in the vague direction of Grosvenor Square. Like pointing at something filthy.

Mother won't say her name, Eliza realised. 'I...I hardly know what to tell her.'

Mrs Farren leaned across the table. 'Oh, I think you do.'

Eliza felt trapped. There was a hair on her mother's chin she'd never noticed before. 'I'm sure she's as distraught as I am, after last night.'

The older woman's arms folded up like penknives. 'That's neither here nor there. Madam can wall herself up like an empress if she pleases. You're the one whose prospects hang by a thread.'

Eliza could hardly breathe. Did her mother mean her career, or Derby, or both? Last night's crowd hissed in her ears like a vast kettle. 'But Anne's done nothing—'

'It's not what she's done, is it? It's what she is.'

Wordless, Eliza lurched up from the table.

She sat in her room for hours, preparing. It was like the time Dora Jordan had gone into early labour and Eliza had had to learn the part of Claramintha in a single day to replace her.

When she came down the stairs her mother was standing in the hall. Had she been there all morning, like a statue of Cerberus? 'His Lordship's carriage isn't out there,' Mrs Farren remarked accusingly. Eliza ignored that. She let her mother help her on with her summer cloak. 'Put this on.' It was a narrow hat with a thick veil.

Eliza flinched, but she knew it was a good idea; there might be journalists lurking about. Mrs Farren had always had the knack of rising to a crisis; that was what came of being married to a drunkard.

It was only a matter of walking round the corner to no. 8 Grosvenor Square. How closely she and Anne lived; it made her shake. She wondered how many passers-by could recognise her through her veil. She was too tall, too slim to be anyone else. Suddenly celebrity seemed a frightening thing.

In Anne's parlour Eliza paused with her hand on the back of a chair. 'Can you trust your servants?'

Anne cleared her throat. 'I believe so.'

Eliza opened the door again to check no one was listening, then shut it and sat, without waiting to be asked. She began her speech. 'I've no intention of discussing the events of yesterday evening.'

'My dear, such a nightmare! How persecution swoops on the innocent like an eagle on young lambs!' Anne produced a miserable half-smile. 'Have you heard from Derby yet? He didn't answer my note. I've been longing to write to you—to come to you—'

Eliza shook her head.

'Mine is perhaps the only heart in England that can understand what mortification yours is suffering.'

This was too much. 'Your *understanding* helps me not at all,' said Eliza through her teeth. 'What I require is an explanation of the facts.'

'Oh, yes. Have you seen this thing called *The Whig Club*?' Anne shuffled through her pocketbook and held up a small pamphlet.

'No.' Eliza's stomach sank at the sight. Not just the buzzing gossip of a theatre audience, then, but cold print.

'Well, I'll lend it to you and then we can plan our campaign,' said Anne, pressing it into her hand. 'Without going into horrid detail—'

'I don't want details, I want an answer,' Eliza interrupted, as she stuffed the thing into her cotton reticule without looking. 'What is it about you?'

'Wait one moment—'

'I've waited five years already.'

Anne stared at her, suddenly every inch the Honourable Mrs Damer.

She's not my better, said Eliza in her head. *I'm entitled to an answer.* She tried to speak slowly and clearly, like a lady. 'Why does this particular rumour, out of all possible slurs, keep resurfacing and clinging to your skirts?'

'I've no idea.' The tone was cool.

'Oh, come on,' Eliza roared. 'People don't make these things up for no reason at all. I've repeatedly given you the benefit of the doubt, but I'm beginning to wonder. Is it true you've turned down several good proposals?'

'Where did you hear that?' Anne's eyes were blazing. 'And what if I have? I've been married once already, unlike you; I've nothing to prove.'

'But it's not me who attracts these rumours,' snarled Eliza. 'I'm only smeared when I associate with you. Something must have happened long ago, before ever you met me; something must have set off this whole foul mudslide.'

She noticed a tiny change in the angular features. She leaned closer. 'What? What is it?'

'Nothing.'

'Don't lie to me. Faces are my trade.'

Anne took a ragged breath. 'I admit I was once foolish,' she said, very low, 'but I've never been criminal.'

Yes. 'Tell me.'

'I was in Italy, in mourning for my husband. It was such a small thing—so random, so unlikely. I met this girl,' said Anne, barely audible.

'An Italian girl?'

A nod. The words came out like a sigh. 'There was a kiss.'

At last. Eliza felt a surge of something like relief. 'Where?'

'In Italy, as I said. Under a lemon tree.'

'No, where was the kiss? On the lips?'

Anne gave her a peculiarly disdainful look. Eliza flushed at the vulgarity of her own question, but she needed to know. A kiss on the cheek was not a kiss on the lips; a touching of the mouth to the back of the fingers was not the same as a kiss pressed to the throat. Female friends kissed each other all the time, but Anne's tone had suggested that this kiss was something more. Longer, more passionate, more lingering? Eliza needed to weigh up the evidence. This woman was accused of wanting terrible things. Well, how could desires be weighed but by the actions they led to?

'It was just a kiss.'

'Were you kissed? Or did you kiss?'

'I can't recall. I've spent so long trying to forget it ever happened. It's ludicrous, the skinny little root of all my troubles. A terrible accident of timing.'

'It doesn't sound like an accident,' said Eliza.

'Not the kiss, perhaps, but the fact that it happened to be glimpsed by an English party. I knew none of them and I thought they knew nothing of me, but the English abroad club together so; they must have gossiped until they discovered that I was that young sculptress whose husband had shot himself in a tavern. Well, such a combination of notorious circumstances must have been irresistible,' she added scornfully, 'and the story raced its way back to Grub Street.'

Eliza sat back as far as her chair would allow her. 'So,' she said almost cheerfully, 'it's true.'

Anne's eyes were burning.

'After all your professions of innocence, of bewilderment, it turns out the scribblers had you in a nutshell!'

'Eliza—'

Her name sounded like an indecent endearment. 'If you weren't a Sapphist—a *filthy Tommy*—whyever would you have kissed this Italian, or let her kiss you?'

'I don't know,' said Anne desperately. 'It happened in a blink, it was over and it's shadowed my life ever since.'

Eliza wanted to shake the truth out of her. 'You and she you must have recognised some hidden bias in each other somehow. Kisses don't just happen.'

'But they do.' Her eyes were as warm and bewildered as a dog's.

'Not to me,' said Eliza, fierce. 'Not like that. I've spent a lifetime in the theatre—the most decadent of professions, they say— and kisses don't happen to me.'

'It was only a moment,' Anne pleaded. 'I was confused—the girl was confused—'

'Yes, but what confused you?'

'Oh, it's not as simple as that,' said Anne impatiently. 'Not so black and white. There are strange moments in life.'

Eliza's arms were folded tightly. 'Not in mine.'

Anne let out a yelp of laughter. It sounded incongruously loud in the little parlour. 'Your whole life is strange.'

'What on earth do you mean?'

'Well, you've kept a good man waiting thirteen years so far.' The older woman was on the attack now. 'You walk through the corridors of Drury Lane like a nun in a bordello; you're as hard and chill as marble. You please all and satisfy none; you like to be looked at and desired, but never ever touched—wouldn't you call that strange?'

'Denial is a habit,' said Eliza furiously, 'and a necessary one in my case. I've always had men fawning around me; I know how to deal with their crude overtures and yes, I'll die a virgin if I must, at least it has a certain dignity.' Her lips were wet; she wiped her hand across her mouth. 'But a fawning, secretly lascivious *woman*—now that's peculiar.'

Anne's face was white and red, as if she'd been slapped.

'What did I ever do or say or seem, to make you single me out?'

'How dare you?'

'You've been hanging around me for so long,' Eliza reminded her. 'I tried to push you away five years ago, I thought I'd success-fully ended the friendship—then you came back from Spain, swore blind the scandal was buried and Derby told me not to be afraid of you—so I was stupid enough to take you up again.'

'You must have had your reasons,' snarled Anne. 'I've never forced my friendship on anyone.'

'I can't remember why I risked it. I'm not like you,' Eliza told her; 'there's nothing in me that resonates with your peculiarities. I couldn't be a Sapphist if I lived to be five hundred.'

'Who asked you?'

'I'm not like you, I tell you. One kiss wouldn't change *my* life.' And Eliza seized Anne by the throat and kissed her, held her in a kiss that was long enough so that when they moved apart they stag-gered a little. She tasted rouge. 'So,' she said, for something to say.

The other woman had two patches of hectic red high on her cheekbones. She sucked in her lips as if to hide them. 'I never asked for that.'

Eliza managed to laugh. 'I was just giving you proof.'

'Proof of what?'

'Proof that you leave me cold.' And blindly she made for the door.

THE TORPOR of late July had settled over Grosvenor Square. Most of the houses were empty by now. Anne stayed indoors, out of sight, brooding over what she should have said to the actress, what she might have done. There was still no message from Derby, which could only mean that he, too, blamed Anne for the catastrophe.

An answer finally arrived from Mary in Yorkshire.

My dearest!
Without telling my family what the matter is I can't set off at once, but I've obtained leave to meet you at Park Place at the end of the month. Till then, don't give way to despair. Haven't you often told me that things can't be as bad as they seem?

Anne couldn't remember ever saying that, or what she'd thought she meant by it. Mary's words read like a faded message from a distant world. Anne would read the rest of it later. She lay face down on her bed and the brocaded counterpane pressed her eyes shut

Her mind was working oddly. She supposed it was the broken sleep and the laudanum; she couldn't stomach most of what her cook sent up. The servants sometimes seemed to look at her strangely; she hardly ever rang for them and she flinched when one of them knocked. She found it hard to endure Bet coming in to dress her every morning and undress her every night; she kept her eyes shut and shrank from the warm, humid hands. She wasn't working, was barely reading, read no letters and wrote none, didn't wash.

Her calves ached, and her shoulders. It was probably the lack of exercise; she hadn't had her daily ride in a week. She'd sent to the stables for her horse, once, on the third morning after Eliza's visit, and managed to get into the saddle and turned its head towards Hyde Park as always—but then the thought of being pointed out by strangers made her start to shake all over. Her foot had jammed in the stirrup; she'd needed the groom's help to get down.

Doctor Fordyce had turned up at Mrs Moll's behest—was it yesterday, or the day before?—and tapped on her bedroom door, but Anne had held her breath and pretended not to be there. What was wrong with her was not something that Fordyce could cure with his powders, liniments or bleedings. Before he left he spoke through the door, urging her to take some nourishment at least. The maids put trays outside her door at intervals, she could smell their sickening trail. *Did Clarissa eat,* she wanted to ask the doctor? Did any woman ever eat after she'd been ruined?

Mrs Moll could read and Sam as well, Anne knew; they probably studied the newspapers. Rumour passed like an infection from servant to servant, house to house. She imagined the staff down there in the housekeeper's room, right now, drinking her tea. *There was always something queer about madam, wasn't there?*

*That's right, vastly peculiar in her habits, and such strong hands, for
a woman.*

She tried to read a newspaper herself, to fill up her brain's
yawning vacancy, but once she'd skipped all the doom and gloom
about war and sedition, the first item she came across was about betrayal. The Prince of Wales had finally succumbed to Pitt's offer of
a higher income if he'd break with Mrs Fitzherbert and marry a
princess. Her hold on him had already been weakened by that fascinating serpent, Lady Jersey. Apparently Mrs Fitzherbert—his
wife of nine years—had received, with no warning, a note from
Prinny made up of three words: *Tout est fini.* Did he think it
sounded more graceful in French?

Mad thoughts came to Anne in the hot afternoons. Sometimes
she looked out of the window through a crack in the blinds, watching the empty street. Once she saw the carriage with the Derby
crest go by and thought she counted two heads. Perhaps she'd mis-
judged Eliza Farren all these years by giving her *the benefit of the
doubt,* she thought viciously. That kiss the woman had pressed on
Anne's lips had been so lewd, so violent. Could the whole World
have been taken in by the actress's performance of chastity?

Eliza and Derby lived just round the corner from each other,
after all, and she used his carriage; what could be easier for the
couple than to enjoy themselves in secret and laugh behind their
masks? *Niminy-Piminy* and her *Noble Dwarf* romping behind their
screen of platonic love; *Miss Tittup* and *Lord Doodle,* skirts up and
breeches down, bouncing together in a well-sprung coach under
the watchful leer of the old procuress who called herself a mother.
Perhaps the actress had been the Earl's mistress all these years and
dropped several pups while pretending to be *on tour,* and all in
magnificent hypocrisy!

Anne pressed the heel of her hand into her forehead. She didn't
know what to believe. Life was a whirl of impossibilities and there
was a foul slug stuck to the back of every flower. Honest men
proved traitors and liberty meant heads in a bucket of blood; virgins

played whores on stage, whores played virgins off stage, and French ships might land in London any day. Her brain was addled, her cheeks were so hot that it felt as if they were peeling off. She had no skin anymore; if she stepped out of her house she'd be exposed to the burning gaze of the World.

MARY, ANNE THOUGHT, one afternoon, to force herself out of bed; *Mary wrote that she'd meet me at Park Place.* She caught a glimpse of a grey face in the glass, but looked away. She rang for Bet and asked for her dark-brown travelling costume. Her voice came out faint and mumbling. 'I'll need a trunk packed. And tell Sam to fetch the coachman with the carriage.'

'Where are you off to, madam?'

It's none of your business, Anne would have liked to say, seizing the girl by the ruffle round her neck. 'Park Place.'

'Very good,' said Bet, dropping a casual curtsy.

When Anne got to her childhood home at the end of the long day's drive, her parents treated her as if she'd been ill: gently and asking no questions. They must have heard from Walpole about the resurrection of her *old trouble.* (As if it were gout, or lunacy.) They let her sit in the garden for hours, a book motionless in her lap. They said of course they'd be delighted to have dear Miss Berry visit, she could stay as long as she liked. The wafting scent of the lavender harvest stuck in Anne's throat.

One twilight there was a knock on her bedroom door and she thought it must be Mary, though there'd been no letter announcing her arrival. But it was only the footman with a tightly folded note, sealed with messy black wax. There was no salutation at the top.

I've been sent a copy of a paragraph from a newspaper, in which my name is linked to yours in a manner I need not describe. You'll understand that this changes everything. I'm sorry but I can't come to you now.

    M.B.

Anne felt the most peculiar sensation, like a heavy blow cleaving her ribs in two. *This changes everything.* The servant came back to announce supper, but she didn't go down. *Tout est fini.* She sat on the edge of the bed and watched the dark thicken on the Berkshire hills. *Praxiteles,* Anne thought, *Praxiteles help me now. I smell burning. My house is on fire and what can I save?*

VIII

Armature

*An internal skeleton, usually of wood or metal,
in a sculpture of clay, plaster, or wax. The armature
bears the weight during hardening and
adds strength to the finished work.*

⟍⟋

IT IS now grown common to suspect Impossibilities (as some
call them) whenever two Ladies live too much together. The
late Queen of France was so accused and so was Raucourt,
the famed Actress on the Paris stage. In our own Metropolis it
is now a joke to say that such-a-one takes Tea with Mrs D—r.
We wish to inform our Correspondents that this horrid practice—though veiled in silence in British Law—is nothing new;
do we not sniff it out in Martial's epigrams and in Ovid's
Epistle in which Sappho the poet renounces her guilty love for
the maidens of Lesbos?

Though this and other Vices may be as old as our race, the
present era is marked by a reckless scorn for all laws of
God, Nature and Reason. Too many are the Englishmen now
drowning in the stagnant pool of Atheism or the poisoned well
of Sodom. Women demand their Rights, including the right to
rival the other sex in debauchery. While their husbands defend our Empire on the high seas, how many have set up
housekeeping with lovers, or dropped fatherless children?

The dreadful example of France suggests that when the
bonds of tradition are untied, a whole Pandora's box of crimes

is shaken into the air: have the streets of Paris not been stained by Torture, Rape, Cannibalism and Satanic rites? Some prophesy that we are approaching the Millennium and that when every offence that can be committed has been committed the World will burn.

But enough of such serious stuff. Any Correspondents with an opinion on the gentlemanly craze for Pantaloons are invited to write to the Editor.

—THE BEAU MONDE INQUIRER, *August 1794*

DERBY WAS BENT DOUBLE OVER THE HORSE. HE PULLED UP the eyelid and examined the milky surface. 'Good lad,' he murmured, 'good lad.'

'You agree, M'Lord?'

'I suppose there's nothing else for it.' He straightened up, his back aching. A pearl button had fallen off his new braces; he picked it out of the straw.

'I've tried everything on the hoof, but it just won't mend,' said the stable master who ran the Earl's five stalls at Epsom.

'Very well,' said Derby, too sharp. He could smell the rot from where he stood, by Sir Peter's head. This was the best mount he'd ever run—his Derby winner of '87—and the stallion deserved a long and profitable career at stud, before being put out to grass. Not this, an agonising disintegration on damp straw. 'I'll do it myself,' he said, before he could shrink from the task.

'The muskets are already primed,' the stable master assured him, letting out a whistle.

A boy ran in, two firelocks under his arm.

'You,' snapped Derby, 'never run with a gun.'

The fellow looked barely thirteen; he went purple in the face. 'Beg pardon, M'Lord.'

'You don't want to trip and be blown to bits,' said Derby, trying to sound kinder.

The boy shook his head violently.

Derby cocked a firelock. *Please let the first one work.* He was feeling a peculiar squeamishness; he couldn't bear the idea that Sir Peter would hear the dull click of a misfiring gun at his skull and know what his master meant to do. *Such sentimentality, at forty-two!* A sob welled up in the back of his throat. He put his boot on the long muscular neck—there was no resistance—and set the nose of the gun to Sir Peter's head. At the last moment he let himself look away. The shot was deafening; it sounded as if the whole stable had exploded.

Face to the wall, Derby wiped his spattered boots with a handkerchief.

'Funeral tomorrow?' asked the stable master.

He nodded, speechless, and walked out of the stall.

This had been the worst summer he'd had since his wife had eloped with Lord Dorset sixteen years before. In some ways it was even harder. Being cuckolded by a fellow nobleman could happen to anyone; despite Derby's rage and shame on that occasion, he'd felt himself to be enduring the common fate of modern husbands. Whereas this fantastical scandal that had sent the actress he loved stumbling from the stage of the Haymarket last month stuck under his skin like a splinter of glass.

He sometimes thought he was losing his wits. He felt he'd been an utter dunderhead, that was the thing. In all his life it'd never occurred to him to feel jealous of a woman. Of women, rather; of all of them, the infinite variety of cooing intimacies that went by the name of *female friendship*. Was it a Trojan horse, a mere toy that men never thought to fear? If Sapphists couldn't easily be identified by their mannishness—if any lady might be hiding twisted desires behind a smooth face—all England might be riddled with this rot. Why, if women were a danger to each other then what bedroom, what parlour, what tea shop was safe?

One of the chief attractions that Eliza had always held for Derby was her virginity. She was one of the only women he knew who'd held on to it past girlhood. He'd never doubted it; it was like a pool of shining light about her. Between her and men—himself included—there'd always been a shimmering, unbreakable veil. But what of women? What mysterious carnalities could they indulge in and still preserve their reputations, still carry that virgin shine like a shield? He'd never thought to watch Eliza in that way, never wondered what her letters contained, how she spent all those private hours with a friend like Anne Damer.

To suspect her would drive Derby mad. But after the events of last month—the humiliation at the Haymarket, the hints in newspapers, the explicit details in Pigott's pamphlet—he could no more control his thoughts than a wasps' nest. Those old rumours about Mrs Damer; how could he ever have been such an idiot as to laugh them off? He didn't know what to believe about Eliza's relations with her, but he knew this much: there was no going back to innocence.

When he walked into one of Epson's smaller inns, his nostrils still full of the stink of Sir Peter Teazle's blood, all he wanted was a brandy. But he found a table full of his Party friends, all sozzled; they must have come down for the King's Cup. 'Derby, me old fellow-me-lad,' roared Sheridan in a fake brogue, 'I haven't seen you in an age.'

'I only came down yesterday,' said Derby, not mentioning Sir Peter.

Fox edged his bulk along the bench to make room and clasped Derby's neck with a fond look. *He knows, then.* Everyone knew. Stories travelled fast, especially disgusting ones. 'Any news from Paris?' he said, for something to say.

'All good,' said Grey. 'Since the fall of Robespierre the city's come awake, like the Sleeping Beauty. Thirteen theatres have reopened—papers are rolling off the press again—people are coming out of hiding—'

'Oo, yes,' said Fox, 'I'm vastly reconciled to the French. Now's the perfect time for Pitt to sue for peace.'

The man's optimistic spirits always rebounded, even when circumstances didn't justify it, thought Derby.

'We can't even maintain peace in London, let alone achieving it in Europe,' snorted Bedford. 'Take these crimping riots—'

The war was dragging on so long that there was a shortage of able-bodied men and heavy-handed recruiting agents had sparked off protests from Holborn to Southwark.

'I heard a young man fell to his death while escaping from the crimpers,' remarked Grey.

Derby felt his arm being poked. 'How's the lovely Eliza?' Sheridan was slurring a little.

He thought of saying *Don't you dare call her that.*

'Farren broke her summer contract after she got hissed at the Haymarket last month,' Sheridan explained to the circle. 'Now I hear she's off touring Ireland, where they're less *au fait!*'

Fox tried for a flippant tone. 'Drop it, would you, Sherry?'

'Drop what?' asked one of the youngsters. 'What's the joke?'

'There is none,' said Derby.

'Oh, come on, even you must admit it's rather hilarious,' said Sheridan, his eyes hazy with drink.

'Shall we have some cold ham?' asked Bedford, looking for a waiter.

'I say, drop it,' Derby barked at Sheridan.

The Irishman's eyebrows soared. 'Don't come the despotic *aristo* with me.'

'But what's the joke?' repeated the youngster.

'Really, men, don't you think—' started Bedford.

'It's more of a riddle than a joke, really.' Sheridan played a mischievous drum roll on the table. 'Question: if one's inamorata is scandalously linked with a fellow *female,* can one be said to be a cuckold?'

Derby's teeth were clamped together.

'Sherry,' protested Grey and Fox in chorus.

'Oh, I mean no slur; we're almost all cuckolds here, aren't we, gentlemen? But I persist in asking that old question, do Sapphic seductions, mere tribadic toyings, fricatrice fondlings', he pronounced with relish, 'count as infidelity? I seem to remember that no less an authority than Brantôme claims they only amount to wantonness, since ladies who dabble in female flesh are merely washing the edges of a cut, not truly lancing the wound!'

Derby's head was clanging like a saucepan. His limbs refused to move him out of this ring of staring faces.

'And there's a further difficulty,' Sheridan lectured on, holding up one finger in parliamentary style. 'To be crowned with horns, surely a gentleman has to have possessed the inamorata in the first place? After all, in this case we're talking about the most famous virgin in England, or at least in the annals of the theatre. So perhaps her platonic lover hasn't been technically cuckolded, gentlemen, merely...beaten to the finish?'

In one lunge across the table Derby had him by the throat.

Somebody screamed.

'For God's sake,' Fox roared as he pushed between them. Hands tugged at Derby's wrists, wrenched him away. Sheridan's face was shocked, his nose scarlet.

'I demand satisfaction,' said Derby, very fast, before Sheridan could; his tongue tripped over the words.

'My pleasure,' said Sheridan hoarsely.

Fox clapped his arm round Derby and half dragged him away from the table. They leaned against the wall of the inn, heads together. 'You've every right, of course, but think, for a moment,' Fox whispered in his ear. 'Sherry fought several duels in his youth and lived to boast of them. You've never fought one.'

'That's neither here nor there,' growled Derby.

'My Party's small enough', said Fox, 'without the loss of a fool like you or a rogue like him. You're both entirely necessary to me. I won't have it!'

'You hold my political allegiance,' Derby told him, 'but my honour is my own.'

'Oh, come now—'

Derby felt a tap on his shoulder. He spun round.

Grey was wearing a grave expression. 'Our colleague has something to say.'

Behind him, Sheridan stood with arms crossed. 'I beg your pardon, Derby. I'm rather the worse for some bottles of brandy,' he drawled. 'I believe I got somewhat carried away. No offence intended to you, My Lord, or to the unimpeachable Miss Farren.'

The adjective stuck in Derby's craw. But he'd received a formal apology in front of witnesses—so the matter had to end there.

'Won't you stay?' Fox asked him on his way to the door, but Derby said no, he had a horse to bury.

He stood out in the street, shaking, blinking in the harsh light. He felt as if he'd had a week without sleep. He would have gone ahead with the duel, he told himself, if he hadn't received satisfaction. It was the only time in his life that he had ever issued a challenge, but he'd been ready; everything in his upbringing had prepared him for it. One didn't decide to fight a duel based on one's chances of winning. Derby remembered explaining it to young Edward years ago, as his own father had explained it to him: *to be a gentleman means to be ready to face death on the field of honour at any time.* He'd never forget the child's petrified, wooden face.

ANNE WAS sitting on the floor of a bedroom at an inn, somewhere in Oxfordshire, or possibly Berkshire. She pressed her back against the door; that way, nobody could open it from the outside. The boards were cold through her muslin skirt; her knees were drawn up and her chin rested between them. Her stomach growled.

What have I done?

She hadn't left a forwarding address for her parents when she'd fled from Park Place. She'd gone at first light, the morning after getting Mary's note of rejection. She knew Conway and Lady Ailesbury would be as kind as ever—they'd never believe anything bad of their daughter—but she couldn't bear to stay; she dreaded a soft word as much as any rebuke. Anne couldn't stand to be written to, spoken to, looked at, even. It made her shudder to think that she was being gossiped about, at this moment, by people she'd never met. All England was covered with delicate webs of tittle-tattle: *Mrs Damer this,* people were whispering, *Mrs Damer that, Mrs Damer did you ever?*

She ached all over from the carriage's jolting progression through the countryside. When she wasn't upstairs in an inn, she always wore a veil. Incognito: it was such a glamorous word, but behind the choking layers of gauze Anne's face was sallow and shapeless. She wore a long travelling coat, buttoned up despite the heat of August; it was getting stained under the arms. Her limbs were heavy; she moved like a sleepwalker, or lay face down on the bed and didn't move at all. She hadn't stayed more than two nights anywhere; she didn't want to have to give an account of herself. She avoided the servants' eyes. She kept her trunks locked, to hide the name and address printed inside; when she noticed that one of her handkerchiefs was monogrammed she put it in the fire. The coals were damp; the *A.D.* took a while to burn.

What have I done? Anne asked herself when she woke up every day, and sometimes the question was rhetorical and sometimes it was literal. She hadn't eaten for a couple of days now; that could explain how strange she felt and the way her head seemed to split in two whenever she tried to decide anything. In her dreams she began to wail, but when she woke up her eyes were bone dry.

She had no occupations. She'd brought no books, not even paper and pen. Mary Berry had cut her off in four lines; Mary, the best friend she had in the world. Nothing was safe from the filth, it leaked in everywhere. There was nowhere to hide her face, no refuge left in the world.

Anne thought of suicide. Oddly enough, the idea hadn't struck her before. Perhaps it was the music, rising from the taproom downstairs, that made her think of it now. It was eighteen years since her husband had gone upstairs in the Bedford Arms with the two whores, the two pistols and the blind fiddler. (It sounded like a joke, didn't it?) Anne wondered what was the last tune he'd asked the fiddler for. Something merry—but she hadn't known John well enough to guess the title. She found herself thinking of him almost fondly. He hadn't even been thirty when the bullet had gone into his head and out again. She'd never understood how he could have done such a shocking thing, with so little consideration for his family and friends—for *her*. But now it came to her with the force of a blow that his miserable wife had not been in his mind the day he'd killed himself; she hadn't been real to him at all. John Damer had gone beyond such mortal connections; he was on his own, in deep water, going down.

Anne understood that, now, because she was the same way. There were no parents watching over her any more, no sister, no godfather, no friends. They'd floated out of her grasp. Here she was, nameless and faceless, on the roads of England and not a soul knew where she was or how to bring her home.

She crawled from the floor to the bed, and sat up half the night thinking of ways and means. She'd never owned a pistol. (John's pair had been sold, together with all his other valuables, to set against his debts.) The knives that came with her dinner tray were blunt and in her reticule she had only tiny scissors. These things were so much easier for men. But then it came to her: *laudanum*. Anne weighed the bottle in her hand; still almost half full. Surely if she drank the lot at once that would do the trick?

It wasn't the sinfulness of these thoughts that stopped her; her conscience was quite mute these days. It was the idea of John, meeting her in the underworld and laughing with his snide, silly laugh. No, Anne had never stooped to his level while they'd been married and she'd be damned if she was going to now.

Walking in the woods behind the inn the next morning, Anne considered going abroad. That was the traditional recourse for outcasts, after all. William Beckford, for instance, to pick a famous monster; hadn't he been living in one warm climate or another ever since his banishment? His only problems were with English diplomats, it seemed; foreigners were more tolerant. But how strange it would be to leave England, Anne thought, knowing one could never come back again. Would she find shelter somewhere, and oblivion, for the rest of her life? Would she sculpt foreign faces, and foreign cats and dogs, and would her pieces never go on show at the Royal Academy again? Anne almost laughed, catching herself out in a paradox; here she was, trembling at the thought that a chambermaid might recognise her face, yet still hoping for fame and glory at the annual Exhibition!

No, she wouldn't flee to Italy or Switzerland and for one good reason. To go was to proclaim that what was said of you was true. She'd never give her accusers that satisfaction.

She pictured Charles Pigott, smirking over his inky work. She assumed he was out of gaol by now; perhaps he'd scribbled the lines about her in *The Whig Club*—the work of two minutes—in some garret off the Strand. Was he munching on a pork pie, or scratching a flea bite, as he chose his words, as he rained down destruction on a woman he'd never met?

He'd been in gaol when she'd written him that scornful letter, but wasn't this travelling a gaol too, of a sort? Could she be any more imprisoned behind bars? Anne thought of the eagle caught by Lord Melbourne's gamekeeper, the eagle she'd sculpted. How shocked, how furious his eyes had been as they'd shackled him. He hadn't eaten, she remembered; he'd pined away and died of a moult.

Pigott was a radical, of course; a leveller, a Jacobin anarchist, probably an atheist. It wasn't just Anne's downfall that he longed for, or Eliza's or Mary's or Walpole's, but the complete annihilation of the World. Whoever had enough money to keep his hands clean Pigott would libel as a compound of all vices. When Pigott had finished his dark work there'd be no more kings or countesses, no paying calls or thirty-dish suppers, no painted fans or marble statues. If he and his conspirators had their way they'd turn Anne's homeland into one vast, brutal, democratic camp. She argued with Pigott in her head; she said plain, foolish things: *I'm innocent*, she told him, *I've done nothing*.

But that was hardly the point. Anne leaned against a tree and bit her thumb. Of course she'd done something to arouse Pigott's rage. She'd been a woman of privilege, rank and some fame. And she had loved; she wouldn't deny that, not if her life depended on it. She'd loved Eliza Farren, and lost her in a matter of hours and thought it the worst pain she'd ever felt. She'd loved Mary Berry, too, differently, and had never thought that anything could come between them. It was difficult to tease out the strands of misery but it seemed to Anne, surprisingly, that this second loss was worse.

She'd loved her friends as many women loved each other, as many men loved men, as Derby loved Fox; wasn't friendship generally agreed to be the highest virtue? *I'm innocent,* she said again to the demon Pigott in her head, but it rang false. This didn't feel like innocence. This was like a dream in which she'd committed some terrible crime, but she couldn't remember what, or how. She hadn't done the things Pigott said of her, but what good was a clear conscience? Shame weighed as heavy as guilt. Shame wasn't brought on only by what one said or did—but by what was said of you, done to you.

And whether the accusations were true or not didn't make much difference, because people would believe them anyway. She'd first been called these names in print by William Combe sixteen years ago. The difference now was that people must be starting to believe it. She'd been abused, hissed and laughed at in a public theatre. The actress had accused her of being a *filthy Tommy.* And Mary, did Mary believe the latest dreadful accusations, or did she simply hate Anne for dragging her down? Perhaps it came to the same thing.

It was the end of August now, and Anne knew she should be sensible and go back to her refuge at Park Place. But she seemed to be floating a great way off from her life and she couldn't find the rope to pull herself back in.

She hadn't been to church all summer, but when she found a limp copy of the Psalms in a drawer at the next inn she opened it at random.

They gaped upon me with their Mouths, as a ravening and a roaring Lion. I am poured out like Water, and all my Bones are out of joint; my heart is like Wax.

Her heart contracting like a fist, she turned the page.

For Dogs have compassed me, the assembly of the Wicked have enclosed me; they pierced my Hands and my Feet. I may tell all my Bones; they look and stare...

SEPTEMBER 1794

The Farrens arrived on the packet boat from Dublin after a very successful tour. 'Six nights in Cork,' Eliza told Derby, speaking fast, 'six in Limerick, fifteen in Dublin, clearing £1400 before two excellent benefits. I gave them Beatrice and Lady Teazle.'

He was examining the gold paintwork on the arm of his chair. 'You left London with no warning.'

'Yes.' Eliza's teeth set. For six weeks she'd only sent the most brief and bland notes from Ireland, and the Earl's replies had been the same. Perhaps he'd try to console her, now, or laugh it off. But she thought it more likely that they'd pretend this disastrous episode had never happened. Over the years the two of them had developed a knack of not speaking about delicate things—for instance, Lady Derby's health. Their harmonious relationship depended on a judicious measure of silence.

Derby surprised her. 'Mrs Farren,' he said, turning his head, 'I wonder, if you'd be so good, might your daughter and I have a moment in private?'

Eliza and her mother stared at each other. In all the long years he'd never asked for this.

'Oh, but—' Mrs Farren began.

'Please. You could sit in the long gallery at the end of the corridor.'

Eliza jerked her head, and her mother gathered up her knotting and went out, her shoulders stiff with offence.

'It seems to me', said Derby into the silence, 'that there need to be changes.'

'Changes, My Lord?'

'Between us.'

She bristled at the pronoun.

'I wish you to break off all connection with Mrs Damer.'

Eliza rose to her feet. She thought of telling him that she hadn't spoken or written to Anne since their terrible quarrel at the end of July.

'I don't ask', he went on, raising one hand like a vicar, 'whether there's any truth in the noxious allegations.'

'How dare you!'

'I don't ask,' said Derby, 'because I've no desire to know.'

She realised something. 'You mean you wouldn't believe my denial.'

'I don't ask,' he repeated, almost snarling, 'and I will never ask. But I do demand that you break with Mrs Damer.'

Eliza's head was full of thunder. She twisted the ring on her little finger, rubbed at its ivory eye. 'And what about Lady Milner, my Yorkshire *connection,* according to Pigott,' she said sardonically, 'am I to cut her off too?'

'Don't be silly.'

'Oh, so you accept that the reference to her was pure invention—but you believe the worst of our old friend?'

'I can't tell what to believe, frankly,' said Derby, 'but smoke implies a fire, and Mrs Damer's reputation has been smoking on and off for half her life.'

Eliza pursed her lips at this hypocrisy. 'Three years ago you told me the story was ludicrous nonsense.'

'Everything's changed. There's a print in Holland's window that shows you dithering between a coronet and a *chisel,*' he said, pronouncing the word with revulsion. 'So I don't want you to see her, speak to her or correspond with her again.'

This was too much. 'For a man who has no rights—no claims on me—you go too far.'

'Miss Farren,' said Derby furiously, 'I am hardly an uninvolved party. Must I remind you that, virtuous as you may be, you have dragged me into the muck? I've been satirised in a best-selling broadside as an impotent old fool whose beloved is betraying him with not one, but two, Sapphic lovers.'

Eliza averted her face.

'To defend my honour,' Derby went on, 'I've quarrelled to the verge of bloodshed with a man I thought my friend.'

Whom could he mean?

'The situation is unendurable at every level, public and private. All I ask is that you resolve it by breaking with the woman whose reputation, rightly or wrongly, has stained both of ours.'

'Have you no mercy? You were Anne's friend long before I met either of you,' she reminded him. 'I tell you she never laid a hand on me.'

Derby's face was very pale, like some worm that never saw the light. 'You sound almost as if you regret that.'

Eliza boiled over. 'You disgusting little tyrant. Is there no end to your appetite for power?'

His eyes bulged.

'You speak of stained reputations, but Lady Derby told me you wouldn't give her a divorce, though she begged for it.' His small mouth opened, registering this hit. 'You've kept her and yourself in a ghastly limbo all these years from sheer begrudgery! And as for me, may I remind you I'm not one of your pedigree horses or dogs or cocks? You can't control me.'

There was a terrible pause. She thought he might stalk out of his own gilt-and-white parlour. 'It's true, the only claim I have on you is a future one,' Derby said in a low voice. 'It's a bet I'm offering, I suppose. If you do what I ask, on this one occasion, you have my solemn word that the moment the present Countess of Derby dies I'll ask for your hand.'

Eliza's heart was thudding. He'd never put it so formally before. This was a verbal promise which, when it came to marriage, was almost as good as a signed contract. This was the moment when a sensible woman should say *Yes, yes, yes, My Lord, thank you, whatever you wish.*

'I don't care for ultimata,' she said, and walked towards the door.

OCTOBER 1794

'We'd no notion where to send them on,' said Mrs Moll, pointing accusingly to the pile of letters.

'That's all right,' murmured Anne, sitting down at her *secrétaire*. She waited till the housekeeper had gone downstairs before she looked through the envelopes, sorting them by handwriting, playing for time. Nothing from Eliza, of course. And nothing in Mary's hand, nothing at all. Anne rested her cheek on her knuckles for a long moment.

It had to be done. She began cracking the seals.

Dearest Sister, I hope you're keeping well, Lady Mary had written in late August.

> *Richmond and I haven't seen you in an age. Do grace us with your presence at Goodwood this month, won't you? Any day before the opening of Parliament is convenient, we're so confined here by our various Maladies.*

What a trivial note, thought Anne—but then, her sister never did like to discuss painful or embarrassing subjects. Still, she and Richmond had clearly decided to stand by Anne in this as in former trials, and Anne ought to be grateful.

Her father wrote more forthrightly.

> *Not having heard from you in so long, your Mother's most alarmed. My dear Girl, you mustn't allow these snivelling hacks to disturb your peace of mind. All true Friends turn a deaf ear to these fantastical inventions.*

All true Friends, yes, she thought ironically. But how many were true? And what if she cared for the untrue ones more than the true?

Your Mother's been rather thrown into the Blue Devils by the whole affair. You know how these Things affect her. Do come back to Park Place as soon as you can; no one else has your knack of livening her up.

Anne's stomach was heavy with guilt. The bleak atmosphere of Park Place in winter wouldn't help Lady Ailesbury's depression. Clearly the family would like Anne to spend the rest of the year scuttling between Park Place and Goodwood, listening to their *various Maladies* and staying out of the merciless gaze of the World.

There was a short note from Fox—bless him—simply asking after her health and assuring her of his good wishes, as always. Nothing from Derby and this confirmed what Anne had already suspected: that this old friendship had foundered at last. What an odd hole it would leave in her life. What had Eliza told him? Could he really be sitting darkly obdurate, across the Square at Derby House, picturing his once dear Mrs Damer as a snake in the grass? Her eyes swam, but she blinked away the tears.

A letter from Georgiana came next, asking her to *drop in to Dev. House for a dish of Tea*; the messy scrawl warmed Anne. Then a letter in unfamiliar writing. Her heart lurched; she hadn't been sure if the famous—and now retired—Mr Edmund Burke would reply to a letter from a lady he barely knew. She'd written it on impulse, at three in the morning, somewhere in Hampshire.

Dear Madam,

Let me begin by assuring you that I am honoured to have been the recipient of your Confidences on this painful occasion, & that I understand your shock & distress. However, I trust that the sense & fortitude that have always distinguished you will enable you on reflection perfectly to despise this calumnious Abuse.

It is true that a dozen years ago, when I objected in Parliament to the sentencing of two Sodomites (pardon my frankness) to the pillory, where they were stoned to death by the

*mob, my reputation was subjected to Innuendo in a newspaper,
whereupon I brought a suit of libel & won an Apology. However, in the case of a Lady, my view is that Silence is the only
safe and dignified rebuttal. Your consolation, Mrs Damer, must
be that the malicious lies of the envious will leave no mark on
History's pages.*

  Your most obedient humble servant,
  Edm. Burke

That afternoon she sat in the library at Strawberry Hill. Walpole normally never had a fire lit in here in summer; he must be
pampering her. He apologised for the mess in the Hall, where
workmen were patching up a wall. 'I don't think my dear niece, the
Duchess of Gloucester, looks forward with any enthusiasm to inheriting my fragile plaything.'

'She doesn't want Strawberry Hill, the most charming house in
England?' asked Anne, shocked out of her blank state.

'Oh, tush, you're too kind,' he said. 'She knows it'll take a deal
of looking after, my little castle of straw spun into gold—a joke
that's gone on forty years too long already! No, it'll fall to dust, in
time, and only our letters will remain to tell the ages what delightful days we had.'

Walpole reported that their mutual friend General O'Hara
must be still languishing in a French gaol, or at least his name
hadn't appeared on the execution lists yet. *Le pauvre* Tonton had recently grown stone deaf and blind, he mentioned as he stroked the
dog's black curls, but he still seemed to enjoy his existence.

A heavy silence seemed to fill the room and settle between the
book-filled Gothic arches. 'My dear girl, come and sit a little
nearer,' Walpole said, tapping the chair beside him.

'Girl? I'm forty-five years old,' said Anne, stern.

'Seventy-seven laughs at forty-five.'

She'd been expecting Walpole to increase her gloom today by
shrill fretfulness, but it was going quite the other way. Her cousin

panicked at small things, she realised, but when it came to serious problems he could be a rock.

'I fear you've been vastly unhappy this summer.'

'It shows, then. Is my loveliness quite faded?' asked Anne ironically.

He was shaking his shrunken head. 'It was a nasty thing that happened, but you mustn't take it so hard.'

'It wasn't a splinter in my finger,' she pointed out.

'Mm. The Berrys have been in Broadstairs, on the Kentish coast,' he remarked.

Ah, so Mary had fled from Yorkshire. Had she feared that Anne would pursue her? That thought gave the pain a fresh twist.

'But they're back in North Audley Street since Tuesday.'

Anne nodded, not trusting herself to speak. She watched the fire.

'I saw the piece in the newspaper that wounded her so—'

'Can you tell me what it said?' Immediately Anne regretted asking. How tasteless, to make an old man repeat obscenities! But whom else could she ask?

'If you like,' Walpole said, wary. 'It claimed that there was not only one *prospective countess* whose prospects were being thwarted by an intimacy with a well-known sculptress, but two.'

Anne winced. 'It didn't actually name her?'

'Oh, as good as, I'm afraid. It added that while the Earl who was courting *Miss F.* was the ugliest in the country, *Miss B.*'s was surely the oldest!'

She put her face in her hands.

'I'd hoped to act as a peacemaker, as you did so kindly some years ago when she was so shocked by being linked with me in a newspaper. But when I pump her gently on the subject she runs from the room.'

'Perhaps Mary's shielding me,' said Anne with difficulty. 'Although she no longer wishes to be my friend, because her reputation has been irreparably wounded by association with mine, she may think it dishonourable to speak ill of me to others.'

'Oh, my dear, she's just distressed, in a tizzy. Her wits have gone astray. As yours did, may I say,' Walpole rebuked her fondly. 'What possessed you to go wandering around the countryside, where you knew not a soul?'

'That was the idea.'

He made a grunt of exasperation. 'You and Mary both, you reason most womanishly, if you'll pardon my saying so.'

Her eyebrows went up.

'All this talk of *irreparably wounded reputations*. Haven't you learned from the Ancients that your conscience is your own and so is your honour? Don't mistake the bubble of fame—or infamy, in this case—for anything solid. Don't you know your own heart?'

Anne managed a half-smile. 'I used to think so.'

'Now that I've reached the twilight of my life,' Walpole told her, 'I realise that what the World knows of one is no true evaluation, just some random associations. After my death, for instance, what'll remain of me on this earth?' For once, he spoke without a trace of self-pity. 'People may read *The Castle of Otranto*, perhaps misquote a bon mot or *aperçu* of mine, handle and bid low on one of my bibelots at auction; that's all. But am I to think my life amounts to no more than that?'

Anne shook her head. After a long silence she asked, 'Will you do me a service?'

'Of course, my dear. Anything that lies in my feeble power.' Walpole spread his hands wide.

'Could you find me someone to attend to the newspapers, and keep a sharp eye out and let me know if I'm mentioned or abused again? I mean the low papers.'

Walpole squirmed in his seat. 'Isn't that a somewhat...unhealthy preoccupation?'

'I need to know,' she told him. 'I dread the thought of being ignorant of what's being said about me. I'd be happy to pay—'

Walpole waved that away. 'But in return you must promise me something.'

She knew what he was going to ask.

'Write to Mary,' he said and his face was crumpled like a paper bag.

Miss Farren [said Sheridan's scrawl],
I'm mystified to hear that your strange fever continues & further postpones your first performance of the autumn season at Drury Lane. Surely never in the annals of History did a fever burn so long without extinguishing the life of its fair victim! If you or your loyal physicians feel it's likely to flame on for another fort-night, do be so good as to let me know, so I can distribute your parts (a tempting collection) between Mrs Jordan & a very tal-ented Girl, newly hired. But I can assure you your audience misses its Queen of Comedy keenly—though its memory is short in other respects—& stands ready to welcome you back with lavish (and respectful) Applause.
Yr svt,
R.B.S.

He could banter and bully all he liked, but Eliza was still not ready. Irish audiences were one thing, but she felt sick at the thought of stepping out in front of a London crowd. What if someone shouted out *Tommy* again? A single catcall, a laugh in the wrong place, and she'd know that they hadn't forgotten the filthy story, no matter what Sheridan said about short memories.

For the first time in her career she thought longingly of retire-ment. But since she'd thrown Derby's ultimatum in his face last month, what prospects had she—what option but to go back to Drury Lane and earn her crust? He'd kept his distance since that interview, though his carriage still turned up outside the door of the Bow Window House for the Farrens' use. *He plays me on a loose line, like a fish.*

She looked at Sheridan's letter again and indulged in a moment of pure hatred of Dora Jordan, who was said to have signed a new contract for 30 guineas a week. The worst of it was that Sheridan had somehow found £200 in cash to pay Mrs Inchbald to write

Dora a charming new comedy called *The Wedding Day,* as relief from Kemble's long string of unpopular tragedies.

Mrs Farren came into the room without knocking, with a glass of whey.

'I said I didn't want any,' said Eliza rudely.

Her mother set it down on the *secrétaire.* 'You hardly touched your dinner. You're looking shocking skinny.'

The word set Eliza's teeth on edge.

'This quarrel with Lord Derby—'

'How many times do I have to tell you, Mother, that I won't discuss it?'

The wrinkled lip trembled. Eliza eyed it coldly; Margaret Farren had always been rather a ham. 'Surely His Lordship doesn't believe you guilty of any nastiness?' asked her mother. 'I daren't believe he'd cast you off, after all these years, on such a whim. The whole scandal's the fault of that evil woman, besides!'

Eliza couldn't help being drawn in. 'Anne Damer is not evil.' The ring on her little finger seemed to stare accusingly. She remembered, with scarlet shame, pressing her friend's strong mouth to hers.

A rap at the front door and Mrs Farren scuttled down to see whom the footman was letting in.

'My dear,' said the Queen of Tragedy, advancing to take Eliza's hands.

'Mrs Siddons! Do sit down,' said Eliza. Though they'd moved in some of the same circles, her colleague had never called on her before. 'I hope you'll take some tea.'

'We've missed you sorely at Drury Lane,' said Mrs Siddons. 'Your health, I understand—'

'On that topic, 'said Eliza, to change the subject, 'I don't believe I sent my felicitations on your confinement.' She couldn't for the life of her remember if this one had been a boy or a girl.

'Ah, yes, my dearest Cecilia—named for Mrs Piozzi's daughter, don't you know. She's almost three months old already! My seventh and, I trust, my last.'

The woman sounded tired; she must be forty by now, Eliza calculated.

'If it were not for financial necessity, how glad would I be to retire from the service of Thespis,' Mrs Siddons confided.

'I understand,' said Eliza with a sigh.

'Our New Drury—for all its glories—is not an easy place in which to perform. If I hadn't made my reputation in a smaller theatre, I doubt I ever would here.'

Eliza nodded eagerly. 'I confess, as the glamour's worn off, I've come to think it a wilderness. A circus tent for giants! Do you notice our costumes are getting gaudier? I have to boom to be heard at all—'

'And I've been obliged to change my whole way of moving,' Mrs Siddons complained. 'Every gesture must be from the shoulder, forceful and unmistakable. To command the attention of almost 4000 people—how it drains one's vital energies!'

Mrs Farren came in with the tea, bobbing and smiling, then excused herself again.

Eliza scissored two pieces of sugar cone into her colleague's cup. She was about to make some light conversation about Sheridan's mismanagement, but Mrs Siddons spoke first.

'Miss Farren, my visit today has a more serious purpose. There is something I would never have dreamed of mentioning to you except that it has come to press upon my conscience. Not', Mrs Siddons added rather wildly, 'that I have committed any wrongdoing myself, but since man and wife are considered one being—'

What on earth was she talking about? Eliza put her tea down untasted.

'The calumny you have endured this summer past—I know, and you know, its ultimate origin.' Mrs Siddons's cheeks were purpling. 'Many years ago, in a spirit of reckless and drunken levity, my husband composed a certain rhyme—'

'Yes, Mrs Piozzi told me its authorship,' said Eliza to save her from having to spell it out. Silence. *I may detest William Siddons,* she thought, *but at least I'm not yoked to him.*

'I have always been sorry,' said the other woman, 'but I thought

it best not to pain you further by mentioning it. Now, however, to
see you labouring under the weight of this hideous rumour—
shrinking from the public eye—and all because of my husband's
damnable invention—'

Eliza had never heard Mrs Siddons use a word like *damnable*.

'I've come not only to apologise on his behalf—since I've failed
to persuade him to do so himself—but to encourage you to return
to the stage.'

'You're kind,' said Eliza rather gruffly, 'but—'

'Believe me, my dear, I speak from experience. You remember
Brereton?'

Meek little Pop Kemble's first husband had tried to throttle her,
before being packed off to the asylum where he'd died; of course
Eliza remembered.

'Many years ago', said Mrs Siddons with a shudder, 'Brereton—though a married man—conceived an unholy passion for
me. I attempted to distance myself and declined to perform in his
Ben. When he tried to do away with himself with a razor, I was
widely blamed as the cause!'

'Oh, but that's outrageous,' said Eliza. 'We've all had fools fall
in love with us, despite ourselves. Why should your reputation be
stained by another's madness?'

A shrug, worthy of Cleopatra. 'My point, Miss Farren, is that
every celebrated actress has her season of shame. I survived mine,
though I scarce believed I would, and you will survive yours.'

26 North Audley Street
My dear A.
*—for dear you still are to me, I insist, though your letter suggests
you think all my fondness has turned to hate. It made me cry,
though I was glad to receive it. I've been wanting to write to you
for some time, but was unsure how to begin.*

*Oh, God! How have we deserved this wretchedness? These
are the first tears I've shed in some time & they have relieved my
head a little. My father and sister (from whom I've kept all*

*knowledge of the newspapers as best I can) talk with pleasure of
the bustle of the new Season—but to what can I look forward,
since all my ideas of peace or comfort in this miserable existence
are inseparable from you & our friendship, long the sole solace of
my heart, has become as a forbidden fruit.*

*I do not nor have I ever for an instant doubted the worth of
your heart. I confess that for some time in the summer I gave
way to suspicions about your intimacy with Miss F., but your
letter has set my mind quite at rest on that subject. I would denounce her for her brutal behaviour to you in your time of crisis—except that my own has been no better.*

*I don't, never will, doubt you, I say. But it can't be between
us as it used to be—I mean in the eyes of the World. You must
rein in your warmth of heart, my dear. Don't think that I'm
proposing some dismal scheme in which we're to be utterly separated (God forbid) but we must learn to live somewhat at a distance. I can't bring myself to see you yet & even when that day
comes we must meet less frequently, modify our manners—yours
sometimes have too great an air of fervour about them, I must
tell you. Your friendship is precious to me, but for my sake let me
have it now upon such limited terms as I can give.*

God bless, preserve & support you.
M.B.

A terrible crash from the parlour made Eliza race downstairs.
She found Mrs Farren, red-faced, standing over the toppled bust of
Thalia. 'Mother!'

'Marble's harder than I thought,' said the older woman, breathing heavily. 'The nose hasn't so much as chipped, though it's left a
nasty scrape on the wood.'

'Have you lost your senses?'

'Have you?' she barked back at Eliza.

Only now did Eliza notice the unfolded paper in her mother's
hand, the Derby seal. She snatched at it, but her mother whipped
it out of the way. 'How dare you?'

'I knew if I gave it to you, I'd never hear a word of what was in it.'

'It's my letter,' Eliza shrieked like a child.

'He'd like to know whether you've been considering his offer,' said Mrs Farren, her face ugly with wrath. 'Whether to give up Mrs Damer in exchange for his *solemn word* that he'll make you a countess, or... how does he put it?' She peered at the page. 'Yes, *to cling to your friend—or worse—and bid me an eternal farewell!*'

Eliza was suddenly tired to the point of dizziness. She let herself down on a chair, eyes resting on the milky curls of the fallen bust.

'If this were in a play,' said her mother more calmly, 'you'd notice how absurd it was. One of those ridiculous tussles between a courting couple, put in to spin out a thin plot.'

Eliza spoke with difficulty. 'I haven't *clung* to Anne Damer. I haven't seen her since July.'

'Then tell Derby so, you twit of a girl!'

'It's none of his business.'

'Oh, no? The poor man's been laughed at all over England for wooing such a cold, queer fish as you.'

Eliza was shaking. 'But it's not his right to tell me what to do.'

'He's going to give you a coronet, isn't he?'

'Only if Lady Derby dies and I wouldn't put it past the old yellow hag to outlive me,' snapped Eliza. '*And* only if I accept him.'

'Mother of Christ, *if!*' roared Mrs Farren. 'If you don't mean to marry him, then what in all the seven hells have we been playing at for the past dozen years, while your youth and fruitfulness have been draining away?'

A sob bubbled up in Eliza's mouth.

'Who'll hire you, may I ask, if the crowd roars *Tommy* again, or throws eggs? And even if Sheridan keeps you on, what'll you be earning in ten years when you're bony and wrinkled, and playing Third Witch in *Macbeth*? You know how many actresses go broke and die in squalor, or debtors' gaol; is that your plan for the pair of us?'

'No.' Eliza wept. 'No.'

'Oh, childy, childy, come here.' Mrs Farren enclosed her daughter in a crushing embrace. 'Let's have no more nonsense. Betsy's going to be Countess of Derby and make her old mam proud.'

When Eliza finally straightened up and mopped at her eyes, her mother spoke calmly. 'I'd take that ring off and send it back to her.'

Eliza nodded. She wrestled with her finger. 'It won't come off.' The ivory eye watched her. She wrenched at it and let out a grunt of pain. 'Wretched thing!'

A jerk of the head. 'Upstairs.' In Eliza's bedroom, her mother rubbed the washball into suds and soaped the hand with the ring on it. 'Nearly done,' she murmured, kneading and pulling. Eliza shut her eyes, feeling like a small child. A slithering sensation, a long pull and the gold chimed against the china.

'MRS DAMER,' said Eliza, as she swept into the study at no. 8 Grosvenor Square.

As she'd meant it to, the formality of the address struck home. Anne's mouth opened and shut; her face looked her age, though her hair still didn't have any trace of grey.

Eliza had decided to begin with a concession, to gain the moral high ground. 'I apologise for losing my temper the last time I was here in July. Given the peculiarly distressing circumstances, for which on mature reflection I don't entirely blame you, I think it for the best that I return this.' With her gloved hand she deposited the tiny gold ring on the *secrétaire*. Without having looked at the back of it in years, she knew what it said: *Preuve de mon amitié.* 'Friendship in this world is always subject to difficulties and, in this case,' she wound up her speech, 'I feel the gods have been against us from the start.'

No answer; Anne just looked at her.

Turn round, Eliza told herself, *get out now.* 'You don't agree?'

A slow shrug. 'It seems cowardly to blame it on the gods.'

Eliza's heart was loud in her ribs. Her mother was right, she shouldn't have come.

Anne rested her knotted fingers on her knees and spoke quietly. 'If you're discarding me out of fear of the World, you might have the candour to say so.'

'Derby demands it,' said Eliza hoarsely. And then wished above all things that she hadn't said those words, like some cowed wife.

'Ah,' said the other woman, nodding. 'So the *silly man* has mastered you.'

'No!' *How dare she quote that back to me?*

'You speak like a chattel. I'd been under the misapprehension that you were an independent woman,' Anne baited her, 'but now it's clear you've bound yourself to marry a man you don't love.'

Eliza set her teeth.

'Pigott's dead, did you know that?'

'What?'

'Pigott, who wrote the detestable pamphlet. Here's the comedy of it,' said Anne. 'He died in June, a nasty death in his cell at Newgate, before the thing was ever published; Walpole found that out for me. So all this damage has been done by a ghost.'

'We won't meet again,' said Eliza at the door, a word at a time, to make it real in her own hearing.

November 1794

The first public occasion Anne dared—forced herself—to attend was a breakfast at Chiswick. She fretted all morning over her Grecian dress, one minute thinking it too flirtatiously girlish, the next too severe, almost mannish.

Georgiana was a kind hostess, as always, though her face looked strained; she confided in a whisper that she'd been shattered to learn, in a newspaper, of Charles Grey's engagement to one Miss Ponsonby. What a brute the politician was, thought Anne, not to break the news himself to the woman who'd lost so much by bearing his child! Did love have to evaporate like perfume from an old bottle? Did it always come to weary, squalid betrayal in the end?

Georgiana made a point of strolling arm in arm with Anne through the villa, from one knot of guests to another, as a sign of her protection. Anne clung on, taking one step at a time as if she were seasick; she clutched her open fan like a shield. Several old friends like Fox made a point of shaking her hand; Derby, glimpsed in the next room, stayed out of range. With most people she simply couldn't tell if they seemed less friendly than the last time she'd encountered them. She felt as if she'd lost her ability to read faces.

Anne began to think she might risk sitting down at a table, though she couldn't imagine eating anything from the vast variety of dishes laid out. 'Here's room, now I must find darling Bess,' cried Georgiana, dropping Anne in a chair opposite some Whig ladies clustered in loud discussion of a radical proposal for something called a *minimum wage*.

Viscountess Melbourne, Mrs Crewe, the Duchess of Norfolk; Anne gave them each the customary bow, but with her eyes lowered. 'But of course Pitiless Pitt will shoot it down in a moment,' Lady Melbourne was saying. As her head turned towards Anne, her features took on a peculiarly blank expression.

Anne let her eyes meet her former friend's. The two of them and Georgiana had been giddy brides together in the '60s. They'd all three known disaster and scandal; Lady Melbourne had been linked with one lover after another and accused of poxing the heir to the throne. If anyone was tolerant, unshockable, it should be she.

'Ladies. Shall we?' The Viscountess rose. Three fans went up like disdainful peacocks' tails. The women glided away from the table.

Anne sat very still with her tongue clamped to the roof of her mouth to prevent herself from bursting into tears. She should have known; she should never have hoped. It was all about surfaces, not substance; the reputation, not the heart. What was it Lady Melbourne used to preach to her? *Discretion is the tax we pay the World, or suffer the consequences.* The Viscountess probably didn't care whether Anne Damer was practised at Sapphic vice, or any other kind; all that mattered was that the World had pronounced its judgement.

Anne only let herself fall apart in the curtained privacy of her carriage. By the time she reached Grosvenor Square she'd mopped her eyes and rearranged her hair.

Which was just as well, because the Duke of Richmond was waiting in her parlour, flicking through a volume of Sir William Hamilton's drawings of ancient vases. 'Dear Anne,' he said, enclosing her hands in his, very much the paterfamilias. 'How are you?'

'Well,' she managed.

'I was just telling Walpole how much good sea bathing at Felpham did you after your accident.'

'He claims he's too old to try such a novelty himself,' said Anne, trying for a touch of flippancy.

Richmond's face stayed compassionate. 'Your sister's really not at all well these days; she'd love you to come down. I crave a retired life myself, if only affairs of state and war didn't press upon me so.'

'Well, Goodwood is so very comfortable.'

'Exactly! It's a perfect refuge from the hugger-mugger of city life,' Richmond told her. 'It can provide all the necessities and luxuries too: spacious accommodations, a reliable staff, cordial neighbours, riding, boating, the hunt, a fine art collection...'

She was rather puzzled by this hymn to his own house.

'In fact, Lady Mary was only saying the other day how much you seem to enjoy your visits.'

'I do,' she said, wary as she glimpsed what was coming.

'We were thinking, she and I, that you might consider making your home with us—which would be delightful, needless to say. In middle age one requires peace, doesn't one?' he pushed on. 'Stability, and calm, and a compatible little family, instead of the glittering throng.'

Anne thought of Georgiana's breakfast at Chiswick; the ranks of black suits and white dresses, the fans flashing like knives. 'You're very kind, brother,' she said haltingly, 'but I feel no desire to leave London.'

That wasn't strictly true; there was something undeniably tempting about the image of Goodwood. She could drive down with Richmond this afternoon and set up a workshop in some unused room within the week. She could hide away down there; she never need risk hearing the name *Miss Farren*, or being cut by Lady

Melbourne, or any member of the *glittering throng*, ever again. This was exactly what Richmond had done for his wild sister Sarah, when she'd run away from her husband, Anne remembered suddenly; he'd negotiated her settlement and built her a house on his estate. A refuge for a fallen woman.

'Quite sure, hm?'

For an awful moment she thought the Duke was going to refer to the events of the summer, the mortification she'd caused her relations. To forestall him she insisted, 'I do very well here. I have my friends. My work. I'm grateful for your offer, of course—'

'Oh, well, bear it in mind, that's all,' Richmond said graciously and consulted the gold watch that hung from his fob.

After he'd hurried off to a Cabinet meeting, Anne stared out of the window at the noisy traffic of Grosvenor Square. *Another bridge burnt,* she told herself. She was doing *very well* here in London, was she?

She'd read somewhere that there were 278 papers and periodicals published in this country. Even common labourers began the morning by going to a coffee house to read the latest news. Anne had no way of telling whether the people she met over the course of a day—stable boys, confectioners, marble merchants, literary ladies, country gentlemen—knew all about her monstrous reputation, or had forgotten it already, or had never heard about it in the first place. She couldn't know whether their polite masks covered sympathy or disgust. She would have to live with that, if she stayed in London. *It's a light,* she thought, *a hard light trained on my face that won't burn out till I die.*

DERBY AND Sheridan met Fox at Brooks's to brief him on the upcoming treason trials. (There had been no official rapprochement since the incident at Epsom three months ago, but somehow, in the glow of relief Derby felt at hearing from Eliza that she'd cut all ties with Mrs Damer, he'd let his grudge drop.)

'The Privy Council's now examined all the so-called *traitors* who were arrested last May,' he began.

Sheridan burst out, 'Gad, how do you have the stomach to take part in such a charade?'

'As a token Whig on the Council, Derby provides us with invaluable information,' Fox scolded.

Derby grinned at his leader, then sobered as he consulted his notes. 'The prosecution's somehow drummed up 208 witnesses against poor Tom Holcroft. Once he and Hardy are convicted, as test cases, 800 other warrants are to be served; they're written out already, ready to be signed.'

'What day is Horne Tooke to be tried?' asked Fox.

'Tuesday,' Sheridan told him. 'The old firecracker's acting as his own counsel. He'll call your humble servant as a witness'—tapping his lapel.

'Mm,' said Fox uneasily. 'Remember what I said the other day, Sherry, about perhaps distancing yourself a little from the prisoners?'

'And remember what I told you, Foxy,' Sheridan retorted, 'that the thing's impossible? I don't much like some of these men, but I've worked shoulder to shoulder with them and my speeches have inspired them. I'll testify that Horne Tooke's views are in many ways less extreme than my own.'

'Oh, why not go ahead and offer to swap places with him?' Derby suggested bitterly. 'I see you'll never rest till you reach the Tower.'

Sheridan smirked. 'Don't fret. Then comes the sudden twist,' he said as if describing a play. 'Tooke will pull this out.'

Derby automatically flinched at the sight of a pamphlet with curling edges. 'What is it?'

'Ha ha! The constitution of the London Corresponding Society, which was formed to support the Duke of Richmond's Reform Bill of 1780. Then, Fox, we call your uncle Richmond to acknowledge that these so-called *insurrectionists* are only asking for exactly the same changes as he proposed fourteen years ago!'

'Brilliant,' murmured Derby.

'Awful cheek,' said Fox enjoyably.

'Then Tooke will subpoena one William Pitt,' Sheridan surged on, 'and force him to acknowledge and reminisce about several meetings he and Tooke attended together back in the early '80s.'

'Yes, of course, even the Eunuch began as a Reformer, didn't he? Everyone did, before all sense was scared out of them,' said Fox nostalgically. '*Autres temps, autres moeurs...*'

How the world had turned upside down in fourteen years; in the last four in particular. Derby caught himself thinking guiltily of Anne Damer. Things changed, that was simply how it was. All over the country friendships had melted away like wax.

'I'VE BEEN longing to see you,' said Anne in the parlour at North Audley Street, 'but not until you were ready. To find you cold to me would be worse than nothing.'

For answer Mary gripped Anne's hands in hers. Anne's dread fell away, her shoulders relaxed and it was as it had always been. The winter light coming through the window took on a softer glow; the air seemed more breathable. She could count each of Mary's warm fingertips on the back of her hands.

Then the door opened and Mary sprang back, her face frozen. It was only the maid, bringing the kettle. Anne thought, *I won't cry. I'm a grown woman. What good would crying do?*

They waited for the water to boil and spoke of other things for a little while. '*This trash of tea,*' Anne quoted lightly, '*I don't know why I drink so much of it. Heigho!*'

Mary smiled, but as if she weren't sure of the reference. 'Are you working on a new sculpture?'

'No,' Anne said, 'I've not touched my tools since July.' The word hung between them. 'I was away from my workshop and since I've come back I don't know, I don't quite trust my fingers.' She stretched them out in front of her, considered the wrinkled knuckles.

'It's so good to see you in the flesh,' said Mary suddenly. 'Do my decrees of caution seem harsh?'

'No, no,' Anne lied. 'I'm content to let your kind judgement direct me.'

'It's only a matter of paying a sort of tax to the World—'

Anne flinched: that was Lady Melbourne's old phrase. 'Ah, I believe I've passed the age of delusion. None of society's blandishments can conceal its deformities from me now. What was that other line of mine, in *The Way to Keep Him?*' She called it up. '*I am tired of the World and the World may be tired of me, if it will.*'

Mary was nodding fervently. 'Yet we live in it; what escape is possible?'

'There must be one,' Anne told her. 'A castle on a Scottish mountaintop. Or no, a few rooms in a farmer's house in Spain, near the sea. A cabin under a few trees in Italy!'

'Would such a humble dwelling satisfy a child of Park Place?'

'Oh, yes,' Anne told her. 'Can't one take a stroll with as much pleasure over lands the law hasn't marked for one's own?'

'You and I won't ever be free to seek out those places. Our duties keep us here.'

'I suppose so. But the World and I will never be upon more than civil terms,' Anne warned her.

'Discretion and prudence is all I ask,' said Mary rather despairingly. 'But you mustn't coop yourself up in your house. To live so much alone is bad for you, and the more you see other people and convince them by your conduct that you're not what your enemies call you, the more I can see you too.'

'Well, if I must go out in company I will,' said Anne with a little shudder. 'While I've a dearer interest than mine to consider, I'll attend to the World's whims with scrupulous care.' And she took hold of Mary's hands again, lightly.

They tried to move on to general conversation. 'Can you believe that the treason trials have all ended in acquittal?' asked Mary.

'Oh, I can't tell what to think! Fox maintains the government's been using the long suspension of habeas corpus to jail the innocent, much as the French kings used to. But on the other hand, what if the juries are contaminated with sedition,' Anne agonised, 'and they've set free a brace of revolutionaries who'll come for us with pikes in the night...'

DECEMBER 1794

The Derby carriage toiled up the Liverpool Road; snow clogged its wheels. It was proving one of the worst winters on record. This was their third day on the road. Eliza pulled back the velvet to look out through the frosted window, her eye trying to encompass the undulating Lancashire landscape: the white fields streaked with brown, the woods and pastures, and a faraway glimpse of the Irish Sea. She could hardly believe she was going to see Knowsley at last.

The Farrens had been packing and repacking Eliza's trunk all week. Some clothes looked too ostentatious for a country visit; others too sheer and revealing. But on the other hand, she didn't want to look plain or underbred. She left out her box of face creams, not wanting to seem painted—then thought of the wrinkles that said thirty-two, and threw it back in.

She'd finally nerved herself to go back to Drury Lane for a revival of *The Rivals*; Sheridan had written her a charming prologue in which she'd appealed to the gallantry of the British public to protect her from further insult and calumny. It brought the house down. It had stuck in Eliza's craw to have to ingratiate herself with a mob for whom she was coming to feel nothing but revulsion. She was oddly reminded of Louis and Marie Antoinette in the early days of the Revolution, smiling unconvincingly in their tricolour cockades.

Derby was chatting away about his mines and spinning factories here in the North, 'which provide year-round employment even for children, it's marvellous'.

'Will this be...a very festive Christmas?' Mrs Farren asked nervously.

'Oh, quiet enough. Apart from the Open Days for tenants, which I'm afraid are pretty much compulsory on a large estate.'

'And your three children will be here?'

'Yes; they're very eager to meet you both, as are my four Burgoyne wards, and my agents and neighbours.'

Her bright eyes slid to Eliza. *Very eager to meet the next Countess.*

Eliza stared out of the window again, gripped by a ridiculous kind of stage fright. She knew her job: to convince all these people that she wasn't the painted Jezebel of their imaginings. She knew little about young Lady Charlotte and Lord Edward, and had no reason to believe that they'd greet her with anything other than scorn. She'd met Lady Elizabeth already, of course—though Derby didn't know that and she hoped the girl would never tell him. Eliza remembered that visit to Marylebone as a kind of feverish hallucination; that yellow Countess on what was meant to be her deathbed, saying such terrible things. Now that Eliza had thrown in her lot with Derby—had agreed to his ultimatum and made some peace with herself—why couldn't the raddled invalid die and be done with it?

Her stomach tightened as the carriage slowed, turning off the road on to a zigzag avenue. In the distance the huge walls rose up. Eliza thought of the 500 years of the Stanleys of Knowsley. They were mentioned in Shakespeare, Spenser, Milton; they were soldiers, statesmen, scholars, moulders of history...

'The game here's not bad at all; of course it's all about management,' Derby was saying. 'During the shooting season I make it a rule that no gun may bag more than five brace of partridge in a morning, so there'll still be good sport for the ladies to watch in the afternoon.'

What a bore he can be, thought Eliza so suddenly that it frightened her.

'The Hall's a terrible mishmash,' said Derby fondly, gesturing across the lawns at the approaching walls. 'Those are my stables and kennels on the left. The King's Tower's the oldest piece of the puzzle: fifteenth century or so.' The carriage rolled under a frowning gateway with a turret. 'There's a rather jolly motto,' said Derby, pointing up at some chiselled lettering: *'Bring good news and knock boldly.'*

When they stopped in front of the red brick main façade, Eliza counted: twenty windows across. The Earl jumped down and came round to hand her down himself. Would that look to onlookers like a mark of special respect, she wondered, or a shocking familiarity? She was dizzy with fright. She wished she were back in the narrow parlour on Green Street, sharing an eel pie with her mother.

Faces, lined up in the Great Hall. Eliza paused on the top marble step to gather her forces for her entrance. The heir, first; he mattered most. Lord Edward Smith-Stanley looked younger than nineteen, and nothing like his father; she gave him a slow, dazzling smile. She was expecting reserve, or sulkiness, but what she won from the boy was the most enormous blush. 'An honour,' he said, bending over her outstretched hand.

'Miss Farren,' said Lady Charlotte and gave a very small curtsy.

It all went much better than Eliza had expected. The food was rather overwhelming—turkey Périgueux and roast chine of pork with apple sauce on Christmas Day, wild boar's head in wine on New Year's Eve—but Lord Edward assured her that these particular dishes had always been served at Knowsley.

'The King eats no loaf but potato bread now,' Eliza told him, 'to set a good example while the wheat harvests are so poor.'

'Potato bread?' repeated Lady Charlotte, eyes wide.

'Yes,' Eliza told her, 'horrible stuff' and the girl smiled back faintly.

No one had cut her dead, so far, or roared out *harlot* or, God forbid, *Tommy*. Young Lord Edward was slightly deaf already, but very sweet, and the two girls were at least civil and apparently resigned to her role in their father's life, though she couldn't imagine that he'd stooped to explaining it to them. If there was a certain wariness in the smiles of the local gentry—a confusion about the eyes of the rector—then that was only to be expected. Eliza's position as a visitor to Knowsley was an ambiguous one, to say the least.

When Derby wasn't meeting with his agents and factory managers he delighted in displaying all the charms of the estate to her and her mother: his collection of Stubbs and other sporting paintings, as well as some Van Dycks, Poussins and Veroneses, the chair in the library on which the seventh Earl had knelt to pray on the scaffold in 1651, the rolling parks (excellent cover for red and fallow deer, he assured her) and a frozen lake three miles wide. He took Eliza up a little hill, wrapped in all her furs, to drink hot port in a summer house lined with the estate's own oak, and they looked down on the Hall together; he was like Lucifer, tempting her with this expanse, she thought. Was she here to be impressed, then, as much as to impress? Was Derby saying, *If I've asked much of you, I'm offering even more?*

At times, strolling through the long gallery with her arm on the Earl's, Eliza couldn't help feeling that this was a rehearsal. Would she know what to say, how to act, when—if—they were married? It was not so much a matter of whether she would be happy, as whether she'd fit the role. Eliza liked luxury and fine things, but Mayfair was all she knew. How would she oversee such a vast, complex staff—or could she leave all that to the steward and butler?

Derby even confided in her about the children. Lord Edward's deafness bothered his father—it would debar him from politics—but rather less than his squeamishness about manly sports. In the summer, when Lady Elizabeth turned sixteen, Derby was planning to marry her to a Mr Cole of Twickenham.

'Is she…willing?' asked Eliza, disconcerted by the ways of the aristocracy.

'Oh, willing enough, though girls are so coy it's hard to be sure. I'm only settling £2000 on her, because of her parentage,' he explained, 'whereas Lady Charlotte will get more like £30,000.'

The figures staggered Eliza. And his obstinate insistence that the girl was Dorset's. Should she say something—remark on how clearly she could see Derby's features echoed in Lady Elizabeth's, despite her colouring? *Stay out of it*, she reminded herself, *you're not his wife.*

In the library on New Year's Day, Mrs Farren fussed over the fire screen, tilting it to keep the heat off Eliza's complexion. It was a hideous copy of a Rubens painting, in thick worsted, and Eliza was suddenly convinced that it was one of Lady Ailesbury's; Park

Place had been littered with them. The families were old friends, of course, but still it struck her as a malign coincidence.

Derby was asking her something. 'I do beg your pardon,' she said.

'I merely asked, how are things at New Drury Lane? Sherry *still* seems on the brink of bankruptcy, even though so many of us bought hundred-year subscriptions to get the new theatre open.'

Eliza sighed. 'One problem is that there are enough seats. You see, the old theatre was so overcrowded that people went early, or sent their footmen to hold their places. Nowadays they know there'll be room for everyone, so there's less enthusiasm; people come late, or don't come at all, for fear it'll be a quiet night and the place will have a half-empty, cheerless look.'

'But that's perverse! A rule of the market, I suppose,' Derby corrected himself, 'that people only want what's in short supply...'

'To fill over 3000 seats, and compete with acrobats and balloon flights at Vauxhall Gardens, Kemble and Sheridan have to keep thinking up more spectacular and expensive attractions,' Eliza complained. 'It's all melodrama and pantomime, with special effects. Take this lurid Polish thing, *Lodoiska*; last week Mrs Crouch was playing the damsel in the burning tower and her dress went on fire. She had to hurl herself down into Michael Kelly's arms—and the rescue was so popular with the house, Kemble told the two of them they have to repeat it every night!'

Derby laughed ruefully. 'Well, I'm glad *you're* not obliged to be set alight. I prefer the plain old comedies myself.'

'But I fear my acting's coarsened too,' confessed Eliza. 'We've all worked ourselves up several notches; one has to leer and grimace for one's expressions to be seen.'

Derby blinked at her, perplexed. 'You seem to me to act as perfectly as ever.'

'Which only proves, My Lord, that your critical faculties on the subject of acting have been suspended for the last dozen years.'

Mrs Farren gave her daughter a glare, but Derby laughed and said, 'How true.'

'Have you heard Colman's satire on the new gigantic theatres?'
Eliza struck a pose for recitation.

> *When people appear*
> *Quite unable to hear*
> *'Tis undoubtedly needless to talk…*
> *'Twere better they began*
> *On the new intended plan*
> *And with telegraphs transmitted us the plot!*

'Oh, that's very neat,' said Derby, 'very up to date. I was just talking to a gentleman from Liverpool who wants me to invest in a
telegraph.'

'Sheridan's now so entangled in mortgages and liabilities that
he hasn't paid us in months,' said Eliza grimly. 'The new treasurer's
office was built with a window on to the street, you see, so Peake
can escape on Saturdays when we come looking for our wages.'

'I don't like the sound of that,' said Derby. 'If it's a matter
of substantial arrears, I'd be happy to speak to Sherry on your
behalf—'

'Oh, My Lord, how kind,' cried Margaret Farren.

Eliza darted a repressive look at her mother. 'Thank you, but
no,' she told Derby in a tone that reminded him that he wasn't in
charge of her affairs yet. Why had she been unwise enough to mention money?

When she and her mother were retiring for the night, Derby
reached into the pocket of his jacket. 'I know you too well to offer
you a Christmas present, Miss Farren,' he said awkwardly, 'but perhaps you'd accept this.'

She put up her hand, fearing it was a banknote.

'It's not what you think,' he insisted. 'Read it, I beg you.'

It was a small stiff page; she kept it folded in her hand all the
way upstairs. 'Good night,' she told her mother with a firm kiss and
shut the door in her face. At the mahogany toilette she pulled the
candle close and read the note before she'd even taken off her
Kashmir shawl.

I, Edward Smith-Stanley, twelfth Earl of Derby, do most solemnly swear that on the death of the present Countess I will propose marriage to Miss Elizabeth Farren, of Green Street, Mayfair, on whatever terms of settlement she may choose.

APRIL 1795

8 Grosvenor Square
Oh M., looking back over this arduous year (wh. I have survived only because of your aid), it seems more and more unjust that you and I should have to turn the other cheek to evil gossip, & be careful how often we meet & how we behave. Why, between old friends, need any excuses be made for fervency of affection? Does the warm partiality of two united hearts need to be justified to those who would interpret it with the basest cynicism?
 Yours,
  A. D.

26 North Audley Street
Dear A.,
I do believe we know each other better now—and trust each other more—than before those monsters attacked us. Our lives must be our honest answer. Surely when the World finds that our blameless connection continues with a steady, equal grace, year after year, it won't suppose it founded on the weakness of passionate engouement? So I conclude, after these many months, that I must put aside my trembling qualms & drop the mask of discretion, showing myself publicly to be what I will always be, your loving friend.
 Your own,
  M.B.

DERBY AND Sheridan sat yawning in a pew in the Chapel Royal at St James's. The crowd had been in their places for two hours.

'So it doesn't bode well,' Sheridan continued in a husky murmur.

'Prinny really said that to the Earl of Malmesbury? *I'm not well, pray get me a glass of brandy?*'

'He was overwhelmed, I tell you, with the stench that rose from his bride's armpits.'

Derby covered his mouth, trying not to laugh. 'But Malmesbury's escorted the Princess all the way from Brunswick. Surely he could have found a moment to have a word?'

Sheridan rolled his eyes. 'He swears he told her maids, he told her dressmakers, he told Caroline herself as bluntly as he dared: said the English and the Prince in particular were very strict on the niceties of feminine hygiene. She'd nod and say *ja, ja, oui, oui,* and call for more music.'

'Do you think Prinny will manage to consummate the marriage?' Derby whispered.

'He'd better. He must get a legitimate heir on her,' muttered Sheridan wrathfully, 'or what's the whole charade been for?'

'Now, about his latest round of debts, Sherry—all £630,000 of them—'

'A deal's a deal,' said Sheridan shortly. 'He marries and Parliament pays the lot.'

Derby was exasperated by his friend's desperate attempts to maintain his grip on the Prince's favour, while staying the darling of the radicals. Sherry and Fox both seemed to cling to the slim hope that the obese and increasingly conservative debauchee, somehow outliving his tough old father, would suddenly remember his fondness for the Foxites.

He gazed around the chapel. English fashions were more and more severe these days; the men were all in black or navy, the women almost inevitably in round-necked straight white dresses, only relieved by little jackets or shawls. He missed the bright silks and vast hats of the '80s. The one improvement, in his view, was that there were more bosoms on show—some of them pushed up as hard as apples. There were many cropped heads on daring young men and more dark heads all round, like his own, he noticed with interest; the tax Pitt had slapped on hair powder in the January budget was having its effects. It wasn't that these people couldn't afford a guinea apiece for a licence, God knew—more that it seemed somehow tasteless to parade one's wealth by wearing wheat powder when the poor were starving because, in the worst winter in living memory and with all trade stifled by the war, a quartern loaf had doubled in price to 12 pence.

He curled his lip, glimpsing 'Citizen' Stanhope, the Earl who'd recently found himself in a minority of one on some vote—having alienated his fellow Foxites—and announced that he was seceding from the Lords. Derby had no patience for principle when it was pushed to the edge of absurdity. If one wasn't doing anything concrete to help one's fellow beings, what was the point of being in politics?

'Did you hear,' Sheridan murmured in Derby's ear with a kind of manic zest, 'our former friend Portland has cashiered Fitzwilliam as Lord-Lieutenant of Ireland after a mere two months, for supporting Catholic emancipation?'

'Fitzwilliam was too hasty,' said Derby, shaking his head. 'The King will never let a Catholic sit in Parliament.'

'Fine, so let's embitter every countryman of mine and push him into the hands of the French,' snapped Sheridan. 'Now Holland's fallen to the Patriots, Pitt's talking of an alliance with Russia and Austria, which will bring on war with Prussia, Sweden, Denmark and Turkey. What a truly diabolical character we're showing to the nations of the world—and how they must detest us. I suspect that if we left them alone they'd all be at peace by now.'

'Lower your voice, there's a good fellow.'

Sheridan made a face at him. 'Don't worry, they'd hardly arrest me in the middle of a wedding. Speaking of which,' he added in an odd tone, 'I'm getting married next Tuesday and I thought of honeymooning in a sloop off Southampton—if you could see your way to a loan.'

Derby stared at his friend.

'I know it's sudden, but Miss Ogle's a wild girl, she hates to waste time.'

'Why, congratulations!' Derby tried to remember what little he knew about Miss Hecca Ogle, daughter of the Dean of Winchester. She was radical in her sympathies, he thought he remembered, and not twenty years old, with strange clothes and a taste for headstrong horses. Really, Sherry was a force of nature; in a matter of years he'd broken his heart for one wife, then lost it to another. While Derby moved as slowly as some iceberg.

'I'll write you a draft on my bank,' he said with a noiseless sigh as he reached for his pocketbook. His investments were suffering this year, as everyone's were, but he'd never had to turn down a friend yet. At Brooks's last night he'd had to pay up the stakes he'd laid a year and a half ago, that Fox would have toppled Pitt and brought in Reform by now. It wasn't the 1500 guineas that stung so much as the humiliation; he'd never made such rash bets before, or caused such widespread amusement.

'You're the soul of decency, you really are,' said Sheridan. 'Especially after my piggish behaviour at Epsom—'

Derby cut off the apology: '—of which I don't care to be reminded.'

There was a bustle at the back of the Chapel. The great surge of organ music made Derby, on impulse, double the sum on the draft before he folded it and handed it to Sheridan. The Archbishop of Canterbury entered in full regalia and the crowd rose like a wave.

Princess Caroline was pleasant-looking enough, though rather too free with giddy smiles that showed her bad teeth. She wore silver tissue and lace, with a robe of velvet lined with ermine; Derby found himself memorising the details to tell Eliza afterwards. The Prince looked like some immense creamy-furred seal. Unsteady on his feet—ill, Derby wondered, or just drunk?—he was helped up the aisle by two dukes, like a man going to his execution.

MAY 1795

This year Eliza let Derby escort her to the Royal Academy's exhibition at Somerset House. She walked on his right, because his left arm was in a sling; at Newmarket last week his carriage had been involved in a tangle with those of the Duke of Bedford, Lord Egremont and Old Queensbury. (She suspected brandy was to blame.)

'There was a terrible kerfuffle at the Academy's annual dinner,' he remarked. 'Fox hadn't remembered to reply to the invitation, so when he turned up late there was no seat for him. He lost his temper and finally Farington wangled him a place at High Table. Now the papers are claiming it was a deliberate slight by Tory artists, *the hallowed Academy has succumbed to party spirit,* that sort of thing!'

'The paintings are a poor lot this year,' said Eliza under her breath. 'I see apocalypse and morbidity are all the rage'—gesturing towards Fuseli's *Odysseus Between Scylla and Charybdis* and his *Nightmare,* in which a demon squatted on the arched bosom of a sleeping woman.

Derby shrugged. '*Bella, horrida bella,* as Virgil says of horrid wars. There's Prinny,' he added, waiting for the royal eye to fall on him before he made his bow.

Eliza dipped into a curtsy. 'He hasn't brought his wife.'

'Oh, they see nothing of each other since he managed to make her *enceinte* on the first night,' Derby assured her. 'The verdict's in: Caroline's incorrigibly vulgar as well as dirty, and barely speaks English.'

Eliza had heard worse: that on the wedding night in question the Princess's manners had not been those of a novice. But that might only be a rumour spread by the machinating Lady Jersey, royal lady-in-waiting, who boasted of having picked a bride Prinny would loathe so that disgust for the wife would ensure constancy to the mistress. Did the Prince regret his bargain, Eliza wondered? Was it true that he'd wept for his betrayal of his Mrs Fitz, his true wife, all the way to his wedding? That lady had gone abroad, they said.

Eliza had no right to judge the Prince harshly; she knew all too well that to survive one would trample anyone underfoot. He was being punished already and not just by the flaws of his wife. Though he'd done his duty, the Commons had proved so resistant to the idea of paying off all his debts again that Pitt had been forced to reduce the Prince's income to less than it had been before the marriage.

'Look, there's Lawrence,' she said, nudging Derby. 'He hasn't really lived up to his youthful promise, has he?'

Tom Lawrence, his face toughened into adulthood, nodded at her and Derby as they approached. Eliza wondered whether he was thinking of the day in his studio, the day he'd molested her. These events loomed large in a woman's life, but often they meant little to men; he might have had scores of sluts since then. 'Mr Lawrence,' she said with a bright smile, 'I saw an interesting advertisement in the *Oracle* the other day, claiming that you're the best painter in England.'

The line had a most satisfying effect; the young man went the purple of dried meat. 'I hope I need not assure you, Miss Farren, that it was none of my doing.'

'Some rash but well-intentioned friend?' asked Derby.

'My father,' said Lawrence, very low. 'He'd formed a notion that I was unfairly neglected by this Academy and by the public at large.'

Lawrence Senior was a publican, Eliza remembered. How mortifying! For all the private battles she and her mother had had over the years—and the last had been the worst—Eliza knew she could trust her absolutely.

When Derby excused himself for a few minutes, to have a word with a fellow horsebreeder, Eliza let herself wander into the small sculpture and prints room. She'd intended to avoid it, but it drew her like an itch.

There, not an arm's length away from her, was Anne Damer, deep in conversation with a small lady with dark hair. Eliza froze. The room was crowded; there was no space to escape at her back. The piece which stood in front of her she recognised now; it was the young lady, Miss Berry. A superb piece in terracotta, Eliza could see that; the lines were quiet and strong.

It wasn't the sculptor who felt her gaze and looked up, it was Miss Berry. 'Miss Farren, I believe?'

Eliza nodded once. It was so rare in the World to be accosted by someone to whom one hadn't been introduced—yet she couldn't accuse this woman of vulgar forwardness. Miss Berry had the air of some fierce bird, rather. And after all, they knew enough of each other not to behave like strangers. 'I recognise you by your portrait,' said Eliza with automatic sweetness, gesturing at the bust.

Anne Damer stood there like a statue. Her eyes moved between them, but she made no attempt to speak. *Oh, come, let's have a civil greeting, since we must,* thought Eliza. But no; the older woman's dignity was absolute. *She won't say a word to me.*

The alarming Miss Berry was making some pertinent remarks on the art of sculpture as practised by the ancients. Eliza managed to contribute something about the Gallic virtuosity of Roubiliac. No doubt she'd picked that up from Anne, she thought with a stab of unease. But the sculptor continued to listen to the whole conversation as if it were taking place on the other side of a window and the rules of the game seemed to require that neither Eliza nor Mary Berry refer to her.

Miss Berry had moved on now to the experience of being sculpted; its many pleasures and its uncomfortable qualities.

'You mean the plaster?'

A look of incomprehension.

Eliza saw she'd made a mistake. 'I only meant...I believe it's sometimes a practice, of...it can happen that a sculptor begins by pasting a thin layer of plaster all over the subject's face.' She soldiered on, aware she was blushing, and hoped the face powder would hide it. As she described the technique she remembered from seven years ago, it sounded mildly obscene. 'Pastes it on so as to form a sort of mask, don't you know.'

'Oh?'

'I believe it's called a life mask,' stammered Eliza. 'To distinguish it from—'

'A death mask. Yes,' said Miss Berry.

Eliza felt extremely stupid.

'But of course, Miss Farren, you've had the experience of sitting for your portrait on many occasions. Do you enjoy it? The being looked at, studied, interrogated, as it were?'

'I... That depends.'

'Do you own any of your portraits?'

Eliza thought of the bust called *Thalia* that was now in a trunk in the garret at Green Street, wrapped in an old sheet. 'One or two,' she said as coolly as she could.

'And do you find them true to life?'

She didn't know how to answer these unsettling questions. 'Less so, as the years go by,' she quipped; 'the marble lasts, but the face ages.'

'On the contrary, I believe that in a portrait like this one'—and Miss Berry suddenly turned to contemplate her own bust—'something is captured, the very essence of the woman, the soul. A part of her that becomes clearer, perhaps, as the charms of girlhood fall away. When I look at this I'll always recognise myself till the day I die.'

'How nice for you,' said Eliza faintly.

Miss Berry gave her a long look before Eliza muttered a farewell and turned to fight her way back into the great saloon. It wasn't a withering glare, Eliza thought, there was more to it than that. There was scorn in it and perhaps a hint of jealousy—but something else as well. Could it be pity?

July 1795

Anne ran across the hall at Park Place and Lady Ailesbury fell against her. They were both thickly swaddled in black lustring; it was like a battle of crows. 'Oh, Mother.'

Only sobs for an answer. Anne glanced over her shoulder; Mary was directing the servants about the baggage.

'Dearest Mother. How are you bearing up?'

'Oh, Anne. Such a saint I've lost! I tell you, living and dying he thought only of me!'

Something about the Countess's remark set her daughter's teeth on edge. Field Marshal Conway hadn't been a saint, but a decent man who cared for many things: his wife, yes, but also his daughter, his dogs, his estate, his country and his dinner.

Lady Ailesbury's whole weight lay across Anne's collarbone. Anne staggered slightly and helped her mother into a chair, which one of the men had pulled out for her. She looked up to thank him. The face had more lines in it, but its broad contours were the same. 'O'Hara!'

The General smiled, then remembered the occasion and sobered again. 'I'm here to pay my respects.'

'Oh, but I'd no idea—I thought you were still in France—' And at the image Anne began to cry. She hadn't wept last night when the news of her father's death had come; she'd only felt a dull ache in her chest and an unreasonable irritation with him for sitting around in wet clothes, at seventy-five, and catching a chill. But now the thought of Charles O'Hara shackled in a French gaol for all this time—with his friends sparing him only the occasional thought—made her sob like a child. She was gripping his hand like a rope that could save her. Even when he sat her down on a chair beside her mother she didn't let go. She heard him talking to the servants, giving firm instructions. 'And here's the lovely Miss Berry,' he remarked, 'who's changed not a whit in the ten or more years since we met in Italy. Do you by any chance recall my face?'

'Of course,' Anne heard Mary say distractedly, 'of course, General; ten years isn't long enough to forget.'

Walpole, who hadn't felt up to visiting Park Place in such a long time, had managed it today. His valet Philip carried him in from the Richmonds' coach, wrapped in a blanket. 'I'm afraid we're a party of invalids,' muttered Lady Mary to her sister, 'with our pills and potions and foot warmers...' Richmond and Walpole were both suffering from gout, and Lady Mary from some of her vague and mysterious ailments; she looked sallow about the eyes.

After the funeral service in the chapel, and the burial, they all drove back to Park Place. The Duchess of Richmond escorted her mother straight to her room. Anne hoped Lady Ailesbury wouldn't take too many drops of laudanum.

She sat downstairs with the few guests who were staying at
Park Place. She felt more tired than anything else. Mary's anxious
dark eyes sought her out and Anne gave her a small smile. Whatever would she have done without her friend's support and decisiveness, ever since she'd got the news?

Charles O'Hara was looking no less handsome for all his sufferings; he joked about having strained the hospitality of the
French nation by eating twice a day at their expense for a year and
a half till his gaolers finally tired of him and exchanged him for
General Rochambeau. Anne felt a pang of relief that she'd never
told anyone about his hinted proposal to her, back in the summer
of '91. Imagine how embarrassing it would have been to sit beside
him here at Park Place in front of people who *knew*.

Walpole, looking more pink-cheeked after an unaccustomed
glass of wine, was bringing the General up to date on British politics. 'Ireland's said to be on the brink of eruption,' he said with
melancholy relish.

Richmond broke in. 'My sister Louisa complains that her lifetime of kindness to the local Catholics has been rewarded with the
basest ingratitude—they join secret societies behind her back, and
she and my other sisters Emily and Sarah have taken to sleeping
with pistols under their beds.'

'Even here in England', Anne told O'Hara, 'there've been bread
riots all this summer—attacks on grain carts, burning of flour
mills—and one Reform meeting in London is said to have at-
tracted a crowd of 100,000!'

'I heard they gave out biscuits,' mentioned Mary.

'Biscuits?' asked the General.

'Yes, with anti-war slogans printed on them,' she told him. 'I
suppose it was thought the poor would pay more attention to a
message if it were edible.'

He let out a booming laugh, then stopped himself, glancing
upwards.

'Don't worry,' said Anne, 'my mother's room is in the west wing and she'll be asleep by now.' She smiled at him. Somehow, meeting again under these peculiar circumstances had freed her from any trace of awkwardness with O'Hara; they were the old friends they'd always been.

Richmond, loosened by brandy, told the humiliating story of his dismissal after more than a decade of tireless service. 'That's Pitt's whole first Cabinet purged in a mere six years. Clearly there's not a single ally he wouldn't sink a knife into,' he concluded bitterly.

The Duchess patted his arm like a mother. 'To be honest, O'Hara,' Richmond went on, 'I dream of retiring altogether, just hunting and sailing my sloop and messing about on the farm. *Il faut cultiver notre jardin,* as Diderot put it.'

Voltaire, Anne silently corrected him.

Walpole spoke shakily about the glorious military career of 'Harry Conway, the dearest friend I ever had. His favourite medicine was magnesia, you know, to purify the blood; you should all try it. I take it every morning.'

Anne mentioned that he'd left a tiny Temple of Harmony unfinished, on the hill; that wouldn't please him. 'I wish you'd had the chance to know my father better,' she told Mary, wiping her eyes.

'One had only to meet Conway once or twice', said O'Hara in his deep growl, 'to know him for a sweet, good man.'

The remark filled her with a wave of gratitude. 'How long can you stay with us, General?'

He made polite noises.

'Oh, now you're here, do grant us a fortnight or more.'

'But you and your family—'

'Believe me, company is just the cordial for our spirits,' she said. 'Miss Berry will be staying a while, won't you?'

'As long as you need me,' said Mary, pressing her shoulder.

Much later Anne and Walpole were the only ones left by the fire. 'I shouldn't keep you from your slumbers,' he said. 'I'm a terrible one for sitting up late.'

'That's all right,' she said, staring into the flames. She didn't like the thought of going into her bedroom and shutting the door. She was one step nearer to death now; the firm barricade of her father had been knocked down.

When Walpole broke the silence his tone was curiously tentative. 'Harry and I had some trouble, once.'

'You quarrelled?' Anne wasn't sure she wanted to hear this, not tonight.

'Oh, no, not trouble between us, no; never that. Fuss with the press, I mean. A trouble shared, a trouble halved, or perhaps doubled, that sort of thing.'

Anne's pulse began to hammer. Could he be tipsy? *What fuss with the press?*

'It was political, of course, these things usually are.'

'What happened?' She sounded too accusatory.

'Oh, the pamphlets, mm,' said Walpole, his gaze inward. 'I'd written an address in defence of your dear father, you see, when he was unjustly dismissed from Lord Grenville's government for opposing some measures of the King's. This was '64, if memory serves—what an eternity ago!—and Harry was one of the first Whigs brave enough to stand up against the encroachments of royal power. I had these *visions'*—Walpole produced the word mockingly—'of your father and me leading a truly just government, if we ever got the chance. At any rate my defence of my dear cousin prompted a wave of vileness from Grub Street. One pamphlet called me *hermaphroditical,*' he said with a tiny laugh, 'said our alliance was an *affaire de coeur.*'

Anne stared at him.

'They claimed I was enrolling in the lists in defence of my first love, for whom I'd harboured an unsuccessful passion for twenty years!'

She had to look away. She'd known that there were rumours about Walpole, of course—sly digs at his manhood, *the Honourable Lady Walpole* and all that—but to learn that he and her own bluff father had been connected in the press... 'Did you issue a denial?' she asked a little hoarsely.

'Not a bit of it,' said Walpole with satisfaction. 'I replied in an open letter, saying that I'd loved Conway for more like thirty years than twenty, and that I saw nothing *unsuccessful* about it.'

Anne loosened into laughter. 'What a neat answer.'

'I thought so.'

'What did my father say about it?'

'The attack, or the defence?'

'Either. Both.'

'D'you know,' said Walpole, 'I don't believe we ever discussed the matter.'

Was he simply telling her an old, painful story, or giving her a message? The face of Eliza Farren flashed in front of her eyes like a warning beacon. As a woman, Anne could hardly rattle off a smart riposte in the form of an open letter. 'My situation is rather different.'

'Oh, quite so,' he assured her. 'My only point is that snide calumny should never be allowed to overshadow the unalterable affections of the heart. We who have a talent for friendship are often persecuted. These sensibilities seem to run in families,' he added, as if to himself.

Anne stared at his bent head. What exactly did he mean by *these sensibilities*? But she didn't want to press him; not tonight, when his face looked far more worn with grief than her own.

'YOU'LL HAVE to take Mother.'

The half-sisters in matching charcoal silk were standing at the gallery window, staring out at the rain-sodden terrace. Anne's head shot round. 'Wait one moment.'

'There's nothing to discuss,' said the Duchess of Richmond. 'It's the only solution.'

Was this her playful, easygoing sister? There were irritable lines round her eyes and not from grief; Lady Mary had liked her stepfather, but not immoderately.

'Mother can't stay here,' Lady Mary went on. 'Park Place is a chilly wasteland without Conway—and an expensive one, may I add. She'd sink into one of her glooms, you know she would.'

'But—'

'Are we to buy her one of those new wooden *companions* they sell in furniture shops—a painted cut-out in the shape of a female friend?'

What a macabre image. Anne folded her arms. 'I've no objection to Mother leaving Park Place,' she said, 'if that's her wish.'

'It should be sold, really. I wonder what it would fetch?'

'Must I remind you', said Anne with a shaking voice, 'that my father is only two days in the ground?'

The Duchess looked a little ashamed of herself.

'Mother could use the house in Soho Square.'

'What, live alone in London? She wouldn't dream of it.'

'It's not such a pathetic way of life,' Anne snapped. 'But if you think the country more suitable, the best home for her would surely be Goodwood, with her married daughter, whom she likes so well.' *Married, childless and idle, with plenty of money and space,* Anne added in her head.

Lady Mary stared at her. 'But my dear, what can you be thinking of? Richmond and I are in such poor health these days—the thing's impossible.'

Anne bit her lip. Only last autumn the Duke had claimed that he and Lady Mary would love Anne to live with them. Had that only been duty, and pity?

'I've lost two stone,' said her sister. 'I suffer from constant rumbling and inflammation, with dark bile; my nerves keep me fidgeting all night.'

'I'm sorry to hear it.' Anne was remembering how stylish and serene Lady Mary had been in the old days at Richmond House.

'No, no, Mother must move in with you at Grosvenor Square, Anne, that's the only thing for it. She won't be any trouble.'

Then why not put her up in one of Goodwood's empty wings? Why not leave me my independence, and my friends, and my art?

'She'll like the stimulus of town; she can pay calls and go to parties.'

Anne had a dreadful picture of herself as the unmarried daughter, shunting her mother from occasion to occasion, carrying both their reticules, reminding her of names, listening to all the familiar stories. *I'm too old for this.*

'So that's settled; I'm glad,' said Lady Mary. It struck Anne that her sister's bland mildness had always concealed this quality of steel. This was ridiculous, Anne should fight back—but she felt too battered after the funeral and a sleepless night. Besides, perhaps this was a matter of conscience. How could Lady Ailesbury find any peace with such a selfish daughter as the Duchess?

'Who's that with Miss Berry in the orchard?' murmured Lady Mary.

Anne followed her eyes. 'O'Hara,' she said, making out the broad shoulders. 'She's showing him the new pear and quince trees.'

'Is she, indeed?' The phrase lingered oddly on the air. 'There's something I want to ask you about Miss Berry.'

Anne's heart seemed to stop for a moment. Was the interrogation to begin at last? Had her friendship with Mary Berry, her intensity, her manner, aroused her sister's disapproval? Anne didn't know whether to bark some retort or flee from the room.

The Duchess was wearing rather a silly smile. 'Do you think he's serious?'

'Serious?'

'Or simply whiling away the summer?'

'I'm at a loss; what are we talking about?'

'Oh, Anne! Really, you're like some stern, oblivious goddess, floating through the mortal throng.' Her sister waited. 'Miss Berry and O'Hara, of course! He's been making *de grands yeux* at her for days.'

Anne sat down, rather fast, and laid her hands on her skirts.

'I do like a romance,' murmured Lady Mary, 'it livens up a visit so. And if both parties have the great luck to be unmarried—why, it suggests some interesting consequences.'

Anne played for time. 'So you think it good luck to be unmarried?'

'Oh, not in a general way, no; I find marriage vastly comfortable,' her sister assured her, arranging her skirts as she sat down at the gilt table. 'I only mean that if the parties in the romance are already married to other people, their attraction must remain a mere flirtation, or risk becoming dangerous. Whereas in the case of the General and your friend there's no such barrier. They're both entirely free, I think?'

'I...I can't answer for him,' said Anne, 'but Miss Berry has no suitor. As far as I'm aware.'

'I think you'd know, you're such intimates.' Lady Mary laughed. 'So I return to my question: do you think O'Hara's serious?'

A strange impulse of honesty made Anne say, 'It wouldn't surprise me if he were looking for a wife.'

'Yes, he'll need one where he's going. It seemed at first as if the ministers here were slighting the General, because they gave the governorship of Gibraltar to someone else, but that man's dropped dead, so O'Hara's to have it after all. I wonder how Miss Berry will like the climate?'

Gibraltar. Anne felt it like a blow to the stomach. So far away. She wanted to be alone, in her room, with the door locked. She'd failed to spot the pattern, pick up the signals. It was as if she'd sat through four acts of *Othello* under the impression that it was *Twelfth Night.* Could her sister be imagining the whole thing?

'He's only known Miss Berry a matter of days, of course, but that can be long enough.'

'No,' said Anne, 'my father first introduced them many years ago in Italy.'

SEPTEMBER 1795

When Anne thought of Conway she felt a dull sort of sadness, but she didn't think of him very often. She was more preoccupied with her mother, in whom widowhood was taking the form of a twitching, whining nervousness. Lady Ailesbury—once the supreme patroness of Rousseau and Madame Kauffmann—now couldn't bear to be alone. She had less of a head for business than any woman Anne knew. The aged Countess knew that Park Place had to be sold—and the last thing she wanted to do was to stay on there alone—but it was Anne who had to take the matter in hand and find an interested party: the Earl of Malmesbury. At least it gave her an excuse to go up early to London, where she met with Malmesbury's agent. Lady Ailesbury only agreed to stay in Park Place for the moment once Anne had found a young female cousin to keep her company.

Anne felt suffocated by filial duty. One good thing: it drove her to her workshop again for the first time in a year and she began a clay model for a self-portrait. Her face seemed strange to her, somehow. She worked hard to trace her own sharp contours, struggling to get flexibility back into her fingers.

She rarely went out. She didn't feel like cards, or conversation, and she never went to the theatre now, even Covent Garden, because it conjured up memories of Eliza Farren. The city was uneasy; the windows of no. 10 Downing Street had been smashed, something to do with the harvest. *Lock your doors, I pray you, for my sake,* Walpole wrote from the seclusion of Strawberry Hill. *Have you heard the mob's latest battle-cry? No Famine, no War, no Pitt, no King!*

The Berrys had spent much of September in Cheltenham, taking the waters, for their health; several of Mary's letters mentioned that they'd seen O'Hara there. Anne read the casual phrases again and again. When the Berrys came back to Little Strawberry, Walpole mentioned to Anne that the General had developed a healthful habit of rowing up the river to Twickenham.

One day she was ready. She sat down opposite Mary in the library at Little Strawberry and said, 'You're hurting me.'

Mary jerked in her seat.

'Do you think to spare me by your silence? Candour's the root of friendship; how can I be a true friend if you won't tell me what's in your heart?'

The small woman had gone pale under the hail of questions. 'Is this about...O'Hara?'

'Whom else? Unless you've a whole roster of suitors you've failed to mention,' added Anne viciously.

'Oh, Anne.' Mary's head sank down on to her hands.

She waited.

'I wanted, but I didn't dare to blurt anything out until I was sure; my spirits quailed. It seemed so...so vain and foolish to presume anything till something was said. It's such a peculiar business.'

Anne made herself say it. 'Courtship, you mean?'

Mary shrank from the word. 'I've no experience. No wisdom. I never thought I was at risk, at the advanced age of thirty-two! How it must look—a penniless female—a distinguished war hero—'

She couldn't stand for that. She seized Mary's left hand. 'You worried how it might look to whom—to the World? But why didn't you tell me? I'd never judge you harshly. What do I care whether you've a fortune or not? I'm sure O'Hara doesn't.'

Mary's eyes were huge and inky. 'That's exactly what he said.'

Anne winced. 'When?'

'Yesterday, on the lawn here, under the mulberry tree. That's when it happened.' Her voice was exalted. 'Before that there was nothing definite I could have told you; it was all a matter of sub-tleties of impression; a certain atmosphere.'

'He followed you to Cheltenham,' said Anne flatly, 'then he fol-lowed you back to Twickenham.'

'He was in both places, yes, but I didn't like to draw any con-clusions,' Mary twittered like a schoolgirl. 'But yesterday, under the mulberry tree—oh, Anne!'

She couldn't look into those shining eyes. She stared at the table. There was some old tag singing in her head: *Every man shall have his maid, every Jack his Jill.* One thing she was glad of: that she'd never told Mary about that day, four summers ago, when O'Hara had seemed on the brink of proposing to her. 'He put the question?'

No answer, only a letting out of breath.

'And you accepted him.'

Mary burst out laughing.

Anne stared at her.

'Oh, I'm sorry,' whooped Mary, 'I don't know what's come over me. It's just the relief of telling you, my dearest.'

'Yes.'

'The only proposal I ever received in my life and that it should be from him. From Charles O'Hara!' Her voice was worshipful.

I'm lacking something, Anne thought, *some vital female attribute. I've never said a man's name that way in my life. My best years are over and I've never known this happiness.* Then she shut down her mind and began to perform the role that had been appointed to her. Somehow she knew all the lines. 'I'm so glad, my dear, so very glad,' she said.

It must have sounded convincing, because Mary pulled her hand over and kissed her on the knuckle. 'I thought you would be, Anne. I hoped. I couldn't be sure—'

'How could you have doubted me?'

'Well, it's all so new and uncertain. We've been corresponding, a little, myself and the General, I mean, but it's difficult to do without attracting attention. Our future is one great blank. I'm very much hoping he'll be offered some high command here—'

Mary sounded like a wife already, Anne thought; that tone of proprietorial anxiety. She lashed out. 'Oh, but haven't you heard? It's to be Gibraltar.'

'Gibraltar?'

'They mean to send him back as Governor.' Mary blanched and Anne twisted the knife. 'You must have known that they might send him anywhere in the Empire. In the past he's served all over the globe, from America to India.'

'But—'

'Don't tell me you never thought that this marriage would mean parting from your father, your sister, Walpole—'

'From *you.*' Mary's face was striped with tears. 'Oh, my darling, how could I bear to go so far away from you?'

OCTOBER 1795

Anne was very busy with her investigation. 'Continue corresponding with the General,' she urged Mary, 'but commit yourself no further and ask him for details of his future plans.' Meanwhile she pumped Walpole for old stories about O'Hara, the war hero who'd somehow emerged unscathed from such brutal captivity; she did the same with Richmond when he called for a glass of Madeira on one of his trips to town. (The Duke claimed he was needed at the Lords, but Anne had become aware of something in the air between him and his old friend Lady Bess at Devonshire House. She knew there was no sense in being shocked by this; her sister had never demanded fidelity, even when she'd been in the full of her health.) In Anne's almost daily letters to Lady Ailesbury—who was full of complaints about the wetness of the weather and the laxity of the maids—she encouraged her mother to reminisce about old friends including Lord Tyrawley, O'Hara's father.

After a fortnight Anne was ready. She steeled herself with a line from an old book, she couldn't remember which: *Marriage is the grave of friendship*. She came to North Audley Street at a time when she knew the other Berrys would be out window-shopping and accepted a cup of tea. 'I've been looking into the matter, my dear, and I must tell you: I'm not happy.'

Mary stopped chewing plum cake and put down her fork.

'I don't mean to alarm you,' said Anne, opening her memorandum book, 'but I feel you should make this decision—the most serious of all decisions—with open eyes.'

Mary nodded fervently. 'Tell me. Tell me everything you know.'

Anne consulted her list. 'Well. In many ways, at first, it looks like a good match. You must know about O'Hara's birth.'

'Yes, that it was illegitimate,' said Mary bravely, 'but his father has always acknowledged him.'

'Nothing's known about the mother; you'll have to ask him that yourself.'

Mary's teeth held her small red lip.

'In all justice, the sins of the fathers shouldn't be visited on the children, but it's ever been so.' Anne sighed. 'O'Hara must feel it very much, of course, poor fellow—since your own parentage is impeccable. Now, as to his education…'

'He's a soldier,' said Mary. 'One can't expect him to have the manners or tastes of a gentleman of leisure.'

Anne nodded. 'The question is whether his intrinsically good character has been tarnished by a life in the army.'

'He's told me he used to be careless about money,' Mary volunteered, 'that's why he went abroad in the early '80s.'

'I'm thinking more of…private matters.'

The euphemism made Mary look away.

'Apparently his nickname in Gibraltar is *Old Cock of the Walk*,' Anne pronounced squeamishly. 'Of course, a man of his years can't be expected to come *pure* to his wedding, but it's to be hoped that the General isn't as steeped in vice as the average soldier. I couldn't bear to think of your health, as well as your happiness, being put at risk.'

Mary nodded, faintly purple.

'Also, there was one incident I heard of, I hate to mention it to you and perhaps it's unfair—'

'What? What incident?'

She sighed. 'O'Hara beat a man. The fellow nearly died.'

Mary put her hand over her mouth.

'I'm sorry to be the one to tell you.'

'Perhaps it was a punishment, one he was ordered to give,' she said shakily.

'I wish the General nothing but good and I like him immensely,' Anne told her, tasting treachery sharp on her breath. 'I simply feel it's important for you to know the man you would be marrying.'

'Not *would be*, but *will*,' Mary reminded her. 'I've given him my word.'

Anne kept her mouth shut.

'What else have you got there in your little book?' She was trying to read Anne's handwriting upside down.

Anne snapped it shut. 'The other factors you need to consider are peculiar to your own situation. Are you confident that your father and sister will be able to manage their affairs without you in England, and do without your encouragement and your daily care?'

Mary shook her head and a tear spangled in her eye.

'Then there's Walpole.'

'I fear he'll have an apoplexy when I tell him,' said Mary. 'The very thought of me settling so far off, in a tiny British colony, a fortress really, in wartime...'

'My dear Mary,' Anne said tentatively, as if stroking a wild animal, 'I suspect from your tone that you begin rather to regret having accepted O'Hara's proposal? It was somewhat impulsive,' she rushed on, forestalling an answer, 'some would even say rash; you might have asked him for the usual period to consider the matter. But nothing's quite settled yet, you see. You mustn't feel trapped.'

Mary kept shaking her head.

'Don't let your exquisite scruples lead you astray on this occasion,' Anne urged her. 'Just because you were prevailed upon, hurried into saying yes, it doesn't mean you're honour bound to go through with it. If, after mature reflection, your heart shrinks from this engagement—'

'But it doesn't.' Mary spoke very firmly. 'Anne, you misunderstand me. I admit to qualms—to downright terrors. But I love the man.'

The silence stretched out like a web.

'If this is the worst of him'—she gestured at the notebook—'then it makes no difference. He's won me. You've never asked if I love him,' said Mary with a curious smile. 'We've talked about every other aspect of the thing. Perhaps you know me so well that you haven't needed to ask. Does my face betray me when I speak of him?'

'Your eyes,' said Anne, barely audible. 'And when you sit beside him listening to his stories you look like Desdemona.'

THAT NIGHT Anne sat at her toilette, brushing out her hair, which still hadn't a single streak of grey in it. She met her own gaze. And she thought, *That's what's changed since I was a girl: my forehead is harder.* She would have to put that in her sculpture. Also, her jaw had a leaden angle to it these days; it looked like desperation.

Sick of the sight of herself she turned away and went to sit on the edge of the bed. She heard it like a voice in her head: *I am what they call me.*

It was strange how quickly these revelations could strike when they came at last after years, after decades, after a lifetime. Like the Greek philosopher in his bath, crying out *Eureka, I have found it.* Or no, more like Monsieur Marat in his bath of blood, stabbed to death by a girl. That was what Anne felt like now; one sudden blow and a helpless draining away.

Consider the facts, she told herself like her first tutor, Hume; *never be afraid to expose your ideas to empirical observation.* Fact: she had spent the last several weeks plotting against the happiness of her best friend. Fact: she was motivated not by concern or caution, but by panic and greed. Anne couldn't bear Mary to go off to Gibraltar and leave her behind. She didn't want her to marry at all, come to that, not even a gentleman who lived in Mayfair. She realised now that for years she'd assumed Mary was a natural-born spinster who'd never change her condition. *Assume nothing,* ordered the philosopher in her head. The thought of Mary's wedding filled Anne with a sort of nauseous, shaking chill. *It's all wrong*—but she knew what she really meant was *Don't go. Stay with me, be by my side. What can he give you that I can't?*

She pressed her fingers into her bony forehead. There were words for women like her, women who saw all the natural attractions of a man like Charles O'Hara and were left cold. Women who asked for more than had been allotted to them. Women who became fixated on shallow, glamorous actresses. Women who loved their female friends not generously but with a demanding, jealous ruthlessness; women who got in the way of good marriages and thwarted nature. There were words for such propensities—hidden inclinations—secret tastes—and she knew them all, had heard them all already.

What was it Walpole had murmured after the Field Marshal's funeral? *These sensibilities seem to run in families.* Was that a sort of confession? Did he mean that Anne wasn't just his cousin and his godchild, but his daughter under the skin?

She was very cold. She shed her shoes and got under the blankets, still fully dressed; she shuddered. Was she ill, she wondered, could knowledge act like a poison, throwing the whole body out of joint? *Oh, God, it can't be true.* But how could she deny it? She'd only ever loved women. Such warmth as she'd felt for men—Walpole, O'Hara, Fawkener, Derby even—had been purely comradely. She'd never loved John Damer, nor seriously considered marrying again. It had always been women who stirred her imagination. How abjectly she'd clung to Eliza for all those years. How fierce her grip on Mary now. This wasn't friendship, it was its darker shadow. It had all the qualities of passion; it was as selfish, as unstable, as dangerous as what men felt for women.

No, not that. She rolled over violently, tangling her legs in the sheets. What she felt was unreasonable, but it wasn't carnal. Anne had never done the things the journalists said of her, never gone further than a kiss; she'd never even dreamed of doing them. It wasn't a matter of urges of the flesh, not for her, at least; it wasn't the sordid, simpering thing they hinted about in the papers. But this much she knew: she was experiencing something terrible. She was trying to hold on to Mary, to bind her, to possess her. And for this she would be punished.

THE KING was going to open Parliament today and Derby wanted to park his carriage outside the Banqueting House to get a good view of the procession from St James's as it came down Whitehall. But the traffic was already so clogged that he told the driver to let him off at Charing Cross and pick him up again in an hour.

'Shouldn't you take both the footmen, My Lord?'

'No, no, one will do,' said Derby, stepping down.

Even with the man clearing the way, oak staff in hand, it took Derby some time to walk down Whitehall and he began almost to wish he'd stayed at home in Mayfair. Graffiti spattered every other wall; it was like being trapped in a printing press, he thought absurdly. The streets seemed filthier than ever. Already his white stockings were spattered and these shoes would have to be donated to his valet. The crowd had a sullen and mutinous air, considering they were gathered to watch a procession. But then, this had been the second dreadful harvest in a row, and Derby had had to set up soup kitchens at Preston and Liverpool. A handbill was pushed into his fingers and he glanced at it—*our Commons is corrupt, our Lords useless, our Judges murderous*—before letting it join the muddy morass underfoot. The thing was he would have difficulty rebutting any of the charges.

Derby's footman found him a prime position on the steps of a corner house on Parliament Street, just in time. Already the glinting string of vehicles was making its way down Whitehall. The usual chants were starting to rise: 'Peace not war!'

'Bread not famine!' As the royal carriage turned its golden mass, with difficulty, and rolled into Parliament Street at a snail's pace, the narrow head of George III could be seen in the window, nodding stiffly to his subjects. Derby's ears could pick out some new slogans now: 'Down with tyrants,' roared a man behind him, making him jump. 'No Pitt, No George!'

Come, this is going rather too far, he thought uneasily. It was more like a Parisian crowd than a London one. Where was the usual outpouring of loyal sentiment? he wondered.

'Down with George! Off with his head!' A woman beside Derby was screaming the words at regular intervals, as if in labour. Some clods of mud and miscellaneous turds smacked the royal carriage. Derby's footman cast him an anxious look, but he ignored it; best to sit tight till the fuss was over. He reminded himself of an insight of Fox's, the other night, over a bottle of sherry: freedom of speech could sound alarming, but it was a great valve for releasing pressure in hard times like these. The English liked to have their say, loudly and sometimes rudely, but there was no harm in them.

And then it happened. Quite soundless, or rather, the tiny sound was drowned in the noises of the crowd. All Derby saw was the window of the gold carriage implode. First one pane starred, then another and the puppet profile had disappeared; the King was down.

God Almighty, what have we done?

Derby only had time for that thought before the mob surged like a dirty river bursting its banks and he was knocked to his knees. When he got up from the bottom step, with painful effort, he couldn't find his footman. He brushed vainly at the mud crusted on his breeches. He pushed through the bodies, beginning to panic; he was too short to see his way. Where could his footman have got to? A man with stumps in dirty bandages for arms shoved Derby out of the way. A fat woman spat on his lapel. *Assassination,* the word hissed in his head till it was meaningless. His knees hurt. *The Republic of Britain.*

'Argh!' Derby reeled, almost fell. His hand flew up to his cheek and came away bloody. He couldn't tell who'd struck him, or with what weapon. The pain was staggering; he thought part of his face had been stove in. His blood was as shiny as holly berries. So real. Not cock's blood or horse's blood but Edward Smith-Stanley's, dripping down his cravat, marking the cobbles.

Shock gave way to terror. It could have been anybody who'd hit him. *You're an aristocrat, for Christ's sake,* he told himself, *what are you playing at? You've no friends here.* He spun round desperately, looking for a way out, but ragged coats and red faces hemmed him in on all sides. Chaos smelt of bodies and fish and shit, tasted metallic as his own blood. *Get out, get out,* said a voice in his head, *before they string you from a lamp-post.*

NOVEMBER 1795

'It wasn't even an airgun pellet,' said Sheridan, swigging the vintage brandy like small beer, 'only a few pebbles. And I have it on good information that it wasn't Reformers who threw them, anyway, but Pitt's agents provocateurs.'

'Oh, Sherry, you always blame government agents,' Fox teased him.

Derby sat mutely beside them in the library at Derby House, nursing his drink. The bandages were gone; his cheekbone was navy-blue and green. Grosvenor Square was dark through the gap in the curtains.

'Apparently he reacted with marvellous calmness,' remarked Fox, 'and picked up a pebble from the floor as a souvenir, before being driven on to the Commons. I suppose the old rat quails at nothing, having survived wars, madness and thirty-five years on the throne already!'

'I don't know; I heard he told Lord Eldon he suspects he'll be the last king of England.' Sheridan smirked.

Derby was finding his friends' flippancy revolting. The whole city was the same. Habeas corpus had been suspended again and cavalry brought in from Cornwall, but it made little difference to the cacophony that was London. All down Whitehall boys were selling fragments of what they claimed was the royal carriage's window glass for sixpence apiece.

'But now to business, my lads,' said Fox, pulling a bundle of papers out of his pocketbook. 'These Gagging Acts of Pitt's, to preserve what they're calling *homeland security*—I've obtained the gory details. The Seditious Meetings Bill will be introduced in the Commons and what it boils down to is that if you hold a meeting of more than fifty, a magistrate can send in the troops to shut it down, and it specifies that he'll bear no responsibility for *any deaths that may result!*'

'That's a licence to kill,' said Sheridan, wild-eyed.

'Then, Derby, in the Lords it'll be up to you and Bedford and the others to tackle the Treasonable Practices Bill, which allows transportation or execution for anyone who publishes anything that possibly *could* incite discontent against King or government. I want you to start by proposing a rake of amendments—and meanwhile we'll be organising a national campaign of petitions—'

'I don't think so,' said Derby quietly.

Fox blinked at him. 'You're dubious about our strategy?'

'I'm dubious about letting traitors go free.'

The silence in the study was thick, like smoke.

'Uh-oh,' murmured Sheridan. 'How's that scratch, Derby? Stinging, is it?'

Derby stared at him. 'You weren't there.'

A comical shrug. 'What can I say? Young wives are demanding.'

'Neither of you was there.'

'The King wasn't hurt,' Fox put in gently.

Derby swatted that away like a wasp. 'You didn't see the anarchy, the utter rabid madness of that crowd. It was—what's that new word?—*terrorism*. We've always boasted that there couldn't be an English revolution. Well, let me tell you we've been fools!'

'For a famous cocker your stomach's not so strong after all,' said Sheridan mildly. 'One little riot and you're Torified overnight. I've attended operas where more blood was shed!'

Fox held up his hands to keep the peace. 'Sherry, no need for insults. My dear Derby, I respect your views, now as always.'

A snort from Sheridan.

'But we can't let Pitt take advantage of this distressing incident to turn the country into one great prison. He's the true *terrorist*; he rules by the politics of threat and panic.'

Derby looked into his glass, exhausted.

'I need every man I've got, especially in the Lords. All I ask,' said Fox with a trembling lip, 'all I entreat is that you consider—'

The footman announced Mrs and Miss Farren. The men jumped up to take their leave and Derby didn't stop them.

He tried to rouse himself enough to make chit-chat with Eliza and her mother; they discussed the new comedy she was starring in, opposite Mrs Jordan (quite harmoniously, to her surprise), and his daughter Charlotte's protracted courting by a cousin in Westmoreland. (If the wedding went ahead, Miss Farren was to be bridesmaid; the girl had made the suggestion herself.) He thought he was doing rather well when Eliza broke a brief silence to ask,

'Did we interrupt a quarrel? Fox and Sheridan were scowling on their way out.'

Derby sighed. Her bright eyes waited.

'My dear,' murmured her mother, 'perhaps you shouldn't interfere with the gentlemen's business.'

'Alas, Mrs Farren,' he said, 'politics has become everyone's business.' As briefly as he could he explained what the matter was.

'Your injury's changed you,' observed Eliza.

'Oh, it's only a bruise,' he said, feeling foolish as he scratched his cheek.

'I meant the blow to your pride.'

Derby wasn't sure he liked the sound of that. 'To be caught up in that frenzied attack on the King's carriage', he said unsteadily, 'was one of the most ghastly experiences of my life.'

'Oh, I believe you,' said the actress. 'That's my point. It seems to have done what all the French horrors never managed: scared you out of your love of liberty.'

Sometimes, he thought, *this woman could do with a good smack.*

'Eliza,' said Mrs Farren, getting to her feet, 'His Lordship must be tired...' Her daughter ignored her.

'What I love', he said hoarsely, leaning his elbows on his knees, 'I don't cease to love. No matter what.'

She nodded gravely.

'I'm Fox's man and I'll fight these damned Gagging Acts, but I don't know. I don't know what'll become of us all.'

She was still nodding as she rose to her feet. 'You'll do what's right. Good night, My Lord.'

'Good night, ladies.'

ANNE AND MARY were walking in the orchard at Strawberry Hill, the last fallen leaves like splashes of bright paint on the brown layers beneath. 'These are such uncertain times, what can one trust but one's own heart?' asked Anne. 'Yes, there are obstacles, but such a deserving love will sweep them all aside.'

'Oh, my dear, you've been such a help to me and to the General—Charles—as well,' said Mary. 'Letting us correspond discreetly via your house, and keeping my spirits up, and soothing all my worries about the future…'

'Well,' said Anne, tasting the bile of sacrifice, 'O'Hara's very dear to me.' She felt like a traitor, though God knew she had no treacherous intentions. She'd stamped down the secret, greedy part of herself and to punish it—and as a silent sacrifice to Mary—she was watching over this engagement like a stern guardian angel.

'When those I love, love each other, I feel wrapped in a sort of blissful cocoon,' Mary assured her.

Anne suddenly thought of their first real conversation, in this garden more than five years ago. How tough-minded, how austere the young Mary had seemed. Now she was a tremulous fiancée. Still herself—but declining inevitably towards ordinary womanhood.

'I still don't know how I'll bear to go to Gibraltar when the time comes,' said Mary, shiny-eyed. 'Quite apart from my family— you've been my constant companion for so long, Anne; it'll be very strange and hard to bear.'

'Many authors call correspondence the meat of friendship,' said Anne, looking hard at a wizened apple on a branch. 'We've done it before.'

'But that was only for a year. We knew we'd see each other again,' said Mary miserably.

'Gibraltar's not Timbuktu,' Anne said crisply.

A WEEK later she learned that the protection of the fleet had been arranged, and General O'Hara was to sail for his new post at once.

Oh, my dearest M.,
has the parting lacerated your heart? Don't despair; it won't be too long before your reunion. I'm sure O'H. is not really angry, only disappointed that you won't go with him directly. But he can hardly expect you to take the most serious step of your life with so little notice. I know he was moved that you managed to

come to town (on the excuse of meeting me) to let him press you to him one last time. After you'd left Grosvenor Square he spoke of you with a soldier's tenderest passion. Console yourself that this enforced separation will keenly impress upon O'H. how superior you are to every other woman in the World!

I do agree that you should endeavour to put your father's business affairs on a better footing before you go & also that Ag. requires your care at this difficult juncture. May I ask, do you think the gentleman in question sincere, or is he toying with her affections? It seems strange to me that neither Ag. nor your father has formed the least suspicion of your engagement—but none are so blind as those who won't see. The same could be said for W., who behaves as if you've nothing better to do with your life than polish & label his cabinet of curiosities! Remember what you owe yourself, Mary, after so many years—decades!— of taking care of others. Is it not time to be free?

I'm endeavouring to pack up my parents' possessions here at Park Place, with my best esprit d'ordre. I fear I spent too long on my knees arranging my father's papers, for this morning I found my leg (on which I'd omitted to put the poultice) so bad that I had difficulty getting downstairs. Today I am taking care to sit well wrapped up as I go through the accounts of the Lavender Distillery.

Such a dismal east wind, cutting through the evergreens & pressing against the windows! I won't regret P. P. much. There's something of eternal storm about it in the winter. But it was my dear father's pride. The trees, all planted & improved under his hands, will now perhaps be mangled or felled...

'Do try to eat some beef, Mother,' Anne said at dinner.

'I've no appetite,' said Lady Ailesbury, averting her head. 'How can I eat in such a melancholy situation, when my whole life is being packed into boxes?'

Anne thought of a sharp answer, but swallowed it.

Mary's letter came from Twickenham the next day.

I wake every morning after three or four hours of broken slumber, to the melancholy knowledge of an uncertain & painful absence from O'H. Perhaps I could be ready to go to him in the spring, or join him at his next home leave?

I think I've done right to delay, for the sake of the peace and happiness of my near ones, not for my own. I hope he'll hereafter love me better for knowing me capable of such sacrifice. But in the meantime I am here & he (who's already suffered so much for our country, so bravely) is far away on a dangerous sea. I begged him in case of illness or attack by the French to send me some token that he thought of me to the last.

When I had to rush away from my last meeting with O'H., I knew that you could explain my feelings better than I could. He calls you the Dear Stick, because you're so tall & such a prop—& he wishes there were some way to repay all you've done for us.

A long engagement at least will give us time to test our affection & to plan our future life. I enclose an estimate of our household expenses, as if we were to set up in London, though I hope Gibraltar will be considerably cheaper. Will you cast your eye over it?

Allowance for O'H.	£800
Housekeeping (victuals et cetera)	£480
Rent and taxes	£200
Allowance for me	£200
One pair of horses & coachman's wages	£150
Wine	£100
Liveries for the Menservants	£80
Housekeeper, cook, housemaid, lady's maid	£58
One Upper Manservant	£55
Coals	£50
Two Lower Manservants	£40
Candles	£25
	£2238 per annum

I've tried to be modest but not shabby. I must confess I have no idea whether O'H. (aided by the meagre amount my father will be able to offer) can afford this.

O'H. fears that W. will look unfavourably on the match for O'H.'s lack of birth & wealth; do you agree? I thought of asking you to break the awful news to W. for me, but O'H. says that would be childish, I must do it (but with you to lean on, Dear Stick!)

If only we were not to be parted by this marriage—you & I. I believe I can steel myself to bear anything but that.

Reading the letter for the third time, Anne wondered if she was imagining a sort of message between the lines. *He wishes there were some way to repay you.* For years, now, the war had kept her confined to England; Doctor Fordyce had said only the other day that she'd never be quite well in this damp climate. What about Gibraltar? *If only we were not to be parted by this marriage—you and I.* As Governor, O'Hara would be given a handsome residence; surely there'd be plenty of room for three? It wouldn't be the first time that a married couple had invited a female friend to stay with them, perhaps to make a permanent home with them. *Not to be parted.* There were the Devonshires. Such an arrangement happened in some novels, like Rousseau's *Julie.* The thing was unusual, but not impossible, surely?

For a moment, Anne imagined a paragraph in the newspapers. She was too familiar with that leering language.

We have received intelligence that a certain Sculptress has taken flight to Southern shores. Her most intimate friend, lately Miss B., now wife to the G——r of G——r, has flung wide her Doors...

Anne shoved the thought away. Some time this year she'd come to the conclusion that she'd drive herself mad if she let herself worry about how others saw her.

———

ANNE PROCEEDED very cautiously. She still had no idea whether O'Hara had ever heard the rumours about herself and Mary. Perhaps he'd laughed them off, or discounted them out of loyalty; she knew how much he liked her and he'd believe nothing bad of his beloved Mary. She reread his letters to her.

> *Your soothing care & affectionate solicitude for the dear inim-*
> *itable, places you, my dear Mrs D., in the inmost chamber of my*
> *heart—where the dear Mary, seated* en souveraine, *courts you*
> *to remain with her for ever. There, folded in her arms, her throb-*
> *bing breast pressed to yours will mutely thank you for us both.*

The image unsettled Anne. There was something papist about it: the Virgin on her throne. *Courts you to remain with her for ever.* Was that an invitation? Had O'Hara guessed that Anne wanted to come to Gibraltar and make her home with them? Or was this letter simply a showy bit of rhetoric?

Mary was edgy; the secrecy was weighing on her. Because the war was disrupting shipping, some crucial letters appeared to have got lost en route. This seemed a tumultuous, uncomfortable courtship—but then, what did Anne know of love matches? The couple seemed unable to resolve either practical questions, such as what would be their income, or ineffable ones, such as how O'Hara could make it up to Mary for all the loved ones she'd be leaving behind.

When one day on the Mall Anne finally allowed herself to hint that she would consider moving to Gibraltar, Mary went into a flood of tears. 'Oh, but—it's the most marvellous, most extraordinary idea,' she said, mopping at her eyes. 'Would you really be willing to give up everything—your house, your mother's company, your friends here in England—and come with us, all for the sake of friendship?'

Would she? Without a glance behind. Lady Mary would simply have to take in their mother; Anne could say Fordyce had insisted her health required the move. 'In my experience of friendship,' she said, 'it's as sacred a tie as all those other duties and connections.' It was starting to drizzle again; Anne put up her umbrella over them and tucked her arm into Mary's, though not without the usual prickling feeling that they might be being watched. 'What I feel for you—and for O'Hara', she said, smooth as milk, 'seems to me to outweigh everything else. But you mustn't tell him yet,' she warned.

'Why not?' Mary smiled up at her. 'It would relieve so much of his anxiety about my future happiness.'

'Oh, the General has enough on his mind, preparing a home for *one* lady. Besides, I wouldn't dream of coming till you two are comfortably established. I wouldn't intrude on newlyweds,' she added with a sharp little laugh.

'Must there be an interval, really?' Mary's mouth turned down and she held Anne's arm tightly as the rain fell more heavily. 'My spirits are chafing at all this delay. Let's take the first ship in the morning!'

Anne laughed with her. There was nothing she would rather do. In ten days, given fair winds, she could be at work on the marble version of her self-portrait under the yellow Spanish sun. She would have left England, with all its damps and chills, its sneering newspapers and starving mobs, far behind her.

MARCH 1796

Derby sat in an armchair in Eliza's dressing room, examining the mud stains on his creamy leather boots. 'The new tax on inheritance means that when Edward succeeds me he'll have to pay the government £1 in every £50. That's 2 percent of the entire Derby fortune!'

Mrs Farren, eyes on her needle, made a dutifully shocked hiss.

Eliza didn't see that it was such a terrible thing for a little cream to be skimmed off the top, but of course she wasn't tactless enough to say so. She was preoccupied with her paint; the shadows on her eyelids were too dark for the lovable prattler she was to play, even if it was a turgid melodrama. 'Perhaps by then there'll be a Whig administration and the tax will be repealed.'

'There's less chance of that than of a thaw in Siberia.'

She smiled at that, though it was nothing to smile at, and scrubbed at her cheeks with a sponge.

'By the time Prinny's little Princess Charlotte has learned to walk this government will have become absolute and we'll be forced on to our knees to worship Pitt as the new Caesar. Oh,' said Derby, brightening, 'on a different subject, have you seen our latest brush with fame?' He opened his watered silk pocketbook and drew out an engraving.

She assumed by *our* he meant the Foxites'. But the print showed Derby and herself sitting in a theatre box in old-fashioned clothes, with *Derby and Joan* written over their heads. The play they were watching was identified as *The Constant Couple*.

'Surprisingly mild,' said Eliza, examining it for any crude details she'd missed.

'Isn't it?' said Derby with a grin. 'I think we may have outlived our critics.'

Eliza pulled out her watch. 'I hate to push you out, Derby, but it'll soon be first call—'

'Yes, My Lord,' said Mrs Farren, scolding him like a mother, 'it's time you were in your box.'

'Of course,' he said, hopping up. He was still rather sprightly for a man with a gouty foot. 'Sherry says he's paid Colman through the nose to adapt this *Iron Chest* from *Caleb Williams*, because it's a sure hit.'

'Huh!' Eliza knew he was playing for time, unwilling to leave her dressing room; it was rather endearing. 'The play's well named, for my money; it's going to sink like a lead coffin. Colman's gutted the story of all its radical politics and set it in the early 1600s, so the Lord Chamberlain can't interpret it as a commentary on our unjust society and ban the thing! And everything that could go wrong has. This foul weather gave our brilliant young composer a cold—you know Storace?—but he insisted on crawling up from his sickbed for rehearsal, where he passed it on to Kemble. Who refuses to give up this plum role to Palmer, but insists on playing the morbid Mortimer with a cough like a cat with hairballs,' she added satirically. 'And Colman caught the cold next, so no one's made the necessary cuts and rehearsals have been a complete shambles.'

'I'm sure you exaggerate,' said Derby. 'Besides, your brilliance will pull it all together.'

She sighed. 'If I were you, My Lord, I'd spend the evening tucked up by the fire at your club.'

He laughed and kissed Eliza's cold hand, before he headed off to the boxes corridor.

William Powell, the careworn prompter, put his head in the door. 'Be patient with the musicians tonight, Miss Farren, they don't have a conductor. Storace's dead of his cold.'

'No!'

'A boy just came with a note from the widow.'

He was thirty-three, like me, remembered Eliza. *Poor wretch.* 'Mr Powell,' she said, standing up with sudden decisiveness, 'you know as well as I do that *The Iron Chest* won't play. It's running at almost four hours.'

'Then you'll all have to speak faster,' he said, straight-faced.

'Tell Sheridan he must give out *Much Ado* instead.'

'Kemble says it'll play,' said Powell grimly.

'But he's half delirious from those opium pills he's dosing himself with.'

A tired shrug. 'Oh, we've had to transpose the first two scenes in Act Two,' Powell said over his shoulder, at the door, 'because the carpenters say they need ten minutes to replace the Abbey scene with the Library.'

Eliza put her hand over her face, then remembered her paint and lifted it carefully away.

The wings were crowded; the cast numbered eighteen men and five women. Eliza saw Mrs Jordan among them, pasty-faced after her latest miscarriage. (She'd accepted the role Eliza had passed up in the forthcoming *Vortigern*, the early tragedy of Shakespeare's that Sheridan was sure was going to make his fortune. Eliza didn't know if *Vortigern* was a forgery, but she could tell it was a stinker.)

They all spoke of the brilliant Stephen Storace, in whispers; there'd have to be a benefit for his widow and children. Annamaria Crouch, who'd been the composer's favourite soprano, kept thumbing stray tears off her cheeks. Then *The Iron Chest* began, and they stood in the shadows like passers-by watching carriages smash and pile up in the Strand.

Kemble sleepwalked his way through the first few scenes. The guilt-racked Mortimer's lines came out in the solemn sing-song of a country rector. Then Kemble paused and let out a series of coughs loud enough to be heard in the street.

'Well, at least that woke the crowd up,' groaned Palmer in Eliza's ear.

Her face was tight with shame. Kemble was not only dull tonight, but he dragged all the other players down too. Dodd, usually so funny, was as slow as treacle. 'Get on with it!' roared a heckler.

Young Bannister, playing the hero Wilford, came off with his teeth clamped together. 'Couldn't you liven it up a bit?' Palmer asked.

'You try playing shuttlecock with a zombie,' hissed Bannister.

It was more like swimming while tied to a corpse, Eliza thought after her first two scenes. As the innocent Helen, it was her job to imbue Mortimer with all the thrilling qualities of a Romeo. '*I dreamed last night of the fire he saved me from; and I saw him, all fresh, in manly bloom, bearing me through the flames...*' On the last phrase Eliza let her head fall backwards, as if swooning reminiscently. But what good were all her eloquent gestures when Kemble walked on like some arthritic gravedigger who'd lost his *manly bloom* some time in the reign of the last king?

The first act appeared to be lasting all night. 'Powell says we're twenty minutes over time already,' muttered Palmer.

'Oh, good God.'

'That's your cue coming up, isn't it, Eliza? Go on!'

Eliza jerked and spun round. She hadn't missed a cue in years; she was behaving like some green girl. She rushed on stage—and arrived a line too early.

Instead of glaring at her Kemble kept his stupefied gaze on the boards.

'What could'st thou do to laugh away my sickness?' he asked leadenly and exploded into a cough; Eliza felt a mist of spit on her face.

A chorus of hacking rose from the pit. The wits were imitating him now. *'I'll mimic the physician—wise and all—'* Eliza cried out, throwing herself into a comical mime,

> *—with cane at nose, and nod emphatical,*
> *portentous in my silence; feel your pulse,*
> *with an owl's face...*

And she took the opportunity to seize Kemble's wrist and give him a sharp dig with her thumbnail to rouse him. He'd have a bruise tomorrow, but she didn't care. He jumped and pulled away from her. A roar of laughter went up from the crowd, and harsh catcalls. Eliza was once again trapped on a huge stage trying to please more than 3000 strangers. It struck her like a slap in the face: *This is no life for a grown woman.*

At her left, Kemble was speechifying gloomily. *'It should seem I was not meant to live long.'*

'Nor this play neither!' roared someone from the pit and the whole painted dome rang with mirth.

TONTON HAD died after lunch, in his master's lap. When Anne reached Strawberry Hill she found Walpole with mud under his long nails. 'I've had him buried behind the chapel, with the other animals. It's for the best.' He sobbed. 'I was rather afraid of his surviving me, as he survived Madame du Deffand; it seemed scarce possible he'd meet with a third owner so devoted. No, I shall miss him sorely, but I mustn't have another dog, I'd just be breeding it up to be unhappy after I'm gone. My only pets now will be marble ones—those kittens you carved for me, my dear, I shall talk to them and caress them, while I can,' he said, seizing Anne's hand.

The image was so pathetic that she had to turn her head away.

'Still, I hope the best readiness for death is to live well,' Walpole rebuked himself. 'Sitting with one's arms folded to think about mortality is a very lazy form of preparation.'

'You're not going to die,' said Anne, muffled.

'That's a rather unscientific opinion.'

'I mean, not soon. You're only seventy-eight,' she said. 'Didn't the Earl of Sandgate live to be a hundred and three?'

This wrung a dry laugh from him. 'What an exhausting prospect.' He folded his papery hands in his lap.

In the silence that followed she asked, 'Have you written much in your *Miscellany* recently?'

'Oh, I abandoned that some time ago.'

'But why?'

'There seemed nothing new to say.'

Anne took a deep breath to steady herself. Now, more than ever before, he needed her kindness. 'My dear cousin,' she said, 'how long will you continue to brood over Mary's engagement?'

His pale eyes were wide. 'You misunderstand me,' he said. 'I have surrendered all resentment. I see now that it was impertinent—absurd—of me to attempt to make a young lady more than forty years my junior pander to my senile dependency. My eyes are opened and I condemn myself.'

Anne's throat was sore. 'No one's asking you to—'

'I've no right to enquire into Miss Berry's plans, views, designs, or, least of all, feelings. I won't question her about the date of her departure; I fear I'm too weak to stand any further shocks or disappointments. Pray forgive me if I am, as a consequence, tedious company.'

Her eyes swam with violent tears. She pitied him, but he was a brilliant strategist of war. Clearly he meant to punish her as much as Mary; he would never forgive them for what he called the *conspiracy* of the secret they'd kept all winter.

'What puzzles me', Walpole went on, examining a yellow, cracked thumbnail, 'is that you remain so philosophical. How can you bear the imminent prospect of being bereft of her company, which seems to have become almost as necessary to you as it has been, God knows, to me? Perhaps your extensive readings in the words of the Stoics have borne fruit.'

Anne made no answer.

'Or could it be that you have hopes—impossible for me—that the separation will not be absolute? After all, you've always liked a sultry climate.'

Her head shot up. How could he know Anne's private plans to go to Gibraltar? Had Mary let something slip, or was Walpole simply shrewd to the point of mind-reading? And then it came to her: *He knows what he would feel, what he would do, if he were me.*

The library door was flung open. Mary, with a letter in her hand. 'What is it, dear?' asked Anne, on her feet.

But it was Walpole Mary addressed, with burning eyes. 'I'm sorry to have wounded you unnecessarily, sir,' she said. 'I don't expect I'll ever forgive myself. The engagement is broken.'

MARY LAY face down on her bed in Little Strawberry, and Anne sat on the edge and stroked her friend's hair. She'd been sitting there so long already, at the same angle, that her shoulder was hurting her. She spoke in the soft tones one might use for a child or a dog. 'This is only a misunderstanding.'

'No,' said Mary, muffled, 'it's over.'

She should have married him in November and left on his ship. Anne was shaken, confused, almost guilty. But she tried to rouse herself to say reassuring things. 'If O'Hara knew your character as I do he wouldn't suspect you; he wouldn't doubt that you're entirely serious in your plans to come to him this summer.'

'But he does doubt,' Mary gulped. 'He does suspect. Or else he's pretending to doubt and suspect to hide the fact that he no longer wants me to come; I can't tell! All I know is I've done with it.'

'Write to him, open your heart to him—'

Mary twisted her streaked face towards Anne. 'I've been writing every other day since November. If Charles were a reasonable being my letters would have relieved all his anxieties; instead, he's shuffled and quibbled away his own happiness and mine. In my last

I told him that I'd no wish to be a drag and a shackle on his future, and I assured him I was ready to release him from the engagement.'

'Whyever did you say that?'

'To test his desire,' said Mary between her teeth. 'And in *this*'—the letter was scrunched in her fist—'he writes that I'm to consider myself entirely free.'

'He's just trying to be honourable.'

'No.'

'He's a good man,' said Anne feebly into the silence. 'Once you're married you'll make him perfectly happy.' *And me,* she thought, *this is my future too, my salvation. Or was.* The cliffs, the sweeping gulls, the dazzling sun of Gibraltar.

The small dark head shook violently. 'I doubt we'll meet again.'

'Oh, Mary!' The sound came out of Anne's mouth like a wail.

IX

Relict Cast

*A unique bronze cast, usually made some time
after the original statue, for the artist's own reference
and often recording the model in a damaged state.*

⌒

THE great goddess Fashion governs many aspects of daily life, from the depth of décolletage to the colour of hair, the slimness of a chair leg to the contour of a lake. It is not surprising, then, that Illness too shelters under her golden aegis. Shakespeare's heroes were dominated by their various Humours, whether sanguine, phlegmatic, choleric or melancholic, while two centuries later, judging by the letters of our Correspondents, we are convinced that much of our suffering has a Digestive origin and can be blamed on spiced meat or tea. In our Grandmothers' day nothing was more common than for fine ladies to suffer from the Spleen; our Mothers complained of an excess of Sensibility and our Wives today are laid prostrate by Nerves, or the Blue Devils. Are these distinct afflictions, one may ask, or merely varied names for the same gloomy emotions?

Though depression of spirits is as old as our race, it does seem that there is currently an epidemic sweeping across our country. Having endured for more than three years the cost (in limbs and lives as well as pounds and pence) of this European War, England as a whole could be said to be exhibiting melancholic symptoms. Despite the Government's success in bringing down the price of bread (the poor having impudently refused to switch to potato loaves), there is still widespread Discontent. We hear that Emigrants are now sailing voluntarily to that dread place Botany Bay, simply to get away from these shores.

To all those suffering from griefs and disappointments, may we recommend (on the advice of the best authorities) Sea Bathing. Whether its excellent effects can be credited to the salt in the water, the fresh air and exercise, or simply to a brief escape from one's usual routine is unknown. The other medicine known for its efficacy is a hearty dose of Hope. When Fortune spins her roulette wheel, who knows where the ball will land? All ills must eventually give way to good, as surely as Death is followed by Inheritance. No loyal Britons (and let us assure any prosecuting magistrates that the editors of this publication are such) can doubt that we will beat Bonaparte and his Spanish and Dutch allies in the end. Given the impossibility of knowing what lies ahead, in life's vale of Smiles and Tears, there is nothing to do but to step forward bravely.

—The Beau Monde Inquirer, *September 1796*

IN THE EARLY DAYS OF SUMMER ANNE HAD OFTEN TOLD Mary 'I'm so sorry' or 'I share your grief'. Every time she said the words she felt a tightening in her lips. Was it true? She'd certainly worked to promote this marriage between Mary and O'Hara; she'd poured her plans for the future into it; she'd been devastated when the engagement fell apart in March. But wasn't she also somewhat...relieved?

If she looked deep into her heart Anne could find resentment at the idea of Mary belonging to any man. It annoyed her when Walpole behaved possessively towards his Elderberry; how much worse it would have been with a husband. Yes, in some ways Anne had to admit that she was grateful that the match was off. Perhaps she'd been deluding herself about the possibility of a cordial, harmonious *ménage à trois*. O'Hara's letters to Anne had been gushily fond, but in his own house, on the Rock of Gibraltar, he might have been a stern master. After all, what could Anne ever have been but the outsider, the spare nail, the troublemaker?

No, all her pain came indirectly, from watching Mary. Anne had never seen anyone so sunken. It was worse than any of Lady Ailesbury's *nervous* periods (which seemed a thing of the past, oddly, now the Countess was ensconced in Grosvenor Square and the social round of Mayfair). This looked like someone drowning very slowly.

Mary seemed tinier than ever; she only ate if bullied into it. 'You've always overestimated me, Anne,' she murmured one day. 'My mind is frailer than yours. It was stifled early by my family's circumstances; its ambitions were checked, its hopes lost, its pleasures confined in a narrow space.'

'Friendship is the best medicine for it,' Anne insisted.

Mary didn't seem to hear. 'To be distinguished by nothing at all,' she continued in a faraway voice, 'to perish from the face of the earth without leaving a mark, to live on only in the memory of two or three loving bosoms, but never having done anything to justify their love...'

'Oh, Mary, stop, please stop saying such things!' When Anne watched her friend lie with her face to the wall, she felt sorrow rise up in her throat like a choking catarrh. It wasn't that she wished the marriage had come to pass; it was more like rage that General O'Hara, far away under blue silk skies, had been so careless in communication, so stupid as to break this woman's heart.

By September Anne was still neglecting her sculpture, her other friends and her mother, who complained that she was down in Little Strawberry from noon till night. Anne consulted in whispers with Doctor Fordyce, with timid, red-eyed Mr Berry and with Agnes, who seemed fond of her sister again now that there was no danger of Mary abandoning her. She brought armfuls of flowers and tempting books. 'I can't believe you've never read *The Monk*,' she told Mary, 'it's thrillingly wicked.'

The pale lids didn't stir.

'You didn't sleep well?' Anne asked.

The brown eyes cracked open. 'I haven't had an unbroken night since March.'

'Self-pity is like quicksand,' Anne told her suddenly. 'Believe me, I know what it is to sink into it. When I was at my worst— that dreadful time two years ago—it was you who saved me. You were so brave—'

'Not at first,' Mary objected.

Anne waved that away. 'You held on to our friendship, no matter what it cost you.'

A slow nod.

'You must be brave again now,' Anne told her. 'You mustn't let grief extinguish you.'

'I don't know that it's grief, exactly,' said Mary in a low voice. 'I don't feel anything as vivid as grief. I can't even see his face any more.'

Anne tried to believe that was a good sign. 'What do you feel, then?'

A long silence. 'Not much of anything except tired. And rather blank. Unequal to life's demands.'

One morning Anne marched into the bedroom and took Mary's hands in hers. 'My dearest, you must come away with me. Travel is the best cure for wounded spirits, Fordyce agrees. Change of air, change of scene, change of habits—everything's been arranged and Agnes has kindly packed your bags so all you have to do is get into my carriage.'

'Where are you taking me?' asked Mary when they had been on the road for half an hour.

'Bognor.' After a moment Anne added, 'It's hardly Florence— but since Bonaparte has overrun the Italian states—'

'That's the worst thing about war, it inconveniences one's travelling plans so.' Mary's face was deadpan and it took Anne several seconds to realise it was a joke, the first in half a year.

———

THE LITTLE fishing village of Bognor, sixty miles from London on the south coast (and near enough to Goodwood for Anne to visit her family), was in danger of becoming fashionable. Last year the Devonshire House set had come down, and told all their friends that it was the smallest, quietest, most charming of watering places. The air was mild, the sands were pure, there were exotic trees and interesting geological specimens. This summer there was another famous visitor, staying at the mansion known as the Dome. Lady Jersey, who'd come to be seen as a public enemy for her bad influence over the Prince of Wales and her cruelty towards his poor Princess, had been forced to retreat here after her resignation as lady-in-waiting, for fear of the mob that had stoned her town house. But a visitor came down to Bognor regularly, in an unmarked carriage; despite all his muffling layers, he had the distinctively swollen silhouette of the Prince.

On their second day in the lodgings on West Street Anne came back from paying a duty call on the Countess and her children. 'She's a fount of information. Apparently we must get our provisions in Chichester. She says Georgiana's in the hands of her torturers again, they've applied leeches to her eyeballs.'

Mary nodded, as if nothing could horrify her any more.

'Did you nap while I was out?' Anne asked.

'A little,' said Mary. 'I dreamed I was walking with you on some southern shore. I was married to O'Hara but he wasn't there, he was at sea; you and I were watching his ship on the horizon and waving our handkerchiefs. I was perfectly happy. Then I woke up and I wanted to die before the vision faded.'

'Oh, Mary.' Anne sat down beside her on the sofa. 'If I could do something—anything—to ease your sufferings—'

'But you do,' Mary assured her. 'How much heavier they'd be if I couldn't lay them on your sympathetic bosom every hour of the day.'

Anne stared at the ugly old chinoiserie wallpaper, with its little men and dragons. She made a decision. 'Lady Jersey said something else, something about O'Hara; she has her sources in every town in Europe. I don't know if it will hurt you or help you more to hear it.'

'Tell me,' said Mary.

'You remember you said the other day that what worried you most—what preyed on your heart—was that you felt you'd destroyed a good man's one chance of domestic happiness? That by your prevarications you'd doomed him to a lonely life in Gibraltar, misunderstood by his men and cut off from all congenial company?'

'Yes.'

'Well.' Anne chewed her lip. 'He's already formed a new connection.'

'With a lady,' Mary breathed.

'A woman, rather. She's bearing his child.'

Mary's face contracted with such instinctive pain that Anne hated herself for having been the one to cause it. 'Oh, my darling girl,' she said, throwing her arms round her. 'I thought you should have the facts.'

'Yes.'

'It's not right that you should keep pining for a man who's not worthy of it.'

But Mary's face was unconsoled.

AFTER A WEEK of plain food, sleep and walks around Bognor, Mary seemed to be reviving slightly. She'd taken up sketching again, which was a good sign, though she complained her hands shook.

As the days remain so warm, we've taken to picnicking on the beach, Anne wrote to Walpole,

from which there's a splendid view of the Isle of Wight. You'll be glad to know that the Bognor Rocks seem intimidating enough to keep the French at bay. We've collected several iron pyrites & a small stone we take to be one of the rarer Moss Agates. We've taken one boat trip & two drives on the Downs. Sometimes we visit the library at the Hotel; luckily there are no places of amusement to tempt us to irregular habits of living! M. seems livelier already & I have hopes of bringing her home to you much improved.

She thought of the old man brooding in his treasure house. He had forgiven Mary for her secret engagement, or so he said, and seemed sympathetic when it had been broken off, but things had never been quite the same between them—or between him and Anne, either. To write to him felt like going through the motions. Between his stiff replies and Mary's torpor, sometimes Anne woke up with a lead weight on her chest.

Today it had rained all morning, so the ladies had missed their walk. The afternoon had been spent at their Greek. Now the early evening was darkening; wind battered the panes. Mary laboured to improve a view of the bridge that she'd taken from their bedroom window.

Anne looked up from a slim volume of Voltaire. 'It's getting dusky; how can you see?'

'I can't, really, I suppose.' Mary rubbed her eyes with the back of her hand.

'Shall I ring for the girl to draw the curtains?'

'No need,' said Mary, standing up to tug them shut herself.

It amused Anne that her friend never could get used to the World's habit of asking servants to do what one could very easily do oneself. Through the heavy curtains she could hear the wind begin to moan. Mary was still standing at the window, lost in thought. Anne rose with a great stretch above her head and joined her. She parted the curtains with her hand. The wind was whipping the Union Jack on the hotel. 'I'd bet the sea is rough this evening.'

'Oh, yes,' said Mary, 'it must be.'

Anne thought she heard a note of longing. 'Shall we go and see?'

Mary gave her a startled look.

'We could wrap up very warm indeed,' said Anne, 'in all our furs, with not a chink open to the damp.'

'Oh, my dear. Do you really think we ought, with our constitutions?'

'I never said ought. I said could.'

Afterwards, Anne couldn't remember what had impelled her to such a rash suggestion; it was something about the swiftly gathering darkness, the restlessness in her limbs after being cooped up all day. But ten minutes later, in riding boots and swaddled in shawls and cloaks over their muslin dresses, they were half running down to the harbour. 'Let's pray we meet no one we know, in this gear,' panted Anne, hot under her layerings.

The quay was deserted. The wind was tingling. Fishing boats at anchor bobbed uneasily and their halyards clinked against their masks like a warning. The sea was foaming round the harbour wall; small white waves sprang up out of the darkness and smacked the stones. 'How cold the water must be, yet it looks like hot milk,' said Mary in Anne's ear.

'What?' said Anne, unlacing and pulling back her hood so it fell loosely on her shoulders.

'It looks like hot milk,' roared Mary.

Anne started to laugh. She seized her friend's hand. 'Come, let's walk down the pier.'

'But won't it be slick?'

'We'll take care.'

Their gloved fingers interlaced, they made their way down the very centre of the pier. The summer night was darkened with clouds; Anne felt a hint of rain speckle her cheek. The wind sprang up about them; it seemed to push them along the pier. 'Are you cold?' she said in Mary's ear.

'Not a bit.'

'Nor am I. Strange, I felt the chill more in our lodgings. Oh, smugglers!' she remarked.

'Where?'

She pointed to the light wavering on the coast. 'Well, it could be. How else does Lady Jersey get her French wine?'

Halfway along the pier a wave that was higher than the others slapped the side, sending up a spray as white as snow, and water sloshed across the stones, touching their shoes.

'Oh!'

'Would you rather go back?' asked Anne.

'Not yet,' Mary told her. Her face was pink as if with embarrassment; her smile was broad.

'You must say, whenever you want to.'

They linked arms tightly. The wind had a grip on their heavy skirts. Ten yards from the end of the pier there was a great stone bollard with a rope round it and the two women sat down without a word. All around them the sea boiled, like the foam on black coffee. The waves were arching higher every minute. The wind roared. It was raining in earnest now and Anne had hardly noticed.

'You're not afraid?' she mouthed at Mary.

A shake of the head. Shining eyes.

They never saw the great wave building; the first they knew was when with a terrible boom it broke on the end of the pier and shattered, pluming in the sky above them like a vast angel, and the women shrieked. As the silver needles of spray fell, the two of them squeezed their eyes shut and clung to the bollard and to each other. Afterwards they gasped, wet-cheeked, as the carpet of dark water rolled off the pier.

'I thought we were going to die,' Anne told Mary, wiping her eyelids with the inside of her furred hood.

Her friend nodded.

Anne licked her lips. 'Taste.'

'Very salty,' said Mary, copying her. 'Promise me—'

'What?' Anne felt ready to promise anything. This was her old Mary, her ever-young Mary, rather.

'Promise me we'll never tell Walpole.'

They both screamed with laughter. 'Never!'

'Never never never!'

'It would snuff him out entirely,' said Anne more soberly.

'Think of the letters he'd write upon the subject,' said Mary.

'Such eloquence, such pathos, such agony!'

'We must carry our secret to the grave.'

And at that word they fell silent. Anne felt her wet cloak grow heavy on her shoulders. Another wave, as big as the last, cracked apart on the stones in front of them and splintered like a firework, like the rays of a white sun, and this time the women screamed less in fear than in delight.

'A BATTLE ROYAL', Derby explained, 'is a very rare event, because of the degree of wastage. Now Rex, for instance—' He indicated the black-breasted red bird in his handler's arms.

'Oh, do you name them, like dogs?' Fox, sitting beside him in the front row of the Preston Cockpit, was clearly trying to take an interest in the details.

'Not usually,' said Derby, a little sheepish, 'but this one's a champion, perhaps the pluckiest I've ever bred; I believe he's unbeatable. Last Michaelmas at the Royal Cockpit I matched him against Old Q.'s Grey and won 100 guineas.'

Fox whistled. 'Did your Rex kill the other bird?'

'No, no, only robbed him of a few feathers; that was a very genteel match, won on technicalities. Since then he's triumphed twice more by wounding and he's had the whole summer resting up at Knowsley.'

'Hang on,' said Fox, his forehead wrinkled, 'you mean to say your four-year-old cock has never killed?'

Derby shrugged. 'He hasn't needed to.'

'Yet you're putting him for a Battle Royal today—eight birds in the pit and only one to come out alive?'

'Oh, but killing comes instinctively to a cock with bottom. And speaking of birds, can't you speak to Grey about this foolish motion to do away with the Game Laws?'

'Mm, I warned him you wouldn't like it,' said Fox. 'But we're only talking about the odd hare for the pot of some hungry family—'

Derby's jaw was set. 'If anyone could march into Knowsley and shoot a deer, in what sense would it be my land any more? And if it weren't my land, passed down by my grandsires' grandsires, why should I feel responsible for it and everyone who lives on it; why should I feel it my duty to represent them in the Lords?' He knew he was beginning to harangue. 'Grey and Sherry make me feel like some stern old Tory sometimes,' he added ruefully. 'We quarrelled half the night at Brooks's last month, and Sherry pushed his point till he was claiming that men of birth, of ancient lineage, are no better qualified to govern their country than shoemakers or hairdressers!'

'Well,' said Fox, hedging, 'individual merit is the thing of course, but I've always thought of the aristocracy as Parliament's backbone—'

'We lords speak for the country because we care for it—because we own most of it,' said Derby pragmatically. 'Why, Sherry even disputed my right to have put my son into a safe seat in Preston this summer—claimed *all* boroughs should be free, and young Edward should have had to fight it out on the hustings with every Tom, Dick and Harry!'

Fox's grin was uneasy. He seemed relieved when the Master started making the announcements in a hoarse roar.

'Gentlemen, quieten down, if you'd be so kind. Today we have a Battle Royal, five matchable cocks and three outsize Shakebags, to fight with fair spurs, sickles, launcels and penknife spurs. Places, please.'

'Which birds are kept in there?' asked Fox, pointing out a large hanging cage.

Derby sniggered. 'That's for any man who makes a wager and can't pay.'

'I mustn't bet a shilling, then!' The cocks were on the sods and feathers were starting to fly. 'Where's your Rex?'

'There, on the far left. He's downed three already,' said Derby pleasurably. Rex was doing superbly; his heels arced down with no warning. There was blood on his clipped wattles, but Derby didn't think it was his own. The only other real contender was Mr Jones's Dun. Several men in the front row had blood spattered across their faces.

'Isn't it a mite...barbaric?' murmured Fox.

Rex had got the Dun in a hard grip. 'At least it's fast. A Welsh Main—where they fight it out in rounds—can go on all day.' Derby looked back at the pit, but he'd missed it, the crucial blow. *Damnation!* Mr Jones's bird lay in a mess of bloody feathers. That was it, Rex was the only bird moving.

Derby jumped to his feet, and received bows and congratulations. He leaned into the pit to accept the heavy purse from the Master's hand. Sitting down again he murmured to Fox, 'I'm afraid this will confirm my feeder, Busley, in his superstition. He smuggled a bit of consecrated bread home from church under his tongue and fed it to Rex this morning!'

Fox's expression was half amused, half horrified.

Derby watched Rex stagger sideways, avoiding the handler's grasp. He looked more closely. Stabbed in the left thigh, he reckoned; the bird would never be fit to fight again. Derby felt misery come over his head like a dark wave.

'I'M SHOWING my age,' said Anne, looking at herself in the small tarnished mirror in their bedroom at Bognor.

'Rubbish,' said Mary, 'your hair's as brown as ever.'

'It's the skin that gives it away.'

'Where?' asked Mary, coming closer.

Anne pointed to various soft faint lines on her face and places where her neck looked stretched.

'That's only your...what's the word? What does one say of statues when they've gained in charm over the years?'

'Patina?' said Anne, amused. 'Like the yellowing of ivory.'

'Exactly,' said Mary. 'Who wants their masterpiece to look new?'

Anne turned and looked at Mary, whose face had new lines of its own and shadows under the eyes. 'You're not quite repaired yet.'

The smile was a little bitter. 'I assure you, dear nurse, I'm mending as fast as I can. Men have an advantage in this respect; a man can gallop and drive and game away till he's forgotten everything, while a poor helpless woman nourishes her passion like a monster in her bosom.'

Anne was stern. 'You're not a poor helpless woman.'

'Well. Rich in friendship, at least.'

'And you're unjust to the opposite sex,' Anne pointed out. 'What about Walpole? He's a martyr to sensibility if ever anyone was. Men can suffer as long and hard as we can.' She found herself thinking of the actress and her *unalterable Earl*. Galloping and driving and gaming had done nothing to free Derby from his long devotion. Was it a weakness, she wondered, or his greatest strength? He'd loved the actress enough to take his old friendship for Anne, for instance, and break it like a twig.

The September day was Italian; at six in the evening the white sands of Bognor still glinted like mica under the weight of the sun. Mary, eyes shut, settled her shoulder blades against the rented chair and rotated her parasol. They'd dined early and lightly, then gone out for more air.

'I'm almost too hot,' said Anne wonderingly.

'Mm.'

Anne pulled out her watch. 'According to our landlady, ladies may bathe on the far side of those rocks before eight and after six.'

Mary's eyes fluttered open. 'You don't propose—'

'I do,' said Anne. 'It's healthy water; Fordyce recommends it.'

'You'd go in alone?'

'Need I?'

'Oh, but I don't bathe, you know,' said Mary, struggling to sit up.

'What, thirty-three years old and never had a bath?'

Mary blushed faintly. 'The things that fall from your tongue!'

'I was only remarking, in the six years and one month since first we met—'

'Only six years?' marvelled Mary.

'I'll take that in a complimentary spirit,' said Anne, rueful. 'I was saying, you've always seemed to me a perfectly clean creature, considering what you now confess.'

'Oh, stop it. All I meant was I've never been in the sea.'

'Then it's high time. Come along,' said Anne, levering herself out of her chair.

'But we've no costumes—' protested Mary.

'One hires them from the attendants in the huts.'

'—and I don't know that I want to make the experiment at this time of life.'

'This time of life,' scoffed Anne. She narrowed her eyes at her friend and held out a hand to pull her out of her chair. 'This time of life can be a very good time of life.' She had been going to say *our time of life,* but there were fourteen years between them, as there always would be. Odd, how the difference between forty-one and twenty-seven had stretched so yawningly when they'd first met, but forty-seven and thirty-three had quite a different ring. They were both in their middle years now, she supposed.

Mary followed her over the sands mutely.

There were a few bathing machines, but Anne didn't like them; it seemed ridiculously elaborate to be towed out to sea in such an apparatus. She and Mary changed in a hut. When they emerged they were cumbrous in calico: bloomers, skirts, boned bodices all salt-stiff and sharp against their hot skin. The huge cap containing Mary's hair was tilting at an odd angle. Mary stared down at herself, then scanned the rocks.

'What are you looking for—prying gentlemen?'

'I suppose,' Mary said with a little laugh. 'I've never been out in such a mad ensemble. What do they wear—the men?'

'Nothing at all,' Anne told her.

'No!'

'That's why we're banned from here between eight and six.' Anne was halfway down the beach by now, in the path of the sinking sun. She called over her shoulder, 'The water should be delightfully warmed by now.'

There were a couple of other female figures immersed in the shining water, or coming out in their heavy draperies. No one they knew. The sand was hot and gritty under Anne's soles.

Mary caught up with her. 'I'm trying to remember the last time

I walked barefoot. Not since I was very small, I think, in my grand-mother's garden in Yorkshire.'

Anne strode into the water, up to her knees.

'I really don't—I think, on the whole—'

Anne went back and held out her hand. Mary grasped it and took one step on to the wet brown sand. Another, and another, and then a wave ran in and seized her by the ankles. 'Oh, the cold!' Her voice was high with shock. The wave slid back.

'It's a strange feeling, isn't it?'

'As if the ground is sucking me in. It is!' she added, looking at her half-buried feet.

'Don't be alarmed.' Anne tugged gently and Mary took a few more steps. 'Isn't it delicious?'

'You said the sun would have warmed it.'

'It has,' Anne assured her. 'I bathed at Brighton one April morning when I was a girl; now *that* was cold.'

Mary clung to Anne's hand and lurched on. The water was like a knife against Anne's thighs, a silvery pain, inch after inch. The reddening sun dazzled her eyes.

'Halfway in. You won't fall, it shelves very gently.' Anne squeezed her fingers.

Mary talked fast, as if to distract herself. 'Oh, it's as if I'm being cut in two. I can't feel my legs,' she said, as much in wonder as re-proach. 'It's like a burning hoop round my waist.'

'*Those friends thou hast,*' Anne quoted merrily, '*and their adoption tried…*'

'*…grapple them to thy soul with hoops of steel,*' finished Mary, breathless. 'Oh!' The water had her by the ribs now, Anne could see the dark line. Because she was so much shorter than Anne it had almost reached her narrow shoulders. It lapped at her corset, out-lining the curves that were still as firm as a girl's. 'I don't believe—' she gasped.

'Oh, you can, you can,' Anne assured her, letting herself sink. 'We're there,' she said, her head tilted up to the dying sun, the water sweet against her throat.

'Don't let go of my hand.'

'I won't.'

Mary stood very still. Then she subsided into the water and it reached her white chin.

'Think how much good this is doing you,' Anne told her. 'All that medicinal salt is refreshing your skin and stimulating your organs.'

Mary didn't answer. Was she fighting the temptation to let go of her friend's hand and stagger back to shore?

'The Greeks, of course, considered water holy,' Anne told her. 'They had their sacred springs and pools. What was it Homer said of water? *Clean, light, precious, most desirable.*'

A wave wet Mary's mouth. 'Oh!'

'Kick your legs.'

Mary jerked out of the water like a seal. She'd dropped Anne's hand. She bounded up and down, waving her arms as if trying to put out a fire. 'It's—it's so—I can't bear—'

Anne joined in the wild laughter. Two mature ladies, wearing grotesque calico sacks, leaping about like sprats in a net! She plunged down for a long moment to let the water possess her entirely: her hot cheeks, the small chambers of her ears. It lifted her sack of hair and parted every strand at the root. She emerged with a shriek of pleasure, her eyes stinging.

Mary was splashing like a dog. 'I thought you were drowning!'

'Just take a big breath and hold it,' Anne told her. Her cap had come loose, and was hanging on her shoulder like bladderwrack; she tugged at it.

Mary gulped the air, then went down. When she rebounded her eyes were huge. 'What an extraordinary sensation.'

'Isn't it? I'll bet you're not cold any more, are you?'

'No,' said Mary. 'No, not any more.'

Between waves Anne took a mouthful of the water. The salt made her shudder. 'Powerful stuff,' she said when she could speak. 'Fordyce says if I could get down a glass of it every morning I'd never know a day's indisposition.'

Mary tried a sip, but her face puckered up like a baby's. 'It's abominable!'

'Oh, I'd pick it over that foul, sulphurous Spa water any time.' Anne took another long gulp of it, then wiped her mouth.

'Can you swim?' said Mary.

'No, I make sure never to go beyond my depth. But there is one thing I know how to do—if you'll help—' She found Mary's hand in the water and placed it against the small of her own back. 'Bear me up, just here, and I'll try to float.' Anne heaved herself backwards and felt the silvery water infiltrate her ears. Somehow it worked, the magic trick of buoyancy. Her costume trailed weightily, but Mary's firm hand was under her.

'Splendid,' cried Mary. 'Let me.'

Reluctantly Anne found her feet again with a great splash, and put out her hand. 'Lie back all at once,' she said, 'arch like a cat. Don't be scared.'

Mary smiled as she floated; her arms were spread like an angel's. Her cap had floated off; her dark curls relaxed on the water. No, not an angel but the statue of an angel, or something like it; the Winged Victory of Samothrace, which Anne went to see whenever she was in Paris. The calico clung to Mary's narrow limbs like carved drapery. She was a Sybil in white marble, a gleaming monument. Like someone who'd leapt from a cliff and now floated, free of her despair. Her eyes opened, and she and Anne were looking at each other.

When they came out of the water it was into a different world, or rather, it was they who'd changed, Anne thought, and they walked through the streets of Bognor like strangers. It was as if the waters had gone over their heads and worked a metamorphosis.

At midnight, when they should have been asleep, Anne was lying so close to Mary that tendrils of nape hair—still damp—touched her lips. Her breath was hot between them. Mary turned over, like a fish, and their faces were touching. 'Anne?'

'Yes,' she said and the word was a great falling.

'You must teach me,' Mary whispered.

A long silence, how long, ten beats of a sure and terror-struck heart? 'I can't.'

Mary moved as if to turn away, but Anne took her by the shoulder with her free hand. 'Don't mistake me,' she said, very low, 'please don't mistake me. I only mean I know no more than you.'

'But—' Mary lay still.

Did she think Anne was lying? For all their talk of candour and sincerity, the two of them had tangled themselves up in lies, it occurred to Anne now: the unsaid, the veiled, the unnameable. Six years, thousands of letters, murmured conversations, professions of faith and attestations of virtue, and what did it all amount to? She lay in the darkness, she and Mary breathing the same inch of fragrant air. It occurred to her that whenever Mary had said *I have full confidence in your frankness*, what she'd meant was more like *Don't tell me*. Now, after all these years, Anne was trying to tell the truth, but perhaps Mary thought she was lying. Was it impossible to say anything that wasn't some kind of lie?

Mary kissed her on the mouth.

Shock kept Anne where she was for a moment, then she kissed back, and slid her arm under Mary's waist and kissed her again, as if sealing a pact, though she couldn't have named the terms.

THE MORNING was grey, but shimmered when the light pushed at the gauzy cloud from behind. At breakfast they were alone in the small dining room; the other lodgers had gone out already. Anne put down her piece of toast, thinking she should be the first to speak, and Mary flinched slightly. After a moment, Anne started eating again.

It was remarkable how life went on. It was as if nothing had happened, except that they were baggy-eyed from lack of sleep and kept hiding yawns behind their fans. They wrote letters and showed them to each other, as if by some silent agreement: *The weather has been fine on the whole*, Mary told her sister, and *My dear Walpole, we both continue to improve in health*, wrote Anne. The hours went by as they always had. They talked about the merits of Richardson versus those of Rousseau and debated whether Palladio's influence on English architecture had been entirely beneficial. For a minute at a time Anne forgot, then remembered, which was like falling over a cliff. They walked to the shop at the hotel, in the afternoon, so Mary could buy a new comb, because her old one had some broken teeth. For dinner there was jugged hare.

All the time Anne was talking to herself. *Is this evil, then?* Was this the thing she'd feared and loathed all her life, shrinking from its touch? She found herself thinking of her sceptical tutor Hume: *Put it to the test.* How did one know the sun would rise tomorrow? Was it just a habitual assumption? *Assume nothing.* Empirically speaking, was last night evil? In what aspect did the evil lie? In the irrationality of this passion? But many things were irrational; Anne sometimes longed for an orange even when she wasn't hungry. In its turning against nature? Well, she and Mary were past all that, surely; nature, in her wisdom, had not made wives and mothers of them, had in fact turned them loose. In its excess? True, this was a strange and overwhelming feeling, a sort of whirlwind, but where was the real harm in that? Anne wasn't reasoning like Hume any more, she was pleading like a child. *Why mayn't I have this?* It was a sin, she knew that much. But what exactly was a sin? Who was damaged by this? *There are no universally agreed crimes,* Hume had told her once, *only things of which various people disapprove.*

'Mrs Damer?'

She jumped. 'I beg your pardon,' she said.

'The gentleman asked you to pass the salt,' murmured Mary.

She gave the cellar to him so fast that it thumped the table.

At the end of the day the two ladies were sitting on a stone bench on the pier, watching the sun go down, as it had the day before when they'd bathed, unknowing, in the cold sea. Anne felt older. No, that wasn't right, she felt younger. Tired, and confused, and triumphant, like a girl. She thought, *I've become a girl again.*

She remembered her wedding night, when she'd been just nineteen. It hadn't occurred to her to think of it until now; the two experiences had nothing in common. But she recalled her mother

kissing her on the cheekbone the next day and murmuring something odd: *You're a woman now.* The bride had been struck by guilt
that she was failing to feel the appropriate sentiments; she had no
sense that she'd been changed by John Damer's brisk, muscular at-
tentions. Whereas today...the very thought of the night she and
Mary had spent, now she let herself dwell on it, made her stomach
twist and her temples sweat. Now it was—nearly three decades
after her wedding—that she'd been truly changed.

'May we...not speak of it?' Mary, beside her on the pier, spoke
so quietly that Anne wasn't sure she'd heard the words.

'Of course we may,' she said at once, marshalling her nerve. 'I'm
willing to speak of it, of anything.'

'No, but—I meant, may we, is it possible for us...*not* to speak
of it for now? Please,' she said, after a pause.

Anne's heart had clenched.

'It's only that to speak of things changes them,' said Mary,
watching Anne like a cat. 'All day I've been waiting as if for a
storm—'

'What kind of storm?'

'Guilt, I suppose. Shame. Self-loathing. All that wretchedness.'
Anne's mouth tightened over each word.

'But the storm hasn't come,' Mary assured her. 'Only, I fear it
may if we speak.'

And were they not speaking now, Anne wondered, speaking of
the very thing? Were they not reliving in their mind's eye every
silken line and curve, hearing again each whispered word, feeling
again every wild, appalling touch? Was she the only one wondering
what would happen this evening after the sun had sunk, after supper, after the candle was snuffed in their little room? 'Certainly,' she
said, looking away. 'Let's just sit here and admire the view.'

They stared out to sea.

NOTHING STOPPED them. They got little sleep. On Wednesday
Anne banged her bad leg against a lamp-post because she wasn't
looking where she was going. After church on Sunday Mary shut

herself up in their bedroom for half an hour before she emerged for dinner, red-eyed but witty. They bathed in the sea four times that week. They never spoke of what they did at night, but it was as if they were speaking of it all the time; in every *Good morning,* every *Such heat, for September!*

How little she'd known, thought Anne—and how little she'd known herself. It seemed she wasn't naturally ascetic or born to solitude. She was no good at renunciation after all. It was as if her virgin heart had been fasting all her life, building up an endless appetite, and now she couldn't have enough of pleasure. She was glutting herself on love. She was unshockable; there was nothing she didn't like, nothing she could do without. Under her fichu the soft skin of her neck was purple with kisses.

She looked back over the years and saw that she'd always wanted this but hadn't seen it for what it was. She'd been confused, terrorised by the grotesqueries of the pamphleteers, the obscene silhouettes on black sofas. This was a private, pure astonishment. *I am this way,* she thought, *as simply as a stream flows down a hill. It has always been women. How many years of my life have I spent chiselling their beautiful cheeks?* This wasn't evil, this wasn't debauchery. It was love made flesh.

At dinner with two watercolourists and a curate, Anne found herself considering Mary's wrist, resting beside her plate, as a tender fruit; her mouth ached to close round it. That night as Mary reached over her to snuff the candle, Anne found herself saying, 'Don't.'

Mary didn't.

This is ridiculous, Anne thought. *I'm nearly fifty years old.* It had taken her all this time to weave and stumble into understanding. It might be ridiculous—but it wasn't too late.

She'd begun to wonder about other women she knew. Had the Devonshire House ladies, for instance, ever known this bliss? It was not something she could ever imagine asking Georgiana. She could well believe that Georgiana and Bess had shared this secret for ten years—or had never thought of such a thing. Who could tell? Every love had its own peculiar story.

Three in the morning, by the tall clock that stood in the corner of their room, and Mary lay awake, pillowed on Anne's arm, and stared at the dragon wallpaper. 'Hideous,' she murmured.

'Isn't it?'

'I'd never stand for it in any home of mine.'

'Nor I.'

The word *home* seemed to linger. The clock ticked loudly for a moment, then faded away again. Five days before they were due to go home, or rather, each to her own, Anne to Grosvenor Square and Mary to join her father and sister in North Audley Street. Five minutes apart, but an unendurable distance, especially in the night.

Mary was about to say something, Anne could tell, though no words had been spoken; it was a matter of a slight tensing, flesh against flesh, an intake of breath. 'What is it?' she asked.

'I was just wondering,' murmured Mary. 'Were you glad when my match was broken off?'

'No.' Anne pulled away. Her heart was noisy in her chest. She'd almost managed to forget all that. 'Mary, I swear I did everything I could to help you and O'Hara. I wanted you to be happy.'

'I know.' Mary nestled back against her, wrapping Anne's arms round her more tightly. 'But you're glad now.'

Anne didn't know what to say.

'You wouldn't want me to be married,' said Mary, looking over her shoulder.

'No,' said Anne, letting out her breath.

'No,' murmured Mary.

The church bell belatedly rang out the hour. Anne looked down at Mary, who was fast asleep, curled into the crook of Anne's elbow. Now how could she move in order to put out the light? Well, it was burnt down to a stub already; it would die in an hour or so. They'd have to ask their landlady for another candle, not three days after the last; it would sound odd. *We read till all hours,* Anne imagined announcing; *we're vastly devoted to the life of the mind.* She watched Mary, though her own eyes were fluttering with fatigue. She thought of a saying that Plutarch ascribed to Heraclitus: that everyone while awake was in the same world, but that all of them, while asleep, were in worlds of their own.

NOVEMBER 1796

Eliza sat in the dressing room with Mrs Siddons, discussing the recent rash of resignations, the most serious of which was Kemble's. 'I'm very sorry for his departure to Ireland, but hardly surprised.'

Mrs Siddons nodded tragically. 'Sheridan had made my brother's position as manager a constant torment.'

'Pop Kemble's retired, too,' said Eliza, counting on her fingers. 'Well, she's not much of a loss, if you don't mind my saying so of your sister-in-law—but her mother Mrs Hopkins and Mrs Powell, too—and Moody, Dodd and Roaring Bob Bensley!'

'The unfortunate young Mr Benson,' Mrs Siddons added, 'if death can be counted as a kind of retirement that makes eight.'

Benson had died of brain fever, which was a tactful way of saying he'd climbed naked out his garret window and split his head open on the stones of Bridges Street. There'd been a Ben for his widow and orphans, but rumour had it that Sheridan hadn't passed on a penny to them yet. 'The Drury Lane Theatrical Fund will be drained, with so many needing pensions at once,' Eliza pointed out.

'Even more worryingly,' said Mrs Siddons, 'we've no one left to play an old man but Mr King and what play has ever been written without two or three hoar sages in the cast?'

'Or a brace of doddering old fools!' Mrs Siddons always brought out cheekiness in Eliza. 'Well, there's nothing else for it: Jack Palmer will have to tie on a beard.'

The other actress smiled wanly at the image.

'I believe Jack's nearly as old as Dodd and Bensley, anyway— well past fifty, though you'd never know it from his swagger. But what I don't understand is', Eliza went on more bitterly, 'how can there be no money for our wages when hundreds of pounds are taken in every night?'

'Nor did my poor brother understand, but then Kemble's a child in business,' Mrs Siddons told her. 'Out of the purest love of the theatre he signed personal guarantees to workmen who didn't trust that Treasurer Westley would pay them—and ended up being arrested for debt in the street!'

The more fool he, thought Eliza.

Mrs Siddons cocked one ear. 'Do I hear a bustle?'

'It seems early, for Sheridan—'

The women hurried along the corridor. By the time they reached the Treasurer's office they were pushing through a crowd. Most of the actors, singers and dancers were there, together with the carpenters and scene shifters, and the dressers; it was like a meeting of the whole company. Voices rose as the proprietor walked smartly along the corridor. 'Mr Sheridan!'

'Sir—'

'Our salaries—'

'Please consider—'

'Certainly, certainly!' Sheridan broadcast his smile. He was arm in arm with Richard Wroughton, the bland, diplomatic actor who'd been suddenly raised to the status of manager on Kemble's departure.

'Look us in the eye, sir, if you dare,' intoned Mrs Siddons, 'and tell us our time of waiting is at an end.'

Jack Palmer spoke from the back wall, effortlessly enlarging his voice: 'For God's sake, man, pay up.'

'My good people, you shall be attended to directly,' said Sheridan. 'You must understand, the affairs of the nation have been pre-occupying me and all my fellow Members. Can you believe this monster Pitt? After shedding oceans of blood and breaking thousands of widows' hearts, he's now suddenly suing for peace with France, which our Party has been urging for the past four years!' This news caused some distraction and a hum of conversation rose from the crowd. The Treasurer's door suddenly opened and let Sheridan and Wroughton in.

There was a rush of bodies. A painter banged on the wood. 'Leave the door open,' he roared.

There was no answer.

'Westley's sweeping the treasury clean of the whole week's receipts,' Eliza murmured to Mrs Siddons, 'then the three of them will hop out through the window.'

'But he promised me,' said the tragedienne confusedly. 'When I threatened to resign with my brother, Sheridan soothed me and gave me his word to pay me in full this very week.'

Eliza smiled at her colleague's *naïveté*. 'He promises everyone— he's uncertainty personified. My mother heard that Dora Jordan's refusing to do any new roles till he stumps up. And has poor Storace's widow seen any of the £500 we raised for her, I wonder?'

'It really is astonishing how we all go on, how much we can bear for love of our art.'

'I shall write Sheridan a nasty note,' said Eliza, turning away; 'it seems more dignified than banging on the door.'

A FEW DAYS after their return from Bognor Mary met Anne at the door of the library at Strawberry Hill. 'He's in a moo,' she whispered.

Anne steeled herself as they went in. She greeted Walpole very pleasantly. 'I'm sorry I'm late, but Mother's only just arrived from Goodwood.'

His pouched eyes were on the fantastically painted ceiling. After a long moment he said, 'So Bognor was all it promised, then.'

'Yes,' she said, gulping a little on the word. 'Very healthful.' This was going to be more difficult than she thought.

'Our Elderberry seems raised from the dead, if I may put it so blasphemously.' His tone was not cheerful. 'What do you say, Miss Mary, have you undergone some *sea change, into something rich and strange?*'

Mary went the colour of a plum. It happened all at once; there was no gradual pinking, but a startling rush of blood from her throat to her hairline. Anne, staring at her, willed her to say something, give some credible explanation. 'Excuse me,' said Mary and ran from the room.

In the silence Anne thought, *He knows.* She sat down by the fire as calmly as she could manage. *Somehow he can do the impossible, see right into our hearts.* 'I'm afraid she's still not quite herself.'

'Evidently.'

Walpole was looking at her so piercingly, so knowledgeably, with those weasel's eyes. *He knows, damn him.* Anne didn't dare say a word; if she spoke of Mary, or if she avoided speaking of her, either would give her away. 'And how have you yourself been? Since your last letter, I mean.'

'That of the third?'

She could never remember the dates of letters. 'I think so. You mentioned in it—something about the builders having finished the New Offices.' Her eyes were straying towards the window.

'That was my letter of the twenty-ninth,' Walpole told her. 'Didn't you receive my next, of the third?'

'I'm sure we did, I'm sure I did,' she corrected herself.

'Do check, won't you, and let me know; you really must keep better track of your correspondence. I hate it when letters go missing,' he snapped. 'There's no excuse for it in this day and age, unless shipping routes are in question.'

'No,' said Anne guiltily. 'So...now the Offices are complete, what will you build next?'

'I'm finished,' he said, looking into the fire.

'What—couldn't Strawberry Hill benefit from another tower or two, or a hermitage in the garden?'

He shook his head. 'My labours are accomplished.'

The phrase chilled her. 'Have you been well?' she said. She'd already asked that.

He gave one slow shrug, like a crow adjusting its wings. 'What does that mean, *well*, to a man of seventy-nine?'

Anne was about to correct him, then she remembered. 'Your birthday! Your seventy-ninth. How could we have let it slip by without sending congratulations?'

'It hardly matters.'

'Mary will be so distressed.'

Walpole gave her a sharp look. 'You speak for her, now?'

'I know what she feels on many matters, that's all,' she said as firmly as she could.

'I'm sure you do, since the two of you have spent the summer entirely secluded from society, writing to me barely once a week. I'm all too aware who holds the first place in her affections these days. Of course, your company has so much to offer her that mine lacks.'

Anne stared at him.

'Health and energy, to name but two,' Walpole said violently, 'all the sensibility and sweetness of your own sex, combined with the strength and vigour of the other.'

She rose to her feet. 'I seem to have come at a bad time.'

Silence.

'I'll put up with much,' said Anne, 'because you're my god-father, my cousin and my dear friend. But you're overstepping the mark. Now, have you finished with your jealous insinuations, or do you want to accuse me of something?' The question hung in the air and she was terribly afraid. 'Should I leave?'

How Walpole must have been tempted to say, *As you wish.* She watched his lips. They formed, at last, into a *No.*

Greatly relieved, Anne ploughed on. 'I'm most dreadfully sorry—that we missed your birthday, I mean. We'll make a great fuss of you next year, for your eightieth. Perhaps a party!'

'I'm afraid I can't promise to attend,' said Walpole dryly.

She caught his eye and started laughing; she couldn't help it. *Oh, please God, let him not demand that I explain what's so funny about the prospect of his death!* That made her laugh all the harder.

A creaking sound, like a gate in a high wind. To her enormous relief, Walpole had joined in. When he stopped laughing he said, 'William Beckford is back in England.'

'Oh, yes?' Anne was startled by the change of tone.

'He wanted a diplomatic mission, of all things, but Loughbor-ough and Portland have blocked him.'

Lord Loughborough was the boy's uncle, Anne remembered, the boy who'd grown up to be Viscount 'Kitty' Courteney.

'Once an exile, always an exile. The verdict of society went against Beckford back in '84 and against that sentence there is no appeal,' said Walpole.

Was he trying to tell her something?

'He means to build an abbey at Fonthill, out-Gothicise Strawberry Hill,' said Walpole disdainfully. 'I hear he calls this place a little mousetrap.'

'The cheek of him!'

'He's told his agents to stay poised to buy up all my best antiquities at auction, the moment I'm dead.' A heavy pause. 'I shall have to live to be ninety at least, to thwart him.'

'I hope so,' said Anne, her throat sore.

IT WAS A COLD November night in Grosvenor Square; Anne and Mary lay knotted up in each other's arms under heavy blankets. They rarely had this opportunity; only when Mary's family could spare her. It still felt strange to Anne. They weren't in Bognor any more, cut off from the World in their private bubble; they were in her house, with her mother sleeping two rooms away. Anne had been afraid that perhaps once they were in London everything would go back to the way it had been before—but no. She hadn't lost Mary, this new, wild Mary; nothing had been lost. She smiled in the darkness.

'What did you mean', came a whisper, 'when you said you knew no more than I did?'

'When?'

'At the start,' said Mary, betraying a little awkwardness.

'Ah,' said Anne, remembering that night in Bognor after their sea bathe. 'I thought you wanted *never to speak of it*,' she added teasingly.

A thoughtful silence. 'I'm ready now. So what did you mean?'

'When I said I knew no more than you? Just that.'

'But Anne—that can't be so.'

'Why can't it?' asked Anne in her ear.

'Because you've always—it's been quite clear to me that you…
knew what to do,' said Mary.

Anne laughed shyly. 'No more than you.'

'But didn't you—hadn't you already'—Mary was a little gruff
now—'oh, don't make me spell it out!'

'My love,' said Anne, a phrase that made her shake now,
though she used to say it without thinking before Bognor.

'I think…I was not the first,' said Mary rather formally.

'Indeed you are.'

Mary's head twisted towards her. 'But—'

Anne cut in before Mary could form the syllables of *Miss Farren*. She didn't want that name spoken in this bed. 'Those I desired,
without knowing it—I can say that now, as I never could before,'
she added with difficulty, '—they didn't desire me. Or, perhaps they
may have,' she said, thinking of that extraordinary scene in which
the actress had forced a defiant kiss on her, 'but not enough to risk
admitting it. I can't be sure.'

After a long pause Mary said, 'I think that was my own situation. So you're telling me that even before—'

'The person in question,' said Anne stiffly.

'Yes, before that, there was nothing?'

'A kiss, once, in Italy,' she added, scrupulous, 'that was all.'

'Then when you told me those rumours were pure invention—'

'I was speaking the literal truth, yes,' said Anne, a little irked.
'Didn't you believe me?'

'I thought I did,' said Mary, 'but now it seems that in some dark
little corner of my heart I didn't.'

'You thought me an accomplished Sapphist, in fact.' Anne
threw the word into the darkness.

Mary twitched at that. 'I suppose I must have done.'

'Why weren't you afraid of me?'

'Oh, I was,' Mary assured her. 'And afraid of what you brought
out in me. I think now that may be why I succumbed so quickly to
O'Hara.'

The name still had a strange power; Anne could almost feel the solidity of him in the room.

'I did love him. I thought he'd save me. But then I couldn't bear to leave you behind. That should have told me something.' And Mary curled her head into the curve of Anne's shoulders.

'You're happier now, aren't you? Happier than before, I mean.'

'So much. Need you ask? But don't expect ever to see me *perfectly* happy,' said Mary, rueful, 'since by nature I'm such a prey to emotion. I worry about the future.'

'Our future?'

'No, no. When my father's taken from us—the fact is, Agnes and I will have no more that £350 a year apiece.'

My God, Anne thought, *I spend that much on marble.* She spoke firmly. 'When that day comes I can't think you'd break my heart by refusing to share my fortune.'

'Oh, my dearest. I wasn't asking—'

'Mary, I would have offered years ago, but I thought it needed no saying.'

A hush between them now, the pressing of cheek to cheek.

There was a hammering at the front door. Anne was out of bed and into her dressing gown before she knew it. Her pulse pounded. *How can anyone have guessed?* she thought. *What can have given us away?*

She met the sleepy-eyed maid on the landing. 'A note from Goodwood, madam.'

Goodwood? Anne tore it open, puzzled. It was very short.

I am sorry to tell you that the Duchess died at twenty-five minutes past ten. Can you come down in the morning and bring your mother?
In haste,
Richmond.

When she'd read it through twice she went back to her room. 'What is it?' hissed Mary. 'Shall I light the lamp?'

'No, no,' said Anne, climbing into the creaking bed. 'My sister's dead,' she said, and laid her head on Mary's breasts and shut her eyes tightly.

Mary held her without saying anything for a long time, so long that Anne thought she might have fallen asleep. 'I knew she was ill,' Anne said at last into the soft cotton of Mary's nightgown.

'Yes.'

'But no particular disease, nothing the doctors could identify. I didn't realise she was in danger.'

'Of course you didn't,' said Mary, as if hushing a child.

'I should have visited Goodwood more these last years.'

'Everyone thinks that when someone dies.'

'No, but—' Anne felt the tears swimming up through her head. 'We were so unlike. I never cared for Lady Mary, not enough, not as a sister should.'

Mary was honest enough not to deny that.

One couldn't pick whom to love, thought Anne. The woman beside her was friend and sister and lover and many things besides. One could only hope to recognise love where it grew, and get a grip on it and hold on.

JANUARY 1797

> Dear Mr Wroughton,
> I'm afraid I can't think of playing Lady Dorville in The Force of Ridicule tonight [Eliza scribbled, at her narrow secrétaire in Green Street] till I receive word that you or Mr Sheridan has given an order for Westley's payment to me of at least £400 of the Amount owing.
> Yours,
> E. Farren

She wasn't claiming to be ill this time; the quarrel was out in the open. Richard Wroughton had turned out to be all steel, under his mild surface, and rumour had it that he'd only agreed to replace Kemble after bargaining Sheridan up to the extraordinary salary of

800 guineas a year. *Guineas, like a gentleman,* thought Eliza vindictively. She was nostalgic for the old days; Wroughton had none of Kemble's ambition or daring and the playbills made dull reading. But the real problem was money. Eliza had been on £18 a week for many years now and hadn't pushed for an increase, even though her bills at Green Street seemed to mount all the time. Did this delicacy win her respect or special treatment? Anything but; Drury Lane now owed her the fantastical sum of £1100. Why, one could buy a house with that! It was time to do what Mrs Jordan had done long ago and stand firm.

She sat and waited; to calm her nerves she read Miss Burney's *Camilla,* as everyone was, this season. At half past four she got Wroughton's tetchy answer and a blunter one from Sheridan.

> *Miss Farren,*
> *I've just come from the Commons & found your latest Note. Getting you £400 tomorrow is out of the question. If I find you £100, will you give over this nonsense?*
> *R. B. S.*

She made the messenger wait for her brief response.

> *Finding you don't take my claim seriously, I am obliged to put the matter in the capable hands of Shawe, my lawyer.*

'I saw Gillray's latest cartoon in a window today,' Mrs Farren mentioned, looking up from her knotting. 'It shows your dear Fox as a revolutionary in shirtsleeves, firing a pistol at a target marked *Crown, Lords and Commons.*'

'Well, no one pays any attention to Gillray's views any more, Mother,' said Eliza sharply, 'since he's been gagged by a pension from Pitt.'

After dinner she sat wrapped up warm against the draughts, ploughing through her novel—but she couldn't concentrate: her eyes went back to the top of the page. Would they have pulled *The*

Force of Ridicule already and given out an old play? Or would Wroughton be counting on her to turn up ten minutes before the curtain rose? She'd only done this—missed a performance—a handful of times in her whole career; it made her feel sick.

The messenger knocked at the door, as she'd been expecting, at ten past six. Her mother sent him away.

Eliza was still in her undress robe the next morning when Jack Palmer was shown up. 'Jack,' she said with startled pleasure.

He wasn't smiling. He threw himself into a chair beside Mrs Farren. 'What do you think you're doing, Eliza?'

She didn't know how to answer him.

'Last night was ghastly. After the orchestra'd dragged through every tune Handel ever wrote, I had to announce that you were too ill to leave your bed and the audience could have their money back at the doors, or stay to see Siddons in *The Fatal Marriage*. We had to yank the poor woman out of a box at Covent Garden for that; by the time she'd driven to Drury Lane and dressed, most of the crowd had gone home.'

'I'm sorry,' said Eliza, 'but she must understand: I'm using an actress's only weapon.'

He snorted. 'Your situation's not unique. All our wages are in arrears.'

'By £1100?'

He was jolted by the figure, she could tell, but he pressed on. 'For God's sake don't act the pauperess when you're a countess-in-waiting. You know it, we all know it, the entire British public knows it. You can draw on the resources of the richest man in England.'

Her mother had risen to her feet, mouth quivering, as if she was trying to find the nerve to order the actor out. Eliza pointed her fan at Palmer. 'I have never accepted a penny from the Earl of Derby. Not presents, not so much as a bracelet. Not that it's any of your business.'

'All I mean is that you can't possibly fear poverty. You've never heard your brats wail because they're hungry,' growled Palmer. 'So don't pretend this is about money.'

'It's about dignity, then.'

'There we go. Your foolish, feminine, damnable pride.'

'How dare you!'

'Mr Palmer—' began her mother.

'You're wasting the little bit of your career you have left. We expect to lose you at a day's notice,' Palmer told Eliza, 'whenever the paralytic Lady D. shrugs off her mortal coil. We're resigned to that. But in the meantime, don't muck about and pose and pout. The theatre needs you.'

'And you need to learn some manners, late in life,' she told him. 'Barging in here—'

'Eliza, I've known you nearly twenty years,' he said, 'and I've slapped out the flames when your dress caught fire in the middle of the *Spanish Barber*. What, am I to leave my card at the door like a stranger?'

She didn't know what to say.

'Come back with me. Let's open this comedy tonight; it could be the hit we all need.'

'I'm sorry, Jack. Not till this is settled.'

In the window, watching the tall, pot-bellied fellow stalk down Green Street, she felt a ridiculous urge to cry. None of them was young any more. Mrs Farren began to complain of the fellow's manners, but Eliza refused to talk about it.

The day dragged by, with no note from Sheridan or Wroughton; it was another brutally cold one. The papers were full of stories of beasts freezing to death in the fields, mothers and babies found stiff in ditches. The army and navy were running out of soldiers, because so many had died in the war, or through fever in the West Indies, or had been discharged unfit; all over the city, hard-faced amputees begged for pennies. *The Times* was urging ladies to refuse to patronise any shops (especially milliners) that employed men to do what women could; in these dark times such men were a disgrace to their sex and should go to war immediately, leaving the jobs for the many distressed females who needed them.

Her mother was clucking over something in the paper.

'What is it?'

'It says here a dressmaker was looking after her poor crippled mother, a Mrs Lamb, when suddenly she upped and stabbed the old woman to death in a frenzical fit!'

'Amazing,' murmured Eliza, hiding a smile.

In the late afternoon the messenger brought Sheridan's letter. *Farren,* it began brusquely,

> *I think this the dirtiest trick you've ever yet played. These coercive measures are unworthy of a lady* (soi-disant) *and contrary to your Articles of Engagement. £150 is the very limit of my resources at the moment & you shall immediately have a draft at a short date on our firm for that sum. May I give out* The Force of Ridicule *for tonight?*

Eliza steeled herself and sent back a single line: *My answer remains the same.* She went to bed early.

On the third morning, Sunday, the messenger brought a draft for £300 on Coutts the banker, signed by Westley, the treasurer. Eliza looked at it wearily. Well, she supposed it would have to do for now. Every day she stayed away from Drury Lane she felt further adrift.

FEBRUARY 1797

Berkeley Square was quiet, that Tuesday morning, except for the rustle of the plane trees. Derby's coachman drew up at no. 11, where the street was thickly strewn with straw and the door knocker was muffled in cloth: two bad signs. 'I may be some time,' Derby said to the driver. 'Why don't you see if Miss Farren needs the carriage? If my business is finished before you come back I'll take a hackney.'

'Very good, M'Lord.'

Derby tapped the knocker gently. The door was opened by a footman, almost at once.

When he was shown into the dark room he couldn't see a thing. 'Your Lordship, what an honour you do me,' came a creaking voice from the bed.

'I wasn't sure you'd be up to receiving visitors, sir.'

Walpole's valet dragged him up a little on the pillows. Derby's eyes were adjusting to the dim. 'Oh, when I'm not in pain I'm still capable of being amused,' drawled the old man, 'which is not to say that every visitor achieves it.'

Derby laughed under his breath as he took a seat. 'I must do my best.' He had only got around to paying this visit because he'd heard at Brooks's that Walpole was on his deathbed. He wondered whether to ask after his health or not.

'Oh, I have great hopes of you,' said the small voice. 'Most of my visitors these days are charitable elders, together with about fourscore nephews and nieces of various ages, brought along to stare at me as the Methuselah of the family.' His words came out slow and faint, but he seemed quite coherent, which was a relief to Derby. 'They never troubled themselves much about me before, but now they begin to see me in the light of a legator they grow very attentive, and send game and sweetmeats, none of which I can eat. They can speak only of their own contemporaries, which interests me no more than if they chattered of their dolls or bats and balls.'

'I hope I'm old enough, at least, to provide congenial conversation. Who was your last amusing visitor?' asked Derby.

'Hm. Mr Lysons the clergyman is not very amusing in himself, but he did tell me about a Welsh sportsman who recently had his daughter christened—let me get this right—*Louisa Victoria Maria Sobieski Foxhunter Moll Boycott.*'

'I congratulate you on your memory.'

'That'll be the last faculty to go,' said Walpole, 'some days I feel like a great sack of memory. Now what can you tell me about politics?' he asked almost briskly. 'Really, these days I see nobody who knows anything.'

'Well, the story that's flying round Brooks's this week', Derby began, 'is of Pitt's broken engagement.'

'Engagement?' Walpole's eyes bulged in their sallow sockets. 'Has the man not enough to do to keep this country out of the abyss, in these mad times, but he must go looking for a wife?'

'I believe it was the other way round. Pitt's such a gloomy monk, he barely sees his friends, let alone going a-wooing. No, it was his neighbour Lord Auckland who tried to foist his eldest daughter on to our PM, but Pitt seems finally to have made his excuses and fled.' Derby was going to go further and report that Pitt was said to have blamed his withdrawal on *certain insurmountable obstacles* that he wasn't willing to discuss with Auckland. According to Sheridan, this was proof positive that Pitt was the molly he'd always thought him. But it occurred to Derby just in time that Walpole himself had been dogged by such rumours for most of his life.

'Tell me, what information have you on the French fleet?' asked the old man.

There'd been several alarming attempts at invasion. At Christmas General Hoche had tried to land 15,000 men on the south-west coast of Ireland in a high gale. 'Have you heard about Wales, sir?'

'What about Wales?'

'Well, I don't mean to alarm you in your present state of health—'

'Tush,' said Walpole, waving one claw.

'—but a legion of French convicts landed there last week.'

'How alarming!'

'It seems they hoped to attract the locals to their standard,' Derby explained, 'having read exaggerated reports of the rebellious state of the Welsh. But they were quickly routed by a band of Pembrokeshire females! Can't you just picture the women, in their red cloaks and black top hats, waving pitchforks and reaping hooks?'

Walpole let out a gasp of mirth. 'Clearly the crimpers have been recruiting the wrong sort of Britons.'

'So the invaders surrendered on Friday,' Derby told him, 'all 1400 of them. They're to be jailed on the Isle of Man. Now there are outbreaks of panic all round the country whenever someone spots an innocent merchantman or fishing vessel on the horizon. It does seem as if only luck has protected us from invasion so far—luck and weather.'

'Of course, you and your radical friends might welcome such visitors.'

The sly line came out so faintly that Derby took a few seconds to recognise it for a quip; Walpole's famous delivery had deserted him. 'Aha,' said Derby, erring on the side of flippancy, 'but no one's safe in a revolution. Sheridan was just saying the other day that if the French landed in numbers, Pitt would declare martial law and start hanging all troublemakers—the remains of our Party included. And on the other hand, if General Bonaparte added these islands to his string of conquests, I suspect I'd be among the first aristos to face the Guillotine.'

'What a peculiar position you find yourself in,' commented Walpole pleasantly.

'Oh, but it'll never happen,' Derby said, as he always did. Despite the bad fright he'd had when the mob had attacked the royal carriage last winter, he'd clung to his Foxite principles; he couldn't afford to change his mind at this stage. As Lord-Lieutenant of Lancashire he steadfastly refused to supply the Home Office with details of *seditious activities* in the area. 'Pitt's new hobby-horse is a Loyalty Loan, as he calls it. There was a very persuasive story going round Brooks's that any man of property who didn't volunteer to lend the government vast amounts would find the same sum demanded in the form of a tax—so we all lined up to subscribe to the Loan on its opening day.'

Walpole chuckled feebly.

'And speaking of money, sir, have you heard that all our gold has turned to paper?'

'Whatever can you mean?'

'Well, cash has been running short and after the news from Pembrokeshire there was a frenzied run on the Bank of England. So the Cabinet decided—in the absence of a visit from King

Midas—that the only solution was to suspend payments in gold. Anything above 20 shillings will now come in the form of paper. There've been shrieks of protest, of course, and some hoarding...'

'Gad, it's as bad as the French and their worthless *assignats*,' wheezed the old man. 'What, you mean that were I to have myself carried into the Bank to withdraw £3 of my own gold they'd refuse me?'

'They'd give you a banknote, which is worth the same.'

Walpole snorted disapprovingly. 'It doesn't feel like the same thing. Not at all as heavy in the pockets.'

'Well, then, you'd save on your tailor's bill,' Derby told him.

The old man let out a terrible cackle of mirth. 'Young man, I haven't had a new suit since 1779!' He coughed and struggled to catch his breath. Opening his mouth, he let out a long, strange sound; Derby thought it was a cry of pain, but it turned out to be a yawn. 'I'd best hurry up and die. All my gold is turned to paper, as it were. Being so bereft of all my forces and decayed in spirits and understanding, I naturally dread being a burden.'

'I'm sure no one thinks of you as one.'

'Things become apparent', whispered the old man, 'when one lies on one's back in the dark waiting for pains to approach or recede. My best friends are all dead; I cling to young people who try to shake me off. My servants think more of their own comfort than mine. I'm become a nuisance and a bore.'

'Mr Walpole!' Derby protested. 'Never a bore.'

'You're kind. Perhaps that could be my epitaph: *Never a bore*,' murmured Walpole with a sort of pleasure.

Standing in the hall, waiting for the footman to bring his great-coat and hat, Derby heard light footsteps on the stairs. He turned.

She was looking very handsome in a simple blue wrapping gown; she seemed just as shocked as he was. 'Lord Derby.'

'Mrs Damer.'

'Are you here to—' She saw the servant come up with his things. 'Ah, your visit is over.'

'I arrived an hour ago,' said Derby, absurdly defensive.

'How good of you.' She sounded as if she meant it. 'He'll have appreciated it.'

Derby knew he should bow and leave. Considering how abruptly and coldly he had ended their friendship, almost three years ago, he had no right to expect a civil conversation. 'What's wrong with him?'

'Age,' said Anne Damer, 'simply the weakness of age. It's not the gout, not in itself, though that adds to his pain. He's losing strength all the time and his pulse is at eighty. He coughs and vomits violently, doesn't eat, and he has inflamed abscesses in both legs.'

Derby winced.

'You chose a lucky day,' she added; 'yesterday he had no voice at all and was suffering from delusions.'

'What kind of delusions?'

'He gets it into his head that we've all abandoned him,' she said, her face blank; 'myself, Miss Berry, all his intimates. We're here every day, but he speaks as if we've gone abroad. He complains that we never write.'

'BUT HOW did it feel, to meet the Earl again by accident?' In the parlour at Berkeley Square Mary examined her fingertips.

Anne shrugged. 'It doesn't matter any more.'

She was tired; they were both tired from staying up at night with Walpole and taking shifts in his dark bedroom all day. There were so many papers to go over; Mary (behind the cover of her father's name) was to be the literary executrix, and Anne and her uncle Lord Frederick Campbell were joint executors of the estate.

'All you can think of is Walpole. I know, I'm the same,' said Mary. 'It's a curious numbness. A suspension.'

'I want Walpole to survive this illness, I do,' insisted Anne, 'and he still may; if ever there was a man likely to defy his doctors and live out a whole century it's he. But in another way I suppose I'm… waiting.'

'For it to be over,' said Mary, almost whispering.

'It's not the pain; I'm used to seeing him in pain. It's the confusion.' Walpole's or hers? she wondered. 'I can't stand his bitter reflections, the accusations of conspiracy. He looks me in the eye and tells me I've deserted him in his hour of greatest need.'

'Oh, my darling.' Mary's hand was warm on the nape of Anne's neck. 'He doesn't mean it; it's just his sickness talking, or the drugs.'

'I'm not so sure. I think he's beyond politeness. He knows about us,' Anne said, finally letting it out.

'How can he?'

'Not everything, perhaps—not the details—but he knows there's been some sort of contest and he's lost it. Lost you.'

She thought Mary would deny it, but the answer surprised her. 'And you, if it comes to that.'

Anne stared at her.

'It's true,' said Mary. 'You were his favourite long before I came on the scene.'

'There's no comparison,' she began irritably. 'The minute he met you—all you Berrys, come to that—he was besotted.'

'But Agnes and I are like children to him,' said Mary, 'whereas you're Walpole's peer, not in age but in other ways. I think he counted on you to stay unattached, the great artist, by his side.'

'Perhaps a little, but it's—'

Mary had put her face in her hands. 'Are we really arguing about whom a dying man has loved more?'

A dying man. The phrase froze Anne. How ridiculous of her to resent Walpole's preference. After all, wouldn't she choose Mary over Walpole? Hadn't she already? Love did that. It cut through everything else; it was the chisel that carved people into its own preferred shape. 'Come to that,' she said ruefully, 'we've only been the preoccupations of his later years. He loved and lost other friends before either of us was born.'

'THESE LAST few weeks,' remarked Walpole, 'I believe I may have mislaid my sense of humour. I do apologise.'

Anne looked up from her book, startled. Soon he was dozing again. She watched the hard wrinkles of his monkey face relax.

That morning Mary brought in Mr Lawrence, the King's painter, who wanted to take a sketch of the old man. Walpole slept right through it. The painter looked like any other busy gentleman in a navy-blue frock coat these days; so unlike the sulky boy who'd painted that remarkable portrait of Eliza Farren in her furs. 'What are you working on now, Mr Lawrence?'

'A vast canvas,' he told her shortly, '*Satan Calling up his Legions.*'

'Where has all our gaiety gone?' she wondered.

Lawrence gave a small shrug and returned to his drawing.

After the painter had left, Walpole woke and murmured, 'I miss my treasure house.'

'As soon as the weather warms a little,' Mary said, 'we'll wrap you up and drive you down to Twickenham.'

He gave her a wry look, as if to say he knew she didn't believe her own words. 'I thought I heard booming, last night, unless it was some fancy or vagrant memory?'

'No,' Anne told him, 'the Tower guns were firing to celebrate Sir John Jervis having beaten the Spanish fleet at St Vincent.'

She thought this news might cheer him, but his face was neutral. 'I sometimes think I've lived a dozen lives,' he murmured. 'I knew James II's mistress, and the courtiers who served under King William and then Queen Anne. I've witnessed half a dozen wars, the Jacobite Rising and the loss of America. I spent thirteen months at Florence, seven months at Paris, twenty-five years in Parliament. As a child I was carried to the first opera performed in England and I kissed the hand of George I, and now I groan over the frolics of his great-great-grandson...No, this can't all have happened in one life! All this and yet I'm not one fifth as old as Methuselah.'

'Not a dozen lives but one, lived fully,' Anne told him, watching Mary carry his untouched tray out of the room.

'Well, I've had to keep myself busy. I've been little loved,' he said suddenly.

'Walpole!'

'It's true, my dear, regrettably true. I've been the World's favourite acquaintance. A great fellow for rounding out a dinner.'

'But you've had so many priceless friendships—' she protested.

'Oh, I've loved, yes; I have a gift for it. Loved often and hard and long. But in return...well, I've been liked, shall we say. Men and women have been vastly *fond* of me,' he said, 'but I'm not so easily fooled.'

She didn't know what to say. If that was how his life had seemed to Walpole then no arguing would change his mind. And after all, what evidence could she offer? No one had ever *cleaved* to him, as the Scriptures put it.

'Mind you, I've sometimes appreciated the pretence,' he went on, almost whispering. 'Everybody wears a mask. Hadn't you noticed? We put them on for one very good reason: we dislike our own faces.'

Anne stared at him, troubled.

'It's not hypocrisy so much as aspiration. We wear them to persuade ourselves as much as others.' A long noisy breath, taken in and released. 'Friendship, fairness, loyalty, dignity—what are they but lovely masks, which we wear till they begin to pinch and then let fall?'

An hour after that there was a long episode of coughing. When Philip the valet came in, Anne said she could deal with it herself, which seemed to annoy him. Walpole vomited into his basin, producing little but clear mucous. He was very weak. 'What a great deal of killing I'm taking. It's not so easy to die as it's commonly imagined.' Somehow he got to talking about his soul. 'To be perfectly honest, my dear, I have my doubts about its exact destination.'

'You can't fear...descent,' said Anne, resorting to a flippant euphemism.

'I suppose not,' he murmured, 'but nor am I entirely confident of exaltation. And I wouldn't fancy harps and sofas made of cloud. In fact, though I have a great respect for Christian ethics, I must tell you in confidence that the more supernatural doctrines of the Church have always left me sceptical.'

'Oh,' she said, helpless.

'But I've always hoped that there might be...somewhere, in some ineffable sense, perhaps, you know, somewhere that we all might meet again,' said Walpole. 'Well, not quite *all* of us, obviously, or it would be such a scrum. Worse than one of Georgiana's routs in the old days.'

Anne laughed weakly.

'A select company, a happy few, with our animals, of course; Fidelle chasing her tail by the door, Tonton asleep on the rug.'

'Oh, dear, do you suppose the celestial rugs already bear the marks of Tonton's little accidents?'

'No, no,' he assured her, 'all that will have been swabbed away by angels. I declare, it doesn't frighten me, when I think of those who've gone before me. They're all dead, you know, all my dear fellows,' he murmured, shutting his papery eyelids. The names came out one at a time, as if pulled up from a well. 'Gray, yes...and Bentley, and Chute, who helped me build my fairy castle, and Littleton too...and Montagu. West. Ashton. Lord Lincoln, who was famed for the biggest member in London.'

Anne blinked. Had she misheard the whispered words? Did Walpole know he was speaking aloud, did he even remember she was there, know who she was? Or was he casting off propriety at last?

'Harry, my dearest Harry Conway, gone before me,' he murmured. 'All the men are dead; there are only women left now. How can I still be here when the men are all gone?'

Anne wanted to weep.

'He was very sweet this morning,' she told Mary much later, when they passed in the corridor; 'we spoke of heaven and old friends.'

Mary was carrying a covered basin and her face was drawn. 'He's delirious again now.'

'Oh, no.' She'd hoped he'd emerged from that dark maze.

Sometimes she thought souls were lazy, or befuddled; they didn't seem to know their way out. 'I'll go to him.'

'It's all right, my love,' said Mary, 'you need your rest.' A maid passed by just then and Mary handed over the basin.

Anne walked back with her. The room was fetid with sickness. 'It's Anne,' she said, stooping over him.

Walpole's crusted eyes looked back at her balefully. 'She's in Gibraltar.'

'No, no.'

'She never came home from Lisbon. Her nose was shockingly broken.' His voice was a tiny insect in the stuffy room. 'I am neglected and deserted by the only friends I have left.'

'But dear Walpole,' said Mary on the other side of him, 'I'm Mary, the broken nose was mine. We're here, right here by your side; we haven't left you.'

'Abandoned', he insisted, 'by those to whom I unwisely clung. Hedged about with cruel strangers!'

'We were only out of your room for five minutes,' Anne told him.

'With the brave General, I fancy,' he wheezed, spitting a little.

That took her aback. Did he mean O'Hara?

He paused for so long she thought he'd fallen asleep. 'Conway, the bravest of them all,' he said at last, very faint. 'Brave Harry. Horry and Harry.'

Anne was overwhelmed with exhaustion. She sat down. Mary settled herself beside her and gripped her hand. Anne was too tired to squeeze back. Walpole was like a wailing baby; nothing could satisfy him.

In his sleep he looked a trifle healthier; there was a warmer tinge to his cheeks.

MARCH 1797

A mild breeze came over the meadow to Strawberry Hill. 'I wonder might I see the death mask?' asked Richmond.

'Certainly.' Anne led him upstairs to the library where it lay, very white and hard, on a black velvet cushion. Richmond approached it with the firm look of the connoisseur. The face was an extraordinary one, narrow and alien; Anne took no credit for it. 'I can't imagine why I never sculpted him while he was with us. Somehow it never occurred to me.' But the only man she'd ever immortalised was King George; that was a strange thing. 'This is only the plaster cast of the mask, of course. I'll have to begin the marble version as soon as I have some time.'

'There's no hurry, surely,' said the Duke.

'Plaster's more brittle than it looks,' she told him, 'the slightest thing could chip or crack it.' Then all at once she was blinded by tears, staggering. Richmond pressed her face to his shoulder. She sobbed harshly. 'It was the abscess in his throat that finished him; he couldn't swallow a thing for the last week. He starved to death.'

Her brother-in-law patted her back stiffly. Anne remembered that she hadn't cried like this at her sister's funeral; did Richmond resent it? It seemed impossible not to hurt people with every step, every word. The world was bruised all over. Richmond had been wearing mourning for four months now and he seemed lost without Lady Mary; who else had ever really known him? Despite the rumours that he might propose to Lady Bess Foster—who'd recently been freed to remarry by the death of her long absent husband—he'd made no moves to put the *affaire* on any official footing.

And Georgiana, Anne wondered, downstairs in the milling crowd again, what did the poor disfigured Duchess think about her beloved Bess's new liaison? Was it possible to love someone without jealousy? 'You seem much better these days,' Anne told her in a murmur, not quite honestly.

Georgiana produced her famous smile. 'I'm half blind and as dependent as a child, but Bess makes the best of mothers. One's glory days can't last for ever, I suppose. Did I ever tell you about the Irishman who came to Devonshire House once? *By Gob, your la'ship*, he said, *I could light me pipe at dem gorgeous eyes!*'

Anne laughed with her, wanting to cry.

They talked about the surreal prospect of invasion, as every-body did these days. Every attic was rumoured to conceal quantities of arms and gunpowder, every sullen servant in London was watched for signs of membership in a secret army, like the United Irishmen that were causing such alarm across the water. (Richmond's nephew and Sheridan's bosom friend, Lord Edward Fitzgerald, was said to be on the brink of arrest for treason.)

Mary detached herself gently from her waiting, red-faced sister and came over to take Anne's elbow whispering, 'It's time for the reading of the Will.'

Oh, God, Anne had forgotten the last part of the ritual. She and Mary walked along the corridor slowly, arm in arm. She didn't worry how it might look; she couldn't care less if their manner was too intense. 'Your letter, last night, was the only thing that did me any good in the absence of your healing hands,' she whispered in Mary's ear. 'I thought I'd go mad, all alone in that melancholy house in Berkeley Square.'

Mary smiled faintly. 'We were both born to suffer in this world—but at least we may suffer together.'

Anne caught herself looking at the painted glass, memorising the angles of arches. This might be the last time she would ever be at Strawberry Hill. She barely knew the Duchess of Gloucester, the favourite niece who was to inherit the house; besides, would she ever want to visit it with its creator gone?

The crowd squeezed into the dark refectory, making a com-motion. There weren't enough chairs; Reynolds's paintings of the dead man's friends looked down on the crowd. Anne sat on a bench and tried to concentrate on the droning voice of the lawyer, Mr Blake.

The deceased Earl of Orford (how strange to hear him called that) had left his estates in Norfolk and Houghton to Lord Chol-mondeley, and £10,000 to the Duchess of Gloucester. Mr Berry was to inherit his manuscripts, the Berry sisters £4000 each—*bless him*, thought Anne—and the use, for as long as they remained unmarried, of the building, grounds and furniture of the house known as Little Strawberry Hill. Sir Horace Mann got £5000, Lady Ailesbury £4000, nineteen nieces and nephews got £500 each, Philip the valet got £1500, and for some reason the poor secretary Kirgate received only £100. There were inconsistencies and omissions; some of his best friends were not mentioned in the Will.

'The sum of £6000 outright, and the buildings, grounds and furniture of the house known as Strawberry Hill, for her lifetime, is bequeathed to Mrs Anne Seymour Conway Damer.'

She jerked in her seat. 'What?' she said. 'No, that's a mistake.'

'It goes to you first, Mrs Damer, until your death,' explained Mr Blake, 'and only then does it pass to the Duchess of Gloucester.'

The Duchess nodded at her civilly.

'Did the deceased not mention the matter to you?'

Anne shook her head. She looked to Mary; the younger woman's dark eyes were glittering with tears. *Strawberry Hill?* Anne was too bewildered to begin to understand this gift. Walpole had been angry with her ever since Bognor, or before; hadn't she betrayed him, over and over, and hadn't he known it?

We regret to announce the departure from this life, at forty-four years, on the fourteenth of this month, at her home on Gloucester Street in the parish of Marylebone, of that famous beauty of a former age, the Countess of Derby.

'She's not buried yet,' Mrs Farren told her daughter with an awful fascination.

Eliza didn't look up from the letter she was writing. 'Why on earth not?'

'Debts. It says the Countess asked to be buried with all the pomp of her rank, but her corpse can't be released till her family discharge what's owing, which amounts to £5000.'

'That's not so very much for a citizen of the Beau Monde,' said Eliza, trying for a light tone. 'Why, Georgiana's never owed less than £50,000.'

She wasn't acting that night; *Much Ado* had closed and she'd begged Wroughton to give her some breathing space before her next role. The truth was that since the news of her rival's death Eliza had felt strangely sunken, unequal to the task of stepping on stage.

Her mother was sitting very close to her; Eliza curved her arm to make sure her writing couldn't be read.

> *My lord,*
> *I hope it won't seem hypocritical of me to offer you my sympa-*
> *thies. The death of a person with whose life yours has been so*
> *long & so intimately connected must be a shock to the nerves.*

Was Derby feeling guilty now, she wondered, or relieved, or a pe-culiar mixture of the two? Were his friends congratulating him, or teasing him for his readiness to jump from one trap to the next? A bitter resentment bubbled up in Eliza. It would be said that the ac-tress had reeled in her big fish at last. She couldn't stop the gossip, and the paragraphs, and the caricatures, but she could at least keep things absolutely clear between herself and Derby.

> *Don't be injured by my enclosure of the Document you were gal-*
> *lant enough to present me with at Knowsley three Christmases*
> *past. I make no claim on you. It may strike you that I've kept you*
> *waiting too long & I'm no longer in my first youth.*

No, that line sounded pathetic; she inked it out.

> *You've given me no reason to suspect that your feelings have*
> *changed, but perhaps I've lived among actors too long to have*
> *any faith in my power to read a face. Which of us in this World*
> *never wears a disguise, for kind reasons as often as cruel?*

The pen skidded and the page flew out of her hands. 'Mother!'

Margaret Farren backed away, peering at the letter, her furious lip jutting. 'I knew it. You mean to throw it all away in the last act.'

Eliza was on her feet. 'Give it back.'

'What devilish little fool is this that calls itself my daughter?' cried Mrs Farren. 'Such a troublesome and wanton spirit you've always had, Betsy, behind that smooth face!'

Eliza reeled at the accusation. 'Wanton?' she repeated. 'I've lived like some anchoress. You've chaperoned my every waking minute since I was a child.'

'Wanton, I say,' ranted the old woman, 'because the best of men's not good enough for you. What, would you throw the Earl's signed promise back in his face? Hasn't he waited on you longer than Jacob in the Scripture?'

'The long delay, that's my point exactly—'

But Mrs Farren stormed on. 'So Derby's plug-ugly; what's that in a man? Is it so dull to be adored and worshipped? Who are you pining for, some fierce Oriental sultan on a flying carpet?'

Eliza stared.

The woman's face was darkening to purple. 'Or maybe it's not a man you want at all.'

As Eliza stepped closer—while her arm was flying up of its own accord to backhand her mother across the cheek hard enough to raise a green bruise for a week—she already knew how it would go. She acknowledged in her bones that she was going to marry Lord Derby and spend the rest of her mother's life silently begging her pardon. But she hit her anyway.

. . . Which of us in this World never wears a disguise, for kind reasons as often as cruel? This is why I'm returning your Promise. If you wish you may destroy it & we'll not speak of it again. I will always be glad to call myself
  your friend,
  E. F.

Derby, halfway through breakfast, crumpled the letter and its enclosure in his fist. *Christ, how long does she mean to torment me?* But he didn't want the servants to read the letter, or, God forbid, sell it to a newspaper; he never liked to leave temptation in their way. He

walked over to the fire and stuffed the paper ball in, watched till it
was ash.

'But M'Lord, the carriage—'

'I don't need it, I'll walk.'

The man goggled at him. It seemed to fill him with shame that
his master, a peer of the realm, would be seen walking down the
street. Derby could have explained that he was only going round
the corner to Green Street, but there was just one person in this
world to whom he was willing to explain himself today. He knew
he shouldn't be doing this at all—approaching Eliza Farren's house
in the broad light of day not a week after his bereavement—but he
was beyond such scruples.

The butler was instructing the footman to fetch His Lordship's
mourning greatcoat, the one with the black squirrel trim. 'I'm very
well as I am,' said Derby with vast impatience and opened the front
door himself.

The April day wasn't as mild as it had looked from the window;
the breeze tightened Derby's calves as he walked and got in under
his black cloth frock coat. He felt a twinge of gout in his elbow. He
told himself to stop thinking like an old man.

Up North Audley Street and left on to Green Street. He stood
outside the house for a moment, catching his breath, and became
aware that a carriage had slowed to a halt. He'd been seen; would
this be in the evening papers? *A certain widowed Peer was glimpsed
on G——n St today, panting outside the Bow Window of his theatrical Inamorata...* It didn't matter.

He turned; the face in the window was framed in a handsome
black hood trimmed with fur. 'Mrs Damer,' he said with a bow. 'My
commiserations on your loss,' he added, remembering Walpole.

'And mine on yours.' Were those eyes ironical or merely grave?
She held his gaze a moment longer, then said a word to the driver.
She pulled the curtain across and the carriage surged on down the
street towards Grosvenor Square.

He was rattled; he was thrown. Was Anne Damer some kind of
witch to haunt him so? Behind him the door scraped open and he

spun round. It wasn't Mrs Farren but the manservant, who muttered something about the mistress inviting him to step up.

Eliza was waiting for him in the parlour. She was alone, for once, thank Christ. Derby came in the door full of wrathful recriminations, but they all fell away at the sight of her face. It was the same perfect oval as it had always been, but there was something uncertain in her azure eyes. She hadn't meant her letter to be cruel, he realised, she was only nervous; a filly shying at the big jump. Her face was like a child's, but it also gave him some hint, for the first time since he'd known her, of what she would look like when she was old. He felt irritable with tenderness. He got down on one cold, aching knee.

She didn't say a word.

'Will you marry me?' Having rehearsed the line for sixteen years, Derby thought he knew how to say it so it would express everything he felt. But it came out quite formal.

Her tone was just as plain: 'I will.'

APRIL 1797

The softly handsome Lord Edward Smith-Stanley drove her to the theatre. His father had asked the young MP to be Miss Farren's escort this month, to save the couple some embarrassment until the first month of mourning was over. 'What do you think of these peace talks between France and Austria, Miss Farren?' he asked. 'I very much wish that *our* government hadn't missed its moment to make peace with France, too.'

'So do I,' she assured him, speaking very clearly because of his bad hearing. He was a sweet fellow and she'd be glad to be his stepmother, absurd though that sounded. All that worried Eliza was a paragraph in one of the newspapers about young Lord Stanley's *aspirations to supplant his Father in a certain Actress's heart...*

She managed to catch Sheridan in the corridor and ask for a few moments in his office. 'I'm to marry Lord Derby on the first of May.'

'Felicitations,' he said blandly.

She was glad the date was soon; the situation was so awkward—almost farcical, with Derby having to go about in mourning clothes over his blithe heart—that she wanted it to be over.

'Now some claimed the Derby stallion would shy at the final ditch,' remarked Sheridan, 'but I always said there'd be no stopping him. The betting was high at Brooks's on this point, I can tell you—and I'll have heavy pockets tonight.'

'I've no idea what you mean,' said Eliza with a wintry smile.

'Well, you must admit it's not a very common event, is it?—an actress catching such a plum? In the whole annals of the theatre', said Sheridan, looking almost fondly around him, 'I can't think of more than one or two examples.'

'I intend to retire after my performance next week,' she told him.

'Ah, yes,' he said with a sigh. 'When I married the first Mrs Sheridan we could have done with her earnings, but I wouldn't have dreamed of being disgraced by having my wife perform for hire. She got £100 by her last concert, but I made her lay it in the plate at church.'

'What a gracious gesture,' said Eliza sardonically. *He thinks we theatre folk are all whores,* she realised. *Himself included.*

'Well, we'll miss you, Miss Farren, I must say,' said Sheridan. 'You're a perverse nymph and you've given me a few grey hairs over the years, but you can certainly act. You'll need all your talent where you're going. I dare say you'll find Knowsley like one long elegant comedy—though short on jokes. Luxurious costumes, superb scenery, but never a moment to step out of role and take a breather.'

Eliza hated him at that moment. She and Sheridan had never sat down and had a conversation in their lives—but he knew her well. 'Now, about my arrears,' she said with a sharp smile. 'The debt still amounts to more than £800. If you prefer, you can take the matter up with Derby; I know you're more used to talking of money with *him*.'

That dart seemed to bounce off Sheridan. 'Now, this is too bad,' he teased, 'the richest lord in England means to rob us of our brightest star and then quarrel with us for a little dust she leaves sprinkled behind her.'

'Gold dust,' she said.

'Dust all the same.'

But she found herself grinning unwillingly. Sheridan had won this final round.

THE EVENING before her last performance Eliza sat at her *secrétaire*, studying the latest prints. A crude one called *The Dance of Death* showed herself and Derby dancing round Lady Derby in her coffin. (Perhaps the Earl was right when he'd speculated the other day that satire released tension; perhaps because the British upper ranks had submitted to the vicious engraving knives of Rowlandson, Gillray and their ilk, they'd avoided the literal Guillotine. So far, at least.) Here was another called *Contemplations upon a Coronet* that showed Eliza at her dressing table in an ecstasy:

> —*hey for my Lady Niminy-Piminy*—*O, Gemini!*—*no more straw beds in Barns*—*no more scowling Managers!*—*& curtsying to a dirty Public!*—*but a Coronet up on my coach*—*dashing at the opera!*—*shining at the Court!*—*oh, dear! dear! what shall I come to!*

That one almost made her laugh. It had been such a long time since *straw beds in barns*. She thought back and tried to remember how that had felt: the scratchiness of old straw under sacking. No, the memory was out of reach now; that was little Betsy who'd slept on straw, not Miss Eliza Farren.

Well, tomorrow she'd be saying farewell to *scowling Managers* and making her last curtsy to the *dirty Public*. She was to give them Lady Teazle in the *School for Scandal*—not so much her favourite as theirs. As she lay awake in the dark night, her mind was clogged with the names of all the women she'd played over the years. *Lady Fanciful, Lady Modish, Lady Paragon, Lady Plotwell, Lady Rustic, Lady Sadlife, Lady Townly, Lady Trifle*: they lined up like some ghost battalion in old-fashioned hoops and lace ruffles. *Mrs Sullen,*

Mrs Simper, Mrs Freelove, Miss Loveless, Miss Lovely, Miss Languish. Alcmena, Alinda, Almeida, she thought, starting to work her way through the alphabet in the hopes that it would send her to sleep; *several Belindas, Berinthia, Bisarre,* and the *Baroness of Bruchsal.*

She yawned, the following evening, as she pulled on the turban and plumes that she'd worn for Teazle ever since big hats went out of fashion. She darkened her eyebrows and shaded the lids with blue; used a dab of rouge to enlarge her lower lip, which had always been a trifle too thin.

There was nothing about her retirement on the playbills, but all London knew. Jack Palmer, in his Joseph Surface costume, popped his head in to say that the crowd was the biggest for years; the doorkeepers had never taken in so high a sum on a non-Ben night. Several carriages had collided outside and three people had been hurt while attempting to squeeze into their boxes.

'Not badly?' Eliza stared at him, thinking of the terrible night at the Haymarket when a dozen people had been trampled to death.

'Nothing to worry about. And your Earl appeared in his box at the end of my scene and got a big cheer,' he assured her.

'Jack?' she said as he was going.

He cocked an eyebrow.

'Thanks.'

'For what?'

'For twenty years.'

He sketched a mocking bow and the boy came to say that Act Two was about to begin.

Eliza tripped on stage as young Lady Teazle, to scoff at her grouchy old husband, played by Tom King. He attempted to an-swer—but they were silenced by a deafening hail of applause. She stood there, smiling and curtsying. The clapping only got louder; the crowd wouldn't let her begin. She felt a tightness in her throat. This was the same audience who'd hissed her when she missed per-formances, howled with laughter when she'd been called a *Tommy.* Was it her departure that was making them so fond, or her story, the fairy tale of a poor girl lifted to a glittering rank?

She found the Derby box and gave him a private smile. The Richmond box was usually empty these days; tonight it was occupied by Anne Damer. Eliza stared at her; her heart appeared to squeeze shut for a moment, before it beat again.

'*Lady Teazle, Lady Teazle, I'll not bear it,*' began Tom King, shaking his head.

'*Sir Peter, Sir Peter, you may bear it or not, as you please,*' she cried merrily, '*but I ought to have my own way in everything, and what's more, I will too.*'

After her first few scenes had passed Eliza found that the familiar lines—not just hers, but her fellow actors' too—were playing rather strangely. The sparkling wit was still there, but also other tones. It was tragic, really, that Sir Peter loved his wife but couldn't tell her so for fear she'd laugh at him; awful, the way these gossips tore apart their so-called friends.

By the end of the play Eliza's throat had a swollen feeling, as if she'd been speaking for days on end. When she came out to take her bows she saw that Anne Damer had already gone. This gave her a peculiar pang: *She might at least have stayed to the end.*

Lady Teazle's epilogue was an old piece, by Colman, but Sheridan thought it suited Eliza's present circumstances perfectly. '*I, who was late so volatile and gay,*' she began,

> *Like a trade wind must now blow all one way,*
> *Bend all my cares, my studies, and my vows,*
> *To one dull rusty weathercock—my spouse!*

Here she bobbed a sulky curtsy in the direction of the Derby box, which won her a great laugh. And now she began a mime of rural boredom.

> *In a lone rustic hall for ever pounded,*
> *With dogs, cats, rats and squalling brats surrounded...*

'Lots of little Derbys!' crowed a Cockney in the pit. Eliza ignored that, but it caused great hilarity.

Farewell all quality of high renown,
Pride, pomp, and circumstance of glorious town!
Farewell! your revels I partake no more,
And Lady Teazle's occupation's o'er...
No more in vice or error to engage,
Or play the fool at large on life's great stage.

Now at last it was over. She curtsied to left and right and centre, left and right and centre again, as she'd been taught by her mother before she'd stepped on her very first ramshackle provincial stage. But Eliza had never heard such deafening cheers in her life. Women fluttered their fans overhead; men tossed their hats and handkerchiefs in the air. Tulips and violets flew on to the stage. When she left this stage, Eliza realised with wet eyes, she'd be losing a self. She'd never be Lady Teazle again, nor any of the rustling, silken crew.

MAY 1797

The wedding day went by in rather a blur for Derby. The Reverend Hornby had come up from Knowsley to conduct the service in the smallest drawing room at Derby House. It was a quiet ceremony; Derby wanted nothing to remind him of the vainglorious *fête champêtre* with which he'd celebrated his first wedding. He thought of his younger self, dressed up as Rubens; what a nincompoop!

Today he was still in light mourning, as a concession to the World; his coat was silver grey with bands of black. After they'd gone through the marriage articles with the lawyer in an ante-room it was time for him to walk into the drawing room with Eliza's hand light as snow on his arm. She was wearing white and silver, something quite simple with long sleeves. 'First it was ordained for the procreation of children,' the vicar intoned.

Derby glanced at his grown-up son and two daughters, sitting together to his left. Did they find it strange to witness their old father going through these promises again at forty-five?

'Secondly it was ordained for a remedy against sin and to avoid fornication.'

Well, he and Eliza had certainly avoided fornication all these years, he thought with dark amusement.

'Thirdly it was ordained for the mutual society, help and comfort that the one ought to have for the other.'

He stole a quick look; Eliza was staring straight ahead. How well she carried herself always, Derby thought; nothing seemed to fluster her.

His cue, all of a sudden: 'I will,' he said hoarsely. He slid the Derby wedding ring on to her slim finger. His mother had worn it till she'd died when he was seven. The first Lady Derby should really have sent it back to him when they'd separated, but her executors had delivered it to him only last week. The blessing came next, then the prayers. They signed the register; she wrote *Eliza Smith-Stanley, Countess of Derby* and the words gave him an unspeakable thrill. Mrs Farren, sniffling as tradition demanded, was the witness. *I must see about settling an annuity on her,* he thought. He'd ordered suites of rooms to be refurbished for his mother-in-law, both at Derby House and at Knowsley; he'd spent enough evenings with Margaret Farren over the years to long for a bit of privacy at last.

The whole ceremony had gone by so fast, that Derby didn't have time to feel like the happiest man in the world. If anything, his state was a little flat. What was that *pensée* of Pascal's about preferring the hunt to the capture, the contest to the victory?

Afterwards, when the bride was resting in her room, Bunbury popped into Derby House to offer his warmest congratulations. 'A prime filly, to my eye, and good breeding stock too. Has she begun her visits?'

'No, she's sent her excuses till we come back from Knowsley.' Derby wished Eliza could be spared that, but it was impossible. A new bride had to call on every person of note in London and spend at least a quarter of an hour with each; Georgiana reckoned she'd done twenty-eight a day for three weeks.

After Bunbury had gone, Fox came by with Sheridan. He had an excited, guilty expression. 'I'm going to do it, old chap. I'm going to secede.'

Taken aback, Derby simply stared.

'When Grey's motion for Reform is defeated next month, I shall stand up and announce that to persevere in Opposition is to contribute to the hoodwinking of the people by maintaining the imposture that this government is a free and representative one. Then Grey and I will lead our remaining followers from the House.'

Disappointment mingled with a sort of relief. Another curtain falling. 'Well. If that's what you think right—I can't blame you,' Derby told him.

'Georgiana says Parliament's like an abused wife,' drawled Sheridan, 'with Pitt as the brutal husband who cows her. She clings to him only because she's given up all her jointure and even pin money into his hands, and the divorce would ruin her. Foxy here is the lover, d'you see, who has Dame Parliament's secret sympathies.'

Fox chuckled. 'Perhaps she'll pine more passionately for me if I walk away. Sherry's not coming, though.'

'Oh, I sympathise and I'll envy your retirement,' Sheridan assured him. 'This old manor house I've bought, Polesden Lacey—I dream of retreating there with Hecca and little Charlie.'

The new baby—a compensation for the last Mrs Sheridan's baby daughter, who hadn't long outlived her mother—had been named for his two godfathers, Fox and Grey. Despite all their combats over the years, Derby thought, this shrunken Party was held together by love.

'But secession's not in my nature. There's still the mutineering sailors to be defended and my poor Ireland...'

Fox patted Sheridan on the back. 'You're tireless. Whereas I wouldn't care if I were condemned never to stir a mile beyond St Anne's Hill for the rest of my days. I'm going to read Liz all the great epics, from the *Iliad* through to *Paradise Lost*.'

Is this the end of the story? Derby wondered. *Has Pitt won our war?* But the Eunuch couldn't last for ever, surely. 'Rest while you can, old Fox,' he said, 'because it won't be for ever. I intend to see you Prime Minister before I die.' It came out so sternly that they all started laughing.

THE CORRIDORS of Derby House were dim; the lamp on the wall outside Derby's bedroom had burnt down. In his nightshirt, cap and slippers, he fumbled his way down four doors and tapped on the wood, praying he'd got the right room. Under his nightshirt he was almost painfully erect. For some reason he found himself remembering a tactless remark of Busley's, the other day in the cock sheds: *You shouldn't breed from old stock, it stands to reason.*

The tapping was meant to warn his bride of his arrival, but it had a tentative timbre to it. No answer. Hadn't Eliza heard his knock? He found himself thinking of the motto over the gateway at Knowsley: *Bring good news and knock boldly.* He turned the handle and went in.

The Etruscan room had been Robert Adam's initial try at that style for the first Lady Derby; she'd hated it. It was painted all over with Etruscan motifs, like one great Wedgwood plate. Eliza was sitting up, very still, in his mother's bed. Only her head was showing, high on the pillows; her fair hair was down, spilling round her face. She smiled at him and lifted her sleeves out of the sheets. He thought he might burst with excitement at the sight of her. 'Are you cold?' he asked. 'Eliza,' he added, daring himself to use the long-forbidden name.

'No, no, I'm perfectly well.'

Derby went up the steps and crawled into the high bed. He wondered whether to snuff the candle, but it was on her side; he would have had to lean across her to do it. This was ridiculous, he was as timid as a boy. How many women had he had? he asked himself. Dozens; a dozen at least. Though more in the early part of his life than in the past ten years but never mind that now, never mind. What was he afraid of? Eliza was dazzling, as beautiful as she'd always been, perfect in all her lines, *age has not withered her*, he quoted in his head. It was just so strange to be here with her, alone in a room, allowed. He undid the ribbons at her bosom and she didn't lift her hands to stop him, made no objection, said not a single cold word, that was the really strange thing. It occurred to Derby that it would be easier to be bold if she fought him off a little. A gulp of laughter rose up in his throat.

'What is it?'

'Nothing,' Derby said and kissed her. That went well; her lips were as firm as an apple. He and she slid down in the bed and it creaked reassuringly. Eliza's bosom was startlingly soft, warm as a spaniel's mane. He was on top of her now. His toes touched her shins and he remembered how much shorter he was. Ugly, unworthy in every way. He told himself it didn't matter; none of that had ever mattered. He kissed her again and bruised his lip against her tooth. *This is it,* he told himself, spurring himself on; *this is the moment I've waited for, panted for.* He thought of the times he'd lain alone in his bed four rooms away and the thought of merely glimpsing Eliza's ankle had made his prick spring up hard as metal in his own fist. Would she be shocked if she knew that, or would she expect no better? She was worldly wise and a virgin; she was an actress who'd lived like a nun. He was bewildered, flustered, aroused and deflated. *Damn, damn, damn, damn your eyes*, he told himself.

After a while Derby moved away from her. She lay still, but he could hear her breathing. Was she excited or distressed? Against the light of the candle her face was shadowed black; he couldn't tell what she thought of him.

'You need your rest,' he said, his voice hoarse with the hypocrisy of it, and slid from the bed.

THE JOURNEY to Knowsley took two days, as the roads weren't as bad in summer. Mrs Farren was brimming over with excitement; she'd even adopted the irritating habit of calling Eliza *Your Ladyship*. Derby was civil but abstracted; he read a book the Duke of Bedford had given him on agricultural improvement and looked out of the window for hours on end, as if he'd never seen the English countryside before. Eliza ransacked her mind for the right thing to say. If only she could be frank and tell him not to worry about last night. It hadn't much alarmed her; it was only a kind of stage fright, surely? The two of them had to break the long habit of prohibition, that was all. It stood to reason that a new life took practice.

Outside Stoke, on the second day, Eliza found herself thinking of all the worldly, sophisticated characters she'd played, Lady Who and Mrs Whatsit, who never saw their husbands from breakfast till night. She remarked, 'I don't want to be a city countess.'

Derby and her mother both looked at her in puzzlement.

'Flirting and shopping and going to the play, I mean.'

'I thought you liked London,' he said.

'I did once, but this will be a new life, with a new name and a transformed circle of acquaintance. A fresh start is what I need,' she reassured him. 'I've seen enough and had enough of the World.'

Derby nodded in agreement. 'Happy he who retires from business to till the fields that were his father's, as Horace puts it.'

'Besides,' Eliza added, 'I expect I'll have new duties to keep me at home.' She was trying for a coy tone, with this hint at children, but it came out stiff.

The Earl shut his eyes and leaned back against the cushions. *Wonderful,* Eliza congratulated herself, *now you've really made him feel impotent.* Nearly thirty-five wasn't too old for her to begin breeding, surely? But Derby probably had no clear idea what age she was, she remembered; he'd taken her in marriage without any guarantees on that score. He was the best of men and she wanted to be the best of wives to him, but it was all going wrong.

THAT NIGHT in the strange, grand bedroom at Knowsley, scented by a bowl of early roses, she unpinned her hair, and glanced through a letter from Wales. Mrs Piozzi, after all this time.

May I offer my most humble congratulations? All the poor of Knowsley will be as much in love with you as the Earl has been for ten years past. Having come through all trials of delay &

calumny, you must be the happiest woman in the world—unless
your mother is. I hope your good reception at Court will make an
aristocrate *of your husband!*

Eliza couldn't read any more; she let the letter drop and stared at
her face in the mirror. She couldn't bear to get into bed and wait for
a re-enactment of last night. Or worse, what if Derby didn't come
to her room at all? How could they climb out of the awful abyss?

Decisive, she picked up her candle and opened the door. In the
corridor her feet stung with cold. She couldn't remember which
door was Derby's. This was ludicrous. What if she walked in on her
mother, or young Lord Edward?

She stole from door to door, listening, peering through the keyhole for a light. *There.* Derby at his desk in his shirtsleeves, looking
through some papers. How strange to see him through a keyhole,
quite oblivious of her; how mysterious the little man looked. She
turned the handle and went in before she could lose her nerve.

He looked up, owlish. 'My dear!'

'I know this isn't customary,' Eliza told him in a whisper, as she
advanced across the Turkish carpet. She almost said *My Lord,* as
usual. 'I'm sorry to invade your chamber,' she added, very pert,
coming close to him on the excuse of setting down her candlestick.
It was time to play the strumpet.

'You're quite welcome.' Derby's hand found the small of her
back.

'I simply wanted to say that I like it here.'

'At Knowsley?'

'Yes. And here.' She let herself down till she was sitting in his lap.

His arms were firm round her and his mouth was on her collarbone; his breath scalded her.

'I think I'll be happy. Very happy,' Eliza said a little desperately.
Was this working? She couldn't tell. How little she knew of this
sealed world to which she was a latecomer; how ignorant she was
for a woman of her age. Derby moved as if to get up and she
thought she might be hurting him; she leapt to her feet.

'Come,' he said, his eyes peculiarly shining, and he tugged her to the bed. There was no time to pull back the covers. He was heavy on top of her and fumbling with his breeches. It was all going to fall apart again, any minute now, she knew it. 'My Lord,' she said, then bit her lip.

He froze. 'What is it?'

She would deliver this line as teasingly, as sweetly as she knew how. 'You've courted me for sixteen years,' she said. 'Why the rush?'

He stared at her and for a moment she thought she'd offended him. Then he broke into a laugh. She let herself join in. Their laughter rippled; she was sure it could be heard all through the house. What an absurd pair they were. *Darby and Joan Go to It, or, The Follies of a Night.* They clung together and giggled like children. She'd known him so long. His ear was against her bare breast, his hand had a grip on her hip. 'I'm yours,' she said into his thinning hair, 'and you're mine.'

'Mm.'

'Sweet Ned,' she improvised. 'Come here to me, Ned, come under the covers.'

Derby was still laughing under his breath, but she could feel his prick against her now, a hard-nosed, eager snake. She found herself clamping her legs shut, by an old instinct, but then she told herself to loosen them. There was no need for waiting, refusing, holding at bay any more. The man who was her husband was lifting her night-gown an inch at a time, he was kissing her knees. He knew what to do and no doubt she would learn. Eliza felt a peculiar sort of nostalgia in advance. It was going to happen at last, it was happening. Any minute now she'd no longer be a virgin, and then who would she be?

Dear A.,

I look round this blank World [the letter said], *full of duties, embarrassments & disappointments, & see not a single being but you on whom I can depend for strength & comfort. What home on earth has my heart but yours? We've both been dogged*

by more than our share of misfortune, but I think the luck of
happening upon each other in this wide world must make up for
all we've suffered. At last I understand Plato's notion of souls
being created in pairs but axed apart & sent spinning into the
world, & only those blessed enough to meet with their tally
again can ever know true happiness.

In the jolting phaeton Anne copied it into the tiny notebook. She'd recently taken to transcribing her favourite passages from Mary's letters, with any names, places and compromising details removed.

She'd also made her Will; the complicated duties involved in being Walpole's executrix had made her aware of how important it was to be ready. (His finances were a mess; his legacies had been calculated before the stocks had started plummeting, and unless the war ended and the market revived within the year they'd all have to be reduced.) Not that Anne had any plans to die for another thirty years at least, but when it came she meant to make a tidy and discreet end. Her Will specified that her chisels, hammer and the little japanned box of Fidelle's ashes were to be put in her coffin with her. It was a pagan touch, perhaps, but she liked the thought of going equipped with her tools. All her papers were to be burnt—except for these little black notebooks. Somehow she couldn't bear them to go on the bonfire. Perhaps Mary would want them as a memento.

'We're almost there,' remarked Lady Ailesbury, angling her parasol to keep the sun off her face. 'Really, when the road's free of mud, Twickenham's a bare forty-five minutes from Mayfair.'

'You're right,' said Anne, tidying away her portable writing desk.

When Anne had first learned of her extraordinary inheritance she'd thought—*well, admit it, hoped*—that her mother might resist the move to Strawberry Hill. Why shouldn't Lady Ailesbury stay in Grosvenor Square all year round and Anne could join her there on visits to London? But no; the company of her remaining daughter was clearly more necessary to Lady Ailesbury than the bustle of the city. And quite apart from filial duty, Anne thought, she could probably do with her mother's company in her new home, which was several times the size of the house in Grosvenor Square. So here they were, the two of them, in a rented phaeton with the breeze in their hair and a weighed-down carriage full of trunks coming along behind.

As they drove into the courtyard Anne looked up and saw the Latin motto. *The skies above the traveller change,* she translated, *but not the traveller.* It seemed so wrong to enter this house in the absence of its master. But she mustn't go into her new home in tears.

Mrs Margaret Young, the long-faced housekeeper, walked them through the rooms, and Anne and her mother made suggestions as to what might be moved or needed refurbishing. Lady Ailesbury was touched to see one of her own worsted pictures in the refectory; Anne, knowing how much Walpole had disliked it, came very close to hysterical laughter.

Alone in the library for a few minutes, while the Countess took Mrs Young to task for the general dustiness, Anne sat on Walpole's favourite chaise longue. She shivered. Then she relaxed into it and let her head fall back on the greasy velvet. *You wanted me to have all this,* she said in her head, *you wanted me to sit there.* Of course Walpole had loved her; she was his cousin, his beloved Harry's daughter, his goddaughter and his friend. But in the last ten years of his life so much had come between them: politics, secrets and, most of all, Mary. He'd died confused and bitter, she knew that, though she could never decide exactly what he'd known, what he'd resented, what he'd understood.

How had he been able to make the grand gesture of entrusting her with Strawberry Hill, a house like no other, a bejewelled haven in a war-torn world? And he'd given Mary Little Strawberry, just across the meadow, which struck Anne now as being as clear a blessing on the pair of them as they could ever have asked for. The two houses were so near each other, with only grass between them, that the residents would have to be on intimate terms. It was as if, with exquisite tact, Walpole had thought of a way for Anne and Mary to be as close to each other as possible, given that they'd probably never be free to leave their families and live together. *Perhaps that's why he thought of me as his heir.* He knew what it was to love one's own sex and to be vilified for it, maybe, but not ashamed. She could feel him in the library with her now; she didn't look up.

'Anne? My dear, you must see the state of these curtains.'

'Coming, Mother.'

'Mr Walpole didn't object to dust,' the housekeeper was insisting, 'he considered it Gothic.'

As soon as she could get away, Anne went out into the gardens and surveyed her territory. The grass slid down to the row of lime trees and the blue river. The lilacs were in full bloom, and she saw jonquils, acacias and syringas. Her future spread out in front of her. She'd set up her workshop tomorrow, perhaps in the former printing house. She'd waste no time getting back to her self-portrait again. She needed to get her hands dirty. Work was like the iron blocks in the hull of a ship, for balance: hard and heavy and life-saving. At Strawberry Hill she would carve pieces so extraordinary that they'd outlive all the scandal of her life; she meant to be remembered as the first serious woman sculptor in the world.

But life wasn't all work. Anne would have dinners, put on plays, perhaps; what about Mary's comedy? She'd take care of this shabby, beautiful little house, in memory of its maker. She'd leave it for the pleasure of coming back to it; she'd spend the worst of the winter in London and travel further, too. She and Mary had promised each other that the day this awful war ended they'd set out for Paris. Perhaps Italy, even Spain. As far as the Pyramids?

She had something in her reticule for Mary: a tiny gold locket. It had a plaited lock of Anne's dark hair inside and for a motto a single word: *Fidèle*. 'It's not a ring,' she was meaning to say, 'nothing to bind you. Just a gift.' She looked up, now, and recognised the small figure coming across the meadow.

Author's Note

This novel is fiction, but the kind that walks arm in arm with fact. *Life Mask* began in my head many years ago when I came across a passage in Hester Thrale Piozzi's commonplace book, known as her *Thraliana*.

> *Wensday 9 Decr [1795] 'tis now grown common to suspect Impossibilities (such I think 'em) whenever two Ladies live too much together* [footnote: *'that horrible Vice...has a Greek name now & is call'd Sapphism'*]—*the Queen of France was all along accused, so was Raucoux the famous Actress on the Paris Stage; & 'tis a Joke in London now to say such a one visits Mrs Damer. Lord Derby certain insisted on Miss Farren keeping her at Distance & there was a droll but bitter Epigram made while they used to see one another often—*
>
> > *Her little Stock of private Fame*
> > *Will fall a Wreck to public Clamour,*
> > *If Farren herds with her whose Name*
> > *Approaches very near to Damn her.*
>
> *When every Offence tow'rds God & Reason, & Religion & Nature has been committed, that can be committed, I suppose the World will burn.*

In piecing together the intricate puzzle of the three lives that Mrs Piozzi wrote about with such glib relish I've tried to stick to the truth where it seemed to matter most. Apart from some servants,

my character are all historical people who lived and died more or
less as I've shown. Almost all the satirical pamphlets and prints
mentioned or quoted are real, except for the passages from the fic-
titious *Beau Monde Inquirer.* Most of the deliberate changes I've
made in order to shape the story are small—a matter of moving
events forward or back a few months or occasionally years, or
changing a location, or simplifying something complicated (such as
the management of Drury Lane). For the private relations between
all these people, of course, I've had to rely on educated guesswork.

In the case of each of my three protagonists I drew on one extremely limited or outdated biography: Percy Noble's *Anne Seymour
Damer: A Woman of Art and Fashion,* Millard Cox's *Derby: The Life
and Times of the 12th Earl of Derby* and Susanna Bloxam's *Walpole's
Queen of Comedy: Elizabeth Farren, Countess of Derby.* The sources I
found far more useful were the surviving published papers of the
three, as well as those of many of my other characters, and contemporaries such as Edward Jerningham and Thomas Creevey. I owe a
great deal to three brilliant biographies: Fintan O'Toole's *A Traitor's
Kiss: The Life of Richard Brinsley Sheridan,* Amanda Foreman's *Georgiana, Duchess of Devonshire* and Stella Tillyard's *Aristocrats: Caroline, Emily, Louisa and Sarah Lennox 1740–1812.* The best scholarly
investigation of Anne Damer is a chapter in Andrew Elfenbein's
Romantic Genius: The Prehistory of a Homosexual Role; her art is doc-
umented in a 1986 Ph.D. thesis by Susan Benforado. The Lewis
Walpole Library in Farmington, Connecticut gave me a fellowship
that allowed me to spend a wonderful week there studying Anne
Damer's notebooks (which proved to be composed of excerpts from
Mary Berry's letters) and their collection of Walpoliana. I'm also
grateful to the staff of Strawberry Hill, the British Library, Cam-
bridge University Library, the Robarts Library (University of
Toronto) and the Weldon Library (University of Western Ontario).

AND WHAT happened next, you may ask?

The twelfth Earl of Derby remained a passionate supporter of
Fox, though his background role meant that he barely earned a

mention in the history books. After a four-year secession, Fox roused his energies to return to Parliament and, on Pitt's premature death in 1806, he finally got into power as Foreign Secretary in the short-lived Ministry of All Talents, with Sheridan, Grey and Fitz-patrick. He managed to set in motion the abolition of the slave trade, but died of cirrhosis of the liver within the year, before he could achieve his second goal, peace with France (which would take another eight years). Derby was one of a stubborn handful of Whig peers who kept the flame of Foxite liberalism alive; well into the nineteenth century he was signing protests in the Lords on the sub-jects of Ireland, Catholics, peace and France. When George III went mad again, Prinny came to the throne as regent, then as king, but never invited his old Whig friends back into government; a Re-form Act wasn't passed until the reign of his brother William IV (Mrs Jordan's former keeper, the Duke of Clarence) in 1832, when Grey was Prime Minister.

Though Derby's long-awaited second wedding in 1797 pro-duced a brief flurry of dirt-digging pamphlets, none of them men-tioned the Sapphist rumours that had dogged Eliza on and off between 1789 and 1794; clearly, by marrying Derby she had restored her sexual reputation. The couple had their first baby (stillborn) ten months after the wedding and Mrs Farren died later the same year; of the three children born to them in the next three years a girl and a boy died at ten and seventeen respectively, and only Lady Mary Smith-Stanley (later Countess of Wilton) survived to adulthood. At Knowsley the couple had a busy country life with their children and grandchildren, local politics, charity, sport and entertaining on a grand scale (a hundred to luncheon every Monday, according to one report). Their many guests described the marriage as a very happy one. The Countess, it was said, never liked to be reminded of her former career, but she didn't forget old friends; when Jack Palmer died on stage, for instance, she sent £50 (about £3000 in today's money) to his widow and children. Eliza died in 1829, at the age of sixty-six, and her epitaph—as if to silence all the old sneers—said *She kept herself unspotted from the world.*

Derby lived five more years, cared for by his daughter Mary, long enough to see his eldest grandson, Edward Geoffrey Stanley (later the fourteenth Earl) launched on a brilliant career as a Whig politician—but not long enough, luckily, to see him change sides and become Tory leader from 1846 to 1868 and three times Prime Minister under Victoria. According to one story, on Derby's deathbed at the age of eighty-one he had his favourite cocks brought into his bedroom for one last fight. It would probably have gratified him to know that his name would live on, worldwide, as that of a horse race.

Anne Damer, too, outlasted her tormentors and seems to have found happiness. She settled in Strawberry Hill with her mother, and there she and Mary Berry staged Mary's play, *Fashionable Friends*. In 1802 they went to Paris during the Peace of Amiens and met Napoleon. Anne published at least one novel, *Belmour*, anonymously, while Mary's work on Walpole's papers launched her career as a woman of letters. In 1811, unable to afford the upkeep of Strawberry Hill, Anne passed it on to Walpole's relations. Living near each other in Mayfair, Anne and Mary remained close for the rest of their lives and though the painter Joseph Farington in his diary sneered at their intense intimacy, they seem to have avoided any further public scandal, or damage to their hectic social lives. Anne was now carving proto-Romantic busts of her male heroes and friends, such as the one of Fox she presented to Napoleon; she exhibited at the Royal Academy till she was sixty-nine. She died ten years later, in 1828, still sculpting; on her orders, all her papers were burnt, except for the notebooks containing passages from Mary's letters.

But Mary saved and published much of their correspondence. Addressing her dead friend, she referred to her own *entirely widowed Soul that has thus long survived Thee, wandering through the world*. Mary lived another twenty-four years with her sister Agnes, achieving celebrity as a sort of salon hostess, and they both died in 1852.

Thomas Lawrence's portrait of Eliza Farren hangs in New York's Metropolitan Museum of Art, and Anne Damer's busts of Eliza Farren and Mary Berry stand in the National Portrait Gallery in London.

Dramatis Personae

The following are the real people who appear or are referred to more than once in Life Mask. *Important characters are highlighted in bold.*

Signor Agostino, head keeper at the Royal Academy of Arts.

Caroline Campbell, **Countess of Ailesbury,** mother of Anne Damer and Lady Mary, wife of the Earl of Ailesbury, then Field Marshal Conway.

Major William Arabin, involved in the Richmond House theatricals.

Mrs Elizabeth 'Liz' Armistead, courtesan to many including the Duke of Dorset, Derby, Prinny; lover and then wife of Fox.

Mr John Bannister (the Younger), actor.

Mr Charles Bannister (the Elder), actor.

Mr William Beckford, MP, traveller, writer and collector.

Duke of Bedford, Foxite Peer, landlord of Drury Lane. Sometime lover of Lady Melbourne.

Miss Mary Berry, elder sister of Agnes, later a woman of letters.

Miss Agnes Berry, younger sister of Mary.

Mr Robert Berry, father of Mary and Agnes Berry.

Mrs Bruce, involved in Richmond House theatricals.

Mrs Blouse, involved in Richmond House theatricals.

Sir Thomas Charles Bunbury, former husband of Lady Sarah Lennox (sister of Richmond). Former MP, president of the Jockey Club.

General John Burgoyne, playwright, uncle of Derby, Foxite MP.

Mr Edmund Burke, sometime Foxite MP, orator, writer.

Busley, cock feeder to Derby.

Princess Caroline of Brunswick, wife of Prinny.

Queen Charlotte, wife of George III.

William, Duke of Clarence, later William IV, younger brother of the Prince of Wales, lover of Mrs Jordan.

Mr George Colman the Younger, playwright, proprietor of the Little Theatre (summer seasons) at the Haymarket.

Philip Columb, valet to Walpole.

Mr William Combe, journalist and satirist.

Field Marshal Henry Seymour Conway, father of Anne Damer, husband of Lady Ailesbury, cousin of Walpole. Former Leader of the House of Commons, Secretary of State, Commander in Chief, Lord-Lieutenant of Ireland. Governor of Jersey.

Mr Richard Cumberland, playwright.

The Honourable Mrs Anne Seymour Conway Damer, widow of the Honourable John Damer, half-sister of the Duchess of Richmond, daughter of Field Marshal Conway and Lady Ailesbury, cousin of Walpole. Sculptor, honorary exhibitor at Royal Academy, sometime Foxite campaigner.

Edward Smith-Stanley, twelfth Earl of Derby, separated husband of Lady 'Betty' Derby, former lover of Mrs Armistead. Foxite peer, Privy Counsellor, Lord-Lieutenant of Lancashire, sportsman.

Elizabeth 'Betty' Hamilton Stanley, Countess of Derby, separated wife of Derby, sometime lover of several including the Duke of Dorset.

Georgiana Spencer Cavendish, Duchess of Devonshire, wife of Devonshire, sister of Lady Duncannon, sometime (possibly) lover of Fox, the Duke of Dorset and Charles Grey, companion of Lady Bess Foster. Foxite hostess and campaigner.

Mr John Downman, artist and scene painter at Drury Lane.

William Cavendish, Duke of Devonshire, husband of Lady Georgiana Spencer, lover of several including Lady Bess Foster, brother-in-law of Portland. Foxite peer.

Duke of Dorset, sometime British ambassador to France, sometime lover of many including Lady Derby, Lady Bess Foster, Georgiana.

Harriet Spencer Ponsonby, Lady Duncannon, later Countess of Bess-borough, sister of Georgiana, wife of Lord Duncannon, sometime lover of several including Sheridan.

The Honourable Mr Richard Edgcumbe, involved in the Richmond House theatricals.

Sir Harry Englefield, involved in the Richmond House theatricals.

Miss Elizabeth ('Eliza') Farren, daughter of Mrs Farren, sister of Peggy. Actress.

Mrs Margaret Farren, widow of George Farren, mother of Eliza, Peggy and two dead daughters, one called Kitty. Former actress.

Mrs Peggy Farren Wright, sister of Eliza, actress.

Mr William Augustus Fawkener, former husband of Georgiana 'Jockey' Poyntz, quarter-nephew of Walpole. Sometime diplomat, Clerk of the Privy Council, sometime lover of several including Lady Jersey.

Lord Edward Fitzgerald, nephew of Richmond, cousin of Fox, a founder of the Friends of the People, sometime lover of Mrs Eliza Sheridan, husband of Pamela Égalité, Irish revolutionary.

Mrs Maria Smythe Fitzherbert, wife of the Prince of Wales.

Colonel Richard 'Dick' Fitzpatrick, Foxite MP.

William Wentworth, Earl Fitzwilliam, sometime Foxite MP, sometime Pittite Cabinet Minister and briefly Lord-Lieutenant of Ireland.

Dr George Fordyce, doctor to Anne Damer.

Lady Elizabeth ('Bess') Hervey Foster, daughter of the Earl of Bristol, separated wife of Mr John Thomas Foster, companion of Georgiana, sometime lover of many including Devonshire and Richmond.

Mr Charles James Fox, nephew of Richmond, sometime lover of Mrs Robinson and (possibly) Georgiana, lover and then husband of Mrs Armistead. MP, former Foreign Secretary, former Lord of the Admiralty, leader of the Foxite (Whig) Party.

George III, King of Great Britain and Ireland, Canada, Gibraltar, Sierra Leone, parts of India, much of the West Indies. Former king of America. Husband of Queen Charlotte, father of thirteen princes and princesses, including the Prince of Wales, Duke of York, Duke of Clarence.

Mr Charles Grey, sometime lover of Georgiana. Foxite MP, a founder of the Friends of the People.

Sir William Hamilton, archaeologist and collector, British envoy at Naples from 1764, later husband of Miss Emma Hart (Nelson's Emma).

The Honourable Mrs Albinia Hobart, Pittite campaigner, involved in Richmond House theatricals.

Mr Thomas Holcroft, radical playwright.

Mrs Elizabeth Hopkins, mother of Mrs Priscilla 'Pop' Kemble, mother-in-law of Kemble. Actress.

The Reverend John Horne Tooke, radical MP.

Mr David Hume, Scottish philospher, sometime secretary to Field Marshal Conway.

Frances Villiers, Countess of Jersey, sometime lover of many including Devonshire, Fawkener, Prinny.

Mrs Dorothy 'Dora' Jordan, sometime lover of Mr Richard Ford and the Duke of Clarence. Actress.

Mr John Philip Kemble, brother of Mrs Siddons, husband of Mrs Priscilla Hopkins Brereton. Actor, sometime manager of Drury Lane.

Mrs Priscilla 'Pop' Hopkins Brereton, later Kemble, daughter of Mrs Hopkins, wife of Brereton, then of Kemble. Actress.

Mr Tom King, actor, sometime manager of Drury Lane.

Thomas Kirgate, secretary and printer to Walpole.

Mr Thomas Lawrence, painter.

Baron Loughborough, sometime Foxite peer, then Pittite Lord Chancellor.

Louis XIV, King of France.

Marie Antoinette, Queen of France.

Lady Elizabeth Milbanke Lamb, **Viscountess Melbourne,** wife of Lord Melbourne, sometime lover of the Prince of Wales, Lord Coleraine, Lord Egremont, Earl of Bedford. Foxite hostess.

General Charles O'Hara, natural son of Lord Tyrawley. Lieutenant-Governor and later Governor of Gibraltar.

Mr John 'Plausible Jack' Palmer, actor, and proprietor of short-lived Royalty Theatre.

Mr Charles Pigott, radical journalist.

Mrs Hester Thrale Piozzi, widow of Mr Henry Thrale, wife of Signor Gabriel Piozzi. Writer.

Mr William Pitt (the Younger), Prime Minister.

William Cavendish-Bentinck, Duke of Portland, brother-in-law of Devonshire. Collector, Foxite peer, nominal leader of Opposition, then leader of 'Portland Whigs', then Pittite Cabinet Minister.

Mr William Powell, under-prompter and stage manager at Drury Lane. Prompter from 1793, husband of actress Mrs Jane Farmer Powell.

George, Prince of Wales, later George IV, known as Prinny, son of George III and Queen Charlotte, sometime lover of many including Mrs Robinson, Mrs Armistead, Lady Melbourne, Lady Jersey; husband of Mrs Fitzherbert, then of Princess Caroline.

Sir Joshua Reynolds, painter, first president of Royal Academy of Arts.

Mr Samuel Richardson, printer and novelist.

Charles Lennox, Duke of Richmond, husband of Lady Mary, brother-in-law of Anne Damer, uncle of Fox, sometime lover of Madame de Cambis and Lady Bess Foster. Pittite peer, Master-General of the Ordnance, Cabinet Minister and Privy Counsellor.

Lady Mary Bruce Lennox, Duchess of Richmond, half-sister of Anne Damer, daughter of Lady Ailesbury's first marriage.

Monsieur Jean-Jacques Rousseau, Swiss philosopher and writer.

Mr Richard Brinsley Sheridan, husband of Eliza Linley, then of Hecca Ogle, sometime lover of Mrs Crewe and Lady Duncannon. Foxite MP, founder of the Friends of the People and proprietor of Theatre Royal, Drury Lane.

Mrs Sarah Kemble Siddons, sister of Kemble, wife of Mr William Siddons. Actress.

Lord Edward Smith-Stanley, later MP, then thirteenth Earl of Derby, Derby's son and heir.

Lady Charlotte Smith-Stanley, Derby's elder daughter.

Lady Elizabeth Smith-Stanley, Derby's younger daughter.

Madame Anne-Louise-Germaine de Staël, French writer and hostess.

Earl Stanhope, Pittite, then radical Foxite peer, brother-in-law of Pitt.

Mr Horace Walpole, later Earl of Orford, second cousin and god-father of Anne Damer, cousin of Conway, quarter-uncle of Fawkener. Former MP, writer and collector.

Mr Robert Walpole, British Minister at Lisbon, cousin of Horace Walpole.

Mr Richard Wroughton, actor, manager of Drury Lane from 1796.

Frederick, Duke of York, younger brother of Prince of Wales.

Mrs Margaret Young, housekeeper to Walpole at Strawberry Hill.